Unstoppable "BRAINY HEROINE" (*New York Times*)
KAY SCARPETTA is . . .

"A character as strong as any in popular fiction."

—*The Wall Street Journal*

"A feisty, independent powerhouse whose capacity to concentrate and observe rivals Sherlock Holmes's."

—*Publishers Weekly*

PRAISE FOR #1 *NEW YORK TIMES* BESTSELLING AUTHOR PATRICIA CORNWELL'S "BONE-RATTLING" (*Publishers Weekly*) NOVEL, *ALL THAT REMAINS*

"You'll probably stay up all night turning the pages."

—*The Denver Post*

"Riveting. . . . Compelling. . . . Scarpetta uses a microscope in her forensic lab the way Sherlock Holmes wielded a magnifying glass."

—*Cosmopolitan*

"A heckuva good thriller."

—*USA Today*

"Intense. . . . Patricia Cornwell writes with grisly authenticity."

—*Los Angeles Times*

"Master prose, a labyrinthian puzzle, a multidimensional protagonist with a credible supporting cast and an authentic milieu. . . . After reading Cornwell's thriller, most others will pale in comparison."

—*Milwaukee Journal Sentinel*

"Powerful. . . . Harrowing. . . . The story is compelling, the prose spare, and Cornwell's depictions of the crime scenes chilling."

—*Harper's Bazaar*

"Colorful. . . . Sensational. . . . Dead on."

—*Newsweek*

. . . AND FOR HER "FRESH AND TRIUMPHANT" (*Washington Post Book World*) THRILLER, *CRUEL AND UNUSUAL*

"Morbidly entertaining . . . The elaborate plot shows expert engineering, and the lucid descriptions of forensic procedures that make her story so grimly fascinating are delivered in an authoritative voice."

—*The New York Times Book Review*

"Disturbing . . . Compelling . . . The best work yet from Patricia Cornwell."

—*People*

"Engrossing . . . an extremely effective novel of suspense, in all its varieties."

—*Entertainment Weekly*

"Classic Cornwell. . . . chilling . . . riveting . . . utterly convincing."

—*Richmond-Times Dispatch*

"Taut, high tech, and eerily credible."

—*Newsweek*

"A first-rate thriller . . . as taut and terrifying as *The Silence of the Lambs*. . . . Cornwell's boldest, darkest work to date."

—*Baltimore Sun*

"A page-turner."

—Larry King, *USA Today*

"Chilling . . . a fine example of crime fiction, one that sets out to claim a little more territory for itself than merely finding out whodunit."

—*Houston Chronicle*

"Unusually good."

—*Charlotte Observer*

"Eerie . . . intriguingly complex. . . . A mesmerizing blend of forensic pathology, investigative technology . . . and throat-constricting tension. . . . Cornwell's plotting is flawless, her pacing is pitch perfect, and even her minor characters are well-drawn."

—*Lexington Herald-Leader*

MORE CRITICAL ACCLAIM FOR PATRICIA CORNWELL AND HER "UTTERLY CHILLING" (*Entertainment Weekly*) KAY SCARPETTA NOVELS

"[Cornwell] makes looking through a microscope as exciting as a hot-pursuit chase."

—*The Washington Post Book World*

"Cornwell's instincts are dead-on."

—*Chicago Sun-Times*

"Gruesome and suspenseful."

—*New York Daily News*

"Cornwell brings [compulsive murderers] to full, frightening life."

—*The New York Times*

"A walloping, riveting mix of mystery, adventure, and psychology."

—*Forbes*

IN THE KAY SCARPETTA SERIES

Scarpetta

Book of the Dead

Predator

Trace

Blow Fly

The Last Precinct

Black Notice

Point of Origin

Unnatural Exposure

Cause of Death

From Potter's Field

The Body Farm

Cruel & Unusual

All That Remains

Body of Evidence

Postmortem

IN THE WIN GARANO SERIES

The Front

At Risk

IN THE ANDY BRAZIL SERIES

Isle of Dogs

Southern Cross

Hornet's Nest

OTHER BOOKS

Portrait of a Serial Killer: Jack the Ripper—Case Closed

Scarpetta's Winter Tale

Food to Die For

Ruth, A Portrait

Life's Little Fable

Patricia Cornwell

THE SCARPETTA COLLECTION

VOLUME II

All That Remains

AND

Cruel & Unusual

POCKET BOOKS

NEW YORK LONDON TORONTO SYDNEY

Pocket Books
A Division of Simon & Schuster, Inc.
1230 Avenue of the Americas
New York, NY 10020

These titles were previously published individually by Scribner.

This Pocket Books trade paperback edition September 2009

Manufactured in the United States of America

1 3 5 7 9 10 8 6 4 2

Library of Congress Cataloging-in-Publication Data is available for the hardcover edition.

ISBN 978-1-4391-7205-6
ISBN 978-1-4391-7206-3 (ebook)

ALL THAT REMAINS

This book is for
Michael Congdon.
As always, thanks.

1

Saturday, the last day of August, I started work before dawn. I did not witness mist burning off the grass or the sky turning brilliant blue. Steel tables were occupied by bodies all morning, and there are no windows in the morgue. Labor Day weekend had begun with a bang of car crashes and gunfire in the city of Richmond.

It was two o'clock in the afternoon when I finally returned to my West End home and heard Bertha mopping in the kitchen. She cleaned for me every Saturday and knew from past instruction not to bother with the phone, which had just begun to ring.

"I'm not here," I said loudly as I opened the refrigerator.

Bertha stopped mopping. "It was ringing a minute ago," she said. "Rang a few minutes before that, too. Same man."

"No one's home," I repeated.

"Whatever you say, Dr. Kay." The mop moved across the floor again.

I tried to ignore the disembodied answering machine message intruding upon the sun-washed kitchen. The Hanover tomatoes I took for granted during the summer I began to hoard with the approach of fall. There were only three left. Where was the chicken salad?

A beep was followed by the familiar male voice. "Doc? It's Marino . . ."

Oh, Lord, I thought, shoving the refrigerator door shut with a hip. Richmond homicide detective Pete Marino had been on the street since midnight, and I had just seen him in the morgue as I was picking bullets out of one of his cases. He was supposed to be on his way to Lake Gaston for what was left of a weekend of fishing. I was looking forward to working in my yard.

"I've been trying to get you, am heading out. You'll have to try my pager . . ."

Marino's voice sounded urgent as I snatched up the receiver.

"I'm here."

"That you or your goddam machine?"

"Take a guess," I snapped.

"Bad news. They found another abandoned car. New Kent, the Sixty-four rest stop, westbound. Benton just got hold of me—"

"Another couple?" I interrupted, my plans for the day forgotten.

"Fred Cheney, white male, nineteen. Deborah Harvey, white female, nineteen. Last seen around eight last night when they drove off from the Harveys' Richmond house, on their way to Spindrift."

"And the car's in the *westbound* lane?" I inquired, for Spindrift, North Carolina, is three and a half hours east of Richmond.

"Yo. Appears they was heading in the opposite direction, back into the city. A trooper found the car, a Jeep Cherokee, about an hour ago. No sign of the kids."

"I'm leaving now," I told him.

Bertha had not stopped mopping, but I knew she had picked up every word.

"Be on my way soon as I finish up in here," she assured me. "I'll lock up and set the alarm. Don't you worry, Dr. Kay."

Fear was running along my nerves as I grabbed my purse and hurried out to my car.

There were four couples so far. Each had disappeared, eventually to be found murdered within a fifty-mile radius of Williamsburg.

The cases, dubbed by the press as The Couple Killings, were inexplicable, and no one seemed to have a clue or credible theory, not even the FBI and its Violent Criminal Apprehension Program, or VICAP, which featured a national data base run on an artificial intelligence computer capable of connecting missing persons with unidentified bodies and linking serial crimes. After the first couple's bodies were found more than two years ago, a VICAP regional team, comprising FBI Special Agent Benton Wesley and veteran Richmond homicide detective Pete Marino, was invited by local police to assist. Another couple would disappear, then two more. In each instance, by the time VICAP could be notified, by the time the National Crime Information Center, or NCIC, could even wire descriptions to police departments across America, the missing teenagers were already dead and decomposing in woods somewhere.

Turning off the radio, I passed through a tollbooth and picked up speed on I-64 East. Images, voices suddenly came back to me. Bones and rotted clothing scattered with leaves. Attractive, smiling faces of missing teenagers printed in the newspapers, and bewildered, distraught families interviewed on television and calling me on the phone.

"I'm so sorry about your daughter."

"Please tell me how my baby died. Oh, God, did she suffer?"

"Her cause of death is undetermined, Mrs. Bennett. There's nothing else I can tell you at this time."

"What do you mean you *don't know?*"

"All that remains is his bones, Mr. Martin. When soft tissue is gone, gone with it is any possible injury . . ."

"I don't want to hear your medical bullshit! I want to know what killed my boy! The cops are asking about drugs! My boy's never been drunk in his life, much less taken drugs! You hear me, lady? He's dead, and they're making him out to be some sort of punk . . ."

"CHIEF MEDICAL EXAMINER BAFFLED: Dr. Kay Scarpetta Unable to Tell Cause of Death."

Undetermined.

Over and over again. Eight young people.

It was awful. It was, in fact, unprecedented for me.

Every forensic pathologist has undetermined cases, but I had never had so many that appeared to be related.

I opened the sunroof and my spirits were lifted somewhat by the weather. The temperature was in the low eighties, leaves would be turning soon. It was only in the fall and spring that I did not miss Miami. Richmond summers were just as hot, without benefit of ocean breezes to sweep the air clean. The humidity was horrible, and in winter I fared no better, for I do not like the cold. But spring and fall were intoxicating. I drank in the change, and it went straight to my head.

The I-64 rest stop in New Kent County was exactly thirty-one miles from my house. It could have been any rest stop in Virginia, with picnic tables, grills and wooden trash barrels, brick-enclosed bathrooms and vending machines, and newly planted trees. But there was not a traveler or a truck driver in sight, and police cars were everywhere.

A trooper, hot and unsmiling in his blue-gray uniform, walked toward me as I parked near the ladies' room.

"I'm sorry, ma'am," he said, leaning close to my open window. "This rest area's closed today. I'm going to have to ask you to drive on."

"Dr. Kay Scarpetta," I identified myself, switching off the ignition. "The police asked me to come."

"For what purpose, ma'am?"

"I'm the chief medical examiner," I replied.

As he looked me over, I could see the skeptical glint in his eyes. I supposed I did not look particularly "chiefly." Dressed in a stone-washed denim skirt, pink oxford cloth shirt, and leather walking shoes, I was without the accouterments of authority, including my state car, which was in the state garage awaiting new tires. At a glance, I was a not-so-young yuppie running errands in her dark gray Mercedes, a distracted ash-blonde en route to the nearest shopping mall.

"I'll need some identification."

Digging inside my purse, I produced a thin black wallet and displayed my brass medical examiner's shield, then handed over my driver's license, both of which he studied for a long moment. I sensed he was embarrassed.

"Just leave your car here, Dr. Scarpetta. The folks you're looking for are in back." He pointed in the direction of the parking area for trucks and buses. "Have a nice one," he added inanely, stepping away.

I followed a brick walk. When I rounded the building and passed beneath the shade of trees, I was greeted by several more police cars, a tow truck with light bar flashing, and at least a dozen men in uniforms and plain clothes. I did not see the red Jeep Cherokee until I was almost upon it. Midway along the exit ramp, it was well off the pavement in a dip and obscured by foliage. Two-door, it was coated with a film of dust. When I looked in the driver's window I could see that the beige leather interior was very clean, the backseat neatly packed with various items of luggage, a slalom ski, a coiled yellow nylon ski rope, and a red-and-white plastic ice chest. Keys dangled from the ignition. Windows were partly rolled down. Depressed tire tracks leading from the pavement were clearly visible in the sloping grass, the front chrome grille nudged up against a clump of pines.

Marino was talking to a thin, blond man, someone he introduced as Jay Morrell with the state police, whom I did not know. He seemed to be in charge.

"Kay Scarpetta," I volunteered, since Marino identified me only as "Doc."

Morrell fixed dark green Ray Bans on me and nodded. Out of uniform and sporting a mustache that was little more than teenage fuzz, he exuded the all-business bravado I associated with investigators brand-new on the job.

"Here's what we know so far." He was glancing around nervously. "The Jeep belongs to Deborah Harvey, and she and her boyfriend, uh, Fred Cheney, left the Harveys' residence last night at approximately eight P.M. They were heading to Spindrift, where the Harvey family owns a beach house."

"Was Deborah Harvey's family home when the couple left Richmond?" I inquired.

"No, ma'am." He briefly turned his shades my way. "They were already at Spindrift, had left earlier in the day. Deborah and Fred wanted to go in a separate car because they planned to return to Richmond on Monday. Both of them are sophomores at Carolina, and needed to come back early to get ready to return to school."

Marino explained as he got out his cigarettes, "Right before they left the Harvey house last night, they called up Spindrift, told one of Deborah's brothers they was heading out and would be arriving sometime between midnight and one A.M. When they didn't show up by four o'clock this morning, Pat Harvey called the police."

"Pat Harvey?" I looked at Marino in disbelief.

It was Officer Morrell who replied, "Oh, yeah. We got us a good one, all right. Pat Harvey's on her way here even as we speak. A chopper picked her up"—he glanced at his watch—"about a half hour ago. The father, uh, Bob Harvey, he's on the road. Was in Charlotte on business and was supposed to get to Spindrift sometime tomorrow. As far as we know, he hasn't been reached yet, doesn't know what's happened."

Pat Harvey was the National Drug Policy Director, a position the media had dubbed Drug Czar. A presidential appointee who not so long ago had been on the cover of *Time* magazine, Mrs. Harvey was one of the most powerful and admired women in America.

"What about Benton?" I asked Marino. "Is he aware Deborah Harvey is Pat Harvey's daughter?"

"He didn't say nothing about it to me. When he called, he'd just landed in Newport News—the Bureau flew him in. He was in a hurry to find a rental car. We didn't talk long."

That answered my question. Benton Wesley would not be rushing here in a Bureau plane unless he knew who Deborah Harvey was. I wondered why he had not said anything to Marino, his VICAP partner, and I tried to read Marino's broad, impassive face. His jaw muscles were flexing, the top of his balding head flushed and beaded with sweat.

"What's going on now," Morrell resumed, "is I got a lot of men stationed around to keep out traffic. We've looked in the bathrooms, poked around a little, to make sure the kids aren't in the immediate area. Once Peninsula Search and Rescue get here, we'll start in on the woods."

Immediately north of the Jeep's front hood the well-attended landscaping of the rest stop was overcome by brush and trees that within an acre became so dense I could see nothing but sunlight caught in leaves and a hawk making circles over a distant stand of pines. Though shopping malls and housing developments continued their encroachment upon I-64, this stretch between Richmond and Tidewater so far had remained unspoiled. The scenery, which I would have found reassuring and soothing in the past, now seemed ominous to me.

"Shit," Marino complained as we left Morrell and began walking around.

"I'm sorry about your fishing trip," I said.

"Hey. Ain't it the way it always goes? Been planning this damn trip for months. Screwed again. Nothing new."

"I noticed that when you pull off the Interstate," I observed, ignoring his irritation, "the entrance ramp immediately divides into two ramps, one leading back here, the other to the front of the rest stop. In other words, the ramps are one-way. It's not possible to pull into the front area for cars, then change your mind and drive back here without going a considerable distance the wrong way on the ramp and risk hitting someone. And I would guess there was a fair amount of travelers on the road last night, since it's Labor Day weekend."

"Right. I know that. It don't take a rocket scientist to figure out that somebody intended to ditch the Jeep exactly where it is because there were probably a lot of cars parked in front last night. So he takes the ramp for trucks and buses. Probably was pretty deserted back here. Nobody sees him, and he splits."

"He may also not have wanted the Jeep found right away, explaining why it's well off the pavement," I said.

Marino stared off toward the woods and said, "I'm getting too old for this."

A perpetual complainer, Marino had a habit of arriving at a crime scene and acting as if he did not want to be there. We had worked with each other long enough for me to be used to it, but this time his attitude struck me as more than an act. His frustration went deeper than the canceled fishing trip. I wondered if he had had a fight with his wife.

"Well, well," he mumbled, looking toward the brick building. "The Lone Ranger's arrived."

I turned around as the lean, familiar figure of Benton Wesley emerged from the men's room. He barely said "hello" when he got to us, his silver hair wet at the temples, the lapels of his blue suit speckled with water as if he had just washed his face. Eyes fixed impassively on the Jeep, he slipped a pair of sunglasses from his breast pocket and put them on.

"Has Mrs. Harvey gotten here yet?" he asked.

"Nope," Marino replied.

"What about reporters?"

"Nope," Marino said.

"Good."

Wesley's mouth was firmly set, making his sharp-featured face seem harder and more unreachable than usual. I would have found him handsome were it not for his imperviousness. His thoughts and emotions were impossible to read, and of late he had become such a master at walling off his personality that I sometimes felt I did not know him.

"We want to keep this under wraps as long as possible," he went on. "The minute the word's out all hell is going to break loose."

I asked him, "What do you know about this couple, Benton?"

"Very little. After Mrs. Harvey reported them missing early this morning, she called the Director at home and then he called me. Apparently, her daughter and Fred Cheney met at Carolina and had been dating since their freshman year. Both of them supposedly good, clean-cut kids. No history of any sort of trouble that might account for them getting tangled up with the wrong type of person out here—at least according to Mrs. Harvey. One thing I did pick up on was she had some ambivalence about the relationship, thought Cheney and her daughter spent too much time alone."

"Possibly the real reason for their wanting to drive to the beach in a separate car," I said.

"Yes," Wesley replied, glancing around. "More than likely that was the real reason. I got the impression from the Director that Mrs. Harvey wasn't keen on Deborah's bringing her boyfriend to Spindrift. It was family time. Mrs. Harvey lives in D.C. during the week and hadn't seen much of her daugher and two sons all summer. Frankly, I have the feeling that Deborah and her mother may not have been getting along very well of late, and may have had an argument right before the family headed off to North Carolina yesterday morning."

"What about the chance the kids might have run off together?" Marino said. "They was smart, right? Would read the papers, watch the news, maybe saw the stuff about these couples on that TV special the other week. Point is, they probably knew about the cases around here. Who's to say they didn't pull something? A pretty slick way to stage a disappearance and punish your parents."

"It's one of many scenarios we need to consider," Wesley replied. "And it's all the more reason I hope we can keep this from the media as long as possible."

Morrell joined us as we walked along the exit ramp back toward the Jeep. A pale blue pickup truck with a camper shell pulled up, and a man and a woman in dark jumpsuits and boots got out. Opening the tailgate, they let two panting, tail-wagging bloodhounds out of their crate. They snapped long leads to rings on the leather belts around their waists and grabbed each dog by its harness.

"Salty, Neptune, heel!"

I didn't know which dog was which. Both were big and light tan with wrinkled faces and floppy ears. Morrell grinned and put out his hand.

"Howya doin', fella?"

Salty, or maybe it was Neptune, rewarded him with a wet kiss and a nuzzle to the leg.

The dog handlers were from Yorktown, their names Jeff and Gail. Gail was as tall as her partner and looked just about as strong. She reminded me of women I've seen who have spent their lives on farms, their faces lined by hard work and the sun, a stolid patience about them that comes from understanding nature and accepting its gifts and punishments. She was the search-and-rescue team captain, and I could tell from the way she was eyeing the Jeep that she was surveying it for any sign that the scene, and therefore the scents, had been disturbed.

"Nothing's been touched," Marino told her, bending over to knead one of the dogs behind the ears. "We haven't even opened the doors yet."

"Do you know if anybody else has been inside it? Maybe the person who found it?" Gail inquired.

Morrell began to explain, "The plate number went out over teletype, BOLOs, early this morning—"

"What the hell are BOLOs?" Wesley interrupted.

"Be On the Lookouts."

Wesley's face was granite as Morrell went on, tediously, "Troopers don't go through lineup, so they're not always going to see a teletype. They just get in their cars and mark on. The dispatchers started sending BOLOs over the air the minute the couple was reported missing, and around one P.M. a trucker spotted the Jeep, radioed it in. The trooper who responded said that other than looking through the windows to make sure nobody was inside, he didn't even get close."

I hoped this was true. Most police officers, even those who know better, can't seem to resist opening doors and at least rummaging through the glove compartment in search of the owner's identification.

Taking hold of both harnesses, Jeff took the dogs off to "use the potty" while Gail asked, "You got anything the dogs can scent off of?"

"Pat Harvey was asked to bring along anything Deborah might have been wearing recently," Wesley said.

If Gail was surprised or impressed by whose daughter she was looking for, she did not show it but continued to regard Wesley expectantly.

"She's flying in by chopper," Wesley added, glancing at his watch. "Should be here any minute."

"Well, just don't be landing the big bird right here," Gail commented, approaching the Jeep. "Don't need anything stirring up the place." Peering through the driver's window, she studied the inside of the doors, the dash, taking in every inch of the interior. Then she backed away and took a long look at the black plastic door handle on the outside of the door.

"Best thing's probably going to be the seats," she decided. "We'll let Salty scent off one, Neptune off the other. But first, we got to get in without screwing up anything. Anybody got a pencil or pen?"

Snatching a ballpoint Mont Blanc pen out of the breast pocket of his shirt, Wesley presented it to her.

"Need one more," she added.

Amazingly, nobody else seemed to have a pen on his person, including me. I could have sworn I had several inside my purse.

"How about a folding knife?" Marino was digging in a pocket of his jeans.

"Perfect."

Pen in one hand and Swiss army knife in the other, Gail simultaneously depressed the thumb button on the outside of the driver's door and pried back the handle, then caught the door's edge with the toe of her boot to gently pull it open. All the while I heard the faint, unmistakable thud-thud of helicopter blades growing louder.

Moments later, a red-and-white Bell Jet Ranger circled the rest stop, then hovered like a dragonfly, creating a small hurricane on the ground. All sound was drowned out, trees shaking and grass rippling in the roar of its terrible wind. Eyes squeezed shut, Gail and Jeff were squatting by the dogs, holding harnesses tight.

Marino, Wesley, and I had retreated close to the buildings, and from this vantage we watched the violent descent. As the helicopter slowly nosed around in a maelstrom of straining engines and beating air, I caught a glimpse of Pat Harvey staring down at her daughter's Jeep before sunlight whited out the glass.

She stepped away from the helicopter, head bent and skirt whipping around her legs as Wesley waited a safe distance from the decelerating blades, necktie fluttering over his shoulder like an aviator's scarf.

Before Pat Harvey had been appointed the National Drug Policy Director, she had been a commonwealth's attorney in Richmond, then a U.S. attorney for the Eastern District of Virginia. Her prosecution of high-profile drug cases in the federal system had occasionally involved victims I had autopsied. But I had never been called to testify; only my reports had been subpoenaed. Mrs. Harvey and I had never actually met.

On television and in newspaper photographs she came across as all business. She was, in the flesh, both feminine and strikingly attractive, slender, her features perfectly wrought, the sun finding hints of gold and red in her short auburn hair. Wesley made brief introductions, and Mrs. Harvey shook each of our hands with the politeness and self-assurance of a practiced politician. But she did not smile or meet anyone's eyes.

"There's a sweatshirt inside," she explained, handing a paper bag to Gail. "I found it in Debbie's bedroom at the beach. I don't know when she wore it last, but I don't think it's been recently washed."

"When's the last time your daughter was at the beach?" Gail inquired without opening the bag.

"Early July. She went there with several friends for a weekend."

"And you're sure she was the one wearing this? Possible one of her friends might have?" Gail asked casually, as though she were inquiring about the weather.

The question caught Mrs. Harvey by surprise, and for an instant doubt clouded her dark blue eyes. "I'm not sure." She cleared her throat. "I would assume Debbie was the one wearing it last, but obviously I can't swear to it. I wasn't there."

She stared past us through the Jeep's open door, her attention briefly fixed on the keys in the ignition, the silver "D" dangling from the keychain. For a long moment no one spoke, and I could see the struggle of mind against emotion as she warded off panic with denial.

Turning back to us, she said, "Debbie would have been carrying a purse. Nylon, bright red. One of those sports purses with a Velcro-lined flap. I'm wondering if you found it inside?"

"No, ma'am," Morrell replied. "At least we haven't seen anything like that yet, not from looking through the windows. But we haven't searched the interior, couldn't until the dogs got here."

"I would expect it to be on the front seat. Perhaps on the floor," she went on.

Morrell shook his head.

It was Wesley who spoke. "Mrs. Harvey, do you know if your daughter had much money with her?"

"I gave her fifty dollars for food and gas. I don't know what she might have had beyond that," she replied. "She also, of course, had charge cards. Plus her checkbook."

"You know what she had in her checking account?" Wesley asked.

"Her father gave her a check last week," she replied matter-of-factly. "For college—books, and so on. I'm fairly certain she's already deposited it. I suppose she should have at least a thousand dollars in her account."

"You might want to look into that," Wesley proposed. "Make certain the money wasn't recently withdrawn."

"I will do so immediately."

As I stood by and watched, I could sense hope blossoming in her mind. Her daughter had cash, charge cards, and access to money in a checking account. It did not appear that she had left her purse inside the Jeep, meaning she might still have it with her. Meaning she might still be alive and well and off somewhere with her boyfriend.

"Your daughter ever threaten to run away with Fred?" Marino asked her bluntly.

"No." Staring again at the Jeep, she added what she wanted to believe, "But that doesn't mean it isn't possible."

"What was her mood when you talked to her last?" Marino went on.

"We exchanged words yesterday morning before my sons and I left for the beach," she replied in a detached, flat tone. "She was upset with me."

"She know about the cases around here? The missing couples?" Marino asked.

"Yes, of course. We have discussed them, wondered about them. She knew."

Gail said to Morrell, "We ought to get started."

"Good idea."

"One last thing." Gail looked at Mrs. Harvey. "You got any idea who was driving?"

"Fred, I suspect," she answered. "When they went places together, he usually drove."

Nodding, Gail said, "Guess I'm going to need that pocketknife and pen again."

Collecting them from Wesley and Marino, she went around to the passenger's side and opened the door. She grasped one of the bloodhounds' harnesses. Eagerly, he got up and moved in perfect accord with his mistress's feet, snuffling along, muscles rippling beneath his loose, glossy coat, ears dragging heavily, as if lined with lead.

"Come on, Neptune, let's put that magic nose of yours to work."

We watched in silence as she directed Neptune's nose at the bucket seat where Deborah Harvey was presumed to have been sitting yesterday. Suddenly he yelped as if he had encountered a rattlesnake, jerking back from the Jeep, practically wrenching the harness from Gail's hand. He tucked his tail between his legs and the fur literally stood up on his back as a chill ran up my spine.

"Easy, boy. Easy!"

Whimpering and quivering all over, Neptune squatted and defecated in the grass.

2

I woke up the next morning, exhausted and dreading the Sunday paper.

The headline was bold enough to be read from a block away:

DRUG CZAR'S DAUGHTER, FRIEND MISSING—
POLICE FEAR FOUL PLAY

Not only had reporters gotten hold of a photograph of Deborah Harvey, but there was a picture of her Jeep being towed from the rest stop and a file photograph, I presumed, of Bob and Pat Harvey, hand in hand, walking a deserted beach in Spindrift. As I sipped coffee and read, I could not help but think about Fred Cheney's family. He was not from a prominent family. He was just "Deborah's boyfriend." Yet he, too, was missing; he, too, was loved.

Apparently, Fred was the son of a Southside businessman, an only child whose mother had died last year when a berry aneurysm ruptured in her brain. Fred's father, the story read, was in Sarasota visiting relatives when the police finally tracked him down late last night. If there were a remote possibility that his son had "run off" with Deborah, the story read, it would have been very much out of character for Fred, who was described as "a good student at Carolina and a member of the varsity swim team." Deborah was an honor student and a gymnast gifted enough to be an Olympic hopeful. Weighing no more than a hundred pounds, she had shoulder-length dark blond hair and her mother's handsome features. Fred was broad-shouldered and lean, with wavy black hair and hazel eyes. They were a couple described as attractive and inseparable.

"Whenever you saw one, you always saw the other," a friend was quoted as saying. "I think it had a lot to do with Fred's mother dying. Debbie met him right about that time, and I don't think he would have made it through without her."

Of course, the story went on to regurgitate the details of the other four Virginia couples missing and later found dead. My name was mentioned several times. I was described as frustrated, baffled, and avoiding comment. I wondered if it occurred to anyone that I continued to autopsy the victims of homicides, suicides, and accidents every week. I routinely talked to families, testified in court, and gave lectures to paramedics and police academies. Couples or not, life and death went on.

I had gotten up from the kitchen table, was sipping coffee and staring out at the bright morning when the telephone rang.

Expecting my mother, who often called at this hour on Sunday to inquire about my well-being and if I had been to Mass, I pulled out a nearby chair as I picked up the receiver.

"Dr. Scarpetta?"

"Speaking." The woman sounded familiar, but I could not place her.

"It's Pat Harvey. Please forgive me for bothering you at home." Behind her steady voice, I detected a note of fear.

"You certainly aren't bothering me," I replied kindly. "What can I do for you?"

"They searched all through the night and are still out there. They brought in more dogs, more police, several aircraft." She began to speak rapidly. "Nothing. No sign of them. Bob has joined the search parties. I'm home." She hesitated. "I'm wondering if you could come over? Perhaps you're free for lunch?"

After a long pause, I reluctantly agreed. As I hung up the telephone I silently berated myself, for I knew what she wanted from me. Pat Harvey would ask about the other couples. If I were her, it was exactly what I would do.

I went upstairs to my bedroom and got out of my robe. Then I took a long, hot bath and washed my hair while my answering machine began intercepting calls that I had no intention of returning unless they were emergencies. Within the hour I was dressed in a khaki skirt suit and tensely playing back messages. There were five of them, all from reporters who had learned that I had been summoned to the New Kent County rest stop, which did not bode well for the missing couple.

I reached for the phone, intending to call Pat Harvey back and cancel our lunch. But I could not forget her face when she had arrived by helicopter with her daughter's sweatshirt, I could not forget the faces of any of the parents. Hanging up the phone, I locked the house and got into my car.

People in public service can't afford the accoutrements privacy demands unless they have some other means of income. Obviously, Pat Harvey's federal salary was a meager sliver of her family's worth. They lived near Windsor on the James in a palatial Jeffersonian house overlooking the river. The estate, which I guessed to be at least five acres, was surrounded by a high brick wall posted with "Private Property" signs. When I turned into a long drive shaded by trees, I was stopped by a sturdy wrought-iron gate that slid open electronically before I could roll down my window to reach for the intercom. The gate slid shut behind me as I drove through. I parked near a black Jaguar sedan before a Roman portico of unfluted columns, old red brick, and white trim.

As I was getting out of my car, the front door opened. Pat Harvey, drying her hands on a dish towel, smiled bravely at me from the top of the steps. Her face was pale, her eyes lusterless and tired.

"It's so good of you to come, Dr. Scarpetta." She motioned for me to enter. "Please come in."

The foyer was as spacious as a living room, and I followed her through a formal sitting room to the kitchen. Furniture was eighteenth century, Oriental rugs wall to wall, and there were original Impressionist paintings and a fireplace with beechwood logs artfully piled on the hearth. At least the kitchen looked functional and lived in, but I did not get the impression that anyone else was home.

"Jason and Michael are out with their father," she explained when I asked. "The boys drove in this morning."

"How old are they?" I inquired, as she opened the oven door.

"Jason is sixteen, Michael fourteen. Debbie is the oldest." Looking around for the potholders, she turned off the oven, then set a quiche on top of a burner. Her hands trembled as she got a knife and spatula from a drawer. "Would you like wine, tea, coffee? This is very light. I did throw together a fruit salad. Thought we'd sit out on the porch. I hope that will be all right."

"That would be lovely," I replied. "And coffee would be fine."

Distracted, she opened the freezer and got out a bag of Irish Creme, which she measured into the drip coffeemaker. I watched her without speaking. She was desperate. Husband and sons were not home. Her daughter was missing, the house empty and silent.

She did not begin to ask questions until we were on the porch, sliding glass doors open wide, the river curving beyond us glinting in the sun.

"What the dogs did, Dr. Scarpetta," she began, picking at her salad. "Can you offer an interpretation?"

I could, but I did not want to.

"Obviously, the one dog got upset. But the other one didn't?" Her observation was posed as a question.

The other dog, Salty, had indeed reacted very differently than Neptune had. After he sniffed the driver's seat, Gail hooked the lead on his harness and commanded, "Find." The dog took off like a greyhound. He snuffled across the exit ramp and up through the picnic area. Then he tugged Gail across the parking lot toward the Interstate and would have gotten a nose full of traffic had she not yelled, "Heel!" I had watched them trot along the wooded strip separating west lanes from east, then across pavement, heading straight for the rest stop opposite the one where Deborah's Jeep had been found. The bloodhound finally lost the scent in the parking lot.

"Am I to believe," Mrs. Harvey continued, "that whoever was driving Debbie's Jeep last got out, cut through the westbound rest stop, and crossed the Interstate? Then this person most likely got into a car parked in the eastbound rest stop and drove away?"

"That is one possible interpretation," I replied, picking at my quiche.

"What other possible interpretation is there, Dr. Scarpetta?"

"The bloodhound picked up a scent. As for the scent of who or what, I don't know. It could have been Deborah's scent, Fred's scent, the scent of a third person—"

"Her Jeep was sitting out there for hours," Mrs. Harvey interrupted, staring off at the river. "I suppose anybody could have gotten in to look for money, valuables. A hitchhiker, transient, someone on foot who crossed over to the other side of the Interstate afterward."

I did not remind her of the obvious. The police had found Fred Cheney's wallet in the glove compartment, complete with credit cards and thirty-five dollars cash. It did not appear that the young couples' luggage had been gone through. As far as anyone could tell, nothing was missing from the Jeep except its occupants and Deborah's purse.

"The way the first dog acted," she went on matter-of-factly. "I assume this is unusual. Something frightened him. Upset him, at any rate. A different smell—not the same scent the other dog picked up. The seat where Debbie may have been sitting . . ." Her voice trailed off as she met my eyes.

"Yes. It appears that the two dogs picked up different scents."

"Dr. Scarpetta, I'm asking you to be direct with me." Her voice trembled. "Don't spare my feelings. Please. I know the dog wouldn't have gotten so upset unless there was a reason. Certainly, your work has exposed you to search-and-rescue efforts, to bloodhounds. Have you ever seen this before, the way the dog reacted?"

I had. Twice. Once was when a bloodhound sniffed a car trunk that, as it turned out, had been used to transport a murder victim whose body had been found inside a Dumpster. The other was when a scent led to an area along a hiking trail where a woman had been raped and shot.

What I said was "Bloodhounds tend to have strong reactions to pheromonal scents."

"I beg your pardon?" She looked bewildered.

"Secretions. Animals, insects, secrete chemicals. Sex attractants, for example," I dispassionately explained. "You're familiar with dogs marking their territory or attacking when they smell fear?"

She just stared at me.

"When someone is sexually aroused, anxious, or afraid, there are various hormonal changes that occur in the body. It is theorized that scent-discriminating animals, such as bloodhounds, can smell the pheromones, or chemicals, that special glands in our bodies secrete—"

She cut me off. "Debbie complained of cramps shortly before Michael, Jason, and I left for the beach. She had just started her period. Could that explain . . . ? Well, if she were sitting in the passenger's seat, perhaps this was the scent the dog picked up?"

I did not reply. What she was suggesting could not account for the dog's extreme distress.

"It's not enough." Pat Harvey looked away from me and twisted the linen napkin in her lap. "Not enough to explain why the dog started whining, the fur stood up on his back. Oh, dear God. It's like the other couples, isn't it?"

"I can't say that."

"But you're thinking it. The police are thinking it. If it hadn't been on everybody's mind from the start, you never would have been called yesterday. I want to know what happened to them. To those other couples."

I said nothing.

"According to what I've read," she pushed, "you were present at every scene, called there by the police."

"I was."

Reaching into a pocket of her blazer, she withdrew a folded sheet of legal paper and smoothed it open.

"Bruce Phillips and Judy Roberts," she began to brief me, as if I needed it. "High school sweethearts who disappeared two and a half years ago on June first when they drove away from a friend's house in Gloucester and never arrived at their respective homes. The next morning Bruce's Camaro was found abandoned off U.S. Seventeen, keys in the ignition, doors unlocked, and windows rolled down. Ten weeks later, you were called to a wooded area one mile east of the York River State Park, where hunters had discovered two partially skeletonized bodies facedown in the leaves, approximately four miles from where Bruce's car had been found ten weeks earlier."

I recalled that it was at this time VICAP was asked by local police to assist. What Marino, Wesley, and the detective from Gloucester did not know was that a second couple had been reported missing in July, a month after Bruce and Judy had vanished.

"Next we have Jim Freeman and Bonnie Smyth." Mrs. Harvey glanced up at me. "They disappeared the last Saturday in July after a pool party at the Freemans' Providence Forge home. Late that evening Jim gave Bonnie a ride home, and the following day a Charles City police officer found Jim's Blazer abandoned some ten miles from the Freeman home. Four months after that, on November twelfth, hunters in West Point found their bodies. . . ."

What I suspected she did not know, I thought, unpleasantly, was that despite my repeated requests, I was not given copies of the confidential sections of the police reports, scene photographs, or inventories of evidence. I attributed the apparent lack of cooperation to what had become a multijurisdictional investigation.

Mrs. Harvey continued relentlessly. In March of the following year, it happened again. Ben Anderson had driven from Arlington to meet his girlfiend, Carolyn Bennett, at her family's home in Stingray Point on the Chesapeake Bay. They pulled away from the Andersons' house shortly before seven o'clock to begin the drive back to Old Dominion University in Norfolk, where they were juniors. The next night a state trooper contacted Ben's parents and reported that their son's Dodge pickup truck had been found abandoned on the shoulder of I-64, approximately five miles east of Buckroe Beach. Keys were in the ignition, the doors unlocked, and Carolyn's pocketbook was beneath the passenger's seat. Their partially skeletonized bodies were discovered six months later during deer season in a wooded area three miles south of Route 199 in York County. This time, I did not even get a copy of the police report.

When Susan Wilcox and Mike Martin disappeared this past February, I found out about it from the morning newspaper. They were heading to Mike's house in Virginia Beach to spend spring break together when, like the couples before them, they vanished. Mike's blue van was found abandoned along the Colonial Parkway near Williamsburg, a white handkerchief tied to the antenna signaling engine trouble that did not exist when the police went over the van later. On May 15 a father and son out turkey hunting discovered the couples' decomposed bodies in a wooded area between Route 60 and I-64 in James City County.

I remembered, once again, packing up bones to send to the Smithsonian's forensic anthropologist for one final look. Eight young people, and despite the countless hours I had spent on each one of them, I could not determine how or why they had died.

"If, God forbid, there is a next time, don't wait until the bodies turn up," I finally had instructed Marino. "Let me know the minute the car is found."

"Yo. May as well start autopsying the cars since the bodies ain't telling us nothing," he had said, trying unsuccessfully to be funny.

"In all cases," Mrs. Harvey was saying, "doors were unlocked, keys in the ignition, there was no sign of a struggle, and it did not appear anything was stolen. The MOs were basically the same."

She folded her notes and slipped them back into a pocket.

"You're well informed" was all I said. I didn't ask, but presumed she had gotten her staff to research the previous cases.

"My point is, you've been involved since the beginning," she said. "You examined all of the bodies. And yet, as I understand it, you don't know what killed these couples."

"That's right. I don't know," I replied.

"You *don't know*? Or is it that you aren't saying, Dr. Scarpetta?"

Pat Harvey's career as a prosecutor in the federal system had earned her national respect, if not awe. She was gutsy and aggressive, and I felt as if her porch suddenly had turned into a courtroom.

"If I knew their cause of death, I would not have signed them out as undetermined," I said calmly.

"But you believe they were murdered."

"I believe that young, healthy people don't suddenly abandon their cars and die of natural causes in the woods, Mrs. Harvey."

"What about the theories? What do you have to say about those? I assume they aren't new to you."

They weren't.

Four jurisdictions and at least that many different detectives were involved, each one with numerous hypotheses. The couples, for example, were recreational drug users and had met up with a dealer selling some new and pernicious designer drug that could not be detected through routine toxicology tests. Or the occult was involved. Or the couples were all members of some secret society, their deaths actually suicide pacts.

"I don't think much of the theories I've heard," I told her.

"Why not?"

"My findings do not support them."

"What do your findings support?" she demanded. "What *findings?* Based on everything I've heard and read, you don't have any goddam findings."

A haze had dulled the sky, and a plane was a silver needle pulling a white thread beneath the sun. In silence I watched the vapor trail expand and begin to disperse. If Deborah and Fred had met up with the same fate as the others, we would not find them anytime soon.

"My Debbie has never taken drugs," she continued, blinking back tears. "She isn't into any weird religions or cults. She has a temper and sometimes gets depressed like every other normal teenager. But she wouldn't—" She suddenly stopped, struggling for control.

"You must try to deal with the here and now," I said quietly. "We don't know what has happened to your daughter. We don't know what has happened to Fred. It may be a long time before we know. Is there anything else you can tell me about her—about them? Anything at all that might help?"

"A police officer came by this morning," she replied with a deep, shaky breath. "He went inside her bedroom, took several articles of her clothing, her hairbrush. Said they were for the dogs, the clothes were, and he needed some of her hair to compare with any hairs they might find inside her Jeep. Would you like to see it? See her bedroom?"

Curious, I nodded.

I followed her up polished hardwood steps to the second floor. Deborah's bedroom was in the east wing, where she could see the sun rise and storms gather over the James. It was not the typical teenager's room. Furniture was Scandinavian, simple in design and built of gorgeous light teakwood. A comforter in shades of cool blue and green covered the queen-size bed, and beneath it was an Indian rug dominated by designs in rose and deep plum. Encyclopedias and novels filled a bookcase, and above the desk two shelves were lined with trophies and dozens of medals attached to bright cloth ribbons. On a top shelf was a large photograph of Deborah on a balance beam, back arched, hands poised like graceful birds, the expression on her face, like the details of her private sanctum, that of pure discipline and grace. I did not have to be Deborah Harvey's mother to know that this nineteen-year-old girl was special.

"Debbie picked out everything herself," Mrs. Harvey said as I looked around. "The furniture, rug, the colors. You'd never know she was in here days ago packing for school." She stared at suitcases and a trunk in a corner and cleared her throat. "She's so organized. I suppose she gets this from me." Smiling nervously, she added, "If I am nothing else, I am organized."

I remembered Deborah's Jeep. It was immaculate inside and out, luggage and other belongings arranged with deliberation.

"She takes wonderful care of her belongings," Mrs. Harvey went on, moving to the window. "I often worried that we indulged her too much. Her clothes, her car, money. Bob and I have had many discussions on the subject. It's difficult with my being in Washington. But when I was appointed last year, we decided, all of us did, that it was too much to uproot the family, and Bob's business is here. Easier if I took the apartment, came home on weekends when I could. Waited to see what would happen with the next election."

After a long pause, she went on. "I suppose what I'm trying to say is that I've never been very good at saying no to Debbie. It's difficult to be sensible when you want the best for your children. Especially when you remember your desires when you were their age, your insecurities about the way you dressed, your physical appearance. When you knew your parents couldn't afford a dermatologist, an orthodontist, a plastic surgeon. We have tried to exercise moderation." She crossed her arms at her waist. "Sometimes I'm not so sure we made the right choices. Her Jeep, for example. I was opposed to her having a car, but I didn't have the energy to argue. Typically, she was practical, wanting something safe that would get her around in any kind of weather."

Hesitantly, I inquired, "When you mention a plastic surgeon, are you referring to something specific concerning your daughter?"

"Large breasts are incompatible with gymnastics, Dr. Scarpetta," she said, not turning around. "By the time Debbie was sixteen she was overendowed. Not only was this rather embarrassing to her, but it interfered with her sport. The problem was taken care of last year."

"Then this photograph is recent," I said, for the Deborah I was looking at was an elegant sculpture of perfectly formed muscle, breasts and buttocks firm and small.

"It was taken last April in California."

When a person is missing and possibly dead, it is not uncommon for people like me to be interested in anatomical detail—whether it be a hysterectomy, a root canal, or scars from plastic surgery—that might assist in the identification of the body. They were the descriptions I reviewed in NCIC missing person forms. They were the mundane and very human features that I depended on, because jewelry and other personal effects, I had learned over the years, can't always be trusted.

"What I've just told you must never go outside this room," Mrs. Harvey said. "Debbie is very private. My family is very private."

"I understand."

"Her relationship with Fred," she continued. "It was private. Too private. As I'm sure you've noted, there are no photographs, no visible symbols of it. I have no doubt they have exchanged pictures, gifts, mementoes. But she has always been secretive about them. Her birthday was last February, for example. I noticed shortly after that she was wearing a gold ring on the pinky of her right hand. A narrow band with a floral design. She never said a word, nor did I ask. But I'm sure it was from him."

"Do you consider him a stable young man?"

Turning around, she faced me, eyes dark and distracted. "Fred is very intense, somewhat obsessive. But I can't say that he's unstable.

I really can't complain about him. I simply have worried that the relationship is too serious, too . . ." She looked away, groping for the right word. "Addictive. That's what comes to mind. It's as if they are each other's drug." Shutting her eyes, she turned away again and leaned her head against the window. "Oh, God. I wish we'd never bought her that goddam Jeep."

I did not comment.

"Fred doesn't have a car. She would have had no choice . . ." Her voice trailed off.

"She would have had no choice," I said, "but to drive with you to the beach."

"And this wouldn't have happened!"

Suddenly she walked out the door to the hallway. She could not bear to be inside her daughter's bedroom one moment longer, I knew, and I followed her down the stairs and to the front door. When I reached for her hand, she turned away from me as her tears fell.

"I'm so sorry." How many times on this earth would I say that?

The front door shut quietly as I went down the steps. While driving home I prayed that if I ever encountered Pat Harvey again, it would not be in my official capacity of chief medical examiner.

3

A week passed before I heard again from anyone connected to the Harvey-Cheney case, the investigation of which had gone nowhere, as far as I knew. Monday, when I was up to my elbows in blood in the morgue, Benton Wesley called. He wanted to talk to Marino and me without delay, and suggested we come for dinner.

"I think Pat Harvey's making him nervous," Marino said that evening. Tentative drops of rain bounced off his car windshield as we headed to Wesley's house. "I personally don't give a rat's ass if she talks to a palm reader, rings up Billy Graham or the friggin' Easter Bunny."

"Hilda Ozimek is not a palm reader," I replied.

"Half those Sister Rose joints with a hand painted on the sign are just fronts for prostitution."

"I'm aware of that," I said wearily.

He opened the ashtray, reminding me what a filthy habit smoking was. If he could cram one more butt in there, it would be a Guinness record.

"I take it you've heard of Hilda Ozimek, then," he went on.

"I really don't know much about her, except that I think she lives somewhere in the Carolinas."

"South Carolina."

"Is she staying with the Harveys?"

"Not anymore," Marino said, turning off the windshield wipers as the sun peeked out from behind clouds. "Wish the damn weather would make up its mind. She went back to South Carolina yesterday. Was flown in and out of Richmond in a private plane, if you can believe that."

"You mind telling me how anybody knows about it?" If I was surprised that Pat Harvey would resort to a psychic, I was even more surprised that she would tell anyone.

"Good question. I'm just telling you what Benton said when he called. Apparently, Broom Hilda found something in her crystal ball that got Mrs. Harvey mighty upset."

"What, exactly?"

"Beats the shit outta me. Benton didn't go into detail."

I did not inquire further, for discussing Benton Wesley and his tight-lipped ways made me ill at ease. Once he and I had enjoyed working together, our regard for each other respectful and warm. Now I found him distant, and I could not help but worry that the way Wesley acted toward me had to do with Mark. When Mark had walked away from me by taking an assignment in Colorado, he had also walked away from Quantico, where he had enjoyed the privileged role of running the FBI National Academy's Legal Training Unit. Wesley had lost his colleague and companion, and in his mind it was probably my fault. The bond between male friends can be stronger than marriage, and brothers of the badge are more loyal to each other than lovers.

A half hour later Marino turned off the highway, and soon after I lost track of the lefts and rights he took on rural routes that led us deeper into the country. Though I had met with Wesley many times in the past, it had always been at my office or his. I had never been invited to his house, located in the picturesque setting of Virginia farmland and forests, pastures surrounded by white fences, and barns and homes set back far from the roads. When we turned into his subdivision, we began to pass long driveways leading to large modern houses on generous lots, with European sedans parked before two- and three-car garages.

"I didn't realize there were Washington bedroom communities this close to Richmond," I commented.

"What? You've lived around here for four, five years and never heard of northern aggression?"

"If you were born in Miami, the Civil War isn't exactly foremost on your mind," I replied.

"I guess not. Hell, Miami ain't even in this country. Any place where they got to vote on whether English is the official language don't belong in the United States."

Marino's digs about my birthplace were nothing new.

Slowing down as he turned into a gravel drive, he said, "Not a bad crib, huh? Guess the feds pay a little better than the city."

The house was shingle style with a fieldstone foundation and projecting bay windows. Rosebushes lined the front, east and west wings shaded by old magnolias and oaks. As we got out, I began to look for clues that might give me more insight into Benton Wesley's private life. A basketball hoop was above the garage door, and near a woodpile covered with plastic was a red rider mower sprayed with cut grass. Beyond, I could see a spacious backyard impeccably landscaped with flower beds, azaleas, and fruit trees. Several chairs were arranged close together near a gas grill, and I envisioned Wesley and his wife having drinks and cooking steaks on leisurely summer nights.

Marino rang the bell. It was Wesley's wife who opened the door. She introduced herself as Connie.

"Ben went upstairs for a minute," she said, smiling, as she led us into a living room with wide windows, a large fireplace, and rustic furniture. I had never heard Wesley referred to as "Ben" before. Nor had I ever met his wife. She appeared to be in her mid-forties, an attractive brunette with hazel eyes so light they were almost yellow, and sharp features very much like her husband's. There was a gentleness about her, a quiet reserve suggesting strength of character and tenderness. The guarded Benton Wesley I knew, no doubt, was a very different man at home, and I wondered how familiar Connie was with the details of his profession.

"Will you have a beer, Pete?" she asked.

He settled into a rocking chair. "Looks like I'm the designated driver. Better stick to coffee."

"Kay, what may I get for you?"

"Coffee would be fine," I replied. "If it's no trouble."

"I'm so glad to finally meet you," she added sincerely. "Ben's spoken of you for years. He regards you very highly."

"Thank you." The compliment disconcerted me, and what she said next came as a shock.

"When we saw Mark last, I made him promise to bring you to dinner next time he comes to Quantico."

"That's very kind," I said, managing a smile. Clearly, Wesley did not tell her everything, and the idea that Mark might have been in Virginia recently without so much as calling me was almost more than I could bear.

When she left us for the kitchen, Marino asked, "You heard from him lately?"

"Denver's beautiful," I replied evasively.

"It's a bitch, you want my opinion. They bring him in from deep cover, hole him up in Quantico for a while. Next thing, they're sending his ass out west to work on something he can't tell nobody about. Just one more reason why you couldn't pay me enough to sign on with the Bureau."

I did not respond.

He went on, "The hell with your personal life. It's like they say, 'If Hoover wanted you to have a wife and kids, he would've issued them with your badge.' "

"Hoover was a long time ago," I said, staring out at trees churning in the wind. It looked like it was about to rain again, this time seriously.

"Maybe so. But you still ain't got a life of your own."

"I'm not sure any of us do, Marino."

"That's the damn truth," he muttered under his breath.

Footsteps sounded and then Wesley walked in, still in suit and tie, gray trousers and starched white shirt slightly wrinkled. He seemed tired and tense as he asked if we had been offered drinks.

"Connie's taking care of us," I said.

Lowering himself into a chair, he glanced at his watch. "We'll eat in about an hour." He clasped his hands in his lap.

"Haven't heard shit from Morrell," Marino started in.

"I'm afraid there are no new developments. Nothing hopeful," Wesley replied.

"Didn't assume there was. I'm just telling you that I ain't heard from Morrell."

Marino's face was expressionless, but I could sense his resentment. Though he had yet to voice any complaints to me, I suspected that he was feeling like a quarterback sitting out the season on the bench. He had always enjoyed a good rapport with detectives from other jurisdictions, and that, frankly, had been one of the strengths of VICAP's efforts in Virginia. Then the missing couple cases had begun. Investigators were no longer talking to each other. They weren't talking to Marino, and they weren't talking to me.

"Local efforts have been halted," Wesley informed him. "We didn't get any farther than the eastbound rest stop where the dog lost the scent. Only other thing to turn up is a receipt found inside the Jeep. It appears that Deborah and Fred stopped off at a Seven-Eleven after leaving the Harvey house in Richmond. They bought a six-pack of Pepsi and a couple other items."

"Then it's been checked out," Marino said, testily.

"The clerk on duty at the time has been located. She remembers them coming in. Apparently, this was shortly after nine P.M."

"And they was alone?" Marino inquired.

"It would seem so. No one else came in with them, and if there was someone waiting for them inside the Jeep, there was no evidence, based on their demeanor, to suggest that anything was wrong."

"Where is this Seven-Eleven located?" I asked.

"Approximately five miles west of the rest stop where the Jeep was found," Wesley replied.

"You said they bought a few other items," I said. "Can you be more specific?"

"I was getting to that," Wesley said. "Deborah Harvey bought a box of Tampax. She asked if she could use a bathroom, and was told it was against policy. The clerk said she directed them to the eastbound rest stop on Sixty-four."

"Where the dog lost the scent," Marino said, frowning as if confused. "Versus where the Jeep was found."

"That's right," Wesley replied.

"What about the Pepsi they bought?" I asked. "Did you find it?"

"Six cans of Pepsi were in the ice chest when the police went through the Jeep."

He paused as his wife appeared with our coffee and a glass of iced tea for him. She served us in gracious silence, then was gone. Connie Wesley was practiced at being unobtrusive.

"You're thinking they hit the rest stop so Deborah could take care of her problem, and that's where they met up with the squirrel who took them out," Marino interpolated.

"We don't know what happened to them," Wesley reminded us. "There are a lot of scenarios we need to consider."

"Such as?" Marino was still frowning.

"Abduction."

"As in kidnapping?" Marino was blatantly skeptical.

"You have to remember who Deborah's mother is."

"Yeah, I know. Mrs. Got-Rocks-the-Drug-Czar who got sworn in because the President wanted to give the women's movement something to chew on."

"Pete," Wesley said calmly, "I don't think it wise to dismiss her as a plutocratic figurehead or token female appointee. Though the position sounds more powerful than it really is because it was never given Cabinet status, Pat Harvey does answer directly to the President. She does, in fact, coordinate all federal agencies in the war against drug crimes."

"Not to mention her track record when she was a U.S. attorney," I added. "She was a strong supporter of the White House's efforts to make drug-related murders and attempted murders punishable by death. And she was quite vocal about it."

"Her and a hundred other politicians," Marino said. "Maybe I'd be more concerned if she was one of these liberals wanting to legalize the shit. Then I'd have to wonder about some right-wing Moral Majority type who thinks God's told him to snatch Pat Harvey's kid."

"She's been very aggressive," Wesley said, "succeeded in getting convictions on some of the worst in the lot, has been instrumental in getting important bills passed, has withstood death threats, and several years ago even had her car bombed—"

"Yeah, an unoccupied Jag parked at the country club. And it made her a hero," Marino interrupted.

"My point," Wesley went on patiently, "is that she's made her share of enemies, especially when it comes to the efforts she's directed at various charities."

"I've read something about that," I said, trying to recall the details.

"What the public knows at present is just a scratch on the surface," Wesley said. "Her latest efforts have been directed at ACTMAD. The American Coalition of Tough Mothers Against Drugs."

"You gotta be kidding," Marino said. "That's like saying UNICEF's dirty."

I did not volunteer that I sent money to ACTMAD every year and considered myself an enthusiastic supporter.

Wesley went on, "Mrs. Harvey has been gathering evidence to prove that ACTMAD has been serving as a front for a drug cartel and other illegal activities in Central America."

"Geez," Marino said, shaking his head. "Good thing I don't give a dime to nobody except the FOP."

"Deborah and Fred's disappearance is perplexing because it seems connected to the other four couples," Wesley said. "But this could also be deliberate, someone's attempt to make us assume there is a link, when in fact there may not be. We may be dealing with a serial killer. We may be dealing with something else. Whatever the case, we want to work this as quietly as possible."

"So I guess what you're waiting for now is a ransom note or something, huh?" Marino said. "You know, some Central American thugs will return Deborah to her mother for a price."

"I don't think that's going to happen, Pete," Wesley replied. "It may be worse than that. Pat Harvey is due to testify in a congressional hearing early next year—and again, this all has to do with the illegitimate charities. There isn't anything much worse that could have happened right now than to have her daughter disappear."

My stomach knotted at the thought. Professionally, Pat Harvey did not seem particularly vulnerable, having enjoyed a spotless reputation throughout her career. But she was also a mother. The welfare of her children would be more precious to her than her own life. Her family was her Achilles' heel.

"We can't dismiss the possibility of political kidnapping," Wesley remarked, staring out at his yard thrashed by the wind.

Wesley had a family, too. The nightmare was that a crime family boss, a murderer, someone Wesley had been instrumental in bringing down would go after Wesley's wife or children. He had a sophisticated burglar alarm system in his house and an intercom outside the front door. He had chosen to live in the far-removed setting of the Virginia countryside, telephone number unlisted, address never given to reporters or even to most of his colleagues and acquaintances. Until today, even I had not known where he lived, but had assumed his home was closer to Quantico, perhaps in McLean or Alexandria.

Wesley said, "I'm sure Marino's mentioned to you this business about Hilda Ozimek."

I nodded. "Is she genuine?"

"The Bureau has used her on a number of occasions, though we don't like to admit it. Her gift, power, whatever you want to call it, is quite genuine. Don't ask me to explain. This sort of phenomenon goes beyond my immediate experience. I can tell you, however, that on one occasion she helped us locate a Bureau plane that had gone down in the mountains of West Virginia. She also predicted Sadat's assassination, and we might have had a little more forewarning about the attempt on Reagan had we listened to her words more carefully."

"You're not going to tell me she predicted Reagan's shooting," Marino said.

"Almost to the day. We didn't pass along what she'd said. Didn't, well, take it seriously, I suppose. That was our mistake, weird as it may seem. Ever since, whenever she says anything, the Secret Service wants to know."

"The Secret Service reading horoscopes, too?" Marino asked.

"I believe that Hilda Ozimek would consider horoscopes rather generic. And as far as I know, she doesn't read palms," Wesley said pointedly.

"How did Mrs. Harvey find out about her?" I asked.

"Possibly from someone within the Justice Department," Wesley said. "In any event, she flew the psychic to Richmond on Friday and apparently was told a number of things that have succeeded in making her . . . well, let's just say that I'm viewing Mrs. Harvey as a loose cannon. I'm concerned that her activities may prove to do a lot more harm than good."

"What exactly did this psychic tell her?" I wanted to know.

Wesley looked levelly at me and replied, "I really can't go into that. Not now."

"But she discussed it with you?" I inquired. "Pat Harvey volunteered to you that she had resorted to a psychic?"

"I'm not at liberty to discuss it, Kay," Wesley said, and the three of us were silent for a moment.

It went through my mind that Mrs. Harvey had not divulged this information to Wesley. He had found out in some other way.

"I don't know," Marino finally said. "Could be a random thing. I don't want to count that out."

"We can't count anything out," Wesley said firmly.

"It's been going on for two and a half years, Benton," I said.

"Yeah," Marino said. "A friggin' long time. Still strikes me as the work of some squirrel out there who fixes on couples, a jealousy-type thing because he's a loser, can't have relationships and hates other people who can."

"Certainly that's one strong possibility. Someone who routinely cruises around looking for young couples. He may frequent lovers' lanes, rest stops, the watering holes where kids park. He may go through a lot of dry runs before he strikes, then replay the homicides for months before the urge to kill again becomes irresistible and the perfect opportunity presents itself. It may be coincidence—Deborah Harvey and Fred Cheney may simply have been in the wrong place at the wrong time."

"I'm not aware there's evidence to suggest that any of the couples were parking, engaged in sexual activity, when they met up with an assailant," I pointed out.

Wesley did not respond.

"And other than Deborah and Fred, the other couples didn't appear to have pulled off at a rest stop or any other sort of 'watering hole,' as you put it," I went on. "It appears they were en route to some destination when something happened to make them pull off the road and either let someone in their car or get into this person's vehicle."

"The killer cop theory," Marino muttered. "Don't think I haven't heard it before."

"It could be someone posing as a cop," Wesley replied. "Certainly that would account for the couples pulling over and, perhaps, getting into someone else's car for a routine license check or whatever. Anybody can walk into a uniform store and buy a bubble light, uniform, badge, you name it. Problem with that is a flashing light draws attention. Other motorists notice it, and if there is a real cop in the area, he's likely to at least slow down, perhaps even pull over to offer assistance. So far, there hasn't been a single report of anyone noticing a traffic stop that might have occurred in the area and at the time that these kids disappeared."

"You would also have to wonder why wallets and purses would be left inside their cars—with the exception of Deborah Harvey, whose purse has not been found," I said. "If the young people were told to get inside a so-called police vehicle for a routine traffic violation, then why would they leave car registrations and driver's licenses behind? These are the first items an officer asks to see, and when you get inside his car, you have these personal effects with you."

"They may not have gotten into this person's vehicle willingly, Kay," Wesley said. "They think they're being stopped by a police officer, and when the guy walks up to their window, he pulls out a gun, orders them into his car."

"Risky as shit," Marino argued. "If it was me, I'd throw the damn car in gear and floorboard it the hell out of there. Always the chance someone driving by might see something, too. I mean, how do you force two people at gunpoint into your car on four, maybe five different occasions and not have anyone passing by notice a goddam thing?"

"A better question," Wesley said, looking unemphatically at me, "is how do you murder eight people without leaving any evidence, not so much as a nick on a bone or a bullet found somewhere near the bodies?"

"Strangulation, garroting, or throats cut," I said, and it was not the first time he had pressed me on this. "The bodies have all been badly decomposed, Benton. And I want to remind you that the cop theory implies the victims got inside the assailant's vehicle. Based on the scent the bloodhound followed last weekend, it seems plausible that if someone did something bad to Deborah Harvey and Fred Cheney, this individual may have driven off in Deborah's Jeep, abandoned it at the rest stop, and then taken off on foot across the Interstate."

Wesley's face was tired. Several times now he had rubbed his temples as if he had a headache. "My purpose in talking to both of you is that there may be some angles to this thing that require us to act very carefully. I'm asking for direct and open channels among the three of us. Absolute discretion is imperative. No loose talk to reporters, no divulging of information to anyone, not to close friends, relatives, other medical examiners, or cops. And no radio transmissions." He looked at both of us. "I want to be land lined immediately if and when Deborah Harvey's and Fred Cheney's bodies are found. And if Mrs. Harvey tries to get in touch with either of you, direct her to me."

"She's already been in contact," I said.

"I'm aware of that, Kay," Wesley replied without looking at me.

I did not ask him how he knew, but I was unnerved and it showed.

"Under the circumstances, I can understand your going to see her," he added. "But it's best if it doesn't happen again, better you don't discuss these cases with her further. It only causes more problems. It goes beyond her interfering with the investigation. The more she gets involved, the more she may be endangering herself."

"What? Because she turns up dead?" Marino asked skeptically.

"More likely because she ends up out of control, irrational."

Wesley's concern over Pat Harvey's psychological well-being may have been valid, but it seemed flimsy to me. And I could not help but worry as Marino and I were driving back to Richmond after dinner that the reason Wesley had wanted to see us had nothing to do with the welfare of the missing couple.

"I think I'm feeling handled," I finally confessed as the Richmond skyline came into view.

"Join the club," Marino said irritably.

"Do you have any idea what's really going on here?"

"Oh, yeah," he replied, punching in the cigarette lighter. "I got a suspicion, all right. I think the Friggin' Bureau of Investigation's caught a whiff of something that's going to make someone who counts look bad. I got this funny feeling someone's covering his ass, and Benton's caught in the middle."

"If he is, then so are we."

"You got it, Doc."

It had been three years since Abby Turnbull had appeared in my office doorway, arms laden with fresh-cut irises and a bottle of exceptional wine. That had been the day when she had come to say good-bye, having given the Richmond *Times* notice. She was on her way to work in Washington as a police reporter for the *Post*. We had promised to keep in touch as people always do. I was ashamed I could not remember the last time I had called or written her a note.

"Do you want me to put her through?" Rose, my secretary, was asking. "Or should I take a message?"

"I'll talk to her," I said. "Scarpetta," I announced out of habit before I could catch myself.

"You still sound so damn *chiefly,*" the familiar voice said.

"Abby! I'm sorry." I laughed. "Rose told me it was you. As usual, I'm in the middle of about fifty other things, and I think I've completely lost the art of being friendly on the phone. How are you?"

"Fine. If you don't count the fact that the homicide rate in Washington has tripled since I moved up here."

"A coincidence, I hope."

"Drugs." She sounded nervous. "Cocaine, crack, and semiautomatics. I always thought a beat in Miami would be the worst. Or maybe New York. But our lovely nation's capital is the worst."

I glanced up at the clock and jotted the time on a call sheet. Habit again. I was so accustomed to filling out call sheets that I reached for the clipboard even when my hair-dresser called.

"I was hoping you might be free for dinner tonight," she said.

"In Washington?" I asked, perplexed.

"Actually, I'm in Richmond."

I suggested dinner at my house, packed up my briefcase, and headed out to the grocery store. After much deliberation as I pushed the cart up and down aisles, I selected two tenderloins and the makings for salad. The afternoon was beautiful. The thought of seeing Abby was improving my mood. I decided that an evening spent with an old friend was a good excuse to brave cooking out again.

When I got home, I began to work quickly, crushing fresh garlic into a bowl of red wine and olive oil. Though my mother had always admonished me about "ruining a good steak," I was spoiled by my own culinary skills. Honestly, I made the best marinade in town, and no cut of meat could resist being improved by it. Rinsing Boston lettuce and draining it on paper towels, I sliced mushrooms, onions, and the last Hanover tomato as I fortified myself to tend to the grill. Unable to put off the task any longer, I stepped out onto the brick patio.

For a moment, I felt like a fugitive on my own property as I surveyed the flower gardens and trees of my backyard. I fetched a bottle of 409 and a sponge and began vigorously to scrub the outdoor furniture before taking a Brillo pad to the grill, which I had not used since the Saturday night in May when Mark and I last had been together. I attacked sooty grease until my elbows hurt. Images and voices invaded my mind. Arguing. Fighting. Then a retreat into angry silence that ended with making frantic love.

I almost did not recognize Abby when she arrived at my front door shortly before six-thirty. When she had worked the police beat in Richmond, her hair had been to her shoulders and streaked with gray, giving her a washed-out, gaunt appearance that made her seem older than her forty-odd years. Now the gray was gone. Her hair was cut short and smartly styled to emphasize the fine bones of her face and her eyes, which were two different shades of green, an irregularity I had always found intriguing. She wore a dark blue silk suit and ivory silk blouse, and carried a sleek black leather briefcase.

"You look very Washingtonian," I said, giving her a hug.

"It's *so good* to see you, Kay."

She remembered I liked Scotch and had brought a bottle of Glenfiddich, which we wasted no time in uncorking. Then we sipped drinks on the patio and talked nonstop as I lit the grill beneath a dusky late summer sky.

"Yes, I do miss Richmond in some ways," she was explaining. "Washington is exciting, but the pits. I indulged myself and bought a Saab, right? It's already been broken into once, had the hubcaps stolen, the hell beaten out of the doors. I pay a hundred and fifty bucks a month to park the damn thing, and we're talking four blocks from my apartment. Forget parking at the *Post*. I walk to work and use a staff car. Washington's definitely not Richmond." She added a little too resolutely, "But I don't regret leaving."

"You're still working evenings?" Steaks sizzled as I placed them on the grill.

"No. It's somebody else's turn. The young reporters race around after dark and I follow up during the day. I get called after hours only if something really big goes down."

"I've been keeping up with your byline," I told her. "They sell the *Post* in the cafeteria. I usually pick it up during lunch."

"I don't always know what you're working on," she confessed. "But I'm aware of some things."

"Explaining why you're in Richmond?" I ventured, as I brushed marinade over the meat.

"Yes. The Harvey case."

I did not reply.

"Marino hasn't changed."

"You've talked to him?" I asked, glancing up at her.

She replied with a wry smile, "Tried to. And several other investigators. And, of course, Benton Wesley. In other words, forget it."

"Well, if it makes you feel any better, Abby, nobody's talking much to me, either. And that's off the record."

"This entire conversation is off the record, Kay," she said seriously. "I didn't come to see you because I wanted to pick your brain for my story." She paused. "I've been aware of what's been going on here in Virginia. I was a lot more concerned about it than my editor was until Deborah Harvey and her boyfriend disappeared. Now it's gotten hot, real hot."

"I'm not surprised."

"I'm not quite sure where to begin." She looked unsettled. "There are things I've not told anybody, Kay. But I have a sense that I'm walking on ground somebody doesn't want me on."

"I'm not sure I understand," I said, reaching for my drink.

"I'm not sure I do, either. I ask myself if I'm imagining things."

"Abby, you're being cryptic. Please explain."

Taking a deep breath as she got out a cigarette, she replied, "I've been interested in the deaths of these couples for a long time. I've been doing some investigating, and the reactions I've gotten from the beginning are odd. It's gone beyond the usual reluctance I often run into with the police. I bring up the subject and people practically hang up on me. Then this past June, the FBI came to see me."

"I beg your pardon?" I stopped basting and looked hard at her.

"You remember that triple homicide in Williamsburg? The mother, father, and son shot to death during a robbery?"

"Yes."

"I was working on a feature about it, and had to drive to Williamsburg. As you know, when you get off Sixty-four, if you turn right you head toward Colonial Williamsburg, William and Mary. But if you turn left off the exit ramp, in maybe two hundred yards you dead-end at the entrance of Camp Peary. I wasn't thinking. I took the wrong turn."

"I've done that once or twice myself," I admitted.

She went on, "I drove up to the guard booth and explained I'd taken a wrong turn. Talk about a creepy place. God. All these big warning signs saying things like 'Armed Forces Experimental Training Activity,' and 'Entering This Facility Signifies Your Consent to the Search of Your Person and Personal Property.' I was half expecting a SWAT team of Neanderthals in camouflage to bolt out of the bushes and haul me away."

"The base police are not a friendly lot," I said, somewhat amused.

"Well, I wasted no time getting the hell out of there," Abby said, "and, in truth, forgot all about it until four days later when two FBI agents appeared in the lobby of the *Post* looking for me. They wanted to know what I'd been doing in Williamsburg, why I'd driven to Camp Peary. Obviously, my plate number had been recorded on film and traced back to the newspaper. It was weird."

"Why would the FBI be interested?" I asked. "Camp Peary is CIA."

"The CIA has no enforcement powers in the United States. Maybe that's why. Maybe the jerks were really CIA agents posing as FBI. Who can say what the hell is going on when you're dealing with those spooks? Besides, the CIA has never admitted that Camp Peary is its main training facility, and the agents never mentioned the CIA when they interrogated me. But I knew what they were getting at, and they knew I knew."

"What else did they ask?"

"Basically, they wanted to know if I was writing something about Camp Peary, maybe trying to sneak in. I told them if I had intended to sneak in, I would have been a little more *covert* about it than driving straight to the guard booth, and though I wasn't currently working on anything about, and I quote, 'the CIA,' maybe now I ought to consider it."

"I'm sure that went over well," I said dryly.

"The guys didn't bat an eye. You know the way they are."

"The CIA is paranoid, Abby, especially about Camp Peary. State police and emergency medical helicopters aren't allowed to fly over it. Nobody violates that airspace or gets beyond the guard booth without being cleared by Jesus Christ."

"Yet you've made that same wrong turn before, as have hundreds of tourists," she reminded me. "The FBI's never come looking for you, have they?"

"No. But I don't work for the *Post*."

I removed the steaks from the grill and she followed me into the kitchen. As I served the salads and poured wine, she continued to talk.

"Ever since the agents came to see me, peculiar things have been happening."

"Such as?"

"I think my phones are being tapped."

"Based on what?"

"It started with my phone at home. I'd be talking to someone and hear something. This has also happened at work, especially of late. A call will be transferred, and I have this strong sense that someone else is listening in. It's hard to explain." She nervously rearranged her silverware. "A static, a noisy silence, or however you want to describe it. But it's there."

"Any other peculiar things?"

"Well, there was something several weeks ago. I was standing out in front of a People's Drug Store off Connecticut, near Dupont Circle. A source was supposed to meet me there at eight P.M., then we were going to find some place quiet to have dinner and talk. And I saw this man. Clean-cut, dressed in a windbreaker and jeans, nice looking. He walked by twice during the fifteen minutes I was standing on the corner, and I caught a glimpse of him again later when my appointment and I were going into the restaurant. I know it sounds crazy, but I had the feeling I was being followed."

"Had you ever seen this man before?"

She shook her head.

"Have you seen him since?"

"No," she said. "But there's something else. My mail. I live in an apartment building. All the mailboxes are downstairs in the lobby. Sometimes I get things with postmarks that don't make sense."

"If the CIA were tampering with your mail, I can assure you that you wouldn't know about it."

"I'm not saying my mail *looks* tampered with. But in several instances, someone—my mother, my literary agent—will swear they mailed something on a certain day, and when I finally get it, the date on the postmark is inconsistent with what it should be. Late. By days, a week. I don't know." She paused. "I probably would just assume it had to do with the ineptitude of the postal service, but with everything else that's been going on, it's made me wonder."

"Why would anyone be tapping your phone, tailing you, or tampering with your mail?" I asked the critical question.

"If I knew that, maybe I could do something about it." She finally got around to eating. "This is wonderful." Despite the compliment, she didn't appear the least bit hungry.

"Any possibility," I suggested bluntly, "that your encounter with these FBI agents, the episode at Camp Peary, might have made you paranoid?"

"Obviously it's made me paranoid. But look, Kay. It's not like I'm writing another *Veil* or working on a Watergate. Washington is one shoot-out after another, the same old shit. The only big thing brewing is what's going on here. These murders, or possible murders, of these couples. I start poking around and run into trouble. What do you think?"

"I'm not sure." I uncomfortably recalled Benton Wesley's demeanor, his warnings from the night before.

"I know the business about the missing shoes," Abby said.

I did not respond or show my surprise. It was a detail that, so far, had been kept from reporters.

"It's not exactly normal for eight people to end up dead in the woods without shoes and socks turning up either at the scenes or inside the abandoned cars." She looked expectantly at me.

"Abby," I said quietly, refilling our wineglasses, "you know I can't go into detail about these cases. Not even with you."

"You're not aware of anything that might clue me in as to what I'm up against?"

"To tell you the truth, I probably know less than you do."

"That tells me something. The cases have been going on for two and a half years, and you may know less than I do."

I remembered what Marino said about somebody "covering his ass." I thought of Pat Harvey and the congressional hearing. My fear was kicking in.

Abby said, "Pat Harvey is a bright star in Washington."

"I'm aware of her importance."

"There's more to it than what you read in the papers, Kay. In Washington, what parties you get invited to mean as much as votes. Maybe more. When it comes to prominent people included on the elite guest lists, Pat Harvey is right up there with the First Lady. It's been rumored that come the next presidential election, Pat Harvey may successfully conclude what Geraldine Ferraro started."

"A vice-presidential hopeful?" I asked dubiously.

"That's the gossip. I'm skeptical, but if we have another Republican President, I personally think she's at least got a shot at a Cabinet appointment or maybe even becoming the next Attorney General. Providing she holds together."

"She's going to have to work very hard at holding herself together through all this."

"Personal problems can definitely ruin your career," Abby agreed.

"They can, if you let them. But if you survive them, they can make you stronger, more effective."

"I know," she muttered, staring at her wineglass. "I'm pretty sure I never would have left Richmond if it hadn't been for what happened to Henna."

Not long after I had taken office in Richmond, Abby's sister, Henna, was murdered. The tragedy had brought Abby and me together professionally. We had become friends. Months later she had accepted the job at the *Post*.

"It still isn't easy for me to come back here," Abby said. "In fact, this is my first time since I moved. I even drove past my old house this morning and was halfway tempted to knock on the door, see if the current owners would let me in. I don't know why. But I wanted to walk through it again, see if I could handle going upstairs to Henna's room, replace that horrible last image of her with something harmless. It didn't appear that anyone was home. And it probably was just as well. I don't think I could have brought myself to do it."

"When you're truly ready, you'll do it," I said, and I wanted to tell her about my using the patio this evening, about how I had not been able to before now. But it sounded like such a small accomplishment, and Abby did not know about Mark.

"I talked to Fred Cheney's father late this morning," Abby said. "Then I went to see the Harveys."

"When will your story run?"

"Probably not until the weekend edition. I've still got a lot of reporting to do. The paper wants a profile of Fred and Deborah and anything else I can come up with about the investigation—especially any connection to the other four couples."

"How did the Harveys seem to you when you talked to them earlier today?"

"Well, I really didn't talk to him, to Bob. As soon as I arrived, he left with his sons. Reporters are not his favorite people, and I have a feeling being 'Pat Harvey's husband' gets to him. He never gives interviews." She pushed her half-eaten steak away and reached for her cigarettes. Her smoking was a lot worse than I remembered it. "I'm worried about Pat. She looks as if she's aged ten years in the last week. And it was strange. I couldn't shake the sensation she knows something, has already formulated her own theory about what's happened to her daughter. I guess that's what made me most curious. I'm wondering if she's gotten a threat, a note, some sort of communication from whomever's involved. And she's refusing to tell anyone, including the police."

"I can't imagine she would be that unwise."

"I can," Abby said. "I think if she thought there was any chance Deborah might return home unharmed, Pat Harvey wouldn't tell God what was going on."

I got up to clear the table.

"I think you'd better make some coffee," Abby said. "I don't want to fall asleep at the wheel."

"When do you need to head out?" I asked, loading the dishwasher.

"Soon. I've got a couple of places to go before I drive back to Washington."

I glanced over at her as I filled the coffeepot with water.

She explained, "A Seven-Eleven where Deborah and Fred stopped after they left Richmond—"

"How did you know about that?" I interrupted her.

"I managed to pry it out of the tow truck operator who hung around the rest stop, waiting to haul away the Jeep. He overheard the police discussing a receipt they found in a wadded-up paper bag. It required one hell of a lot of trouble, but I managed to figure out which Seven-Eleven and what clerk would have been working around the time Deborah and Fred would have stopped in. Someone named Ellen Jordan works the four-to-midnight shift Monday through Friday."

I was so fond of Abby, it was easy for me to forget that she had won more than her share of investigative reporting awards for a very good reason.

"What do you expect to find out from this clerk?"

"Ventures like this, Kay, are like looking for the prize inside a box of Crackerjacks. I don't know the answers—in fact, I don't even know the questions—until I start digging."

"I really don't think you should wander around out there alone late at night, Abby."

"If you'd like to ride shotgun," she replied, amused, "I'd love the company."

"I don't think that's a very good idea."

"I suppose you're right," she said.

I decided to do it anyway.

4

The illuminated sign was visible half a mile before we reached the exit, a "7-Eleven" glowing in the dark. Its cryptic red-and-green message no longer meant what it said, for every 7-Eleven I knew of was open twenty-four hours a day. I could almost hear what my father would say.

"Your grandfather left Verona for *this*?"

That was his favorite remark when he would read the morning paper, shaking his head in disapproval. It was what he said when someone with a Georgia accent treated us as if we weren't "real Americans." It was what my father would mumble when he heard tales of dishonesty, "dope," and divorce. When I was a child in Miami, he owned a small neighborhood grocery and was at the dinner table every night talking about his day and asking about ours. His presence in my life was not long. He died when I was twelve. But I was certain that were he still here, he would not appreciate convenience stores. Nights, Sundays, and holidays were not to be spent working behind a counter or eating a burrito on the road. Those hours were for family.

Abby checked her mirrors again as she turned off on the exit. In less than a hundred feet, she was pulling into the 7-Eleven's parking lot, and I could tell she was relieved. Other than a Volkswagen near the double glass front doors, it seemed we were the only customers.

"Coast is clear so far," she observed, switching off the ignition. "Haven't passed a single patrol car, unmarked or otherwise, in the last twenty miles."

"At least not that you know of," I said.

The night was hazy, not a star in sight, the air warm but damp. A young man carrying a twelve-pack of beer passed by us as we went inside the air-conditioned coolness of America's favorite fixes, where video games flashed bright lights in a corner and a young woman was restocking a cigarette rack behind the counter. She didn't look a day over eighteen, her bleached blonde hair billowing out in a frizzy aura around her head, her slight figure clad in an orange-and-white-checked tunic and a pair of tight black jeans. Her fingernails were long and painted bright red, and when she turned around to see what we wanted, I was struck by the hardness of her face. It was as if she had skipped training wheels and gone straight to a Harley-Davidson.

"Ellen Jordan?" Abby inquired.

The clerk looked surprised, then wary. "Yeah? So who wants to know?"

"Abby Turnbull." Abby presented her hand in a very businesslike fashion. Ellen Jordan shook it limply. "From Washington," Abby added. "The *Post.*"

"What *Post?*"

"The *Washington Post,*" Abby said.

"Oh." Instantly, she was bored. "We already carry it. Right over there." She pointed to a depleted stack near the door.

There was an awkward pause.

"I'm a *reporter* for the *Post,*" Abby explained.

Ellen's eyes lit up. "No kidding?"

"No kidding. I'd like to ask you a few questions."

"You mean for a story?"

"Yes. I'm doing a story, Ellen. And I really need your help."

"What do you want to know?" She leaned against the counter, her serious expression reflecting her sudden importance.

"It's about the couple that came in here Friday night a week ago. A young man and woman. About your age. They came in shortly after nine P.M., bought a six-pack of Pepsi, several other items."

"Oh. The ones missing," she said, animated now. "You know, I shoulda never told 'em to go to that rest stop. But one of the first things they tell us when we're hired is nobody gets to use the bathroom. Personally, I wouldn't mind, especially not when the girl and boy came in. I felt so sorry for her. I mean, I sure understood."

"I'm sure you did," Abby said sympathetically.

"It was sort of embarrassing," Ellen went on. "When she bought the Tampax and asked if she could please use the bathroom, her boyfriend standing right there. Wow, I sure do wish I'd let her now."

"How did you know he was her boyfriend?" Abby asked.

For an instant, Ellen looked confused. "Well, I just assumed. They was looking around in here together, seemed to like each other a lot. You know how people act. You can tell if you're paying attention. And when I'm in here all hours by myself, I get pretty good at telling about people. Take married couples. Get 'em all the time, on a trip, kids in the car. Most of 'em come in here and I can tell they're tired and not getting along good. But the two you're talking about, they was real sweet with each other."

"Did they say anything else to you, other than needing to find a rest room?"

"We talked while I was ringing them up," Ellen replied. "Nothing special. I said the usual. 'Nice night for driving,' and 'Where ya headin'?' "

"And did they tell you?" Abby asked, taking notes.

"Huh?"

Abby glanced up at her. "Did they tell you where they were heading?"

"They said the beach. I remember that because I told 'em they was lucky. Seems whenever everybody else's heading off to fun places, I'm always stuck right here. Plus, me and my boyfriend had just broke up. It was getting to me, you know?"

"I understand." Abby smiled kindly. "Tell me more about how they were acting, Ellen. Anything jump out at you?"

She thought about this, then said, "Uh-uh. They was real nice, but in a hurry. I guess because she wanted to find a bathroom pretty bad. Mostly I remember how polite they was. You know, people come in here all the time wanting to use the bathroom and get nasty when I tell 'em they can't."

"You mentioned you directed them to the rest stop," Abby said. "Do you remember exactly what you told them?"

"Sure. I told 'em there's one not too far from here. Just get back on Sixty-four East"—she pointed—"and they'd see it in about five, ten minutes, couldn't miss it."

"Was anybody else in here when you told them this?"

"People were in and out. Lot of folks on the road." She thought for a minute. "I know there was a kid in back playing Pac Man. Same little creep always in here."

"Anybody else who might have been near the counter when the couple was?" Abby asked.

"There was this man. He came in right after the couple came in. Was looking through the magazines, ended up buying a cup of coffee."

"Was this while you were talking to the couple?" Abby relentlessly pursued the details.

"Yeah. I remember because he was real friendly and said something to the guy about the Jeep being a nice one. The couple drove up in a red Jeep. One of those fancy kinds. It was parked right in front of the doors."

"Then what happened?"

Ellen sat down on the stool in front of the cash register. "Well, that was pretty much it. Some other customers came in. The guy with the coffee left, and then maybe five minutes later, the couple left, too."

"But the man with the coffee—he was still near the counter when you were directing the couple to the rest stop?" Abby wanted to know.

She frowned. "It's hard to remember. But I think he was looking through the magazines when I was telling them that. Then it seems like the girl went off down one of the aisles to find what she needed, got back to the counter just as the man was paying for his coffee."

"You said the couple left maybe five minutes after the man did," Abby went on. "What were they doing?"

"Well, it took a couple minutes," she replied. "The girl set a six-pack of Coors on the counter, you know, and I had to card her, saw she was under twenty-one, so I couldn't sell her beer. She was real nice about it, sort of laughed. I mean, all of us were laughing about it. I don't take it personal. Hell, I used to try it, too. Anyway, she ended up buying a six-pack of sodas. Then they left."

"Can you describe this man, the one who bought the coffee?"

"Not real good."

"White or black?"

"White. Seems like he was dark. Black hair, maybe brown. Maybe in his late twenties, early thirties."

"Tall, short, fat, thin?"

Ellen stared off toward the back of the store. "Medium height, maybe. Sort of well built but not big, I think."

"Beard or mustache?"

"Don't think so. . . . Wait a minute." Her face lit up. "His hair was short. Yeah! In fact, I remember it passed through my mind he looked military. You know, there's a lot of military types around here, come in all the time on their way to Tidewater."

"What else made you think he might be military?" Abby asked.

"I don't know. But maybe it was just his way. It's hard to explain, but when you've seen enough military guys, it gets to where you can pick 'em out. There's just something about 'em. Like tattoos, for example. A lot of 'em have tattoos."

"Did this man have a tattoo?"

Her frown turned to disappointment. "I didn't notice."

"How about the way he was dressed?"

"Uhhhh . . ."

"A suit and tie?" Abby asked.

"Well, he wasn't in a suit and tie. Nothing fancy. Maybe jeans or dark pants. He might've been wearing a zip-up jacket. . . . Gee, I really can't be sure."

"Do you, by chance, remember what he was driving?"

"No," she said with certainty. "I never saw his car. He must've parked off to the side."

"Did you tell the police all this when they came to talk to you, Ellen?"

"Yeah." She was eyeing the parking lot out front. A van had just pulled up. "I told 'em pretty much the same things I told you. Except for some of the stuff I couldn't remember then."

When two teenage boys sauntered in and headed straight for the video games, Ellen returned her attention to us. I could tell she had nothing more to say and was beginning to entertain doubts about having said too much.

Apparently, Abby was getting the same message. "Thank you, Ellen," she said, backing away from the counter. "The story will run on Saturday or Sunday. Be sure you watch for it."

Then we were out the door.

"Time to get the hell out of here before she starts screaming that everything was *off the record*."

"I doubt she'd even know what the term meant," I replied.

"What surprises me," Abby said, "is that the cops didn't tell her to keep her mouth shut."

"Maybe they did but she couldn't resist the possibility of seeing her name in print."

The I-64 East rest stop where the clerk had directed Deborah and Fred was completely deserted when we pulled in.

Abby parked in front, near a cluster of newspaper vending machines, and for several minutes we sat in silence. A small holly tree directly in front of us was silver in the car's headlights, and lamps were smudges of white in the fog. I couldn't imagine getting out to use the rest room were I alone.

"Creepy," Abby muttered under her breath. "God. I wonder if it's always this deserted on a Tuesday night, or if the news releases have scared people away."

"Possibly both," I replied. "But you can be sure it wasn't deserted the Friday night Deborah and Fred pulled in."

"They may have been parked right about where we are," she mused. "Probably people all over the place, since it was the beginning of the Labor Day weekend. If this is where they encountered someone bad, then he must be a brash son of a bitch."

"If there were people all over the place," I said, "then there would have been cars all over the place."

"Meaning?" She lit a cigarette.

"Assuming this is where Deborah and Fred encountered someone, and assuming that for some reason they let him in the Jeep, then what about his car? Did he arrive here on foot?"

"Not likely," she replied.

"If he drove in," I went on, "and left his car parked out here, that wasn't going to work very well unless there was a lot of traffic."

"I see what you're suggesting. If his was the only car in this lot, and it remained out here for hours late at night, chances are a trooper might have spotted it and called it in."

"That's a big chance to take if you're in the process of committing a crime," I added.

She thought for a moment. "You know, what bothers me is that the entire scenario is random but not random. Deborah and Fred's stopping at the rest stop was random. If they happened to encounter someone bad here—or even inside the Seven-Eleven, such as the guy buying coffee—that seems random. But there's premeditation, too. Forethought. If someone abducted them, it seems like he knew what he was doing."

I did not respond.

I was thinking about what Wesley had said. A political connection. Or an assailant who went through a lot of dry runs. Assuming that the couple had not chosen to disappear, then I did not see how the outcome could be anything but tragic.

Abby put the car in gear.

It wasn't until we were on the Interstate and she was setting the cruise control that she spoke again. "You think they're dead, don't you?"

"Are you asking for a quote?"

"No, Kay. I'm not asking for a quote. You want to know the truth? Right now I don't give a damn about this story. I just want to know what the hell's going on."

"Because you're worried about yourself."

"Wouldn't you be?"

"Yes. If I thought my phones were tapped, that I was being tailed, I would be worried, Abby. And speaking of worried, it's late. You're exhausted. It's ridiculous for you to drive back to Washington tonight."

She glanced over at me.

"I've got plenty of room. You can head out first thing in the morning."

"Only if you've got an extra toothbrush, something I can sleep in, and don't mind if I pillage your bar."

Leaning back in the seat, I shut my eyes and muttered, "You can get drunk, if you want. In fact, I might just join you."

When we walked into my house at midnight, the telephone started ringing, and I answered it before my machine could.

"Kay?"

At first, the voice did not register because I was not expecting it. Then my heart began to pound.

"Hello, Mark," I said.

"I'm sorry to call so late—"

I could not keep the tension out of my voice as I interrupted. "I have company. I'm sure you remember my mentioning my friend Abby Turnbull, with the *Post?* She's here staying the night. We've been having a wonderful time catching up."

Mark did not respond. After a pause, he said, "Maybe it would be easier for you to call me, when it suits."

When I hung up, Abby was staring at me, startled by my obvious distress.

"Who in God's name was that, Kay?"

My first months at Georgetown I was so overwhelmed by law school and feelings of alienation that I kept my own counsel and distance from others. I was already an M.D., a middle-class Italian from Miami with very little exposure to the finer things in life. Suddenly I found myself cast among the brilliant and beautiful, and though I am not ashamed of my heritage, I felt socially common.

Mark James was one of the privileged, a tall, graceful figure, self-assured and self-contained. I was aware of him long before I knew his name. We first met in the law library between dimly lit shelves of books, and I will never forget his intense green eyes as we began to discuss some tort I cannot recall. We ended up drinking coffee in a bar and talking until early in the morning. After that, we saw each other almost every day.

For a year we did not sleep, it seemed, for even when we slept together our lovemaking did not permit many hours of rest. No matter how much we got of each other it was never enough, and foolishly, typically, I was convinced we would be together forever. I refused to accept the chill of disappointment that settled over the relationship during our second year. When I graduated wearing someone else's engagement ring, I had convinced myself that I had gotten over Mark, until he mysteriously reappeared not so long ago.

"Maybe Tony was a safe harbor," Abby considered, referring to my ex-husband as we drank Cognac in my kitchen.

"Tony was practical," I replied. "Or so it seemed at first."

"Makes sense. I've done it before in my own pathetic love life." She reached for her snifter. "I'll have some passionate fling, and God knows there have been few and they never last long. But when it ends, I'm like a wounded soldier limping home. I wind up in the arms of some guy with the charisma of a slug who promises to take care of me."

"That's the fairy tale."

"Right out of Grimm's," she agreed, bitterly. "They say they'll take care of you, but what they mean is they want you to be there fixing dinner and washing their shorts."

"You've just described Tony to a T," I said.

"What ever happened to him?"

"I haven't talked to him in too many years to count."

"People at least ought to be friends."

"He didn't want to be friends," I said.

"Do you still think about him?"

"You can't live six years with somebody and not think about him. That doesn't mean I want to be with Tony. But a part of me will always care about him, hope he's doing well."

"Were you in love with him when you got married?"

"I thought I was."

"Maybe so," Abby said. "But it sounds to me as if you never stopped loving Mark."

I refilled our glasses. Both of us were going to feel like hell in the morning.

"I find it incredible that you got together again after so many years," she went on. "And no matter what's happened, I suspect Mark has never stopped loving you, either."

When he came back into my life, it was as if we had lived in foreign countries during our years apart, the languages of our pasts indecipherable to each other. We communicated openly only in the dark. He did tell me he had married and his wife had been killed in an automobile accident. I later found out he had forsaken his law practice and signed on with the FBI. When we were together it was euphoric, the most wonderful days I had known since our first year at Georgetown. Of course, it did not last. History has a mean habit of repeating itself.

"I don't suppose it's his fault he was transferred to Denver," Abby was saying.

"He made a choice," I said. "And so did I."

"You didn't want to go with him?"

"I'm the reason he requested the assignment, Abby. He wanted a separation."

"So he moves across the country? That's rather extreme."

"When people are angry, their behavior can be extreme. They can make big mistakes."

"And he's probably too stubborn to admit he made a mistake," she said.

"He's stubborn, I'm stubborn. Neither of us win any prizes for our skills in compromising. I have my career and he has his. He was in Quantico and I was here—that got old fast, and I had no intention of leaving Richmond and he had no intention of moving to Richmond. Then he started contemplating going back on the street, transferring to a field office somewhere or taking a position at Headquarters in D.C. On and on it went, until it seemed that all we did was fight." I paused, groping to explain what would never be clear. "Maybe I'm just set in my ways."

"You can't be with someone and continue to live as you always did, Kay."

How many times had Mark and I said that to each other? It got to where we rarely said anything new.

"Is maintaining your autonomy worth the price you're paying, the price both of you are paying?"

There were days when I was no longer so sure, but I did not tell Abby this.

She lit a cigarette and reached for the bottle of Cognac.

"Did the two of you ever try counseling?"

"No."

What I told her was not entirely true. Mark and I had never gone to counseling, but I had gone alone and was still seeing a psychiatrist, though infrequently now.

"Does he know Benton Wesley?" Abby asked.

"Of course. Benton trained Mark in the Academy long before I came to Virginia," I replied. "They're very good friends."

"What's Mark working on in Denver?"

"I have no idea. Some special assignment."

"Is he aware of the cases here? The couples?"

"I would assume so." Pausing, I asked, "Why?"

"I don't know. But be careful what you say to Mark."

"Tonight was the first time he's called in months. Obviously, I say very little to him."

She got up and I led her to her room.

As I gave her a gown and showed her the bath, she went on, the effects of the Cognac becoming apparent, "He'll call again. Or you're going to call him. So be careful."

"I'm not planning on calling him," I said.

"You're just as bad as he is, then," she said. "Both of you hard-headed and unforgiving as hell. So there. That's my assessment of the situation, whether you like it or not."

"I have to be at the office by eight," I said. "I'll make sure you're up by seven."

She hugged me good night and kissed my cheek.

The following weekend I went out early and bought the *Post* and could not find Abby's story. It did not come out the next week or the week after that, and I thought this strange. Was Abby all right? Why had I not heard a word from her since our visit in Richmond?

In late October I called the *Post*'s newsroom.

"I'm sorry," said a man who sounded harried. "Abby's on leave. Won't be back until next August."

"Is she still in town?" I asked, stunned.

"Got no idea."

Hanging up, I flipped through my address book and tried her home number. I was answered by a machine. Abby did not return that call or any of the others I made during the next few weeks. It wasn't until shortly after Christmas that I began to realize what was going on. On Monday, January sixth, I came home to find a letter in my mailbox. There was no return address, but the handwriting was unmistakable. Opening the envelope, I discovered inside a sheet of yellow legal paper scribbled with "FYI. Mark," and a short article clipped from a recent issue of the *New York Times.* Abby Turnbull, I read with disbelief, had signed a book contract to write about the disappearance of Fred Cheney and Deborah Harvey, and the "frightening parallels" between their cases and those of four other couples in Virginia who had vanished and turned up dead.

Abby had warned me about Mark, and now he was warning me about her. Or was there some other reason for his sending me the article?

For a long interval I sat in my kitchen, tempted to leave an outraged message on Abby's machine or to call Mark. I finally decided to call Anna, my psychiatrist.

"You feel betrayed?" she asked when I got her on the phone.

"To put it mildly, Anna."

"You've known Abby is writing a newspaper story. Is writing a book so much worse?"

"She never told me she was writing a book," I said.

"Because you feel betrayed doesn't mean you truly have been," Anna said. "This is your perception at the moment, Kay. You will have to wait and see. And as for why Mark sent you the article, you may have to wait and see about that, too. Perhaps it was his way of reaching out."

"I'm wondering if I should consult a lawyer," I said. "See if there's something I should do to protect myself. I have no idea what might end up in Abby's book."

"I think it would be wiser to take her words at face value," Anna advised. "She said your conversations were off the record. Has she ever betrayed you before?"

"No."

"Then I suggest you give her a chance. Give her an opportunity to explain. Besides," she added, "I'm not sure how much of a book she can write. There have been no arrests, and there is no resolution as to what happened to the couple. They have yet to turn up."

The bitter irony of that remark would hit me exactly two weeks later, on January twentieth, when I was on the Capitol grounds waiting to see what happened when a bill authorizing the Forensic Science Bureau to create a DNA data bank went before the Virginia General Assembly.

I was returning from the snack bar, cup of coffee in hand, when I spotted Pat Harvey, elegant in a navy cashmere suit, a zip-up black leather portfolio under her arm. She was talking to several delegates in the hall, and glancing my way, she immediately excused herself.

"Dr. Scarpetta," she said, offering her hand. She looked relieved to see me, but drawn and stressed.

I wondered why she wasn't in Washington, and then she answered my unspoken question. "I was asked to lend my support to Senate Bill One-thirty," she said, smiling nervously. "So I suppose both of us are here today for the same reason."

"Thank you. We need all the support we can get."

"I don't think you have a worry," she replied.

She was probably right. The testimony of the national drug policy director and the publicity it would generate would put considerable pressure on the Courts of Justice Committee.

After an awkward silence, with both of us glancing at the people milling about, I asked her quietly, "How are you?"

For an instant her eyes teared up. Then she gave me another quick, nervous smile and stared off down the hall. "If you'll please excuse me, I see someone I need to have a word with."

Pat Harvey was barely out of earshot when my pager went off. A minute later I was on the phone.

"Marino's on his way," my secretary was explaining.

"So am I," I said. "Get my scene kit, Rose. Make sure everything's in order. Flashlight, camera, batteries, gloves."

"Will do."

Cursing my heels and the rain, I hurried down steps and along Governor Street, the wind tearing at my umbrella as I envisioned Mrs. Harvey's eyes that split second when they had revealed her pain. Thank God she had not been standing there when my pager had sounded its dreadful alert.

5

The odor was noticeable from a distance. Heavy drops of rain smacked loudly against dead leaves, the sky as dark as dusk, winter-bare trees drifting in and out of the fog.

"Jesus," Marino muttered as he stepped over a log. "They must be ripe. No other smell like it. Always reminds me of pickled crabs."

"It gets worse," promised Jay Morrell, who was leading the way.

Black mud sucked at our feet, and every time Marino brushed against a tree I was showered with freezing water. Fortunately, I kept a hooded Gore-tex coat and heavy rubber boots in the trunk of my state car for scenes like this one. What I had been unable to find were my thick leather gloves, and it was impossible to navigate through the woods and keep branches out of my face if my hands were in my pockets.

I had been told there were two bodies, suspected to be a male and a female. They were less than four miles from the rest stop where Deborah Harvey's Jeep had been found last fall.

You don't know that it's them, I thought to myself with every step.

But when we reached the perimeter of the scene, my heart constricted. Benton Wesley was talking to an officer working a metal detector, and Wesley would not have been summoned unless the police were sure. He stood with military erectness, exuding the quiet confidence of a man in charge. He seemed bothered neither by the weather nor by the stench of decomposing human flesh. He was not looking around and taking in the details the way Marino and I were, and I knew why. Wesley had already looked around. He had been here long before I was called.

The bodies were lying next to each other, facedown in a small clearing about a quarter of a mile from the muddy logging road where we had left our cars. They were so badly decomposed they were partially skeletonized. The long bones of arms and legs protruded like dirty gray sticks from rotted clothing scattered with leaves. Skulls were detached and had been nudged or rolled, probably by small predators, a foot or two away.

"Did you find their shoes and socks?" I asked, not seeing either.

"No, ma'am. But we found a purse." Morrell pointed to the body on the right. "Forty-four dollars and twenty-six cents in it. Plus a driver's license, Deborah Harvey's driver's license." He pointed again, adding, "We're assuming the body there on the left is Cheney."

Yellow crime scene tape glistened wetly against the dark bark of trees. Twigs snapped beneath the feet of men moving about, their voices blending into an indistinguishable babble beneath the relentless, dreary rain. Opening my medical bag, I got out a pair of surgical gloves and my camera.

For a while I did not move as I surveyed the shrunken, almost fleshless bodies before me. Determining the sex and race of skeletal remains cannot always be done at a glance. I would not swear to anything until I could look at the pelves, which were obscured by what appeared to be dark blue or black denim jeans. But based on the characteristics of the body to my right—small bones, small skull with small mastoids, nonprominent brow ridge, and strands of long blondish hair clinging to rotted fabric—I had no reason to think anything other than white female. The size of her companion, the robustness of the bones, prominent brow ridge, large skull, and flat face were good for white male.

As for what might have happened to the couple, I could not tell. There were no ligatures indicating strangulation. I saw no obvious fractures or holes that might have meant blows or bullets. Male and female were quietly together in death, the bones of her left arm slipped under his right as if she had been holding on to him in the end, empty eye sockets gaping as rain rolled over their skulls.

It wasn't until I moved in close and got down on my knees that I noticed a margin of dark soil, so narrow it was barely perceptible, on either side of the bodies. If they had died Labor Day weekend, autumn leaves would not have fallen yet. The ground beneath them would be relatively bare. I did not like what was going through my mind. It was bad enough that the police had been tramping around out here for hours. Dammit. To move or disturb a body in any way before the medical examiner arrives is a cardinal sin, and every officer out here knew that.

"Dr. Scarpetta?" Morrell was towering over me, his breath smoking. "Was just talking to Phillips over there." He glanced in the direction of several officers searching thick underbrush about twenty feet east of us. "He found a watch and an earring, some change, all right about here where the bodies are. The interesting thing is, the metal detector kept going off. He had it right over the bodies and it was beeping. Could be from a zipper or something. Maybe a metal snap or button on their jeans. Thought you should know."

I looked up into his thin, serious face. He was shivering beneath his parka.

"Tell me what you did with the bodies in addition to running the metal detector over them, Morrell. I can see they've been moved. I need to know if this is the exact position they were in when they were discovered this morning."

"I don't know about when the hunters found them, though they claim they didn't get very close," he said, eyes probing the woods. "But yes, ma'am, this is the way they looked when we got here. All we did was check for personal effects, went into their pockets and her purse."

"I assume you took photographs before you moved anything," I said evenly.

"We started taking pictures as soon as we arrived."

Getting out a small flashlight, I began the hopeless task of looking for trace evidence. After bodies have been exposed to the elements for so many months, the chance of finding significant hairs, fibers, or other debris was slim to none. Morrell watched in silence, uneasily shifting his weight from one foot to the other.

"Have you found out anything else from your investigation that might be of assistance, assuming this is Deborah Harvey and Fred Cheney?" I asked, for I had not seen Morrell or talked to him since the day Deborah's Jeep had been found.

"Nothing but a possible drug connection," he said. "We've been told Cheney's roommate at Carolina was into cocaine. Maybe Cheney fooled around with cocaine too. That's one of the things we're considering, if maybe he and the Harvey girl met up with someone who was selling drugs and came out here."

That didn't make any sense.

"Why would Cheney leave the Jeep at a rest stop and go off with a drug dealer, taking Deborah with him, and come out here?" I asked. "Why not just buy the drugs at the rest stop and be on their way?"

"They may have come out here to party."

"Who in his right mind would come out here after dark to party or do anything else? And where are their shoes, Morrell? Are you suggesting they walked through the woods barefoot?"

"We don't know what happened to their shoes," he said.

"That's very interesting. So far, five couples have been found dead and we don't know what happened to their shoes. Not one shoe or sock has turned up. Don't you find that rather odd?"

"Oh, yes, ma'am. I think it's odd, all right," he said, hugging himself to get warm. "But right now I've got to work these two cases here without thinking about the other four couples. I've got to go with what I've got. And all I've got at the moment is a possible drug connection. I can't allow myself to get sidetracked by this serial murder business or who the girl's mother is, or I might be wrong and miss the obvious."

"I certainly wouldn't want you to miss the obvious."

He was silent.

"Did you find any drug paraphernalia inside the Jeep?"

"No. Nothing out here so far to suggest drugs, either. But we've got a lot of soil and leaves to go through—"

"The weather's awful. I'm not sure it's a good idea to begin sifting through the soil." I sounded impatient and irritable. I was put out with him. I was put out with the police. Water was trickling down the front of my coat. My knees hurt. I was losing feeling in my hands and feet. The stench was overpowering, and the loud smacking of the rain was getting on my nerves.

"We haven't started digging or using the sieves. Thought we might wait on that. It's too hard to see. The metal detector's all we've used so far, that and our eyes."

"Well, the more all of us walk around out here, the more we risk destroying the scene. Small bones, teeth, other things, get stepped on and pushed down into the mud." They had already been here for hours. It was probably too damn late to preserve the scene.

"So, you want to move them today or hold off until the weather clears?" he asked.

Under ordinary circumstances, I would have waited until the rain stopped and there was more light. When bodies have been in the woods for months, leaving them covered with plastic and in place for another day or two isn't going to make any difference. But when Marino and I had parked on the logging road, there were already several television news trucks waiting. Reporters were sitting in their cars, others braving the rain and trying to coax information out of police officers standing sentry. The circumstances were anything but ordinary. Though I had no right to tell Morrell what to do, by Code I had jurisdiction over the bodies.

"There are stretchers and body bags in the back of my car," I said, digging out my keys. "If you could have somebody get them, we'll move the bodies shortly and I'll take them on in to the morgue."

"Sure thing. I'll take care of it."

"Thanks." Then Benton Wesley was crouching next to me.

"How did you find out?" I asked. The question was ambiguous, but he knew what I meant.

"Morrell reached me in Quantico. I came right away." He studied the bodies, his angular face almost haggard in the shadow of his dripping hood. "You seeing anything that might tell us what happened?"

"All I can tell you at the moment is their skulls weren't fractured and they weren't shot in the head."

He did not respond, his silence adding to my tension.

I began unfolding sheets as Marino walked up, hands jammed into his coat pockets, shoulders hunched against the cold and rain.

"You're going to catch pneumonia," Wesley remarked, getting to his feet. "Is Richmond PD too cheap to buy you guys hats?"

"Shit," Marino said, "you're lucky they put gas in your damn car and furnish you with a gun. The squirrels in Spring Street got it better than we do."

Spring Street was the state penitentiary. It was true that it cost the state more money each year to house some inmates than a lot of police officers got paid for keeping them off the street. Marino loved to complain about it.

"I see the locals drug your ass out here from Quantico. Your lucky day," Marino said.

"They told me what they'd found. I asked if they'd called you yet."

"Yeah, well, they got around to it eventually."

"I can see that. Morrell told me he's never filled out a VICAP form. Maybe you can give him a hand."

Marino stared at the bodies, his jaw muscles flexing.

"We need to get this into the computer," Wesley went on as rain drummed the earth.

Tuning out their conversation, I arranged one of the sheets next to the female's remains and turned her on her back. She held together nicely, joints and ligaments still intact. In a climate like Virginia's, it generally takes at least a year of being exposed to the elements before a body is fully skeletonized, or reduced to disarticulated bones. Muscle tissue, cartilage, and ligaments are tenacious. She was petite, and I recalled the photograph of the lovely young athlete posed on a balance beam. Her shirt, I noted, was some sort of pullover, possibly a sweatshirt, and her jeans were zipped up and snapped. Unfolding the other sheet, I went through the same procedure with her companion. Turning over decomposed bodies is like turning over rocks. You never know what you'll find underneath, except that you can usually count on insects. My flesh crawled as several spiders skittered off, vanishing beneath leaves.

Shifting positions in a fruitless attempt to get more comfortable, I realized Wesley and Marino were gone. Kneeling alone in the rain, I began feeling through leaves and mud, searching for fingernails, small bones, and teeth. I noticed at least two teeth missing from one of the mandibles. Most likely, they were somewhere near the skulls. After fifteen or twenty minutes of this, I had recovered one tooth, a small transparent button, possibly from the male's shirt, and two cigarette butts. Several cigarette butts had been found at each of the scenes, though not all of the victims were known to smoke. What was unusual was that not one of the filters bore a manufacturer's brand mark or name.

When Morrell returned, I pointed this out to him.

"Never been to a scene where there aren't cigarette butts," he replied, and I wondered just how many scenes he could swear he had been to. Not many, I guessed.

"It's as if part of the paper has been peeled away or the end of the filter nearest the tobacco pinched off," I explained, and when this evoked no response from him, I dug in the mud some more.

Night was falling when we headed back to our cars, a somber procession of police officers gripping stretchers bearing bright orange body bags. We reached the narrow unpaved logging road as a sharp wind began to kick in from the north and the rain began to freeze. My dark blue state station wagon was equipped as a hearse. Fasteners in the plyboard floor in back locked stretchers into place so they did not slide around during transport. I positioned myself behind the wheel and buckled up as Marino climbed in, Morrell slammed shut the tailgate, and photographers and television cameramen recorded us on film. A reporter who wouldn't give up rapped on my window, and I locked the doors.

"God bless it. I hope like hell I ain't called to another one of these," Marino exclaimed, turning on the heat full blast.

I drove around several potholes.

"What a bunch of vultures." Eyeing his side mirror, he watched journalists scurrying into their cars. "Some asshole must've run his mouth over the radio. Probably Morrell. The dumb-ass. If he was in my squad, I'd send his ass back to traffic, get him transferred to the uniform room or information desk."

"You remember how to get back on Sixty-four from here?" I asked.

"Hang a left at the fork straight ahead. Shit." He cracked the window and got out his cigarettes. "Nothing like driving in a closed-up car with decomposed bodies."

Thirty miles later I unlocked the back door to the OCME and pushed a red button on the wall inside. The bay door made a loud grating noise as it opened, light spilling onto the wet tarmac. Backing in the wagon, I opened the tailgate. We slid out the stretchers and wheeled them inside the morgue as several forensic scientists got off the elevator and smiled at us without giving our cargo more than a glance. Body-shaped mounds on stretchers and gurneys were as common as the cinder-block walls. Blood drips on the floor and foul odors were unpleasantnesses you learned to step around and quietly hurry past.

Producing another key, I opened the padlock on the refrigerator's stainless-steel door, then went to see about toe tags and signing in the bodies before we transferred them to a double-decker gurney and left them for the night.

"You mind if I stop by tomorrow to see what you figure out about these two?" Marino asked.

"That would be fine."

"It's them," he said. "Gotta be."

"I'm afraid that's the way it looks, Marino. What happened to Wesley?"

"On his way back to Quantico, where he can prop his Florsheim shoes on top of his big desk and get the results over the phone."

"I thought you two were friends," I said warily.

"Yeah, well, life's funny like that, Doc. It's like when I'm supposed to go fishing. All the weather reports predict clear skies, and the minute I put the boat in the water it begins to friggin' rain."

"Are you on evening shift this weekend?"

"Not last I heard."

"Sunday night—how about coming over for dinner? Six, six-thirty?"

"Yeah, I could probably manage that," he said, looking away, but not before I caught the pain in his eyes.

I had heard his wife supposedly had moved back to New Jersey before Thanksgiving to take care of her dying mother. Since then I had had dinner with Marino several times, but he had been unwilling to talk about his personal life.

Letting myself into the autopsy suite, I headed for the locker room, where I always kept personal necessities and a change of clothes for what I considered hygienic emergencies. I was filthy, the stench of death clinging to my clothing, skin, and hair. I quickly stuffed my scene clothes inside a plastic garbage bag and taped a note to it instructing the morgue supervisor to drop it by the cleaners first thing in the morning. Then I got into the shower, where I stayed for a very long time.

One of many things Anna had advised me to do after Mark moved to Denver was to make an effort to counteract the damage I routinely inflicted upon my body.

"*Exercise.*" She had said that frightful word. "The endorphins relieve depression. You will eat better, sleep better, feel so much better. I think you should take up tennis again."

Following her suggestion had proved a humbling experience. I had scarcely touched a racket since I was a teenager, and though my backhand had never been good, over the decades it ceased to exist at all. Once a week I took a lesson late at night, when I was less likely to be subjected to the curious stares of the cocktail and happy hour crowd lounging in the observation gallery of Westwood Racquet Club's indoor facility.

After leaving the office, I had just enough time to drive to the club, dash into the ladies' locker room, and change into tennis clothes. Retrieving my racket from my locker, I was out on the court with two minutes to spare, muscles straining as I fell into leg stretches and bravely tried to touch my toes. My blood began to move sluggishly.

Ted, the pro, appeared from behind the green curtain shouldering two baskets of balls.

"After hearing the news, I didn't think I'd be seeing you tonight," he said, setting the baskets on the court and slipping out of his warm-up jacket. Ted, perennially tan and a joy to look at, usually greeted me with a smile and a wisecrack. But he was subdued tonight.

"My younger brother knew Fred Cheney. I knew him, too, though not well." Staring off at people playing several courts away, he said,

"Fred was one of the nicest guys I've ever met. And I'm not just saying that because he's . . . Well. My brother's really shook up about it." He bent over and picked up a handful of balls. "And it sort of bothers me, if you want to know the truth, that the newspapers can't get past who Fred was dating. It's like the only person who disappeared was Pat Harvey's daughter. And I'm not saying that the girl wasn't terrific and what happened to her isn't just as awful as what happened to him." He paused. "Well. I think you know what I mean."

"I do," I said. "But the other side of that is Deborah Harvey's family is being subjected to intense scrutiny, and they will never be permitted to grieve privately because of who Deborah's mother is. It's unfair and tragic any way you look at it."

Ted thought about this and met my eyes. "You know, I hadn't considered it that way. But you're right. I don't think being famous would be a whole lot of fun. And I don't think you're paying me by the hour to stand out here and talk. What would you like to work on tonight?"

"Ground strokes. I want you to run me corner to corner so I can remind myself how much I hate smoking."

"No more lectures from me on that subject." He moved to the center of the net.

I backed up to the baseline. My first forehand wouldn't have been half bad had I been playing doubles.

Physical pain is a good diversion, and the harsh realities of the day were pushed aside until the phone rang at home later as I was peeling off my wet clothes.

Pat Harvey was frantic. "The bodies they found today. I have to know."

"They have not been identified, and I have not examined them yet," I said, sitting on the edge of the bed and nudging off my tennis shoes.

"A male and a female. That's what I heard."

"So it appears at this point. Yes."

"Please tell me if there's *any* possibility it isn't them," she said.

I hesitated.

"Oh, God," she whispered.

"Mrs. Harvey, I can't confirm—"

She cut me off in a voice that was getting hysterical. "The police told me they found Debbie's purse, her driver's license."

Morrell, I thought. The half-brained bastard.

I said to her, "We can't make identifications solely from personal effects."

"She's my daughter!"

Next would follow threats and profanity. I had been through this before with the other parents who under ordinary circumstances were as civilized as Sunday school. I decided to give Pat Harvey something constructive to do.

"The bodies have not been identified," I repeated.

"I want to see her."

Not in a million years, I thought. "The bodies aren't visually identifiable," I said. "They're almost skeletonized."

Her breath caught.

"And depending on you, we might establish identity with certainty tomorrow or it might take days."

"What do you want me to do?" she asked shakily.

"I need X rays, dental charts, anything pertaining to Deborah's medical history that you can get your hands on."

Silence.

"Do you think you could track these down for me?"

"Of course," she said. "I'll see to it immediately."

I suspected she would have her daughter's medical records before sunrise, even if she had to drag half of the doctors in Richmond out of bed.

* * *

The following afternoon, I was removing the plastic cover from the OCME's anatomical skeleton when I heard Marino in the hall.

"I'm in here," I said loudly.

He stepped inside the conference room, a blank expression on his face as he stared at the skeleton, whose bones were wired together, a hook in the vertex of his skull attached to the top of an L-shaped bar. He stood a little taller than I was, feet dangling over a wooden base with wheels.

Gathering paperwork from a table, I said, "How about rolling him out for me?"

"You taking Slim for a stroll?"

"He's going downstairs, and his name's Haresh," I replied.

Bones and small wheels clattered quietly as Marino and his grinning companion followed me to the elevator, attracting amused glances from several members of my staff. Haresh did not get out very often, and as a rule, when he was spirited away from his corner, his abductor was not motivated by serious intent. Last June I had walked into my office on the morning of my birthday to find Haresh sitting in my chair, glasses and lab coat on, a cigarette clamped between his teeth. One of the more preoccupied forensic scientists from upstairs—or so I had been told—had walked past my doorway and said good morning without noticing anything odd.

"You're not going to tell me he talks to you when you're working down here," Marino said as the elevator doors shut.

"In his own way he does," I said. "I've found having him on hand is a lot more useful than referring to diagrams in *Gray's*."

"What's the story on his name?"

"Apparently, when he was purchased years ago, there was an Indian pathologist here named Haresh. The skeleton is also Indian. Male, fortyish, maybe older."

"As in Little Bighorn Indian or the other kind that paint dots on their foreheads?"

"As in the Ganges River in India," I said as we got out on the first floor. "The Hindus cast their dead upon the river, believing they will go straight to heaven."

"I sure as hell hope this joint ain't heaven."

Bones and wheels clattered again as Marino rolled Haresh into the autopsy suite.

On top of a white sheet covering the first stainless-steel table were Deborah Harvey's remains, gray dirty bones, clumps of muddy hair, and ligaments as tan and tough as shoe leather. The stench was relentless but not as overpowering, since I had removed her clothes. Her condition was made all the more pitiful by the presence of Haresh, who bore not so much as a scratch on his bleached white bones.

"I have several things to tell you," I said to Marino. "But first I want your promise that nothing leaves this room."

Lighting a cigarette, he looked curiously at me. "Okay."

"There's no question about their identities," I began, arranging clavicles on either side of the skull. "Pat Harvey brought in dental X rays and charts this morning—"

"In person?" he interrupted, surprised.

"Unfortunately," I said, for I had not expected Pat Harvey to deliver the records herself—a miscalculation on my part, and one I wasn't likely to forget.

"That must've created quite a stir," he said.

It had.

When she pulled up in her Jaguar, she had left it illegally parked by the curb and appeared full of demands and on the verge of tears. Intimidated by the presence of the famous public official, the receptionist let her in, and Mrs. Harvey promptly set off down the hall in search of me. I think she would have come down to the morgue had my administrator not intercepted her at the elevator and ushered her into my office, where I found her moments later. She was sitting rigidly in a chair, her face as white as chalk. On top of my desk were death certificates, case files, autopsy photographs, and an excised stab wound suspended in a small bottle of formalin tinted pink by blood. Hanging on the back of the door were bloodstained clothes I was intending to take upstairs when I made evidence rounds later in the day. Two facial reconstructions of unidentified dead females were perched on top of a filing cabinet like decapitated clay heads.

Pat Harvey had gotten more than she had bargained for. She had run head-on into the hard realities of this place.

"Morrell also brought me Fred Cheney's dental records," I said to Marino.

"Then it's definitely Fred Cheney and Deborah Harvey?"

"Yes," I said, and then I directed his attention to X rays clipped to a view box on the wall.

"That ain't what I think it is." A look of amazement passed over his face as he fixed on a radiopaque spot within the shadowy outline of lumbar vertebrae.

"Deborah Harvey was shot." I picked up the lumbar in question. "Caught right in the middle of the back. The bullet fractured the spinous process and the pedicles and lodged in the vertebral body. Right here." I showed him.

"I don't see it." He leaned closer.

"No, you can't see it. But you see the hole?"

"Yeah? I see a lot of holes."

"This is the bullet hole. The others are vascular foramina, holes for the vascular vessels that supply blood to bone and marrow."

"Where are the fractured pedestals you mentioned?"

"Pedicles," I said patiently. "I didn't find them. They would be in pieces and are probably still out there in the woods. An entrance and no exit. She was shot in the back versus the abdomen."

"You find a bullet hole in her clothes?"

"No."

On a nearby table was a white plastic tray in which I had placed Deborah's personal effects, including her clothing, jewelry, and red nylon purse. I carefully lifted up the sweatshirt, tattered, black, and putrid.

"As you can see," I pointed out, "the back of it, in particular, is in terrible shape. Most of the fabric's completely rotted away, torn by predators. The same goes for the waistband of her jeans in back, and that makes sense, since these areas of her clothing would have been bloody. In other words, the area of fabric where I would expect to have found a bullet hole is gone."

"What about distance? You got any idea about that?"

"As I've said, the bullet didn't exit. This would make me suspect we're not dealing with a contact gunshot wound. But it's hard to say. As for caliber, and again I'm conjecturing, I'm thinking a thirty-eight or better, based on the size of this hole. We won't know with certainty until I crack open the vertebra and take the bullet upstairs to the firearms lab."

"Weird," Marino said. "You haven't looked at Cheney yet?"

"He's been rayed. No bullets. But no, I haven't examined him yet."

"Weird," he said again. "It don't fit. Her being shot in the back don't fit with the other cases."

"No," I agreed. "It doesn't."

"So that's what killed her?"

"I don't know."

"What do you mean, you don't know?" He looked at me.

"This injury isn't immediately fatal, Marino. Since the bullet didn't go right on through, it didn't transect the aorta. Had it done so at this lumbar level, she would have hemorrhaged to death within minutes. What's significant is that the bullet had to have transected her cord, instantly paralyzing her from the waist down. And of course, blood vessels were hit. She was bleeding."

"How long could she have survived?"

"Hours."

"What about the possibility of sexual assault?"

"Her panties and brassiere were in place," I answered. "This doesn't mean that she wasn't sexually assaulted. She could have been allowed to put her clothes back on afterward, assuming she was assaulted before she was shot."

"Why bother?"

"If you're raped," I said, "and your assailant tells you to put your clothes back on, you assume you're going to live. A sense of hope serves to control you, make you do as you're told because if you struggle with him, he might change his mind."

"It don't feel right." Marino frowned. "I just don't think that's what happened, Doc."

"It's a scenario. I don't know what happened. All I can tell you with certainty is that I didn't find any articles of her clothing torn, cut, inside out, or unfastened. And as for seminal fluid, after so many months in the woods, forget it." Handing him a clipboard and a pencil, I added, "If you're going to hang around, you might as well scribe for me."

"You plan to tell Benton about this?" he asked.

"Not at the moment."

"What about Morrell?"

"Certainly, I'll tell him she was shot," I said. "If we're talking about an automatic or semiautomatic, the cartridge case may still be at the scene. If the cops want to run their mouths, that's up to them. But nothing's coming from me."

"What about Mrs. Harvey?"

"She and her husband know their daughter and Fred have been positively identified. I called the Harveys and Mr. Cheney as soon as I was sure. I will be releasing nothing further until I've concluded the examinations."

Ribs sounded like Tinker Toys quietly clacking together as I separated left from right.

"Twelve on each side," I began to dictate. "Contrary to legend, women don't have one more rib than men."

"Huh?" Marino looked up from the clipboard.

"Have you never read Genesis?"

He stared blankly at the ribs I had arranged on either side of the thoracic vertebrae.

"Never mind," I said.

Next I began looking for carpals, the small bones of the wrist that look very much like stones you might find in a creek bed or dig up in your garden. It is hard to sort left from right, and this is where the anatomical skeleton was helpful. Moving him closer, I propped his bony hands on the edge of the table and began comparing. I went through the same process with the distal and proximal phalanges, or bones of the fingers.

"Looks like she's missing eleven bones in her right hand and seventeen in her left," I reported.

Marino scribbled this down. "Out of how many?"

"There are twenty-seven bones in the hand," I replied as I worked. "Giving the hand its tremendous flexibility. It's what makes it possible for us to paint, play the violin, love each other through touch."

It is also what makes it possible for us to defend ourselves.

It was not until the following afternoon that I realized Deborah Harvey had attempted to ward off an assailant who had been armed with more than a gun. It had gotten considerably warmer out, the weather had cleared, and the police had been sifting through soil all day. At not quite four P.M., Morrell stopped by my office to deliver a number of small bones recovered from the scene. Five of them belonged to Deborah, and on the dorsal surface of her left proximal phalange—or the top of the shaft, the longest of the index finger bones—I found a half-inch cut.

The first question when I find injury to bone or tissue is whether it is pre- or postmortem. If one is not aware of the artifacts that can occur after death, he can make serious mistakes.

People who burn up in fires come in with fractured bones and epidural hemorrhages, looking for all practical purposes as if someone worked them over and then torched the house to disguise a homicide, when the injuries are actually postmortem and caused by extreme heat. Bodies washed up on the beach or recovered from rivers and lakes often look as if a deranged killer mutilated faces, genitals, hands, and feet, when fish, crabs, and turtles are to blame. Skeletal remains get gnawed, chewed on, and torn from limb to limb by rats, buzzards, dogs, and raccoons.

Predators of the four-legged, winged, or finned variety inflict a lot of damage, but blessedly, not until the poor soul is already dead. Then nature simply begins recycling. Ashes to ashes. Dust to dust.

The cut on Deborah Harvey's proximal phalange was too neat and linear to have been caused by tooth or claw, it was my opinion. But this still left much open to speculation and suspicion, including the inevitable suggestion that I might have nicked the bone myself with a scalpel at the morgue.

By Wednesday evening the police had released Deborah's and Fred's identities to the press, and within the next forty-eight hours there were so many calls that the clerks in the front office could not manage their regular duties because all they did was answer the phone. Rose was informing everyone, including Benton Wesley and Pat Harvey, that the cases were pending while I stayed in the morgue.

By Sunday night, there was nothing more I could do. Deborah's and Fred's remains had been defleshed, degreased, photographed from every angle, the inventory of their bones completed. I was packing them in a cardboard box when the buzzer went off in back. I heard the night watchman's footsteps down the hall and the bay door open. Then Marino was walking in.

"You sleeping down here or what?" he asked.

Glancing up at him, I was surprised to note that his overcoat and hair were wet.

"It's snowing." He pulled off his gloves and set his portable radio on the edge of the autopsy table where I was working.

"That's all I need," I said, sighing.

"Coming down like a bitch, Doc. Was driving by and saw your ride in the lot. Figured you'd been in this cave since the crack of dawn and had no idea."

It occurred to me as I tore off a long strip of tape and sealed the box. "I thought you weren't on evening shift this weekend."

"Yeah, and I thought you was having me in for dinner."

Pausing, I stared curiously at him. Then I remembered. "Oh, no," I muttered, glancing up at the clock. It was past eight P.M. "Marino, I'm so sorry."

"Don't matter. Had a couple of things to follow up on, anyway."

I always knew when Marino was lying. He wouldn't look me in the eye and his face got red. It wasn't coincidence that he had seen my car in the lot. He had been looking for me, and not simply because he wanted dinner. Something was on his mind.

Leaning against the table, I gave him my full attention.

"Thought you might want to know that Pat Harvey was in Washington over the weekend, went to see the Director," he said.

"Did Benton inform you of this?"

"Yo. He also said he'd been trying to get hold of you but you ain't returning his calls. The Drug Czar's complaining that you ain't returning her calls either."

"I'm not returning anybody's calls," I replied wearily. "I've been rather preoccupied, to say the least, and I don't have anything to release at this point."

Looking at the box on the table, he said, "You know Deborah was shot, a homicide. What are you waiting for?"

"I don't know what killed Fred Cheney or if there's any possibility drugs might have been involved. I'm waiting for tox reports, and I don't intend to release a thing until those are in and I've had a chance to talk to Vessey."

"The guy at the Smithsonian?"

"I'm seeing him in the morning."

"Hope you got four-wheel drive."

"You haven't explained the purpose of Pat Harvey's going to see the Director."

"She's accusing your office of stonewalling, says the FBI is stonewalling her, too. She's pissed. Wants her daughter's autopsy report, police reports, the whole nine yards, and is threatening to get a court order and raise hell if her demands aren't met right away."

"That's crazy."

"Bingo. But if you don't mind a little advice, Doc, I think you might consider calling Benton before the night's out."

"Why?"

"I don't want you getting burned, that's why."

"What are you talking about, Marino?" I untied my surgical gown.

"The more you avoid everybody right now, the more you're adding fuel to the fire. According to Benton, Mrs. Harvey's convinced there's some sort of cover-up and all of us are involved."

When I did not reply he said, "Are you listening?"

"Yes. I've listened to every word you said."

He picked up the box.

"Incredible to think there's two people inside this thing," he marveled.

It was incredible. The box wasn't much bigger than a microwave oven and weighed ten or twelve pounds. As he placed it in the trunk of my state car, I said under my breath, "Thank you for everything."

"Huh?"

I knew he'd heard me, but he wanted me to say it again.

"I appreciate your concern, Marino. I really do. And I'm so sorry about dinner. Sometimes I really screw up."

The snow was falling fast, and as usual, he wasn't wearing a hat. Cranking the engine and turning on the heat full blast, I looked up at him and thought how odd it was that I should find him such a comfort. Marino got on my nerves more than anyone I knew, and yet I could not imagine him not being around.

Locking my door, he said, "Yeah, well you owe me."

"Semifreddo di cioccolato."

"I love it when you talk dirty."

"A dessert. My specialty, you big jerk. Chocolate mousse with ladyfingers."

"Ladyfingers?" He stared pointedly in the direction of the morgue, feigning horror.

It seemed to take forever to get home. I crept along snow-covered roads, concentrating so fiercely my head was splitting by the time I was in my kitchen pouring myself a drink. Sitting at the table, I lit a cigarette and gave Benton Wesley a call.

"What have you found?" he asked immediately.

"Deborah Harvey was shot in the back."

"Morrell told me. Said the bullet was unusual. Hydra-Shok, nine millimeter."

"That's correct."

"What about her boyfriend?"

"I don't know what killed him. I'm waiting on tox results, and I need to confer with Vessey at the Smithsonian. I'm pending both cases for now."

"The longer you pend them, the better."

"I beg your pardon?"

"I'm saying that I'd like you to pend the cases for as long as possible, Kay. I don't want reports going out to anyone, not even to the parents, and especially not to Pat Harvey. I don't want anyone knowing that Deborah was shot—"

"Are you telling me that the Harveys don't know?"

"When Morrell informed me, I made him promise to keep the

information under wraps. So, no, the Harveys haven't been told. Uh, the police haven't told them. They know only that their daughter and Cheney are dead." He paused, adding, "Unless you've released something that I don't know about."

"Mrs. Harvey has tried to get hold of me a number of times, but I haven't talked to her or hardly anybody else during the past few days."

"Keep it that way," Wesley said firmly. "I'm asking you to release information only to me."

"There will come a point, Benton," I said just as firmly, "when I will have to release cause and manner of death. Fred's family, Deborah's family, are entitled to that by Code."

"Hold off as long as possible."

"Would you be so kind as to tell me why?"

Silence.

"Benton?" I was about to wonder if he was still on the line.

"Just don't do anything without conferring with me first." He hesitated again. Then, "I presume you're aware of this book Abby Turnbull is under contract to write."

"I saw something about it in the paper," I answered, getting angry.

"Has she contacted you again? Uh, recently?"

Again? How did Wesley know Abby had come to see me last fall? Damn you, Mark, I thought. When he had telephoned me, I had mentioned that Abby was with me that night.

"I haven't heard from her," I replied curtly.

6

Monday morning the road in front of my house was blanketed in deep snow, the sky gray and threatening more bad weather to come. I fixed a cup of coffee and debated the wisdom of my driving to Washington. On the verge of scrapping my plans, I called the state police and learned that I-95 North was clear, the snow tapering off to less than an inch by Fredericksburg. Deciding that my state car wasn't likely to make it out of my driveway, I loaded the cardboard box in my Mercedes.

As I turned off on the Interstate, I realized that if I had a wreck or were pulled over by the police, it wasn't going to be easy explaining why I was heading north in an unofficial car with human skeletons in the trunk. Sometimes flashing my medical examiner shield wasn't enough. I never would forget flying to California carrying a large briefcase packed with sadomasochistic sexual paraphernalia. The briefcase got as far as the X-ray scanner, and the next thing I knew airport security was squiring me away for what was nothing less than an interrogation. No matter what I said, they couldn't seem to get it through their heads that I was a forensic pathologist en route to the National Association of Medical Examiners' annual meeting, where I was to give a presentation on autoerotic asphyxiation. The handcuffs, studded collars, leather bindings, and other unseemly odds and ends were evidence from old cases and did not *belong* to me.

By ten-thirty I was in D.C. and had managed to find a parking place within a block of Constitution Avenue and Twelfth. I had not been to the Smithsonian's National Museum of Natural History since attending a forensic anthropology course there several years before. When I carried the cardboard box inside a lobby fragrant with potted orchids and noisy with the voices of tourists, I wished I could leisurely peruse dinosaurs and diamonds, mummy cases and mastodons, and never know the bleaker treasures housed within these walls.

Rising from ceiling to floor in every available inch of space not visible to guests were green wooden drawers containing, among other dead things, more than thirty thousand human skeletons. Bones of every description arrived by registered mail every week for Dr. Alex Vessey to examine. Some remains were archaeological, others turned out to be bear or beaver paws or the hydrocephalic skulls of calves, human-looking artifacts found along the wayside or turned up by plows, and feared, at first, to be what was left of a person who had met a violent end. Other parcels truly did contain bad news, the bones of someone murdered. In addition to being a natural scientist and curator, Dr. Vessey worked for the FBI and assisted people like me.

Gaining clearance from the unsmiling security guard, I clipped on my visitor's pass and headed for the brass elevator that took me up to the third floor. As I passed walls of drawers inside a dimly lit, crowded corridor, the sounds of people levels below looking at the great stuffed elephant faded. I began to feel claustrophobic. I remembered being so desperate for sensory input after eight hours of class inside this place that when I finally escaped at the end of the day, crowded sidewalks were welcome, the noise of traffic a relief.

I found Dr. Vessey where I had seen him last, inside a laboratory cluttered with steel carts bearing skeletons of birds and animals, teeth, femurs, mandibles. Shelves were covered with more bones and other unhappy human relics such as skulls and shrunken heads. Dr. Vessey, white haired and wearing thick glasses, was sitting behind his desk talking on the phone. While he concluded his call, I opened the box and got out the plastic envelope containing the bone from Deborah Harvey's left hand.

"The Drug Czar's daughter?" he asked right off, taking the envelope from me.

It seemed a strange question. But, in a way, it was correctly posed, for Deborah had been reduced to a scientific curiosity, a piece of physical evidence.

"Yes," I said as he took the phalange out of the envelope and began gently turning it under the light.

"I can tell you without hesitation, Kay, that this is not a postmortem cut. Though some old cuts can look fresh, fresh cuts can't look old," he said. "The inside of the cut is discolored from the environment in a manner consistent with the rest of the bone's surface. In addition, the way the lip of the cut is bent back tells me this wasn't inflicted on dead bone. Green bone bends. Dead bone doesn't."

"My conclusion exactly," I replied, pulling up a chair. "But you know the question will be asked, Alex."

"And it should be," he said, peering at me over the rim of his glasses. "You wouldn't believe the things that come through here."

"I suspect I would," I said, unpleasantly reminded that the degree of forensic competence dramatically varied from state to state.

"A coroner sent me a case a couple months ago, a chunk of soft tissue and bone he told me was a newborn child found in the sewer. The question was sex and race. The answer was male beagle, two weeks old. Not long before that, another coroner who didn't know pathology from plants sent in a skeleton found in a shallow grave. He had no idea how the person had died. I counted forty-some cuts, lips bent back, textbook examples of green bone plasticity. Definitely not a natural death." He cleaned his glasses with the hem of his lab coat. "Of course, I get the other, too. Bones cut during autopsy."

"Any chance this was caused by a predator?" I said, even though I didn't see how it could have been.

"Well, cuts aren't always easy to distinguish from marks made by carnivores. But I'm fairly certain we're talking about some sort of blade." Getting up, he added cheerfully, "Let's take a look."

The anthropological minutiae that drove me to distraction gave Dr. Vessey joy, and he was energized and animated as he moved to the dissecting microscope on a countertop and centered the bone on the stage. After a long, silent moment of peering through the lenses and turning the bone in the field of light, he commented, "Now, that's interesting."

I waited.

"And this was the only cut you found?"

"Yes," I said. "Perhaps you'll find something else when you conduct your own examination. But I found nothing else except the bullet hole I mentioned. In her lumbar spine."

"Yes. You said the bullet hit the spinal cord."

"Right. She was shot in the back. I recovered the slug from her vertebra."

"Any idea of the location of the shooting?"

"We don't know where she was in the woods—or if she was even *in* the woods—when she was shot."

"And she has this cut to her hand," Dr. Vessey mused, peering into the scope again. "No way to know which came first. She would have been paralyzed from the waist down after being shot, but she still could have moved her hands."

"A defense injury?" I asked what I suspected.

"A very unusual one, Kay. The cut is dorsal versus palmar." He leaned back in the chair and looked up at me. "Most defense injuries to the hands are palmar." He held up his hands palm out. "But she took this cut to the *top* of her hand." He turned his hands palm in. "I usually associate cuts on the top of the hand with someone who is aggressive in defending himself."

"Punching," I said.

"Right. If I'm coming at you with a knife and you're punching away, you're likely to get cut on the top of your hand. Certainly, you're not going to receive a cut to your palmar surfaces, unless you unclench your fists at some point. But what's more significant is that most defense injuries are slices. The perpetrator is swinging or stabbing, and the victim raises his hands or forearms to ward off the blade. If the cut goes deep enough to strike bone, I'm usually not going to be able to tell you much about the cutting surface."

"If the cutting surface is serrated," I interpolated, "with a slice, the blade covers its own tracks."

"That's one reason this cut is so interesting," he said. "There's no question it was inflicted by a serrated blade."

"Then she wasn't sliced but *hacked?*" I asked, puzzled.

"Yes." He returned the bone to its envelope. "The pattern of serrations means that at least a half an inch of the blade must have struck the top of her hand." Returning to his desk, he added, "I'm afraid that's as much information as I can give you about the weapon and what might have occurred. As you know, there's so much variability. I can't tell you the size of the blade, for example, whether the injury occurred before or after she was shot, and what position she was in when she received the cut."

Deborah could have been on her back. She could have been kneeling or on her feet, and as I returned to my car, I began to analyze. The cut to her hand was deep and would have bled profusely. This most likely placed her on the logging road or in the woods when she received the injury, because there was no blood inside her Jeep. Did this hundred-pound gymnast struggle with her assailant? Did she try to punch him, was she terrified and fighting for her life because Fred already had been murdered? And where did the gun fit in? Why did the killer use two weapons when it did not seem he had needed a gun to kill Fred?

I was willing to bet that Fred's throat was cut. Quite likely, after Deborah was shot, her throat was cut or else she was strangled. She was not shot and left to die. She did not drag herself, half paralyzed, to Fred's side and slip her arm under his. Their bodies had been positioned this way deliberately.

Turning off Constitution, I finally found Connecticut, which eventually led me to a northwest section of the city that I suspected would have been little better than a slum were it not for the Washington Hilton. Rising from a grassy slope that covered a city block, the hotel was a magnificent white luxury liner surrounded by a troubled sea of dusty liquor stores, laundromats, a nightclub featuring "live dancers," and dilapidated row houses with broken windows boarded up and cement front stoops almost on the street. Leaving my car in the hotel's underground parking deck, I crossed Florida Avenue and climbed the front steps of a dingy tan brick apartment building with a faded blue awning in front. I pressed the button for Apartment 28, where Abby Turnbull lived.

"Who is it?"

I barely recognized the disembodied voice blaring out of the intercom. When I announced myself, I wasn't sure what Abby muttered, or maybe she simply gasped. The electronic lock clicked open.

I stepped inside a dimly lit landing with soiled tan carpet on the floor and a bank of tarnished brass mailboxes on a wall paneled in Masonite. I remembered Abby's fear about someone tampering with her mail. It certainly did not appear that one could easily get past the apartment building's front door without a key. The mailboxes required keys as well. Everything she had said to me in Richmond last fall rang false. By the time I climbed the five flights to her floor, I was out of breath and angry.

Abby was standing in her doorway.

"What are you doing here?" she whispered, her face ashen.

"You're the only person I know in this building. So what do you think I'm doing here?"

"You didn't come to Washington just to see me." Her eyes were frightened.

"I was here on business."

Through her open doorway I could see arctic white furniture, pastel throw pillows, and abstract monotype Gregg Carbo prints, furnishings I recognized from her former house in Richmond. For an instant I was unsettled by images from that terrible day. I envisioned her sister's decomposing body on the bed upstairs, police and paramedics moving about as Abby sat on a couch, her hands trembling so violently she could barely hold a cigarette. I did not know her then except by reputation, and I had not liked her at all. When her sister was murdered, Abby at least had gotten my sympathy. It wasn't until later that she had earned my trust.

"I know you won't believe me," Abby said in the same hushed tone, "but I was going to come see you next week."

"I have a phone."

"I couldn't," she pleaded, and we were having this conversation in the hall.

"Are you going to ask me in, Abby?"

She shook her head.

Fear tingled up my spine.

Glancing past her, I asked quietly, "Is someone in there?"

"Let's walk," she whispered.

"Abby, for God's sake . . ."

She stared hard at me and raised a finger to her lips.

I was convinced she was losing her mind. Not knowing what else to do, I waited in the hall as she went inside to get her coat. Then I followed her out of the building, and for the better part of half an hour we walked briskly along Connecticut Avenue, neither of us speaking. She led me into the Mayflower Hotel and found a table in the darkest corner of the bar. Ordering espresso, I leaned back in the leather chair and regarded her tensely across the polished table.

"I know you don't understand what's going on," she began, glancing around. At this early hour in the afternoon, the bar was almost empty.

"Abby? Are you all right?"

Her lower lip trembled. "I couldn't call you. I can't even talk to you inside my own fucking apartment! It's like I told you in Richmond, only a thousand times worse."

"You need to see someone," I said very calmly.

"I'm not crazy."

"You're an inch away from being completely unglued."

Taking a deep breath, she met my eyes fiercely. "Kay, I'm being followed. I'm positive my phone is being tapped, and I can't even be sure there aren't listening devices planted inside my place—which is why I couldn't ask you in. There, go ahead. Conclude that I'm paranoid, psychotic, whatever you want to think. But I live in my world and you don't. I know what I've been going through. I know what I know about these cases and what's been happening ever since I got involved in them."

"What, exactly, has been happening?"

The waitress returned with our order. After she left, Abby said, "Less than a week after I'd been in Richmond talking to you, my apartment was broken into."

"You were burglarized?"

"Oh, no." Her laugh was hollow. "Not hardly. The person—or persons—were much too clever for that. Nothing was stolen."

I looked quizzically at her.

"I have a computer at home for my writing, and on the hard disk is a file about these couples, their strange deaths. I've been keeping notes for a long time, writing them into this file. The word processing package I use has an option that automatically backs up what you're working on, and I have it set to do this every ten minutes. You know, to make sure I don't lose anything should the power go out or something. Especially in my building—"

"Abby," I interrupted. "What in God's name are you talking about?"

"What I'm saying is that if you go into a file on my computer, if you're in there for ten minutes or more, not only is a backup created, but when you save the file, the date and time are recorded. Are you following me?"

"I'm not sure." I reached for my espresso.

"You remember when I came to see you?"

I nodded.

"I took notes when I talked to the clerk at the Seven-Eleven."

"Yes. I remember."

"And I talked to a number of other people, including Pat Harvey. I intended to put the notes from these interviews into the computer after I got home. But things went haywire. As you recall, I saw you on a Tuesday night and drove back here the next morning. Well, that day, Wednesday, I talked to my editor around noon, and he was suddenly uninterested, said he wanted to hold off on the Harvey-Cheney story because the paper was going to run a series over the weekend about AIDS.

"It was strange," she went on. "The Harvey-Cheney story was hot, the *Post* was in one big hurry for it. Then I return from Richmond and suddenly have a new assignment?" She paused to light a cigarette. "As it turned out, I didn't have a free moment until Saturday, which was when I finally sat down in front of my computer to pull up this file, and there was a date and time listed after it that I didn't understand. Friday, September twentieth, two-thirteen in the afternoon *when I wasn't even home.* The file had been opened, Kay. Someone went into it, and I know it wasn't me because I didn't touch my computer—not even once—until that Saturday, the twenty-first, when I had some free time."

"Perhaps the clock in your computer was off. . . ."

She was already shaking her head. "It wasn't. I checked."

"How could anybody do that?" I asked. "How could someone break into your apartment without anyone seeing them, without your knowing?"

"The FBI could."

"Abby," I said, exasperated.

"There's a lot you don't know."

"Then fill me in, please," I said.

"Why do you think I took a leave of absence from the *Post?*"

"According to the *New York Times,* you're writing a book."

"And you're assuming I already knew I was going to write this book when I was with you in Richmond."

"It's more than an assumption," I said, feeling angry again.

"I wasn't. I swear." Leaning forward, she added in a voice trembling with emotion, "My beat was changed. Do you understand what that means?"

I was speechless.

"The only thing worse would have been to be fired, but they couldn't do that. There was no cause. Jesus Christ, I won an investigative reporting award last year, and all of a sudden they want to switch me over to features. Do you hear me? *Features.* Now, you tell me what you make of that."

"I don't know, Abby."

"I don't know, either." She blinked back tears. "But I have my self-respect. I know there's something big going on, a story. And I sold it. There. Think what you want, but I'm trying to survive. I have to live and I had to get away from the paper for a while. Features. Oh, God. Kay, I'm so scared."

"Tell me about the FBI," I said firmly.

"I've already told you a lot. About the wrong turn I took, about ending up at Camp Peary, and the FBI agents coming to see me."

"That's not enough."

"The jack of hearts, Kay," she said as if she were telling me something I already knew.

When it dawned on her that I had no idea what she was talking about, her expression changed to astonishment.

"You don't know?" she asked.

"What jack of hearts?"

"In each of these cases, a playing card has been found." Her incredulous eyes were fixed on mine.

I vaguely remembered something from one of the few transcripts of police interviews I had seen. The detective from Gloucester had talked to a friend of Bruce Phillips and Judy Roberts, the first couple. What was it the detective had asked? I recalled it had struck me as rather peculiar. Cards. Did Judy and Bruce ever play cards? Had the friend ever seen any cards inside Bruce's Camaro?

"Tell me about the cards, Abby," I said.

"Are you familiar with the ace of spades, with how it was used in Vietnam?"

I told her I wasn't.

"When a particular outfit of American soldiers wanted to make a point after making a kill, they would leave an ace of spades on the body. In fact, a company that manufactures playing cards supplied this unit with boxes of the cards just for this purpose."

"What does this have to do with Virginia?" I asked, baffled.

"There's a parallel. Only we're not talking about an ace of spades, but a jack of hearts. In each of the first four cases, a jack of hearts was found in the abandoned car."

"Where did you get this information?"

"You know I can't tell you that, Kay. But we're talking about more than one source. That's why I'm so sure of it."

"And did one of your *sources* also tell you that a jack of hearts was found in Deborah Harvey's Jeep?"

"Was one found?" She idly stirred her drink.

"Don't toy with me," I warned.

"I'm not." She met my eyes. "If a jack of hearts was found inside her Jeep or anywhere else, I don't know about it. Obviously, it's an important detail because it would definitely link Deborah Harvey's and Fred Cheney's deaths with those of the first four couples. Believe me, I'm looking hard for that link. I'm not sure it's there. Or if it is, what it means."

"What does this have to do with the FBI?" I asked reluctantly, for I was not sure I wanted to hear her reply.

"They've been preoccupied with these cases almost from the start, Kay. And it goes way beyond VICAP's usual participation. The FBI's known about the cards for a long time. When a jack of hearts was found inside the first couple's Camaro—on the dash—no one paid much attention. Then the second couple disappeared, and there was another card, this one on the passenger seat. When Benton Wesley found out, he immediately started controlling things. He went back to the detective in Gloucester County and told him not to say a word about the jack of hearts found inside the Camaro. He told the investigator in the second case the same thing. Each time another abandoned car turned up, Wesley was on the phone with that investigator."

She paused, studying me as if trying to read my thoughts. "I guess I shouldn't be surprised you didn't know," she added. "I don't suppose it would be that hard for the police to withhold from you what was discovered inside the cars."

"It wouldn't be hard for them to do that," I replied. "Were the cards found with the bodies, that would be another matter. I don't know how that could be kept from me."

Even as I heard myself say the words, doubt whispered in the back of my mind. The police had waited hours before calling me to the scene. By the time I got there, Wesley had arrived, and Deborah Harvey's and Fred Cheney's bodies had been tampered with, searched for personal effects.

"I would expect the FBI to keep quiet about this," I continued to reason. "The detail could be critical to the investigation."

"I'm so sick of hearing shit like that," Abby said angrily. "The detail about the killer leaving a calling card, so to speak, is critical to the investigation only if the guy comes forward and confesses, says he left a card in each couple's car when there's no way for him to know about that unless he really did it. I don't think that's going to happen. And I don't think the FBI is sitting on this thing just because they want to make sure nothing screws up the investigation."

"Then why?" I asked uneasily.

"Because we're not just talking about serial murders. We're not just talking about some fruitcake out there who's got a thing about couples. This thing's political. It's got to be."

Falling silent, she caught the waitress's eye. Abby did not say another word until a second round of drinks was placed on our table and she had taken several sips.

"Kay," she continued, and she was calmer, "does it surprise you that Pat Harvey talked to me when I was in Richmond?"

"Yes, frankly."

"Have you given any thought as to why she agreed to it?"

"I suppose she would have done anything to bring her daughter back," I said. "And sometimes publicity can help."

Abby shook her head. "When I talked to Pat Harvey, she told me a lot of things that I would never have put in the paper. And it's not the first encounter I'd had with her, not by a long shot."

"I don't understand." I was feeling shaky, and it was due to more than the espresso.

"You know about her crusade against illegal charities."

"Vaguely," I replied.

"The tip that alerted her about all that originally came from me."

"From *you?*"

"Last year I began work on a big investigative piece about drug trafficking. As I was going along, I began to uncover a lot of things I couldn't verify, and this is where the fraudulent charities come in. Pat Harvey has an apartment here, at the Watergate, and one evening I went there to interview her, to get a couple quotes for my story. We got to talking. I ended up telling her about the allegations I'd heard to see if she could corroborate any of them. That's how it began."

"What allegations, exactly?"

"About ACTMAD, for example," Abby said. "Allegations that

some of these antidrug charities are really fronts for drug cartels and other illegal activities in Central America. I told her I'd been informed by what I considered to be reliable sources that millions of dollars donated each year were ending up in the pockets of people like Manuel Noriega. Of course, this was before Noriega was arrested. But it's believed that funds from ACTMAD and other so-called charities are being used to buy intelligence from U.S. agents and facilitate the heroin trade through Panamanian airports, customs offices, in the Far East and the Americas."

"And Pat Harvey, prior to your coming to her apartment, had heard nothing about this?"

"No, Kay. I don't think she had a clue, but she was outraged. She started investigating, and then finally went before Congress with a report. A special subcommittee was formed to investigate, and she was invited to serve as a consultant, as you probably know. Apparently, she's uncovered a great deal and a hearing has been set for this April. Some people aren't happy about it, including the Justice Department."

I was beginning to see where this was going.

"There are informants involved," Abby went on, "that the DEA, FBI, and CIA have been after for years. And you know how it works. When Congress gets involved, they have the power to offer special immunity in exchange for information. Once these informants testify in this congressional hearing, the game's over. No way the Justice Department will be able to prosecute."

"Meaning that Pat Harvey's efforts are not exactly appreciated by the Justice Department."

"Meaning that the Justice Department would be secretly thrilled if her entire investigation fell apart."

"The National Drug Policy Director, or Drug Czar," I said, "is subservient to the Attorney General, who commands the FBI and DEA. If Mrs. Harvey is having a conflict of interests with the Justice Department, why doesn't the AG reign her in?"

"Because it's not the AG she's having a problem with, Kay. What she's doing is going to make him look good, make the White House look good. Their Drug Czar is making a dent in drug crimes. What your average citizen won't understand is that as far as the FBI and DEA are concerned, the consequences of this congressional hearing aren't great enough. All that will occur is a full disclosure, the names of these charities and the truth about what they've been doing. The publicity will put groups like ACTMAD out of business, but the scumbags involved will suffer nothing more than a slap on the wrist. The agents working the cases end up with an empty bag because nobody gets put away. Bad people don't stop doing bad things. It's like closing down a nip joint. Two weeks later, it's reopened on another corner."

"I fail to see how this is connected to what's happened to Mrs. Harvey's daughter," I said again.

"Start with this. If you were at cross-purposes with the FBI," Abby said, "and maybe even doing battle with them, how would you feel if your daughter disappeared and the FBI was working the case?"

It was not a pleasant thought. "Justified or not, I would feel very vulnerable and paranoid. I suppose it would be hard for me to trust."

"You've just skimmed the surface of Pat Harvey's feelings. I think she really believes that someone used her daughter to get to her, that Deborah's not the victim of a random crime, but a hit. And she's not sure that the FBI isn't involved—"

"Let me get this straight," I said, stopping her. "Are you implying that Pat Harvey is suspicious the *FBI* is behind the deaths of her daughter and Fred?"

"It's entered her mind that the feds are involved."

"Are you going to tell me that you're entertaining this notion yourself?"

"I'm to the point of believing anything."

"Good God," I muttered under my breath.

"I know how off-the-wall it sounds. But if nothing else, I believe the FBI knows what's going on and maybe even knows who's doing it, and that's why I'm a problem. The feds don't want me snooping around. They're worried I might turn over a rock and find out what's really crawling underneath it."

"If that's the case," I reminded her, "then it would seem to me the *Post* would be offering you a raise, not sending you over to features. It's never been my impression that the *Post* is easily intimidated."

"I'm not Bob Woodward," she replied bitterly. "I haven't been there very long, and the police beat is chicken shit, usually where rookies get their feet wet. If the Director of the FBI or someone in the White House wants to talk lawsuits or diplomacy with the powers to be at the *Post,* I'm not going to be invited in on the meeting or necessarily told what's going on."

She was probably right about that, I thought. If Abby's demeanor in the newsroom was anything like it was now, it was unlikely anyone was eager to deal with her. In fact, I wasn't sure I was surprised she had been relieved of her beat.

"I'm sorry, Abby," I said. "Maybe I could understand politics being a factor in Deborah Harvey's case, but the others? How do the other couples fit? The first couple disappeared two and a half years before Deborah and Fred did."

"Kay," she said fiercely, "I don't know the answers. But I swear to God something is being covered up. Something the FBI, the government, doesn't want the public ever to find out. You mark my words, even if these killings stop, the cases will never be solved if the FBI has its way about it. That's what I'm up against. And that's what you're up against." Finishing her drink, she added, "And maybe that would be all right—as long as the killings stopped. But the problem is, *when* will they stop? And could they have been stopped before now?"

"Why are you telling me all this?" I asked bluntly.

"We're talking about innocent teenage kids who are turning up dead. Not to mention the obvious—I trust you. And maybe I need a friend."

"You're going to continue with the book?"

"Yes. I just hope there will be a final chapter to write."

"Please be careful, Abby."

"Believe me," she said, "I know."

When we left the bar it was dark out and very cold. My mind was in turmoil as we were jostled along crowded sidewalks, and I felt no better as I made the drive back to Richmond. I wanted to talk to Pat Harvey, but I did not dare. I wanted to talk to Wesley, but I knew he would not divulge his secrets to me, were there any, and more than ever I was unsure of our friendship.

The minute I was home, I called Marino.

"Where in South Carolina does Hilda Ozimek live?" I asked.

"Why? What did you find out at the Smithsonian?"

"Just answer my question, please."

"Some little armpit of a town called Six Mile."

"Thank you."

"Hey! Before you hang up, you mind telling me what went down in D.C.?"

"Not tonight, Marino. If I can't find you tomorrow, you get hold of me."

7

At 5.45 A.M., Richmond International Airport was deserted. Restaurants were closed, newspapers were stacked in front of locked-up gift shops, and a janitor was slowly wheeling a trash can around, a somnambulist picking up gum wrappers and cigarette butts.

I found Marino inside the USAir terminal, eyes shut and raincoat wadded behind his head as he napped in an airless, artificially lit room of empty chairs and dotted blue carpet. For a fleeting moment I saw him as if I did not know him, my heart touched in a sad, sweet way. Marino had aged.

I don't think I had been in my new job more than several days when I met him for the first time. I was in the morgue performing an autopsy when a big man with an impassive face walked in and positioned himself on the other side of the table. I remembered feeling his cool scrutiny. I had the uncomfortable sensation he was dissecting me as thoroughly as I was dissecting my patient.

"So you're the new chief." He had posed the comment as a challenge, as if daring me to acknowledge that I believed I could fill a position never before held by a woman.

"I'm Dr. Scarpetta," I had replied. "You're with Richmond City, I assume?"

He had mumbled his name, then waited in silence while I removed several bullets from his homicide case and receipted them to him. He strolled off without so much as a "good-bye" or "nice to meet you," by which point our professional rapport had been established. I perceived he resented me for no cause other than my gender, and in turn I dismissed him as a dolt with a brain pickled by testosterone. In truth, he had secretly intimidated the hell out of me.

It was hard for me to look at Marino now and imagine I had ever found him threatening. He looked old and defeated, shirt straining across his big belly, wisps of graying hair unruly, brow drawn in what was neither a scowl nor a frown but a series of deep creases caused by the erosion of chronic tension and displeasure.

"Good morning." I gently touched his shoulder.

"What's in the bag?" he muttered without opening his eyes.

"I thought you were asleep," I said, surprised.

He sat up and yawned.

Settling next to him, I opened the paper sack and got out Styrofoam cups of coffee and cream cheese bagels I had fixed at home and heated in the microwave oven just before heading out in the dark.

"I assume you haven't eaten?" I handed him a napkin.

"Those look like real bagels."

"They are," I said, unwrapping mine.

"I thought you said the plane left at six."

"Six-thirty. I'm quite sure that's what I told you. I hope you haven't been waiting long."

"Yeah, well I have been."

"I'm sorry."

"You got the tickets, right?"

"In my purse," I replied. There were times when Marino and I sounded like an old married couple.

"You ask me, I'm not sure this idea of yours is worth the price. It wouldn't come out of my pocket, even if I had it. But it don't thrill me that you're getting soaked, Doc. It would make me feel better if you at least tried to get reimbursed."

"It wouldn't make me feel better." We had been through this before. "I'm not turning in a reimbursement voucher, and you aren't, either. You turn in a voucher and you leave a paper trail. Besides," I added, sipping my coffee, "I can afford it."

"If it would save me six hundred bucks, I'd leave a paper trail from here to the moon."

"Nonsense. I know you better than that."

"Yeah. Nonsense is right. This whole thing's goofy as shit." He dumped several packs of sugar into his coffee. "I think Abby *Turncoat* scrambled your brains."

"Thank you," I replied shortly.

Other passengers were filing in, and it was amazing the power Marino had to make the world tilt slightly on its axis. He had chosen to sit in an area designated as nonsmoking, then had carried an upright ashtray from rows away and placed it by his chair. This served as a subliminal invitation for other semiawake smokers to settle near us, several of whom carried over additional ashtrays. By the time we were ready to board there was hardly an ashtray to be found in the smoking area and nobody seemed quite sure where to sit. Embarrassed and determined to have no part in this unfriendly takeover, I left my pack in my purse.

Marino, who disliked flying more than I did, slept to Charlotte, where we boarded a commuter prop plane that reminded me unpleasantly of how little there is between fragile human flesh and empty air. I had worked my share of disasters and knew what it was like to see an aircraft and passengers scattered over miles of earth. I noted there was no rest room or beverage service, and when the engines started, the plane shook as if it were having a seizure. For the first part of the trip, I had the rare distinction of watching the pilots chat with each other, stretching and yawning until a stewardess made her way up the aisle and yanked the curtain shut. The air was getting more turbulent, mountains drifting in and out of fog. The second time the plane suddenly lost altitude, sending my stomach into my throat, Marino gripped both armrests so hard his knuckles went white.

"Jesus Christ," he muttered, and I began to regret bringing him breakfast. He looked as if he were about to get sick. "If this bucket ever makes it on the ground in one piece, I'm having a drink. I don't friggin' care what time it is."

"Hey, I'll buy," a man in front of us turned around and said.

Marino was staring at a strange phenomenon occurring in a section of the aisle directly ahead of us. Rolling up from a metal strip at the edge of the carpet was a ghostly condensation that I had never seen on any previous flight. It looked as if clouds were seeping inside the plane, and when Marino pointed this out with a loud "What the hell?" to the stewardess, she completely ignored him.

"Next time I'm going to slip phenobarbital in your coffee," I warned him between clenched teeth.

"Next time you decide to talk to some wild-ass gypsy who lives in the sticks, I ain't coming along for the ride."

For half an hour we circled Spartanburg, bumped and tossed, fits of freezing rain pelting the glass. We could not land because of the fog, and it honestly occurred to me that we might die. I thought about my mother. I thought about Lucy, my niece. I should have gone home for Christmas, but I was so weighted down by my own concerns, and I had not wanted to be asked about Mark. *I'm busy, Mother. I simply can't get away right now.* "But it's Christmas, Kay." I could not remember the last time my mother had cried, but I always knew when she felt like it. Her voice got funny. Words were spaced far apart. "Lucy will be so disappointed," she had said. I had mailed Lucy a generous check and called her Christmas morning. She missed me terribly, but I think I missed her more.

Suddenly, clouds parted and the sun lit up windows. Spontaneously, all of the passengers, including me, gave God and pilots a round of applause. We celebrated our survival by chatting up and down the aisle as if all of us had been friends for years.

"So maybe Broom Hilda's looking out for us," Marino said sarcastically, his face covered with sweat.

"Maybe she is," I said, taking a deep breath as we landed.

"Yeah, well, be sure to thank her for me."

"You can thank her yourself, Marino."

"Yo," he said, yawning and fully recovered.

"She seems very nice. Maybe for once, you might consider having an open mind."

"Yo," he said again.

When I had gotten Hilda Ozimek's number from directory assistance and given her a call, I was expecting a woman shrewd and suspicious who bracketed every comment in dollar signs. Instead, she was unassuming and gentle, and surprisingly trusting. She did not ask questions or want proof of who I was. Her voice sounded worried only once, and this was when she mentioned that she could not meet us at the airport.

Since I was paying and in a mood to be chauffeured, I told Marino to pick out what he wanted. Like a sixteen-year-old on his first test drive to manhood, he selected a brand-new Thunderbird, black, with a sunroof, a tape deck, electric windows, leather bucket seats. He drove west with the sunroof open and the heat turned on as I went into more detail about what Abby had said to me in Washington.

"I know Deborah Harvey's and Fred Cheney's bodies were moved," I was explaining. "And now I suspect I understand why."

"I'm not sure I do," he said. "So why don't you lay it out for me one point at a time."

"You and I got to the rest stop before anyone went through the Jeep," I began. "And we didn't see a jack of hearts on the dash, on a seat, or anywhere else."

"Don't mean the card wasn't in the glove compartment or something, and the cops didn't find it until after the dogs was finished sniffing." Setting the cruise control, he added, "*If* this card business is true. Like I said, it's the first I've heard of it."

"Let's for the sake of argument assume it is true."

"I'm listening."

"Wesley arrived at the rest stop after we did, so he didn't see a card, either. Later, the Jeep was searched by the police, and you can be sure that Wesley was either on hand or he called Morrell and wanted to know what was found. If there was no sign of a jack of hearts, and I'm willing to bet that's the case, this had to have thrown Wesley a curve. His next thought may have been that either Deborah's and Fred's disappearance was unrelated to the other couples' disappearances and deaths, or else if Deborah and Fred were already dead, then it was possible that this time a card may have been left at the scene, left with the bodies."

"And you're thinking this was why their bodies was moved before you got there. Because the cops was looking for the card."

"Or Benton was. Yes, that's what I'm considering. Otherwise it doesn't make much sense to me. Benton and the police *know* not to touch a body before the medical examiner arrives. But Benton also wouldn't want to take the chance that a jack of hearts might come into the morgue with the bodies. He wouldn't want me or anyone else to find it or know about it."

"Then it would make more sense for him to just tell us to keep our mouths shut instead of him screwing around with the scene," Marino argued. "It's not like he was out there in the woods alone. There was other cops around. They would have noticed if Benton found a card."

"Obviously," I said. "But he would also realize that the fewer people who know, the better. And if I found a playing card among Deborah's or Fred's personal effects, that would go into my written report. Commonwealth's attorneys, members of my staff, families, insurance companies—other people are going to see the autopsy reports eventually."

"Okay, okay." Marino was getting impatient. "But so what? I mean, what's the big deal?"

"I don't know. But if what Abby's implying is true, these cards turning up must be a very big deal to someone."

"No offense, Doc, but I never liked Abby Turnbull worth a

damn. Not when she was working in Richmond, and I sure as hell don't think better of her now that she's at the *Post*."

"I've never known her to lie," I said.

"Yeah. You've never *known* it."

"The detective in Gloucester mentioned playing cards in a transcript I read."

"And maybe that's where Abby picked up the ball. Now she's running around the block with it. Making assumptions. Hoping. All she gives a shit about is writing her book."

"She's not herself right now. She's frightened, angry, but I don't agree with you about her character."

"Right," he said. "She comes to Richmond, acts like your long-lost friend. Says she don't want nothing from you. Next thing, you have to read the *New York Times* to find out she's writing a friggin' book about these cases. Oh, yeah. She's a real friend, Doc."

I shut my eyes and listened to a country-music song playing softly on the radio. Sunlight breaking through the windshield was warm on my lap, and the early hour I had gotten out of bed hit me like a stiff drink. I dozed off. When I came to, we were bumping slowly along an unpaved road out in the middle of nowhere.

"Welcome to the big town of Six Mile," Marino announced.

"What town?"

There was no skyline, not so much as a single convenience store or gas station in sight. Roadsides were dense with trees, the Blue Ridge a haze in the distance, and houses were poor and spread so far apart a cannon could go off without your neighbor hearing it.

Hilda Ozimek, psychic to the FBI and oracle to the Secret Service, lived in a tiny white frame house with white-painted tires in the front yard where pansies and tulips probably grew in the spring. Dead cornstalks leaned against the porch, and in the drive was a rusting Chevrolet Impala with flat tires. A mangy dog began to bark, ugly as sin and big enough to give me pause as I considered getting out of the car. Then he trotted off on three legs, favoring his right front paw, as the front screen door screeched open and a woman squinted at us in the bright, cold morning.

"Be still, Tootie." She patted the dog's neck. "Now go on around back." The dog hung his head, tail wagging, and limped off to the backyard.

"Good morning," Marino said, his feet heavy on the front wooden steps.

At least he intended to be polite, and there had been no guarantee of that.

"It is a fine morning," Hilda Ozimek said.

She was at least sixty and looked as country as corn bread. Black polyester pants were stretched over wide hips, a beige sweater buttoned up to her neck, and she wore thick socks and loafers. Her eyes were light blue, hair covered by a red head rag. She was missing several teeth. I doubted Hilda Ozimek ever looked in a mirror or gave a thought to her physical self unless she was forced to by discomfort or pain.

We were invited into a small living room cluttered with musty furniture and bookcases filled with a variety of unexpected volumes not arranged in any sort of sensible order. There were books on religion and psychology, biographies and histories, and a surprising assortment of novels by some of my favorite authors: Alice Walker, Pat Conroy, and Keri Hulme. The only hint of our hostess's otherworldly inclinations was several works by Edgar Cayce and half a dozen or so crystals placed about on tables and shelves. Marino and I were seated on a couch near a kerosene heater, Hilda across from us in an overstuffed chair, sunlight from the window behind her shining through the open blinds and painting white bars across her face.

"I hope you had no trouble, and I am so sorry I couldn't come get you. But I don't drive anymore."

"Your directions were excellent," I reassured her. "We had no problem finding your house."

"If you don't mind my asking," Marino said, "how do you get around? I didn't see a store or nothing within walking distance."

"Many people come here for readings or just to talk. Somehow, I always have what I need or can get a ride."

A telephone rang in another room, and was instantly silenced by an answering machine.

"How may I help you?" Hilda asked.

"I brought photographs," Marino replied. "The Doc said you wanted to see them. But there's a couple things I want to clear up first. No offense or nothing, Miss Ozimek, but this mind-reading stuff is something I've never put much stock in. Maybe you can help me understand it better."

For Marino to be so forthright without a trace of combativeness in his tone was uncommon, and I glanced over at him, rather startled. He was studying Hilda with the openness of a child, his expression an odd mix of curiosity and melancholy.

"First, let me say that I'm not a mind reader," Hilda replied matter-of-factly. "And I don't even feel comfortable with being called a psychic, but for lack of a better term, I suppose, that is how I am referred to and how I refer to myself. All of us have the capability. Sixth sense, some part of our brain most people choose not to use. I explain it as an enhanced intuition. I feel energy coming from people and just relay the impressions that come into my mind."

"Which is what you did when Pat Harvey was with you," he said.

She nodded. "She took me into Debbie's bedroom, showed me photographs of her, and then she took me to the rest stop where the Jeep was found."

"What impressions did you get?" I inquired.

Staring off, she thought hard for a moment. "I can't remember all of them. That's the thing. It's the same when I give readings. People come back to me later and tell me about something I said and what's happened since. I don't always remember what I've said until I'm reminded."

"Do you remember anything you said to Mrs. Harvey?" Marino wanted to know, and he sounded disappointed.

"When she showed me Debbie's picture, I knew right away the girl was dead."

"What about the boyfriend?" Marino asked.

"I saw his picture in the newspaper and knew he was dead. I knew both of them were dead."

"So you been reading about these cases in the newspaper," Marino then said.

"No," Hilda answered. "I don't take the newspaper. But I saw the boy's picture because Mrs. Harvey had clipped it out to show me. She didn't have a photograph of him, only of her daughter, you see."

"You mind explaining how you knew they was dead?"

"It was something I felt. An impression I got when I touched their pictures."

Reaching into his back pocket and pulling out his wallet, Marino said, "If I give you a picture of someone, can you do the same thing? Give me your impressions?"

"I'll try," she said as he handed her a snapshot.

Closing her eyes, she rubbed her fingertips over the photograph in slow circles. This went on for at least a minute before she spoke again. "I'm getting guilt. Now, I don't know if it's because this woman was feeling guilty when the picture was taken, or if it's because she's feeling that way now. But that's coming in real strong. Conflict, guilt. Back and forth. She's made up her mind one minute, then doubting herself the next. Back and forth."

"Is she alive?" Marino asked, clearing his throat.

"I feel that she is alive," Hilda replied, still rubbing. "I'm also getting the impression of a hospital. Something medical. Now I don't know if this means that she's sick or if someone close to her is. But something medical is involved, a concern. Or maybe it will be involved at some future point."

"Anything else?" Marino asked.

She shut her eyes again and rubbed the photograph a little longer. "A lot of conflict," she repeated. "It's as if something's past but it's hard for her to let it go. Pain. And yet she feels she has no choice. That's all that's coming to me." She looked up at Marino.

When he retrieved the photograph, his face was red. Returning the wallet to his pocket without saying a word, he unzipped his briefcase and got out a microcassette tape recorder and a manila envelope containing a series of retrospective photographs that began at the logging road in New Kent County and ended in the woods where Deborah Harvey's and Fred Cheney's bodies had been found. Hilda spread them out on the coffee table and began rubbing her fingers over each one. For a very long time she said nothing, eyes closed as the telephone continued to ring in the other room. Each time the machine intervened, and she did not seem to notice. I was deciding that her skills were in more demand than those of any physician.

"I'm picking up fear," she began talking rapidly. "Now, I don't know if it's because someone was feeling fear when these pictures were taken, or if it's because someone was feeling fear in these places at some earlier time. But fear." She nodded, eyes still shut. "I'm definitely picking it up with each picture. All of them. Very strong fear."

Like the blind, Hilda moved her fingers from photograph to photograph, reading something that seemed as tangible to her as the features of a person's face.

"I feel death here," she went on, touching three different photographs. "I feel that strong." They were photographs of the clearing where the bodies were found. "But I don't feel it here." Her fingers moved back to photographs of the logging road and a section of woods where I had walked when being led to the clearing in the rain.

I glanced over at Marino. He was leaning forward on the couch, elbows on his knees, his eyes fixed on Hilda. So far, she wasn't telling us anything dramatic. Neither Marino nor I had ever assumed that Deborah and Fred had been murdered on the logging road, but in the clearing where their bodies were found.

"I see a man," Hilda went on. "Light-complected. He's not real tall. Not short. Medium height and slender. But not skinny. Now, I don't know who it is, but since nothing is coming to me strongly, I'll have to assume it was someone who had an encounter with the couple. I'm picking up friendliness. I'm hearing laughter. It's like he was, you know, friendly with the couple. Maybe they met him somewhere, and I can't tell you why I'm thinking this, but I'm feeling as if they were laughing with him at some point. Trusted him."

Marino spoke. "Can you see anything else about him? About the way he looked?"

She continued rubbing the photographs. "I'm seeing darkness. It's possible he has a dark beard or something dark over part of his face. Maybe he's dressed in dark clothing. But I'm definitely picking him up in connection with the couple and with the place where the pictures were taken."

Opening her eyes, she stared up at the ceiling. "I'm feeling that the first meeting was a friendly encounter. Nothing to make them worry. But then there's fear. It's so strong in this place, the woods."

"What else?" Marino was so intense, the veins were standing out in his neck. If he leaned forward another inch, he was going to fall off the couch.

"Two things," she said. "They may not mean anything but they're coming to me. I have a sense of another place that's not in these pictures, and I'm feeling this in connection with the girl. She might have been taken somewhere or gone somewhere. Now this place could be close by. Maybe it's not. I don't know, but I'm getting a sense of crowdedness, of things grabbing. Of panic, a lot of noise and motion. Nothing about these impressions is good. And then there is something lost. I'm seeing this as something metal that has to do with war. I'm not getting anything more about that except I don't feel anything bad—I'm not picking up that the object itself is harmful."

"Who lost whatever this metal thing is?" Marino inquired.

"I have a sense that this is a person who is still alive. I'm not getting an image, but I feel this is a man. He perceives the item as lost versus discarded and is not real worried about it, but there is some concern. As if whatever he has lost enters his mind now and then."

She fell silent as the telephone rang again.

I asked, "Did you mention any of this to Pat Harvey last fall?"

"When she wanted to see me," Hilda replied, "the bodies had not been found. I didn't have these pictures."

"Then you did not get any of these same impressions."

She thought hard. "We went to the rest stop and she led me right over to where the Jeep was found. I stood there for a while. I remember there was a knife."

"What knife?" Marino asked.

"I saw a knife."

"What kind of knife?" he asked, and I recalled that Gail, the dog handler, had borrowed Marino's Swiss army knife when opening the Jeep's doors.

"A long knife," Hilda said. "Like a hunting knife or maybe some kind of military knife. It seems there was something about the handle. Black and rubbery, maybe, with one of those blades I associate with cutting through hard things like wood."

"I'm not sure I understand," I said, even though I had a good idea what she meant. I did not want to lead her.

"With teeth. Like a saw. I guess serrated is what I'm trying to say," she replied.

"This is what came into your mind when you was standing out there at the rest stop?" Marino asked, staring at her in disbelief.

"I did not feel anything that was frightening," she said. "But I saw the knife, and I knew it was not the couple who had been in the Jeep when it was left where it was. I did not feel their presence at that rest stop. They were never there." She paused, closing her eyes again, brow furrowed. "I remember feeling anxiety. I had the impression of someone anxious and in a hurry. I saw darkness. Like it was night. Then someone was walking quickly. I couldn't see who it was."

"Can you see this individual now?" I asked.

"No. I can't see him."

"Him?" I said.

She paused again. "I believe my feeling was that it was a man."

It was Marino who spoke. "You told Pat Harvey all this when you was with her at the rest stop?"

"Some of it, yes," Hilda replied. "I don't remember everything I said."

"I need to walk around," Marino muttered, getting up from the couch. Hilda did not seem surprised or concerned as he went out, the screen door slamming shut behind him.

"Hilda," I said, "when you met with Pat Harvey, did you pick up anything about her? Did you get any sense that she knew something, for example, about what might have happened to her daughter?"

"I picked up guilt real strong, like she was feeling responsible. But this would be expected. When I deal with the relatives of someone who has disappeared or been killed, I always pick up guilt. What was a little more unusual was her aura."

"Her *aura?*"

I knew what an aura was in medicine, a sensation that can precede the onset of a seizure. But I did not think this was what Hilda meant.

"Auras are invisible to most people," she explained. "I see them as colors. An aura surrounding a person. A color. Pat Harvey's aura was gray."

"Does that mean something?"

"Gray is neither death nor life," she said. "I associate it with illness. Someone sick of body, mind, or soul. As if something is draining the color from her life."

"I suppose that makes sense when you consider her emotional state at the time," I pointed out.

"It might. But I remember that it gave me a bad feeling. I picked up that she might be in some sort of danger. Her energy wasn't good, wasn't positive or healthy. I felt she was at risk for opening herself up to harm, or maybe bringing harm upon herself through her own doings."

"Have you ever seen a gray aura before?"

"Not often."

I could not resist asking, "Are you picking up a color from me?"

"Yellow with a little brown mixed in."

"That's interesting," I said, surprised. "I never wear either color. In fact, I don't believe I have anything yellow or brown inside my house. But I love sunlight and chocolate."

"Your aura has nothing to do with colors or foods you like." She smiled. "Yellow can mean spiritual. And brown I associate with good sense, practical. Someone grounded in reality. I see your aura as being very spiritual but also very practical. Now mind you, that is my interpretation. For each person, colors mean a different thing."

"And Marino?"

"A thin margin of red. That's what I see around him," she said. "Red often means anger. But he needs more red, I think."

"You're not serious," I said, for the last thing I would have thought that Marino needed was more anger.

"When someone is low on energy, I tell them they need more red in their life. It gives energy. Makes you get things done, fight against your troubles. Red can be real good if channeled properly. But I get the sense he is afraid of what he is feeling, and this is what is weakening him."

"Hilda, have you seen pictures of the other couples who disappeared?"

She nodded. "Mrs. Harvey had their pictures. From the newspaper."

"And did you touch them, read them?"

"I did."

"What did you perceive?"

"Death," she said. "All of the young people were dead."

"What about the light-complected man who may have a beard or something dark over part of his face?"

She paused. "I don't know. But I do remember picking up this friendliness I mentioned. Their initial encounter was not one of fear. I had the impression that none of the young people were afraid at first."

"I want to ask you about a card now," I said. "You mentioned that you read people's cards. Are you talking about playing cards?"

"You can use most anything. Tarot cards, a crystal ball. It doesn't matter. These things are tools. It's whatever makes it easy for you to concentrate. But yes, I use a deck of playing cards."

"How does that work?"

"I ask the person to cut the cards, then I begin to pick one at a time and tell what impressions come to mind."

"Were you to pick the jack of hearts, would there be any special significance?" I asked.

"It all depends on the person I'm dealing with, what energy I'm picking up from this individual. But the jack of hearts is equal to the knight of cups in tarot cards."

"A good card or a bad card?"

"It depends on who the card represents in relation to the individual whose reading I'm doing," she said. "In tarot cards, cups are love and emotion cards, just as swords and pentacles are business and money cards. The jack of hearts would be a love and emotion card. And this could be very good. It could also be very bad if the love has gone sour or turned vengeful, hateful."

"How would a jack of hearts be different from a ten of hearts or queen of hearts, for example?"

"The jack of hearts is a face card," she said. "I would say this is a card that represents a man. Now a king of hearts is also a face card, but I would associate a king with power, someone who is perceived or perceives himself as in control, in charge, possibly a father or boss, something like that. A jack, like a knight, might represent someone who is perceived or perceives himself as a soldier, a defender, a champion. He might be someone who is out in the world doing battle on the business front. Maybe he's into sports, a competitor. He could be a lot of things, but since hearts are emotion, love cards, that would make me say that whoever this card represents, there is an emotional element versus a money or work element."

Her telephone rang again.

She said to me, "Don't always trust what you hear, Dr. Scarpetta."

"About what?" I asked, startled.

"Something that matters a great deal to you is causing unhappiness, grief. It has to do with a person. A friend, a romantic interest. It could be a member of your family. I don't know. Definitely someone of great importance in your life. But you are hearing and maybe even imagining many things. Be careful what you believe."

Mark, I thought, or maybe Benton Wesley. I couldn't resist asking, "Is this someone currently in my life? Someone I'm having encounters with?"

She paused. "Since I'm sensing confusion, much that is unknown, I'll have to say that it isn't someone you are currently close to. I'm feeling a distance, you know, not necessarily geographical, but emotional. Space that is making it hard for you to trust. My advice is to let it go, don't do anything about this now. A resolution will come, and I can't tell you when this will be, but it will be all right if you relax, don't listen to the confusion, or act impulsively.

"And there's something else," she went on. "Look beyond what is before you, and I don't know what this is about. But there is something you aren't seeing and it has to do with the past, something of importance that happened in the past. It will come to you and lead you to the truth, but you will not recognize its significance unless you open yourself first. Let your faith guide you."

Wondering what had happened to Marino, I got up and looked out the window.

Marino drank two bourbon and waters in the Charlotte airport, then had one more when we were in the air. He had very little to say during the trip back to Richmond. It wasn't until we were walking to our cars in the parking lot that I decided to take initiative.

"We need to talk," I said, getting out my keys.

"I'm beat."

"It's almost five o'clock," I said. "Why don't you come to my house for dinner?"

He stared off across the parking lot, squinting in the sun. I could not tell if he was in a rage or on the verge of tears, and I wasn't sure I'd ever seen him this out of sorts.

"Are you angry with me, Marino?"

"No, Doc. Right now I just want to be alone."

"Right now, I don't think you should be."

Fastening the top button of his coat, he muttered, "See ya later," and walked off.

I drove home, absolutely drained, and was mindlessly puttering in the kitchen when my doorbell rang. Looking through the peephole, I was amazed to see Marino.

"I had this in my pocket," he explained the instant I opened the door. He handed me his canceled plane ticket and inconsequential paperwork from the rental car. "Thought you might need it for your tax records or whatever."

"Thank you," I said, and I knew this was not why he had come. I had charge card receipts. Nothing he had given to me was necessary. "I was just fixing dinner. You might as well stay since you're already here."

"Maybe for a little while." He would not meet my eyes. "Then I got things to do."

Following me into the kitchen, he sat at the table while I resumed slicing sweet red peppers and adding them to chopped onions sautéing in olive oil.

"You know where the bourbon is," I said, stirring.

He got up, heading to the bar.

"While you're at it," I called after him, "would you please fix me a Scotch and soda?"

He did not reply, but when he came back he set my drink on the counter nearby and leaned against the butcher's block. I added the onions and peppers to tomatoes sautéing in another pan, then began browning sausage.

"I don't have a second course," I apologized as I worked.

"Don't look to me like you need one."

"Spring lamb with white wine, breast of veal, or roast pork would be perfect." I filled a pot with water and set it on the stove. "I'm pretty amazing with lamb, but I'll have to give you a rain check."

"Maybe you ought to forget cutting up dead bodies and open a restaurant."

"I'll assume you mean that as a compliment."

"Oh, yeah." His face was expressionless, and he was lighting a cigarette. "So what do you call this?" He nodded at the stove.

"I call it yellow and green broad noodles with sweet peppers and sausage," I replied, adding the sausage to the sauce. "But if I really wanted to impress you, I would call it *le papardelle del Cantunzein.*"

"Don't worry. I'm impressed."

"Marino." I glanced over at him. "What happened this morning?"

He replied with a question, "You mention to anyone what Vessey told you about the hack mark's being made with a serrated blade?"

"So far, you're the only person I've told."

"Hard to figure how Hilda Ozimek came up with that, with the hunting knife with a serrated edge she claims popped into her mind when Pat Harvey took her to the rest stop."

"It is hard to understand," I agreed, placing pasta in the boiling water. "There are some things in life that can't be reasoned away or explained, Marino."

Fresh pasta takes only seconds to cook, and I drained it and transferred it to a bowl kept warm in the oven. Adding the sauce, I tossed in butter and grated fresh Parmesan, then told Marino we were ready to eat.

"I've got artichoke hearts in the refrigerator." I served our plates. "But no salad. I do have bread in the freezer."

"This is all I need," he said, his mouth full. "It's good. Real good."

I had barely touched my meal when he was ready for a second helping. It was as though Marino had not eaten in a week. He was not taking care of himself, and it was showing. His tie was in serious need of a dry cleaner, the hem on one leg of his trousers had unraveled, and his shirt was stained yellow under the arms. Everything about him cried out that he was needy and neglected, and I was as repelled by this as I was disturbed. There was no reason why an intelligent grown man should allow himself to fall into poor repair like an abandoned house. Yet I knew his life was out of control, that in a way he could not help himself. Something was terribly wrong.

I got up and retrieved a bottle of Mondavi red wine from the wine rack.

"Marino," I said, pouring each of us a glass, "whose photograph did you show to Hilda? Was it your wife?"

He leaned back in his chair and would not look at me.

"You don't have to talk about it if you don't want to. But you haven't been yourself for quite a while. It's very apparent."

"What she said freaked me out," he replied.

"What Hilda said?"

"Yeah."

"Would you like to tell me about it?"

"I haven't told no one about it." He paused, reaching for his wine. His face was hard, eyes humiliated. "She went back to Jersey last November."

"I'm not sure you've ever told me your wife's name."

"Wow," he muttered bitterly. "Ain't that a comment."

"Yes, it is. You keep an awful lot to yourself."

"I've always been that way. But I guess being a cop has made it worse. I'm so used to hearing the guys bitch and moan about their wives, girlfriends, kids. They cry on your shoulder, you think they're your brothers. Then when it's your turn to have a problem, you make the mistake of spilling your guts and next thing it's all the hell over the police department. I learned a long time ago to keep my mouth shut."

He paused, getting out his wallet. "Her name's Doris." He handed me the snapshot he had shown Hilda Ozimek this morning.

Doris had a good face and a round, comfortable body. She was standing stiffly, dressed for church, her expression self-conscious and reluctant. I had seen her a hundred times, for the world was full of Dorises. They were the sweet young women who sat on porch swings dreaming of love as they stared into nights magic with stars and the smells of summer. They were mirrors, their images of themselves reflections of the significant people in their lives. They derived their importance from the services they rendered, survived by killing off their expectations in inches, and then one day woke up mad as hell.

"We would've been married thirty years this June," Marino said as I returned the photograph. "Then suddenly she ain't happy. Says I work too much, never around. She don't know me. Things like that. But I wasn't born yesterday. That's not the real story."

"Then what is?"

"It got started last summer when her mother had a stroke. Doris went to look after her. Was up north for almost a month, getting her mother out of the hospital and into a nursing home, taking care of everything. When Doris came home, she was different. It's like she was somebody else."

"What do you think happened?"

"I know she met this guy up there whose wife died a couple years back. He's into real estate, was helping sell her mother's house. Doris mentioned him once or twice like it was no big deal. But something was going on. The phone would ring late, and when I answered it, the person would hang up. Doris would rush out to get the mail before I did. Then in November, she suddenly packs up and leaves, says her mother needs her."

"Has she been home since?" I asked.

He shook his head. "Oh, she calls now and then. She wants a divorce."

"Marino, I'm sorry."

"Her mother's in this home, you see. And Doris is looking after her, seeing this real estate guy, I guess. Upset one minute, happy the next. Like she wants to come back, but don't want to. Guilty, then don't give a damn. It's just like Hilda said when she was looking at her picture. Back and forth."

"Very painful for you."

"Hey." He tossed his napkin on the table. "She can do what she wants. Screw her."

I knew he did not mean that. He was devastated, and my heart ached for him. At the same time, I could not help but feel sympathy for his wife. Marino would not be easy to love.

"Do you want her to come home?"

"I've been with her longer than I was alive before we met. But let's face it, Doc." He glanced at me, his eyes frightened. "My life sucks. Always counting nickels and dimes, called out on the street in the middle of the night. Plan vacations and then something goes down and Doris unpacks and waits at home—like Labor Day weekend when the Harvey girl and her boyfriend disappeared. That was the last straw."

"Do you love Doris?"

"She don't believe I do."

"Maybe you should make sure she understands how you feel," I said. "Maybe you should show that you want her a lot and don't need her so much."

"I don't get it." He looked bewildered.

He would never get it, I thought, depressed.

"Just take care of yourself," I told him. "Don't expect her to do that for you. Maybe it will make a difference."

"I don't earn enough bucks, and that's it, chapter and verse."

"I'll bet your wife doesn't care so much about money. She'd rather feel important and loved."

"He's got a big house and a Chrysler New Yorker. Brand-new, with leather seats, the whole nine yards."

I did not reply.

"Last year he went to Hawaii for his vacation." Marino was getting angry.

"Doris spent most of her life with you. That was her choice, Hawaii or not—"

"Hawaii's nothing but a tourist trap," he cut in, lighting a cigarette. "Me, I'd rather go to Buggs Island and fish."

"Has it occurred to you that Doris might have grown weary of being your mother?"

"She ain't my mother," he snapped.

"Then why is it that since she left, you've begun looking like you desperately need a mother, Marino?"

"Because I don't got time to sew buttons on, cook, and clean, do shit like that."

"I'm busy, too. I find time for shit like that."

"Yeah, you also got a maid. You also probably earn a hundred G's a year."

"I would take care of myself if I earned only ten G's a year," I said. "I would do it because I have self-respect and because I *don't want* anyone to take care of me. I simply want to be cared for, and there's a very big difference between the two."

"If you got all the answers, Doc, then how come you're divorced? And how come your friend Mark's in Colorado and you're here? Don't sound to me like you wrote the book on relationships."

I felt a flush creeping up my neck. "Tony did not truly care for me, and when I finally figured that out, I left. As for Mark, he has a problem with commitments."

"And you were committed to him?" Marino almost glared at me.

I did not respond.

"How come you didn't go out west with him? Maybe you're only committed to being a chief."

"We were having problems, and certainly part of it was my fault. Mark was angry, went out west . . . maybe to make a point, maybe just to get away from me," I said, dismayed that I could not keep the emotion out of my voice. "Professionally, my going with him wouldn't have been possible, but it was never an option."

Marino suddenly looked ashamed. "I'm sorry. I didn't know that."

I was silent.

"Sounds like you and me are in the same boat," he offered.

"In some ways," I said, and I did not want to admit to myself what those ways were. "But I'm taking care of myself. If Mark ever reappears, he won't find me looking like hell, my life down the drain. I want him, but I don't *need* him. Maybe you ought to try that with Doris?"

"Yeah." He seemed encouraged. "Maybe I will. I think I'm ready for coffee."

"Do you know how to fix it?"

"You gotta be kidding," he said, surprised.

"Lesson number one, Marino. Fixing coffee. Step this way."

While I showed him the technical wonders of a drip coffeemaker that required nothing more than a fifty IQ, he resumed contemplating this day's adventures.

"A part of me don't want to take what Hilda said seriously," he explained. "But another part of me has to. I mean, it sure gave me second thoughts."

"In what way?"

"Deborah Harvey was shot with a nine-millimeter. They never found the shell. Kind of hard to believe the squirrel could collect the shell out there in the dark. Makes me think Morrell and the rest of them wasn't looking in the right place. Remember, Hilda wondered if there wasn't another place, and she mentioned something lost. Something metal that had to do with war. That could be a spent shell."

"She also said this object wasn't harmful," I reminded him.

"A spent shell couldn't hurt a fly. It's the bullet that's harmful, and only when it's being fired."

"And the photographs she looked at were taken last fall," I went on. "Whatever this lost item is may have been out there then but isn't there now."

"You thinking the killer came back during daylight to look for it?"

"Hilda said the person who lost this metal object was concerned about it."

"I don't think he went back," Marino said. "He's too careful for that. Be a big damn risk. The area was crawling with cops and bloodhounds right after the kids disappeared. You can bet the killer laid low. He's got to be pretty cool to have gotten away with what he's doing for so long, whether we're talking about a psychopath or a paid hit man."

"Maybe," I said as the coffee began to drip.

"I think we should go back out there and poke around a little. You up for it?"

"Frankly, the idea has crossed my mind."

8

In the light of a clear afternoon, the woods did not seem so ominous until Marino and I drew closer to the small clearing. Then the faint, foul odor of decomposing human flesh was an insidious reminder. Pine tags and leaves had been displaced and piled in small mounds by the scraping of shovels and emptying of sieves. It would take time and hard rains before the tangible remnants of murder were no longer to be found in this place.

Marino had brought a metal detector and I carried a rake. He got out his cigarettes and looked around.

"Don't see any point in scanning right here," he said. "It's been gone over half a dozen times."

"I assume the path's been gone over thoroughly as well," I said, staring back at the trail we had followed from the logging road.

"Not necessarily, because the path didn't exist when the couple was taken out here last fall."

I realized what he was saying. The trail of displaced leaves and hard-packed dirt had been made by police officers and other interested parties going back and forth from the logging road to the scene.

Surveying the woods, he added, "The fact is, we don't even know where they was parked, Doc. It's easy to assume it's close to where we parked, and that they got here pretty much the same way we did. But it depends on whether the killer was actually *heading* here."

"I have a feeling the killer knew where he was going," I replied. "It doesn't make sense to think he randomly turned down the logging road and then ended up out here after haphazardly wandering around in the dark."

Shrugging, Marino switched on the metal detector. "Can't hurt to give it a try."

We began at the perimeter of the scene, scanning the path, sweeping yards of undergrowth and leaves on either side as we slowly made our way back toward the logging road. For almost two hours we probed any opening in trees and brush that looked remotely promising for human passage, the detector's first high-frequency tone rewarding our efforts with an Old Milwaukee beer can, the second with a rusty bottle opener. The third alert did not sound until we were at the edge of the woods, within sight of our car, where we uncovered a shotgun shell, the red plastic faded by the years.

Leaning against the rake, I stared dismally back down the path, thinking. I pondered what Hilda had said about another place being involved, perhaps somewhere that the killer had taken Deborah, and I envisioned the clearing and the bodies. My first thought had been that if Deborah had broken free of the killer at some point, it may have been when she and Fred were being led in the dark from the logging road to the clearing. But as I looked through the woods, this theory didn't really make sense.

"Let's accept as a given that we're dealing with one killer," I said to Marino.

"Okay, I'm listening." He wiped his damp forehead on his coat sleeve.

"If you were the killer and had abducted two people and then forced them, perhaps at gunpoint, to come out here, who would you kill first?"

"The guy's going to be a bigger problem," he said without pause. "Me, I'm going to take him out first and save the little girl for last."

It was still difficult to imagine. When I tried to envision one person forcing two hostages to walk through these woods after dark, I continued to draw a blank. Did the killer have a flashlight? Did he know this area so well he could find the clearing blindfolded? I voiced these questions aloud to Marino.

"I've been trying to see the same thing," he said. "A couple ideas come to mind. First, he probably restrained them, tied their hands behind their back. Second, if it was me, I'd hold on to the girl, have the gun to her ribs while we're walking through the woods. This would make the boyfriend as gentle as a lamb. One false move, and his girl gets blown away. As for a flashlight? He had to have had some way of seeing out here."

"How are you going to hold a gun, a flashlight, and the girl at the same time?" I asked.

"Easy. Want me to show you?"

"Not particularly." I backed away as he reached toward me.

"The rake. Geez, Doc. Don't be so damn jumpy."

He handed me the metal detector and I gave him the rake.

"Pretend the rake's Deborah, okay? I'm yoking her around the neck with my left arm, the flashlight in my left hand, like this." He demonstrated. "In my right hand I've got the gun, which is stuck against her ribs. No problem. Fred's gonna be a couple feet in front of us, following the beam of the flashlight while I watch him like a hawk." Pausing, Marino stared down the path. "They're not going to be moving very fast."

"Especially if they're barefoot," I pointed out.

"Yeah, and I'm thinking they were. He can't tie up their feet if he's going to walk them out here. But if he makes them take off their shoes, then that's going to slow them down, make it harder for them to run. Maybe after he whacks them, he keeps the shoes as souvenirs."

"Maybe." I was thinking about Deborah's purse again.

I said, "If Deborah's hands were bound behind her back, then how did her purse get out here? It didn't have a strap, no way to loop it over her arm or shoulder. It wasn't attached to a belt, in fact it doesn't appear she was wearing a belt. And if someone were forcing you out into the woods at gunpoint, why would you take your purse with you?"

"Got no idea. That's been bothering me from the start."

"Let's give it one last try," I said.

"Oh, shit."

By the time we got back to the clearing, clouds had passed over the sun and it was getting windy, making it seem that the temperature had dropped ten degrees. Damp beneath my coat from exertion, I was cold, the muscles in my arms trembling from raking. Moving to the perimeter farthest from the path, I studied an area beyond which stretched a terrain so uninviting that I doubted even hunters ventured there. The police had dug and sifted maybe ten feet in this direction before running into an infestation of kudzu that had metastasized over the better part of an acre. Trees covered in the vine's green mail looked like prehistoric dinosaurs rearing up over a solid green sea. Every living bush, pine, and plant was slowly being strangled to death.

"Good God," Marino said as I waded out with my rake. "You're not serious."

"We won't go very far," I promised.

We did not have to.

The metal detector responded almost immediately. The tone got louder and higher pitched as Marino positioned the scanner over an area of kudzu less than fifteen feet from where the bodies had been found. I discovered that raking kudzu was worse than combing snarled hair and finally resorted to dropping to my knees and ripping off leaves and feeling around roots with fingers sheathed in surgical gloves until I felt something cold and hard that I knew wasn't what I was hoping for.

"Save it for the tollbooth," I said dejectedly, tossing Marino a dirty quarter.

Several feet away the metal detector signaled us again, and this time my rooting around on hands and knees paid off. When I felt the unmistakable hard, cylindrical shape, I gently parted kudzu until I saw the gleam of stainless steel, a cartridge case still as shiny as polished silver. I gingerly plucked it out, touching as little of its surface as possible, while Marino bent over and held open a plastic evidence bag.

"Nine-millimeter, Federal," he said, reading the head stamp through plastic. "I'll be damned."

"He was standing right around here when he shot her," I muttered, a strange sensation running along my nerves as I recalled what Hilda had said about Deborah's being in a place "crowded" with things "grabbing" at her. *Kudzu.*

"If she was shot at close range," Marino said, "then she went down not too far from here."

Wading out a little farther as he followed me with the metal detector, I said, "How the hell did he *see* to shoot her, Marino? Lord. Can you imagine this place at night?"

"The moon was out."

"But it wasn't full," I said.

"Full enough so it wouldn't have been pitch-dark."

The weather had been checked months ago. The Friday night of August thirty-first when the couple had disappeared, the temperature had been in the upper sixties, the moon three-quarters full, the sky clear. Even if the killer had been armed with a powerful flashlight, I still could not understand how he could force two hostages out here at night without being as disoriented and vulnerable as they were. All I could imagine was confusion, a lot of stumbling about.

Why didn't he just kill them on the logging road, drag their bodies several yards into the woods, and then drive away? Why did he want to bring them out here?

And yet the pattern was the same with the other couples. Their bodies also had been found in remote, wooded areas like this.

Looking around at the kudzu, an unpleasant expression on his face, Marino said, "Glad as hell this ain't snake weather."

"That's a lovely thought," I said, unnerved.

"You want to keep going?" he asked in a tone that told me he had no interest in venturing an inch farther into this gothic wasteland.

"I think we've had enough for one day." I waded out of the kudzu as quickly as possible, my flesh crawling. The mention of snakes had done me in. I was on the verge of a full-blown anxiety attack.

It was almost five, the woods gloomy with shadows as we headed back to the car. Every time a twig snapped beneath Marino's feet, my heart jumped. Squirrels scampering up trees and birds flying off branches were startling intrusions upon the eerie silence.

"I'll drop this off at the lab first thing in the morning," he said. "Then I gotta be in court. Great way to spend your day off."

"Which case?"

"The case of Bubba shot by his friend named Bubba, the only witness was another drone named Bubba."

"You're not serious."

"Hey," he said, unlocking the car doors, "I'm as serious as a sawed-off shotgun." Starting the engine, he muttered, "I'm starting to hate this job, Doc. I swear, I really am."

"At the moment you hate the whole world, Marino."

"No, I don't," he said, and he actually laughed. "I like you all right."

The last day of January began when the morning's mail brought an official communication from Pat Harvey. Brief and to the point, it stated that if copies of her daughter's autopsy and toxicology reports were not received by the end of the following week, she would get a court order. A copy of the letter had been sent to my immediate boss, the Commissioner of Health and Human Services, whose secretary was on the phone within the hour summoning me to his office.

While autopsies awaited me downstairs, I left the building and made the short walk along Franklin to Main Street Station, which had been vacant for years, then converted into a short-lived shopping mall before the state had purchased it. In a sense, the historic red building with its clock tower and red tile roof had become a train station again, a temporary stop for state employees forced to relocate while the Madison Building was stripped of asbestos and renovated. The Governor had appointed Dr. Paul Sessions commissioner two years before, and though face-to-face meetings with my new boss were infrequent, they were pleasant enough. I had a feeling today might prove a different story. His secretary had sounded apologetic on the phone, as if she knew I were being called in to be gaffed.

The commissioner resided in a suite of offices on the second level, accessible by a marble stairway worn smooth by travelers scuffing up and down steps in an era long past. The spaces the commissioner had appropriated had once been a sporting goods store and a boutique selling colorful kites and wind socks. Walls had been knocked out, plate glass windows filled in with brick, his offices carpeted, paneled, and arranged with handsome furnishings. Dr. Sessions was familiar enough with the sluggish workings of government to have settled into his temporary headquarters as if the relocation were permanent.

His secretary greeted me with a sympathetic smile that made me feel only worse as she swiveled around from her keyboard and reached for the phone.

She announced that I was here, and immediately the solid oak door across from her desk opened and Dr. Sessions invited me in.

An energetic man with thinning brown hair and large-framed glasses that swallowed his narrow face, he was living proof that marathon running was never intended for human beings. His chest was tubercular, body fat so low he rarely took his suit jacket off and frequently wore long sleeves in the summer because he was chronically cold. He still wore a splint on the left arm he had broken several months ago while running a race on the West Coast and getting tangled up in a coathanger that had eluded the feet of runners ahead of him and sent him crashing to the street. He was, perhaps, the only contender not to finish the race and end up in the newspapers anyway.

He seated himself behind his desk, the letter from Pat Harvey centered on the blotter, his face unusually stern.

"I assume you've already seen this?" He tapped the letter with an index finger.

"Yes," I said. "Understandably, Pat Harvey is very interested in the results of her daughter's examination."

"Deborah Harvey's body was found eleven days ago. Am I to conclude you don't yet know what killed her or Fred Cheney?"

"I know what killed her. His cause of death is still undetermined."

He looked puzzled. "Dr. Scarpetta, would you care to explain to me why this information has not been released to the Harveys or to Fred Cheney's father?"

"My explanation is simple," I said. "Their cases are still pending as further special studies are conducted. And the FBI has asked me to withhold releasing anything to anyone."

"I see." He gazed at the wall as if it contained a window to look out of, which it did not.

"If you direct me to release my reports, I will do so, Dr. Sessions. In fact, I would be relieved if you would order me to meet Pat Harvey's request."

"Why?" He knew the answer, but he wanted to hear what I had to say.

"Because Mrs. Harvey and her husband have a right to know what happened to their daughter," I said. "Bruce Cheney has a right to hear what we do or don't know about his son. The wait is anguish for them."

"Have you talked to Mrs. Harvey?"

"Not recently."

"Have you talked to her since the bodies were found, Dr. Scarpetta?" He was fidgeting with his sling.

"I called her when the identifications were confirmed, but I haven't talked with her since."

"Has she tried to reach you?"

"She has."

"And you have refused to talk to her?"

"I've already explained why I'm not talking to her," I said. "And I don't believe it would be politic for me to get on the phone and tell her that the FBI doesn't want me to release information to her."

"You haven't mentioned the FBI's directive to anyone, then."

"I just mentioned it to you."

He recrossed his legs. "And I appreciate that. But it would be inappropriate to mention this business to anybody else. Especially reporters."

"I've been doing my best to avoid reporters."

"The *Washington Post* called me this morning."

"Who from the *Post*?"

He began sorting through message slips as I waited uneasily. I did not want to believe that Abby would go behind my back and over my head.

"Someone named Clifford Ring." He glanced up. "Actually, it's not the first time he's called, nor am I the only person he's attempted to milk for information. He's also been badgering my secretary and other members of my staff, including my deputy and the Secretary of Human Resources. I assume he's called you as well, which was why he finally resorted to administration, because, as he put it, 'the medical examiner won't talk to me.' "

"A lot of reporters have called. I don't remember most of their names."

"Well, Mr. Ring seems to think there's some sort of cover-up going on, something conspiratorial, and based on the direction of his questioning, he seems to have information that buttresses this."

Strange, I thought. It didn't sound to me as if the *Post* was holding off on investigating these cases, as Abby had stated so emphatically.

"He's under the impression," the commissioner continued, "that your office is stonewalling, and that it's therefore part of this so-called conspiracy."

"And I suppose we are." I worked hard to keep the annoyance out of my voice. "And that leaves me caught in the middle. Either I defy Pat Harvey or the Justice Department, and frankly, given a choice, I would prefer to accommodate Mrs. Harvey. Eventually, I will have to answer to her. She is Deborah's mother. I don't have to answer to the FBI."

"I'm not interested in antagonizing the Justice Department," Dr. Sessions said.

He did not have to outline why. A substantial portion of the commissioner's departmental budget was supplied by money from federal grants, some of which trickled down to my office to subsidize the collection of data needed by various injury prevention and traffic safety agencies. The Justice Department knew how to play hardball. If antagonizing the feds did not dry up much-needed revenues, we could at least count on our lives being made miserable. The last thing the commissioner wanted was to account for every pencil and sheet of stationery purchased with grant money. I knew how it worked. All of us would be nickel-and-dimed, papered to death.

The commissioner reached for the letter with his good arm and studied it for a moment.

He said, "Actually, the only answer may be for Mrs. Harvey to go through with her threat."

"If she gets a court order, then I will have no choice but to send her what she wants."

"I realize that. And the advantage is the FBI can't hold us accountable. The disadvantage, obviously, will be the negative publicity," he thought aloud. "Certainly, it won't shine a good light on the Department of Health and Human Services if the public knows we were forced by a judge to give Pat Harvey what she is entitled to by law. I suppose it may corroborate our friend Mr. Ring's suspicions."

The average citizen didn't even know that the Medical Examiner's Office was part of Health and Human Services. I was the one who was going to look bad. The commissioner, in good bureaucratic fashion, was setting me up to take it on the nose because he had no intention of aggravating the Justice Department.

"Of course," he considered, "Pat Harvey will come across as rather heavy-handed, as using her office to throw her weight around. She may be bluffing."

"I doubt it," I said tersely.

"We'll see." He got up from his desk and showed me to the door. "I'll write Mrs. Harvey, saying you and I talked."

I'll just bet you will, I thought.

"Let me know if I can be of any assistance." He smiled, avoiding my eyes.

I had just let him know I needed assistance. He might as well have had two broken arms. He wasn't going to lift a finger.

As soon as I got back to the office, I asked the clerks up front and Rose if a reporter from the *Post* had been calling. After searching memories and digging through old message slips, no one could come up with a Clifford Ring. He couldn't exactly accuse me of stonewalling if he'd never tried to reach me, I reasoned. All the same, I was perplexed.

"By the way," Rose added as I headed down the hall, "Linda's been looking for you, says she needs to see you right away."

Linda was a firearms examiner. Marino must have been by with the cartridge case, I thought. Good.

The toolmarks and firearms laboratory was on the third floor and could have passed for a used-gun shop. Revolvers, rifles, shotguns, and pistols covered virtually every inch of counter space, and evidence wrapped in brown paper was stacked chest high on the floor. I was about to decide that everyone was at lunch when I heard the muffled explosions of a gun discharging behind closed doors. Adjoining the lab was a small room used to test-fire weapons into a galvanized steel tank filled with water.

Two rounds later Linda emerged, .38 Special in one hand, spent bullets and cartridge cases in the other. She was slender and feminine, with long brown hair, good bones, and wide-spaced hazel eyes. A lab coat protected a flowing black skirt and pale yellow silk blouse with a gold circle pin at the throat. Were I sitting next to her on a plane and trying to guess her profession, teaching poetry or running an art gallery would have come to mind.

"Bad news, Kay," she said, setting the revolver and spent ammunition on her desk.

"I hope it doesn't pertain to the cartridge case Marino brought in," I said.

"Afraid it does. I was about to etch my initials and a lab number on it when I got a little surprise." She moved over to the comparison microscope. "Here." She offered me the chair. "A picture's worth a thousand words."

Seating myself, I peered into the lenses. In the field of light to my left was the stainless-steel cartridge case.

"I don't understand," I muttered, adjusting the focus.

Etched inside the cartridge case's mouth were the initials "J.M."

"I thought Marino receipted this to you." I looked up at her.

"He did. He came by about an hour ago," Linda said. "I asked him if he etched these initials, and he said he didn't. Not that I really thought he had. Marino's initials are P.M., not J.M., and he's been around long enough to know better."

Though some detectives initialed cartridge cases just as some medical examiners initialed bullets recovered from bodies, the firearms examiners discouraged the practice. Taking a stylus to metal is risky because there's always the threat one might scratch breech block, firing pin, ejector marks, or other features, such as lands and grooves, suitable for identification. Marino did know better. Like me, he always initialed the plastic bag and left the evidence inside untouched.

"Am I to believe these initials were *already* on this cartridge case when Marino brought it in?" I asked.

"Apparently so."

J.M. *Jay Morrell,* I thought, mystified. Why would a cartridge case left at the scene be marked with his initials?

Linda proposed, "I'm wondering if a police officer working the scene out there had this in his pocket for some reason, and inadvertently lost it. If he had a hole in his pocket, for example?"

"I'd find that hard to believe," I said.

"Well, I've got one other theory I'll toss out. But you aren't going to like it, and I don't like it much, either. The cartridge case could have been reloaded."

"Then why would it be marked with an investigator's initials? Who on earth would reload a cartridge case marked as evidence?"

"It's happened before, Kay, and you didn't hear this from me, all right?"

I just listened.

"The number of weapons and the amount of ammunition and cartridge cases collected by the police and submitted to the courts are astronomical and worth a lot of money. People get greedy, even judges. They take the stuff for themselves or sell it to gun dealers, other enthusiasts. I suppose it's remotely possible this cartridge case was collected by a police officer or submitted to the courts as evidence at some point, and ended up reloaded. It may be that whoever fired it had no idea someone's initials were etched inside it."

"We can't prove that this cartridge case belongs to the bullet I found in Deborah Harvey's lumbar spine, and won't be able to do so unless we recover the pistol," I reminded her. "We can't even say with certainty it's from a Hydra-Shok cartridge. All we know is it's nine-millimeter, Federal.

"True. But Federal holds the patent for Hydra-Shok ammunition, has since the late eighties. For whatever that's worth."

"Does Federal sell Hydra-Shok bullets for reloading?" I asked.

"That's the problem. No. Only the cartridges are available on the market. But that doesn't mean someone couldn't get hold of the bullets in some other way. Steal them from the factory, have a contact who steals them from the factory. I could get them, for example, if I claimed I were working on a special project. Who knows?" She retrieved a can of Diet Coke from her desk, adding, "Nothing much surprises me anymore."

"Is Marino aware of what you found?"

"I called him."

"Thank you, Linda," I said, getting up, and I was formulating my own theory, which was quite different from hers and, unfortunately, more probable. Just the thought of it made me furious. In my office I snatched up the phone and dialed Marino's pager number. He returned my call almost immediately.

"The little fuckhead," he said right off.

"Who? Linda?" I asked, startled.

"Morrell, that's who. The lying son of a bitch. Just got off the phone with him. Said he didn't know what I was talking about until I accused him of stealing evidence for reloads—asked him if he was stealing guns and live ammo, too. Said I'd have his ass investigated by Internal Affairs. Then he started singing."

"He etched his initials in the cartridge case and left it out there deliberately, didn't he, Marino?"

"Oh, yeah. They found the goddam cartridge case last week. The real one. Then the asshole leaves this goddam plant, starts whining that he was just doing what the FBI told him to do."

"Where is the real cartridge case?" I demanded, blood pounding in my temples.

"The FBI lab's got it. You and yours truly spent an entire afternoon in the woods, and guess what, Doc? The whole goddam time we was being watched. The place is under physical surveillance. Just a damn good thing neither one of us wandered behind a bush to take a piss, right?"

"Have you talked to Benton?"

"Hell, no. As far as I'm concerned, he can screw himself." Marino slammed down the receiver.

9

There was something reassuring about the Globe and Laurel that made me feel safe. Brick, with simple lines and not a hint of ostentation, the restaurant occupied a sliver of northern Virginia real estate in Triangle, near the U.S. Marine Corps base. The narrow strip of lawn in front was always tidy, boxwoods neatly pruned, the parking lot orderly, every car within the painted boundaries of its allotted space.

Semper Fidelis was over the door, and stepping inside I was welcomed by the cream of the "always faithful" crop: police chiefs, four-star generals, secretaries of defense, directors of the FBI and CIA, the photographs so familiar to me that the men sternly smiling in them seemed a host of long-lost friends. Major Jim Yancey, whose bronzed combat boots from Vietnam were on top of the piano across from the bar, strode across red Highland tartan carpet and intercepted me.

"Dr. Scarpetta," he said, grinning as he shook my hand. "I was afraid you didn't like the food when last you were here, and that's why you waited so long to come back."

The major's casual attire of turtleneck sweater and corduroy trousers could not camouflage his former profession. He was as military as a campaign hat, posture proudly straight, not an ounce of fat, white hair in a buzz cut. Past retirement age, he still looked fit enough for combat, and it wasn't hard for me to imagine him bumping over rugged terrain in a Jeep or eating rations from a can in the jungle while monsoon rains hammered down.

"I've never had a bad meal here, and you know it," I said warmly.

"You're looking for Benton, and he's looking for you. The old boy's around there"—he pointed—"in his usual foxhole."

"Thank you, Jim. I know the way. And it's so good to see you again."

He winked at me and returned to the bar.

It was Mark who had introduced me to Major Yancey's restaurant when I drove to Quantico two weekends every month to see him. As I walked beneath a ceiling covered with police patches and passed displays of old Corps memorabilia, recollections tugged at my heart. I could pick out the tables where Mark and I had sat, and it seemed odd to see strangers there now, engaged in their own private conversations. I had not been to the Globe in almost a year.

Leaving the main dining room, I headed for a more secluded section where Wesley was waiting for me in his "foxhole," a corner table before a window with red draperies. He was sipping a drink and did not smile as we greeted each other formally. A waiter in a black tuxedo appeared to take my drink order.

Wesley looked up at me with eyes as impenetrable as a bank vault, and I responded in kind. He had signaled the first round, and we were going to come out swinging.

"I am very concerned that we're having a problem with communication, Kay," he began.

"My sentiments exactly," I said with the iron-hard calm I had perfected on the witness stand. "I, too, am concerned by our problem with communication. Is the Bureau tapping my phone, tailing me as well? I hope whoever was hiding in the woods got good photographs of Marino and me."

Wesley said just as calmly, "You, personally, are not under surveillance. The wooded area where you and Marino were spotted yesterday afternoon is under surveillance."

"Perhaps if you had kept me informed," I said, holding in my anger, "I might have told you in advance when Marino and I had decided to go back out there."

"It never occurred to me you might."

"I routinely pay retrospective visits to scenes. You've worked with me long enough to be aware of that."

"My mistake. But now you know. And I would prefer that you not go back out there again."

"I have no plans to do so," I said testily. "But should the need arise, I will be happy to give you advance warning. Might as well, since you'll find out anyway. And I certainly don't need to waste my time picking up evidence that has been planted by your agents or the police."

"Kay," he said in a softer tone, "I'm not trying to interfere with your job."

"I'm being lied to, Benton. I'm told no cartridge case was recovered from the scene, only to discover it was receipted to the Bureau's laboratory more than a week ago."

"When we decided to set up surveillance, we didn't want word of it to leak," he said. "The fewer people told about what we were up to the better."

"Obviously, you must be assuming the killer might return to the scene."

"It's a possibility."

"Did you entertain this possibility with the first four cases?"

"It's different this time."

"Why?"

"Because he left evidence, and he knows it."

"If he were so worried about the cartridge case, he had plenty of time to go back and look for it last fall," I said.

"He may not know we would figure out Deborah Harvey was shot, that a Hydra-Shok bullet would be recovered from her body."

"I don't believe the individual we're dealing with is stupid," I said.

The waiter returned with my Scotch and soda.

Wesley went on, "The cartridge case you recovered was planted.

I won't deny that. And yes, you and Marino walked into an area under physical surveillance. There were two men hiding in the woods. They saw everything the two of you did, including picking up the cartridge case. Had you not called me, I would have called you."

"I'd like to think you would have."

"I would have explained. Would have had no choice, really, because you inadvertently upset the apple cart. And you're right." He reached for his drink. "I should have let you know in advance; then none of this would have happened and we wouldn't have been forced to call things off, or better put, postpone them."

"What have you postponed, exactly?"

"Had you and Marino not stumbled upon what we were doing, tomorrow morning's news would have carried a story targeted at the killer." He paused. "Disinformation to draw him out, make him worry. The story will run, but not until Monday."

"And the point of it?" I asked.

"We want him to think that something turned up during the examination of the bodies. Something to make us believe he left important evidence at the scene. Alleged this, alleged that, with plenty of denials and no comments from the police. All of it intended to imply that whatever this evidence is, we've had no luck finding it yet. The killer knows he left a cartridge case out there. If he gets sufficiently paranoid and returns to look for it, we'll be waiting, watching him pick up the one we planted, get it on film, and then grab him."

"The cartridge case is worthless unless you have him and the gun. Why would he risk returning to the scene, especially if it appears that the police are busy looking around out there for this evidence?" I wanted to know.

"He may be worried about a lot of things, because he lost control of the situation. Had to have, or it would not have been necessary to shoot Deborah in the back. It might not have been necessary to shoot her at all. It appears he murdered Cheney without using a gun. How does he know what we're really looking for, Kay? Maybe it's a cartridge case. Maybe it's something else. He isn't going to be certain about the exact condition of the bodies when they were found. We don't know what he did to the couple, and he doesn't really know what you may have discovered while doing the autopsies. And he might not go back out there the day after the story runs, but he might try it a week or two later if everything seems quiet."

"I doubt your disinformation tactic will work," I said.

"Nothing ventured, nothing gained. The killer left evidence. We'd be foolish not to act on that."

The opening was too wide for me to resist walking through it. "And have you acted on evidence found in the first four cases, Benton? It's my understanding that a jack of hearts was recovered inside each of the vehicles. A detail you apparently have worked very hard to suppress."

"Who told you this?" he asked, the expression on his face unchanged. He did not even look surprised.

"Is it true?"

"Yes."

"And did you find a card in the Harvey-Cheney case?"

Wesley stared off across the room, nodding at the waiter. "I recommend the filet mignon." He opened his menu. "That or the lamb chops."

I placed my order as my heart pounded. I lit a cigarette, unable to relax, my mind frenetically groping for a way to break through.

"You didn't answer my question."

"I don't see how it is relevant to your role in the investigation," he said.

"The police waited hours before calling me to the scene. The bodies had been moved, tampered with, by the time I got there. I'm being stonewalled by investigators, you've asked me to indefinitely pend the cause and manner of Fred's and Deborah's deaths. Meanwhile, Pat Harvey is threatening to get a court order because I won't release my findings." I paused. He remained unflappable.

"Finally," I concluded, my words beginning to bite, "I make a retrospective visit to a scene without knowing it's under surveillance or that the evidence I collected was planted. And you don't think the details of these cases are relevant to my role in the investigation? I'm no longer sure I even have a role in the investigation. Or at least you seem determined to make sure I don't have one."

"I'm not doing anything of the sort."

"Then someone is."

He did not reply.

"If a jack of hearts was found inside Deborah's Jeep or somewhere near their bodies, it's important for me to know. It would link the deaths of all five couples. When there's a serial killer on the loose in Virginia, it is of great concern to me."

Then he caught me off guard. "How much have you been telling Abby Turnbull?"

"I haven't been telling her anything," I said, my heart pounding harder.

"You've met with her, Kay. I'm sure you won't deny that."

"Mark told you, and I'm sure you won't deny that."

"Mark would have no reason to know you saw Abby in Richmond or Washington unless you told him. And in any event, he would have no reason to pass this along to me."

I stared at him. How could Wesley have known I had seen Abby in Washington unless she really was being watched?

"When Abby came to see me in Richmond," I said, "Mark called and I mentioned she was visiting. Are you telling me he said nothing to you?"

"He didn't."

"Then how did you find out?"

"There are some things I can't tell you. And you're just going to have to trust me."

The waiter set down our salads, and we ate in silence. Wesley did not speak again until our main courses arrived.

"I'm under a lot of pressure," he said in a quiet voice.

"I can see that. You look exhausted, run-down."

"Thank you, Doctor," he said ironically.

"You've changed in other ways as well." I pushed the point.

"I'm sure that is your perception."

"You're shutting me out, Benton."

"I suppose I keep my distance because you ask questions that I can't answer; so does Marino. And then I feel even more pressure. Do you understand?"

"I'm trying to understand," I said.

"I can't tell you everything. Can you let it go at that?"

"Not quite. Because that's where we're at cross-purposes. I have information you need. And you have information I need. I'm not going to show you mine unless you show me yours."

He surprised me by laughing.

"Do you think we can strike a deal under these terms?" I persisted.

"It looks like I don't have much of a choice."

"You don't," I said.

"Yes, we did find a jack of hearts in the Harvey-Cheney case. Yes, I did have their bodies moved before you arrived at the scene, and I know that was poor form, but you have no idea why the cards are so significant or the problems that would be precipitated by word of them leaking. If it made the newspapers, for example. I'm not going to say anything further about that right now."

"Where was the card?" I asked.

"We found it inside Deborah Harvey's purse. When a couple of the cops helped me turn her over, we found the purse under her body."

"Are you suggesting that the killer carried her purse out into the woods?"

"Yes. It wouldn't make any sense to think that Deborah carried her purse out there."

"In the other cases," I pointed out, "the card was left in plain sight inside the vehicle."

"Exactly. Where the card was found is just one more inconsistency. Why *wasn't* it left inside the Jeep? Another inconsistency is that the cards left in the other cases are Bicycle playing cards. The one left with Deborah is a different brand. Then there's the matter of fibers."

"What fibers?" I asked.

Though I had collected fibers from all of the decomposed bodies, most of them were consistent with the victims' own clothing or the upholstery of their vehicles. Unknown fibers—what few I had found—had supplied no link between the cases, had proved useless so far.

"In the four cases preceding Deborah's and Fred's murders," Wesley said, "white cotton fibers were recovered from the driver's seat of each abandoned car."

"That's news to me," I said, irritation flaring again.

"The fiber analysis was done by our labs," he explained.

"And what is your interpretation?" I asked.

"The pattern of fibers recovered is interesting. Since the victims weren't wearing white cotton clothing at the time of their deaths, I have to assume that the fibers were left by the perpetrator, and this places him driving the victims' cars after the crimes. But we've been assuming that all along. One has to consider his clothing. And a possibility is that he was wearing some type of uniform when he encountered the couples. White cotton trousers. I don't know. But no white cotton fibers were recovered from the driver's seat of Deborah Harvey's Jeep."

"What did you find inside her Jeep?" I asked.

"Nothing that tells me anything right now. In fact, the interior was immaculate." He paused, cutting his steak. "The point is, the

MO's different enough in this case to worry me a lot, because of the other circumstances."

"Because one of the victims is the Drug Czar's daughter, and you're still considering that what happened to Deborah may have been politically motivated, related to her mother's antidrug endeavors," I said.

He nodded. "We can't rule out that the murders of Deborah and her boyfriend were disguised to resemble the other cases."

"If their deaths aren't related to the others, and were a hit," I asked skeptically, "then how do you explain their killer knowing about the cards, Benton? Even I didn't find out about the jack of hearts until recently. Certainly it hasn't been in the newspapers."

"Pat Harvey knows," he startled me by saying.

Abby, I thought. And I was willing to bet that Abby had divulged the detail to Mrs. Harvey, and that Wesley knew this.

"How long has Mrs. Harvey known about the cards?" I asked.

"When her daughter's Jeep was found, she asked me if we'd recovered a card. And she called me about it again after the bodies turned up."

"I don't understand," I said. "Why would she have known last fall? It sounds to me as if she knew the details of the other cases *before* Deborah and Fred disappeared."

"She knew some of the details. Pat Harvey was interested in these cases long before she had personal motivation."

"Why?"

"You've heard some of the theories," he said. "Drug overdoses. Some new weird designer drug on the street, the kids going out in the woods to party and ending up dead. Or some drug dealer who gets his thrills by selling bad stuff in some remote place, then watching the couples die."

"I've heard the theories, and there is nothing to support them. Toxicology results were negative for drugs in the first eight deaths."

"I remember that from the reports," he said thoughtfully. "But I also assumed this didn't necessarily mean the kids hadn't been involved in drugs. Their bodies were almost skeletonized. Doesn't seem there was much left to test."

"There was some red tissue left, muscle. That's enough for testing. Cocaine or heroin, for example. We, at least, would have expected to find their metabolites of benzoyle-cogonine or morphine. As for designer drugs, we tested for analogues of PCP, amphetamines."

"What about China White?" he proposed, referring to a very potent synthetic analgesic popular in California. "From what I understand, it doesn't take much for an overdose and is difficult to detect."

"True. Less than one milligram can be fatal, meaning the concentration is too low to detect without using special analytical procedures such as RIA." Noting the blank expression on his face, I explained, "Radioimmunoassay, a procedure based on specific drug antibody reactions. Unlike conventional screening procedures, RIA can detect small levels of drugs, so it's what we resort to when looking for China White, LSD, THC."

"None of which you found."

"That's correct."

"What about alcohol?"

"Alcohol's a problem when bodies are badly decomposed. Some of those tests were negative, others less than point oh-five, possibly the result of decomposition. Inconclusive, in other words."

"With Harvey and Cheney as well?"

"No trace of drugs so far," I told him. "What is Pat Harvey's interest in the early cases?"

"Don't get me wrong," he replied. "I'm not saying it was a major preoccupation. But she must have gotten tips back when she was a U.S. attorney, inside information, and she asked some questions. Politics, Kay. I suppose if it had turned out that these deaths of couples in Virginia were related to drugs—either accidental deaths or drug homicides—she would have used the information to buttress her antidrug efforts."

That would explain why Mrs. Harvey seemed well informed when I had lunch at her house last fall, I thought. No doubt she had information on file in her office because of her early interest in the cases.

"When her inquiries into this didn't go anywhere," Wesley continued, "I think she pretty much let it go until her daughter and Fred disappeared. Then it all came back to her, as you can imagine."

"Yes, I can imagine. And I can also imagine the bitter irony had it turned out that drugs killed the Drug Czar's daughter."

"Don't think that hasn't crossed Mrs. Harvey's mind," Wesley said grimly.

The reminder made me tense again. "She has a right to know, Benton. I can't pend these cases forever."

He nodded to the waiter that we were ready for coffee.

"I need you to buy me more time, Kay."

"Because of your disinformation tactics?"

"We need to give that a shot, let the stories run without interference. The minute Mrs. Harvey gets anything from you, all hell's going to break loose. Believe me, I know how she'll react better than you do at this point. She'll go to the press, and in the process screw up everything we've been setting up to lure the killer."

"What happens when she gets her court order?"

"That will take time. It won't happen tomorrow. Will you stall a little longer, Kay?"

"You haven't finished explaining about the jack of hearts," I reminded him. "How could a hit man have known about the cards?"

Wesley replied reluctantly, "Pat Harvey doesn't gather information or investigate situations alone. She has aides, a staff. She talks to other politicians, any number of people, including constituents. It all depends on who she divulged information to, and who out there might have wished to destroy her, assuming that's the case, and I'm not saying it is."

"A paid hit disguised to look like the early cases," I considered. "Only the hit man made a mistake. He didn't know to leave the jack of hearts in the car. He left it with Deborah's body, inside her purse. Someone perhaps involved with the fraudulent charities Pat Harvey is supposed to testify against?"

"We're talking about bad people who know other bad people. Drug dealers. Organized crime." He idly stirred his coffee. "Mrs. Harvey's not faring too well through all this. She's very distracted. This congressional hearing isn't exactly foremost on her mind, at the moment."

"I see. And I suspect she's not exactly on friendly terms with the Justice Department, because of this hearing."

Wesley carefully set his teaspoon on the edge of his saucer. "She's not," he said, looking up at me. "What she's trying to bring about isn't going to help us. It's fine to put ACTMAD and other scams like it out of business. But it's not enough. We want to prosecute. In the past, there's been some friction between her and the DEA, FBI, also the CIA."

"And now?" I continued to probe.

"It's worse, because she's emotionally involved, has to rely on the Bureau to assist in solving her daughter's homicide. She's uncooperative, paranoid. She's trying to work around us, take matters into her own hands." Sighing, he added, "She's a problem, Kay."

"She probably says the same thing about the Bureau."

He smiled wryly. "I'm sure she does."

I wanted to continue the mental poker game to see if Wesley was keeping anything else from me, so I gave him more. "It appears that Deborah received a defensive injury to her left index finger. Not a cut, but a hack, inflicted by a knife with a serrated blade."

"Where on her index finger?" he asked, leaning forward a little.

"Dorsal." I held up my hand to show him. "On top, near her first knuckle."

"Interesting. Atypical."

"Yes. Difficult to reconstruct how she got it."

"So we know he was armed with a knife," he thought out loud. "That makes me all the more suspicious that something went wrong out there. Something happened he wasn't expecting. He may have resorted to a gun to subdue the couple, but intended to kill them with the knife. Possibly by cutting their throats. But then something went haywire. Deborah somehow got away and he shot her in the back, then maybe cut her throat to finish her off."

"And then positioned their bodies to look like the others?" I asked. "Arm in arm, facedown, and fully clothed?"

He stared at the wall above my head.

I thought of the cigarette butts left at each scene. I thought of the parallels. The fact that the playing card was a different brand and left in a different place this time proved nothing. Killers are not machines. Their rituals and habits are not an exact science or set in stone. Nothing that Wesley had divulged to me, including the absence of white cotton fibers in Deborah's Jeep, was enough to validate the theory that Fred's and Deborah's homicides were unrelated to the other cases. I was experiencing the same confusion that I felt whenever I visited Quantico, where I was never sure if guns were firing bullets or blanks, if helicopters carried marines on real business or FBI agents simulating maneuvers, or if buildings in the Academy's fictitious town of Hogan's Alley were functional or Hollywood facades.

I could push Wesley no further. He wasn't going to tell me more.

"It's getting late," he commented. "You have a long drive back."

I had one last point to make.

"I don't want friendship to interfere with all this, Benton."

"That goes without saying."

"What happened between Mark and me—"

"That's not a factor," he interrupted, and his voice was firm but not unkind.

"He was your best friend."

"I'd like to think he still is."

"Do you blame me for why he went to Colorado, left Quantico?"

"I know why he left," he said. "I'm sorry he left. He was very good for the Academy."

The FBI's strategy of drawing out the killer by way of disinformation did not materialize the following Monday. Either the Bureau had changed its mind, or it was preempted by Pat Harvey, who held a press conference the same day.

At noon, she faced cameras in her Washington office, adding to the pathos by having Bruce Cheney, Fred's father, by her side. She looked awful. Weight added by the camera and makeup could not hide how thin she had gotten or the dark circles under her eyes.

"When did these threats begin, Mrs. Harvey, and what was the nature of them?" a reporter asked.

"The first one came shortly after I began investigating the charities. And I suppose this was a little over a year ago," she said without emotion. "This was a letter mailed to my home in Richmond. I won't divulge the specific nature of what it said, but the threat was directed at my family."

"And you believe this was connected to your probe into fraudulent charities like ACTMAD?"

"There's no question about that. There were other threats, the last one as recent as two months before my daughter and Fred Cheney disappeared."

Bruce Cheney's face flashed on the screen. He was pale, blinking in the blinding haze of TV lights.

"Ms. Harvey . . ."

"Mrs. Harvey . . ."

Reporters were interrupting each other, and Pat Harvey interrupted them, the camera swinging back her way.

"The FBI was aware of the situation, and it was their opinion that the threats, the letters, were originating from one source," she said.

"Mrs. Harvey . . ."

"Ms. Harvey"—a reporter raised her voice above the commotion—"it's no secret that you and the Justice Department have different agendas, a conflict of interests arising from the investigation of the charities. Are you suggesting the FBI knew that the safety of your family was in jeopardy and *didn't do anything?*"

"It's more than a suggestion," she stated.

"Are you accusing the Justice Department of incompetence?"

"What I'm accusing the Justice Department of is conspiracy," Pat Harvey said.

Groaning, I reached for a cigarette as the din, the interruptions reached a crescendo. You've lost it, I thought, staring in disbelief at the TV inside the small medical library in my downtown office.

It got only worse. And my heart was filled with dread as Mrs. Harvey turned her cool stare to the camera and one by one ran her sword through everyone involved in the investigation, including me. She spared no one, and there was nothing sacred, including the detail of the jack of hearts.

It had been a gross understatement when Wesley had said she was uncooperative and a problem. Beneath her armor of reason was a woman crazed by rage and grief. Numbly I listened as she plainly and without reservation indicted the police, the FBI, and the Medical Examiner's Office for complicity in a "cover-up."

"They are deliberately burying the truth about these cases," she concluded, "when the act of doing so serves only their self-interest at the unconscionable expense of human lives."

"What a lot of shit," muttered Fielding, my deputy chief, sitting nearby.

"*Which* cases?" a reporter demanded loudly. "The deaths of your daughter and her boyfriend or are you referring to the four other couples?"

"All of them," Mrs. Harvey replied. "I'm referring to all of the young men and women hunted down like animals and murdered."

"What is being covered up?"

"The identity or identities of those responsible," she said as if she knew. "There has been no intervention on the part of the Justice Department to stop these killings. The reasons are political. A certain federal agency is protecting its own."

"Could you please be more specific?" a voice shot back.

"When my investigation is concluded, I will make a full disclosure."

"At the hearing?" she was asked. "Are you suggesting that the murder of Deborah and her boyfriend . . ."

"His name is Fred."

It was Bruce Cheney who had spoken, and suddenly his livid face filled the television screen.

The room went silent.

"Fred. His name is *Frederick Wilson Cheney.*" The father's voice trembled with emotion. "He's not just Debbie's *boyfriend*. He's dead, murdered, too. My *son!*" Words caught in his throat, and he hung his head to hide his tears.

I turned off the television, upset and unable to sit still.

Rose had been standing in the doorway, watching. She looked at me and slowly shook her head.

Fielding got up, stretched, tightened the drawstring of his surgical greens.

"She just screwed herself in front of the whole damn world," he announced, walking out of the library.

I realized as I was pouring myself a cup of coffee what Pat Harvey had said. I began to really hear it as it replayed inside my head.

"Hunted down like animals and murdered . . ."

Her words had the sound of something scripted. They did not strike me as glib, off the cuff, or a figure of speech. *A federal agency protecting its own?*

Hunt.

A jack of hearts like a knight of cups. Someone who is perceived or perceives himself as a competitor, a defender. One who does battle, Hilda Ozimek had said to me.

A knight. A soldier.

Hunt.

Their murders were meticulously calculated, methodically planned. Bruce Phillips and Judy Roberts disappeared in June. Their bodies were found in mid-August, when hunting season opened.

Jim Freeman and Bonnie Smyth disappeared in July, their bodies found the opening day of quail and pheasant season.

Ben Anderson and Carolyn Bennett disappeared in March, their bodies found in November during deer season.

Susan Wilcox and Mike Martin disappeared in late February, their bodies discovered in mid-May, during spring gobbler season.

Deborah Harvey and Fred Cheney vanished Labor Day weekend and were not found until months later when the woods were crowded with hunters after rabbit, squirrel, fox, pheasant, and raccoon.

I had not assumed the pattern meant anything because most of the badly decomposed and skeletonized bodies that end up in my office are found by hunters. When someone drops dead or is dumped in the woods, a hunter is the most likely person to stumble upon the remains. But when and where the couples' bodies were discovered could have been planned.

The killer wanted his victims found, but not right away, so he killed them off season, knowing that it was probable his victims would not be discovered until hunters were out in the woods again.

By then the bodies were decomposed. Gone with the tissue were the injuries he had inflicted. If rape was involved, there would be no seminal fluid. Most trace evidence would be dislodged by wind and washed away by rain. It may even be that it was important to him that the bodies be found by hunters because in his fantasies he, too, was a hunter. The greatest hunter of all.

Hunters hunted animals, I thought as I sat at my downtown desk the following afternoon. Guerrillas, military special agents, and soldiers of fortune hunted human beings.

Within the fifty-mile radius where the couples had vanished and turned up dead were Fort Eustis, Langley Field, and a number of other military installations, including the CIA's West Point, operated under the cover of a military base called Camp Peary. "The Farm," as Camp Peary is referred to in spy novels and investigative nonfiction books about intelligence, was where officers were trained in the paramilitary activities of infiltration, exfiltration, demolitions, nighttime parachute jumps, and other clandestine operations.

Abby Turnbull took a wrong turn and ended up at the entrance of Camp Peary, and days later FBI agents came looking for her.

The feds were paranoid, and I had a suspicion I might know why. After reading the newspaper accounts of Pat Harvey's press conference, I had become only more convinced.

A number of papers, including the *Post,* were on my desk, and I had studied the write-ups several times. The byline on the *Post*'s story was Clifford Ring, the reporter who had been pestering the commissioner and other personnel of the Department of Health and Human Services. Mr. Ring mentioned me only in passing when he implied that Pat Harvey was inappropriately using her public office to intimidate and threaten all involved into releasing details about her daughter's death. It was enough to make me wonder if Mr. Ring was Benton Wesley's media source, the FBI's conduit for planted releases, and that would not have been so bad, really. It was the point of the stories that I found disturbing.

What I had assumed would be dished out as the sensational exposé of the month was, instead, being bruited about as the colossal degradation of a woman who, just weeks before, had been talked of by some as a possible Vice President of the United States. I would be the first to say that Pat Harvey's diatribe at the press conference was reckless in the least, premature at best. But I found it odd that there was no evidence of a serious attempt at corroborating her accusations. Reporters in this case did not seem inclined to get the usual incriminating "no comments" and other double-talk evasions from the governmental bureaucrats that journalists typically pursue with enthusiasm.

The media's only quarry, it seemed, was Mrs. Harvey, and she was shown no pity. The headline for one editorial was SLAUGHTERGATE? She was being ridiculed, not only in print but in political cartoons. One of the nation's most respected officials was being dismissed as a hysterical female whose "sources" included a South Carolina psychic. Even her staunchest allies were backing away, shaking their heads, her enemies subtly finishing her off with attacks softly wrapped in sympathy. "Her reaction is certainly understandable in light of her terrible personal loss," said one Democratic detractor, adding, "I think it wise to overlook her imprudence. Consider her accusations the slings and arrows of a deeply troubled mind." Said another, "What's happened to Pat Harvey is a tragic example of self-destruction brought on by personal problems too overwhelming to endure."

Rolling Deborah Harvey's autopsy report into my typewriter, I whited out "pending" in the manner and cause of death spaces. I typed in "homicide" and "exsanguination due to gunshot wound to lower back and cutting injuries." Amending her death certificate and CME-1 report, I went up front and made photocopies. These I enclosed with a cover letter explaining my findings and apologizing for the delay, which I attributed to the long wait for toxicology results, which were still provisional. I would give Benton Wesley that much. Pat Harvey would not hear from me that I had been strong-armed by him to indefinitely pend the results of her daughter's medicolegal examination.

The Harveys were going to get it all—my findings on gross and microscopically, the fact that the first rounds of toxicology tests were negative, the bullet in Deborah's lower lumbar, the defense injury to her hand, and, pathetically, the detailed description of her clothing, or what had been left of it. The police had recovered her earrings, watch, and the friendship ring given to her by Fred for her birthday.

I also mailed copies of Fred Cheney's reports to his father, though I could go no further than saying that his son's manner of death was homicide, the cause "undetermined violence."

I reached for the phone and dialed Benton Wesley's office, only to be told he wasn't in. Next, I tried his home.

"I'm releasing the information," I said when he got on the line. "I wanted you to know."

Silence.

Then he said very calmly, "Kay, you heard her press conference?"

"Yes."

"And you've read today's paper?"

"I watched her press conference, and I've read the papers. I'm well aware that she shot herself in the foot."

"I'm afraid she shot herself in the head," he said.

"Not without some help."

A pause, then Wesley asked, "What are you talking about?"

"I'll be happy to spell it out in detail. Tonight. Face-to-face."

"Here?" He sounded alarmed.

"Yes."

"Uh, it's not a good idea, not tonight."

"I'm sorry. But it can't wait."

"Kay, you don't understand. Trust me—"

I cut him off. "No, Benton. Not this time."

10

A frigid wind wreaked havoc with the dark shapes of trees, and in the scant light of the moon the terrain looked foreign and foreboding as I drove to Benton Wesley's house. There were few streetlights, and the rural routes were poorly marked. I finally stopped at a country store with a single island of gas pumps in front. Switching on the overhead lamp, I studied my scribbled directions. I was lost.

I could see the store was closed but spotted a pay phone near the front door. Pulling close, I got out, leaving headlights burning and the engine on. I dialed Wesley's number and his wife, Connie, answered.

"You've really gotten tangled up," she said after I did my best to describe where I was.

"Oh, God," I said, groaning.

"Well, it's really not that far. The problem is it's complicated getting from where you are to here." She paused, then decided, "I think the wise thing would be for you to stay put, Kay. Lock your doors and sit tight. Better if we come and you follow us. Fifteen minutes, all right?"

Backing out, I parked closer to the road, turned on the radio, and waited. Minutes passed like hours. Not a single car went by. My headlights illuminated a white fence girdling a frosty pasture across the road. The moon was a pale sliver floating in the hazy darkness. I smoked several cigarettes, my eyes darting around.

I wondered if it had been like this for the murdered couples, what it would be like to be forced barefoot and bound into the woods. They had to have known they were going to die. They had to have been terrified by what he would do to them first. I thought of my niece, Lucy. I thought of my mother, my sister, my friends. Fearing for the pain and death of one you loved would be worse than fearing for your own life. I watched as headlights grew brighter far down the dark, narrow road. A car I did not recognize turned in and stopped not far from mine. When I caught a glimpse of the driver's profile, adrenaline rushed through my blood like electricity.

Mark James climbed out of what I assumed was a rental car. I rolled down the window and stared at him, too shocked to speak.

"Hello, Kay."

Wesley had said this was not a good night, had tried to talk me out of it, and now I understood why. Mark was visiting. Perhaps Connie had asked Mark to meet me, or he had volunteered. I could not imagine my reaction had I walked through Wesley's front door and found Mark sitting in the living room.

"It's a maze to Benton's house from here," Mark said. "I suggest you leave your car. It will be safe. I'll drive you back later so you won't have a problem finding your way."

Wordlessly, I parked closer to the store, then got in his car.

"How are you?" he asked quietly.

"Fine."

"And your family? How's Lucy?"

Lucy still asked about him. I never knew what to say.

"Fine," I said again.

As I looked at his face, his strong hands on the wheel, every contour, line, and vein familiar and wonderful to me, my heart ached with emotion. I hated and loved him at the same time.

"Work's all right?"

"Please stop being so goddam polite, Mark."

"Would you rather I be rude like you?"

"I'm not being rude."

"What the hell do you want me to say?"

I replied with silence.

He turned on the radio and we drove deeper into the night.

"I know this is awkward, Kay." He stared straight ahead. "I'm sorry. Benton suggested I meet you."

"That was very thoughtful of him," I said sarcastically.

"I didn't mean it like that. I would have insisted had he not asked. You had no reason to think I might be here."

We rounded a sharp bend and turned into Wesley's subdivision.

As we pulled into Wesley's driveway, Mark said, "I guess I'd better warn you that Benton's not in a very good mood."

"I'm not either," I replied coldly.

A fire burned in the living room, and Wesley was sitting near the hearth, a briefcase open and resting against the leg of his chair, a drink on the table nearby. He did not get up when I walked in, but nodded slightly as Connie invited me to the couch. I sat on one end, Mark the other.

Connie left to get coffee, and I started in. "Mark, I know nothing of your involvement in all this."

"There isn't much to know. I was in Quantico for several days and am spending the night with Benton and Connie before returning to Denver tomorrow. I'm not involved in the investigation, not assigned to the cases."

"All right. But you're aware of the cases." I wondered what Wesley and Mark had discussed in my absence. I wondered what Wesley had said to Mark about me.

"He's aware of them," Wesley answered.

"Then I'll ask both of you," I said. "Did the Bureau set up Pat Harvey? Or was it the CIA?"

Wesley did not move or change the expression on his face. "What leads you to suppose she's been set up?"

"Obviously, the Bureau's disinformation tactics went beyond luring the killer. It was someone's intention to destroy Pat Harvey's credibility, and the press has done this quite successfully."

"Even the President doesn't have that much influence over the media. Not in this country."

"Don't insult my intelligence, Benton," I said.

"What she did was anticipated. Let's put it that way." Wesley recrossed his legs and reached for his drink.

"And you laid the trap," I said.

"No one spoke for her at her press conference."

"It doesn't matter because no one needed to. Someone made sure her accusations would come across in print as the ravings of a lunatic. Who primed the reporters, the politicians, her former allies, Benton? Who leaked that she consulted a psychic? Was it you?"

"No."

"Pat Harvey saw Hilda Ozimek last September," I went on. "It never made the news until now, meaning the press didn't know about it until now. That's pretty low, Benton. You told me yourself that the FBI and Secret Service have resorted to Hilda Ozimek on a number of occasions. That's probably how Mrs. Harvey found out about her, for God's sake."

Connie returned with my coffee, then left again as quickly as she had appeared.

I could feel Mark's eyes on me, the tension. Wesley continued staring into the fire.

"I think I know the truth." I made no effort to disguise my outrage. "I intend to have it out in the open now. And if you can't accommodate me this way, then I don't think it will be possible for me to continue accommodating you."

"What are you implying, Kay?" Wesley looked over at me.

"If it happens again, if another couple dies, I can't guarantee that reporters won't find out what's really going on—"

"Kay." It was Mark who interrupted, and I refused to look at him. I was doing my best to block him out. "You don't want to trip up like Mrs. Harvey."

"She didn't exactly trip up on her own," I said. "I think she's right. Something *is* being covered up."

"You sent her your reports, I presume," Wesley said.

"I did. I will no longer play a part in this manipulation."

"That was a mistake."

"My mistake was not sending them to her earlier."

"Do the reports include information about the bullet you recovered from Deborah's body? Specifically, that it was nine-millimeter Hydra-Shok?"

"The caliber and brand would be in the firearms report," I said. "I don't send out copies of firearms reports any more than I send out copies of police reports, neither of which are generated by my office. But I'm interested in why you're so concerned over that detail."

When Wesley did not reply, Mark intervened. "Benton, we need to smooth this out."

Wesley remained silent.

"I think she needs to know," Mark added.

"I think I already know," I said. "I think the FBI has reason to fear the killer is a federal agent gone bad. Quite possibly, someone from Camp Peary."

Wind moaned around the eaves, and Wesley got up to tend to the fire. He put on another log, rearranged it with the poker, and swept ashes off the hearth, taking his time. When he was seated again, he reached for his drink and said, "How did you come to this conclusion?"

"It doesn't matter," I said.

"Did someone say this to you directly?"

"No. Not directly." I got out my cigarettes. "How long has this been your suspicion, Benton?"

Hesitating, he replied, "I believe you are better off not knowing the details. I really do. It's only going to be a burden. A very heavy one."

"I'm already carrying a very heavy burden. And I'm tired of stumbling over disinformation."

"I need your assurance nothing discussed leaves here."

"You know me too well to worry about that."

"Camp Peary entered into it not long after the cases began."

"Because of the close proximity?"

He looked at Mark. "I'll let you elaborate," Wesley said to him.

I turned and confronted this man who once had shared my bed and dominated my dreams. He was dressed in navy blue corduroy trousers and a red-and-white-striped oxford shirt that I had seen him wear in the past. He was long legged and trim. His dark hair was gray at the temples, eyes green, chin strong, features refined, and he still gestured slightly with his hands and leaned forward when he talked.

"In part, the CIA got interested," Mark explained, "because the cases were occurring close to Camp Peary. And I'm sure it comes as no surprise to you that the CIA is privy to most of what goes on around their training facility. They know a lot more than anyone might imagine, and in fact, local settings and citizens are routinely incorporated into maneuvers."

"What sorts of maneuvers?" I asked.

"Surveillance, for example. Officers in training at Camp Peary often practice surveillance, using local citizens as guinea pigs, for lack of a better term. Officers set up surveillance operations in public places, restaurants, bars, shopping centers. They tail people in cars, on foot, take photographs, and so on. No one is ever aware this is going on, of course. And there's no harm done, I suppose, except that local citizens wouldn't be keen on knowing they were being tailed, watched, or captured on film."

"I shouldn't think so," I said uncomfortably.

"These maneuvers," he continued, "also include going through dry runs. An officer might feign car trouble and stop a motorist for assistance, see how far he can go in getting this individual to trust him. He might pose as a law enforcement officer, tow truck operator, any number of things. It's all practice for overseas operations, to train people how to spy and avoid being spied upon."

"And it's an MO that may parallel what's been going on with these couples," I interpolated.

"That's the point," Wesley interjected. "Someone at Camp Peary got worried. We were asked to help monitor the situation. Then when the second couple turned up dead, and the MO was the same as the first case, the pattern had been established. The CIA began to panic. They're a paranoid lot anyway, Kay, and the last thing they needed was to discover that one of their officers at Camp Peary was practicing *killing* people."

"The CIA has never admitted that Camp Peary is its main training facility," I pointed out.

"It's common knowledge," Mark said, meeting my eyes. "But you're right, the CIA has never admitted it publicly. Nor do they wish to."

"Which is all the more reason they wouldn't want these murders connected to Camp Peary," I said, wondering what he was feeling. Maybe he wasn't feeling anything.

"That and a long list of other reasons," Wesley took over. "The publicity would be devastating, and when was the last time you read anything positive about the CIA? Imelda Marcos was accused of theft and fraud, and the defense claimed that every transaction the Marcoses made was with the full knowledge and encouragement of the CIA. . . ."

He wouldn't be so tense, so afraid to look at me, if he felt nothing.

". . . Then it came out that Noriega was on the CIA's payroll," Wesley continued making his case. "Not long ago it was publicized that CIA protection of a Syrian drug smuggler made it possible for a bomb to be placed on a Pan Am seven-forty-seven that exploded over Scotland, killing two hundred and seventy people. Not to mention the more recent allegation that the CIA is financing certain drug wars in Asia to destabilize governments over there."

"If it turned out," Mark said, shifting his eyes away from me, "that teenage couples were being murdered by a CIA officer at Camp Peary, you can imagine the public's reaction."

"It's unthinkable," I said, willing myself to concentrate on the discussion. "But why would the CIA be so sure these murders are being committed by one of their own? What hard evidence do they have?"

"Most of it's circumstantial," Mark explained. "The militaristic touch of leaving a playing card. The similarities between the patterns in these cases and the maneuvers that go on both inside the Farm and on streets of nearby cities and towns. For example, the wooded areas where the bodies have been turning up are reminiscent of the 'kill zones' inside Camp Peary, where officers practice with grenades, automatic weapons, utilizing all the trade craft, such as night vision equipment, allowing them to see in the woods after dark. They also receive training in defense, how to disarm someone, maim and kill with their bare hands."

"When there was no apparent cause of death with these couples," Wesley said, "one had to wonder if they were being murdered without the use of weapons. Strangulation, for example. Or even if their throats were cut, this is associated with guerrilla warfare, taking out an enemy swiftly and in silence. You cut through his airway and he's not going to be making any noise."

"But Deborah Harvey was shot," I said.

"With an automatic or semiautomatic weapon," Wesley replied. "Either a pistol or something like an Uzi. The ammunition uncommon, associated with law enforcement, mercenary soldiers, people whose targets are human beings. You don't associate exploding bullets or Hydra-Shok ammo with deer hunting." Pausing, he added, "I would think this gives you a better idea why we don't want Pat Harvey cognizant of the type of weapon and ammunition that was used on her daughter."

"What about the threats Mrs. Harvey mentioned in her press conference?" I asked.

"That is true," Wesley said. "Not long after she was appointed National Drug Policy Director, someone did send communications threatening her and her family. It isn't true that the Bureau didn't take them seriously. She's been threatened before and we've always taken it seriously. We have an idea who's behind the more recent threats and don't believe they're related to Deborah's homicide."

"Mrs. Harvey also implicated a 'federal agency,' " I said. "Was she referring to the CIA? Is she aware of what you've just told me?"

"That concerns me," Wesley admitted. "She's made comments to suggest she has an idea, and what she said in the press conference only increases my anxiety. She might have been referring to the CIA. Then again, maybe she wasn't. But she has a formidable network. For one thing, she has access to CIA information, providing it's relevant to the drug trade. More worrisome is that she's close friends with an ex-United Nations ambassador who is a member of the President's Foreign Intelligence Advisory Board. Members of the board are entitled to top secret intelligence briefings on any subject at any time. The board knows what's going on, Kay. It's possible Mrs. Harvey knows everything."

"So she's set up Martha Mitchell–style?" I asked. "To make sure she comes off as irrational, unreliable, so that no one takes her seriously, so that if she does blow the lid, no one will believe her?"

Wesley was running his thumb around the rim of his glass. "It's unfortunate. She's been uncontrollable, uncooperative. And the irony is, we want to know who murdered her daughter more than she does, for obvious reasons. We're doing everything within our power, have mobilized everything we can think of to find this individual—or individuals."

"What you're telling me seems patently inconsistent with your earlier suggestion that Deborah Harvey and Fred Cheney may have been a paid hit, Benton," I said angrily. "Or was that just a lot of smoke you were blowing out to hide the Bureau's real fears?"

"I don't know if they were a paid hit," he said grimly. "Frankly, there's so little we really know. Their murders could be political, as I've already explained. But if we're dealing with a CIA officer gone haywire, someone like that, the cases of the five couples may, in fact, be connected, may be serial killings."

"It could be an example of escalation," Mark offered. "Pat Harvey's been in the news a lot, especially over the past year. If we're looking for a CIA officer who's practicing homicidal maneuvers, he may have decided to target a presidential appointee's daughter."

"Thus adding to the excitement, the risk," Wesley explained. "And making the kill similar to the sorts of operations you associate with Central America, the Middle East, political neutralizations. Assassinations, in other words."

"It's my understanding that the CIA is not supposed to be in the business of assassinations, not since the Ford administration," I said. "In fact, the CIA's not even supposed to engage in coup attempts in which a foreign leader is in danger of being killed."

"That's correct," Mark replied. "The CIA's not supposed to be in that business. American soldiers in Vietnam weren't supposed to kill civilians. And cops aren't supposed to use excessive force on suspects and prisoners. When it's all reduced to individuals, sometimes things get out of control. Rules get broken."

I could not help but wonder about Abby Turnbull. How much of this did she know? Had Mrs. Harvey leaked something to her? Was this the true nature of the book Abby was writing? No wonder she suspected her phones were being bugged, that she was being followed. The CIA, the FBI, and even the President's Foreign Intelligence Advisory Board, which had a backdoor entrée straight into the Oval Office, had very good reason to be nervous about what Abby was writing, and she had very good reason to be paranoid. She may have placed herself in real danger.

The wind had died down, a light fog settling over treetops as

Wesley closed the door behind us. Following Mark to his car, I felt a sense of resolution and validation because of what had been said, and yet I was more unsettled than before.

I waited to speak until we left the subdivision. "What's happening to Pat Harvey is outrageous. She loses her daughter, now her career and reputation are being destroyed."

"Benton's had nothing to do with leaks to the press, any sort of 'setup,' as you put it." Mark kept his eyes on the dark, narrow road.

"It's not a matter of how I *put it,* Mark."

"I'm just referring to what you said," he replied.

"You know what's going on. Don't act naive with me."

"Benton's done everything he can for her, but she's got a vendetta against the Justice Department. To her, Benton's just another federal agent out to get her."

"If I were her, I might feel the same way."

"Knowing you, you probably would."

"And what's that supposed to mean?" I asked, as my anger, which went far deeper than Pat Harvey, surfaced.

"It doesn't mean a thing."

Minutes passed in silence as the tension grew. I did not recognize the road we were on, but I knew our time together was nearing an end. Then he turned into the store's parking lot and pulled up next to my car.

"I'm sorry we had to see each other under these circumstances," he said quietly.

I did not reply, and he added, "But I'm not sorry to see you, not sorry it happened."

"Good night, Mark." I started to get out of the car.

"Don't, Kay." He put his hand on my arm.

I sat still. "What do you want?"

"To talk to you. Please."

"If you're so interested in talking to me, then why haven't you gotten around to it before now?" I replied with emotion, pulling my arm away. "You've made no effort to say a goddam thing to me for months."

"That works both ways. I called you last fall and you never called me back."

"I knew what you were going to say, and I didn't want to hear it," I replied, and I could feel his anger building, too.

"Excuse me. I forgot that you have always had the uncanny ability of reading my mind." He placed both hands on the wheel and stared straight ahead.

"You were going to announce that there was no chance of reconciliation, that it was over. And I wasn't interested in having you put into words what I already assumed."

"Think what you want."

"It has nothing to do with what I *want* to think!" I hated the power he had to make me lose my temper.

"Look." He took a deep breath. "Do you think there's any chance we can declare a truce? Forget the past?"

"Not a chance."

"Great. Thanks for being so reasonable. At least I tried."

"Tried? It's been what? Eight, nine months since you left? What the hell have you tried, Mark? I don't know what it is you're asking, but it's impossible to forget the past. It's impossible for the two of us to run into each other and pretend there was never anything between us. I refuse to act that way."

"I'm not asking that, Kay. I'm asking if we can forget the fights, the anger, what we said back then."

I really could not remember exactly what had been said or explain what had gone wrong. We fought when we weren't sure what we were fighting about until the focus became our injuries and not the differences that had caused them.

"When I called you last September," he went on with feeling, "I wasn't going to tell you there was no hope of reconciliation. In fact, when I dialed your number I knew I was running the risk of hearing *you* say that. And when you never called me back, I was the one who made assumptions."

"You're not serious."

"The hell I'm not."

"Well, maybe you were wise to make assumptions. After what you did."

"After what *I* did?" he asked, incredulous. "What about what *you* did?"

"The only thing I did was to get sick and tired of making concessions. You never really tried to relocate to Richmond. You didn't know what you wanted and expected me to comply, concede, uproot myself whenever you figured everything out. No matter how much I love you, I can't give up what I am and I never asked you to give up what you are."

"Yes, you did. Even if I could have transferred to the field office in Richmond, that's not what I wanted."

"Good. I'm glad you pursued what you wanted."

"Kay, it's fifty-fifty. You're to blame, too."

"I'm not the one who left." My eyes filled with tears, and I whispered, "Oh, shit."

Getting out a handkerchief, he gently placed it on my lap.

Dabbing my eyes, I moved closer to the door, leaning my head against the glass. I did not want to cry.

"I'm sorry," he said.

"Your being sorry doesn't change anything."

"Please don't cry."

"I will if I want," I said, ridiculously.

"I'm sorry," he said again, this time in a whisper, and I thought he was going to touch me. But he didn't. He leaned back in the seat and stared up at the roof.

"Look," he said, "if you want to know the truth, I wish *you* had been the one who left. Then you could have been the one who screwed up instead of me."

I did not say anything. I did not dare.

"Did you hear me?"

"I'm not sure," I said to the window.

He shifted his position. I could feel his eyes on me.

"Kay, look at me."

Reluctantly, I did.

"Why do you think I've been coming back here?" he asked in a low voice. "I'm trying to get back to Quantico, but it's tough. The timing's bad with the federal budget cuts, the economy, the Bureau's being hit hard. There are a lot of reasons."

"You're telling me you're professionally unhappy?"

"I'm telling you I made a mistake."

"I regret any professional mistakes you've made," I said.

"I'm not referring just to that, and you know it."

"Then what are you referring to?" I was determined to make him say it.

"You know what I'm referring to. Us. Nothing's been the same."

His eyes were shining in the dark. He looked almost fierce.

"Has it been for you?" he pushed.

"I think both of us have made a lot of mistakes."

"I'd like to start undoing some of them, Kay. I don't want it to end this way with us. I've felt that for a long time but . . . well, I just didn't know how to tell you. I didn't know if you wanted to hear from me, if you were seeing someone else."

I did not admit that I had been wondering the same about him and was terrified of the answers.

He reached for me, taking my hand. This time I could not pull away.

"I've been trying to sort through what went wrong with us," he said. "All I know is I'm stubborn, you're stubborn. I wanted my way and you wanted yours. So here we are. I can't say what your life has been like since I left, but I'm willing to bet it hasn't been good."

"How arrogant of you to bet on such a thing."

He smiled. "I'm just trying to live up to your image of me. One of the last things you called me before I left was an arrogant bastard."

"Was that before or after I called you a son of a bitch?"

"Before, I believe."

"As I remember it, you called me a few rather choice names as well. And I thought you just suggested that we forget what was said back then."

"And you just said *no matter how much I love you.*"

"I beg your pardon?"

" 'Love,' as in present tense. Don't try to take it back. I heard it."

He pressed my hand to his face, his lips moving over my fingers.

"I've tried to stop thinking about you. I can't." He paused, his face close to mine. "I'm not asking you to say the same thing."

But he was asking that, and I answered him.

I touched his cheek and he touched mine, then we kissed the places our fingers had been until we found each other's lips. And we said nothing more. We stopped thinking entirely until the windshield suddenly lit up and the night beyond was throbbing red. We frantically rearranged ourselves as a patrol car pulled up and a deputy climbed out, flashlight and portable radio in hand.

Mark was already opening his door.

"Everything all right?" the deputy asked, bending over to peer inside. His eyes wandered disconcertingly over the scene of our passion, his face stern, an unseemly bulge in his right cheek.

"Everything's fine," I said, horrified as I not so subtly probed the floor with my stocking foot. Somehow I had lost a shoe.

He stepped back and spat out a stream of tobacco juice.

"We were having a conversation," Mark offered, and he had the presence of mind not to display his badge. The deputy knew damn well we had been doing a lot of things when he pulled up. Conversing was not one of them.

"Well, now, if y'all intend to continue your *conversation,*" he said, "I'd 'preciate it if you'd go someplace else. You know, it ain't safe to be sitting out here late at night in a car, been some problems. And if you're not from around here, maybe you hadn't heard about the couples disappearing."

He went on with his lecture, my blood running cold.

"You're right, and thank you," Mark finally said. "We're leaving now."

Nodding, the deputy spat again, and we watched him climb into his car. He pulled out onto the road and slowly drove away.

"Jesus," Mark muttered under his breath.

"Don't say it," I replied. "Let's not even get into how stupid we are. Lord."

"Do you see how damn easy it is?" He said it anyway. "Two people out at night and someone pulls up. Hell, my damn gun's in the glove compartment. I never even thought about it until he was right in my face, and then it would have been too late—"

"Stop it, Mark. Please."

He startled me by laughing.

"It's not funny!"

"Your blouse is buttoned crooked," he gasped.

Shit!

"You better hope like hell he didn't recognize you, Chief Scarpetta."

"Thank you for the reassuring thought, Mr. FBI. And now I'm going home." I opened the door. "You've gotten me into enough trouble for one night."

"Hey. You started it."

"I most certainly did not."

"Kay?" He got serious. "What do we do now? I mean, I'm going back to Denver tomorrow. I don't know what's going to happen, what I can make happen or if I should try to make anything happen."

There were no easy answers. There never had been with us.

"If you don't try to make anything happen, nothing will."

"What about you?" he asked.

"There's a lot of talking we need to do, Mark."

He turned on the headlights and fastened his seat belt. "What about you?" he asked again. "It takes two to try."

"Funny you should say that."

"Kay, don't. Please don't start in."

"I need to think." I got out my keys. I was suddenly exhausted.

"Don't jerk me around."

"I'm not jerking you around, Mark," I said, touching his cheek.

We kissed one last time. I wanted the kiss to go on for hours, and yet I wanted to get away. Our passion had always been reckless. We had always lived for moments that never seemed to add up to any sort of future.

"I'll call you," he said.

I opened my car door.

"Listen to Benton," he added. "You can trust him. What you're involved in is very bad stuff."

I started the engine.

"I wish you'd stay out of it."

"You always wish that," I said.

Mark did call late the following night and again two nights after that. When he called a third time, on February tenth, what he said sent me out in search of the most recent issue of *Newsweek*.

Pat Harvey's lusterless eyes stared out at America from the magazine's cover. A headline in bold, black letters read THE MURDER OF THE DRUG CZAR'S DAUGHTER, the "exclusive" inside a rehashing of her press conference, her charges of conspiracy, and the cases of the other teenagers who had vanished and been found decomposed in Virginia woods. Though I had declined to be interviewed for the story, the magazine had found a file photograph of me climbing the steps of Richmond's John Marshall Court House. The caption read,

"Chief Medical Examiner releases findings under threat of court order."

"It just goes with the turf. I'm fine," I reassured Mark when I called him back.

Even when my mother rang me up later that same night, I remained calm until she said, "There's someone here who's dying to talk to you, Kay."

My niece, Lucy, had always had a special talent for doing me in.

"How come you got in trouble?" she asked.

"I didn't get in trouble."

"The story says you did, that someone threatened you."

"It's too complicated to explain, Lucy."

"It's really awesome," she said, unfazed. "I'm going to take the magazine to school tomorrow and show it to everybody."

Great, I thought.

"Mrs. Barrows," she went on, referring to her homeroom teacher, "has already asked if you can come for career day in April . . . ?"

I had not seen Lucy in a year. It did not seem possible she was already a sophomore in high school, and though I knew she had contact lenses and a driver's license, I still envisioned her as a pudgy, needy child wanting to be tucked into bed, an *enfant terrible* who, for some strange reason, had bonded to me before she could crawl. I would never forget flying to Miami the Christmas after she was born and staying with my sister for a week. Lucy's every conscious minute, it seemed, was spent watching me, eyes following my every move like two luminous moons. She would smile when I changed her diapers and howl the instant I walked out of the room.

"Would you like to spend a week with me this summer?" I asked.

Lucy hesitated, then said disappointedly, "I guess that means you can't come for career day."

"We'll see, all right?"

"I don't know if I can come this summer." Her tone had turned petulant. "I've got a job and might not be able to get away."

"It's wonderful you have a job."

"Yeah. In a computer store. I'm going to save enough to get a car. I want a sports car, a convertible, and you can find some of the old ones pretty cheap."

"Those are death traps," I said before I could stop myself. "Please don't get something like that, Lucy. Why don't you come see me in Richmond? We'll go around and shop for cars, something nice and safe."

She had dug a hole, and as usual, I had fallen in it. She was an expert at manipulation, and it didn't require a psychiatrist to figure out why. Lucy was the victim of chronic neglect by her mother, my sister.

"You are a bright young lady with a mind of your own," I said, changing tactics. "I know you'll make a good decision about what to do with your time and money, Lucy. But if you can fit me in this summer, maybe we can go somewhere. The beach or mountains, wherever you'd like. You've never been to England, have you?"

"No."

"Well, then, that's a thought."

"Really?" she asked suspiciously.

"Really. I haven't been in years," I said, warming up to the idea. "I think it's time for you to see Oxford and Cambridge, the museums in London. I'll arrange a tour of Scotland Yard, if you'd like, and if we could manage to get away as early as June, we might be able to get tickets for Wimbledon."

Silence.

Then she said cheerfully, "I was just teasing. I don't really want a sports car, Aunt Kay."

The next morning there were no autopsies, and I sat at my desk trying to diminish piles of paperwork. I had other deaths to investigate, classes to teach, and trials demanding my testimony, yet I could not concentrate. Every time I turned to something else, my attention was drawn back to the couples. There was something important I was overlooking, something right under my nose.

I felt it had to do with Deborah Harvey's murder.

She was a gymnast, an athlete with superb control of her body. She may not have been as strong as Fred, but she would have been quicker and more agile. I believed the killer had underestimated her athletic potential, and this was why he momentarily lost control of her in the woods. As I stared blankly at a report I was supposed to be reviewing, Mark's words came back to me. He had mentioned "kill zones," officers at Camp Peary utilizing automatic weapons, grenades, and night vision equipment to hunt each other down in fields and woods. I tried to imagine this. I began toying with a gruesome scenario.

Perhaps when the killer abducted Deborah and Fred and took them to the logging road, he had a terrifying game in store for them. He told them to take off their shoes and socks, and bound their hands behind their backs. He may have been wearing night vision goggles, which enhanced moonlight, making it possible for him to see quite well as he forced them into the woods, where he intended to track them down, one at a time.

I believed Marino was right. The killer would have gotten Fred out of the way first. Perhaps he told him to run, gave him a chance to get away, and all the while Fred was stumbling through trees and brush, panicking, the killer was watching, able to see and move about with ease, knife in hand. At the opportune moment, it would not have been very difficult for him to ambush his victim from behind, yoke arm under chin and jerk the head back, then slash through the windpipe and carotid arteries. This commando style of attack was silent and swift. If the bodies were not discovered for a while, the medical examiner would have difficulty finding a cause of death because tissue and cartilage would have decomposed.

I took the scenario further. Part of the killer's sadism might have been to force Deborah to witness her boyfriend being tracked and murdered in the dark. I was considering that once they were in the woods, the killer held her captive audience by binding her feet at the ankles, but what he did not anticipate was her flexibility. It was possible that while he was occupied with Fred, she managed to bring her bound hands under her buttocks and work her legs through her arms, thus getting her hands in front of her. This would have allowed her to untie her feet and defend herself.

I held my hands in front of me, as if they were bound at the wrists. Had Deborah locked her fingers together in a double fist and swung, and had the killer's reflex been to defensively raise his hands, in one of which he was holding the knife he had just used to murder Fred, then the hack to Deborah's left index finger made sense. Deborah ran like hell, and the killer, knocked off guard, shot her in the back.

Was I right? I could not know. But the scenario continued to play in my mind without a hitch. What didn't fit were several presuppositions. If Deborah's death was a paid hit carried out by a professional or the work of a psychopathic federal agent who had selected her in advance because she was Pat Harvey's daughter, then did this individual not know that Deborah was an Olympic-caliber gymnast? Would he not have considered that she would be unusually quick and agile and have incorporated this into his premeditations?

Would he have shot her *in the back*?

Was the manner in which she was killed consistent with the cold, calculating profile of a professional killer?

In the back.

When Hilda Ozimek had studied the photographs of the dead teenagers, she continued to pick up fear. Obviously, the victims had felt fear. But it had never occurred to me before this moment that the killer may have felt fear, too. Shooting someone in the back is cowardly. When Deborah resisted her assailant, he was unnerved. He lost control. The more I thought about it, the more I was convinced that Wesley and perhaps everybody else was wrong about this character. To hunt bound, barefoot teenagers in the woods after dark, when you have weapons, are familiar with the terrain, and are perhaps equipped with a night vision scope or goggles would be like shooting fish in a barrel. It's cheating. It's too damn easy. It did not strike me as the modus operandi I would expect were the killer an expert who thrived on taking risks.

And then there was the matter of his weapons.

If I were a CIA officer hunting human prey, what would I use? An Uzi? *Maybe.* More likely I would pick a nine-millimeter pistol, something that would do the job, nothing more, nothing less. I would use commonplace cartridges, something unremarkable. Everyday hollowpoints, for example. What I would not use was anything unusual like Exploder bullets or Hydra-Shoks.

The ammunition. Think hard, Kay! I could not remember the last time I had recovered Hydra-Shok bullets from a body.

The ammunition was originally designed with law enforcement officers in mind, the bullets having greater expansion upon impact than any other round fired from a two-inch barrel. When the lead projectile with its hollowpoint construction and distinctive raised central post enters the body, hydrostatic pressure forces the peripheral rim to flare like the petals of a flower. There's very little recoil, making it easier for one to fire repeat shots. The bullets rarely exit the body; the disruption to soft tissue and organs is devastating.

This killer was into specialized ammunition. He, no doubt, had sighted his gun by his cartridges of choice. To select one of the most lethal types of ammunition probably gave him confidence, made him feel powerful and important. He might even be superstitious about it.

I picked up the phone and told Linda what I needed.

"Come on up," she said.

When I walked into the firearms lab, she was seated before a computer terminal.

"No cases so far this year, except for Deborah Harvey, of course," she said, moving the cursor down the screen. "One for last year. One the year before that. Nothing else for Federal. But I did find two cases involving Scorpions."

"Scorpions?" I puzzled, leaning over her shoulder.

She explained, "An earlier version. Ten years before Federal bought the patent, Hydra-Shok Corporation was manufacturing basically the same cartridges. Specifically, Scorpion thirty-eights and Copperhead three-fifty-sevens." She hit several keys, printing out what she had found. "Eight years ago, we got in one case involving Scorpion thirty-eights. But it wasn't human."

"I beg your pardon?" I asked, baffled.

"Appears this victim was of the canine variety. A dog. Shot, let's see . . . three times."

"Was the shooting of the dog connected with some other case? A suicide, homicide, burglary?"

"Can't tell from what I've got here," Linda replied apologetically. "All I've got is that three Scorpion bullets were recovered from the dead dog. Never matched up with anything. I guess the case was never solved."

She tore off the printout and handed it to me.

The OCME, on rare occasions, did perform autopsies on animals. Deer shot out of season were sometimes sent in by game wardens, and if someone's pet was shot during the commission of a crime or if the pet was found dead along with its owners, we took a look, recovered bullets or tested for drugs. But we did not issue death certificates or autopsy reports for animals. It wasn't likely I was going to find anything on file for this dog shot eight years ago.

I rang up Marino and filled him in.

"You gotta be kidding," he said.

"Can you track it down without making a commotion? I don't want this raising any antennas. It may be nothing, but the jurisdiction is West Point, and that's rather interesting. The bodies of the second couple were found in West Point."

"Yeah, maybe. I'll see what I can do," he said, and he didn't sound thrilled about it.

The next morning Marino appeared while I was finishing work on a fourteen-year-old boy thrown out of the back of a pickup truck the afternoon before.

"That ain't something you got on, I hope." Marino moved closer to the table and sniffing.

"He had a bottle of aftershave in a pocket of his pants. It broke when he hit the pavement, and that's what you're smelling." I nodded at clothing on a nearby gurney.

"Brut?" He sniffed again.

"I believe so," I replied absently.

"Doris used to buy me Brut. One year she got me Obsession, if you can believe that."

"What did you find out?" I continued to work.

"The dog's name was Dammit, and I swear that's the truth," Marino said. "Belonged to some old geezer in West Point, a Mr. Joyce."

"Did you find out why the dog came into this office?"

"No connection to any other cases. A favor, I think."

"The state veterinarian must have been on vacation," I replied, for this had happened before.

On the other side of my building was the Department of Animal Health, complete with a morgue where examinations were conducted on animals. Normally, the carcasses went to the state veterinarian. But there were exceptions. When asked, the forensic pathologists indulged the cops and pitched in when the veterinarian was unavailable. During my career I had autopsied tortured dogs, mutilated cats, a sexually assaulted mare, and a poisoned chicken left in a judge's mailbox. People were just as cruel to animals as they were to each other.

"Mr. Joyce don't got a phone, but a contact of mine says he's still in the same crib," Marino said. "Thought I might run over there, check out his story. You want to come along?"

I snapped in a new scalpel blade as I thought about my cluttered desk, the cases awaiting my dictation, the telephone calls I had yet to return and the others I needed to initiate.

"Might as well," I said hopelessly.

He hesitated, as if waiting for something.

When I looked up at him, I noticed. Marino had gotten his hair cut. He was wearing khaki trousers held up by suspenders and a tweed jacket that looked brand new. His tie was clean, so was his pale yellow shirt. Even his shoes were shined.

"You look downright handsome," I said like a proud mother.

"Yeah." He grinned, his face turning red. "Rose whistled at me when I was getting on the elevator. It was kinda funny. Hadn't had a woman whistle at me in years, except Sugar, and Sugar don't exactly count."

"Sugar?"

"Hangs out on the corner of Adam and Church. Oh yeah, found Sugar, also known as Mad Dog Mama, down in an alleyway, passed out drunk as a skunk, practically ran over her sorry ass. Made the mistake of bringing her to. Fought me like a damn cat and cussed me all the way to lockup. Every time I pass within a block of her, she yells, whistles, hitches up her skirt."

"And you were worrying that you were no longer attractive to women," I said.

11

Dammit's origin was undetermined, though it was patently clear that every genetic marker he had picked up from every dog in his lineage was the worst of the lot.

"Raised him from a pup," said Mr. Joyce as I returned to him a Polaroid photograph of the dog in question. "He was a stray, you know. Just appeared at the back door one morning and I felt sorry for him, threw him some scraps. Couldn't get rid of him to save my life after that."

We were sitting around Mr. Joyce's kitchen table. Sunlight seeped wanly through a dusty window above a rust-stained porcelain sink, the faucet dripping. Ever since we had arrived fifteen minutes ago, Mr. Joyce had not had a kind word to offer about his slain dog, and yet I detected warmth in his old eyes, and the rough hands thoughtfully stroking the rim of his coffee mug looked capable of tender affection.

"How did he get his name?" Marino wanted to know.

"Never did give him a name, you see. But I was always hollering at him. 'Dammit, shut up! Come here, dammit! Dammit, if you don't stop yapping, I'm gonna wire your mouth shut.' " He smiled sheepishly. "Got to where he thought his name was Dammit. So that's what I took to calling him."

Mr. Joyce was a retired dispatcher for a cement company, his tiny house a monument to rural poverty out in the middle of farmland. I suspected the house's original owner had been a tenant farmer, for on either side of the property were vast expanses of fallow fields that Mr. Joyce said were thick with corn in the summer.

And it had been summer, a hot, sultry July night, when Bonnie Smyth and Jim Freeman had been forced to drive along the sparsely populated dirt road out front. Then November had come, and I passed over the same road, passed right by Mr. Joyce's house, the back of my station wagon packed with folded sheets, stretchers, and body pouches. Less than two miles east of where Mr. Joyce lived was the dense wooded area where the couple's bodies had been found some two years before. An eerie coincidence? What if it wasn't?

"So tell me what happened to Dammit," Marino was saying as he lit a cigarette.

"It was a weekend," Mr. Joyce began. "Middle of August, it seems. Had all the windows open and was sitting in the living room watching TV. 'Dallas.' Funny I can remember that. Guess it means it was a Friday. Nine o'clock's when it came on."

"Then it was between nine and ten when your dog was shot," Marino said.

"That's my guess. Couldn't have been shot much before that or he'd never made it home. I'm watching TV, and next thing I hear him scratching at the door, whimpering. I knew he was hurt, just figured he'd gotten tangled up with a cat or something until I opened the door and got a good look at him."

He got out a pouch of tobacco and began to roll a cigarette in expert, steady hands.

Marino prodded him. "What did you do after that?"

"Put him in my truck and drove him to Doc Whiteside's house. About five miles northwest."

"A veterinarian?" I asked.

He slowly shook his head. "No, ma'am. Didn't have a vet or even know one. Doc Whiteside took care of my wife before she passed on. A mighty nice fellow. Didn't know where else to go, to tell you the truth. Course, it was too late. Wasn't a thing the doc could do by the time I carried the dog in. He said I ought to call the police.

Only thing in season in the middle of August is crow, and no good reason in the world anybody should be out late at night shooting at crow or anything else. I did what he said. Called the police."

"Do you have any idea who might have shot your dog?" I asked.

"Like I said, Dammit was bad about chasing folks, going after cars like he was going to chew the tires off. You want my personal opinion, I've always halfway suspected it might have been a cop who done it."

"Why?" Marino asked.

"After the dog was examined, I was told the bullets came from a revolver. So maybe Dammit chased after a police car and that's how it happened."

"Did you see any police cars on your road that night?" Marino asked.

"Nope. Don't mean there wasn't one, though. And I can't be sure where the shooting happened. I know it wasn't nearby. I would've heard it."

"Maybe not if you had your TV turned up loud," Marino said.

"I would've heard it, all right. Not much sound around here, specially late at night. You live here awhile, you get to where you hear the smallest thing out of the ordinary. Even if your TV's on, the windows shut tight."

"Did you hear any cars on your road that night?" Marino asked.

He thought for a moment. "I know one went by not long before Dammit started scratching on the door. The police asked me that. I got the feeling whoever was in it is the one who shot the dog. The officer who took the report sort of thought that, too. Least, that's what he suggested." He paused, staring out the window. "Probably just some kid."

A clock gonged off-key from the living room, then silence, the passing empty seconds measured by water clinking in the sink. Mr. Joyce had no phone. He had very few neighbors, none of whom were close by. I wondered if he had children. It didn't appear he had gotten another dog or found himself a cat. I saw no sign that anybody or anything lived here except him.

"Old Dammit was worthless as hell, but he sort of grew on you. Used to give the mailman a fit. I'd stand there in the living room looking out the window, laughing so hard my eyes was streaming. The sight of it. A puny little fellow, looking around, scared to death to get out of his little mail truck. Old Dammit running in circles snapping at the air. I'd give it a minute or two before I'd start hollering, then out I'd go in the yard. All I had to do was point my finger, and off Dammit would go, tail 'tween his legs." He took a deep breath, the cigarette forgotten in the ashtray. "Lot of meanness out there."

"Yes, sir," Marino agreed, leaning back in his chair. "Meanness everywhere, even in a nice, quiet area like this. Last time I was out this way must've been two years ago, a few weeks before Thanksgiving, when that couple was found in the woods. You remember that?"

"Sure do." Mr. Joyce nodded deeply. "Never seen so much commotion. I was out getting firewood when all of a sudden these police cars come thundering past, lights flashing. Must have been a dozen of them and a couple ambulances, too." He paused, eyeing Marino thoughtfully. "Don't recall seeing you out there." Turning his attention to me, he added, "Guess you were out there, too?"

"I was."

"Thought so." He seemed pleased. "Thought you looked familiar and I've been raking my brain the whole time we've been talking, trying to figure out where I might have seen you before."

"Did you go down to the woods where the bodies were?" Marino asked casually.

"With all those police cars going right past my house, wasn't a way in the world I could just sit here. I couldn't imagine what was going on. No neighbors down that way, just woods. And I was thinking, well, if it's a hunter who got shot, then that don't make sense either. Too many cops for that. So I got in my truck and headed down the road. Found an officer standing by his car and asked him what was going on. He told me some hunters had found a couple bodies back there. Then he wanted to know if I lived nearby. Said I did, and next thing there's a detective at my door asking questions."

"Do you remember the detective's name?" Marino asked.

"Can't say I do."

"What sorts of questions did he ask?"

"Mostly wanted to know if I'd seen anybody in the area, specially around the time this young couple was thought to have disappeared. Any strange cars, things like that."

"Had you?"

"Well, I got to thinking about it after he left, and it's entered my mind now and again ever since," Mr. Joyce said. "Now, the night the police think this couple was taken out here and killed, I didn't hear a thing that I remember. Sometimes I turn in early. Could be I was asleep. But there was something that I remembered a couple months back, after this other couple was found the first of the year."

"Deborah Harvey and Fred Cheney?" I asked.

"The girl whose mother's important."

Marino nodded.

Mr. Joyce went on, "Those murders got me to thinking again about the bodies found out here, and it popped into my mind. If you noticed when you drove up, I have a mailbox out front. Well, I had a bad spell maybe a couple weeks before they think that girl and boy was killed out here several years back."

"Jim Freeman and Bonnie Smyth," Marino said.

"Yes, sir. I had the flu, was throwing up, felt like I had a toothache from head to toe. Stayed in bed what must've been two days and didn't even have the strength to go out and fetch the mail. This night I'm talking about, I was finally up and around, made myself some soup and kept it down all right. So I went out to get the mail. Must have been nine, ten o'clock at night. And right as I was walking back toward the house, I heard this car. Black as tar out and the person was creeping along with his headlights off."

"Which direction was the car going?" Marino asked.

"That way." Mr. Joyce pointed west. "In other words, he was heading away from the area down there where the woods are, back toward the highway. Could be nothing, but I remember it crossed my mind that it was strange. For one thing, there's nothing down there but farmland and woods. I just figured it was kids drinking or parking or something."

"Did you get a good look at the car?" I inquired.

"Seems like it was mid-size, dark in color. Black, dark blue, or dark red, maybe."

"New or old?" Marino asked.

"Don't know if it was brand new, but it wasn't old. Wasn't one of these foreign cars, either."

"How could you tell?" Marino asked.

"By the sound," Mr. Joyce replied easily. "These foreign cars don't sound the same as American ones. The engine's louder, chugs more, don't know exactly how to describe it, but I can tell. Just like when you were pulling up earlier. I knew you were in an American car, probably a Ford or Chevy. This car that went by with its headlights off, it was real quiet, smooth sounding. The shape of it reminded me of one of these new Thunderbirds, but I can't swear to it. Might have been a Cougar."

"It was sporty, then," Marino said.

"Depends on how you look at it. To me, a Corvette's sporty. A Thunderbird or Cougar's fancy."

"Could you tell how many people were inside this car?" I asked.

He shook his head. "Now, I got no idea about that. It was mighty dark out, and I didn't stand there staring."

Marino got a notepad out of his pocket and began flipping through it.

"Mr. Joyce," he said, "Jim Freeman and Bonnie Smyth disappeared July twenty-ninth on a Saturday night. You sure when you saw this car it was before then? Sure it wasn't later on?"

"Sure as I'm sitting here. Reason I know's because I got sick, like I told you. Started coming down with whatever it was the second week of July. I remember that because my wife's birthday's July thirteenth. I always go to the cemetery on her birthday and put flowers on her grave. Had just come home from doing that when I started feeling a little funny. The next day I was too sick to get out of bed." He stared off for a moment. "Must'ave been the fifteenth or sixteenth I went out to get the mail and saw the car."

Marino got out his sunglasses, ready to leave.

Mr. Joyce, who wasn't born yesterday, asked him, "You thinking there's something about these couples dying that's got to do with my dog being shot?"

"We're looking into a lot of things. And it's best if you don't mention this conversation to anyone."

"Won't breathe a word of it, no, sir."

"I'd appreciate it."

He walked us to the door.

"Drop by again when you can," he said. "Come July the tomatoes will be in. Got a garden out back there, best tomatoes in Virginia. But you don't have to wait till then to visit. Anytime. I'm always here."

He watched us from the porch as we drove off.

Marino gave me his opinion as we followed the dirt road back to the highway.

"I'm suspicious about the car he saw two weeks before Bonnie Smyth and Jim Freeman was killed out here."

"So am I."

"As for the dog, I have my doubts. If the dog had been shot weeks, even months, before Jim and Bonnie disappeared, I'd think we were on to something. But hell, Dammit got whacked a good five years before these couples started dying."

Kill zones, I thought. Maybe we were on to something, anyway.

"Marino, have you considered that we may be dealing with someone for whom the place of death is more important than victim selection?"

He glanced over at me, listening.

"This individual may spend quite a long time finding just the right spot," I went on. "When that is done, he hunts, brings his quarry to this place he has carefully chosen. The place is what is most important, and the time of year. Mr. Joyce's dog was killed in mid-August. The hottest time of the year, but off season as far as hunting goes, except for crow. Each of these couples has been killed off season. In every instance, the bodies have been found weeks, months later, in season. By hunters. It's a pattern."

"Are you suggesting this killer was out scouting the woods for a place to commit murders when the dog trotted up and spoiled his plan?" He glanced over at me, frowning.

"I'm just throwing out a lot of things."

"No offense, but I think you can throw that idea right out the window. Unless the squirrel was fantasizing about whacking couples for years, then finally got around to it."

"My guess is this individual's got a very active fantasy life."

"Maybe you should take up profiling," he said. "You're beginning to sound like Benton."

"And you're beginning to sound as if you've written Benton off."

"Nope. Just not in a mood to deal with him right now."

"He's still your VICAP partner, Marino. You and I are not the only ones under pressure. Don't be too hard on him."

"You sure are into handling out free advice these days," he said.

"Just be glad it's free, because you need all the advice you can get."

"You want to grab some dinner?"

It was getting close to six P.M.

"Tonight I exercise," I replied dismally.

"Geez. Guess that's what you'll be telling *me* to do next."

Just the thought of it made both of us reach for our cigarettes.

I was late for my tennis lesson, despite my doing everything short of running red lights to get to Westwood on time. One of my shoelaces broke, my grip was slippery, and there was a Mexican buffet in progress upstairs, meaning the observation gallery was full of people with nothing better to do than eat tacos, drink margaritas, and witness my humiliation. After sending five backhands in a row sailing well beyond the baseline, I started bending my knees and slowing my swing. The next three shots went into the net. Volleys were pathetic, overheads unmentionable. The harder I tried, the worse I got.

"You're opening up too soon and hitting everything late." Ted came around to my side of the net. "Too much back-swing, not enough follow-through. And what happens?"

"I consider taking up bridge," I said, my frustration turning to anger.

"Your racket face is open. Take your racket back early, shoulder turned, step, hitting the ball out front. And keep it on your strings as long as you can."

Following me to the baseline, he demonstrated, stroking several balls over the net as I watched jealously. Ted had Michelangelo muscle definition, liquid coordination, and he could, without effort, put enough spin on a ball to make it bounce over your head or die at your feet. I wondered if magnificent athletes had any concept of how they made the rest of us feel.

"Most of your problem's in your head, Dr. Scarpetta," he said. "You walk out here and want to be Martina when you'd be much better off being yourself."

"Well, I sure as hell can't be Martina," I muttered.

"Don't be so determined to win points when you ought to be working at not losing them. Playing smart, setting up, keeping the ball in play until your opponent misses or gives you an easy opening to put the ball away. Out here that's the game. Club-level matches aren't won. They're lost. Someone beats you not because they win more points than you but because you lose more points than them." Looking speculatively at me, he added, "I'll bet you're not this impatient in your work. I'll bet you hit every ball back, so to speak, and can do it all day long."

I wasn't so sure about that, but Ted's coaching did the opposite of what he had intended. It took my mind off tennis. Playing smart. Later, I pondered this at length while soaking in the tub.

We weren't going to beat this killer. Planting bullets and newspaper stories were offensive tactics that had not worked. A little defensive strategy was in order. Criminals who escape apprehension are not perfect but lucky. They make mistakes. All of them do. The problem is recognizing the errors, realizing their significance, and determining what was intentional and what was not.

I thought of the cigarette butts we'd been finding near the bodies. Had the killer intentionally left them? Probably. Were they a mistake? No, because they were worthless as evidence and we could not determine their brand. The jacks of hearts left in the vehicles were intentional, but they were not a mistake either. No fingerprints had been recovered from them, and if anything, their purpose may be to make us think what the person who had left them wanted us to think.

Shooting Deborah Harvey I was sure was a mistake.

Then there was the perpetrator's past, which was what I was considering now. He didn't suddenly go from being a law-abiding citizen to becoming an experienced murderer. What sins had he committed before, what acts of evil?

For one thing, he may have shot an old man's dog eight years ago. If I was right, then he had made another mistake, because the incident suggested he was local, not new to the area. It made me wonder if he had killed before.

* * *

Immediately after staff meeting the following morning, I had my computer analyst, Margaret, give me a printout of every homicide that had occurred within a fifty-mile radius of Camp Peary over the past ten years. Though I wasn't necessarily looking for a double homicide, that was exactly what I found.

Numbers C0104233 and C0104234. I had never heard of the related cases, which had occurred several years before I moved to Virginia. Returning to my office, I shut the doors and reviewed the files with growing excitement. Jill Harrington and Elizabeth Mott had been murdered eight years ago in September, a month after Mr. Joyce's dog was shot.

Both women were in their early twenties when they disappeared eight years before on the Friday night of September fourteenth, their bodies found the next morning in a church cemetery. It wasn't until the following day that the Volkswagen belonging to Elizabeth was located in a motel parking lot off Route 60 in Lightfoot, just outside of Williamsburg.

I began studying autopsy reports and body diagrams. Elizabeth Mott had been shot once in the neck, after which, it was conjectured, she was stabbed once in the chest, her throat cut. She was fully clothed, with no evidence of sexual assault, no bullet was recovered, and there were ligature marks around her wrists. There were no defense injuries. Jill's records, however, told another story. She bore defense cuts to both forearms and hands, and contusions and lacerations to her face and scalp consistent with being "pistol whipped," and her blouse was torn. Apparently, she had put up one hell of a struggle, ending with her being stabbed eleven times.

According to newspaper clips included in their files, the James City County police said the women were last seen drinking beer in the Anchor Bar and Grill in Williamsburg, where they stayed until approximately ten P.M. It was theorized that it was here they met up with their assailant, a "Mr. Goodbar" situation, in which the two women left with him and followed him to the motel where Elizabeth's car was later found. At some point he abducted them, perhaps in the parking lot, and forced them to drive him to the cemetery where he murdered them.

There was a lot about the scenario that didn't make sense to me. The police had found blood in the backseat of the Volkswagen that could not be explained. The blood type did not match up with either woman's. If the blood was the killer's, then what happened? Did he struggle with one of the women in the backseat? If so, why wasn't her blood found as well? If both women were up front and he was in back, then how did he get injured? If he cut himself while struggling with Jill in the cemetery, then that didn't make sense, either. After the murders, he would have had to drive their car from the cemetery to the motel, and his blood should have been in the driver's area, not in the backseat. Finally, if the man intended to murder the women after engaging in sexual activity, why didn't he just kill them inside the motel room? And why were the women's physical evidence recovery kits negative for sperm? Had they engaged in intercourse with this man and then cleaned up afterward? *Two* women with one man? A ménage à trois? Well, I supposed, there wasn't much I hadn't seen in my line of work.

Buzzing the computer analyst's office, I got Margaret on the line.

"I need you to run something else for me," I said. "A list of all drug-positive homicide cases worked by James City County Detective R. P. Montana. And I need the information right away, if you can manage it."

"No problem." I could hear her fingers clicking over the keyboard.

When I got the printout there were six drug-positive homicides investigated by Detective Montana. The names of Elizabeth Mott and Jill Harrington were on the list, because their postmortem blood was positive for alcohol. The result in each instance was insignificant, less than .05. In addition, Jill was positive for chlordiazepoxide and clidinium, the active drugs found in Librax.

Reaching for the phone, I dialed the James City County Detective Division and asked to speak to Montana. I was told he was a captain now in Internal Affairs, and my call was transferred to his desk.

I intended to be very careful. If it were perceived I was considering that the murders of the two women might be related to the deaths of the other five couples, I feared Montana would back off, not talk.

"Montana," a deep voice answered.

"This is Dr. Scarpetta," I said.

"How'ya doing, Doc? Everybody in Richmond's still shooting each other, I see."

"It doesn't seem to get much better," I agreed. "I'm surveying for drug-positive homicides," I explained. "And I wonder if I could ask you a question or two about several old cases of yours I came across in our computer."

"Fire away. But it's been a while. I may be a little fuzzy on the details."

"Basically, I'm interested in the scenarios, the details surrounding the deaths. Most of your cases occurred before I came to Richmond."

"Oh, yeah, back in the days of Doc Cagney. Working with him was something." Montana laughed. "Never forget the way he used to sometimes dig around in bodies without gloves. Nothing fazed him except kids. He didn't like doing kids."

I began reviewing the information from the computer printout, and what Montana recalled about each case didn't surprise me. Hard drinking and domestic problems had culminated in husband shooting wife or the other way around—the Smith & Wesson divorce, as it was irreverently referred to by the police. A man tanked to the gills was beaten to death by several drunk companions after a poker game went sour. A father with a .30 blood alcohol level was shot to death by his son. And so on. I saved Jill's and Elizabeth's cases for last.

"I remember them real well," Montana said. "Weird's all I got to say about what happened to those two girls. Wouldn't have thought they were the type to go off to a motel with some guy who picked them up in a bar. Both of them college graduates, had good jobs, smart, attractive. It's my opinion the guy they met up with had to be mighty slick. We're not talking about some redneck type. I've always suspected it was someone just passing through, not from around here."

"Why?"

"Because if it was someone local, I think we might have had a little luck developing a suspect. Some serial killer, it's my opinion. Picks up women in bars and murders them. Maybe some guy on the road a lot, hits in different cities and towns, then moves on."

"Was robbery involved?" I asked.

"Didn't appear to be. My first thought when I got the cases was maybe the two girls were into recreational drugs, went off with someone to make a buy, maybe agreed to meet him at the motel to party or exchange cash for coke. But no money or jewelry was missing, and I never found out anything to make me think the girls had a history of snorting or shooting up."

"I notice from the toxicology reports that Jill Harrington tested positive for Librax, in addition to alcohol," I said. "Do you know anything about that?"

He thought for a moment. "Librax. Nope. Doesn't ring a bell."

I asked him nothing else and thanked him.

Librax is a versatile therapeutic drug used as a muscle relaxant and to relieve anxiety and tension. Jill may have suffered from a bad back or soreness due to sports injuries, or she may have had psychosomatic problems such as spasms in her gastrointestinal tract. My next chore was to find her physician. I began by calling one of my medical examiners in Williamsburg and asking him to fax the section in his Yellow Pages that listed pharmacies in his area. Then I dialed Marino's pager number.

"Do you have any police friends in Washington? Anyone you trust?" I said when Marino rang me back.

"I know a couple of guys. Why?"

"It's very important I talk to Abby Turnbull. And I don't think it's a good idea for me to call her."

"Not unless you want to take the risk of someone knowing about it."

"Exactly."

"You ask me," he added, "it's not a good idea for you to talk to her anyway."

"I understand your point of view. But that doesn't change my mind, Marino. Could you contact one of your friends up there and send him to her apartment, have him see if he can locate her?"

"I think you're making a mistake. But yeah. I'll take care of it."

"Just have him tell her I need to talk to her. I want her to contact me immediately." I gave Marino her address.

By this time, the copies of the Yellow Pages I was interested in had come off the fax machine down the hall and Rose placed them on my desk. For the rest of the afternoon, I called every pharmacy that Jill Harrington might have patronized in Williamsburg. I finally located one that had her listed in their records.

"Was she a regular customer?" I asked the pharmacist.

"Sure was. Elizabeth Mott was, too. Both of them didn't live too far from here, in an apartment complex just down the road. Nice young women, never will forget how shocked I was."

"Did they live together?"

"Let me see." A pause. "Wouldn't appear so. Different addresses and phone numbers, but the same apartment complex. Old Towne, about two miles away. Nice enough place. A lot of young people, William and Mary students out there."

He went on to give me Jill's medication history. Over a period of three years, Jill had brought in prescriptions for various antibiotics, cough suppressants, and other medications associated with the mundane flu bugs and respiratory or urinary tract infections that commonly afflict the hoi polloi. As recently as a month before her murder, she had been in to fill a prescription for Septra, which she apparently was no longer on when she died, since trimethoprim and sulfamethoxazole were not detected in her blood.

"Did you ever dispense Librax to her?" I asked.

I waited while he looked.

"No, ma'am. No record of that."

Perhaps the prescription was Elizabeth's, I considered.

"What about her friend Elizabeth Mott?" I asked the pharmacist. "Did she ever come in with a prescription for Librax?"

"No."

"Was there any other pharmacy either woman patronized that you're aware of?"

"Afraid I can't help you on that one. Got no idea."

He gave me the names of other pharmacies close by. I had already called most of them, and calls to the rest confirmed neither woman had brought in a prescription for Librax or any other drug. The Librax itself wasn't necessarily important, I reasoned. But the mystery of who had prescribed it and why bothered me considerably.

12

Abby Turnbull had been a crime reporter in Richmond when Elizabeth Mott and Jill Harrington were murdered. I was willing to bet that Abby not only remembered the cases, but probably knew more about them than Captain Montana did.

The next morning she called from a pay phone and left a number where she told Rose she would wait for fifteen minutes. Abby insisted that I call her back from a "safe place."

"Is everything all right?" Rose asked quietly as I peeled off my surgical gloves.

"God only knows," I said, untying my gown.

The nearest "safe place" I could think of was a pay phone outside the cafeteria in my building. Breathless and somewhat frantic to meet Abby's deadline, I dialed the number my secretary had given me.

"What's going on?" Abby asked immediately. "Some Metro cop came by my apartment, said you'd sent him."

"That's correct," I reassured her. "Based on what you've told me, I didn't think it a good idea to call you at home. Are you all right?"

"Is that why you wanted me to call?" She sounded disappointed.

"One of the reasons. We need to talk."

There was a long silence on the line.

"I'll be in Williamsburg on Saturday," she then said. "Dinner, The Trellis at seven?"

I did not ask her why she was going to be in Williamsburg. I wasn't sure I wanted to know, but when I parked my car in Merchant's Square Saturday, I found my apprehensions diminishing with each step I took. It was hard to be preoccupied with murder and other acts of incivility while sipping hot apple cider in the sharp wintry air of one of my favorite places in America.

It was a low season for tourists, and there were still plenty of people about, strolling, browsing inside the restored shops, and riding past in horse-drawn carriages driven by liverymen in knee breeches and three-cornered hats. Mark and I had talked about spending a weekend in Williamsburg. We would rent one of the eighteenth-century carriage houses inside the Historic District, follow cobblestone sidewalks beneath the glow of gaslights and dine in one of the taverns, then drink wine before the fire until falling asleep in each other's arms.

Of course, none of it had come to pass, the history of our relationship more wishes than memories. Would it ever be different from this? Recently, he had promised me on the phone that it would. But he had promised before, and so had I. He was still in Denver and I was still here.

Inside the Silversmith's Shop, I bought a handwrought sterling silver pineapple charm and a handsome chain. Lucy would get a late Valentine's Day present from her negligent aunt. A forage inside the Apothecary Shop brought forth soaps for my guest room, spicy shaving cream for Fielding and Marino, and potpourri for Bertha and Rose. At five minutes before seven, I was inside The Trellis looking for Abby. When she arrived half an hour later, I was impatiently waiting at a table nestled against a planter of wandering jew.

"I'm sorry," she said with feeling, slipping out of her coat. "I got delayed. Got here as fast as I could."

She looked keyed up and exhausted, her eyes nervously darting about. The Trellis was doing a brisk business, people talking in low voices in the wavering shadows of candlelight. I wondered if Abby felt she had been followed.

"Have you been in Williamsburg all day?" I asked.

She nodded.

"I don't suppose I dare ask what you've been doing."

"Research" was all she said.

"Nowhere near Camp Peary, I hope." I looked her in the eye.

She got my meaning very well. "You know," she said.

The waitress arrived and then went off to the bar to get Abby a Bloody Mary.

"How did you find out?" Abby asked, lighting a cigarette.

"A better question is how did *you* find out?"

"I can't tell you that, Kay."

Of course she couldn't. But I knew. Pat Harvey.

"You have a source," I said carefully. "Let me just ask you this. Why would this source want you to know? Information wasn't passed on to you without there being motive on the source's part."

"I'm well aware of that."

"Then why?"

"The truth is important." Abby stared off. "I'm also a source."

"I see. In exchange for information, you pass on what you dig up."

She did not respond.

"Does this include me?" I asked.

"I'm not going to screw you, Kay. Have I ever?" She looked hard at me.

"No," I said sincerely. "So far, you never have."

Her Bloody Mary was set before her, and she absently stirred it with the stalk of celery.

"All I can tell you," I went on, "is you're walking on dangerous ground. I don't need to elaborate. You should realize this better than anyone. Is it worth the stress? Is your book worth the price, Abby?"

When she made no comment, I added with a sigh, "I don't guess I'm going to change your mind, am I?"

"Have you ever gotten into something you can't get out of?"

"I do it all the time." I smiled wryly. "That's where I am now."

"That's where I am, too."

"I see. And what if you're wrong, Abby?"

"I'm not the one who can be wrong," she replied. "Whatever the truth is about who's committing these murders, the fact remains that the FBI and other interested agencies are acting on certain suspicions and making decisions based on them. That's reportable. If the feds, the police, are wrong, it just adds another chapter."

"That sounds awfully cold," I said uneasily.

"I'm being professional, Kay. When you talk professionally, sometimes you sound cold, too."

I had talked to Abby directly after the body of her murdered sister was discovered. If I hadn't sounded cold on that horrible occasion, at best I had come across as clinical.

"I need your help with something," I said. "Eight years ago, two women were murdered very close to here. Elizabeth Mott and Jill Harrington."

She looked curiously at me. "You don't think—"

"I'm not sure what I'm thinking," I interrupted. "But I need to know the details of the cases. There's very little in my office reports. I wasn't in Virginia then. But there are news clips in the files. Several of them have your byline."

"It's hard for me to imagine that what happened to Jill and Elizabeth is connected to the other cases."

"So you remember them," I said, relieved.

"I will never forget them. It was one of the few times working on something actually gave me nightmares."

"Why is it hard for you to imagine a connection?"

"A number of reasons. There was no jack of hearts found. The car wasn't found abandoned on a roadside, but in a motel parking lot, and the bodies didn't turn up weeks or months after the fact decomposing in the woods. They were found within twenty-four hours. Both victims were women, and they were in their twenties, not teenagers. And why would the killer strike and then not do it again until some five years later?"

"I agree," I said. "The timing doesn't fit with the profile of your typical serial killer. And the MO seems inconsistent with the others. The victim selection seems inconsistent as well."

"Then why are you so interested?" She sipped her drink.

"I'm groping, and I'm troubled by their cases, which were never solved," I admitted. "It's unusual for two people to be abducted and murdered. There was no evidence of sexual assault. The women were killed around here, in the same area where the other murders have occurred."

"And a gun and a knife were used," Abby mused.

She knew about Deborah Harvey, then.

"There are some parallels," I said evasively.

Abby looked unconvinced but interested.

"What do you want to know, Kay?"

"Anything you might remember about them. Anything at all."

She thought for a long moment, toying with her drink.

"Elizabeth was working in sales for a local computer company and doing extremely well," she said. "Jill had just finished law school at William and Mary and had gone to work with a small firm in Williamsburg. I never did buy the notion that they went off to a motel to have sex with some creep they met in a bar. Neither of the women struck me as the type. And two of them with one man? I always thought it was strange. Also, there was blood in the backseat of their car. It didn't match either Jill's or Elizabeth's blood types."

Abby's resourcefulness never ceased to amaze me. Somehow she had gotten hold of the serology results.

"I assume the blood belonged to the killer. There was a lot of it, Kay. I saw the car. It looked as if someone had been stabbed or cut in the backseat. Possibly, this would place the killer there, but it was hard to come up with a good interpretation of what might have occurred. The police were of the opinion the women met up with this animal in the Anchor Bar and Grill. But if he rode off with them in their car and was planning to kill them, then how was he going to get back to his car later on?"

"Depends on how far the motel is from the bar. He could have walked back to his car after the murders."

"The motel is a good four or five miles from the Anchor Bar, which isn't around anymore, by the way. The women were last seen inside the bar at around ten P.M. If the killer had left his car there, it probably would have been the only one in the lot by the time he got back to it, and that wouldn't have been very bright. A cop might have noticed the car, or at least the night manager would have as he was locking up to go home."

"This doesn't preclude the killer leaving his car at the motel and abducting them in Elizabeth's, then returning later, getting into his car, and driving off," I pointed out.

"No, it doesn't. But if he drove his own car to the motel, then when did he get inside hers? The scenario of the three of them being inside a motel room together, and then forcing them to drive him to the cemetery, has never set well with me. Why go to all the trouble, the risk? They could have started screaming in the parking lot, could have resisted. Why not just murder them inside the room?"

"Was it verified that the three of them were ever inside one of the rooms?"

"That's the other thing," she said. "I questioned the clerk who was on duty that night. The Palm Leaf, a low-rent motel off Route Sixty in Lightfoot. Doesn't exactly do a thriving business. But the clerk didn't remember either woman. Nor did he remember some guy coming in and renting a room near where the Volkswagen was found. In fact, most of the rooms in that section of the motel were vacant at the time. More important, no one checked in and then left without turning in the key. Hard to believe this guy would have had opportunity or inclination to check out. Certainly not after committing the crimes. He would have been bloody."

"What was your theory when you were working on your stories?" I asked.

"The same as it is now. I don't think they met up with their killer inside the bar. I think something happened shortly after Elizabeth and Jill left."

"Such as?"

Frowning, Abby was stirring her drink again. "I don't know. They definitely weren't the type to pick up a hitchhiker, certainly not at that late hour. And I never believed there was a drug connection. Neither Jill nor Elizabeth was found to have used coke, heroin, or anything like that, and no paraphernalia was found inside their apartments. They didn't smoke, weren't heavy drinkers. Both of them jogged, were health nuts."

"Do you know where they were heading after they left the bar? Were they going straight home? Might they have stopped somewhere?"

"No evidence if they did."

"And they left the bar alone?"

"Nobody I talked to remembered seeing them with another person while they were in the bar drinking. As I remember it, they had a couple of beers, were at a corner table talking. Nobody recalled seeing them leave with anyone."

"They might have met someone in the parking lot when they left," I said. "This individual might even have been waiting in Elizabeth's car."

"I doubt they would have left the car unlocked, but I suppose it's possible."

"Did the women frequent this bar?"

"As I remember it, they didn't frequent it, but they'd gone there before."

"A rough place?"

"That was my expectation since it was a favorite watering hole for military guys," she replied. "But it reminded me of an English pub. Civilized. People talking, playing darts. It was the sort of place I could have gone with a friend and felt quite comfortable and private. The theory was that the killer was either someone passing through town or else a military person temporarily stationed in the area. It wasn't someone they knew."

Perhaps not, I thought. But it must have been someone they felt they could trust, at least initially, and I recalled what Hilda Ozimek had said about the encounters being "friendly" at first. I wondered what would come to her if I showed her photographs of Elizabeth and Jill.

"Did Jill have any medical problems you're aware of?" I asked.

She thought about this, her face perplexed. "I don't recall."

"Where was she from?"

"Kentucky comes to mind."

"Did she go home often?"

"I didn't get that impression. I think she made it home for holidays and that was about it."

Then it wasn't likely she had a prescription for Librax filled in Kentucky where her family lived, I thought.

"You mentioned she had just begun practicing law," I went on. "Did she travel much, have reason to be in and out of town?"

She waited as our chef's salads were served, then said, "She had a close friend from law school. I can't remember his name, but I talked to him, asked him about her habits, activities. He said he was suspicious Jill was having an affair."

"What made him suspect that?"

"Because during their third year of law school she drove to Richmond almost every week, supposedly because she was job hunting, liked Richmond a lot, and wanted to find an opening in a firm there. He told me she often needed to borrow his notes because her out-of-town excursions caused her to miss classes. He thought it was strange, especially since she ended up going with a firm here in Williamsburg right after graduation. He went on and on about it because he was afraid her trips might be related to her murder, if she were seeing a married man in Richmond, for example, and perhaps threatened to expose their affair to his wife. Maybe she was having an affair with someone prominent, a successful lawyer or judge, who couldn't afford the scandal, so he silenced Jill forever. Or got someone else to, and it just so happened Elizabeth had the misfortune of being around at the time."

"What do you think?"

"The lead went nowhere, like ninety percent of the tips I get."

"Was Jill romantically involved with the student who told you this?"

"I think he would have liked for her to have been," she said. "But no, they weren't involved. I got the impression this was, in part, the reason for his suspicions. He was pretty sure of himself and figured the only reason Jill never succumbed to his charms was because she had somebody else nobody knew about. A secret lover."

"Was he ever a suspect, this student?" I asked.

"Not at all. He was out of town when the murders occurred, and that was verified beyond a doubt."

"Did you talk to any of the other lawyers in the firm where Jill worked?"

"I didn't get very far with that," Abby answered. "You know how lawyers are. In any event, she'd been with the firm only a few months before she was murdered. I don't think her colleagues knew her very well."

"Doesn't sound as if Jill was an extrovert," I remarked.

"She was described as charismatic, witty, but self-contained."

"And Elizabeth?" I asked.

"More outgoing, I think," she said. "Which I suppose she had to have been to be good in sales."

The glow of gaslight lamps pushed the darkness back from cobblestone sidewalks as we walked to the Merchant's Square parking lot. A heavy layer of clouds obscured the moon, the damp, cold air penetrating.

"I wonder what these couples would be doing now, if they'd still be with each other, what difference they might have made," Abby said, chin tucked into her collar, hands in her pockets.

"What do you think Henna would be doing?" I gently asked about her sister.

"She'd probably still be in Richmond. I guess both of us would be."

"Are you sorry you moved?"

"Some days I'm sorry about everything. Ever since Henna died, it's as if I've had no options, no free will. It's as if I've been propelled along by things out of my control."

"I don't see it that way. You chose to take the job at the *Post,* move to D.C. And now you've chosen to write a book."

"Just as Pat Harvey chose to hold that press conference and do all the other things she's done that have burned her so badly," she said.

"Yes, she has made choices, too."

"When you're going through something like this, you don't know what you're doing, even if you think you do," she went on. "And no one can really understand what it's like unless they've suffered the same thing. You feel isolated. You go places and people avoid you, are afraid to meet your eyes and make conversation because they don't know what to say. So they whisper to each other. 'See her over there? Her sister was the one murdered by the strangler.' Or 'That's Pat Harvey. Her daughter was the one.' You feel as if you're living inside a cave. You're afraid to be alone, afraid to be with others, afraid to be awake, and afraid to go to sleep because of how awful it feels when morning comes. You run like hell and wear yourself out. As I look back, I can see that everything I've done since Henna died was half crazy."

"I think you've done remarkably well," I said sincerely.

"You don't know the things I've done. The mistakes I've made."

"Come on. I'll drive you to your car," I said, for we had reached Merchant's Square.

I heard a car engine start in the dark lot as I got out my keys. We were inside my Mercedes, doors locked and seat belts on when a new Lincoln pulled up beside us and the driver's window hummed down.

I opened my window just enough to hear what the man wanted. He was young, clean cut, folding a map and struggling with it.

"Excuse me." He smiled helplessly. "Can you tell me how to get back on Sixty-four East from here?"

I could feel Abby's tension as I gave him quick directions.

"Get his plate number," she said urgently as he drove away. She dug in her pocketbook for a pen and notepad.

"E-N-T-eight-nine-nine," I read quickly.

She wrote it down.

"What's going on?" I asked, unnerved.

Abby looked left and right for any sign of his car as I pulled out of the lot.

"Did you notice his car when we got to the parking lot?" she asked.

I had to think. The parking lot was nearly empty when we had gotten there. I had been vaguely aware of a car that might have been the Lincoln parked in a poorly lit corner.

I told Abby this, adding, "But I assumed no one was in it."

"Right. Because the car's interior light wasn't on."

"I guess not."

"Reading a map in the dark, Kay?"

"Good point," I said, startled.

"And if he's from out of town, then how do you explain the parking sticker on his rear bumper?"

"Parking sticker?" I repeated.

"It had the Colonial Williamsburg seal on it. The same sticker I was given years ago when the skeletal remains were discovered at that archaeology dig, Martin's Hundred. I did a series, was out here a lot, and the sticker permitted me to park inside the Historic District and at Carter's Grove."

"The guy works here and needed directions to Sixty-four?" I muttered.

"You got a good look at him?" she asked.

"Pretty good. Do you think it was the man who followed you that night in Washington?"

"I don't know. But maybe . . . Damn it, Kay! This is making me crazy!"

"Well, enough is enough," I said firmly. "Give me that license number. I intend to do something about it."

The next morning Marino called with the cryptic message, "If you haven't read the *Post*, better go out and get a copy."

"Since when do you read the *Post*?"

"Since never, if I can help it. Benton alerted me about an hour ago. Call me later. I'm downtown."

Putting on a warm-up suit and ski jacket, I drove through a downpour to a nearby drugstore. For the better part of half an hour I sat inside my car, heater blasting, windshield wipers a monotonous metronome in the hard, cold rain. I was appalled by what I read. Several times it entered my mind that if the Harveys didn't sue Clifford Ring, I should.

The front page carried the first in a three-part series about Deborah Harvey, Fred Cheney, and the other couples who had died. Nothing sacred was spared, Ring's reporting so comprehensive it included details even I did not know.

Not long before Deborah Harvey was murdered, she had confided to a friend her suspicions that her father was an alcoholic and having an affair with an airline flight attendant half his age. Apparently, Deborah had eavesdropped on a number of telephone conversations between her father and his alleged mistress. The flight attendant lived in Charlotte, and according to the story, Harvey was with her the night his daughter and Fred Cheney disappeared, which was why the police and Mrs. Harvey were unable to reach him. Ironically, Deborah's suspicions did not make her bitter toward her father but her mother, who, consumed with her career, was never home, and therefore, in Deborah's eyes, to blame for her father's infidelity and alcohol abuse.

Column after column of vitriolic print added up to paint a pathetic portrait of a powerful woman bent on saving the world while her own family disintegrated from neglect. Pat Harvey had married into money, her home in Richmond was palatial, her quarters at the Watergate filled with antiques and valuable art, including a Picasso and a Remington. She wore the right clothes, went to the right parties, her decorum impeccable, her policies and knowledge of world affairs brilliant.

Yet lurking behind this plutocratic, flawless facade, Ring concluded, was "a driven woman born in a blue-collar section of Baltimore, someone described by her colleagues as tormented by insecurity that perpetually propelled her into proving herself." Pat Harvey, he said, was a megalomaniac. She was irrational—if not rabid—when threatened or put to the test.

His treatment of the homicides that had occurred in Virginia over the past three years was just as relentless. He disclosed the fears of the CIA and FBI that the killer might be someone at Camp Peary, and served up this revelation with such a wild spin that it made everyone involved look bad.

The CIA and the Justice Department were involved in a cover-up, their paranoia so extreme they had encouraged investigators in Virginia to withhold information from each other. False evidence had been planted at a scene. Disinformation had been "leaked" to reporters, and it was even suspected that some reporters were under surveillance. Pat Harvey, meanwhile, was supposedly privy to all this, and her indignation was not exactly depicted as righteous, as evidenced by her demeanor during her infamous press conference. Engaged in a turf battle with the Justice Department, Mrs.

Harvey had exploited sensitive information to incriminate and harass those federal agencies with which she had become increasingly at odds due to her campaign against fraudulent charities such as ACTMAD.

The final ingredient in this poisonous stew was me. I had stonewalled and withheld case information at the request of the FBI until forced by threat of a court order to release my reports to the families. I had refused to talk to the press. Though I had no formal obligation to answer to the FBI, it was suggested by Clifford Ring that it was possible my professional behavior was influenced by my personal life. "According to a source close to Virginia's Chief Medical Examiner," the article read, "Dr. Scarpetta has been romantically involved with an FBI Special Agent for the past two years, has frequently visited Quantico and is on friendly terms with the Academy's personnel, including Benton Wesley, the profiler involved in these cases."

I wondered how many readers would conclude from this that I was having an affair with Wesley.

Impeached along with my integrity and morals was my competence as a forensic pathologist. In the ten cases in question, I had been unable to determine a cause of death in all of them but one, and when I discovered a cut on one of Deborah Harvey's bones, I was so worried that I had inflicted this myself with a scalpel, claimed Ring, that I "drove to Washington in the snow, Harvey's and Cheney's skeletons in the trunk of her Mercedes, and sought the advice of a forensic anthropologist at the Smithsonian's National Museum of Natural History."

Like Pat Harvey, I had "consulted a psychic." I had accused investigators of tampering with Fred Cheney's and Deborah Harvey's remains at the scene, and then returned to the wooded area to search for a cartridge case myself because I did not trust the police to find it. I had also taken it upon myself to question witnesses, including a clerk at a 7-Eleven, where Fred and Deborah were last seen alive. I smoked, drank, had a license to carry my .38 concealed, had "almost been killed" on several occasions, was divorced and "from Miami." The latter somehow seemed an explanation for all of the above.

The way Clifford Ring made it sound, I was an arrogant, gun-slinging wild woman who, when it came to forensic medicine, didn't know her ass from a hole in the ground.

Abby, I thought, as I sped home over rain-slick streets. Was this what she meant last night when she referred to mistakes she had made? Had she fed information to her colleague Clifford Ring?

"That wouldn't add up," Marino pointed out later as we sat in my kitchen drinking coffee. "Not that my opinion about her's changed. I think she'd sell her grandmother for a story. But she's working on this big book, right? Don't make sense that she'd share information with the competition, especially since she's pissed off at the *Post.*"

"Some of the information had to have come from her." It was hard for me to admit. "The bit about the Seven-Eleven clerk, for example. Abby and I were together that night. And she knows about Mark."

"How?" Marino looked curiously at me.

"I told her."

He just shook his head.

Sipping my coffee, I stared out at the rain. Abby had tried to call twice since I'd gotten home from the drugstore. I had stood by my machine listening to her tense voice. I wasn't ready to talk to her yet. I was afraid of what I might say.

"How's Mark going to react?" Marino asked.

"Fortunately, the story didn't mention his name."

I felt another wave of anxiety. Typical of FBI agents, especially those who had spent years under deep cover, Mark was secretive about his personal life to the point of paranoia. The paper's allusion to our relationship would upset him considerably, I feared. I had to call him. Or maybe I shouldn't. I didn't know what to do.

"Some of the information, I suspect, came from Morrell," I went on, thinking aloud.

Marino was silent.

"Vessey must have talked, too. Or at least someone at the Smithsonian did," I said. "And I don't know how the hell Ring found out that we went to see Hilda Ozimek."

Setting down his cup and saucer, Marino leaned forward and met my eyes.

"My turn to give advice."

I felt like a child about to be scolded.

"It's like a cement truck with no brakes going down a hill. You ain't going to stop it, Doc. All you can do is get out of the way."

"Would you care to translate?" I said impatiently.

"Just do your work and forget it. If you get questioned, and I'm sure you will, just say you never talked to Clifford Ring, don't know nothing about it. Brush it off, in other words. You get into a pissing match with the press and you're going to end up like Pat Harvey. Looking like an idiot."

He was right.

"And if you got any sense, don't talk to Abby anytime soon."

I nodded.

He stood up. "Meanwhile, I got a few things to run down. If they pan out, I'll let you know."

That reminded me. Fetching my pocketbook, I got out the slip of paper with the plate number Abby had taken down.

"Wonder if you could check NCIC. A Lincoln Mark Seven, dark gray. See what comes back."

"Someone tailing you?" He tucked the slip of paper in his pocket.

"I don't know. The driver stopped to ask directions. I don't think he was really lost."

"Where?" he asked as I walked him to the door.

"Williamsburg. He was sitting in the car in an empty parking lot. This was around ten-thirty, eleven last night at Merchant's Square. I was getting into my car when his headlights suddenly went on and he drove over, asked me how to get to Sixty-four."

"Huh," Marino said shortly. "Probably some dumb-shit detective working under cover, bored, waiting for someone to run a red light or make a U-turn. Might have been trying to hit on you, too. A decent-looking woman out at night alone, climbing into a Mercedes."

I didn't offer that Abby had been with me. I didn't want another lecture.

"I wasn't aware that many detectives drive new Lincolns," I said.

"Would you look at the rain. Shit," he complained as he ran to his car.

Fielding, my deputy chief, was never too preoccupied or busy to glance at any reflective object he happened to pass. This included plate-glass windows, computer screens, and the bulletproof security partitions separating the lobby from our inner offices. When I got off the elevator on the first floor, I spotted him pausing before the morgue's stainless-steel refrigerator door, smoothing back his hair.

"It's getting a little long over your ears," I said.

"And yours is getting a little gray." He grinned.

"Ash. Blondes go ash, never gray."

"Right." He absently tightened the drawstring of his surgical greens, biceps bulging like grapefruits. Fielding couldn't blink without flexing something formidable. Whenever I saw him hunched over his microscope, I was reminded of a steroid version of Rodin's *The Thinker.*

"Jackson was released about twenty minutes ago," he said, referring to one of the morning's cases. "That's it, but we've already got one for tomorrow. The guy they had on life support from the shootout over the weekend."

"What's on your schedule for the rest of the afternoon?" I asked. "And that reminds me, I thought you had court in Petersburg."

"The defendant pleaded." He glanced at his watch. "About an hour ago."

"He must have heard you were coming."

"Micros are stacked up to the ceiling in the cinder-block cell the state calls my office. That's my agenda for the afternoon. Or at least it was." He looked speculatively at me.

"I've got a problem I'm hoping you can help me with. I need to track down a prescription that may have been filled in Richmond eight or so years ago."

"Which pharmacy?"

"If I knew that," I said as we took the elevator to the second floor, "then I wouldn't have a problem. What it amounts to is we need to organize a telethon, so to speak. As many people as possible on the lines calling every pharmacy in Richmond."

Fielding winced. "Jesus, Kay, there's got to be at least a hundred."

"A hundred and thirty-three. I've already counted. Six of us with a list of twenty-two, twenty-three, each. That's fairly manageable. Can you help me out?"

"Sure." He looked depressed.

In addition to Fielding, I drafted my administrator, Rose, another secretary, and the computer analyst. We assembled in the conference room with lists of the pharmacies. My instructions were quite clear. Discretion. Not a word about what we were doing to family, friends, or the police. Since the prescription had to be at least eight years old and Jill was deceased, there was a good chance the records were no longer in the active files. I told them to ask the pharmacist to check the drugstore's archives. If he was uncooperative or reluctant to release the information, roll that call over to me.

Then we disappeared into our respective offices. Two hours later, Rose appeared at my desk, tenderly massaging her right ear.

She handed me a call sheet and could not suppress a triumphant smile. "Boulevard Drug Store at Boulevard and Broad. Jill Harrington had two prescriptions for Librax filled." She gave me the dates.

"Her physician?"

"Dr. Anna Zenner," she answered.

Good God.

Hiding my surprise, I congratulated her. "You're wonderful, Rose. Take the rest of the day off."

"I leave at four-thirty anyway. I'm late."

"Then take a three-hour lunch tomorrow." I felt like hugging her. "And tell the others mission accomplished. They can put down the phones."

"Wasn't Dr. Zenner the president of the Richmond Academy of Medicine not so long ago?" Rose asked, pausing thoughtfully in my doorway. "Seems I read something about her. Oh! She's the musician."

"She was the president of the Academy year before last. And yes, she plays the violin for the Richmond Symphony."

"Then you know her." My secretary looked impressed.

All too well, I thought, reaching for the phone.

That evening, when I was home, Anna Zenner returned my call.

"I see from the papers you have been very busy lately, Kay," she said. "Are you holding up?"

I wondered if she had read the *Post.* This morning's installment had included an interview with Hilda Ozimek and a photograph of her with the caption: "Psychic Knew All of Them Were Dead." Relatives and friends of the slain couples were quoted, and half of a page was filled with a color diagram showing where the couples' cars and bodies had been found. Camp Peary was ominously positioned in the center of this cluster like a skull and crossbones on a pirate's map.

"I'm doing all right," I told her. "And I'll be doing even better if you can assist me with something." I explained what I needed, adding, "Tomorrow I will fax you the form citing the Code giving me statutory rights to Jill Harrington's records."

It was pro forma. Yet it seemed awkward reminding her of my legal authority.

"You can bring the form in person. Dinner at seven on Wednesday?"

"It's not necessary for you to go to any trouble—"

"No trouble, Kay," she interrupted warmly. "I have missed seeing you."

13

The art deco pastels of uptown reminded me of Miami Beach. Buildings were pink, yellow, and Wedgwood blue with polished brass door knockers and brilliant handmade flags fluttering over entrances, a sight that seemed even more incongruous because of the weather. Rain had turned to snow.

Traffic was rush-hour awful, and I had to drive around the block twice before spotting a parking place within a reasonable walk of my favorite wine shop. I picked out four good bottles, two red, two white.

I drove along Monument Avenue, where statues of Confederate generals on horses loomed over traffic circles, ghostly in the milky swirl of snow. Last summer I had traveled this route once a week on my way to see Anna, the visits tapering off by fall and ending completely this winter.

Her office was in her house, a lovely old white frame where the street was blacktopped cobblestone and gas carriage lamps glowed after dark. Ringing the bell to announce my arrival just as her patients did, I let myself into a foyer that led into what was Anna's waiting room. Leather furniture surrounded a coffee table stacked with magazines, and an old Oriental rug covered the hardwood floor. There were toys in a box in a corner for her younger patients, a receptionist's desk, a coffeemaker, and a fireplace. Down a long hallway was the kitchen, where something was cooking that reminded me I had skipped lunch.

"Kay? Is that you?"

The unmistakable voice with its strong German accent was

punctuated by brisk footsteps, and then Anna was wiping her hands on her apron and giving me a hug.

"You locked the door after you?"

"I did, and you know to lock up after your last patient leaves, Anna." I used to say this every time.

"You are my last patient."

I followed her to the kitchen. "Do all of your *patients* bring you wine?"

"I wouldn't permit it. And I don't cook for or socialize with them. For you I break all the rules."

"Yes." I sighed. "How will I ever repay you?"

"Certainly not with your services, I hope." She set the shopping bag on a countertop.

"I promise I would be very gentle."

"And I would be very naked and very dead, and I wouldn't give a damn how gentle you were. Are you hoping to get me drunk or did you run into a sale?"

"I neglected to ask what you were cooking," I explained. "I didn't know whether to bring red or white. To be on the safe side, I got two of each."

"Remind me to never tell you what I'm cooking, then. Goodness, Kay!" She set the bottles on the counter. "This looks marvelous. Do you want a glass now, or would you rather have something stronger?"

"Definitely something stronger."

"The usual?"

"Please." Looking at the large pot simmering on the stove, I added, "I hope that's what I think it is." Anna made fabulous chili.

"Should warm us up. I threw in a can of the green chilies and tomatoes you brought back last time you were in Miami. I've been hoarding them. There's sourdough bread in the oven, and coleslaw. How's your family, by the way?"

"Lucy has suddenly gotten interested in boys and cars but I won't take it seriously until she's more interested in them than in her computer," I said. "My sister has another children's book coming out next month, and she's still clueless about the child she's supposedly raising. As for my mother, other than her usual fussing and fuming about what's become of Miami, where no one speaks English anymore, she's fine."

"Did you make it down there for Christmas?"

"No."

"Has your mother forgiven you?"

"Not yet," I said.

"I can't say that I blame her. Families should be together at Christmas."

I did not reply.

"But this is good," she surprised me by saying. "You did not feel like going to Miami, so you didn't. I have told you all along that women need to learn to be selfish. So perhaps you are learning to be selfish?"

"I think selfishness has always come pretty easily to me, Anna."

"When you no longer feel guilty about it, I will know you are cured."

"I still feel guilty, so I suppose I'm not cured. You're right."

"Yes. I can tell."

I watched her uncork a bottle to let it breathe, the sleeves of a white cotton blouse rolled up to her elbows, forearms as firm and strong as those of a woman half her age. I did not know what Anna had looked like when she was young, but at almost seventy, she was an eye-catcher with strong Teutonic features, short white hair, and light blue eyes. Opening a cupboard, she reached for bottles and in no time was handing me a Scotch and soda and fixing herself a manhattan.

"What has happened since I saw you last, Kay?" We carried our drinks to the kitchen table. "That would have been before Thanksgiving? Of course, we have talked on the phone. Your worries about the book?"

"Yes, you know about Abby's book, at least know as much as I do. And you know about these cases. About Pat Harvey. All of it." I got out my cigarettes.

"I've been following it in the news. You're looking well. A little tired, though. Perhaps a little too thin?"

"One can never be too thin," I said.

"I've seen you look worse, that's my point. So you are handling the stress from your work."

"Some days better than others."

Anna sipped her manhattan and stared thoughtfully at the stove. "And Mark?"

"I've seen him," I said. "And we've been talking on the phone. He's still confused, uncertain. I suppose I am, too. So maybe nothing's new."

"You have seen him. That is new."

"I still love him."

"That isn't new."

"It's so difficult, Anna. Always has been. I don't know why I can't seem to let it go."

"Because the feelings are intense, but both of you are afraid of commitment. Both of you want excitement and want your own way. I noticed he was alluded to in the newspaper."

"I know."

"And?"

"I haven't told him."

"I shouldn't think you would need to. If he didn't see the paper himself, certainly someone from the Bureau has called him. If he's upset, you would hear, no?"

"You're right," I said, relieved. "I would hear."

"You at least have contact, then. You are happier?"

I was.

"You are hopeful?"

"I'm willing to see what will happen," I replied. "But I'm not sure it can work."

"No one can ever be sure of anything."

"That is a very sad truth," I said. "I can't be sure of anything. I know only what I feel."

"Then you are ahead of the pack."

"Whatever the pack is, if I am ahead of it, then that's another sad truth," I admitted.

She got up to take the bread out of the oven. I watched her fill earthenware bowls with chili, toss coleslaw, and pour the wine. Remembering the form I had brought, I got it out of my pocketbook and placed it on the table.

Anna did not even glance at it as she served us and sat down.

She said, "Would you like to review her chart?"

I knew Anna well enough to be sure she would not record details of her counseling sessions. People like me have statutory rights to medical records, and these documents can also end up in court. People like Anna are too shrewd to put confidences in print.

"Why don't you summarize," I suggested.

"I diagnosed her as having an adjustment disorder," she said.

It was the equivalent of my saying that Jill's death was due to respiratory or cardiac arrest. Whether you are shot or run over by a train, you die because you stop breathing and your heart quits. The diagnosis of adjustment disorder was a catchall straight out of the *Diagnostic and Statistical Manual of Mental Disorders.* It qualified a patient for insurance coverage without divulging one scrap of useful information about his history or problems.

"The entire human race has an adjustment disorder," I said to Anna.

She smiled.

"I respect your professional ethics," I said. "And I have no intention of amending my own records by adding information that you consider confidential. But it's important for me to know anything about Jill that might give me insight into her murder. If there was something about her lifestyle, for example, that might have placed her at risk."

"I respect your professional ethics as well."

"Thank you. Now that we've established our mutual admiration for each other's fairness and integrity, might we push formalities aside and hold a conversation?"

"Of course, Kay," she said gently. "I remember Jill vividly. It is hard not to remember an unusual patient, especially one who is murdered."

"How was she special?"

"Special?" She smiled sadly. "A very bright, endearing young woman. So much in her favor. I used to look forward to her appointments. Had she not been my patient, I would have liked to know her as a friend."

"How long had she been seeing you?"

"Three to four times a month for more than a year."

"Why you, Anna?" I asked. "Why not someone in Williamsburg, someone closer to where she lived?"

"I have quite a number of patients from out of town. Some come from as far away as Philadelphia."

"Because they don't want anyone to know they are seeing a psychiatrist."

She nodded. "Unfortunately, many people are terrified by the prospect of others knowing. You would be surprised at the number of people who have been in this office and left by way of the back door."

I had never told a soul I was seeing a psychiatrist, and had Anna not refused to charge me, I would have paid for the sessions in cash. The last thing I needed was for someone in Employee Benefits to get hold of my insurance claims and spread gossip throughout the Department of Health and Human Services.

"Obviously, then, Jill did not want anyone to know she was seeing a psychiatrist," I said. "And this might also explain why she had her prescriptions for Librax filled in Richmond."

"Before you called, I did not know she filled the prescriptions in Richmond. But I'm not surprised." She reached for her wine.

The chili was spicy enough to bring tears to my eyes. But it was outstanding, Anna's best effort, and I told her so. Then I explained to her what she probably already suspected.

"It's possible Jill and her friend, Elizabeth Mott, were murdered by the same individual killing these couples," I said. "Or at least, there are some parallels between their homicides and the others that cause me concern."

"I'm not interested in what you know about the cases you are involved in now, unless you feel it necessary to tell me. So I'll let you ask me questions and I'll do my best to recall what I can about Jill's life."

"Why was she so worried about anyone knowing she was seeing a psychiatrist? What was she hiding?" I asked.

"Jill was from a prominent family in Kentucky, and their approval and acceptance were very important to her. She went to the right schools, did well, and was going to be a successful lawyer. Her family was very proud of her. They did not know."

"Know what? That she was seeing a psychiatrist?"

"They did not know that," Anna said. "More importantly, they did not know she was involved in a homosexual relationship."

"Elizabeth?" I knew the answer before I asked. The possibility had crossed my mind.

"Yes. Jill and Elizabeth became friends during Jill's first year in law school. Then they became lovers. The relationship was very intense, very difficult, rife with conflict. It was a first for both of them, or at least this was how it was presented to me by Jill. You must remember that I never met Elizabeth, never heard her side. Jill came to see me, initially, because she wanted to change. She did not want to be homosexual, was hoping therapy might redeem her heterosexuality."

"Did you see any hope for that?" I asked.

"I don't know what would have happened eventually," Anna said. "All I can tell you is that based on what Jill said to me, her bond with Elizabeth was quite strong. I got the impression that Elizabeth was more at peace with the relationship than Jill, who intellectually could not accept it but emotionally could not let it go."

"She must have been in agony."

"The last few times I saw Jill it had become more acute. She had just finished law school. Her future was before her. It was time to make decisions. She began suffering psychosomatic problems. Spastic colitis. I prescribed Librax."

"Did Jill ever mention anything to you that might have given you a hint as to who might have done this to them?"

"I thought about that, studied the matter closely after it happened. When I read about it in the papers, I could not believe it. I had just seen Jill three days before. I can't tell you how hard I concentrated on everything she had ever said to me. I hoped I would recall something, any detail that might help. But I never have."

"Both of them hid their relationship from the world?"

"Yes."

"What about a boyfriend, someone Jill or Elizabeth dated from time to time? For appearances?"

"Neither dated, I was told. Not a jealousy situation, therefore, unless there was something I did not know." She glanced at my empty bowl. "More chili?"

"I couldn't."

She got up to load the dishwasher. For a while we did not speak. Anna untied her apron and hung it on a hook inside the broom closet. Then we carried our glasses and the bottle of wine into her den.

It was my favorite room. Shelves of books filled two walls, a third centered by a bay window through which she could monitor from her cluttered desk flowers budding or snow falling over her small backyard. From that window I had watched magnolias bloom in a fanfare of lemony white, I had watched the last bright sparks of autumn fade. We had talked about my family, my divorce, and

Mark. We had talked about suffering and we had talked about death. From the worn leather wing chair where I sat, I had awkwardly led Anna through my life, just as Jill Harrington had done.

They had been lovers. This linked them to the other murdered couples and made the "Mr. Goodbar" theory that much more implausible, and I pointed this out to Anna.

"I agree with you," she said.

"They were last seen in the Anchor Bar and Grill. Did Jill ever mention this place to you?"

"Not by name. But she mentioned a bar they occasionally went to, a place where they talked. Sometimes they went to out-of-the-way restaurants where people would not know them. Sometimes they went on drives. Generally, these excursions occurred when they were in the midst of emotionally charged discussions about their relationship."

"If they were having one of these discussions that Friday night at the Anchor, they were probably upset, one or the other possibly feeling rejected, angry," I said. "Is it possible either Jill or Elizabeth might have gone through the motions of picking up a man, flirting, to jerk the other around?"

"I can't say that's impossible," Anna said. "But it would surprise me a great deal. I never got the impression that Jill or Elizabeth played games with each other. I'm more inclined to suspect that when they were talking that night, the conversation was very intense and they were probably unaware of their surroundings, focused only on each other."

"Anyone observing them might have overheard."

"That is the risk if one has personal discussions in public, and I had mentioned this to Jill."

"If she were so paranoid about anyone suspecting, then why did she take the risk?"

"Her resolve was not strong, Kay." Anna reached for her wine. "When she and Elizabeth were alone, it was too easy to slip back into intimacy. Hugging, comforting, crying, and no decisions were made."

That sounded familiar. When Mark and I had discussions either at his place or mine, inevitably we ended up in bed. Afterward, one of us would leave, and the problems were still there.

"Anna, did you ever consider that their relationship might have been connected to what happened to them?" I asked.

"If anything, their relationship made it seem all the more unusual. I should think that a woman alone in a bar looking to be picked up is in much greater danger than two women together who are not interested in drawing attention to themselves."

"Let's return to the subject of their habits and routines," I said.

"They lived in the same apartment complex but did not live together, and again, this was for the sake of appearances. But it was convenient. They could lead their separate lives, and then get together late at night at Jill's apartment. Jill preferred to be in her own place. I remember her telling me that if her family or other people repeatedly tried to call her late at night and she was never home, there would have been questions." She paused, thinking. "Jill and Elizabeth also exercised, were very fit. Running, I think, but they didn't always do this together."

"Where did they run?"

"I believe there was a park near where they lived."

"Anything else? Theaters, shops, malls they may have frequented?"

"Nothing comes to mind."

"What does your intuition tell you? What did it tell you at the time?"

"I felt that Jill and Elizabeth were having a stressful conversation in the bar. They probably wanted to be left alone and would have resented an intrusion."

"Then what?"

"Clearly they encountered their killer at some point that evening."

"Can you imagine how that might have happened?"

"It has always been my opinion it was someone they knew, or at least were well enough acquainted with so that they had no reason not to trust him. Unless they were abducted at gunpoint by one or more persons, either in the bar's parking lot or somewhere else they might have gone."

"What if a stranger had approached them in the bar's parking lot, asked them for a lift somewhere, claimed to have car trouble . . . ?"

She was already shaking her head. "It is inconsistent with my impressions of them. Again, unless it was someone with whom they were acquainted."

"And if the killer was impersonating a police officer, perhaps pulled them over for a routine traffic stop?"

"That's another matter. I suppose even you and I might be vulnerable to that."

Anna was looking tired, so I thanked her for dinner and her time. I knew our conversation was difficult for her. I wondered how I would feel were I in her position.

Minutes after I walked through my front door, the phone rang.

"One last thing that I remember but probably does not matter," Anna said. "Jill mentioned something about the two of them working crossword puzzles when they wanted to stay in, just the two of them, on Sunday mornings, for example. Insignificant, perhaps. But a routine, something they did together."

"A book of puzzles? Or the ones in the newspapers?"

"I don't know. But Jill did read a variety of newspapers, Kay. She usually had something with her to read while waiting for her appointment. The *Wall Street Journal,* the *Washington Post.*"

I thanked her again and said next time it was my turn to cook. Then I called Marino.

"Two women were murdered in James City Country eight years ago." I went straight to the point. "It's possible there's a connection. Do you know Detective Montana out there?"

"Yeah. I've met him."

"We need to get with him, review the cases. Can he keep his mouth shut?"

"Hell if I know," Marino said.

Montana looked like his name, big, rawboned, with hazy blue eyes set in a rugged, honest face topped by thick gray hair. His accent was that of a native Virginian, his conversation peppered with "yes, ma'am"s. The following afternoon he, Marino, and I met at my home, where we were ensured privacy and no interruptions.

Montana must have depleted his annual film budget on Jill and Elizabeth's case, for covering my kitchen table were photographs of their bodies at the scene, the Volkswagen abandoned at the Palm Leaf Motel, the Anchor Bar and Grill, and, remarkably, of every room inside the women's apartments, including pantries and closets. He had a briefcase bulging with notes, maps, interview transcriptions, diagrams, evidence inventories, logs of telephone tips. There is something to be said for detectives who rarely have homicides in their jurisdictions. Cases like these come along once or twice in their careers, and they work them meticulously.

"The cemetery is right next to the church." He moved a photograph closer to me.

"It looks quite old," I said, admiring weathered brick and slate.

"It is and it isn't. Was built in the seventeen-hundreds, did all right until maybe twenty years ago, when bad wiring did it in. I remember seeing the smoke, was on patrol, thought one of my neighbor's farmhouses was burning. Some historical society took an interest. It's supposed to look just like it used to inside and out.

"You get to it by this secondary road right here"—he tapped another photograph—"which is less than two miles west of Route Sixty and about four miles west of the Anchor Bar, where the girls were last seen alive the night before."

"Who discovered the bodies?" Marino asked, eyes roaming the photograph spread.

"A custodian who worked for the church. He came in Saturday morning to clean up, get things ready for Sunday. Says he had just pulled in when he spotted what looked like two people sleeping in the grass about twenty feet inside the cemetery's front gate. The bodies were visible from the church parking lot. Doesn't seem whoever did it was concerned about anybody finding them."

"Am I to assume there was no activity at the church that Friday night?" I asked.

"No, ma'am. It was locked up tight, nothing going on."

"Does the church ever have activities scheduled for Friday nights?"

"They do on occasion. Sometimes the youth groups get together on Friday nights. Sometimes there's choir practice, things like that. The point is, if you selected this cemetery in advance to kill someone, it wouldn't make a whole lot of sense. There's no guarantee the church would be deserted, not on any night of the week. That's one of the reasons I figured from the start that the murders were random, the girls just met up with someone, maybe in the bar. There isn't much about these cases to make me think the homicides were carefully planned."

"The killer was armed," I reminded Montana. "He had a knife and a handgun."

"The world's full of folks carrying knives, guns in their cars or even on their person," he said matter-of-factly.

I collected the photographs of the bodies in situ and began to study them carefully.

The women were less than a yard from each other, lying in the grass between two tilting granite headstones. Elizabeth was facedown, legs slightly spread, left arm under her stomach, right arm straight and by her side. Slender, with short brown hair, she was dressed in jeans and a white pullover sweater stained dark red around the neck. In another photograph, her body had been turned over, the front of her sweater soaked with blood, eyes the dull stare of the dead. The cut to her throat was shallow, the gunshot wound to her neck not immediately incapacitating, I recalled from her autopsy report. It was the stab wound to her chest that had been lethal.

Jill's injuries had been much more mutilating. She was on her back, face so streaked by dried blood that I could not tell what she had looked like in life, except that she had short black hair and a straight, pretty nose. Like her companion, she was slender. She was dressed in jeans and a pale yellow cotton shirt, bloody, untucked, and ripped open to her waist, exposing multiple stab wounds, several of which had gone through her brassiere. There were deep cuts to her forearms and hands. The cut to her neck was shallow and probably inflicted when she was already dead or almost dead.

The photographs were invaluable for one critical reason. They revealed something that I had not been able to determine from any of the newspaper clippings or reports I had reviewed in their cases on file in my office.

I glanced at Marino and our eyes met.

I turned to Montana. "What happened to their shoes?"

14

You know, it's interesting you should mention that," Montana replied. "I never have come up with a good explanation for why the girls took their shoes off, unless they were inside the motel, got dressed when it was time to leave, and didn't bother. We found their shoes and socks inside the Volkswagen."

"Was it warm that night?" Marino asked.

"It was. All the same, I would have expected them to put their shoes back on when they got dressed."

"We don't know for a fact they ever went inside a motel room," I reminded Montana.

"You're right about that," he agreed.

I wondered if Montana had read the series in the *Post,* which had mentioned that shoes and socks were missing in the other murder cases. If he had, it did not seem he had made the connection yet.

"Did you have much contact with the reporter Abby Turnbull when she was covering Jill's and Elizabeth's murders?" I asked him.

"The woman followed me like tin cans tied to a dog's tail. Everywhere I went, there she was."

"Do you recall if you told her that Jill and Elizabeth were barefoot? Did you ever show Abby the scene photographs?" I asked, for Abby was too smart to have forgotten a detail like that, especially since it was so important now.

Montana said without pause, "I talked to her, but no, ma'am. I never did show her these pictures. Was right careful what I said, too. You read what was in the papers, didn't you?"

"I've seen some of the articles."

"Nothing in there about the way the girls were dressed, about Jill's shirt being torn, their shoes and socks off."

So Abby didn't know, I thought, relieved.

"I notice from the autopsy photographs that both women had ligature marks around their wrists," I said. "Did you recover whatever might have been used to bind them?"

"No, ma'am."

"Then apparently he removed the ligatures after killing them," I said.

"He was right careful. We didn't find any cartridge cases, no weapon, nothing he might have used to tie them up. No seminal fluid. So it doesn't appear he got around to raping them, or if he did, no way to tell. And both were fully clothed. Now, as far as this girl's blouse being ripped"—he reached for a photograph of Jill—"that might have happened when he was struggling with her."

"Did you recover any buttons at the scene?"

"Several. In the grass near her body."

"What about cigarette butts?"

Montana began calmly looking through his paperwork. "No cigarette butts." He paused, pulling out a report. "Tell you what we did find, though. A lighter, a nice silver one."

"Where?" Marino asked.

"Maybe fifteen feet from where the bodies were. As you can see, an iron fence surrounds the cemetery. You enter through this gate." He was showing us another photograph. "The lighter was in the grass, five, six feet inside the gate. One of these expensive, slim lighters shaped like an ink pen, the kind people use to light pipes."

"Was it in working order?" Marino asked.

"Worked just fine, polished up real nice," Montana recalled. "I'm pretty sure it didn't belong to either of the girls. They didn't smoke, and no one I talked to remembered seeing either one of them with a lighter like that. Maybe it fell out of the killer's pocket, no way to know. Could have been anybody who lost it, maybe someone out there a day or two earlier sightseeing. You know how folks like to wander in old cemeteries looking at the graves."

"Was this lighter checked for prints?" Marino asked.

"The surface wasn't good for that. The silver's engraved with these crisscrosses, like you see with some of these fancy silver fountain pens." He stared off thoughtfully. "The thing probably cost a hundred bucks."

"Do you still have the lighter and the buttons you found out there?" I asked.

"I've got all the evidence from these cases. Always hoped we might solve them someday."

Montana didn't hope it half as much as I did, and it wasn't until after he left some time later that Marino and I began to discuss what was really on our minds.

"It's the same damn bastard," Marino said, his expression incredulous. "The damn squirrel made them take their shoes off just like he done with the other couples. To slow them down when he led them off to wherever it was he planned to kill them."

"Which wasn't the cemetery," I said. "I don't believe that was the spot he had selected."

"Yo. I think he took on more than he could handle with those two. They weren't cooperating or something went down that freaked him out—maybe having to do with the blood in the back of the Volkswagen. So he made them pull over at the earliest opportunity, which just happened to be a dark, deserted church with a cemetery. You got a map of Virginia handy?"

I went back to my office and found one. Marino spread it open on the kitchen table and studied it for a long moment.

"Take a look," he said, his face intense. "The turnoff for the church is right here on Route Sixty, about two miles before you get to the road leading to the wooded area where Jim Freeman and Bonnie Smyth were killed five, six years later. I'm saying we drove right past the damn road leading to the church where the two women was whacked when we went to see Mr. Joyce the other day."

"Good God," I muttered. "I wonder—"

"Yeah, I'm wondering, too," Marino interrupted. "Maybe the squirrel *was* out there casing the woods, selecting the right spot when Dammit surprised him. He shoots the dog. About a month later, he's abducted his first set of victims, Jill and Elizabeth. He intends to force them to drive him to this wooded area, but things get out of control. He ends the trip early. Or maybe he's confused, rattled, and tells Jill or Elizabeth the wrong road to turn off on. Next thing, he sees this church and now he's really freaked, realizes they didn't turn where they were supposed to. He may not have even known where the hell they were."

I tried to envision it. One of the women was driving and the other was in the front passenger's seat, the killer in the back holding a gun on them. What had happened to cause him to lose so much blood? Had he accidentally shot himself? That was highly unlikely. Had he cut himself with his knife? Maybe, but again, it was hard for me to imagine. The blood inside the car, I had noted from Montana's photographs, seemed to begin with drips on the back of the passenger's headrest. There were also drips on the back of the seat with a lot of blood on the floor mat. This placed the killer directly behind the passenger's seat, leaning forward. Was his head or face bleeding?

A *nosebleed?*

I proposed this to Marino.

"Must'ave been one hell of a one. There was a lot of blood." He thought for a moment. "So maybe one of the women threw back an elbow and hit him in the nose."

"How would you have responded if one of the women had done that to you?" I said. "Provided you were a killer."

"She wouldn't have done it again. I probably wouldn't have shot her inside the car, but I might have punched her, hit her in the head with the gun."

"There was no blood in the front seat," I reminded him. "Absolutely no evidence that either of the women was injured inside the car."

"Hmmmm."

"Perplexing, isn't it?"

"Yeah." He frowned. "He's in the backseat, leaning forward, and suddenly starts bleeding? Perplexing as shit."

I put on a fresh pot of coffee while we began to toss around more ideas. For starters, there continued to be the problem of how one individual subdues two people.

"The car belonged to Elizabeth," I said. "Let's assume she was driving. Obviously, her hands were not tied at this point."

"But Jill's might have been. He might have tied her hands during the drive, made her hold them up behind her head so he could tie them from the backseat."

"Or he could have forced her to turn around and place her arms over the headrest," I proposed. "This might have been when she struck him in the face, if that's what happened."

"Maybe."

"In any event," I went on, "we'll assume that by the time they stopped the car, Jill was already bound and barefoot. Next he orders Elizabeth to remove her shoes and binds her. Then he forces them at gunpoint into the cemetery."

"Jill had a lot of cuts on her hands and forearms," Marino said. "Are they consistent with her warding off a knife with her hands tied?"

"As long as her hands were tied in front of her and not behind her back."

"It would have been smarter to tie their hands behind their backs."

"He probably found that out the hard way and improved his techniques," I said.

"Elizabeth didn't have any defense injuries?"

"None."

"The squirrel killed Elizabeth first," Marino decided.

"How would you have done it? Remember, you've got two hostages to handle."

"I would have made both of them lie facedown in the grass. I would have put the gun to the back of Elizabeth's head to make her behave as I get ready to use the knife on her. If she surprised me by resisting, I might have pulled the trigger, shot her when I wasn't really intending to."

"That might explain why she was shot in the neck," I said. "If he had the gun to the back of her head and she resisted, the muzzle may have slipped. The scenario is reminiscent of what happened to Deborah Harvey, except that I seriously doubt she was lying down when she was shot."

"This guy likes to use a blade," Marino replied. "He uses his gun when things don't go down the way he planned. And so far, that's only happened twice that we know of. With Elizabeth and Deborah."

"Elizabeth was shot, then what, Marino?"

"He finishes her off and takes care of Jill."

"He fought with Jill," I reminded him.

"You can bet she struggled. Her friend's just been killed. Jill knows she don't got a chance, may as well fight like hell."

"Or else she was already fighting with him," I ventured.

Marino's eyes narrowed the way they did when he was skeptical.

Jill was a lawyer. I doubted she was naive about the cruel deeds people perpetrate upon one another. When she and her friend were being forced into the cemetery late at night, I suspected Jill knew both of them were going to die. One or both women may have begun resisting as he opened the iron gate. If the silver lighter did belong to the killer, it may have fallen out of his pocket at this point. Then, and perhaps Marino was right, the killer forced both women to lie facedown, but when he started on Elizabeth, Jill panicked, tried to protect her friend. The gun discharged, shooting Elizabeth in the neck.

"The pattern of Jill's injuries sends a message of frenzy, someone who is angry, frightened, because he's lost control," I said. "He may have hit her in the head with the gun, gotten on top of her and ripped open her shirt and started stabbing. As a parting gesture, he cuts their throats. Then he leaves in the Volkswagen, ditches it at the motel, and heads out on foot, perhaps back to wherever his car was."

"He should have had blood on him," Marino considered. "Interesting there wasn't any blood found in the driver's area, only in the backseat."

"There hasn't been any blood found in the driver's areas of any of the couples' vehicles," I said. "This killer is very careful. He may bring a change of clothing, towels, who knows what, when he's planning to commit his murders."

Marino dug into his pocket and produced his Swiss army knife. He began to trim his fingernails over a napkin. Lord knows what Doris had put up with all these years, I thought. Marino probably never bothered to empty an ashtray, place a dish in the sink, or pick his dirty clothes off the floor. I hated to think what the bathroom looked like after he had been in it.

"Abby *Turncoat* still trying to get hold of you?" he asked without looking up.

"I wish you wouldn't call her that."

He didn't respond.

"She hasn't tried in the last few days, at least not that I'm aware of."

"Thought you might be interested in knowing that she and Clifford Ring have more than a professional relationship, Doc."

"What do you mean?" I asked uneasily.

"I mean that this story about the couples Abby's been working on has nothing to do with why she was taken off the police beat." He was working on his left thumb, fingernail shavings falling on the napkin. "Apparently, she was getting so squirrelly no one in the newsroom could deal with her anymore. Things reached a head last fall, right before she came to Richmond and saw you."

"What happened?" I asked, staring hard at him.

"Way I heard it, she made a little scene right in the middle of the newsroom. Dumped a cup of coffee in Ring's lap and then stormed out, didn't tell her editors where the hell she was going or when she'd be back. That's when she got reassigned to features."

"Who told you this?"

"Benton."

"How would Benton know what goes on in the *Post*'s newsroom?"

"I didn't ask." Marino folded the knife and slipped it back into his pocket. Getting up, he wadded the napkin and put it in the trash.

"One last thing," he said, standing in the middle of my kitchen. "That Lincoln you was interested in?"

"Yes?"

"A 1990 Mark Seven. Registered to a Barry Aranoff, thirty-eight-year-old white male from Roanoke. Works for a medical supply company, a salesman. On the road a lot."

"Then you talked to him," I said.

"Talked to his wife. He's out of town and has been for the past two weeks."

"Where was he supposed to have been when I saw the car in Williamsburg?"

"His wife said she wasn't sure of his schedule. Seems he sometimes hits a different city every day, buzzes all over the place, including out of state. His territory goes as far north as Boston. As best she could remember, around the time you're talking about, he was in Tidewater, then was flying out of Newport News, heading to Massachusetts."

I fell silent, and Marino interpreted this as embarrassment, which it wasn't. I was thinking.

"Hey, what you done was good detective work. Nothing wrong

with writing down a plate number and checking it out. Should make you happy you wasn't being followed by some spook."

I did not respond.

He added, "Only thing you missed was the color. You said the Lincoln was dark gray. Aranoff's ride is brown."

Later that night lightning flashed high over thrashing trees as a storm worthy of summer unloaded its violent arsenal. I sat up in bed, browsing through several journals as I waited for Captain Montana's telephone line to clear.

Either his phone was out of order or someone had been on it for the past two hours. After he and Marino had left, I had recalled a detail from one of the photographs that reminded me of what Anna had said to me last. Inside Jill's apartment, on the carpet beside a La-Z-Boy chair in the living room, was a stack of legal briefs, several out-of-town newspapers, and a copy of the *New York Times Magazine.* I have never bothered with crossword puzzles. God knows I have too many other things to figure out. But I knew the *Times* crossword puzzle was as popular as manufacturer's coupons.

Reaching for the phone, I tried Montana's home number again. This time I was rewarded.

"Have you ever considered getting Call Waiting?" I asked good-naturedly.

"I've considered getting my teenage daughter her own switchboard," he said.

"I've got a question."

"Ask away."

"When you went through Jill's and Elizabeth's apartments, I'm assuming you went through their mail."

"Yes, ma'am. Checked out their mail for quite a while, seeing what all came in, seeing who wrote them letters, went through their charge card bills, that sort of thing."

"What can you tell me about Jill's subscriptions to newspapers that were delivered by mail?"

He paused.

It occurred to me. "I'm sorry. Their cases would be in your office. . . ."

"No, ma'am. I came straight home, have 'em right here. I was just trying to think, it's been a long day. Can you hold on?"

I heard pages turning.

"Well, there were a couple of bills, junk mail. But no newspapers."

Surprised, I explained Jill had several out-of-town newspapers in her apartment. "She had to have gotten them from somewhere."

"Maybe vending machines," he offered. "Lots of them around the college. That would be my guess."

The *Washington Post* or the *Wall Street Journal,* maybe, I thought. But not the Sunday *New York Times.* Most likely that had come from a drugstore or a newsstand where Jill and Elizabeth may routinely have stopped when they went out for breakfast on Sunday mornings. I thanked him and hung up.

Switching off the lamp, I got in bed, listening as rain drummed the roof in a relentless rhythm. I pulled the covers more tightly around me. Thoughts and images drifted, and I envisioned Deborah Harvey's red purse, damp and covered with dirt.

Vander, in the fingerprints lab, had finished examining it and I had looked over the report the other day.

"What are you going to do?" Rose was asking me. Oddly, the purse was in a plastic tray on Rose's desk. "You can't send it back to her family like that."

"Of course not."

"Maybe we could just take out the charge cards and things, wash them off and send those?" Rose's face twisted in anger. She shoved the tray across her desk and screamed, "Get it out of here! I can't stand it!"

Suddenly I was in my kitchen. Through the window I saw Mark

drive up, only the car was unfamiliar, but I recognized it somehow. Rummaging in my pocketbook for a brush, I frantically fixed my hair. I started to run to the bathroom to brush my teeth, but there wasn't time. The doorbell rang, just once.

He took me in his arms, whispering my name, like a small cry of pain. I wondered why he was here, why he was not in Denver.

He kissed me as he pushed the door with his foot. It slammed shut with a tremendous bang.

My eyelids flew open. Thunder cracked. Lightning lit up my bedroom again and then again as my heart pounded.

The next morning I performed two autopsies, then went upstairs to see Neils Vander, section chief of the fingerprints examination lab. I found him inside the Automated Fingerprint Identification System computer room deep in thought in front of a monitor. In hand was my copy of the report detailing the examination of Deborah Harvey's purse, and I placed it on top of his keyboard.

"I need to ask you something." I raised my voice over the computer's pervasive hum.

He glanced down at the report with preoccupied eyes, unruly gray hair wisping over his ears.

"How did you find anything after the purse had been in the woods so long? I'm amazed."

He returned his gaze to the monitor. "The purse is nylon, waterproof, and the credit cards were protected inside plastic windows, which were inside a zipped-up compartment. When I put the cards in the superglue tank, a lot of smudges and partials popped up. I didn't even need the laser."

"Pretty impressive."

He smiled a little.

"But nothing identifiable," I pointed out.

"Sorry about that."

"What interests me is the driver's license. Nothing popped up on it."

"Not even a smudge," he said.

"Clean?"

"As a hound's tooth."

"Thank you, Neils."

He was off somewhere again, gone in his land of loops and whorls.

I went back downstairs and looked up the number for the 7-Eleven Abby and I had visited last fall. I was told that Ellen Jordan, the clerk we had talked to, would not be in until nine P.M. I mowed through the rest of the day without stopping for lunch, unaware of the passing hours. I wasn't the slightest bit tired when I got home.

I was loading the dishwasher when the doorbell rang at eight P.M. Drying my hands on a towel, I walked anxiously to the front door.

Abby Turnbull was standing on the porch, coat collar turned up around her ears, face wan, eyes miserable. A cold wind rocked dark trees in my yard and lifted strands of her hair.

"You didn't answer my calls. I hope you won't refuse me entrance into your house," she said.

"Of course not, Abby. Please." I opened the door wide and stepped back.

She did not take off her coat until I invited her to do so, and when I offered to hang it up, she shook her head and draped it over the back of a chair, as if to reassure me that she did not intend to stay very long. She was dressed in faded denim jeans and a heavy-knit maroon sweater flecked with lint. Brushing past her to clear paperwork and newspapers off the kitchen table, I detected the stale odor of cigarette smoke and a pungent hint of sweat.

"Something to drink?" I asked, and for some reason I could not feel angry with her.

"Whatever you're having would be fine." She got out her cigarettes while I fixed both of us a drink.

"It's hard to start," she said when I was seated. "The articles were unfair to you, to say the least. And I know what you must be thinking."

"It's irrelevant what I'm thinking. I'd rather hear what's on your mind."

"I told you I've made mistakes." Her voice trembled slightly. "Cliff Ring was one of them."

I sat quietly.

"He's an investigative reporter, one of the first people I got to know after moving to Washington. Very successful, exciting. Bright and sure of himself. I was vulnerable, having just moved to a new city, having been through . . . well, what happened to Henna." She glanced away from me.

"We started out as friends, then everything went too fast. I didn't see what he was like because I didn't want to see it." Her voice caught and I waited in silence while she steadied herself.

"I trusted him with my life, Kay."

"From which I am to conclude that the details in his story came from you," I said.

"No. They came from my reporting."

"What does that mean?"

"I don't talk to anybody about what I'm writing," Abby said. "Cliff was aware of my involvement in these cases, but I never went into detail about them. He never seemed all that interested." She was beginning to sound angry. "But he was, more than a little. That's the way he operates."

"If you didn't go into detail with him," I said, "then how did he get the information from you?"

"I used to give him keys to my building, my apartment, when I'd go out of town so he could water my plants, bring the mail in. He could have had copies made."

Our conversation at the Mayflower came back to me. When Abby had talked about someone breaking into her computer and had gone on to accuse the FBI or CIA, I had been skeptical. Would an experienced agent open a word processing file and not realize that the time and date might be changed? Not likely.

"Cliff Ring went into your computer?"

"I can't prove it, but I know he did," Abby said. "I can't prove he's been going through my mail, but I know he has. It's no big deal to steam open a letter, reseal it, and then place it back in the box. Not if you've made a copy of the mailbox key."

"Were you aware he was writing the story?"

"Of course not. I didn't know a damn thing about it until I opened the Sunday paper! He'd let himself into my apartment when he knew I wouldn't be there. He was going through my computer, anything he could find. Then he followed up by calling people, getting quotes and information, which was pretty easy, since he knew exactly where to look and what he was looking for."

"Easy because you had been relieved of your police beat. When you thought the *Post* had backed off from the story, what your editors had really backed away from was you."

Abby nodded angrily. "The story was passed into what they viewed as more reliable hands. Clifford Ring's hands," she said.

I realized why Clifford Ring had made no effort to contact me. He would know that Abby and I were friends. Had he asked me for details about the cases, I might have said something to Abby, and he had wanted to keep Abby in the dark about what he was doing for as long as possible. So Ring had avoided me, gone around me.

"I'm sure he . . ." Abby cleared her throat and reached for her drink. Her hand shook. "He can be very convincing. He'll probably win a prize. For the series."

"I'm sorry, Abby."

"It's nobody's fault but my own. I was stupid."

"We take risks when we allow ourselves to love—"

"I'll never take a risk like that again," she cut me off. "It was always a problem with him, one problem after another. I was always the one making concessions, giving him a second chance, then a third and a fourth."

"Did the people you work with know about you and Cliff?"

"We were careful." She got evasive.

"Why?"

"The newsroom is a very incestuous, gossipy place."

"Certainly your colleagues must have seen the two of you together."

"We were very careful," she repeated.

"People must have sensed something between you. Tension, if nothing else."

"Competition. Guarding my turf. That's what he would say if asked."

And jealousy, I thought. Abby never had been good at hiding her emotions. I could imagine her jealous rages. I could imagine those observing her in the newsroom misconstruing, assuming she was ambitious and jealous of Clifford Ring, when that was not the case. She was jealous of his other commitments.

"He's married, isn't he, Abby?"

She could not stop the tears this time.

I got up to refresh our drinks. She would tell me he was unhappy with his wife, contemplating divorce, and Abby had believed he would leave it all for her. The story was as threadbare and predictable as something in Ann Landers. I had heard it a hundred times before. Abby had been used.

I set her drink on the table and gently squeezed her shoulder before I moved back to my chair.

She told me what I expected to hear, and I just looked at her sadly.

"I don't deserve your sympathy," she cried.

"You've been hurt much more than I have."

"Everybody has been hurt. You. Pat Harvey. The parents, friends of these kids. If the cases hadn't happened, I'd still be working cops.

At least I'd be all right professionally. No one person should have the power to cause such destruction."

I realized she was no longer thinking about Clifford Ring. She was thinking of the killer.

"You're right. No one should have the power. And no one will if we don't allow it."

"Deborah and Fred didn't allow it. Jill, Elizabeth, Jimmy, Bonnie. All of them." She looked defeated. "They didn't want to be murdered."

"What will Cliff do next?" I asked.

"Whatever it is, it won't involve me. I've changed all my locks."

"And your fears that your phones are bugged, that you're being followed?"

"Cliff's not the only one who wants to know what I'm doing. I can't trust anyone anymore!" Her eyes filled with angry tears. "You were the last person I wanted to hurt, Kay."

"Stop it, Abby. You can cry all year and it won't do me any good."

"I'm sorry. . . ."

"No more apologies." I was very firm but gentle.

She bit her bottom lip and stared at her drink.

"Are you ready to help me now?"

She looked up at me.

"First, what color was the Lincoln we saw in Williamsburg last week?"

"Dark gray, the interior leather dark, maybe black," she said, her eyes coming alive.

"Thank you. That's what I thought."

"What's going on?"

"I'm not sure. But there's more."

"More what?"

"I've got an *assignment* for you," I said, smiling. "But first, when are you returning to D.C.? Tonight?"

"I don't know, Kay." She stared off. "I can't be there now."

Abby felt like a fugitive, and in a sense she was. Clifford Ring had run her out of Washington. It probably wasn't a bad idea for her to disappear for a while.

She explained, "There's a bed and breakfast in the Northern Neck, and—"

"And I have a guest room," I interrupted. "You can stay with me for a while."

She looked uncertain, then confessed, "Kay, do you have any idea how that would look?"

"Frankly, I don't care at the moment."

"Why not?" She studied me closely.

"Your paper has already fried me in deep fat. I'm going for broke. Things will either get worse or better, but they won't stay the same."

"At least you haven't been fired."

"Neither have you, Abby. You had an affair and acted inappropriately in front of your colleagues when you dumped coffee in your lover's lap."

"He deserved it."

"I'm quite sure he did. But I wouldn't advise your doing battle with the *Post*. Your book is your chance to redeem yourself."

"What about you?"

"My concern is these cases. You can help because you can do things I can't do."

"Such as?"

"I can't lie, hoodwink, finagle, cheat, badger, sneak, snipe, snoop, and pretend to be something or somebody I'm not because I'm an officer of the Commonwealth. But you have great range of motion. You're a reporter."

"Thanks a lot," she protested as she walked out of the kitchen. "I'll get my things from the car."

* * *

It was not very often I had houseguests, and the bedroom downstairs was usually reserved for Lucy's visits. Covering the hardwood floor was an Iranian Dergezine rug with a brightly colored floral design that turned the entire room into a garden, in the midst of which my niece had been a rosebud or a stinkweed, depending on her behavior.

"I guess you like flowers," Abby said absently, laying the suit bag on top of the bed.

"The rug is a little overpowering in here," I apologized. "But when I saw it I had to buy it, and there was no place else to put it. Not to mention, it's virtually indestructible, and since this is where Lucy stays, that point is important."

"Or at least it used to be." Abby went to the closet and opened the door. "Lucy's not ten years old anymore."

"There should be plenty of hangers in there." I moved closer to inspect. "If you need more . . ."

"This is fine."

"There are towels, toothpaste, soap in the bath." I started to show her.

She had begun unpacking and wasn't paying any attention.

I sat down on the edge of the bed.

Abby carried suits and blouses into the closet. Coat hangers screeched along the metal bar. I watched her in silence, experiencing a prick of impatience.

This went on for several minutes, drawers sliding, more coat hangers screeching, the medicine cabinet in the bathroom wheezing open and clicking shut. She pushed her suit bag inside the closet and glanced around, as if trying to figure out what to do next. Opening her briefcase, she pulled out a novel and a notebook, which she placed on the table by the bed. I watched uneasily as she then tucked a .38 and boxes of cartridges into the drawer.

* * *

It was midnight when I finally went upstairs. Before settling into bed, I dialed the number for the 7-Eleven again.

"Ellen Jordan?"

"Yeah? That's me. Who's this?"

I told her, explaining, "You mentioned to me last fall that when Fred Cheney and Deborah Harvey came in, Deborah tried to buy beer, and you carded her."

"Yeah, that's right."

"Can you tell me exactly what you did when you carded her?"

"I just said I needed to see her driver's license," Ellen said, and she sounded puzzled. "You know, I asked to see it."

"Did she get it out of her purse?"

"Sure. She had to get it out so I could look at it."

"She handed it to you, then," I said.

"Uh-huh."

"Was it inside anything? Inside a plastic window?"

"It wasn't in nothing," she said. "She just handed it over and I looked at it, then I gave it back to her." A pause. "Why?"

"I'm trying to determine if you touched Deborah Harvey's driver's license."

"Sure I did. I had to touch it to look at it." She sounded frightened. "I'm not in trouble or anything, am I?"

"No, Ellen," I replied reassuringly. "You're not in any trouble at all."

15

Abby's assignment was to see what she could find out about Barry Aranoff, and she left for Roanoke in the morning. The following evening, she returned just minutes before Marino appeared at my front door. I had invited him to dinner.

When he discovered Abby in the kitchen, his pupils contracted. His face turned red.

"Jack Black?" I inquired.

I returned from the bar to find Abby smoking at the table while Marino stood before the window. He had cracked the blinds and was staring sullenly out at the feeder.

"You won't see any birds at this hour, unless you're interested in bats," I said.

He did not reply or turn around.

I began to serve the salad. It wasn't until I was pouring Chianti that Marino finally took his chair.

"You didn't tell me you had company," he said.

"If I had told you, you wouldn't have come," I replied just as bluntly.

"She didn't tell me either," Abby said, testily. "So now that it's been established that we're all happy to be together, let's enjoy dinner."

If I had learned nothing else from my failed marriage to Tony, it was never to engage in confrontations if it's late at night or time to eat. I did the best I could to fill the silence with light conversation. I waited until coffee was served before speaking my mind.

"Abby's going to be staying with me for a while," I said to Marino.

"It's your business." He reached for the sugar.

"It's your business, too. We're all in this together."

"Maybe you ought to explain what it is we're all into, Doc. But first"—he looked at Abby—"I'd like to know where this little dinner scene is going to show up in your book. Then I won't have to read the whole damn thing. I can just turn to the right page."

"You know, Marino, you really can be a jerk," Abby said.

"I can be an asshole, too. You ain't had that pleasure yet."

"Thank you for giving me something to look forward to."

Snatching a pen out of his breast pocket, he tossed it across the table. "Better start writing. Wouldn't want you to quote me wrong."

Abby glared at him.

"Stop it," I said angrily.

They looked at me.

"You're acting no better than the rest of them," I added.

"Who?" Marino's face was blank.

"Everybody," I said. "I'm sick to death of lies, jealousy, power plays. I expect more of my friends. I thought you were my friends."

I pushed back my chair.

"If the two of you wish to continue taking potshots at each other, go ahead. But I've had enough."

Without looking at either of them, I carried my coffee into the living room, turned on the stereo, and closed my eyes. Music was my therapy, and I had been listening to Bach last. His Sinfonia Two, Cantata No. 29 began midflight, and I began to relax. For weeks after Mark left, I would come downstairs when I couldn't sleep, put the headphones on, and surround myself with Beethoven, Mozart, Pachelbel.

Abby and Marino had the sheepish expressions of a squabbling couple that have just made up when they joined me fifteen minutes later.

"Uh, we've been talking," Abby said as I turned off the stereo. "I explained things as best I could. We've begun to reach a level of understanding."

I was delighted to hear it.

"May as well pitch in, the three of us," Marino said. "What the hell. Abby ain't really a reporter right now, anyway."

The remark stung her a little, I could tell, but they were going to cooperate, miracle of miracles.

"By the time her book comes out, this will probably be over with. That's what matters, that it's over with. It's been almost three years now, ten kids. You include Jill and Elizabeth, we're talking twelve." He shook his head, his eyes getting hard. "Whoever's whacking these kids ain't going to retire, Doc. He'll keep on until he gets nailed. And in investigations like this, that usually happens because someone gets lucky."

"We may already have gotten lucky," Abby said to him. "Aranoff's not the man who was driving the Lincoln."

"You sure?" Marino asked.

"Positive. Aranoff's got gray hair, what little hair he has left. He's maybe five-foot-eight and must weigh two hundred pounds."

"You telling me you met him?"

"No," she said. "He was still out of town. I knocked on the door and his wife let me in. I was wearing work pants, boots. I told her I was with the power company and needed to check their meter. We got to chatting. She offered me a Coke. While I was inside, I looked around, saw a family photograph, asked her about the photo to be sure. That's how I found out what Aranoff looks like. It wasn't him, the man we saw. Not the man tailing me in Washington, either."

"I don't guess there's any possibility you read the plate number wrong," Marino asked me.

"No. Even if I had," I said, "the coincidence would be incredible. Both cars 1990 Lincoln Mark Sevens? Aranoff just happens to be traveling in the Williamsburg-Tidewater area around the same time I *erroneously* record a plate number that just happens to be his?"

"Looks like Aranoff and me are going to have to have a little discussion," Marino said.

* * *

Marino called my office later that week and said right off, "You sitting down?"

"You talked with Aranoff."

"Bingo. He left Roanoke Monday, February tenth, and hit Danville, Petersburg, and Richmond. On Wednesday the twelfth, he was in the Tidewater area, and this is where it gets real interesting. He was due in Boston on Thursday the thirteenth, which is the night you and Abby was in Williamsburg. The day before that, Wednesday the twelfth, Aranoff left his car in long-term parking at the Newport News airport. From there he flew to Boston, was up in that area buzzing around in a rental car for the better part of a week. Returned to Newport News yesterday morning, got into his car, and headed home."

"Are you suggesting someone may have stolen the tags off his car while it was in long-term parking, then returned them?" I asked.

"Unless Aranoff's lying, and I don't see any reason for that, there's no other explanation, Doc."

"When he retrieved his car, did he notice anything that might have made him think it had been tampered with?"

"Nope. We went into his garage and took a look at it. Both tags were there, screwed on nice and tight. The tags were dirty like the rest of the car and they were smudged, which may or may not mean anything. I didn't lift any prints, but whoever borrowed the tags was probably wearing gloves, which could account for the smudges. No tool or pry marks that I could see."

"Was the car in a conspicuous place in the parking lot?"

"Aranoff said he left it in pretty much in the middle of the lot, which was almost full."

"You would think if his car had been sitting out there for several days without license plates, Security or someone would have noticed," I said.

"Not necessarily. People aren't all that observant. When they leave their ride at the airport or are returning from a trip, the only thing on their mind is hauling their bags, catching their plane, or getting the hell home. Even if someone noticed, it's not likely he's going to report it to Security. Security couldn't do nothing anyway until the owner returned, then it would be up to him to report the stolen plates. As for the actual theft of the plates, that wouldn't be very hard. You go to the airport after midnight and there's not going to be anybody around. If it was me, I'd just walk into the lot like I was looking for my car, then five minutes later I'd be heading out of there with a set of plates in my briefcase."

"And that's what you think happened?"

"My theory is this," he said. "The guy who asked you directions last week wasn't no detective, FBI agent, or spook out spying. He was somebody up to no good. Could be a drug dealer, could be almost anything. I think the dark gray Mark Seven he was in is his personal car, and to be on the safe side, when he goes out to do whatever he's into, he switches plates in the event his ride is spotted in the area, maybe by cops out on patrol, whatever."

"Rather risky if he gets pulled for running a red light," I pointed out. "The license number would come back to someone else."

"True. But I don't think he plans on getting pulled. I think he's more worried about his car being spotted because he's out to break the law, something's going to go down and he don't want to take the chance his own tag number's going to be on the street when it does."

"Why doesn't he just use a rental car, then?"

"That's just as bad as having his own plate number out there. Any cop knows a rental car when he sees it. All tag numbers in Virginia begin with R. And if you track it down, it's going to come back to whoever rented it. Switching tags is a better idea if you're smart enough to figure out a safe routine. It's what I'd do, and I'd probably resort to a long-term parking lot. I'd use the tags, then take them off my car and put my tags back on. I'd drive to the airport, walk out into the lot after dark, make sure no one's looking, and put the tags back on the car I'd stolen them from."

"What if the owner's already returned and found his tags stolen?"

"If the ride's no longer in the lot, I'd just pitch the tags in the nearest Dumpster. Either way I can't lose."

"Good Lord. The man Abby and I saw that night might be the killer, Marino."

"The squirrel you saw wasn't no businessman who was lost or fruitcake tailing you," he said. "He was up to something illegal. That don't mean he's a killer."

"The parking sticker . . ."

"I'm gonna track that down. See if Colonial Williamsburg can supply me with a list of everybody who's been issued one."

"The car Mr. Joyce saw going down his road with the headlights off could have been a Lincoln Mark Seven," I said.

"Could have been. Mark Sevens came out in 1990. Jim and Bonnie was murdered in the summer of 1990. And in the dark, a Mark Seven wouldn't look all that different from a Thunderbird, which was what Mr. Joyce said the car he saw looked like."

"Wesley will have a field day with this," I muttered, incredulous.

"Yeah," Marino said. "I got to call him."

March came in with a whispered promise that winter would not last forever. The sun was warm on my back as I cleaned the windshield of my Mercedes while Abby pumped gas. The breeze was gentle, freshly scrubbed from days of rain. People were out washing cars and riding bikes, the earth stirring but not quite awake.

Like a lot of service stations these days, the one I frequented doubled as a convenience store, and I bought two cups of coffee to go when I went inside to pay. Then Abby and I drove off to Williamsburg, windows cracked, Bruce Hornsby singing "Harbor Lights" on the radio.

"I called my answering machine before we left," Abby said.

"And?"

"Five hang-ups."

"Cliff?"

"I'm willing to make a bet," she said. "Not that he wants to talk to me. I suspect he's just trying to figure out if I'm home, has probably cruised past my parking lot a number of times, too, looking for my car."

"Why would he do that if he's not interested in talking to you?"

"Maybe he doesn't know that I've changed my locks."

"Then he must be stupid. One would think he would realize you would put two and two together when his series ran."

"He's not stupid," Abby said, staring out the side window.

I opened the sunroof.

"He knows I know. But he's not stupid," she said again. "Cliff's fooled everyone. They don't know he's crazy."

"Hard to believe he could have gotten as far as he has if he's crazy," I said.

"That's the beauty of Washington," she replied cynically. "The most successful, powerful people in the world are there and half of them are crazy, the other half neurotic. Most of them are immoral. Power does it. I don't know why Watergate surprised anyone."

"What has power done to you?" I asked.

"I know how it tastes, but I wasn't there long enough to get addicted."

"Maybe you're lucky."

She was silent.

I thought of Pat Harvey. What was she doing these days? What was going through her mind?

"Have you talked to Pat Harvey?" I asked Abby.

"Yes."

"Since the articles ran in the *Post?*"

She nodded.

"How is she?"

"I once read something written by a missionary to what was then the Congo. He recalled encountering a tribesman in the jungle who looked perfectly normal until he smiled. His teeth were filed to points. He was a cannibal."

Her voice was flat with anger, her mood suddenly dark. I had no idea what she was talking about.

"That's Pat Harvey," she went on. "I dropped by to see her before heading out to Roanoke the other day. We talked briefly about the stories in the *Post,* and I thought she was taking it all in stride until she smiled. Her smile made my blood run cold."

I didn't know what to say.

"That's when I knew Cliff's stories had pushed her over the edge. Deborah's murder pushed Pat as far as I thought she could go. But the stories pushed her further. I remember when I talked to her I had this sense that something wasn't there anymore. After a while I figured out what's not there is Pat Harvey."

"Did she know her husband was having an affair?"

"She does now."

"If it's true," I added.

"Cliff wouldn't write something that he couldn't back up, attribute to a credible source."

I wondered what it would take to push me to the edge. Lucy, Mark? If I had an accident and could no longer use my hands or went blind? I did not know what it would take to make me snap. Maybe it was like dying. Once you were gone you didn't know the difference.

We were at Old Towne shortly after noon. The apartment complex where Jill and Elizabeth had lived was unremarkable, a honeycomb of buildings that all looked the same. They were brick with red awnings announcing block numbers over the main entrances; the landscaping was a patchwork of winter-brown grass and narrow margins of flower beds covered in woodchips. There were areas for cookouts with swing sets, picnic tables, and grills.

We stopped in the parking lot and stared up at what had been Jill's balcony. Through wide spaces in the railing two blue-and-white-webbed chairs rocked gently in the breeze. A chain dangled from a hook in the ceiling, lonely for a potted plant. Elizabeth had lived on the other side of the parking lot. From their respective residences the two friends would have been able to check on each other. They could watch lights turn on and off, know when the other got up and went to bed, when one was home or not.

For a moment, Abby and I shared a depressed silence.

Then she said, "They were more than friends, weren't they, Kay?"

"To answer that would be hearsay."

She smiled a little. "To tell you the truth, I wondered about it when I was working on the stories. It crossed my mind, at any rate. But no one ever suggested it or even hinted." She paused, staring out. "I think I know what they felt like."

I looked at her.

"It must have been the way I felt with Cliff. Sneaking, hiding, spending half your energy worrying about what people think, fearing they somehow suspect."

"The irony is," I said, putting the car in gear, "that people don't really give a damn. They're too preoccupied with themselves."

"I wonder if Jill and Elizabeth would ever have figured that out."

"If their love was greater than their fear, they would have figured it out eventually."

"Where are we going, by the way?" She looked out her window at the roadside streaming past.

"Just cruising," I said. "In the general direction of downtown."

I had never given her an itinerary. All I had said was that I wanted to "look around."

"You're looking for that damn car, aren't you?"

"It can't hurt to look."

"And just what are you going to do if you find it, Kay?"

"Write the plate number down, see who it comes back to this time."

"Well"—she started to laugh—"if you find a 1990 charcoal Lincoln Mark Seven with a Colonial Williamsburg sticker on the rear bumper, I'll pay you a hundred dollars."

"Better get your checkbook out. If it's here, I'm going to find it."

And I did, not half an hour later, by following the age-old rule of how you find something lost. I retraced my steps. When I returned to Merchant's Square the car was sitting there big as life in the parking lot, not far from where we had spotted it the first time when its driver had stopped to ask directions.

"Jesus Christ," Abby whispered. "I don't believe it."

The car was unoccupied, sunshine glinting off the glass. It looked as if it had just been washed and waxed. There was a parking sticker on the left side of the rear bumper, the plate number ITU-144. Abby wrote it down.

"This is too easy, Kay. It can't be right."

"We don't know that it's the same car." I was being scientific now. "It looks the same, but we can't be sure."

I parked some twenty spaces away, tucking my Mercedes between a station wagon and a Pontiac, and sat behind the wheel scanning the storefronts. A gift shop, a picture-framing shop, a restaurant. Between a tobacco shop and a bakery was a bookstore, small, inconspicuous, books displayed in the window. A wooden sign hung over the door, with the name "The Dealer's Room" painted on it in Colonial-style calligraphy.

"Crossword puzzles," I said under my breath, and a chill ran up my spine.

"What?" Abby was still watching the Lincoln.

"Jill and Elizabeth liked crossword puzzles. They often went out to breakfast on Sunday mornings and picked up the *New York Times.*" I was opening my door.

Abby put a hand on my arm, restraining me. "No, Kay. Wait a minute. We've got to think about this."

I settled back into the seat.

"You can't just walk in there," she said, and it sounded like an order.

"I want to buy a paper."

"What if he's in there? Then what are you going to do?"

"I want to see if it's him, the man who was driving. I think I'd recognize him."

"And he might recognize you."

" 'Dealer' could refer to cards," I thought out loud as a young woman with short curly black hair walked up to the bookstore, opened the door, and disappeared inside.

"The person who deals cards, deals the jack of hearts," I added, my voice trailing off.

"You talked to him when he asked directions. Your picture's been in the news." Abby was taking charge. "You're not going in there. I will."

"We both will."

"That's crazy!"

"You're right." My mind was made up. "You're staying put. I'm going in."

I was out of the car before she could argue. She got out, too, and just stood there, looking lost, as I walked with purpose in that direction. She did not come after me. She had too much sense to make a scene.

When I put my hand on the cold brass handle of the door, my heart was hammering. When I walked inside, I felt weak in the knees.

He was standing behind the counter, smiling and filling out a charge card receipt while a middle-aged woman in an Ultrasuede suit prattled on, ". . . That's what birthdays are for. You buy your husband a book *you* want to read . . ."

"As long as you both enjoy the same books, that's all right." His voice was very soft, soothing, a voice you could trust.

Now that I was inside the shop, I was desperate to leave. I wanted to run. There were stacks of newspapers to one side of the counter, including the *New York Times.* I could pick one up, quickly pay for it, and be gone. But I did not want to look him in the eye.

It was him.

I turned around and walked out without glancing back.

Abby was sitting in the car smoking.

"He couldn't work here and not know his way to Sixty-four," I said, starting the engine.

She got my meaning precisely. "Do you want to call Marino now or wait until we get back to Richmond?"

"We're going to call him now." I found a pay phone and was told Marino was on the street. I left him the message, "ITU-144. Call me."

Abby asked me a lot of questions, and I did my best to answer them. Then there were long stretches of silence as I drove. My stomach was sour. I considered pulling off somewhere. I thought I might throw up.

She was staring at me. I could feel her concern.

"My God, Kay. You're white as a sheet."

"I'm all right."

"You want me to drive?"

"I'm fine. Really."

When we got home, I went straight up to my bedroom. My hands trembled as I dialed the number. Mark's machine answered after the second ring, and I started to hang up but found myself mesmerized by his voice.

"I'm sorry, there's no one to answer your call right now . . ."

At the beep I hesitated, then quietly returned the receiver to its cradle. When I looked up, I found Abby in my doorway. I could tell by the look on her face that she knew what I had just done.

I stared at her, my eyes filling with tears, and then she was sitting next to me on the edge of the bed.

"Why didn't you leave him a message?" she whispered.

"How could you possibly know who I was calling?" I fought to steady my voice.

"Because it's the same impulse that overwhelms me when I'm terribly upset. I want to reach for the phone. Even now, after all of it. I still want to call Cliff."

"Have you?"

She slowly shook her head.

"Don't. Don't ever, Abby."

She studied me closely. "Was it walking into the bookstore and seeing him?"

"I'm not sure."

"I think you know."

I glanced away from her. "When I get too close, I know it. I've gotten too close before. I ask myself why it happens."

"People like us can't help it. We have a compulsion, something drives us. That's why it happens," she said.

I could not admit to her my fear. Had Mark answered the phone, I didn't know if I could have admitted it to him, either.

Abby was staring off, her voice distant when she asked, "As much as you know about death, do you ever think about your own?"

I got off the bed. "Where the hell is Marino?" I picked up the phone to try him again.

16

Days turned into weeks while I waited anxiously. I had not heard from Marino since giving him the information about The Dealer's Room. I had not heard from anyone. With each hour that passed the silence grew louder and more ominous.

On the first day of spring, I emerged from the conference room after being deposed for three hours by two lawyers. Rose told me I had a call.

"Kay? It's Benton."

"Good afternoon," I said, adrenaline surging.

"Can you come up to Quantico tomorrow?"

I reached for my calendar. Rose had penciled in a conference call. It could be rescheduled.

"What time?"

"Ten, if that's convenient. I've already talked to Marino."

Before I could ask questions, he said he couldn't talk and would fill me in when we met.

It was six o'clock before I left my office. The sun had gone down and the air felt cold. When I turned into my driveway, I noticed the lights were on. Abby was home.

We had seen little of each other of late, both of us in and out, rarely speaking. She never went to the grocery store, but would leave a fifty-dollar bill taped to the refrigerator every now and then, which more than covered what little she ate. When wine or Scotch got low, I would find a twenty-dollar bill under the bottle. Several days ago, I had discovered a five-dollar bill on top of a depleted box of laundry soap. Wandering through the rooms of my house had turned into a peculiar scavenger hunt.

When I unlocked the front door, Abby suddenly stepped into the doorway, startling me.

"I'm sorry," she said. "I heard you drive in. Didn't mean to scare you."

I felt foolish. Ever since she had moved in, I had become increasingly jumpy. I supposed I wasn't adjusting well to my loss of privacy.

"Can I fix you a drink?" she asked. Abby looked tired.

"Thanks," I said, unbuttoning my coat. My eyes wandered into the living room. On the coffee table, beside an ashtray filled with cigarette butts, were a wineglass and several reporter's notepads.

Taking off my coat and gloves, I went upstairs and tossed them on my bed, pausing long enough to play back the messages on the answering machine. My mother had tried to reach me. I was eligible to win a prize if I dialed a certain number by eight P.M., and Marino had called to tell me what time he would pick me up in the morning. Mark and I continued missing each other, talking to each other's machines.

"I've got to go to Quantico tomorrow," I told Abby when I entered the living room.

She pointed to my drink on the coffee table.

"Marino and I have a meeting with Benton," I said.

She reached for her cigarettes.

"I don't know what it's about," I continued. "Maybe you do."

"Why would I know?"

"You haven't been here much. I don't know what you've been doing."

"When you're at your office, I don't know what you're doing either."

"I haven't been doing anything remarkable. What would you like to know?" I offered lightly, trying to dispel the tension.

"I don't ask because I know how private you are about your work. I don't want to pry."

I assumed she was implying that if I asked about what she was doing *I* would be prying.

"Abby, you seem distant these days."

"Preoccupied. Please don't take it personally."

Certainly she had plenty to think about, with the book she was writing, what she was going to do with her life. But I had never seen Abby this withdrawn.

"I'm concerned, that's all," I said.

"You don't understand what I'm like, Kay. When I get into something, I'm consumed by it. Can't get my mind off it." She paused. "You were right when you said this book was my chance to redeem myself. It is."

"I'm glad to hear it, Abby. Knowing you, it will be a bestseller."

"Maybe. I'm not the only one interested in writing a book about these cases. My agent's already hearing rumors about other deals out there. I've got a head start, will be all right if I work fast."

"It's not your book I care about, it's you."

"I care about you, too, Kay," she said. "I appreciate what you've done for me by letting me stay here. And that won't go on much longer, I promise."

"You can stay as long as you like."

She collected her notepads and drink. "I've got to start writing soon, and I can't do that until I have my own space, my computer."

"Then you're simply doing research these days."

"Yes. I'm finding a lot of things I didn't know I was looking for," she said enigmatically as she headed for her bedroom.

When the Quantico exit came into view the following morning, traffic suddenly stopped. Apparently there had been an accident somewhere north of us on I-95, and cars weren't moving. Marino flipped on his grille lights and veered off onto the shoulder, where we bumped along, rocks pelting the undercarriage of the car, for a good hundred yards.

For the past two hours he had been giving me a complete account of his latest domestic accomplishments, while I wondered what Wesley had to tell us and worried about Abby.

"Never had any idea venetian blinds was such a bitch," Marino complained as we sped past Marine Corps barracks and a firing range. "I'm spraying them with 409, right?" He glanced over at me. "And it's taking me a minute per slat, paper towels shredding the hell all over the place. Finally I get an idea, just take the damn things out of the windows and dump them in the tub. Fill it with hot water and laundry soap. Worked like a charm."

"That's great," I muttered.

"I'm also in the process of tearing down the wallpaper in the kitchen. It came with the house. Doris never liked it."

"The question is whether *you* like it. You're the one who lives there now."

He shrugged. "Never paid it much mind, you want to know the truth. But I figure if Doris says it's ugly, it probably is. We used to talk about selling the camper and putting in an above-the-ground pool. So I'm finally getting around to that, too. Ought to have it in time for summer."

"Marino, be careful," I said gently. "Make sure what you're doing is for you."

He did not answer me.

"Don't hang your future on a hope that may not be there."

"It can't hurt nothing," he finally said. "Even if she never comes back, it can't hurt nothing for things to look nice."

"Well, you're going to have to show me your place sometime," I said.

"Yeah. All the times I've been to your crib and you've never seen mine."

He parked the car and we got out. The FBI Academy had continued to metastasize over the outer fringes of the U.S. Marine Corps base. The main building with its fountain and flags had been turned into administrative offices, and the center of activity had been moved into a new tan brick building next door. What looked like another dormitory had gone up since I had visited last. Gunfire in the distance sounded like firecrackers popping.

Marino checked his .38 at the desk. We signed in and clipped on visitor passes, then he took me on another series of shortcuts, avoiding the enclosed brick-and-glass breezeways, or gerbil tubes. I followed him through a door that led outside the building, and we walked over a loading dock, through a kitchen. We finally emerged from the back of the gift shop, which Marino strolled right through without a glance in the direction of the young female clerk holding a stack of sweatshirts. Her lips parted in unspoken protest as she viewed our unorthodox passage. Out of the store and around a corner, we entered the bar and grill called The Boardroom, where Wesley was waiting for us at a corner table.

He wasted no time getting down to business.

The owner of The Dealer's Room was Steven Spurrier. Wesley described him as "thirty-four years old, white, with black hair, brown eyes. Five-eleven, one hundred and sixty pounds." Spurrier had not yet been picked up or questioned, but he had been under constant surveillance. What had been observed so far was not exactly normal.

On several occasions he had left his two-story brick home at a late hour and driven to two bars and one rest stop. He never seemed to stay in one place very long. He was always alone. The previous week he had approached a young couple emerging from a bar called Tom-Toms. It appeared he asked for directions again. Nothing happened. The couple got in their car and left. Spurrier got into his Lincoln and eventually meandered back home. His license tags remained unchanged.

"We've got a problem with the evidence," Wesley reported, looking at me through rimless glasses, his face stern. "We've got a cartridge case in our lab. You've got the bullet from Deborah Harvey in Richmond."

"I don't have the bullet," I replied. "The Forensic Science Bureau does. I presume you've started the DNA analysis on the blood recovered from Elizabeth Mott's car."

"It will be another week or two."

I nodded. The FBI DNA lab used five polymorphic probes. Each probe had to stay in the X-ray developer for about a week, which was why I had written Wesley a letter some time ago suggesting that he get the bloody swatch from Montana and begin its analysis immediately.

"DNA's not worth a damn without a suspect's blood," Marino reminded us.

"We're working on that," Wesley said stoically.

"Yeah, well, seems like we could pop Spurrier because of the license plate. Ask his sorry ass to explain why he was driving around with Aranoff's tags several weeks back."

"We can't prove he was driving around with them. It's Kay and Abby's word against his."

"All we need is a magistrate who will sign a warrant. Then we start digging. Maybe we turn up ten pairs of shoes," Marino said. "Maybe an Uzi, some Hydra-Shok ammo, who knows what we'll find?"

"We're planning to do so," Wesley continued. "But one thing at a time."

He got up for more coffee, and Marino took my cup and his and followed him. At this early hour The Boardroom was deserted. I looked around at empty tables, the television in a corner, and tried to envision what must go on here late at night. Agents in training lived like priests. Members of the opposite sex, booze, and cigarettes were not allowed inside the dormitory rooms, which also could not be locked. But The Boardroom served beer and wine. When there were blowouts, confrontations, indiscretions, this was where it happened. I remembered Mark telling me he had broken up a free-for-all in here one night when a new FBI agent went too far with his homework and decided to "arrest" a table of veteran DEA agents. Tables had crashed to the floor, beer and baskets of popcorn everywhere.

Wesley and Marino returned to the table, and setting down his coffee, Wesley slipped out of his pearl-gray suit jacket and hung it neatly on the back of his chair. His white shirt scarcely had a wrinkle, I noticed, his silk tie was peacock blue with tiny white fleur-de-lis, and he was wearing peacock blue suspenders. Marino served as the perfect foil to this Fortune 500 partner of his. With his big belly, Marino couldn't possibly do justice to even the most elegant suit, but I had to give him credit. These days he was trying.

"What do you know about Spurrier's background?" I asked. Wesley was writing notes to himself while Marino reviewed a file, both men seeming to have forgotten there was a third person at the table.

"He doesn't have a record," Wesley replied, looking up. "Never been arrested, hasn't gotten so much as a speeding ticket in the past ten years. He bought the Lincoln in February of 1990 from a dealer in Virginia Beach, traded in an '86 Town Car, paid the rest in cash."

"He must have some bucks," Marino commented. "Drives high-dollar cars, lives in a nice crib. Hard to believe he makes that much from his bookstore."

"He doesn't make that much," Wesley said. "According to what he filed last year, he cleared less than thirty thousand dollars. But he's got assets of over half a million, a money market account, waterfront real estate, stocks."

"Jeez." Marino shook his head.

"Any dependents?" I asked.

"No," Wesley said. "Never married, both parents dead. His

father was very successful in real estate in the Northern Neck. He died when Steven was in his early twenties. I suspect this is where the money comes from."

"What about his mother?" I asked.

"She died about a year after the father did. Cancer. Steven came along late in life. His mother had him when she was forty-two. The only other sibling is a brother named Gordon. He lives in Texas, is fifteen years older than Steven, married, with four kids."

Skimming his notes again, Wesley brought forth more information. Spurrier was born in Gloucester, attended the University of Virginia, where he received a bachelor's degree in English. Afterward he joined the navy, where he lasted less than four months. The next eleven months were spent working at a printing press, where his primary responsibility was to maintain the machinery.

"I'd like to know more about his months in the navy," Marino said.

"There's not much to know," Wesley answered. "After enlisting, he was sent to boot camp in the Great Lakes area. He chose journalism as his speciality and was assigned to the Defense Information School at Fort Benjamin Harrison in Indianapolis. Later he was assigned his duty station, working for the Commander-in-Chief of the Atlantic Fleet in Norfolk." He looked up from his notes. "About a month later his father died, and Steven received a hardship discharge so he could return to Gloucester to take care of his mother, who was already ill with cancer."

"What about the brother?" Marino asked.

"Apparently he couldn't get away from his job and family responsibilities in Texas." He paused, glancing at us. "Maybe there are other reasons. Obviously, Steven's relationship with his family is of interest to me, but I'm not going to know a whole lot more about it for a while."

"Why not?" I asked.

"It's too risky for me to confront the brother directly at this point. I don't want him calling Steven, tipping my hand. It's unlikely Gordon would cooperate, anyway. Family members tend to stick together in matters like this, even if they don't get along."

"Well, you've been talking to someone," Marino said.

"A couple of people from the navy, UVA, his former employer at the printing press."

"What else did they have to say about this squirrel?"

"A loner," Wesley said. "Not much of a journalist. Was more interested in reading than interviewing anyone or writing stories. Apparently, the printing press suited him rather well. He stayed in the back, had his nose in a book when things were slow. His boss said Steven loved to tinker with the presses, various machines, and kept them spotless. Sometimes he would go for days without talking to anyone. His boss described Steven as peculiar."

"His boss offer any examples?"

"Several things," Wesley said. "A woman employed by the press took off her fingertip with a paper cutter one morning. Steven got angry because she bled all over a piece of equipment he had just cleaned. His response to his mother's death was abnormal as well. Steven was reading during a lunch break when the call came from the hospital. He showed no emotion, just returned to his chair and resumed reading his book."

"A real warmhearted guy," Marino said.

"No one has described him as warmhearted."

"What happened after his mother died?" I asked.

"Then, I would assume, Steven got his inheritance. He moved to Williamsburg, leased the space at Merchant's Square, and opened The Dealer's Room. This was nine years ago."

"A year before Jill Harrington and Elizabeth Mott were murdered," I said.

Wesley nodded. "He was in the area, then. He's been in the area during all of these murders. He's been working in his bookstore since it opened, except for a period of about five months back, uh, seven years ago. The store was closed during that time. We don't know why or know where Spurrier was."

"He runs his bookstore by himself?" Marino asked.

"It's a small operation. No other employees. The store is closed on Mondays. It's been noted that when there isn't much business he just sits behind the counter and reads, and if he leaves the store before closing time he either closes early or puts a sign on the door that says he'll be back at such and such an hour. He also has an answering machine. If you're looking for a certain book or want him to search for something out of print, you can leave your request on his machine."

"It's interesting that someone so antisocial would open a business that requires him to have contact with customers, even if the contact is rather limited," I said.

"It's actually very appropriate," Wesley said. "The bookstore would serve as a perfect lair for a voyeur, someone intensely interested in observing people without having to personally interact with them. It has been noted that William and Mary students frequent his store, primarily because Spurrier carries unusual, out-of-print books in addition to popular fiction and nonfiction. He also carries a wide selection of spy novels and military magazines, which attract business from the nearby military bases. If he's the killer, then watching young, attractive couples and military personnel who come into his store would fascinate him in a voyeuristic fashion and at the same time stir up feelings of inadequacy, frustration, rage. He would hate what he envies, envy what he hates."

"I wonder if he suffered ridicule during his time in the navy," I conjectured.

"Based on what I've been told, he did, at least to a degree. Spurrier's peers considered him a wimp, a loser, while his superiors found him arrogant and aloof, even though he was never a disciplinary problem. Spurrier had no success with women and kept to himself, partly by choice and because others did not find his personality particularly attractive."

"Maybe being in the navy was the closest he ever got to being a real man," Marino said, "being what he wanted to be. His father dies and Spurrier has to take care of his sick mother. In his mind, he gets screwed."

"That's quite possible," Wesley agreed. "In any event, the killer we're dealing with would believe that his troubles are the fault of others. He would take no responsibility. He would feel his life was controlled by others, and therefore, controlling others and his environment became an obsession for him."

"Sounds like he's paying back the world," Marino said.

"The killer is showing he has power," Wesley said. "If the military aspects enter into his fantasies, and I think they do, then he believes he's the ultimate soldier. He kills without being caught. He outsmarts the enemy, plays games with them, and wins. It may be possible that he has deliberately set things up in such a way as to make those investigating the murders suspect that the perpetrator is a professional soldier, even someone from Camp Peary."

"His own disinformation campaign," I considered.

"He can't destroy the military," Wesley added, "but he could try to tarnish the image, degrade and defame it."

"Yeah, and all the while he's laughing up his sleeve," Marino said.

"I think the main point is that the killer's activities are the product of violent, sexualized fantasies that existed early on in the context of his social isolation. He believes he lives in an unjust world, and fantasy provides an important escape. In his fantasies he can express his emotions and control other human beings, he can be and get anything he wants. He can control life and death. He has the power to decide whether to injure or kill."

"Too bad Spurrier don't just *fantasize* about whacking couples," Marino said. "Then the three of us wouldn't have to be sitting here having this conversation."

"I'm afraid it doesn't work that way," Wesley said. "If violent, aggressive behavior dominates your thinking, your imagination, you're going to start acting out in ways that move you closer to the actual expression of these emotions. Violence fuels more violent thoughts, and more violent thoughts fuel more violence. After a while, violence and killing are a natural part of your adult life, and you see nothing wrong with it. I've had serial murderers tell me emphatically that when they killed, they were just doing what everybody else thinks of doing."

"Evil to him who evil thinks," I said.

It was then that I offered my theory about Deborah Harvey's purse.

"I think it's possible the killer knew who Deborah was," I said. "Perhaps not when the couple was first abducted, but he may have known by the time he killed them."

"Please explain," Wesley said, studying me with interest.

"Have either of you seen the fingerprints report?"

"Yeah, I've seen it," Marino replied.

"As you know, when Vander examined Deborah's purse he found partials, smudges on her credit cards, but nothing on her driver's license."

"So?" Marino looked perplexed.

"The contents of her purse were well preserved because the nylon purse was waterproof. And the credit cards and her driver's license were inside plastic windows and zipped inside a compartment, thus protected from the elements and the body fluids of decomposition. Had Vander not picked up anything that would be one thing. But I find it interesting that he picked up something on the credit cards but not on her driver's license, when we know that Deborah got out her license when she went inside the Seven-Eleven and tried to buy beer. So she handled the license, and Ellen Jordan, the clerk, also handled it. What I'm wondering is if the killer didn't touch Deborah's driver's license, too, and then wipe it clean afterward."

"Why would he do that?" Marino asked.

"Maybe when he was inside the car with the couple, had the gun out and was abducting them, Deborah told him who she was," I answered.

"Interesting," Wesley said.

"Deborah may have been a modest young woman, but she was well aware of her family's prominence, of her mother's power," I went on. "She may have informed the killer in hopes that he would change his mind, think that in harming them there would be hell to pay. This may have startled the killer considerably, and he may have demanded proof of her identity, at which point he may have gotten hold of her purse to see the name on her driver's license."

"Then how did the purse end up out in the woods, and why did he leave the jack of hearts in it?" Marino asked.

"Maybe to buy himself a little time," I said. "He would have known that the Jeep would be found quickly, and if he realized who Deborah was, then he was also going to know that half the law enforcement world was going to be out looking for them. Maybe he decided to play it safe by not having the jack of hearts found immediately, so he left it with the bodies instead of inside the Jeep. By placing the card inside the purse and putting the purse under Deborah's body, he ensured that the card would be found, but probably not for a long time. He changes the rules a little but still wins the game."

"Not half bad. What do you think?" Marino looked at Wesley.

"I think we may never know exactly what happened," he said. "But it wouldn't surprise me if Deborah did exactly what Kay has proposed. One thing is certain—no matter what Deborah may have said or threatened, it would have been too risky for the killer to free her and Fred because they probably would have been able to identify him. So he went through with the murders, but the unforeseen turn of events could have thrown him off. Yes," he said to me. "This could have caused him to alter his ritual. It may also be that leaving the card in Deborah's purse was his way of showing contempt toward her and who she was."

"Sort of an 'up yours,' " Marino said.

"Possibly," Wesley replied.

Steven Spurrier was arrested the following Friday when two FBI agents and a local detective who had been tailing him all day followed him to the long-term parking lot of the Newport News airport.

When Marino's call woke me before dawn, my first thought was that another couple had disappeared. It took a moment for me to comprehend what he was saying over the phone.

"They popped him while he was lifting another set of tags," he was saying. "Charged him with petit larceny. The best they could do, but at least we got our probable cause to turn him inside out."

"Another Lincoln?" I asked.

"This time a 1991, silver-gray. He's in lockup waiting to see the magistrate, no way they're going to be able to hold him on a nickel-and-dime class one misdemeanor. Best they can do is stall, take their sweet time processing him. Then he's out of there."

"What about a search warrant?"

"His crib's crawling with cops and the feds even as we speak. Looking for everything from *Soldier of Fortune* magazines to Tinker Toys."

"You're heading out there, I guess," I said.

"Yeah. I'll let you know."

It was not possible for me to go back to sleep. Throwing a robe over my shoulders, I went downstairs and switched on a lamp in Abby's room.

"It's just me," I said as she sat straight up in bed. She groaned, covering her eyes.

I told her what had happened. Then we went into the kitchen and put on a pot of coffee.

"I'd pay to be present when they search his house." She was so wired I was surprised she didn't bolt out the door.

But she stayed inside all day, suddenly industrious. She cleaned up her room, helped me in the kitchen, and even swept the patio. She wanted to know what the police had found and was smart enough to realize that driving to Williamsburg would get her nowhere, because she would not be allowed entrance into Spurrier's residence or bookstore.

Marino stopped by early that evening as Abby and I were loading the dishwasher. I knew instantly by the look on his face that his news wasn't good.

"First I'll tell you what we *didn't* find," he began. "We didn't find a friggin' thing that will convince a jury Spurrier's ever killed a housefly. No knives except the ones in his kitchen. No guns or cartridges. No souvenirs such as shoes, jewelry, locks of hair, whatever, that might have belonged to the victims."

"Was his bookstore searched as well?" I asked.

"Oh, yeah."

"And his car of course."

"Nothing."

"Then tell us what you *did* find," I asked, depressed.

"Enough weirdo stuff to make me know it's him, Doc," Marino said. "I mean, this drone ain't no Eagle Scout. He's into skin magazines, violent pornography. Plus, he's got books about the military, especially the CIA, and files filled with newspaper clippings about the CIA. All of it cataloged, labeled. The guy's neater than an old lady librarian."

"Did you find any newspaper clips about these cases?" Abby asked.

"We did, including old stories about Jill Harrington and Elizabeth Mott. We also found catalogs to a number of what I call spy shops, these outfits that sell security-survival shit, everything from bulletproof cars to bomb detectors and night vision goggles. The

FBI's going to check it out, see what all he's ordered over the years. Spurrier's clothes are interesting, too. He must have half a dozen nylon warm-up suits in his bedroom, all of them black or navy blue and never worn, labels cut out of them, like maybe they were intended to be disposable, worn over his clothes and pitched somewhere after the fact."

"Nylon sheds very little," I said. "Windbreakers, nylon warm-ups aren't going to leave many fibers."

"Right. Let's see. What else?" Marino paused, finishing his drink. "Oh, yeah. Two boxes of surgical gloves and a supply of those disposable shoe-covers you wear downstairs."

"Booties?"

"Right. Like you wear in the morgue so you don't get blood on your shoes. And guess what? They found cards, four decks of them, never been opened, still in the cellophane."

"I don't suppose you found an opened deck missing a jack of hearts?" I asked, hopefully.

"No. But that don't surprise me. He probably removes the jack of hearts and then throws the rest of the cards away."

"All the same brand?"

"No. A couple different brands."

Abby was sitting silently in her chair, fingers laced tightly in her lap.

"It doesn't make sense that you didn't find any weapons," I said.

"This guy's slick, Doc. He's careful."

"Not careful enough. He kept the clippings about the murders, the warm-up suits, gloves. And he was caught red-handed stealing license tags, which makes me wonder if he wasn't getting ready to strike again."

"He had stolen tags on his car when he stopped you to ask directions," Marino pointed out. "No couple disappeared that weekend that we've heard about."

"That's true," I mused. "And he wasn't wearing a warm-up suit, either."

"He may save putting that on for last. May even keep it in a gym bag in his trunk. My guess is he has a kit."

"Did you find a gym bag?" Abby asked bluntly.

"No," Marino said. "No murder kit."

"Well, if you ever find a gym bag, or murder kit," Abby added, "then maybe you'll find his knife, gun, goggles, and all the rest of it."

"We'll be looking until the cows come home."

"Where is he now?" I asked.

"Was sitting in his kitchen drinking coffee when I left," Marino replied. "Friggin' unbelievable. Here we are tearing up his house and he's not even sweating. When he was asked about the warm-up suits, the gloves, decks of cards, and so on, he said he wasn't talking to us without his attorney present. Then he took a sip of his coffee and lit a cigarette like we wasn't there. Oh, yeah, I left that out. The squirrel smokes."

"What brand?" I asked.

"Dunhills. Probably buys them in that fancy tobacco shop next to his bookstore. And he uses a fancy lighter, too. An expensive one."

"That would certainly explain his peeling the paper off the butts before depositing them at the scenes, if that's what he did," I said. "Dunhills are distinctive."

"I know," Marino said. "They've got a gold band around the filter."

"You got a suspect's kit?"

"Oh, yeah." He smiled. "That's our little trump card that will beat his jack of hearts hands down. If we can't make these other cases, at least we got the murders of Jill Harrington and Elizabeth Mott to hang him with. DNA ought to nail his ass. Wish the damn tests didn't take so long."

After Marino left, Abby stared coolly at me.

"What do you think?" I asked.

"It's all circumstantial."

"Right now it is."

"Spurrier's got money," she said. "He's going to get the best trial lawyer money can buy. I can tell you exactly how it's going to go. The lawyer's going to suggest that his client was railroaded by the cops and the feds because of the pressure to solve these homicides. It's going to come out that a lot of people are looking for a scapegoat, especially in light of the accusations Pat Harvey has made."

"Abby . . ."

"Maybe the killer *is* someone from Camp Peary."

"You don't really believe that," I protested.

She glanced at her watch. "Maybe the feds already know who it is and have already taken care of the problem. Privately, which would explain why no other couples since Fred and Deborah have disappeared. Someone's got to pay in order to remove the cloud of suspicion, end the matter to the public's satisfaction . . ."

Leaning back in my chair, I turned my face up to the ceiling and shut my eyes while she went on and on.

"No question Spurrier's into something or he wouldn't be stealing license plates. But he could be selling drugs. Maybe he's a cat burglar or gets his jollies from driving around with borrowed tags for a day? He's weird enough to fit the profile, but the world is full of weirdos who don't ever kill anyone. Who's to say the stuff in his house wasn't planted?"

"Please stop," I said quietly.

But she wouldn't. "It's just so goddam neat. The warmup suits, gloves, decks of cards, pornography, and newspaper clips. And it doesn't make sense that no weapons or ammunition were found. Spurrier was caught by surprise, didn't have any idea he was under surveillance. In fact, it not only doesn't make sense, it's very convenient. One thing the feds couldn't plant was the pistol that fired the bullet you recovered from Deborah Harvey."

"You're right. They couldn't plant that." I got up from the table and began wiping the counters because I couldn't sit still.

"Interesting that the one item of evidence they couldn't plant didn't show up."

There had been stories before about the police, federal agents, planting evidence in order to frame someone. The ACLU probably had a file room full of such accusations.

"You're not listening," Abby said.

"I'm going up to take a bath," I replied wearily.

She walked over to the sink where I was wringing out the dishrag.

"Kay?"

I stopped what I was doing and looked at her.

"You want it to be easy," she admonished.

"I've always wanted things to be easy. They almost never are."

"You want it to be easy," she repeated. "You don't want to think that the people you trust could send an innocent man to the electric chair in order to cover their asses."

"No question about that. I wouldn't want to think it. I refuse to think it unless there is proof. And Marino was at Spurrier's house. He would never have gone along with it."

"He was there." She walked away from me. "But he wasn't the first one there. By the time he arrived, he would have seen what they wanted him to see."

17

The first person I saw when I reached the office on Monday was Fielding.

I had come in through the bay, and he was already dressed in scrubs, waiting to get on the elevator. When I noticed the plasticized blue paper booties over his running shoes, I thought of what the police had found inside Steven Spurrier's house. Our medical supplies were on state contract. But there were any number of businesses in any city that sold booties and surgical gloves. One did not need to be a physician to purchase such items any more than one needed to be a police officer to buy a uniform, badge, or gun.

"Hope you got a good night's rest," Fielding warned as the elevator doors parted.

We stepped inside.

"Give me the bad news. What have we got this morning?" I said.

"Six posts, every one of them a homicide."

"Great," I said irritably.

"Yeah, the Knife and Gun Club had a busy weekend. Four shootings, two stabbings. Spring has sprung."

We got off on the second floor and I was already taking off my suit jacket and rolling up my sleeves when I walked into my office. Marino was sitting in a chair, his briefcase on his lap, a cigarette lit. I assumed one of the morning's cases was his until he handed me two lab reports.

"Thought you'd want to see it for yourself," he said.

Typed at the top of one report was the name Steven Spurrier. The serology lab had already completed a workup on his blood.

The other report was eight years old, the results of the workup done on the blood found inside Elizabeth Mott's car.

"Of course, it's going to be a while before the DNA results are in," Marino began to explain, "but so far so good."

Settling behind my desk, I took a moment to study the reports. The blood from the Volkswagen was type O, PGM type 1, EAP type B, ADA type 1, and EsD type 1. This particular combination could be found in approximately 8 percent of the population. The results were consistent with those of the tests conducted on the blood from Spurrier's suspect kit. He also was type O, types in other blood groups the same, but since more enzymes had been tested for, the combination had been narrowed to approximately 1 percent of the population.

"It's not enough to charge him with murder," I said to Marino. "You'd have to have more than the fact that his blood type includes him in a group of thousands of people."

"A damn shame the report from the old blood isn't more complete."

"They didn't routinely test for as many enzymes back then," I replied.

"Maybe they could do it now?" he suggested. "If we could narrow it down, that would be a big help. The damn DNA for Spurrier's blood is going to take weeks."

"They're not going to be able to do it," I told him. "The blood from Elizabeth's car is too old. After this many years the enzymes would have degraded, so the results this time would be less specific than what's on this eight-year-old report. The best you could get now is the ABO grouping, and almost half of the population is type O. We have no choice but to wait for the DNA results. Besides," I added, "even if you could lock him up this minute you know he'd make bail. He's still under surveillance, I hope."

"Being watched like a hawk, and you can bet he knows it. The good news is he's not likely to try whacking anyone. The bad news is he's got time to destroy any evidence we missed. Like the murder weapons."

"The alleged missing gym bag."

"Don't add up that we couldn't find it. We did everything short of tearing up his floorboards."

"Maybe you should have torn up his floorboards."

"Yeah, maybe."

I was trying to think where else Spurrier might have hidden a gym bag when it occurred to me. I don't know why I didn't think of it earlier.

"How is Spurrier built?" I asked.

"He ain't very big, but he looks pretty strong. Not an ounce of fat."

"Then he probably works out, exercises."

"Probably. Why?"

"If he belongs to some place, the YMCA, a fitness club, he might have a locker. I do at Westwood. If I wanted to hide something, that would be a good place to do it. No one would think twice when he walked out of the club with his gym bag in hand or when he returned the bag to his locker."

"Interesting idea," Marino said thoughtfully. "I'll ask around, see what I can find out."

He lit another cigarette and unzipped his briefcase. "I got pictures of his crib, if you're interested."

I glanced up at the clock. "I've got a houseful downstairs. We'll have to make it quick."

He handed me a thick manila envelope of eight-by-tens. They were in order, and going through them was like seeing Spurrier's house through Marino's eyes, beginning with the Colonial brick front lined with boxwoods and a brick walk leading to the black front door. In back was a paved drive leading to a garage that was attached to the house.

I spread out several more photographs and found myself inside his living room. On the bare hardwood floor was a gray leather couch near a glass coffee table. Centered on the table was a jagged brass plant growing out of a chunk of coral. A recent copy of the *Smithsonian* was perfectly aligned with the table's edges. Centered on the magazine was a remote control that I suspected operated the overhead television projector suspended like a spaceship from the whitewashed ceiling. An eighty-inch television screen was retracted into an inconspicuous vertical bar above the bookcase lined with VCR tapes, neatly labeled, and scores of hardbound volumes, the titles of which I could not make out. To one side of the bookcase was a bank of sophisticated electronic equipment.

"The squirrel's got his own movie theater," Marino said. "Got surround sound, speakers in every room. The whole setup probably cost more than your Mercedes, and he wasn't sitting back at night watching *Sound of Music,* either. Those tapes there in the bookcase"—he reached across my desk to point them out. "They're all *Lethal Weapon*–type shit, flicks about Vietnam, vigilantes. Now on the shelf right above is the good stuff. The tapes look like your everyday box office hits, but you pop one of them in the VCR and get a little surprise. The one labeled *On Golden Pond,* for example, should be called *On the Cesspool.* Hardcore violent pornography. Benton and I were together all of yesterday viewing the crap. Friggin' unbelievable. About every other minute, I felt like taking a bath."

"Did you find any home movies?"

"No. Not any photography equipment, either."

I looked at more photographs. In the dining room was another glass table, this one surrounded by transparent acrylic chairs. I noticed that the hardwood floor was bare. I had yet to see a rug or carpet in any room.

The kitchen was immaculate and modern. Windows were shrouded with gray miniblinds. There were no curtains, no draperies in any room I had seen, not even upstairs where this creature slept. The brass bed was king-size, neatly made, sheets white, but no spread. Dresser drawers pulled open revealed the warm-up suits Marino had told me about, and in boxes on the closet floor were packets of surgical gloves and booties.

"There's nothing fabric," I marveled, returning the photographs to their envelope. "I've never before seen a house that didn't have at least one rug."

"No curtains, either. Not even in the shower," Marino said. "It's enclosed in glass doors. Of course, there are towels, sheets, his clothes."

"Which he probably washes constantly."

"The upholstery in his Lincoln is leather," Marino said. "And the carpet's covered with plastic mats."

"He doesn't have any pets?"

"No."

"The way he has furnished his house may have to do with more than his personality."

Marino met my eyes. "Yeah, I'm thinking that."

"Fibers, pet hairs," I said. "He doesn't have to worry about transferring them."

"You ever thought it interesting that all of the abandoned vehicles in these cases was so clean?"

I had.

"Maybe he vacuums them after the crimes," he said.

"At a car wash?"

"A filling station, apartment complex, any place that has a coin-operated car vacuum. The murders were committed late at night. By the time he stopped somewhere to vacuum the car afterward, there wouldn't be many people out to see what he was doing."

"Maybe. Who knows what he did?" I said. "But the picture we're getting is of someone who is obsessively neat and careful. Someone very paranoid and familiar with the types of evidence that are important in forensic examinations."

Leaning back in the chair, Marino said, "The Seven-Eleven

where Deborah and Fred stopped the night they disappeared, I dropped by there over the weekend and talked to the clerk."

"Ellen Jordan?"

He nodded. "I showed her a photo lineup, asked her if anybody in it looked like the man who was buying coffee in the Seven-Eleven the night Fred and Deborah was in there. She picked out Spurrier."

"She was certain?"

"Yes. Said he was wearing a jacket of some sort, dark. All she really recalled was that the guy was in dark clothes, and I'm thinking Spurrier already had on a warm-up suit when he went inside the Seven-Eleven. I've been running a lot of things through my mind. We'll start with two things we do know for a fact. The interiors of the abandoned cars were very clean, and in the four cases before Deborah and Fred, white cotton fibers were recovered from the driver's seat, right?"

"Yes," I agreed.

"Okay. I think this squirrel was out cruising for victims and spotted Fred and Deborah on the road, maybe saw them sitting real close to each other, her head on Fred's shoulder, that sort of thing. It sets him off. He tails them, pulls into the Seven-Eleven right after they do. Maybe he slips into the warm-up suit at this time, changes in his car. Maybe he already has it on. But he goes inside, hangs around looking through magazines, buying coffee and listening to what they're saying to the clerk. He overhears the clerk giving Fred and Deborah directions to the nearest rest stop where there's a bathroom. Then he leaves, speeds east on Sixty-four, turns into the rest stop and parks. He gets his bag that's got his weapons, ligatures, gloves, and so on, and makes himself scarce until Deborah and Fred pull in. He probably waits until she's gone to use the ladies' room, then he approaches Fred, feeds him some story about his car breaking down or whatever. Maybe Spurrier says he was working out at the gym, on his way home, thus explaining why he's dressed the way he is."

"Fred wouldn't recognize him from the Seven-Eleven?"

"I doubt it," Marino said. "But it don't matter. Spurrier might have been bold enough to mention that, say he was just buying coffee at the Seven-Eleven, and his car conked out right after he left. He says he's just called a wrecker and wonders if Fred could give him a lift back to his car so he can wait for the wrecker, promises that his car isn't very far down the road, et cetera. Fred agrees, then Deborah reappears. Once Spurrier's inside the Cherokee, Fred and Deborah are his."

I remembered Fred described as helpful, generous. He probably would have helped a stranger in distress, especially one as smooth and clean-cut as Steven Spurrier.

"When the Cherokee's back on the Interstate, Spurrier leans over and unzips his bag, puts on gloves, booties, and slips out his gun, points it at the back of Deborah's head. . . ."

I thought of the bloodhound's reaction when he had sniffed the seat where it was believed Deborah had been sitting. What the dog had detected was her terror.

". . . He orders Fred to drive to the spot Spurrier's already picked in advance. By the time they stop on the logging road, Deborah's hands have probably already been tied behind her back. Her shoes and socks are off. Spurrier orders Fred to take off his shoes and socks, then binds his hands. Spurrier orders them out of the Cherokee and walks them into the woods. Maybe he's wearing night vision goggles so he can see. He might have had those in his bag, too.

"Then he starts his game with them," Marino went on in a detached voice. "He takes out Fred first, then goes after Deborah. She resists, gets cut, and he shoots her. He drags their bodies to the clearing, positioning them side by side, her arm under his, like they was holding hands, holding on to each other. Spurrier smokes a few cigarettes, maybe sits out there in the dark by the bodies, enjoying the afterglow. Then he heads back to the Cherokee, takes off his warm-up, gloves, booties, puts them in a plastic bag he's got inside his gym bag. Maybe puts the kids' shoes and socks in the bag, too.

He drives away, finds some deserted place with a coin-operated vacuum and cleans out the inside of the Cherokee, especially the driver's area where he's been sitting. All done, and he disposes of the trash bag, maybe in a Dumpster. I'm guessing he put something over the driver's seat at this point. Maybe a folded white sheet, a white towel in the first four cases—"

"Most athletic clubs," I interrupted, "have a linen service. They keep a supply of white towels in the locker rooms. If Spurrier does keep his murder kit in a locker somewhere—"

Marino cut me off. "Yeah, I'm reading you loud and clear. Damn. Maybe I'd better start working on that one pronto."

"A white towel would explain the white cotton fibers found," I added.

"Except he must have used something different with Deborah and Fred. Hell, who knows? Maybe he sat on a plastic trash bag this time. The point is, I'm thinking he sat on something so he didn't leave fibers from his clothes on the seat. Remember, he's not wearing the warm-up suit anymore, no way he would because it would be bloody. He drives off, dumps the Cherokee where we found it, and trots across the Interstate to the eastbound rest stop where his Lincoln's parked. He's out of there. Mission accomplished."

"There were probably a lot of cars in and out of the rest stop that night," I said. "No one was going to notice his Lincoln parked out there. But even if someone had, the tags wouldn't have come back to him because they were 'borrowed.' "

"Right. That's his last task, either returning the tags to the ride he stole them from or, if that isn't possible, just pitching them somewhere." He paused, rubbing his face in his hands. "I've got a feeling Spurrier picked an MO early on and has pretty much stuck to it in all of the cases. He cruises, spots his victims, tails them, and knows he's hit pay dirt if they pull off at some place, a bar, a rest stop, where they're going to be long enough for him to get set up. Then he makes his approach, pulls something to make them trust him. Maybe he strikes only once for every fifty times he goes out cruising. But he's still getting off on it."

"The scenario seems plausible for the five recent cases," I said. "But I don't think it works quite as well for Jill and Elizabeth. If the Palm Leaf Motel was where he'd left his car, that was some five miles from the Anchor Bar and Grill."

"We don't know that Spurrier hooked up with them at the Anchor."

"I have a feeling he did."

Marino looked surprised. "Why?"

"Because the women had been in his bookstore before," I explained. "They were familiar with Spurrier, though I doubt they knew him very well. I'm guessing that he watched them when they came in to buy newspapers, books, whatever. I suspect he sensed immediately that the two women were more than friends, and this pushed his button. He's obsessed with couples. Maybe he'd been contemplating his first killings, and he thought that two women would be easier than a man and a woman. He planned the crime long in advance, his fantasies fed every time Jill and Elizabeth came into his bookstore. He might have followed them, stalked them after hours, gone through a lot of dry runs, practicing. He had already selected the wooded area out near where Mr. Joyce lives and probably was the person who shot the dog. Then one night he follows Jill and Elizabeth to the Anchor, and this is when he decides to do it. He leaves his car somewhere, heads to the bar on foot, his gym bag in hand."

"Are you thinking he went inside the bar and watched them while they drank beer?"

"No," I said. "I think he was too careful for that. I think he hung back, waited until they came out to get into the Volkswagen. Then I think Spurrier approached them and put on the same act. His car had broken down. He was the owner of the bookstore they frequented. They had no reason to fear him. He gets inside, and very soon after his plan begins to unravel. They don't end up in the wooded area, but at the cemetery. The women, Jill, in particular, aren't very cooperative."

"And he bleeds inside the Volkswagen," Marino said. "A nosebleed, maybe. Ain't no vacuum cleaner gonna get blood out of a seat or floor mat."

"I doubt he bothered to vacuum. Spurrier probably was panicking. He probably ditched the car as quickly as he could in the most convenient spot, which turned out to be the motel. As for where his car was parked, who knows? But I'm betting he was in for a little hike."

"Maybe the episode with the two women spooked him so bad he didn't try again for five years."

"I don't think that's it," I said. "Something's missing."

The telephone rang several weeks later when I was home alone working in my study. My recorded message had barely begun when the person hung up. The phone rang again half an hour later, and this time I answered before my machine. I said hello, and the line was disconnected again.

Perhaps someone was trying to reach Abby and did not want to talk to me? Perhaps Clifford Ring had discovered where she was? Distracted, I went to the refrigerator for a snack and settled on several slices of cheese.

I was back in my study paying bills when I heard a car pull in, gravel crunching beneath tires. I assumed it was Abby until the doorbell rang.

I looked through the peephole at Pat Harvey zipped up in a red windbreaker. The hang-ups, I thought. She had made certain I was home because she wanted to speak to me face-to-face.

She greeted me with "I'm sorry to impose," but I could tell she wasn't.

"Please come in," I said reluctantly.

She followed me to the kitchen, where I poured her a cup of coffee. She sat stiffly at the table, coffee mug cradled in her hands.

"I'm going to be very direct with you," she began. "It has come to my attention that this man they arrested in Williamsburg, Steven Spurrier, is believed to have murdered two women eight years ago."

"Where did you hear this?"

"That's not important. The cases were never solved and have now been linked to the murders of the five couples. The two women were Steven Spurrier's first victims."

I noticed that the lower lid of her left eye was twitching. Pat Harvey's physical deterioration since I had seen her last was shocking. Her auburn hair was lifeless; her eyes were dull; her skin was pale and drawn. She looked even thinner than she had been during her televised press conference.

"I'm not sure I'm following you," I said tensely.

"He inspired their trust and they made themselves vulnerable. Which is exactly what he did with the others, with my daughter, with Fred."

She said all this as if she knew it for a fact. Pat Harvey had convicted Spurrier in her mind.

"But he will never be punished for Debbie's murder," she said. "I know that now."

"It is too early to know anything," I replied calmly.

"They have no proof. What was found inside his house is not enough. It will not hold up in any court, if the cases ever go to court. You can't convict someone of capital murder just because you found newspaper clippings and surgical gloves inside his house, especially if the defense claims the evidence was planted to frame his client."

She had been talking to Abby, I thought with a sick feeling.

"The only evidence," she went on coldly, "is the blood found inside the women's car. It will all depend on DNA, and there will be questions because the cases occurred so long ago. The chain of custody, for example. Even if the prints match and the courts accept the evidence, there is no certainty that a jury will, especially since the police have yet to find the murder weapons."

"They're still looking."

"He's had plenty of time to dispose of those by now," she replied, and she was right.

Marino had discovered that Spurrier worked out at a gym not far from where he lived. The police had searched his rented locker, which not only locked with a key but had had a padlock on it. The locker was empty. The blue athletic bag Spurrier had been seen carrying around the gym had never been found, and never would be, I felt sure.

"What do you need from me, Mrs. Harvey?"

"I want you to answer my questions."

"Which questions?"

"If there is evidence I don't know about, I think you'd be wise to tell me."

"The investigation is not over. The police, the FBI are working very hard on your daughter's case."

She stared across the kitchen. "Are they talking to you?"

Instantly, I understood. No one directly involved in the investigation was giving Pat Harvey the time of day. She had become a pariah, perhaps even a joke. She was not going to admit this to me, but that's why she had appeared at my door.

"Do you believe Steven Spurrier murdered my daughter?"

"Why does my opinion matter?" I asked.

"It matters a great deal."

"Why?" I asked again.

"You don't form opinions lightly. I don't think you jump to conclusions or believe something just because you wish to. You're familiar with the evidence"—her voice trembled—"and you took care of Debbie."

I could not think of what to say.

"So I'll ask you again. Do you believe Steven Spurrier murdered them, murdered her?"

I hesitated, just for an instant, but it was enough. When I told her that I could not possibly answer such a question, and indeed, did not know the answer, she did not listen.

She got up from the table.

I watched her dissolve in the night, her profile briefly illuminated by the interior light of her Jaguar as she got in and drove away.

Abby did not come in until after I had given up waiting for her and had gone to bed. I slept fitfully and opened my eyes when I heard water running downstairs. I squinted at the clock. It was almost midnight. I got up and slipped into my robe.

She must have heard me in the hall, for when I reached her bedroom she was standing in the doorway, her pajamas a sweat suit, feet bare.

"You're up late," she said.

"So are you."

"Well, I . . ." She didn't finish her sentence as I walked inside her room and sat on the edge of the bed.

"What's up?" she asked uneasily.

"Pat Harvey came to see me earlier this evening, that's what's up. You've been talking to her."

"I've been talking to a lot of people."

"I know you want to help her," I said. "I know you've been outraged by the way her daughter's death has been used to hurt her. Mrs. Harvey's a fine woman, and I think you genuinely care about her. But she needs to stay out of the investigation, Abby."

She looked at me without speaking.

"For her own good," I added empathically.

Abby sat down on the rug, crossing her legs Indian style, and leaned against the wall.

"What did she say to you?" she asked.

"She's convinced Spurrier murdered her daughter and will never be punished for it."

"I certainly had nothing to do with her reaching such a conclusion," she said. "Pat has a mind of her own."

"Spurrier's arraignment is Friday. Does she plan to be there?"

"It's just a petit larceny charge. But if you're asking if I'm worried Pat might appear and make a scene . . ." She shook her head. "No way. It would serve no purpose for her to show up. She's not an idiot, Kay."

"And you?"

"What? Am I an idiot?" She evaded me again.

"Will you be at the arraignment?"

"Sure. And I'll tell you exactly how it will go. He'll be in and out, will plead guilty to petit larceny and get slapped with a fifteen-hundred-dollar fine. And he's going to spend a little time in jail, maybe a month at most. The cops want him to sweat behind bars for a while, break him down so he'll talk."

"How do you know that?"

"He's not going to talk," she went on. "They're going to lead him out of the courthouse in front of everyone and shove him in the back of a patrol car. It's all meant to scare and humiliate him, but it won't work. He knows they don't have enough on him. He'll bide his time in jail, then be out. A month isn't forever."

"You sound as if you feel sorry for him."

"I don't feel anything for him," she said. "Spurrier was into recreational cocaine, according to his attorney, and the night the cops caught him stealing the license tags, he was planning to make a buy. Spurrier was afraid some drug dealer would turn out to be a snitch, record his plate number, maybe give it to the cops. That's the explanation for the stolen tags."

"You can't believe that," I said heatedly.

Abby straightened out her legs, wincing a little. Without saying a word, she stood up and walked out of the room. I followed her to the kitchen, my frustration mounting. As she began to fill a glass with ice, I placed my hands on her shoulders and turned her around until we were face-to-face.

"Are you listening to me?"

Her eyes softened. "Please don't be angry with me. What I'm doing has nothing to do with you, with our friendship."

"What *friendship*? I feel as if I don't even know you anymore. You leave money around my house as if I'm nothing more than the damn maid. I don't remember the last time we ate a meal together. You never talk to me. You're so obsessed with this damn book. You see what's happened to Pat Harvey. Can't you see that the same thing is happening to you?"

Abby just stared at me.

"It's as if you've made up your mind about something," I continued to plead with her. "Why won't you tell me what it is?"

"There's nothing to make up my mind about," she said quietly, pulling away from me. "Everything's already been decided."

Fielding called early Saturday morning to say there were no autopsies, and exhausted, I went back to bed. It was midmorning when I got up. After a long, hot shower I was ready to deal with Abby and see if we could somehow repair our damaged relationship.

But when I went downstairs and knocked on her door, there was no answer, and when I went out to get the paper I saw her car was gone. Irritated that she had managed to avoid me again, I put on a pot of coffee.

I was sipping my second cup when a small headline caught my attention:

WILLIAMSBURG MAN GIVEN
SUSPENDED SENTENCE

Steven Spurrier had not been cuffed and hauled off to jail following his arraignment the day before as Abby had predicted, I read, horrified. He pleaded guilty to petit larceny, and because he had no prior record and had always been a law-abiding citizen of Williamsburg, he was fined one thousand dollars and had walked out of the courthouse a free man.

Everything's already been decided, Abby had said.

Is this what she had been referring to? If she knew Spurrier would be released, why would she deliberately mislead me?

I left the kitchen and opened the door to her room. The bed was made, curtains drawn. Inside the bath, I noticed drops of water in the sink and the faint scent of perfume. She had not been gone long. I looked for her briefcase and tape recorder, but could not find them. Her .38 was not in its drawer. I went through dressers until I found her notepads, hidden beneath clothes.

Sitting on the edge of the bed, I frantically flipped through them. I streaked through her days and weeks as the meaning became clearer.

What had begun as Abby's crusade to discover the truth about the couples' murders had turned into her own ambitious obsession. She seemed fascinated by Spurrier. If he was guilty, she was determined to make his story the focus of her book, to explore his psychopathic mind. If he was innocent, it would be "another Gainesville," she wrote, referring to the spree murders of university students in which a suspect became a household name and later turned out to be innocent. "Only it would be worse than Gainesville," she added. "Because of what the card implies."

Initially, Spurrier had repeatedly denied Abby's requests for interviews. Then late last week, she had tried again and he had picked up the phone. He had suggested they meet after the arraignment, telling her his attorney had "made a deal."

"He said he had read my stories in the *Post* over the years," Abby had scribbled, "and had recalled my byline from when I was in Richmond. He remembered what I had written about Jill and Elizabeth, too, and remarked that they were 'nice girls' and he'd always hoped the cops would get the 'psycho.' He also knew about my sister, said he'd read about her murder. That's the reason he finally agreed to talk to me, he said. He 'felt' for me, said he realized I understood what it was like to 'be a victim,' because what happened to my sister made me a victim, too.

" 'I am a victim,' he said. 'We can talk about that. Maybe you can help me better understand what that's all about.'

"He suggested I come to his house Saturday morning at eleven, and I agreed, providing all interviews are exclusive. He said that was fine, he had no intention of talking to anybody else as long as I told his side. 'The truth,' as he put it. Thank you, Lord! Screw you and your book, Cliff. You lose."

Cliff Ring was writing a book about these cases, too. Dear Lord. No wonder Abby had been acting so odd.

She had lied when she had told me what was going to happen at Spurrier's arraignment. She did not want me to suspect that she planned to go to his house, and she knew such a thought would never occur to me if I assumed he would be in jail. I remembered her saying that she no longer trusted anyone. She didn't, not even me.

I glanced at my watch. It was eleven-fifteen.

Marino wasn't in, so I left a message on his pager. Then I called the Williamsburg police, and the phone rang forever before a secretary answered. I told her I needed to speak to one of the detectives immediately.

"They're all out on the street right now."

"Then let me speak to whoever's in."

She transferred me to a sergeant.

Identifying myself, I said, "You know who Steven Spurrier is."

"Can't work around here and not know that."

"A reporter is interviewing him at his house. I'm alerting you so you can make sure your surveillance teams know she's there, make sure everything's all right."

There was a long pause. Paper crinkled. It sounded as if the sergeant was eating something. Then, "Spurrier's not under surveillance anymore."

"I beg your pardon?"

"I said our guys have been pulled off."

"Why?" I demanded.

"Now, that I don't know, Doc, been on vacation for the past—"

"Look, all I'm asking is you send a car by his house, make sure everything's all right." It was all I could do not to scream at him.

"Don't you worry about a thing." His voice was as calm as a mill pond. "I'll pass it along."

I hung up as I heard a car pull in.

Abby, thank God.

But when I looked out the window, it was Marino.

I opened the front door before he could ring the bell.

"Was in the area when I got your message on the beeper, so I—"

"Spurrier's house!" I grabbed his arm. "Abby's there! She's got her gun!"

The sky had turned dark and it was raining as Marino and I sped east on 64. Every muscle in my body was rigid. My heart would not slow down.

"Hey, relax," Marino said as we turned off at the Colonial Williamsburg exit. "Whether the cops are watching him or not, he ain't stupid enough to touch her. Really, you know that. He ain't going to do that."

There was only one vehicle in sight when we turned onto Spurrier's quiet street.

"Shit," Marino muttered under his breath.

Parked on the street in front of Spurrier's house was a black Jaguar.

"Pat Harvey," I said. "Oh, God."

He slammed on the brakes.

"Stay here." He was out of the car as if he had been ejected, running up the driveway in the pouring rain. My heart was pounding as he pushed the front door open with his foot, revolver in hand, and disappeared inside.

The doorway was empty when suddenly he filled it again. He stared in my direction, yelling something I could not hear.

I got out of the car, rain soaking my clothes as I ran.

I smelled the burnt gunpowder the instant I entered the foyer.

"I've called for help," Marino said, eyes darting around. "Two of them are in there."

The living room was to the left.

He was hurrying up the stairs leading to the second story as photographs of Spurrier's house crazily flashed in my mind. I recognized the glass coffee table and saw the revolver on top of it. Blood was pooled on the bare wood floor beneath Spurrier's body, a second revolver several feet away. He was facedown, inches from the gray leather couch where Abby lay on her side. She stared at the cushion beneath her cheek through drowsy, dull eyes, the front of her pale blue blouse soaked bright red.

For an instant I didn't know what to do, the roaring inside my head as loud as a windstorm. I squatted beside Spurrier, blood spilling and seeping around my shoes as I rolled him over. He was dead, shot through the abdomen and chest.

I hurried to the couch and felt Abby's neck. There was no pulse. I turned her on her back and started CPR, but her heart and lungs had given up too long ago to remember what they were supposed to do. Holding her face in my hands, I felt her warmth and smelled her perfume as sobs welled up and shook me uncontrollably.

Footsteps on the hardwood floor did not register until I realized they were too light to be Marino's. I looked up as Pat Harvey lifted the revolver off the coffee table.

I stared wide-eyed at her, my lips parting.

"I'm sorry." The revolver shook as she pointed it in my direction.

"Mrs. Harvey." My voice stuck in my throat, hands frozen in front of me, stained with Abby's blood. "Please . . ."

"Just stay there." She backed up several steps, lowering the gun a little. For some bizarre reason it occurred to me she was wearing the same red windbreaker she had worn to my house.

"Abby's dead," I said.

Pat Harvey didn't react, her face ashen, eyes so dark they looked black. "I tried to find a phone. He doesn't have any phones."

"Please put the gun down."

"He did it. He killed my Debbie. He killed Abby."

Marino, I thought. *Oh, God, hurry!*

"Mrs. Harvey, it's over. They're dead. Please put the gun down. Don't make it worse."

"It can't be worse."

"That's not true. Please listen to me."

"I can't be here anymore," she said in the same flat tone.

"I can help you. Put the gun down. Please," I said, getting up from the couch as she raised the gun again.

"No," I begged, realizing what she was going to do.

She pointed the muzzle at her chest as I lunged toward her.

"Mrs. Harvey! No!"

The explosion knocked her back and she staggered, dropping the revolver. I kicked it away and it spun slowly, heavily, across the smooth wood floor as her legs buckled. She reached for something to hold on to, but nothing was there. Marino was suddenly in the room, exclaiming "Holy shit!" He held his revolver in both hands, muzzle pointed at the ceiling. Ears ringing, I was trembling all over as I knelt beside Pat Harvey. She lay on her side, knees drawn, clutching her chest.

"Get towels!" I moved her hands out of the way and fumbled with her clothing. Untucking her blouse and pushing up her brassiere, I pressed bunched cloth against the wound below her left breast. I could hear Marino cursing as he rushed out of the room.

"Hold on," I whispered, applying pressure so the small hole would not suck in air and collapse the lung.

She was squirming and began to groan.

"Hold on," I repeated as sirens wailed from the street.

Red light pulsed through blinds covering the living room windows, as if the world outside Steven Spurrier's house were on fire.

18

Marino drove me home and did not leave. I sat in my kitchen staring out at the rain, only vaguely aware of what was going on around me. The doorbell rang, and I heard footsteps and male voices.

Later, Marino came into the kitchen and pulled out a chair across from me. He perched on the edge of it as if he wasn't planning to sit long.

"Any other places in the house Abby might have put her things, beside her bedroom?" he asked.

"I don't think so," I murmured.

"Well, we've got to look. I'm sorry, Doc."

"I understand."

He followed my gaze out the window.

"I'll make coffee." He got up. "We'll see if I remember what you taught me. My first quiz, huh?"

He moved about in the kitchen, cabinet doors opening and shutting, water running as he filled the pot. He walked out while coffee dripped, and moments later was back with another detective.

"This won't take very long, Dr. Scarpetta," the detective said. "Appreciate your cooperation."

He said something in a low voice to Marino. Then he left and Marino returned to the table, setting a cup of coffee in front of me.

"What are they looking for?" I tried to concentrate.

"We're going through the notebooks you told me about. Looking for tapes, anything that might tell us what led up to Mrs. Harvey shooting Spurrier."

"You're sure she did it."

"Oh, yeah. Mrs. Harvey did it. Damn miracle she's alive. She missed her heart. She was lucky, but maybe she won't think so if she pulls through."

"I called the Williamsburg police. I told them—"

"I know you did." He cut me off gently. "You did the right thing. You did all you could."

"They couldn't be bothered." I closed my eyes, fighting the tears.

"That wasn't it." He paused. "Listen to me, Doc."

I took a deep breath.

Marino cleared his throat and lit a cigarette. "While I was back there in your office, I talked to Benton. The FBI completed the DNA analysis of Spurrier's blood and compared it with the blood found in Elizabeth Mott's car. The DNA don't match."

"What?"

"The DNA don't match," he said again. "The detectives in Williamsburg who had been tailing Spurrier were just told yesterday. Benton had been trying to get hold of me and we kept missing each other, so I didn't know. You understand what I'm saying?"

I stared numbly at him.

"Legally, Spurrier was no longer a suspect. A pervert, yeah. We're talking the land of fruits and nuts. But he didn't murder Elizabeth and Jill. He didn't leave the blood in the car, couldn't have. If he killed these other couples, we've got no proof. To keep tailing him all the hell over the place, watching his house or banging on his door because they see he's got company, was harassment. Well, I mean there comes a point when there aren't enough cops to keep that up, and Spurrier could sue. And the FBI had backed off. So that's the way it went."

"He killed Abby."

Marino looked away from me. "Yeah, it appears so. She had her tape recorder running, we got the whole thing on tape. But that don't prove he killed the couples, Doc. It's looking like Mrs. Harvey gunned down an innocent man."

"I want to hear the tape."

"You don't want to hear it. Take my word for it."

"If Spurrier was *innocent,* then why did he shoot Abby?"

"I got an idea, based on what I heard on the tape and saw at the scene," he said. "Abby and Spurrier was talking in the living room. Abby was sitting on the couch where we found her. Spurrier heard someone at the door and got up to answer it. I don't know why he let Pat Harvey in. You would think he would have recognized her, but maybe he didn't. She had on a windbreaker with a hood, and jeans. Might have been hard to tell who she was. No way to know how she identified herself, what she said to him. We won't know until we can talk to her, and even then we might not know."

"But he let her in."

"He opened the door," Marino said. "Then she had her revolver out, a Charter Arms, the one she later shot herself with. Mrs. Harvey forced him back inside the house, into the living room. Abby's still sitting there, and the tape recorder's still running. Since Abby's Saab was out back in the drive, Mrs. Harvey wouldn't have seen it when she parked in front. She had no idea Abby was there, and this diverted her attention long enough for Spurrier to go for Abby, probably to use her as a shield. Hard to know exactly what went down, but we know Abby had her revolver with her, probably in her purse, which was probably next to her on the couch. She tries to get out her gun, she and Spurrier struggle and she gets shot. Then, before he can shoot Mrs. Harvey, she shoots him. Twice. We checked her revolver. Three spent shells, two live."

"She said something about looking for a phone," I said dully.

"Spurrier's only got two phones. One in his bedroom upstairs, the other in the kitchen, same color as the wall and between two cabinets, hard as shit to see. I almost didn't find it either. It looks like we rolled up to the house maybe minutes after the shootings, Doc.

I think Mrs. Harvey set her gun on the coffee table when she went over to Abby, saw how bad it was and tried to find a phone to call for help. Mrs. Harvey must have been in another room when I walked in, maybe heard me and ducked out of sight. All I know is when I went in, I scanned the immediate area. All I saw was the bodies in the living room, checked their carotids and thought Abby had a faint pulse, but I wasn't sure. I had a choice, had to make a split-second decision. I could start searching Spurrier's crib for Mrs. Harvey, or get you and then look. I mean, I didn't see her when I first came in. I thought she might have gone out the back door or upstairs," he said, obviously distressed he'd put me in jeopardy.

"I want to hear the tape," I said again.

Marino rubbed his face in his hands, his eyes bleary and bloodshot when he looked back at me. "Don't put yourself through it."

"I have to."

Reluctantly, he got up from the table and left. When he returned, he opened a plastic evidence bag that contained a microcassette recorder. He set it upright on the table, briefly rewound a portion of the tape, and depressed the Play button.

The sound of Abby's voice filled the kitchen.

". . . I'm just trying to see your side of it, but that doesn't really explain why you drive around at night, stop and ask people things that you don't really need to know. Such as directions."

"Look, I already told you about the coke. You ever snorted coke?"

"No."

"Try it some time. You do a lot of off-the-wall things when you're high. You get confused and think you know where you're going. Then suddenly you're lost and have to ask directions."

"You said you're not doing coke anymore."

"Not anymore. No way. My big mistake. Never again."

"What about the items the police found in your house . . . ? Uh . . ."

There was the faint chime of a doorbell.

"Yeah. Hold on." Spurrier sounded tense.

Footsteps receded. Voices were indistinguishable in the background. I could hear Abby shifting on the couch. Then Spurrier's disbelieving voice: "Wait. You don't know what you're—"

"I know exactly what I'm doing, you bastard." It was Pat Harvey's voice, increasing in volume. "That was my daughter you took out into the woods."

"I don't know what you're—"

"Pat. Don't!"

A pause.

"Abby? Oh my God."

"Pat. Don't do it, Pat." Abby's voice was tight with fear. She gasped as something hit the couch. "Get away from me!" A commotion, rapid breathing, and Abby screaming, "Stop! Stop!" then what sounded like a cap gun going off.

Again and again.

Silence.

Footsteps clicked across the floor and got louder. They stopped.

"Abby?"

A pause.

"Please don't die. *Abby* . . ." Pat Harvey's voice was quavering so badly I could barely hear it.

Marino reached for the recorder, turned if off, and slipped it back inside the plastic bag as I stared at him in shock.

On the Saturday morning of Abby's graveside service, I waited until the crowd had thinned, then walked along a footpath beneath the shade of magnolias and oaks, dogwoods blazing fuchsia and white in the gentle spring sun.

The turnout for Abby's funeral had been small. I met several of her former Richmond colleagues and tried to comfort her parents. Marino came. So did Mark, who hugged me tight, then left with the promise he would come by my house later in the day. I needed to talk with Benton Wesley, but first I wanted a few moments alone.

Hollywood Cemetery was Richmond's most formidable city for the dead, some forty acres of rolling hills, streams, and stands of hardwood trees north of the James River. Curving streets were paved and named, with speed limits posted, the sloping grass crowded with granite obelisks, headstones, and angels of grief, many of them more than a century old. Buried here were Presidents James Monroe and John Tyler, and Jefferson Davis, and tobacco magnate Lewis Ginter. There was a soldiers' section for the Gettysburg dead, and a family plot of low-lying lawn where Abby had been buried beside her sister, Henna.

I drew upon a break in the trees, the river below glimmering like tarnished copper, muddy from recent rains. It did not seem possible that Abby was now part of this population, a granite marker weathering passing time. I wondered if she had ever gone back to her former house, to Henna's room upstairs as she had told me she intended to do when she could find the courage.

When I heard footsteps behind me, I turned to find Wesley walking slowly in my direction.

"You wanted to talk to me, Kay?"

I nodded.

He slipped off his dark suit jacket and loosened his tie. Staring out at the river, he waited to hear what was on my mind.

"There are some new developments," I began. "I called Gordon Spurrier on Thursday."

"The brother?" Wesley replied, looking at me curiously.

"Steven Spurrier's brother, yes. I didn't want to tell you about it until I'd looked into several other things."

"I haven't talked to him yet," he stated. "But he's on my list. Just a damn shame about the DNA results, that's still a major problem."

"That's my point. There isn't a problem with the DNA, Benton."

"I don't understand."

"During Spurrier's autopsy, I discovered a lot of old therapeutic scars, one of them from a small incision made above the middle of the collarbone that I associate with someone having trouble getting in a subclavian line," I said.

"Meaning?"

"You don't run a subclavian line unless the patient has a serious problem, trauma requiring the dumping of fluids very quickly, an infusion of drugs or blood. In other words, I knew Spurrier had a significant medical problem at some point in the past, and I began contemplating that this might have something to do with the five months he was absent from his bookstore not long after Elizabeth and Jill were murdered. There were other scars, too, over his hip and lateral buttock. Minute scars that made me suspect he'd had samples of bone marrow taken before. So I called his brother to find out about Steven's medical history."

"What did you learn?"

"Around the time he disappeared from his bookstore, Steven was treated for aplastic anemia at UVA," I said. "I've talked with his hematologist. Steven received total lymphoid irradiation, chemotherapy. Gordon's marrow was infused into Steven, and Steven then spent time in a laminar flow room, or a bubble, as most people call it. You may recall Steven's house was like a bubble, in a sense. Very sterile."

"Are you saying that the bone-marrow transplant changed his DNA?" Wesley asked, his face intense.

"For blood, yes. His blood cells had been totally wiped out by his aplastic anemia. He was HLA-typed for a suitable match, which turned out to be his brother, whose ABO type and even types in other blood group systems are the same."

"But Steven's and Gordon's DNA wouldn't be the same."

"No, not unless the brothers are identical twins, which, of course, they aren't," I said. "So Steven's blood type was consistent with the blood recovered from Elizabeth Mott's car. But at the level of DNA a discernible difference would have been noticed because Steven left the blood in the Volkswagen before his marrow transplant. When Steven's blood was recently taken for the suspect kit, what we were getting, in a sense, was Gordon's blood. What was actually compared with the DNA print of the old blood from the Volkswagen was not Steven's DNA, but Gordon's."

"Incredible," he said.

"I want the test run again on tissue from his brain because Steven's DNA in other cells will be the same as it was before the transplant. Marrow produces blood cells, so if you've had a marrow transplant you take on the blood cells of the donor. But brain, spleen, sperm cells don't change."

"Explain aplastic anemia to me," he said as we started walking.

"Your marrow is no longer making anything. It's as if you've already been irradiated, all blood cells wiped out."

"What causes it?"

"It's felt to be idiopathic; nobody really knows. But possibilities are exposure to pesticides, chemicals, radiation, organic phosphates. Significantly, benzene has been associated with aplastic anemia. Steven had worked at a printing press. Benzene is a solvent used to clean printing presses and other machinery. He was exposed to it, so his hematologist said, on a daily basis for almost a year."

"And the symptoms?"

"Fatigue, shortness of breath, fever, possibly infections, and bleeding from the gums and nose. Spurrier was already suffering from aplastic anemia when Jill and Elizabeth were murdered. He may have been having nosebleeds, which would have occurred with very little provocation. Stress always makes everything worse, and he would have been under a great deal of stress while abducting Elizabeth and Jill. If his nose had started bleeding, that would explain the blood in the back of Elizabeth's car."

"When did he finally go to the doctor?" Wesley asked.

"A month after the women were murdered. During his examination, it was discovered that his white count was low, his platelets and hemoglobin low. When your platelets are low you bleed a lot."

"He committed murders while he was that sick?"

"You can have aplastic anemia for a while before it becomes severe," I said. "Some people simply find out during a routine physical."

"Poor health and losing control of his first victims were enough to make him retreat," he thought out loud. "Years went by as he recovered and fantasized, reliving the murders and improving his techniques. Eventually, he was confident enough to start killing again."

"That could explain the long interval. But who knows what went through his mind."

"We'll never really know that," Wesley said grimly.

He paused to study an ancient grave marker before speaking again. "I have some news, too. There's a company in New York, a spy shop whose catalogs were found in Spurrier's house. After some tracking we've ascertained that four years ago he ordered a pair of night vision goggles from them. In addition, we've located a gun store in Portsmouth where he purchased two boxes of Hydra-Shok cartridges less than a month before Deborah and Fred disappeared."

"Why did he do it, Benton?" I asked. "Why did he kill?"

"I can never answer that satisfactorily, Kay. But I've talked with his former roommate at UVA, who indicated that Spurrier's relationship with his mother was unhealthy. She was very critical and controlling, belittled him constantly. He was dependent on her and at the same time probably hated her."

"What about the victimology?"

"I think he spotted young women who reminded him of what he couldn't have, the girls who had never given him the time of day. When he saw an attractive couple, it set him off because he was incapable of relationships. He took possession through murder, fused himself with and overpowered what he envied." Pausing, he added, "If you and Abby hadn't encountered him when you did, I'm not sure we would have gotten him. Scary how it works. Bundy gets pulled because a taillight's out. Son of Sam gets nailed because of a parking ticket. Luck. We were lucky."

I didn't feel lucky. Abby hadn't been lucky.

"You might find it interesting to know that since all of this has been in the news we've received a lot of phone calls from people claiming someone who fits Spurrier's description approached them outside bars, at service stations, convenience stores. It's been reported that on one occasion he actually got a ride with a couple. He claimed his car had broken down. The kids dropped him off. No problem."

"Did he approach only young male-female couples during these dry runs?" I asked.

"Not always. Thus explaining how you and Abby fit that night he stopped to ask directions. Spurrier loved the risk, the fantasy, Kay. The killing was, in a sense, incidental to the game he was playing."

"I still don't completely understand why the CIA was so worried the killer might be from Camp Peary," I told him.

He paused, draping his suit jacket over his other arm.

"It was more than the MO, the jack of hearts," he said. "The police recovered a plastic computerized gas card in the back of Jim and Bonnie's car, on the floor under the seat. It was assumed the card had inadvertently fallen out of the killer's pocket, a jacket pocket, maybe a shirt pocket, while he was abducting the couple."

"And?"

"The company name on the gas card was Syn-Tron. After some tracking, the account came back to Viking Exports. Viking Exports is a cover for Camp Peary. The gas card is issued to Camp Peary personnel for their use at the pumps on base."

"Interesting," I said. "Abby referred to a card in one of her notepads. I assumed she was referring to the jack of hearts. She knew about the gas card, didn't she, Benton?"

"I suspect Pat Harvey told her. Mrs. Harvey had known about the card for quite a while, thus explaining her accusations during the press conference that something was being covered up by the feds."

"Obviously, she no longer believed that when she decided to kill Spurrier."

"The Director briefed her after the press conference, Kay. Had no choice but to inform her that we were suspicious the gas card was left deliberately. We were suspicious from the beginning, but that didn't mean we couldn't take it seriously. Obviously, the CIA took it very seriously."

"And this silenced her."

"If nothing else it made her think twice. Certainly, after Spurrier was arrested, what the Director had said to her made a lot of sense."

"How could Spurrier have gotten hold of a Camp Peary gas card?" I puzzled.

"Camp Peary agents frequented his bookstore."

"You're saying that he somehow stole this card from a Camp Peary customer?"

"Yes. Suppose someone from Camp Peary walked out of the bookstore leaving his wallet on the counter. By the time he came back looking for it, Spurrier could have tucked it away, said he hadn't seen it. Then he left the gas card in Jim and Bonnie's car so we would link the killings to the CIA."

"No identification number on the card?"

"The ID numbers are on stickers that had been peeled off, so we couldn't trace the card back to an individual."

I was getting tired and my feet were beginning to hurt when the parking area where we had left our cars came into view. Those who had come to mourn Abby's death were gone.

Wesley waited until I was unlocking my car before touching my arm and saying, "I'm sorry for those times . . ."

"So am I." I didn't let him finish. "We go on from here, Benton. Do whatever you can to make sure Pat Harvey isn't punished further."

"I don't think a grand jury will have a problem understanding how she's suffered."

"Did she know about the DNA results, Benton?"

"She's had a way of finding out details critical to the investigation, despite our efforts to keep them from her, Kay. I suspect she knew. Certainly, it would help explain why she did what she did. She would have believed Spurrier was never going to be punished."

I got in and put the key in the ignition.

"I'm sorriest about Abby," he added.

I nodded as I shut the door, my eyes filling with tears.

I followed the narrow road to the cemetery's entrance, passing through elaborate wrought-iron gates. The sun shone on downtown office buildings and steeples in the distance, light caught in the trees. I opened the windows and drove west toward home.

CRUEL
& UNUSUAL

This book is for the inimitable Dr. Marcella Fierro.
(You taught Scarpetta well.)

PROLOGUE

(A MEDITATION AT SPRING STREET BY THE DAMNED)

It is two weeks before Christmas. Four days before nothing at all. I lie on my iron bed staring at my dirty bare feet and the white toilet missing its seat, and when cockroaches crawl across the floor I don't jump anymore. I watch them the same way they watch me.

I close my eyes and breathe slow.

I remember raking hay in the heat of day and getting no pay compared to the way white folk live. I dream of roasting peanuts in a tin and when the tomatoes are in eating them like apples. I imagine driving the pickup truck, sweat shining on my face in that no-future place I swore I'd leave.

I can't use the john, blow my nose, or smoke without guards taking notes. There's no clock. I never know the weather. I open my eyes and see a blank wall going on forever. What's a man supposed to feel when he's about to be gone?

Like a sad, sad song. I don't know the words. I can't remember. They say it happened in September when the sky was like a robin's egg and leaves were on fire and falling to the ground. They say a beast got loose in the city. Now there's one less sound.

Killing me won't kill the beast. The dark is his friend, flesh and blood his feast. When you think it's safe to stop looking that's when you'd better start looking, brother.

One sin leads to another.

Ronnie Joe Waddell

1

The Monday I carried Ronnie Joe Waddell's meditation in my pocketbook, I never saw the sun. It was dark out when I drove to work that morning. It was dark again when I drove home. Small raindrops spun in my headlights, the night gloomy with fog and bitterly cold.

I built a fire in my living room and envisioned Virginia farmland and tomatoes ripening in the sun. I imagined a young black man in the hot cab of a pickup truck and wondered if his head had been full of murder back then. Waddell's meditation had been published in the *Richmond Times-Dispatch* and I had taken the clipping to work to add to his growing file. But the business of the day distracted me and his meditation had remained in my pocketbook. I had read it several times. I supposed it would always intrigue me that poetry and cruelty could reside in the same heart.

For the next few hours I paid bills and wrote Christmas cards while the television played mutely. Like the rest of Virginia's citizens, whenever an execution was scheduled I found out from the media whether all appeals had been exhausted or the governor had granted clemency. The news determined whether I went on to bed or drove downtown to the morgue.

At almost ten P.M. my telephone rang. I answered it expecting my deputy chief or some other member of my staff whose evening, like mine, was on hold.

"Hello?" asked a male voice I did not recognize. "I'm trying to reach Kay Scarpetta? Uh, the chief medical examiner, Dr. Scarpetta?"

"Speaking," I said.

"Oh, good. Detective Joe Trent with Henrico County. Found your number in the book. Sorry to bother you at home." He sounded keyed up. "But we've got a situation we really need your help with."

"What's the problem?" I asked, staring tensely at the TV. A commercial was playing. I hoped I wasn't needed at a scene.

"Earlier this evening, a thirteen-year-old white male was abducted after leaving a convenience store on Northside. He was shot in the head and there may be some sexual components involved."

My heart sank as I reached for paper and pen. "Where is the body?" I asked.

"He was found behind a grocery store on Patterson Avenue in the county. I mean, he's not dead. He hasn't regained consciousness but no one's saying right now whether he'll make it. I realize it's not your case since he's not dead. But he's got some injuries that are real odd. They're not like anything I've ever come across. I know you see a lot of different types of injuries. I'm hoping you might have some idea how these were inflicted and why."

"Describe them for me," I said.

"We're talking about two areas. One on his inner right thigh, you know, up high near the groin. The other's in the area of his right shoulder. Chunks of flesh are missing—cut out. And there's weird cuts and scratches around the edges of the wounds. He's at Henrico Doctor's."

"Did you find the excised tissue?" My mind was racing through other cases, looking for something similar.

"Not so far. We've got men out there still searching. But it's possible the assault occurred inside a car."

"Whose car?"

"The assailant's. The grocery store parking lot where the kid was found is a good three or four miles from the convenience store where he was last seen. I'm thinking he got into somebody's car, maybe was forced to."

"You got photographs of the injuries before the doctors started working on him?"

"Yes. But they haven't done much. Because of the amount of skin missing, they'll have to do skin grafts—*full* grafts, is what they said, if that tells you anything."

It told me they had debrided the wounds, had him on intravenous antibiotics, and were waiting to do a gluteal graft. If, however, that was not the case and they had undermined the tissue around the injuries and sutured them, then there wasn't going to be much left for me to see.

"They haven't sutured his wounds," I said.

"That's what I've been told."

"Do you want me to take a look?"

"That would be really great," he said, relieved. "You should be able to see the wounds real well."

"When would you like me to do this?"

"Tomorrow would work."

"All right. What time? The earlier the better."

"Eight hundred hours? I'll meet you in front of the ER."

"I'll be there," I said as the anchorman stared grimly at me. Hanging up, I reached for the remote control and turned up the sound.

". . . Eugenia? Can you tell us if there's been any word from the governor?"

The camera shifted to the Virginia State Penitentiary, where for two hundred years the Commonwealth's worst criminals had been warehoused along a rocky stretch of the James River at the edge of downtown. Sign-carrying protesters and capital punishment enthusiasts gathered in the dark, their faces harsh in the glare of television lights. It chilled my soul that some people were laughing. A pretty, young correspondent in a red coat filled the screen.

"As you know, Bill," she said, "yesterday a telephone line was set up between Governor Norring's office and the penitentiary. Still no word, and that speaks volumes. Historically, when the governor doesn't intend to intervene, he remains silent."

"How are things there? Is it relatively peaceful so far?"

"So far, yes, Bill. I'd say several hundred people are standing vigil out here. And of course, the penitentiary itself is almost empty. All but several dozen of the inmates have already been transported to the new correctional facility in Greensville."

I turned off the TV and moments later was driving east with my doors locked and the radio on. Fatigue seeped through me like anesthesia. I felt dreary and numb. I dreaded executions. I dreaded waiting for someone to die, then running my scalpel through flesh as warm as mine. I was a physician with a law degree. I had been trained to know what gave life and what took it, what was right and what was wrong. Then experience had become my mentor, wiping its feet on that pristine part of myself that was idealistic and analytical. It is disheartening when a thinking person is forced to admit that many clichés are true. There is no justice on this earth. Nothing would ever undo what Ronnie Joe Waddell had done.

He had been on death row nine years. His victim had not been my case because she had been murdered before I had been appointed chief medical examiner of Virginia and had moved to Richmond. But I had reviewed her records. I was well aware of every savage detail. On the morning of September fourth, ten years before, Robyn Naismith called in sick at Channel 8, where she was an anchorwoman. She went out to buy cold remedies and returned home. The next day, her nude, battered body was found in her living room, propped against the TV. A bloody thumbprint recovered from the medicine cabinet was later identified as Ronnie Joe Waddell's.

There were a number of cars parked behind the morgue when I pulled in. My deputy chief, Fielding, was already there. So was my administrator, Ben Stevens, and morgue supervisor, Susan Story. The bay door was open, lights inside dimly illuminating the tarmac beyond, and a capitol police officer was sitting in his marked car smoking. He got out as I parked.

"Safe to keep the bay door open?" I asked. He was a tall, gaunt man with thick white hair. Though I had talked to him many times in the past, I couldn't remember his name.

"Appears okay at the moment, Dr. Scarpetta," he said, zipping up his heavy nylon jacket. "I haven't seen any troublemakers around. But as soon as Corrections gets here I'll close it and make sure it stays closed."

"Fine. As long as you'll be right here in the meantime."

"Yes, ma'am. You can count on that. And we'll have a couple more uniform men back here in case there's a problem. Apparently there's a lot of protesters. I guess you read in the paper about that petition all those people signed and took to the governor. And I heard earlier today some bleeding hearts as far away as California are on a hunger strike."

I glanced around the empty parking lot and across Main Street. A car rushed past, tires swishing over wet pavement. Streetlights were smudges in the fog.

"Hell, not me. I wouldn't even miss a coffee break for Waddell." The officer cupped his hand around his lighter and began puffing on a cigarette. "After what he done to that Naismith girl. You know, I remember watching her on TV. Now, I like my women the same way I like my coffee—sweet and white. But I have to admit, she was the prettiest black girl I ever seen."

I had quit smoking barely two months ago, and it still made me crazy to watch someone else doing it.

"Lord, that must've been close to ten years ago," he went on. "I'll never forget the uproar, though. One of the worst cases we've ever had around here. You'd've thought a grizzly bear got hold of—"

I interrupted him. "You'll let us know what's going on?"

"Yes, ma'am. They'll radio me and I'll give you the word." He headed back to the shelter of his car.

Inside the morgue, fluorescent light bleached the corridor of color, the smell of deodorizer cloying. I passed the small office where funeral homes signed in bodies, then the X-ray room, and the refrigerator, which was really a large refrigerated room with double-decker gurneys and two massive steel doors. The autopsy suite was lit up, stainless steel tables polished bright. Susan was sharpening a long knife and Fielding was labeling blood tubes. Both of them looked as tired and unenthusiastic as I felt.

"Ben's upstairs in the library watching TV," Fielding said to me. "He'll let us know if there are any new developments."

"What's the chance this guy had AIDS?" Susan referred to Waddell as if he already were dead.

"I don't know," I said. "We'll double-glove, take the usual precautions."

"I hope they'll say something if he had it," she persisted. "You know, I don't trust it when they send these prisoners in. I don't think they care if they're HIV positive because it's not their problem. They're not the ones doing the posts and worrying about needle sticks."

Susan had become increasingly paranoid about such occupational hazards as exposure to radiation, chemicals, and diseases. I could not blame her. She was several months pregnant, though it barely showed.

Slipping on a plastic apron, I went back into the locker room and put on greens, covered my shoes with booties, and got two packets of gloves. I inspected the surgical cart parked beside table three. Everything was labeled with Waddell's name, the date, and an autopsy number. The labeled tubes and cartons would go in the trash if Governor Norring interceded at the last minute. Ronnie Waddell would be deleted from the morgue log, his autopsy number assigned to whoever came in next.

At eleven P.M. Ben Stevens came downstairs and shook his head. All of us looked up at the clock. No one spoke. Minutes ticked by.

The capitol police officer walked in, portable radio in hand. I finally remembered his name was Rankin.

"He was pronounced at eleven-oh-five," he said. "Will be here in about fifteen minutes."

The ambulance beeped a warning as it backed into the bay, and when its rear doors swung open, enough Department of Corrections guards hopped out to control a small prison riot. Four of them slid out the stretcher bearing Ronnie Waddell's body. They carried it up the ramp and inside the morgue, metal clacking, feet scuffing, all of us getting out of the way. Lowering the stretcher to the tile floor without bothering to unfold the legs, they propelled it along like a sled on wheels, its passenger strapped in and covered with a bloodstained sheet.

"A nosebleed," one of the guards offered before I could ask the question.

"Who had a nosebleed?" I inquired, noting that the guard's gloved hands were bloody.

"Mr. Waddell did."

"In the ambulance?" I puzzled, for Waddell should not have had a blood pressure by the time he was loaded inside the ambulance.

But the guard was preoccupied with other matters and I did not get an answer. It would have to wait.

We transferred the body to the gurney positioned on top of the floor scale. Busy hands fumbled with unfastening straps and opening the sheet. The door to the autopsy suite quietly shut as the Department of Corrections guards left just as abruptly as they had appeared.

Waddell had been dead exactly twenty-two minutes. I could smell his sweat, his dirty bare feet, and the faint odor of singed flesh. His right pant leg was pushed up above his knee, his calf dressed in fresh gauze applied postmortem to his burns. He was a big, powerful man. The newspapers had called him the *gentle giant,* poetic Ronnie with soulful eyes. Yet there had been a time when he had used the large hands, the massive shoulders and arms before me to rip the life from another human being.

I pulled apart the Velcro fasteners of his light blue denim shirt, checking pockets as I undressed him. Searching for personal effects is pro forma and usually fruitless. Inmates are not supposed to carry anything with them to the electric chair, and I was very surprised when I discovered what appeared to be a letter in the back pocket of his jeans. The envelope had not been opened. Written in bold block letters across the front of it was

EXTREMELY CONFIDENTIAL. PLEASE BURY WITH ME!!

"Make a copy of the envelope and whatever's inside and submit the originals with his personal effects," I said, handing the envelope to Fielding.

He tucked it under the autopsy protocol on a clipboard, mumbling, "Jesus. He's bigger than I am."

"Amazing that anyone could be bigger than you are," Susan said to my bodybuilder deputy chief.

"Good thing he's not been dead long," he added. "Otherwise we'd need the Jaws of Life."

When musclebound people have been dead for hours, they are as uncooperative as marble statues. Rigor had not begun to set in. Waddell was limber as in life. He could have been asleep.

It required all of us to transfer him, facedown, to the autopsy table. He weighed two hundred and fifty-nine pounds. His feet protruded over the table's edge. I was measuring the burns to his leg when the buzzer sounded from the bay. Susan went to see who it was, and shortly Lieutenant Pete Marino walked in, trench coat unbuttoned, one end of the belt trailing along the tile floor.

"The burn to the back of his calf is four by one and a quarter by two and three-eighths," I dictated to Fielding. "It's dry, contracted, and blistered."

Marino lit a cigarette. "They're raising a stink about him bleeding," he said, and he seemed agitated.

"His rectal temp is one hundred and four," Susan said as she removed the chemical thermometer. "That's at eleven-forty-nine."

"You know why his face was bleeding?" Marino asked.

"One of the guards said a nosebleed," I replied, adding, "We need to turn him over."

"You saw this on the inner aspect of his left arm?" Susan directed my attention to an abrasion.

I examined it through a lens under a strong light. "I don't know. Possibly from one of the restraints."

"There's one on his right arm, too."

I took a look while Marino watched me and smoked. We turned the body, shoving a block under the shoulders. Blood trickled out of the right side of his nose. His head and chin had been shaved to an uneven stubble. I made the Y incision.

"There might be some abrasions here," Susan said, looking at the tongue.

"Take it out." I inserted the thermometer into the liver.

"Jesus," Marino said under his breath.

"Now?" Susan's scalpel was poised.

"No. Photograph the burns around his head. We need to measure those. Then remove the tongue."

"Shit," she complained. "Who used the camera last?"

"Sorry," Fielding said. "There was no film in the drawer. I forgot. By the way, it's your job to keep film in the drawer."

"It would help if you'd tell me when the film drawer's empty."

"Women are supposed to be intuitive. I didn't think I needed to tell you."

"I got the measurement of these burns around his head," Susan reported, ignoring his remark.

"Okay."

Susan gave him the measurements, then started work on the tongue.

Marino backed away from the table. "Jesus," he said again. "That always gets me."

"Liver temp's one hundred and five," I reported to Fielding.

I glanced up at the clock. Waddell had been dead for an hour. He hadn't cooled much. He was big. Electrocution heats you up. The brain temperatures of smaller men I had autopsied were as high as a hundred and ten. Waddell's right calf was at least that, hot to the touch, the muscle in total tetanus.

"A little abrasion at the margin. But nothing big-time," Susan pointed out to me.

"He bite his tongue hard enough to bleed that much?" Marino asked.

"No," I said.

"Well, they're already raising a stink about it." His voice rose. "I thought you'd want to know."

I paused, resting the scalpel on the edge of the table as it suddenly occurred to me. "You were a witness."

"Yeah. I told you I was going to be."

Everybody looked at him.

"Trouble's brewing out there," he said. "I don't want no one leaving this joint alone."

"What sort of trouble?" Susan asked.

"A bunch of religious nuts have been hanging out at Spring Street since this morning. Somehow they got word about his bleeding, and when the ambulance drove off with his body they started marching in this direction like a bunch of zombies."

"Did you see it when he started bleeding?" Fielding asked him.

"Oh, yeah. They juiced him twice. The first time he made this loud hiss, like steam coming out of a radiator, and the blood started pouring out from under his mask. They're saying the chair might have malfunctioned."

Susan started the Stryker saw and no one competed with its loud buzzing as she cut through the skull. I continued examining the organs. Heart was good, coronaries terrific. When the saw stopped, I resumed dictating to Fielding.

"You got the weight?" he asked.

"Heart weights five-forty, and he's got a single adhesion of the left upper lobe to the aortic arch. Even found four parathyroids, in case you didn't already get that."

"I got it."

I placed the stomach on the cutting board. "It's almost tubular."

"You sure?" Fielding moved closer to inspect. "That's bizarre. A guy this big needs a minimum of four thousand calories a day."

"He wasn't getting it, not lately," I said. "He doesn't have any gastric contents. His stomach is absolutely empty and clean."

"He didn't eat his last meal?" Marino asked me.

"It doesn't appear that he did."

"Do they usually?"

"Yes," I said, "usually."

We were finished by one A.M., and followed the funeral home attendants out to the bay, where the hearse was waiting. As we walked out of the building, darkness throbbed with red and blue lights. Radio static drifted on the cold, damp air, engines rumbled, and beyond the chain-link fence enclosing the parking lot was a ring of fire. Men, women, and children stood silently, faces wavering in candlelight.

The attendants wasted no time sliding Waddell's body into the back of the hearse and slamming the tailgate shut.

Somebody said something I did not get, and suddenly candles showered over the fence like a storm of falling stars and landed softly on the pavement.

"Goddam squirrels!" Marino exclaimed.

Wicks glowed orange and tiny flames dotted the tarmac. The hearse hastily began to back out of the bay. Flashguns were going off. I spotted the Channel 8 news van parked on Main Street. Someone was running along the sidewalk. Uniformed men were stamping out the candles, moving toward the fence, demanding that everyone clear the area.

"We don't want any problems here," an officer said. "Not unless some of you want to spend the night in lockup—"

"Butchers," a woman screamed.

Other voices joined in and hands grabbed the chain-link fence, shaking it.

Marino hurried me to my car.

A chant rose with tribal intensity. "*Butchers, butchers, butchers . . .*"

I fumbled with my keys, dropped them on the floor mat, snatched them up, and managed to find the right one.

"I'm following you home," Marino said.

I turned the heater on high but could not get warm. Twice I checked to make sure my doors were locked. The night took on a surreal quality, a strange asymmetry of light and dark windows, and shadows moved in the corners of my eyes.

We drank Scotch in my kitchen because I was out of bourbon.

"I don't know how you stand this stuff," Marino said rudely.

"Help yourself to whatever else there is in the bar," I told him.

"I'll tough it out."

I wasn't quite sure how to broach the subject, and it was obvious that Marino wasn't going to make it easy for me. He was tense, his face flushed. Strands of gray hair clung to his moist, balding head, and he was chain-smoking.

"Have you ever witnessed an execution before?" I asked.

"Never had a strong urge to."

"But you volunteered this time. So the urge must have been pretty strong."

"I bet if you put some lemon and soda water in this it wouldn't be half bad."

"If you want me to ruin good Scotch, I'll be glad to see what I can do."

He slid the glass toward me and I went to the refrigerator. "I've got bottled Key Lime juice, but no lemon." I searched shelves.

"That's fine."

I dribbled Key Lime juice into his glass, then added the Schweppes. Oblivious to the strange concoction he was sipping, he said, "Maybe you've forgotten, but the Robyn Naismith case was mine. Mine and Sonny Jones's."

"I wasn't around then."

"Oh, yeah. Funny, it seems like you've been here forever. But you know what happened, right?"

I was a deputy chief medical examiner for Dade County when Robyn Naismith was murdered, and I remembered reading about the case, following it in the news, and later seeing a slide presentation about it at a national meeting. The former Miss Virginia was a stunning beauty with a gorgeous alto voice. She was articulate and charismatic before the camera. She was only twenty-seven years old.

The defense claimed that Ronnie Waddell's intent was burglary, and Robyn's misfortune was to walk in on it after returning home from the drugstore. Allegedly, Waddell did not watch television and was unfamiliar with her name or brilliant future when he was ransacking her residence and brutalizing her. He was so hopped up on drugs, the defense argued, that he didn't know what he was doing. The jurors rejected Waddell's temporary insanity plea and recommended the death penalty.

"I know the pressure to catch her killer was incredible," I said to Marino.

"Friggin' unbelievable. We had this great latent print. We had bite marks. We had three guys doing a cold search through the files morning, noon, and night. I got no idea how many hours I put in on that damn case. Then we catch the bastard because he's driving around North Carolina with an expired inspection sticker." He paused, his eyes hard when he added, "Course, Jones wasn't around by then. Too damn bad he missed out on seeing Waddell get his reward."

"Do you blame Waddell for what happened to Sonny Jones?" I asked.

"Hey, what do you think?"

"He was a close friend."

"We worked Homicide together, fished together, was on the same bowling team."

"I know his death was hard for you."

"Yeah, well, the case wore him down. Working all hours, no sleep, never home, and that sure as hell didn't help matters with his wife. He kept telling me he couldn't take it no more and then he stopped telling me anything. One night he decides to eat his gun."

"I'm sorry," I said gently. "But I'm not sure you can blame Waddell for that."

"I had a score to settle."

"And was it settled when you witnessed his execution?"

At first Marino did not reply. He stared across the kitchen, his jaw rigidly set. I watched him smoke and drain his drink.

"Can I refresh that?"

"Yo. Why not."

I got up and did my thing again as I thought about the injustices and losses that had gone into the making of Marino. He had survived a loveless, impoverished childhood in the wrong part of New Jersey, and nursed an abiding distrust of anyone whose lot had been better. Not long ago his wife of thirty years had left him, and he had a son nobody seemed to know anything about. Regardless of his loyalty to law and order and his record of excellent police work, it was not in his genetic code to get along with the brass. It seemed his life's journey had placed him on a hard road. I feared that what he hoped to find at the end was not wisdom or peace but paybacks. Marino was always angry about something.

"Let me ask you this, Doc," he said to me when I returned to the table. "How would you feel if they caught the assholes who killed Mark?"

His question caught me by surprise. I did not want to think about those men.

"Isn't there a part of you that wants to see the bastards hung?" he went on. "Doesn't a part of you want to volunteer for the firing squad so you could pull the trigger yourself?"

Mark died when a bomb placed in a trash can inside London's Victoria Station exploded at the moment he happened to walk past. My shock and grief had catapulted me beyond revenge.

"It's an exercise in futility for me to contemplate punishing a group of terrorists," I said.

Marino stared intensely at me. "That's what's known as one of your famous bullshit answers. You'd give them free autopsies if you could. And you'd want them alive and would cut real slow. I ever tell you what happened to Robyn Naismith's family?"

I reached for my drink.

"Her father was a doctor in northern Virginia, a real fine man," he said. "About six months after the trial, he came down with cancer and a couple months after that was dead. Robyn was the only child. The mother moves to Texas, gets in a car wreck, and spends her days in a wheelchair with nothing but memories. Waddell killed Robyn Naismith's entire family. He poisoned every life he touched."

I thought of Waddell growing up on the farm, images from his meditation drifting through my mind. I envisioned him sitting on porch steps, biting into a tomato that tasted like the sun. I wondered what had gone through his mind the last second of his life. I wondered if he had prayed.

Marino stubbed out a cigarette. He was thinking about leaving.

"Do you know a Detective Trent with Henrico?" I asked.

"Joe Trent. Used to be with K-Nine and got transferred into the detective division after he made sergeant a couple months ago. Sort of a nervous Nellie, but he's all right."

"He called me about a boy—"

He cut me off. "Eddie Heath?"

"I don't know his name."

"A white male about thirteen years old. We're working on it. Lucky's is in the city."

"Lucky's?"

"The convenience store where he was last seen. It's off Chamberlayne Avenue, Northside. What did Trent want?" Marino frowned. "He gotten word that Heath ain't going to pull through and is making an appointment with you in advance?"

"He wants me to look at unusual injuries, possible mutilation."

"Christ. I hate it when it's kids." Marino pushed back his chair and rubbed his temples. "Damn. Every time you get rid of one toad there's another to take his place."

After Marino left, I sat on the hearth in the living room watching coals shift in the fireplace. I was weary and felt a dull, implacable sadness that I did not have the strength to chase away. Mark's death had left a tear in my soul. I had come to realize, incredibly, just how much of my identity had been tied to my love for him.

The last time I saw him was on the day he flew to London, and we managed a quick lunch downtown before he headed to Dulles Airport. What I remembered most clearly about our last hour together was both of us glancing at our watches as storm clouds gathered and rain began to spit against the window beside our booth. He had a nick on his jaw from where he'd cut himself while shaving, and later, when I would see his face in my mind, I would envision that small injury and for some reason be undone by it.

He died in February while the war was ending in the Persian Gulf, and determined to put the pain behind me, I had sold my house and moved to a new neighborhood. What I accomplished was to uproot myself without really going anywhere, and the familiar plants and neighbors that once had given me comfort were gone. Redecorating my new home or redesigning the yard only added to my stress. Everything I did provided distractions for which I had no time, and I could imagine Mark shaking his head.

"For someone so logical . . ." he would smile and say.

"And what would you do?" I would tell him in my thoughts some nights when I could not sleep. "Just what the hell would *you* do if you were still here instead of me?"

Returning to the kitchen, I rinsed out my glass and went into my study to see what awaited me on my answering machine. Several reporters had called, so had my mother and Lucy, my niece. Three other messages were hang ups.

I would have loved an unlisted number but it was not possible. The police, Commonwealth's Attorneys, and the four hundred or so appointed medical examiners statewide had legitimate reasons to reach me after hours. To counter the loss of privacy, I used my answering machine to screen calls, and anyone who left threatening or obscene messages ran the risk of being tracked by Caller ID.

Pressing the review button on the ID box, I began scrolling through the numbers materializing on the narrow screen. When I found the three calls I was looking for, I was perplexed and unsettled. The number was curiously familiar by now. It had been appearing on my screen several times a week of late when the caller would hang up without leaving a message. Once, I had tried dialing the number back to see who answered and had gotten the high-pitched tone of what sounded like a fax machine or a computer modem. For whatever reason, this individual or thing had called my number three times between ten-twenty and eleven P.M., while I was at the morgue waiting for Waddell's body. That didn't make sense. Computerized telephone solicitations should not occur so frequently and at such a late hour, and if one modem trying to dial another was getting me instead, shouldn't someone have figured out by now that his computer was dialing a wrong number?

I woke up several times during the few hours left of the early morning. Every creak or shift of sound in the house made my pulse pick up. Red lights on the burglar alarm's control panel across from the bed glowed ominously, and when I turned or rearranged the covers, motion sensors I did not arm while I was home watched me silently with flashing red eyes. My dreams were strange. At five-thirty I turned on lamps and got dressed.

It was dark out and there was very little traffic as I drove to the office. The parking lot behind the bay was deserted and littered with dozens of small beeswax candles that brought to mind Moravian love feasts and other religious celebrations. But these candles had been used to protest. They had been used as weapons hours before. Upstairs, I fixed coffee and began going through the paperwork Fielding had left for me, curious about the contents of the envelope I'd found in Waddell's back pocket. I was expecting a poem, perhaps another meditation or a letter from his minister.

Instead, I discovered that what Waddell had considered "extremely confidential" and had wanted buried with him were cash register receipts. Inexplicably, five were for tolls; three others were for meals, including a fried chicken dinner ordered at a Shoney's two weeks earlier.

2

Detective Joe Trent would have looked quite youthful were it not for a beard and receding blond hair that was turning gray. He was trim and tall, a crisp trench coat belted tightly around his waist, his shoes perfectly shined. He blinked nervously as we shook hands and introduced ourselves on the sidewalk in front of Henrico Doctor's Emergency Center. I could tell he was upset by Eddie Heath's case.

"You don't mind if we talk out here a minute," he said, his breath turning white. "For privacy reasons."

Shivering, I tucked my elbows close to my sides as a Medflight helicopter made a terrific noise taking off from the helipad on a grassy rise not far from where we stood. The moon was a shaving of ice melting in the slate-gray sky, cars in the parking lots dirty from road salt and frigid winter rains. The early morning was stark and without color, the wind sharp like a slap, and I observed all this more keenly because of the nature of my business here. Had the temperature suddenly risen forty degrees and the sun begun to blaze I do not think I could have felt warm.

"What we got here is real bad, Dr. Scarpetta." He blinked. "I think you'll agree we don't want the details getting out."

"What can you tell me about this boy?" I asked.

"I've talked to his family and several other people who know him. As best I can ascertain, Eddie Heath is just your average kid—likes sports and has a paper route, has never gotten into any trouble with the police. His father works for the phone company and his mother sews for people out of the home. Apparently, last night, Mrs. Heath needed a can of cream of mushroom soup for a casserole she was fixing for dinner and asked Eddie to run over to the Lucky Convenience Store to get it."

"The store is how far from their house?" I asked.

"A couple of blocks, and Eddie's been there any number of times. The people working the counter know him by name."

"He was last seen at what time?"

"Around five-thirty P.M. He was in the store a few minutes and left."

"It would have been dark out," I said.

"Yes, it was." Trent stared off at the helicopter transfigured by distance into a white dragonfly softly thudding through clouds. "At approximately eight-thirty, an officer on routine patrol was checking the back of buildings along Patterson and saw the kid propped up against the Dumpster."

"Do you have photographs?"

"No, ma'am. When the officer realized the boy was alive, his first priority was getting help. We don't have pictures. But I've got a pretty detailed description based on the officer's observations. The boy was nude, and he was propped up, with his legs straight out and arms by his sides and head bent forward. His clothing was in a moderately neat pile on the pavement, along with a small bag containing a can of cream of mushroom soup and a Snickers bar. It was twenty-eight degrees out. We're thinking he may have been left there anywhere from minutes to half an hour before he was found."

An ambulance halted near us. Doors slammed and metal grated as attendants quickly lowered the legs of a stretcher to the ground and wheeled an old man through opening glass doors. We followed and in silence walked through a bright, antiseptic corridor busy with medical personnel and patients dazed by the misfortunes that had brought them here. As we rode the elevator up to the third floor, I wondered what trace evidence had been scrubbed away and tossed in the trash.

"What about his clothes? Was a bullet recovered?" I asked Trent as the elevator doors parted.

"I've got his clothes in my car and will drop them and his PERK off at the lab this afternoon. The bullet's still in his brain. They haven't gone in there yet. I hope like hell they swabbed him good."

The pediatric intensive care unit was at the end of a polished hallway, panes of glass in the double wooden doors covered with friendly dinosaur paper. Inside, rainbows decorated sky blue walls, and animal mobiles were suspended over hydraulic beds in the eight rooms arranged in a semicircle around the nurses' station. Three young women worked behind monitors, one of them typing on a keyboard and another talking on the phone. A slender brunette dressed in a red corduroy jumper and turtleneck sweater identified herself as the head nurse after Trent explained why we were here.

"The attending physician's not in yet," she apologized.

"We just need to look at Eddie's injuries. It won't take long," Trent said. "His family still in there?"

"They stayed with him all night."

We followed her through soft artificial light, past code carts and green tanks of oxygen that would not be parked outside the rooms of little boys and girls were the world the way it ought to be. When we reached Eddie's room, the nurse went inside and shut the door most of the way.

"Just for a few minutes," I overheard her say to the Heaths. "While we do the exam."

"What kind of specialist is it this time?" the father asked in an unsteady voice.

"A doctor who knows a lot about injuries. She's sort of like a police surgeon." The nurse diplomatically refrained from saying I was a medical examiner, or worse, a coroner.

After a pause, the father quietly said, "Oh. This is for evidence."

"Yes. How about some coffee? Maybe something to eat?"

Eddie Heath's parents emerged from the room, both of them considerably overweight, their clothes badly wrinkled from having been slept in. They had the bewildered look of innocent, simple people who have been told the world is about to end, and when they glanced at us with exhausted eyes I wished there were something I could say that would make it not so or at least a little better. Words of comfort died in my throat as the couple slowly walked off.

Eddie Heath did not stir on top of the bed, his head wrapped in bandages, a ventilator breathing air into his lungs while fluids dripped into his veins. His complexion was milky and hairless, the thin membrane of his eyelids a faint bruised blue in the low light. I surmised the color of his hair by his strawberry blond eyebrows. He had not yet emerged from that fragile prepubescent stage when boys are full-lipped and beautiful and sing more sweetly than their sisters. His forearms were slender, the body beneath the sheet small. Only the disproportionately large, still hands tethered by intravenous lines were true to his fledgling gender. He did not look thirteen.

"She needs to see the areas on his shoulder and leg," Trent told the nurse in a low voice.

She got two packets of gloves, one for her and one for me, and we put them on. The boy was naked beneath the sheet, his skin grimy in creases and fingernails dirty. Patients who are unstable cannot be thoroughly bathed.

Trent tensed as the nurse removed the wet-to-dry dressings from the wounds. "Christ," he said under his breath. "It looks even worse than it did last night. Jesus." He shook his head and backed up a step.

If someone had told me that the boy had been attacked by a shark, I might have gone along with it were it not for the neat edges of the wounds, which clearly had been inflicted by a sharp, linear instrument, such as a knife or razor. Sections of flesh the size of elbow patches had been excised from his right shoulder and right inner thigh. Opening my medical bag, I got out a ruler and measured the wounds without touching them, then took photographs.

"See the cuts and scratches at the edges?" Trend pointed. "That's what I was telling you about. It's like he cut some sort of pattern on the skin and then removed the whole thing."

"Did you find any anal tearing?" I asked the nurse.

"When I did a rectal temperature I didn't notice any tears, and no one noticed anything unusual about his mouth or throat when he was intubated. I also checked for old fractures and bruises."

"What about tattoos?"

"Tattoos?" she asked as if she'd never seen a tattoo.

"Tattoos, birthmarks, scars. Anything that someone may have removed for some reason," I said.

"I have no idea," the nurse said dubiously.

"I'll go ask his parents." Trent wiped sweat from his forehead.

"They may have gone to the cafeteria."

"I'll find them," he said as he passed through the doorway.

"What are his doctors saying?" I asked the nurse.

"He's very critical and unresponsive." She stated the obvious without emotion.

"May I see where the bullet went in?" I asked.

She loosened the edges of the bandage around his head and pushed the gauze up until I could see the tiny black hole, charred around the edges. The wound was through his right temple and slightly forward.

"Through the frontal lobe?" I asked.

"Yes."

"They've done an angio?"

"There's no circulation to the brain, due to the swelling. There's no electroencephalic activity, and when we put cold water in his ears there was no caloric activity. It evoked no brain potentials."

She stood on the other side of the bed, gloved hands by her sides and expression dispassionate as she continued to relate the various tests conducted and maneuvers instigated to decrease intracranial pressure. I had paid my dues in ERs and ICUs and knew very well that it is easier to be clinical with a patient who has never been awake. And Eddie Heath would never be awake. His cortex was gone. That which made him human, made him think and feel, was gone and was never coming back. He had been left with vital functions, left with a brain stem. He was a breathing body with a beating heart maintained at the moment by machines.

I began looking for defense injuries. Concentrating on getting out of the way of his lines, I was unaware I was holding his hand until he startled me by squeezing mine. Such reflex movements are not uncommon in people who are cortically dead. It is the equivalent of a baby grabbing your finger, a reflex involving no thought process at all. I gently released his hand and took a deep breath, waiting for the ache in my heart to subside.

"Did you find anything?" the nurse asked.

"It's hard to look with all these lines," I said.

She replaced his dressings and pulled the sheet up to his chin. I took off my gloves and dropped them in the trash as Detective Trent returned, his eyes a little wild.

"No tattoos," he said breathlessly, as if he had sprinted to the cafeteria and back. "No birthmarks or scars, either."

Moments later we were walking to the parking deck. The sun slipped in and out, and tiny snowflakes were blowing. I squinted as I stared into the wind at heavy traffic on Forest Avenue. A number of cars had Christmas wreaths affixed to their grilles.

"I think you'd better prepare for the eventuality of his death," I said.

"If I'd known that, I wouldn't have bothered you to come out. Damn, it's cold."

"You did exactly the right thing. In several days his wounds would have changed."

"They say all of December's going to be like this. Cold as hell and a lot of snow." He stared down at the pavement. "You have kids?"

"I have a niece," I said.

"I've got two boys. One of 'em's thirteen."

I got out my keys. "I'm over here," I said.

Trent nodded, following me. He watched in silence as I unlocked my gray Mercedes. His eyes took in the details of the leather interior as I got in and fastened my seat belt. He looked the car up and down as if appraising a gorgeous woman.

"What about the missing skin?" he asked. "You ever seen anything like that?"

"It's possible we're dealing with someone predisposed to cannibalism," I said.

I returned to the office and checked my mailbox, initialed a stack of lab reports, filled a mug with the liquid tar left in the bottom of the coffeepot, and spoke to no one. Rose appeared so quietly as I seated myself behind my desk that I would not have noticed her immediately had she not placed a newspaper clipping on top of several others centering the blotter.

"You look tired," she said. "What time did you come in this morning? I got here and found coffee made and you had already gone out somewhere."

"Henrico's got a tough one," I said. "A boy who probably will be coming in."

"Eddie Heath."

"Yes," I said, perplexed. "How did you know?"

"He's in the paper, too," Rose replied, and I noticed that she had gotten new glasses that made her patrician face less haughty.

"I like your glasses," I said. "A big improvement over the Ben Franklin frames perched on the end of your nose. What did it say about him?"

"Not much. The article just said that he was found off Patterson and that he had been shot. If my son were still young, no way I'd let him have a paper route."

"Eddie Heath was not delivering papers when he was assaulted."

"Doesn't matter. I wouldn't permit it, not these days. Let's see."

She touched a finger to the side of her nose. "Fielding's downstairs doing an autopsy and Susan's off delivering several brains to MCV for consultation. Other than that, nothing happened while you were out except the computer went down."

"Is it still down?"

"I think Margaret's working on it and is almost done," Rose said.

"Good. When it's up again, I need her to do a search for me. Codes to look for would be *cutting, mutilation, cannibalism, bite marks.* Maybe a free-format search for the words *excised, skin, flesh*—a variety of combinations of them. You might try *dismemberment,* too, but I don't think that's what we're really after."

"For what part of the state and what time period?" Rose took notes.

"All of the state for the past five years. I'm particularly interested in cases involving children, but let's not restrict ourselves to that. And ask her to see what the Trauma Registry's got. I spoke with the director at a meeting last month and he seemed more than willing for us to share data."

"You mean you also want to check victims who have survived?"

"If we can, Rose. Let's check everything to see if we find any cases similar to Eddie Heath's."

"I'll tell Margaret now and see if she can get started," my secretary said on her way out.

I began going through the articles she had clipped from a number of morning newspapers. Unsurprisingly, much was being made of Ronnie Waddell's allegedly bleeding from "his eyes, nose, and mouth." The local chapter of Amnesty International was claiming that his execution was no less inhumane that any homicide. A spokesman for the ACLU stated that the electric chair "may have malfunctioned, causing Waddell to suffer terribly," and went on to compare the incident to the execution in Florida in which synthetic sponges used for the first time had resulted in the condemned man's hair catching fire.

Tucking the news stories inside Waddell's file, I tried to anticipate what pugilistic rabbits his attorney, Nicholas Grueman, would pull out of his hat this time. Our confrontations, though infrequent, had become predictable. His true agenda, I was about to believe, was to impeach my professional competence and in general make me feel stupid. But what bothered me most was that Grueman gave no indication that he remembered I had once been his student at Georgetown. To his credit, I had despised my first year of law school, had made my only B, and missed out on *Law Review.* I would never forget Nicholas Grueman as long as I lived, and it did not seem right that he should have forgotten me.

I heard from him on Thursday, not long after I had been informed that Eddie Heath was dead.

"Kay Scarpetta?" Grueman's voice came over the line.

"Yes." I closed my eyes and knew from the pressure behind them that a raging front was rapidly advancing.

"Nicholas Grueman here. I've been looking over Mr. Waddell's provisional autopsy report and have a few questions."

I said nothing.

"I'm talking about Ronnie Joe Waddell."

"What can I help you with?"

"Let's start with his so-called *almost tubular* stomach. An interesting description, by the way. I'm wondering if that's your vernacular or a bona fide medical term? Am I correct in assuming Mr. Waddell wasn't eating?"

"I can't say that he wasn't eating at all. But his stomach had shrunk. It was empty and clean."

"Was it, perhaps, reported to you that he may have been on a hunger strike?"

"No such thing was reported to me." I glanced up at the clock and light stabbed my eyes. I was out of aspirin and had left my decongestant at home.

I heard pages flip.

"It says here that you found abrasions on his arms, the inner aspects of both upper arms," Grueman said.

"That's correct."

"And just what, exactly, is an *inner aspect?*"

"The inside of the arm above the antecubital fossa."

A pause. "The *antecubital fossa,*" he said in amazement. "Well, let me see. I've got my own arm turned palm up and am looking at the inside of my elbow. Or where the arm folds, actually. That would be accurate, wouldn't it? To say that the inner aspect is the side where the arm folds, and the antecubital fossa, therefore, is where the arm folds?"

"That would be accurate."

"Well, well, very good. And to what do you attribute these injuries to the inner aspects of Mr. Waddell's arms?"

"Possibly to restraints," I said testily.

"Restraints?"

"Yes, as in the leather restraints associated with the electric chair."

"You said *possibly.* Possibly restraints?"

"That's what I said."

"Meaning, you can't say with certainty, Dr. Scarpetta?"

"There's very little in this life that one can say with certainty, Mr. Grueman."

"Meaning that it would be reasonable to entertain the possibility that the restraints that caused the abrasions could have been of a different variety? Such as the human variety? Such as marks left by human hands?"

"The abrasions I found are inconsistent with injuries inflicted by human hands," I said.

"And are they consistent with the injuries inflicted by the electric chair, with the restraints associated with it?"

"It is my opinion that they would be."

"Your *opinion,* Dr. Scarpetta?"

"I haven't actually examined the electric chair," I said sharply.

This was followed by a long pause, for which Nicholas Grueman had been famous in the classroom when he wanted a student's obvious inadequacy to hang in the air. I envisioned him hovering over me, hands clasped behind his back, his face expressionless as the clock ticked loudly on the wall. Once I had endured his silent scrutiny for more than two minutes as my eyes raced blindly over pages of the casebook opened before me. And as I sat at my solid walnut desk some twenty years later, a middle-aged chief medical examiner with enough degrees and certificates to paper a wall, I felt my face begin to burn. I felt the old humiliation and rage.

Susan walked into my office as Grueman abruptly ended the encounter with "Good day" and hung up.

"Eddie Heath's body is here." Her surgical gown was untied in back and clean, the expression on her face distracted. "Can he wait until the morning?"

"No," I said. "He can't."

The boy looked smaller on the cold steel table than he had seemed in the bright sheets of his hospital bed. There were no rainbows in this room, no walls or windows decorated with dinosaurs or color to cheer the heart of a child. Eddie Heath had come in naked with IV needles, catheter, and dressings still in place. They seemed sad remnants of what had held him to this world and then disconnected him from it, like string tailing a balloon blowing forlornly through empty air. For the better part of an hour I documented injuries and marks of therapy while Susan took photographs and answered the phone.

We had locked the doors leading into the autopsy suite, and beyond I could hear people getting off the elevator and heading home in the rapidly descending dark. Twice the buzzer sounded in the bay as funeral home attendants arrived to bring a body or take one away. The wounds to Eddie's shoulder and thigh were dry and a dark shiny red.

"God," Susan said, staring. "God, who would do something like that? Look at all the little cuts to the edges, too. It's like somebody cut crisscrosses and then removed the whole area of skin."

"That's precisely what I think was done."

"You think someone carved some sort of pattern?"

"I think someone attempted to eradicate something. And when that didn't work, he removed the skin."

"Eradicate what?"

"Nothing that was already there," I said. "He had no tattoos, birthmarks, or scars in those areas. If something wasn't already there, then perhaps something was added and had to be removed because of the potential evidentiary value."

"Something like bite marks."

"Yes," I said.

The body was not yet fully rigorous and was still slightly warm as I began swabbing any area that a washcloth might have missed. I checked axillas, gluteal folds, behind ears and inside them, and inside the navel. I clipped fingernails into clean white envelopes and looked for fibers and other debris in hair.

Susan continued to glance at me, and I sensed her tension. Finally she asked, "Anything special you're looking for?"

"Dried seminal fluid, for one thing," I said.

"In his axilla?"

"There, in any crease in skin, any orifice, anywhere."

"You don't usually look in all those places."

"I don't usually look for zebras."

"For what?"

"We used to have a saying in medical school. If you hear hoof-beats, look for horses. But in a case like this I know we're looking for zebras," I said.

I began going over every inch of the body with a lens. When I got to his wrists, I slowly turned his hands this way and that, studying them for such a long time that Susan stopped what she was doing. I referred to the diagrams on my clipboard, correlating each mark of therapy with the ones I had drawn.

"Where are his charts?" I glanced around.

"Over here." Susan fetched paperwork from a countertop.

I began flipping through charts, concentrating particularly on emergency room records and the report filled in by the rescue squad. Nowhere did it indicate that Eddie Heath's hands had been bound. I tried to remember what Detective Trent had said to me when describing the scene where the boy's body had been found. Hadn't Trent said that Eddie's hands were by his sides?

"You find something?" Susan finally asked.

"You have to look through the lens to see. There. The undersides of his wrists and here on the left one, to the left of the wrist bone. You see the gummy residue? The traces of adhesive? It looks like smudges of grayish dirt."

"Just barely. And maybe some fibers sticking to it," Susan marveled, her shoulder pressed against mine as she stared through the lens.

"And the skin's smooth," I continued to point out. "Less hair in this area than here and here."

"Because when the tape was removed, hairs would have been pulled out."

"Exactly. We'll take wrist hairs for exemplars. The adhesive and fibers can be matched back to the tape, if the tape is ever recovered. And if the tape that bound him is recovered, it can be matched back to the roll."

"I don't understand." She straightened up and looked at me. "His IV lines were held in place with adhesive tape. You sure that's not the explanation?"

"There are no needle marks on these areas of his wrists that would indicate marks of therapy," I said to her. "And you saw what was taped to him when he came in. Nothing to account for the adhesive here."

"True."

"Let's take photographs and then I'm going to collect this adhesive residue and let Trace see what they find."

"His body was outside next to a Dumpster. Seems like that would be a Trace nightmare."

"It depends on whether this residue on his wrists was in contact with the pavement." I began gently scraping the residue off with a scalpel.

"I don't guess they did a vacuuming out there."

"No, I'm sure they wouldn't have. But I think we can still get sweepings if we ask nicely. It can't hurt to try."

I continued examining Eddie Heath's thin forearms and wrists, looking for contusions or abrasions I might have missed. But I did not find any.

"His ankles look okay," Susan said from the far end of the table. "I don't see any adhesive or areas where the hair is gone. No injuries. It doesn't look like he was taped around his ankles. Just his wrists."

I could recall only a few cases in which a victim's tight bindings had left no mark on skin. Clearly, the strapping tape had been in direct contact with Eddie's skin. He should have moved his hands, wriggled as his discomfort had grown and his circulation had been restricted. But he had not resisted. He had not tugged or squirmed or tried to get away.

I thought of the blood drips on the shoulder of his jacket and the soot and stippling on the collar. I again checked around his mouth, looked at his tongue, and glanced over his charts. If he had been gagged, there was no evidence of it now, no abrasions or bruises, no traces of adhesive. I imagined him propped against the Dumpster, naked and in the bitter cold, his clothing piled by his side, moderately neat, not sloppily, from the way it had been described to me.

When I tried to sense the emotion of the crime, I did not detect anger, panic, or fear.

"He shot him first, didn't he?" Susan's eyes were alert like those of a wary stranger you pass on a desolate, dark street. "Whoever did this taped his wrists together after he shot him."

"I'm thinking that."

"But that's so weird," she said. "You don't need to bind someone you've just shot in the head."

"We don't know what this individual fantasizes about." The sinus headache had arrived and I had fallen like a city under siege. My eyes were watering; my skull was two sizes too small.

Susan pulled the thick electrical cord down from its reel and plugged in the Stryker saw. She snapped new blades in scalpels and checked the knives on the surgical cart. She disappeared into the X-ray room and returned with Eddie's films, which she fixed to light boxes. She scurried about frenetically and then did something she had never done before. She bumped hard against the surgical cart she had been arranging and sent two quart jars of formalin crashing to the floor.

I ran to her as she jumped back, gasping, waving fumes from her face and sending broken glass skittering across the floor as her feet almost went out from under her.

"Did it get your face?" I grabbed her arm and hurried her toward the locker room.

"I don't think so. No. Oh, God. It's on my feet and legs. I think on my arm, too."

"You're sure it's not in your eyes or mouth?" I helped her strip off her greens.

"I'm sure."

I ducked inside the shower and turned on the water as she practically tore off the rest of her clothes.

I made her stand beneath a blast of tepid water for a very long time as I donned mask, safety glasses, and thick rubber gloves. I soaked up the hazardous chemical with formalin pillows, supplied by the state for biochemical emergencies like this. I swept up glass and tied everything inside double plastic bags. Then I hosed down the floor, washed myself, and changed into fresh greens. Susan eventually emerged from the shower, bright pink and scared.

"Dr. Scarpetta, I'm so sorry," she said.

"My only concern is you. Are you all right?"

"I feel weak and a little dizzy. I can still smell the fumes."

"I'll finish up here," I said. "Why don't you go home."

"I think I'll just rest for a while first. Maybe I'd better go upstairs."

My lab coat was draped over the back of a chair, and I reached inside a pocket and got out my keys. "Here," I said, handing them to her. "You can lie down on the couch in my office. Get on the intercom immediately if the dizziness doesn't go away or you start feeling worse."

She reappeared about an hour later, her winter coat on and buttoned up to her chin.

"How do you feel?" I asked as I sutured the Y incision.

"A little shaky but okay."

She watched me in silence for a moment, then added, "I thought of something while I was upstairs. I don't think you should list me as a witness in this case."

I glanced up at her in surprise. It was routine for anyone present during an autopsy to be listed as a witness on the official report. Susan's request wasn't of great importance, but it was peculiar.

"I didn't participate in the autopsy," she went on. "I mean, I helped with the external exam but wasn't present when you did the post. And I know this is going to be a big case—if they ever catch anyone. If it ever goes to court. And I just think it's better if I'm not listed, since, like I said, I really wasn't present."

"Fine," I said. "I have no problem with that."

She placed my keys on a counter and left.

* * *

Marino was home when I tried him from my car phone as I slowed at a tollbooth about an hour later.

"Do you know the warden at Spring Street?" I asked him.

"Frank Donahue. Where are you?"

"In my car."

"I thought so. Probably half the truckers in Virginia are listening to us on the their CBs."

"They won't hear much."

"I heard about the kid," he said. "You finished with him?"

"Yes. I'll call you from home. There's something you can do for me in the meantime. I need to look over a few things at the pen right away."

"The problem with looking over the pen is it looks back."

"That's why you're going with me," I said.

If nothing else, after two miserable semesters of my former professor's tutelage I had learned to be prepared. So it was on Saturday afternoon that Marino and I were en route to the state penitentiary. Skies were leaden, wind thrashing trees along the roadsides, the universe in a state of cold agitation, as if reflecting my mood.

"You want my private opinion," Marino said to me as we drove, "I think you're letting Grueman jerk you around."

"Not at all."

"Then why is it every time there's an execution and he's involved, you act jerked around?"

"And how would you handle the situation?"

He pushed in the cigarette lighter. "Same way you are. I'd take a damn look at death row and the chair, document everything, and then tell him he's full of shit. Or better yet, tell the press he's full of shit."

In this morning's paper Grueman was quoted as saying that Waddell had not been receiving proper nourishment and his body bore bruises I could not adequately explain.

"What's the deal, anyway?" Marino went on. "Was he defending these squirrels when you was in law school?"

"No. Several years ago he was asked to run Georgetown's Criminal Justice Clinic. That's when he began taking on death penalty cases pro bono."

"The guy must have a screw loose."

"He's very opposed to capital punishment and has managed to turn whoever he represents into a cause célèbre. Waddell in particular."

"Yo. Saint Nick, the patron saint of dirtbags. Ain't that sweet," Marino said. "Why don't you send him color photos of Eddie Heath and ask if he wants to talk to the boy's family? See how he feels about the pig who committed *that* crime."

"Nothing will change Grueman's opinions."

"He got kids? A wife? Anybody he cares about?"

"It doesn't make any difference, Marino. I don't guess you've got anything new on Eddie."

"No, and neither does Henrico. We've got his clothes and a twenty-two bullet. Maybe the labs will get lucky with the stuff you turned in."

"What about VICAP?" I asked, referring to the FBI's Violent Criminal Apprehension Program, in which Marino and FBI profiler Benton Wesley were regional team partners.

"Trent's working on the forms and will send them off in a couple days," Marino said. "And I alerted Benton about the case last night."

"Was Eddie the type to get into a stranger's car?"

"According to his parents, he wasn't. We're either dealing with a blitz attack or someone who earned the kid's confidence long enough to grab him."

"Does he have brothers and sisters?"

"One of each, both more than ten years older than him. I think Eddie was an accident," Marino said as the penitentiary came into view.

Years of neglect had faded its stucco veneer to a dirty, diluted shade of Pepto-Bismol pink. Windows were dark and covered in thick plastic, tugged and torn by the wind. We took the Belvedere exit, then turned left on Spring Street, a shabby strip of pavement connecting two entities that did not belong on the same map. It continued several blocks past the penitentiary, then simply quit at Gambles Hill, where Ethyl Corporation's white brick headquarters roosted on a rise of perfect lawn like a great white heron at the edge of a landfill.

Drizzle had turned to sleet when we parked and got out of the car. I followed Marino past a Dumpster, then a ramp leading to a loading dock occupied by a number of cats, their insouciance flickering with the wariness of the wild. The main entrance was a single glass door, and stepping inside what purported to be the lobby, we found ourselves behind bars. There were no chairs; the air was frigid and stale. To our right the Communication Center was accessible by a small window, which a sturdy woman in a guard's uniform took her time sliding open.

"Can I help you?"

Marino displayed his badge and laconically explained that we had an appointment with Frank Donahue, the warden. She told us to wait. The window shut again.

"That's Helen the Hun," Marino said to me. "I've been down here more times than I can count and she always acts like she don't know me. But then, I'm not her type. You'll get better acquainted with her in a minute."

Beyond barred gates were a dingy corridor of tan tile and cinder block, and small offices that looked like cages. The view ended with the first block of cells, tiers painted institutional green and spotted with rust. They were empty.

"When will the rest of the inmates be relocated?" I asked.

"By the end of the week."

"Who's left?"

"Some real Virginia gentlemen, the squirrels with segregation status. They're all locked up tight and chained to their beds in C Cell, which is that way." He pointed west. "We won't be walking through there, so don't get antsy. I wouldn't put you through that. Some of these assholes haven't seen a woman in years—and Helen the Hun don't count."

A powerfully built young man dressed in Department of Corrections blues appeared down the corridor and headed our way. He peered at us through bars, his face attractive but hard, with a strong jaw and cold gray eyes. A dark red mustache hid an upper lip that I suspected could turn cruel.

Marino introduced us, adding, "We're here to see the chair."

"Yeah, my name's Roberts and I'm here to give you the royal tour." Keys jingled against iron as he opened the heavy gates. "Donahue's out sick today." The clang of doors shutting behind us echoed off walls. "I'm afraid we got to search you first. If you'll step over there, ma'am."

He began running a scanner over Marino as another barred door opened and "Helen" emerged from the Communication Center. She was an unsmiling woman built like a Baptist church, her shiny Sam Browne belt the only indication she had a waist. Her close-cropped hair was mannishly styled and dyed shoe-polish black, her eyes intense when they briefly met mine. The name tag pinned on a formidable breast read "Grimes."

"Your bag," she ordered.

I handed over my medical bag. She rifled through it, then roughly turned me this way and that as she subjected me to a salvo of probes and pats with the scanner and her hands. In all, the search couldn't have lasted more than twenty seconds, but she managed to acquaint herself with every inch of my flesh, crushing me against her stiffly armored bosom like a wide-bodied spider as thick fingers lingered and she breathed loudly through her mouth. Then she brusquely nodded that I checked out okay as she returned to her lair of cinder block and iron.

Marino and I followed Roberts past bars and more bars, through a series of doors that he unlocked and relocked, the air cold and ringing with the dull chimes of unfriendly metal. He asked us nothing about ourselves and made no references that I would call remotely friendly. His preoccupation seemed to be his role, which this afternoon was tour guide or guard dog, I wasn't sure which.

A right turn and we entered the first cell block, a huge drafty space of green cinder block and broken windows, with four tiers of cells rising to a false roof topped by coils of barbed wire. Sloppily piled along the middle of the brown tile floor were dozens of narrow, plastic-covered mattresses, and scattered about were brooms, mops, and ratty red barber chairs. Leather tennis shoes, blue jeans, and other odd personal effects littered high windowsills, and left inside many of the cells were televisions, books, and footlockers. It appeared that when the inmates had been evacuated they had not been allowed to take all of their possessions with them, perhaps explaining the obscenities scrawled in Magic Marker on the walls.

More doors were unlocked, and we found ourselves outside in the yard, a square of browning grass surrounded by ugly cell blocks. There were no trees. Guard towers rose from each corner of the wall, the men inside wearing heavy coats and holding rifles. We moved quickly and in silence as sleet stung our cheeks. Down several steps, we turned into another opening leading to an iron door more massive than any of the others I had seen.

"The east basement," Roberts said, inserting a key in the lock. "This is the place where no one wants to be."

We stepped inside death row.

Against the east wall were five cells, each furnished with an iron bed and a white porcelain sink and toilet. In the center of the room were a large desk and several chairs where guards sat around the clock when death row was occupied.

"Waddell was in cell two." Roberts pointed. "According to the laws of the Commonwealth, an inmate must be transferred here fifteen days prior to his execution."

"Who had access to him while he was here?" Marino asked.

"Same people who always have access to death row. Legal representatives, the clergy, and members of the death team."

"The death team?" I asked.

"It's made up of Corrections officers and supervisors, the identities of which are confidential. The team becomes involved when an inmate is shipped here from Mecklenburg. They guard him, set up everything from beginning to end."

"Don't sound like a very pleasant assignment," Marino commented.

"It's not an assignment, it's a choice," Roberts replied with the machismo and inscrutability of coaches interviewed after the big game.

"It don't bother you?" Marino asked. "I mean, come on, I saw Waddell go to the chair. It's got to bother you."

"Doesn't bother me in the least. I go home afterward, drink a few beers, go to bed." He reached in the breast pocket of his uniform shirt and pulled out a pack of cigarettes.

"Now, according to Donahue, you want to know everything that happened. So I'm going to walk you through it." He sat on top of the desk, smoking. "On the day of it, December thirteenth, Waddell was allowed a two-hour contact visit with members of his immediate family, which in this case was his mother. We put him in waist chains, leg irons, and cuffs and led him over to the visitors' side around one P.M.

"At five P.M., he ate his last meal. His request was sirloin steak, salad, a baked potato, and pecan pie, which we had prepared for him at Bonanza Steak House. He didn't pick the restaurant. The inmates don't get to do that. And, as is the routine, there were two identical meals ordered. The inmate eats one, a member of the death team eats the other. And this is all to make sure some overly enthusiastic chef doesn't decide to speed up the inmate's journey to the Great Beyond by spicing the food with something extra like arsenic."

"Did Waddell eat his meal?" I asked, thinking about his empty stomach.

"He wasn't real hungry—asked us to save it for him to eat the next day."

"He must have thought Governor Norring was going to pardon him," Marino said.

"I don't know what he thought. I'm just reporting to you what Waddell said when he was served his meal. Afterward, at seven-thirty, personal property officers came to his cell to take an inventory of his property and ask him what he wanted done with it. We're talking about one wristwatch, one ring, various articles of clothing and mail, books, poetry. At eight P.M., he was taken from his cell. His head, face, and right ankle were shaved. He was weighed, showered, and dressed in the clothing he would wear to the chair. Then he was returned to his cell.

"At ten-forty-five, his death warrant was read to him, witnessed by the death team." Roberts got up from the desk. "Then he was led, without restraints, to the adjoining room."

"What was his demeanor at this point?" Marino asked as Roberts unlocked another door and opened it.

"Let's just say that his racial affiliation did not permit him to be white as a sheet. Otherwise, he would've been."

The room was smaller than I had imagined. About six feet from the back wall and centered on the shiny brown cement floor was the chair, a stark, rigid throne of dark polished oak. Thick leather straps were looped around the high slatted back, the two front legs, and the armrests.

"Waddell was seated and the first strap fastened was the chest strap," Roberts continued in the same indifferent tone. "Then the two arm straps, the belly strap, and the straps for the legs." He roughly plucked at each strap as he talked. "It took one minute to strap him in. His face was covered with the leather mask—and I'll show you that in a minute. The helmet was placed on his head, the leg piece attached to his right leg."

I got out my camera, a ruler, and photocopies of Waddell's body diagrams.

"At exactly two minutes past eleven, he received the first current—that's twenty-five hundred volts and six and a half amps. Two amps will kill you, by the way."

The injuries marked on Waddell's body diagrams correlated nicely with the construction of the chair and its restraints.

"The helmet attaches to this." Roberts pointed out a pipe running from the ceiling and ending with a copper wing nut directly over the chair.

I began taking photographs of the chair from every angle.

"And the leg piece attaches to this wing nut here."

The flashbulb going off gave me a strange sensation. I was getting jumpy.

"All this man was, was one big circuit breaker."

"When did he start to bleed?" I asked.

"The minute he was hit the first time, ma'am. And he didn't stop until it was completely over, then a curtain was drawn, blocking him from the view of the witnesses. Three members of the death team undid his shirt and the doc listened with his stethoscope and felt the carotid and pronounced him. Waddell was placed on a gurney and taken into the cooling room, which is where we're headed next."

"Your theory about the chair allegedly malfunctioning?" I said.

"Pure crap. Waddell was six-foot-four, weighed two hundred and fifty-nine pounds. He was cooking long before he sat in the chair, his blood pressure probably out of sight. After he was pronounced, because of the bleeding, the deputy director came over to take a look at him. His eyeballs hadn't popped out. His eardrums hadn't popped out. Waddell had a damn nosebleed, same thing people get when they strain too hard on the toilet."

I silently agreed with him. Waddell's nosebleed was due to the Valsalva maneuver, or an abrupt increase in intrathoracic pressure. Nicholas Grueman would not be pleased with the report I planned to send him.

"What tests had you run to make sure the chair was operating properly?" Marino asked.

"Same ones we always do. First, Virginia Power looks at the equipment and checks it out." He pointed to a large circuit box enclosed in gray steel doors in the wall behind the chair. "Inside this is twenty two-hundred-watt lightbulbs attached to plyboard for running tests. We test this during the week before the execution, three times the day of it, and then once more in front of the witnesses after they've assembled."

"Yeah, I remember that," Marino said, staring at the glass-enclosed witness booth no more than fifteen feet away. Inside were twelve black plastic chairs arranged in three neat rows.

"Everything worked like a charm," Roberts said.

"Has it always?" I asked.

"To my knowledge, yes, ma'am."

"And the switch, where is that?"

He directed my attention to a box on the wall to the right of the witness booth. "A key cuts the power on. But the button's in the control room. The warden or a designee turns the key and pushes the button. You want to see that?"

"I think I'd better."

It wasn't much to look at, just a small cubicle directly behind the back wall of the room housing the chair. Inside was a large G.E. box with various dials to raise and lower the voltage, which went as high as three thousand volts. Rows of small lights affirmed that everything was fine or warned that things were not.

"At Greensville, it will all be computerized," Roberts added.

Inside a wooden cupboard were the helmet, leg piece, and two thick cables, which, he explained as he held them up, "attach to the wing nuts above and to one side of the chair, and then to this wing nut on top of the helmet and the one here on the leg piece." He did this without effort, adding, "Just like hooking up a VCR."

The helmet and leg piece were copper riddled with holes, through which cotton string was woven to secure the sponge lining inside. The helmet was surprisingly light, a patina of green tarnish at the edges of the connecting plates. I could not imagine having such a thing placed on top of my head. The black leather mask was nothing more than a wide, crude belt that buckled behind the inmate's head, a small triangle cut in it for the nose. It could have been on display in the Tower of London and I would not have questioned its authenticity.

We passed a transformer with coils leading to the ceiling, and Roberts unlocked another door. We stepped inside another room.

"This is the cooling room," he said. "We wheeled Waddell in here and transferred him to this table."

It was steel, rust showing at the joints.

"We let him cool down for ten minutes, put sandbags on his leg. That's them right there."

The sandbags were stacked on the floor at the foot of the table.

"Ten pounds each. Call it a knee-jerk reaction, but the leg's severely bent. The sandbags straighten it out. And if the burns are bad, like Waddell's were, we dress them with gauze. All done, and we put Waddell back on the stretcher and carried him out the same way you came in. Only we didn't bother with the stairs. No point in anybody getting a hernia. We used the food elevator and carried him out the front door, and loaded him in the ambulance. Then we hauled him into your place, just like we always do after our children ride the Sparky."

Heavy doors slammed. Keys jangled. Locks clicked. Roberts

continued talking boisterously as he led us back to the lobby. I barely listened and Marino did not say a word. Sleet mixed with rain beaded grass and walls with ice. The sidewalk was wet, the cold penetrating. I felt queasy. I was desperate to take a long, hot shower and change my clothes.

"Lowlifes like Roberts are just one level above the inmates," Marino said as he started the car. "In fact, some of them aren't any better than the drones they lock up."

Moments later he stopped at a red light. Drops of water on the windshield shimmered like blood, were wiped away and replaced by a thousand more. Ice coated trees like glass.

"You got time for me to show you something?" Marino wiped condensation off the windshield with his coat sleeve.

"Depending on how important it is, I suppose I could make time." I hoped my obvious reluctance would inspire him to take me home instead.

"I want to retrace Eddie Heath's last steps for you." He flipped on the turn signal. "In particular, I think you need to see where his body was found."

The Heaths lived east of Chamberlayne Avenue, or on the wrong side of it, in Marino's words. Their small brick house was but several blocks from a Golden Skillet fried chicken restaurant and the convenience store where Eddie had walked to buy his mother a can of soup. Several cars, large and American, were parked in the Heaths' driveway, and smoke drifted out the chimney and disappeared in the smoky gray sky. Aluminum glinted dully as the front screen door opened and an old woman bundled in a black coat emerged, then paused to speak to someone inside. Clinging to the railing as if the afternoon threatened to pitch her overboard, she made her way down the steps, glancing blankly at the white Ford LTD cruising past.

Had we continued east for another two miles, we would have entered the war zone of the federal housing projects.

"This neighborhood used to be all white," Marino said. "I remember when I first came to Richmond this was a good area to live. Lots of decent, hardworking folks who kept their yards real nice and went to church on Sunday. Times change. Me, I wouldn't let any kid of mine walk around out here after dark. But when you live in a place, you get comfortable. Eddie was comfortable walking around, delivering his papers, and running errands for his mother.

"The night it happened he came out the front door of his crib, cut through to Azalea, then took a right like we're doing as I speak. There's Lucky's on our left, next to the gas station." He pointed out a convenience store with a green horseshoe on the lighted sign. "That corner right over there is a popular hangout for drug drones. They trade crack for cash and fade. We catch the cockroaches, and two days later they're on another corner doing the same thing."

"A possibility Eddie was involved in drugs?" My question would have been somewhat farfetched back in the days when I began my career, but no longer. Juveniles now comprised approximately ten percent of all narcotics trafficking arrests in Virginia.

"No indication of it so far. My gut tells me he wasn't," Marino said.

He pulled into the convenience store's parking lot, and we sat gazing out at advertisements taped to plate glass and lights shining garishly through fog. Customers formed a long line by the counter as the harried clerk worked the cash register without looking up. A young black man in high tops and a leather coat stared insolently at our car as he sauntered out with a quart of beer and dropped change in a pay phone near the front door. A man, red-faced and in paint-spattered jeans, peeled cellophane off a pack of cigarettes as he trotted to his truck.

"I'm betting this is where he met up with his assailant," Marino said.

"How?" I said.

"I think it went down simple as hell. I think he came out of the store and this animal came right up to him and fed him a line to gain his confidence. He said something and Eddie went with him and got in the car."

"His physical findings would certainly support that," I said. "He had no defense injuries, nothing to indicate a struggle. No one inside the convenience store saw him with anyone?"

"No one I've talked to so far. But you see how busy this joint is, and it was dark out. If anybody saw anything, it was probably a customer coming in or returning to his car. I plan to get the media to run something so we can appeal to anyone who might have stopped here between five and six that night. And Crime Stoppers is going to do a segment on it, too."

"Was Eddie streetwise?"

"You get a squirrel who's smooth and even kids who know better can fall for it. I had a case back in New York where a ten-year-old girl walked to the local store to buy a pound of sugar. As she's leaving, this pedophile approaches her and says her father's sent him. He says her mom's just been rushed to the hospital and he's supposed to pick the girl up and take her there. She gets in his car and ends up a statistic." He glanced over at me. "All right, white or black?"

"In which case?"

"Eddie Heath's."

"Based on what you've said, the assailant is white."

Marino backed up and waited for a break in traffic. "No question the MO fits for white. Eddie's old man don't like blacks and Eddie didn't trust them, either, so it's unlikely a black guy gained Eddie's confidence. And if people notice a white boy walking with a white man—even if the boy looks unhappy—they think big brother and little brother or father and son." He turned right, heading west. "Keep going, Doc. What else?"

Marino loved this game. It gave him just as much pleasure when I echoed his thoughts as it did when he believed I was flat-out wrong.

"If the assailant is white, then the next conclusion I'd make is he's not from the projects, despite their close proximity."

"Race aside, why else might you conclude that the perp's not from the projects?"

"The MO again," I said simply. "Shooting someone in the head—even a thirteen-year-old—would not be unheard of in a street killing, but aside from that, nothing fits. Eddie was shot with a twenty-two, not with a nine- or ten-millimeter or large-caliber revolver. He was nude and he was mutilated, suggesting the violence was sexually motivated. As far as we know, he had nothing worth stealing and did not appear to have a lifestyle that put him at risk."

It was raining hard now, and streets were treacherous with cars moving at imprudent rates of speed with their headlights on. I supposed many people were headed to shopping malls, and it occurred to me that I had done little to prepare for Christmas.

The grocery store on Patterson Avenue was just ahead on our left. I could not remember its former name, and signs had been removed, leaving nothing but a bare brick shell with a number of windows boarded up. The space it occupied was poorly lit, and I suspected the police would not have bothered to check behind the building at all were there not a row of businesses to the left of it. I counted five of them: pharmacy, shoe repair, dry cleaner, hardware store, and Italian restaurant, all closed and deserted the night Eddie Heath was driven here and left for dead.

"Do you recall when this grocery store went out of business?" I asked.

"About the same time a bunch of other places did. When the war started in the Persian Gulf," Marino said.

He cut through an alleyway, the high beams of his headlights licking brick walls and rocking when the unpaved ground got rough. Behind the store a chain-link fence separated an apron of cracked asphalt from a wooded area stirring darkly in the wind. Through the limbs of bare trees I could see streetlights in the distance and the illuminated sign for a Burger King.

Marino parked, headlights boring into a brown Dumpster cancerous with blistered paint and rust, beads of water running down its sides. Raindrops smacked against glass and drummed the roof, and dispatchers were busy dispatching cars to the scenes of accidents.

Marino pushed his hands against the steering wheel and hunched his shoulders. He massaged the back of his neck. "Christ, I'm getting old," he complained. "I got a rain slicker in the trunk."

"You need it more than I do. I won't melt," I said, opening my door.

Marino fetched his navy blue police raincoat and I turned my collar up to my ears. The rain stung my face and coldly tapped the top of my head. Almost instantly, my ears started getting numb. The Dumpster was near the fence, at the outer limits of the pavement, perhaps twenty yards from the back of the grocery store. I noted that the Dumpster opened from the top, not the side.

"Was the door to the Dumpster open or shut when the police got here?" I asked Marino.

"Shut." The hood of his raincoat made it difficult for him to look at me without turning his upper body. "You notice there's nothing to step up on." He shone a flashlight around the Dumpster. "Also, it was empty. Not a damn thing in it except rust and the carcass of a rat big enough to saddle up and ride."

"Can you lift the door?"

"Only a couple inches. Most of the ones made like this have a latch on either side. If you're tall enough, you can lift the lid a couple inches and slide your hand down along the edge, continuing to raise the lid by bumping the latches in place a little at a time. Eventually you can get it open far enough to stuff a bag of trash inside. Problem is, the latches on this one don't catch. You'd have to open the lid all the way and let it flop over on the other side, and no way you're going to do that unless you climb up on something."

"You're what? Six-one or -two?"

"Yeah. If I can't open the Dumpster, he couldn't either. The favorite theory at the moment is he carried the body out of the car and leaned it up against the Dumpster while he tried to open the door—the same way you put a bag of garbage down for a minute to free your hands. When he can't get the door open, he hauls ass, leaving the kid and his crap right here on the pavement."

"He could have dragged him back there in the woods."

"There's a fence."

"It's not very high, maybe five feet high," I pointed out. "At the very least, he could have left the body *behind* the Dumpster. As it was, if you drove back here, the body was in plain sight."

Marino looked around in silence, shining the flashlight through the chain-link fence. Raindrops streaked through the narrow beam like a million small nails driven down from heaven. I could barely bend my fingers. My hair was soaked and icy water was trickling down my neck. We returned to the car and he switched the heater up high.

"Trent and his guys are all hung up on the Dumpster theory, the location of its door and so on," he said. "My personal opinion is the Dumpster's only role in this is it was a damn easel for the squirrel to prop his work of art against."

I looked out through the rain.

"The point is," he went on in a hard voice, "he didn't bring the kid back here to conceal the body but to make sure it was found. But the guys with Henrico just don't see it. I not only see it, I feel it like something breathing down the back of my neck."

I continued staring out at the Dumpster, the image of Eddie Heath's small body propped against it so vivid it was as if I had been present when he was found. The realization struck me suddenly and hard.

"When was the last time you went through the Robyn Naismith case?" I asked.

"It doesn't matter. I remember everything about it," Marino said, staring straight ahead. "I was waiting to see if it would cross your mind. It hit me the first time I came out here."

3

That night I built a fire and ate vegetable soup in front of it as freezing rain mixed with snow. I had switched off lamps and drawn draperies back from the sliding glass doors. Grass was frosted white, rhododendron leaves curled tight, winter-bare trees backlit by the moon.

The day had drained me, as if a greedy, dark force had sucked the light right out of my being. I felt the invasive hands of a prison guard named Helen, and smelled the stale stench of hovels that once had housed remorseless, hateful men. I remembered holding slides up to lamplight in a hotel bar in New Orleans at the American Academy of Forensic Sciences' annual meeting. Robyn Naismith's homicide was then unsolved, and to discuss what had been done to her as Mardi Gras revelers loudly drifted past had somehow seemed ghastly.

She had been beaten and bullied, and stabbed to death, it was believed, in her living room. But it was Waddell's postmortem acts that had shocked people most, his uncommon and creepy ritual. After she was dead, he undressed her. If he raped her, there was no evidence of it. His preference, it seemed, was to bite and repeatedly penetrate the fleshier parts of her body with a knife. When her friend from work stopped by to check on her, she found Robyn's battered body propped against the television, head drooping forward, arms by her sides, legs straight out, and clothing piled nearby. She looked like a bloody, life-size doll returned to its place after a session of make-believe and play that had turned into a horror.

The court testimony of a psychiatrist was that after Waddell had murdered her, he was overcome by remorse and had sat talking to her body for perhaps hours. A forensic psychologist for the Commonwealth speculated quite the opposite, that Waddell knew Robyn was a television personality and his act of propping her body against the television set was symbolic. He was watching her on TV again and fantasizing. He was returning her to the medium that had brought about their introduction, and this, of course, implied premeditation. The nuances and twists in the endless analyses got only more complicated with time.

The grotesque display of that twenty-seven-year-old anchorwoman's body was Waddell's special signature. Now a little boy was dead ten years later and someone had signed his work—on the eve of Waddell's execution—the same way.

I made coffee, poured it into a thermos, and carried it into my study. Sitting at my desk, I booted up my computer and dialed into the one downtown. I had yet to see the printout of the search Margaret had conducted for me, though I suspected it was one of the reports in the depressingly large stack of paperwork that had been in my box late Friday afternoon. The output file, however, would still be on the hard disk. At the UNIX log-in I typed my user name and password and was greeted by the flashing word *mail*. Margaret, my computer analyst, had sent me a message.

"Check flesh file," it read.

"That's really awful," I muttered, as if Margaret could hear.

Changing to the directory called Chief, where Margaret routinely directed output and copied files I had requested, I brought up the file she had named Flesh.

It was quite large because Margaret had selected from all manners of death and then merged the data with what she had generated from the Trauma Registry. Unsurprisingly, most of the cases the computer had picked up were accidents in which limbs and tissue had been lost in vehicular crashes and misadventures with machines. Four cases were homicides in which the bodies bore bite marks. Two of those victims had been stabbed, the other two strangled. One of the victims was an adult male, two were adult females, and one was a female only six years old. I jotted down case numbers and ICD-9 codes.

Next I began scanning screen after screen of the Trauma Registry's records of victims who had survived long enough to be admitted to a hospital. I expected the information to be a problem, and it was. Hospitals released patient data only after it had been as sterilized and depersonalized as operating rooms. For purposes of confidentiality, names, Social Security numbers, and other identifiers were stripped away. There was no common link as the person traveled through the paperwork labyrinth of rescue squads, emergency rooms, various police departments, and other agencies. The sorry end of the story was that data about a victim might reside in six different agency data bases and never be matched, especially if there had been any entry errors along the way. It was possible, therefore, for me to discover a case that aroused my interest without having much hope of figuring out who the patient was or if he or she had eventually died.

Making a note of Trauma Registry records that might prove interesting, I exited the file. Finally, I ran a list command to see what old data reports, memos, or notes in my directory I could remove to free up space on the hard disk. That was when I spotted a file I did not understand.

The name of it was tty07. It was only sixteen bytes in size and the date and time were December 16, this past Thursday, at 4:26 in the afternoon. The file's contents was one alarming sentence:

I can't find it.

Reaching for the phone, I started to call Margaret at home and then stopped. The directory Chief and its files were secure. Though anyone could change to my directory, unless he logged in with my user name and password, he should not be able to list the files in Chief or read them. Margaret should be the only person besides me who knew my password. If she had gone into my directory, what was it she could not find and who was she saying this to?

Margaret wouldn't, I thought, staring intensely at that one brief sentence on the screen.

Yet I was unsure, and I thought of my niece. Perhaps Lucy knew UNIX. I glanced at my watch. It was past eight on a Saturday night and in a way I was going to be heartbroken if I found Lucy at home. She should be out on a date or with friends. She wasn't.

"Hi, Aunt Kay." She sounded surprised, reminding me that I had not called in a while.

"How's my favorite niece?"

"I'm your only niece. I'm fine."

"What are you doing at home on a Saturday night?" I asked.

"Finishing a term paper. What are you doing at home on a Saturday night?"

For an instant, I did not know what to say. My seventeen-year-old niece was more adept at putting me in my place than anyone I knew.

"I'm mulling over a computer problem," I finally said.

"Then you've certainly called the right department," said Lucy, who was not given to fits of modesty. "Hold on. Let me move these books and stuff out of the way so I can get to my keyboard."

"It's not a PC problem," I said. "I don't guess you know anything about the operating system called UNIX, do you?"

"I wouldn't call UNIX an operating system, Aunt Kay. It's like calling it the weather when it's really the environment, which is comprised of the weather and all the elements and the edifices. Are you using A-T an' T?"

"Good God, Lucy. I don't know."

"Well, what are you running it on?"

"An NCR mini."

"Then it's A-T an' T."

"I think someone might have broken security," I said.

"It happens. But what makes you think it?"

"I found a strange file in my directory, Lucy. My directory and its files are secure—you shouldn't be able to read anything unless you have my password."

"Wrong. If you have root privileges, you're the superuser and can do anything you want and read anything you want."

"My computer analyst is the only superuser."

"That may be true. But there may be a number of users who have root privileges, users you don't even know about that came with the software. We can check that easily, but first tell me about the strange file. What's it called and what's in it?"

"It's called t-t-y-oh-seven and there's a sentence in it that reads: 'I can't find it.'"

I heard keys clicking.

"What are you doing?" I asked.

"Making notes as we talk. Okay. Let's start with the obvious. A big clue is the file's name, t-t-y-oh-seven. That's a device. In other words, t-t-y-oh-seven is probably somebody's terminal in your office. It's possible it could be a printer, but my guess is that whoever was in your directory decided to send a note to the device called t-t-y-oh-seven. But this person screwed up and instead of sending a note, he created a file."

"When you write a note, aren't you creating a file?" I puzzled.

"Not if you're just sending keystrokes."

"How?"

"Easy. Are you in UNIX now?"

"Yes."

"Type cat redirect t-t-y-q—"

"Wait a minute."

"And don't worry about the slash-dev—"

"Lucy, slow down."

"We're deliberately leaving out the dev directory, which is what I'm betting this person did."

"What comes after cat?"

"Okay. Cat redirect and the device—"

"Please slow down."

"You should have a four-eighty-six chip in that thing, Aunt Kay. Why's it so slow?"

"It's not the damn chip that's slow!"

"Oh, I'm sorry," Lucy said sincerely. "I forgot."

Forgot what?

"Back to the problem," she went on. "I'm assuming you don't have a device called t-t-y-q, by the way. Where are you?"

"I'm still on cat," I said, frustrated. "Then it's redirect . . . Damn. That's the caret pointing right?"

"Yes. Now hit return and your cursor will be bumped down to the next line, which is blank. Then you type the message you want echoed to t-t-y-q's screen."

"See Spot run," I typed.

"Hit return and then do a control C," Lucy said. "Now you can do an ls minus one and pipe it to p-g and you'll see your file."

I simply typed "ls" and caught a flash of something flying by.

"Here's what I think happened," Lucy resumed. "Someone was in your directory—and we'll get to that in a minute. Maybe they were looking for something in your files and couldn't find whatever it was. So this person sent a message, or tried to, to the device called t-t-y-oh-seven. Only he was in a hurry, and instead of typing cat redirect slash d-e-v slash t-t-y-oh-seven, he left out the dev directory and typed cat redirect t-t-y-oh-seven. So the keystrokes weren't echoed on t-t-y-oh-seven's screen at all. In other words, instead of sending a message to t-t-y-oh-seven, this person unwittingly created a file called t-t-y-oh-seven."

"If the person had typed in the proper command and sent the keystrokes, would the message have been saved?" I asked.

"No. The keystrokes would have appeared on t-t-y-oh-seven's screen, and would have stayed there until the user cleared it. But you would have seen no evidence of this in your directory or anywhere else. There wouldn't be a file."

"Meaning, we don't know how many times somebody might have sent a message from my directory, saying it was done correctly."

"That's right."

"How could someone have been able to read anything in my directory?" I went back to that basic question.

"You're sure no one else might have your password?"

"No one but Margaret."

"She's your computer analyst?"

"That's right."

"She wouldn't have given it to anyone?"

"I can't imagine that she would," I said.

"Okay. You could get in without the password if you have root privileges," Lucy said. "That's the next thing we'll check. Change to the etc directory and vi the file called Group and look for root group—that's r-o-o-t-g-r-p. See which users are listed after it."

I began to type.

"What do you see?"

"I'm not there yet," I said, unable to keep the impatience out of my voice.

She repeated her instructions slowly.

"I see three log-in names in the root group," I said.

"Good. Write them down. Then colon, q, bang, and you're out of Group."

"Bang?" I asked, mystified.

"An exclamation point. Now you've got to vi the password file—that's p-a-s-s-w-d—and see if any of those log-ins with root privileges maybe don't have a password."

"Lucy." I took my hands off the keyboard.

"It's easy to tell because in the second field you'll see the encrypted form of the user's password, if he has a password. If there's nothing in the second field except two colons, then he's got no password."

"Lucy."

"I'm sorry, Aunt Kay. Am I going too fast again?"

"I'm not a UNIX programmer. You might as well be speaking Swahili."

"You could learn. UNIX is really fun."

"Thank you, but my problem is I don't have time to learn right now. Someone broke into my directory. I keep very confidential documents and data reports in there. Not to mention, if someone is reading my private files, what else is he looking at and who is doing it and why?"

"The who part is easy unless the violator is dialing in by modem from the outside."

"But the note was sent to someone in my office—to a device in my office."

"That doesn't mean that an insider didn't get someone from the outside to break in, Aunt Kay. Maybe the person snooping doesn't know anything about UNIX and needed help to break into your directory, so they got a programmer from the outside."

"This is serious," I said.

"It could be. If nothing else, it sounds to me like your system isn't very secure."

"When's your term paper due?" I asked.

"After the holidays."

"Are you finished?"

"Almost."

"When does Christmas vacation start?"

"It starts Monday."

"How would you like to come up here for a few days and help me out with this?" I asked.

"You're kidding."

"I'm very serious. But don't expect much. I generally don't

bother with much in the way of decorations. A few poinsettias and candles in the windows. Now, I *will* cook."

"No tree?"

"Is that a problem?"

"I guess not. Is it snowing?"

"As a matter of fact, it is."

"I've never seen snow. Not in person."

"You'd better let me talk to your mother," I said.

Dorothy, my only sibling, was overly solicitous when she got on the phone several minutes later.

"Are you still working so hard? Kay, you work harder than anyone I've ever met. People are so impressed when I tell them we're sisters. What's the weather like in Richmond?"

"There's a good chance we'll have a white Christmas."

"How special. Lucy ought to see a white Christmas at least once in her life. I've never seen one. Well, I take that back. There was the Christmas I went skiing out west with Bradley."

I could not remember who Bradley was. My younger sister's boyfriends and husbands were an endless parade I had stopped watching years ago.

"I'd very much like Lucy to spend Christmas with me," I said. "Would that be possible?"

"You can't come to Miami?"

"No, Dorothy. Not this year. I'm in the middle of several very difficult cases and have court scheduled virtually up to Christmas Eve."

"I can't imagine a Christmas without Lucy," she said with great reluctance.

"You've had Christmas without her before. When you went skiing out west with Bradley, for example."

"True. But it was hard," she said, nonplussed. "And every time we've spent a holiday apart, I've vowed to never do it again."

"I understand. Maybe another time," I said, sick to death of my sister's games. I knew she couldn't get Lucy out the door fast enough.

"Actually, I'm on deadline for this newest book and will be spending most of the holiday in front of my computer anyway," she reconsidered quickly. "Maybe Lucy would be better off with you. I won't be much fun. Did I tell you that I now have a Hollywood agent? He's fantastic and knows everybody who's somebody out there. He's negotiating a contract with Disney."

"That's great. I'm sure your books will make terrific movies." Dorothy wrote excellent children's books and had won several prestigious awards. She was simply a failure as a human being.

"Mother's here," my sister said. "She wants to have a word with you. Now listen, it was so good to talk to you. We just don't do it enough. Make sure Lucy eats something besides salads, and I warn you that she'll exercise until it drives you mad. I worry that she's going to start looking masculine."

Before I could say anything, my mother was on the line.

"Why can't you come down here, Katie? It's sunny and you should see the grapefruit."

"I can't do it, Mother. I'm really sorry."

"And now Lucy won't be here, either? Is that what I heard? What am I supposed to do, eat a turkey by myself?"

"Dorothy will be there."

"What? Are you kidding? She'll be with Fred. I can't stand him."

Dorothy had gotten divorced again last summer. I didn't ask who Fred was.

"I think he's Iranian or something. He'll squeeze a penny until it screams and has hair in his ears. I know he's not Catholic, and Dorothy never takes Lucy to church these days. You ask me, that child's going to hell in a hand basket."

"Mother, they can hear you."

"No they can't. I'm in the kitchen by myself staring at a sink full of dirty dishes that I just know Dorothy expects me to do while I'm here. It's just like when she comes to my house, because she hasn't done a thing about dinner and is hoping I'll cook. Does she ever offer to bring anything? Does she care that I'm an old woman and practically a cripple? Maybe you can talk some sense into Lucy."

"In what way is Lucy lacking sense?" I asked.

"She doesn't have any friends except this one girl you have to wonder about. You should see Lucy's bedroom. It looks like something out of a science fiction movie with all these computers and printers and pieces and parts. It's not normal for a teenage girl to live inside her brain all the time like that and not get out with kids her own age. I worry about her just like I used to worry about you."

"I turned out all right," I said.

"Well, you spent far too much time with science books, Katie. You saw what it did to your marriage."

"Mother, I'd like Lucy to fly here tomorrow, if possible. I'll make the reservations from my end and take care of the ticket. Make sure she packs her warmest clothes. Anything she doesn't have, such as a winter coat, we can find here."

"She could probably borrow your clothes. When was the last time you saw her? Last Christmas?"

"I guess it was that long ago."

"Well, let me tell you. She's gotten bosoms since then. And the way she dresses? And did she bother to ask her grandmother's advice before cutting off her beautiful hair? No. Why should she bother telling me that—"

"I've got to call the airlines."

"I wish you were coming here. We could all to be together." Her voice was getting funny. My mother was about to cry.

"I wish I could, too," I said.

Late Sunday morning I drove to the airport along dark, wet roads running through a dazzling world of glass. Ice loosened by the sun slipped from telephone lines, roofs, and trees, shattering to the ground like crystal missiles dropped from the sky. The weather report called for another storm, and I was deeply pleased, despite the inconvenience. I wanted quiet time in front of the fire with my niece. Lucy was growing up.

It did not seem so long ago that she was born. I would never forget her wide, unblinking eyes following my every move in her mother's house, or her bewildering fits of petulance and grief when I failed her in some small way. Lucy's open adoration touched my heart as profoundly as it frightened me. She had caused me to experience a depth of feeling I had not known before.

Talking my way past Security, I waited at the gate, eagerly searching passengers emerging from the boarding bridge. I was looking for a pudgy teenager with long, dark red hair and braces when a striking young woman met my eyes and grinned.

"Lucy," I exclaimed, hugging her. "My God. I almost didn't recognize you."

Her hair was short and deliberately messy, accentuating clear green eyes and good bones I did not know she had. There was not so much as a hint of metal in her mouth, and her thick glasses had been replaced by weightless tortoise-shell frames that gave her the look of a seriously pretty Harvard scholar. But it was the change in her body that astonished me most, for since I had seen her last she had been transformed from a chunky adolescent into a lean, leggy athlete dressed in snug, faded jeans several inches too short, a white blouse, a woven red leather belt, loafers, and no socks. She carried a book satchel, and I caught the sparkle of a delicate gold ankle bracelet. I was fairly certain she was wearing neither makeup nor bra.

"Where's your coat?" I asked as we headed to Baggage.

"It was eighty degrees when I left Miami this morning."

"You'll freeze walking out to the car."

"It's physically impossible for me to freeze while walking to your car unless you're parked in Chicago."

"Perhaps you have a sweater in your suitcase?"

"You ever notice that you talk to me the same way Grans talks to you? By the way, she thinks I look like a 'pet rocker.' That's her malapropism for the month. It's what you get when you cross a pet rock with a punk rocker."

"I've got a couple of ski jackets, corduroys, hats, gloves. You can borrow anything you wish."

She slipped her arm in mine and sniffed my hair. "You're still not smoking."

"I'm still not smoking and I hate being reminded that I'm still not smoking because then I think about smoking."

"You look better and don't stink like cigarettes. And you haven't gotten fat. Geez, this is a dinky airport," said Lucy, whose computer brain had formatting errors in the diplomacy sectors. "Why do they call it Richmond *International*?"

"Because it has flights to Miami."

"Why doesn't Grans ever come see you?"

"She doesn't like to travel and refuses to fly."

"It's safer than driving. Her hip is really getting bad, Aunt Kay."

"I know. I'm going to leave you to get your bags so I can pull the car in front," I said when we got to Baggage. "But first let's see which carousel it is."

"There are only three carousels. I bet I can figure it out."

I left her for the bright, cold air, grateful for a moment alone to think. The changes in my niece had thrown me off guard and I was suddenly more unsure than ever how to treat her. Lucy had never been easy. From day one she had been a prodigious adult intellect ruled by infantile emotions, a volatility accidentally given form when her mother had married Armando. My only advantage had been size and age. Now Lucy was as tall as I was and spoke with the low, calm voice of an equal. She was not going to run to her room and slam the door. She would no longer end a disagreement by screaming that she hated me or was glad I was not her mother. I imagined moods I could not anticipate and arguments I could not win. I had visions of her coolly leaving the house and driving off in my car.

We talked little during the drive, for Lucy seemed fascinated by the winter weather. The world was melting like an ice sculpture as another cold front appeared on the horizon in an ominous band of gray. When we turned into the neighborhood where I had moved since she had visited last, she stared out at expensive homes and lawns, at colonial Christmas decorations and brick sidewalks. A man dressed like an Eskimo was out walking his old, overweight dog, and a black Jaguar gray with road salt sprayed water as it slowly floated past.

"It's Sunday. Where are the children, or aren't there any?" Lucy said as if the observation incriminated me in some way.

"There are a few." I turned on my street.

"No bikes in the yards, no sleds or tree houses. Doesn't anybody ever go outside?"

"This is a very quiet neighborhood."

"Is that why you chose it?"

"In part. It's also quite safe, and hopefully buying a home here will prove to be a good investment."

"Private security?"

"Yes," I said as my uneasiness grew.

She continued staring out at the large homes flowing past. "I bet you can go inside and shut the door and never hear from anyone—never see anyone outside, either, unless they're walking their dog. But you don't have a dog. How many trick-or-treaters did you have on Halloween?"

"Halloween was quiet," I said evasively.

In truth, my doorbell had rung only once, when I was working in my study. I could see in my video monitor the four trick-or-treaters on my porch, and picking up the handset, I started to tell them that I would be right there when I overheard what they were saying to each other.

"No, there isn't a dead body in there," whispered the tiny UVA cheerleader.

"Yes, there is," said Spiderman. "She's on TV all the time because she cuts dead people up and puts them in jars. Dad told me."

I parked inside the garage and said to Lucy, "We'll get you settled in your room and the first order of business after that is for me to build a fire and make a pot of hot chocolate. Then we'll think about lunch."

"I don't drink hot chocolate. Do you have an espresso maker?"

"Indeed I do."

"That would be perfect, especially if you have decaf French roast. Do you know your neighbors?"

"I know who they are. Here, let me get that bag and you take this one so I can unlock the door and deactivate the alarm. Lord, this is heavy."

"Grans insisted I bring grapefruit. They're pretty good but full of seeds." Lucy looked around as she stepped inside my house. "Wow. Skylights. What do you call this style of architecture, besides rich?"

Maybe her disposition would self-correct if I pretended not to notice.

"The guest bedroom is back this way," I said. "I could put you upstairs if you wish, but I thought you'd rather be down here near me."

"Down here is fine. As long as I'm close to the computer."

"It's in my study, which is next door to your room."

"I brought my UNIX notes, books, and a few other things." She paused in front of the sliding glass doors in the living room. "The yard's not as nice as your other one." She said this as if I had let down everyone I had ever known.

"I've got plenty of years to work on my yard. It gives me something to look forward to."

Lucy slowly scanned her surroundings, her eyes finally resting on me. "You've got cameras in your doors, motion sensors, a fence, security gates, and what else? Gun turrets?"

"No gun turrets."

"This is your Fort Apache, isn't it, Aunt Kay? You moved here because Mark's dead and there's nothing left in the world except bad people."

The comment ambushed me with terrific force, and instantly tears filled my eyes. I went into the guest bedroom and set down her suitcase, then checked towels, soap, and toothpaste in the bath. Returning to the bedroom, I opened the curtains, checked dresser drawers, rearranged the closet, and adjusted the heat while my niece sat on the edge of the bed, following my every move. In several minutes, I was able to meet her eyes again.

"When you unpack, I'll show you a closet you can rummage through for winter things," I said.

"You never saw him the way everybody else did."

"Lucy, we need to talk about something else." I switched on a lamp and made certain the telephone was plugged in.

"You're better off without him," she added with conviction.

"Lucy . . ."

"He wasn't there for you the way he should have been. He never would have been there because that's the way he was. And every time things didn't go right, you changed."

I stood in front of the window and looked out at dormant clematis and roses frozen to trellises.

"Lucy, you need to learn a little gentleness and tact. You can't just say exactly what you think."

"That's a funny thing to hear coming from you. You've always told me how much you hate dishonesty and games."

"People have feelings."

"You're right. Including me," she said.

"Have I somehow hurt your feelings?"

"How do you think I felt?"

"I'm not sure I understand."

"Because you didn't think about me at all. That's why you don't understand."

"I think about you all the time."

"That's like saying you're rich and yet you never give me a dime. What difference does it make to me what you've got hidden away?"

I did not know what to say.

"You don't call me anymore. You haven't come to see me once since he got killed." The hurt in her voice had been saved for a long time. "I wrote you and you didn't write back. Then you called me yesterday and asked me to come visit because you needed something."

"I didn't mean it like that."

"It's the same thing Mom does."

I shut my eyes and leaned my forehead against the cold glass. "You expect too much from me, Lucy. I'm not perfect."

"I don't expect you to be perfect. But I thought you were different."

"I don't know how to defend myself when you make a remark like that."

"You can't defend yourself!"

I watched a gray squirrel hop along the top of the fence bordering the yard. Birds were pecking seeds off the grass.

"Aunt Kay?"

I turned to her and never had I seen her eyes look so dejected.

"Why are men always more important than me?"

"They're not, Lucy," I whispered. "I swear."

My niece wanted tuna salad and *caffè latte* for lunch, and while I sat in front of the fire editing a journal article, she rummaged through my closet and dresser drawers. I tried not to think about another human being touching my clothes, folding something in a way I wouldn't or returning a jacket to the wrong hanger. Lucy had a gift for making me feel like the Tinman rusting in the forest. Was I becoming the rigid, serious adult I would have disliked when I was her age?

"What do you think?" she asked when she emerged from my bedroom at half past one. She was wearing one of my tennis warm-up suits.

"I think you spent a long time to come up with only that. And yes, it fits you fine."

"I found a few other things that are okay, but most of your stuff is too dressy. All these lawyerly suits in midnight blue and black, gray silk with delicate pinstripes, khaki and cashmere, and white blouses. You must have twenty white blouses and just as many ties. You shouldn't wear brown, by the way. And I didn't see much in red, and you'd look good in red, with your blue eyes and grayish blonde hair."

"Ash blonde," I said.

"Ashes are gray or white. Just look in the fire. We don't wear the same size shoe, not that I'm into Cole-Haan or Ferragamo. I did find a black leather jacket that's really cool. Were you a biker in another life?"

"It's lambskin and you're welcome to borrow it."

"What about your Fendi perfume and pearls? Do you own a pair of jeans?"

"Help yourself." I started to laugh. "And yes, I have a pair of jeans somewhere. Maybe in the garage."

"I want to take you shopping, Aunt Kay."

"I'd have to be crazy."

"Please?"

"Maybe," I said.

"If it's all right, I want to go to your club to work out for a while. I'm stiff from the plane."

"If you'd like to play tennis while you're here, I'll see if Ted has any time to hit with you. My racquets are in the closet to the left. I just switched to a new Wilson. You can hit the ball a hundred miles an hour. You'll love it."

"No, thanks. I'd rather use the StairMaster and weights or go running. Why don't *you* take a lesson from Ted while I work out, and we can go together?"

Dutifully, I reached for the phone and dialed Westwood's pro shop. Ted was booked solid until ten o'clock. I gave Lucy directions and my car keys, and after she left, I read in front of the fire and fell asleep.

When I opened my eyes, I heard coals shift and wind gently touching the pewter wind chimes beyond the sliding glass doors. Snow was drifting down in large, slow flakes, the sky the color of a dusty blackboard. Lights in my yard had come on, the house so silent I was conscious of the clock ticking on the wall. It was shortly after four and Lucy had not returned from the club. I dialed the number for my car phone and no one answered. She had never driven in snow before, I thought anxiously. And I needed to go to the store to pick up fish for dinner. I could call the club and have her paged. I told myself that was ridiculous. Lucy had been gone barely two hours. She was not a child anymore. When it got to be four-thirty, I tried my car phone again. At five I called the club and they could not find her. I began to panic.

"Are you sure she's not on the StairMaster or maybe in the women's locker room taking a shower? Or maybe she stopped by the mixed grill?" I again asked the young woman in the pro shop.

"We've paged her four times, Dr. Scarpetta. And I've gone around looking. I'll check again. If I locate her, I'll have her call you immediately."

"Do you know if she ever showed up at all? She should have gotten there around two."

"Gosh. I just came on at four. I don't know."

I continued calling my car phone.

"The Richmond Cellular customer you have dialed does not answer. . . ."

I tried Marino and he wasn't home or at headquarters. At six o'clock I stood in the kitchen staring out the window. Snow streaked down in the chalky glow of streetlights. My heart beat hard as I paced from room to room and continued calling my car phone. At half past six I had decided to file a missing person report with the police when the telephone rang. Running back to my study, I was reaching for the receiver when I noticed the familiar number eerily materializing on the Caller ID screen. The calls had stopped after the night of Waddell's execution. I had not thought about them since. Bewildered, I froze, waiting for the expected hang up to follow my recorded message. I was shocked when I recognized the voice that began to speak.

"I hate to do this to you, Doc . . ."

Snatching up the receiver, I cleared my throat and said in disbelief, "Marino?"

"Yeah," he said. "I got bad news."

4

Where are you?" I demanded, my eyes riveted to the number on the screen.

"East End, and it's coming down like a bitch," Marino said. "We got a DOA. White female. At a glance appears to be your typical CO suicide, car inside the garage, hose hooked up to the exhaust pipe. But the circumstances are a little weird. I think you better come."

"Where are you placing this call from?" I asked so adamantly that he hesitated. I could feel his surprise.

"The decedent's house. Just got here. That's the other thing. It wasn't secured. The back was unlocked."

I heard the garage door. "Oh, thank God. Marino, hold on," I said, flooded with relief.

Paper bags crackled as the kitchen door shut.

Placing my hand over the receiver, I called out, "Lucy, is that you?"

"No, Frosty the Snowman. You ought to see it coming down out there! It's awesome!"

Reaching for pen and paper, I said to Marino, "The decedent's name and address?"

"Jennifer Deighton. Two-one-seven Ewing."

I did not recognize the name. Ewing was off Williamsburg Road, not too far from the airport in a neighborhood unfamiliar to me.

Lucy walked into my study as I was hanging up the phone. Her face was rosy from the cold, eyes sparkling.

"Where in God's name have you been?" I snapped.

Her smile faded. "Errands."

"Well, we'll discuss this later. I've got to go to a scene."

She shrugged and returned my irritation. "So what else is new?"

"I'm sorry. It's not as if I have control over people dying."

Grabbing coat and gloves, I hurried out to the garage. I started the engine, buckled up, adjusted the heat, and studied my directions before remembering the automatic door opener attached to the visor. It's amazing how quickly an enclosed space will fill with fumes.

"Good God," I said severely to no one but my own distracted self as I quickly opened the garage door.

Poisoning by motor vehicle exhaust is an easy way to die. Young couples necking in the backseat, engine running and heater on, drift off in each other's arms and never wake up. Suicidal individuals turn cars into small gas chambers and leave their problems for others to solve. I had neglected to ask Marino if Jennifer Deighton lived alone.

The snow was already several inches deep, the night lit up by it. There was no traffic in my neighborhood and very little when I got on the downtown expressway. Christmas music played nonstop on the radio as my thoughts flew in a riot of bewilderment and alighted, one by one, on fear. Jennifer Deighton had been calling my number and hanging up, or someone using her telephone had. Now she was dead. The overpass curved above the east end of downtown, where railroad tracks crisscrossed the earth like sutured wounds, and concrete parking decks were higher than many of the buildings. Main Street station hulked out of the milky sky, tile roof frosted white, the clock in its tower a bleary Cyclops eye.

On Williamsburg Road I drove very slowly past a deserted shopping center, and just before the city turned into Henrico County, I found Ewing Avenue. Houses were small, with pickup trucks and old model American cars parked out front. At the 217 address, police cars were in the drive and on both sides of the street. Pulling in behind Marino's Ford, I got out with my medical bag and walked to the end of the unpaved driveway where the single-car garage was lit up like a Christmas crèche. The door was rolled up, police officers gathered inside around a beat-up beige Chevrolet. I found Marino squatting by the back door on the driver's side, studying a section of green garden hose leading from the exhaust pipe through a partially opened window. The interior of the car was filthy with soot, the smell of fumes lingering on the cold, damp air.

"The ignition's still switched on," Marino said to me. "The car ran out of gas."

The dead woman appeared to be in her fifties or early sixties. She was slumped over on her right side behind the steering wheel, the exposed flesh of her neck and hands bright pink. Dried bloody fluid stained the tan upholstery beneath her head. From where I stood, I could not see her face. Opening my medical bag, I got out a chemical thermometer to take the temperature inside the garage, and put on a pair of surgical gloves. I asked a young officer if he could open the car's front doors.

"We were just about to dust," he said.

"I'll wait."

"Johnson, how 'bout dusting the door handles so the doc here can get in the car." He fixed dark Latin eyes on me. "By the way, I'm Tom Lucero. What we got here is a situation that doesn't completely add up. To begin with, it bothers me there's blood on the front seat."

"There are several possible explanations for that," I said. "One is postmortem purging."

He narrowed his eyes a little.

"When pressure in the lungs forces bloody fluid from the nose and mouth," I explained.

"Oh. Generally, that doesn't happen until the person's started to decompose, right?"

"Generally."

"Based on what we know, this lady's been dead maybe twenty-four hours and it's cold as a morgue fridge in here."

"True," I said. "But if she had her heater running, that in addition to the hot exhaust pouring in would have heated up the inside of the car, and it would have stayed quite warm until the car ran out of gas."

Marino peered through a window opaque with soot and said, "Looks like the heater's pushed all the way to hot."

"Another possibility," I continued, "is that when she became unconscious, she slumped over, striking her face on the steering wheel, the dash, the seat. Her nose could have bled. She could have bitten her tongue or split her lip. I won't know until I examine her."

"Okay, but how about the way she's dressed?" Lucero said. "Strike you as unusual that she'd walk out in the cold, come inside a cold garage, hook up the hose, and get into a cold car with nothing but a gown on?"

The pale blue gown was ankle-length, with long sleeves, and made of what looked like a flimsy synthetic material. There is no dress code for people who commit suicide. It would have been logical for Jennifer Deighton to put on coat and shoes before venturing outside on a frigid winter night. But if she had planned to take her life, she would have known she would not feel the cold long.

The ID officer had finished dusting the car doors. I retrieved the chemical thermometer. It was twenty-nine degrees inside the garage.

"When did you get here?" I asked Lucero.

"Maybe an hour and a half ago. Obviously, it was warmer in here before we opened the door, but not much. The garage isn't heated. Plus, the car hood was cold. I'm guessing the car ran out of gas and the battery went dead a number of hours before we were called."

Car doors opened and I took a series of photographs before going around to the passenger's side to look at her head. I braced myself for a spark of awareness, a detail that might ignite some long-buried memory. But there was not the faintest glimmer. I did not know Jennifer Deighton. I had never seen her before in my life.

Her bleached hair was dark at the roots and tightly wound in small pink curlers, several of which had been displaced. She was grossly overweight, though I could tell from her refined features that she may have been quite pretty in a younger, leaner life. I palpated her head and neck and felt no fractures. I placed the back of my hand against her cheek, then struggled to turn her. She was cold and stiff, the side of her face that had been resting against the seat, pale and blistered from the heat. It did not appear that her body had been moved after death, and the skin did not blanch when pressed. She had been dead at least twelve hours.

It wasn't until I was ready to bag her hands that I noticed something under her right index fingernail. I got out a flashlight for a better look, then retrieved a plastic evidence envelope and a pair of forceps. The tiny fleck of metallic green was embedded in the skin beneath the nail. Christmas glitter, I thought. I also found fibers of a gold tint, and as I studied each of her fingers I found more. Slipping the brown paper bags over her hands and securing them at the wrists with rubber bands, I went around to the other side of the car. I wanted to look at her feet. Her legs were fully rigorous and uncooperative as I pulled them free of the steering wheel and positioned them on the seat. Examining the bottoms of her thick dark socks, I found fibers clinging to the wool that looked similar to the ones I had noticed under her fingernails. Absent was dirt, mud, or grass. An alarm was sounding in the back of my mind.

"Find anything interesting?" Marino asked.

"You found no bedroom slippers or shoes nearby?" I said.

"Nope," Lucero answered. "Like I told you, I thought it unusual she walked out of the house on a cold night with nothing but—"

I interrupted. "We've got a problem. Her socks are too clean."

"Shit," Marino said.

"We need to get her downtown." I backed away from the car.

"I'll tell the squad," Lucero volunteered.

"I want to see the inside of her house," I said to Marino.

"Yeah." He had taken his gloves off and was blowing on his hands. "I want you to see it, too."

While I waited for the squad, I moved about the garage, careful where I stepped and keeping out of the way. There wasn't much to see, just the usual clutter of items needed for the yard and odds and ends that had no other proper storage place. I scanned stacks of old newspapers, wicker baskets, dusty cans of paint, and a rusty charcoal grill that I doubted had been used in years. Sloppily coiled in a corner like a headless green garter snake was the hose from which the segment attached to the exhaust pipe appeared to have been cut. I knelt near the severed end without touching it. The plastic rim did not look sawn but severed at an angle by one hard blow. I spotted a linear cut in the cement floor nearby. Getting to my feet, I surveyed the tools hanging from a pegboard. There was an ax and a maul, both of them rusty and festooned with cobwebs.

The rescue squad was coming in with its stretcher and body pouch.

"Did you find anything inside her house that she might have used to cut the hose?" I asked Lucero.

"No."

Jennifer Deighton did not want to come out of the car, death resisting the hands of life. I moved to the passenger's side to help. Three of us secured her under the arms and waist while an attendant pushed her legs. When she was zipped up and buckled in, they carried her out into the snowy night and I trudged with Lucero along the driveway, sorry that I'd not taken the time to put on boots. We entered the ranch-style brick house through a back door that led into the kitchen.

It looked recently renovated, appliances black, counters and cabinets white, the wallpaper an Oriental pattern of pastel flowers against delicate blue. Heading toward the sound of voices, Lucero and I crossed a narrow hallway with a hardwood floor and stopped at the entrance of a bedroom where Marino and an ID officer were going through dresser drawers. For a long moment, I looked around at the peculiar manifestations of Jennifer Deighton's personality. It was as if her bedroom were a solar cell in which she captured radiant energy and converted it into magic. I thought again of the hang ups I had been getting, my paranoia growing by leaps and bounds.

Walls, curtains, carpet, linens, and wicker furniture were white. Oddly, on the rumpled bed not far from where both pillows were propped against the headboard a crystal pyramid anchored a single blank sheet of white typing paper. On the dresser and bedside tabletops were more crystals, with smaller ones suspended from window frames. I could imagine rainbows dancing in the room and light glancing off prismatic glass when the sun poured in.

"Weird, huh?" Lucero asked.

"Was she a psychic of some sort?" I asked.

"Let's put it this way, she had her own business, most of it carried out right there." Lucero moved closer to an answering machine on a table by the bed. The message light was flashing, the number thirty-eight glowing red.

"*Thirty-eight* messages since eight o'clock last night," Lucero added. "I've skipped through a few of 'em. The lady was into horoscopes. Looks like people would call to find out if they were going to have a good day, win the lottery, or be able to pay off their charge cards after Christmas."

Opening the cover of the answering machine, Marino used his pocket knife to flip out the tape, which he sealed inside a plastic evidence envelope. I was interested in several other items on the small bedside table and moved closer to take a look. Next to a notepad and pen was a glass with an inch of clear liquid inside it. I bent close, smelling nothing. Water, I thought. Nearby were two paperback books, Pete Dexter's *Paris Trout* and Jane Roberts's *Seth Speaks.* I saw no other books in the bedroom.

"I'd like to take a look at these," I said to Marino.

"*Paris Trout,*" he mused. "What's it about, fishing in France?"

Unfortunately, he was serious.

"They might tell me something about her state of mind before she died," I added.

"No problem. I'll have Documents check them for prints, then hand them over to you. And I think we'd better have Documents take a look at the paper, too," he added, referring to the sheet of blank paper on the bed.

"Right," Lucero said drolly. "Maybe she wrote a suicide note in disappearing ink."

"Come on," Marino said to me. "I want to show you a couple things."

He took me into the living room, where an artificial Christmas tree cowered in a corner, bent from copious gaudy ornaments and strangled by tinsel, lights, and angel hair. Gathered near its base were boxes of candy and cheeses, bubble bath, a glass jar of what looked like spiced tea, and a ceramic unicorn with blazing blue eyes and gilded horn. The gold shag carpet, I suspected, was the origin of the fibers I had noticed on the bottom of Jennifer Deighton's socks and under her fingernails.

Marino slipped a small flashlight from a pocket and squatted.

"Take a look," he said.

I got down beside him as the beam of light illuminated metallic glitter and a bit of slender gold cord in the deep pile of the carpet around the base of the tree.

"When I got here, the first thing I checked was to see if she had any presents under the tree," Marino said, switching the flashlight off. "Obviously, she opened them early. And the wrapping paper and cards got disposed of right over there in the fireplace—it's full of paper ash, some pieces of foil-type paper still unburned. The lady across the street says she noticed smoke coming out of the chimney right before it got dark last night."

"Is this neighbor the one who called the police?" I asked.

"Yeah."

"Why?"

"That I'm not clear on. I got to talk to her."

"When you do, see if you can find out anything about this woman's medical history, if she had psychiatric problems, et cetera. I'd like to know who her physician is."

"I'm going over there in a few minutes. You can come with me and ask her yourself."

I thought of Lucy waiting for me at home as I continued taking in details. In the center of the room, my eyes stopped at four small square indentations in the carpet.

"I noticed that, too," Marino said. "Looks like someone brought a chair in here, probably from the dining room. There's four chairs around the dining room table. All of 'em have square legs."

"Another thing you might consider doing," I thought out loud, "is checking her VCR. See if she had programmed it to record anything. That might tell us something more about her, too."

"Good idea."

We left the living room, passing through the small dining room with an oak table and four straight-backed chairs. The braided rug on the hardwood floor looked either new or rarely walked on.

"Looks like the room she pretty much lived in was this one," Marino said as we crossed a hallway and entered what clearly was her office.

The room was crammed with the paraphernalia needed to run a small business, including a fax machine, which I investigated immediately. It was turned off, the line connected to it plugged into a single jack in the wall. I looked around some more as my mystification grew. A personal computer, postage machine, various forms, and envelopes crowded a table and the desk. Encyclopedias and books on parapsychology, astrology, zodiac signs, and Eastern and Western religions lined bookcases. I noted several different translations of the Bible and dozens of ledgers with dates written on the spines.

Near the postage machine was a stack of what appeared to be

subscription forms, and I picked up one. For three hundred dollars a year, you could call as often as once a day and Jennifer Deighton would spend up to three minutes telling you your horoscope "based on personal details, including the alignment of the planets at the moment of your birth." For an additional two hundred dollars a year, she would throw in "a weekly reading." Upon payment of the fee, the subscriber would receive a card with an identification code that was valid only as long as the annual fee continued to be paid.

"What a lot of horseshit," Marino said to me.

"I'm assuming she lived alone."

"That's the way it's looking so far. A woman alone running a business like this—a damn good way to attract the wrong person."

"Marino, do you know how many telephone lines she has?"

"No. Why?"

I told him about the hang ups I had been getting while he stared hard at me. His jaw muscles began to flex.

"I need to know if her fax machine and phone are on the same line," I concluded.

"Jesus Christ."

"If they are and she happened to have her fax machine turned on the night I dialed back the number that appeared on my Caller ID screen," I went on, "that would explain the tone I heard."

"Jesus friggin' Christ," he said, snatching the portable radio out of his coat pocket. "Why the hell didn't you tell me this before?"

"I didn't want to mention it when others were around."

He moved the radio close to his lips. "Seven-ten." Then he said to me, "If you were worried about hang ups, why didn't you say something weeks ago?"

"I wasn't that worried about them."

"Seven-ten," the dispatcher's voice crackled back.

"Ten-five eight-twenty-one."

The dispatcher sent out a broadcast for 821, the code for the inspector.

"Got a number I need you to dial," Marino said when he and the inspector connected on the air. "You got your cellular phone handy?"

"Ten-fo'."

Marino gave him Jennifer Deighton's number and then turned on the fax machine. Momentarily, it began a series of rings, beeps, and other complaints.

"That answer your question?" Marino asked me.

"It answers one question, but not the most important question," I said.

The name of the neighbor across the street who had notified the police was Myra Clary. I accompanied Marino to her small aluminum-sided house with its plastic Santa lit up on the front lawn and lights strung in the boxwoods. Marino barely had rung the bell when the front door opened and Mrs. Clary invited us in without asking who we were. It occurred to me that she probably had watched our approach from a window.

She showed us into a dismal living room where we found her husband huddled by the electric fire, lap robe over his spindly legs, his vacuous stare fixed on a man lathering up with deodorant soap on television. The pitiful custodial care of the years manifested itself everywhere. Upholstery was threadbare and soiled where human flesh had made repeated contact with it. Wood was cloudy from layers of wax, prints on walls yellowed behind dusty glass. The oily smell of a million meals cooked in the kitchen and eaten on TV trays permeated the air.

Marino explained why we were here as Mrs. Clary moved about nervously, plucking newspapers off the couch, turning down the television, and carrying dirty dinner plates into the kitchen. Her husband did not venture forth from his interior world, his head trembling on its stalklike neck. Parkinson's disease is when the machine shakes violently just before it conks out, as if it knows what is ahead and protests the only way it can.

"Nope, we don't need a thing," Marino said when Mrs. Clary offered us food and drink. "Sit down and try to relax. I know this has been a tough day for you."

"They said she was in her car breathing in those fumes. Oh, my," she said. "I saw how smoky the window was, looked like the garage had been on fire. I knew the worst right then."

"Who's *they?*" Marino asked.

"The police. After I called, I was watching for them. When they pulled up, I went straight over to see if Jenny was all right."

Mrs. Clary could not sit still in the wing chair across from the couch where Marino and I had settled. Her gray hair had strayed out of the bun on top of her head, face as wrinkled as a dried apple, eyes hungry for information and bright with fear.

"I know you already talked to the police earlier," Marino said, moving the ashtray closer. "But I want you to go through it chapter and verse for us, beginning with when you saw Jennifer Deighton last."

"I saw her the other day—"

Marino interrupted. "Which day?"

"Friday. I remember the phone rang and I went to the kitchen to answer it and saw her through the window. She was pulling into her driveway."

"Did she always park her car in the garage?" I asked.

"She always did."

"What about yesterday?" Marino inquired. "You see her or her car yesterday?"

"No, I didn't. But I went out to get the mail. It was late, tends to be that way this time of year. Three, four o'clock and still no mail. I guess it was close to five-thirty, maybe a little later, when I remembered to check the mailbox again. It was getting dark and I noticed smoke coming out of Jenny's chimney."

"You sure about that?" Marino asked.

She nodded. "Oh, yes. I remember it went through my mind it was a good night for a fire. But fires were always Jimmy's job. He never showed me how, you see. When he was good at something, that was his. So I quit on the fires and had the electric log put in."

Jimmy Clary was looking at her. I wondered if he knew what she was saying.

"I like to cook," she went on. "This time of year I do a lot of baking. I make sugar cakes and give them to the neighbors. Yesterday I wanted to drop one by for Jenny, but I like to call first. It's hard to tell when someone's in, especially when they keep their car in a garage. And you leave a cake on the doormat and one of the dogs around here gets it. So I tried her and got that machine. All day I tried and she didn't answer, and to tell you the truth, I was a little worried."

"Why?" I asked. "Did she have health problems, any sort of problems you were aware of?"

"Bad cholesterol. Way over two hundred's what's she told me once. Plus high blood pressure, which she said ran in the family."

I had not seen any prescription drugs in Jennifer Deighton's house.

"Do you know who her doctor was?" I asked.

"I can't recall. But Jenny believed in natural cures. She told me when she felt poorly she'd meditate."

"Sounds like the two of you were pretty close," Marino said.

Mrs. Clary was plucking at her skirt, hands like hyperactive children. "I'm here all day except when I go to the store." She glanced at her husband, who was staring at the TV again. "Now and then I'd go see her, you know, just being neighborly, maybe to drop by something I'd been cooking."

"Was she a friendly sort?" Marino asked. "She have a lot of visitors?"

"Well, you know she worked out of the house. I think she handled most of her business over the phone. But occasionally I'd see people going in."

"Anybody you knew?"

"Not that I recall."

"You notice anybody coming by to see her last night?" Marino asked.

"I didn't notice."

"What about when you went out to get your mail and saw the smoke coming out of her chimney? You get any sense she might have had company?"

"I didn't see a car. Nothing to make me think she had company."

Jimmy Clary had drifted off to sleep. He was drooling.

"You said she worked at home," I said. "Do you have any idea what she did?"

Mrs. Clary fixed wide eyes on me. She leaned forward and lowered her voice. "I know what folks said."

"And what was that?" I asked.

She pressed her lips together and shook her head.

"Mrs. Clary," Marino said. "Anything you could tell us might help. I know you want to help."

"There's a Methodist church two blocks away. You can see it. The steeple's lit up at night, has been ever since they built the church three or four years ago."

"I saw the church when I was driving in," Marino replied. "What's that got to do—"

"Well," she cut in, "Jenny moved here, I guess it was early September. And I've never been able to figure it out. The steeple light. You watch when you're driving home. Of course . . ." She paused, her face disappointed. "Maybe it won't do it anymore."

"Do what?" Marino asked.

"Go out and then come back on. The strangest thing I've ever seen. It's lit up one minute, and then you look out your window again and it's dark like the church isn't there. Then next thing you know, you look out again and the steeple's lit up just like it's always been. I've timed it. On for a minute, then off for two, on again for three. Sometimes it will burn for an hour. No pattern to it at all."

"What does this have to do with Jennifer Deighton?" I asked.

"I remember it was not long after she moved in, just weeks before Jimmy had his stroke. It was a cool night so he was building a fire. I was in the kitchen doing dishes and could see the steeple out the window lit up like it always was. And he came in to get himself a drink, and I said, 'You know what the Bible says about being drunk with the Spirit and not with wine.' And he said, 'I'm not drinking wine. I'm drinking bourbon. The Bible's never said a word about bourbon.' Then, right while he was standing there the steeple went dark. It was like the church vanished into thin air. I said, 'There you have it. The Word of the Lord. That's his opinion about you and your bourbon.'

"He laughed like I was the craziest thing, but he never touched another drop. Every night he'd stand in front of the window over the kitchen sink watching. One minute the steeple would be lit up, then it would be dark. I let Jimmy think it was God's doing—anything to keep him off the bottle. The church never behaved like that before Miss Deighton moved across the street."

"Has the light been going on and off lately?" I asked.

"Was still doing it last night. I don't know about now. To tell you the truth, I haven't looked."

"So you're saying that she somehow had an effect on the lights in the church steeple," Marino said mildly.

"I'm saying that more than one person on this street decided about her some time ago."

"Decided what?"

"About her being a witch," Mrs. Clary said.

Her husband had started snoring, making hideous strangling noises that his wife did not seem to notice.

"Sounds to me like your husband there started doing poorly

about the time Miss Deighton moved here and the lights started acting funny," Marino said.

She looked startled. "Well, that's so. He had his stroke the end of September."

"You ever think there might be a connection? That maybe Jennifer Deighton had something to do with it, just like you're thinking she had something to do with the church lights?"

"Jimmy didn't take to her." Mrs. Clary was talking faster by the minute.

"You're saying the two of them didn't get along," Marino said.

"Right after she moved in, she came over a couple of times to ask him to help out with a few things around the house, man's work. I remember one time her doorbell was making a terrible buzzing sound inside the house and she appeared on the doorstep, scared she was about to have an electrical fire. So Jimmy went over there. I think her dishwasher flooded once, too, back then. Jimmy's always been real handy." She glanced furtively at her snoring husband.

"You still haven't made it clear why he didn't get along with her," Marino reminded her.

"He said he didn't like going over there," she said. "Didn't like the inside of her house, with all these crystals everywhere. And the phone would ring all the time. But what really gave him the willies was when she told him she read people's fortunes and would do it for him for nothing if he'd keep fixing things around her house. He said, and I remember this like it was yesterday, 'No, thank you, Miss Deighton. Myra's in charge of my future, plans every minute of it.' "

"I wonder if you might know of anybody who had a big enough problem with Jennifer Deighton to wish something bad on her, hurt her in some way," Marino said.

"You think somebody killed her?"

"There's a lot we don't know at this point. We have to check out every possibility."

She crossed her arms under her sagging bosom, hugging herself.

"What about her emotional state?" I inquired. "Did she ever seem depressed to you? Do you know if she had any problems she couldn't seem to cope with, especially of late?"

"I didn't know her that well." She avoided my eyes.

"Did she go to any doctors that you're aware of?"

"I don't know."

"What about next of kin? Did she have family?"

"I have no idea."

"What about her phone?" I then said. "Did she answer it when she was home or did she always let the machine do it?"

"It's been my experience that when she was home, she answered it."

"Which is why you got worried about her earlier today when she wasn't answering the phone when you called," Marino said.

"That's exactly why."

Myra Clary realized too late what she had said.

"That's interesting," Marino commented.

A flush crept up her neck and her hands went still.

Marino asked, "How did you know she was home today?"

She did not answer. Her husband's breath rattled in his chest and he coughed, eyes blinking open.

"I guess I assumed. Because I didn't see her pull out. In her car . . ." Mrs. Clary's voice trailed off.

"Maybe you went over there earlier in the day?" Marino offered, as if trying to be helpful. "To deliver your cake or say hello and thought her car was in the garage?"

She dabbed tears from her eyes. "I was in the kitchen baking all morning and never saw her go out to get the paper or leave in her car. So mid-morning, when I went out, I went over there and rang the bell. She didn't answer. I peeked inside the garage."

"You telling me you saw the windows all smoked up and didn't think something was wrong?" Marino asked.

"I didn't know what it meant, what to do." Her voice went up several octaves. "Lord, Lord. I wish I'd called somebody then. Maybe she was—"

Marino cut in. "I don't know that she was still alive then, that she would have been." He looked pointedly at me.

"When you looked inside the garage, did you hear the car engine running?" I asked Mrs. Clary.

She shook her head and blew her nose.

Marino got up and tucked his notepad back in his coat pocket. He looked dejected, as if Mrs. Clary's spinelessness and lack of veracity deeply disappointed him. By now, there wasn't a role he played that I did not know well.

"I should have called earlier." Myra Clary directed this at me, her voice quavering.

I did not reply. Marino stared at the carpet.

"I don't feel good. I need to go lie down."

Marino slipped a business card out of his wallet and handed it to her. "Anything else comes to mind that you think I ought to know about, you give me a call."

"Yes, sir," she said weakly. "I promise I will."

"You doing the post tonight?" Marino asked me after the front door shut.

Snow was ankle-deep and still coming down.

"In the morning," I said, fishing keys out of my coat pocket.

"What do you think?"

"I think her unusual occupation put her at great risk for the wrong sort of person to come along. I also think her apparent isolated existence, as Mrs. Clary described it, and the fact that it appears she opened her Christmas presents early makes suicide an easy assumption. But her clean socks are a major problem."

"You got that right," he said.

Jennifer Deighton's house was lit up, and a flatbed truck with chains on its tires had backed into the driveway. Voices of men working were muted by the snow, and every car on the street was solid white and soft around the edges.

I followed Marino's gaze above the roof of Miss Deighton's house. Several blocks away, the church was etched against the pearl gray sky, the steeple shaped weirdly like a witch's hat. Arches in the arcade stared back at us with mournful, empty eyes when suddenly the light blinked on. It filled spaces and painted surfaces a luminescent ocher, the arcade an unsmiling but gentle face floating in the night.

I glanced over at the Clary house as curtains moved in the kitchen window.

"Jesus, I'm out of here." Marino headed across the street.

"You want me to alert Neils about her car?" I called after him.

"Yeah," he yelled back. "That'd be good."

My house was lit up when I got home and good smells came from the kitchen. A fire blazed and two places had been set on the butler's table in front of it. Dropping my medical bag on the couch, I looked around and listened. From my study across the hall came the faint, rapid clicking of keys.

"Lucy?" I called out, slipping off my gloves and unbuttoning my coat.

"I'm in here." Keys continued to click.

"What have you been cooking?"

"Dinner."

I headed for my study, where I found my niece sitting at my desk staring intensely at the computer monitor. I was stunned when I noticed the pound sign prompt. She was in UNIX. Somehow she had dialed into the computer downtown.

"How did you do that?" I asked. "I didn't tell you the dial-in command, user name, password, or anything."

"You didn't have to tell me. I found the file that told me what the *bat* command is. Plus, you've got some programs in here with your user name and password coded in so you don't get prompted for them. A good shortcut but risky. Your user name is Marley and password is *brain*."

"You're dangerous." I pulled up a chair.

"Who's Marley?" She continued to type.

"We had assigned seating in medical school. Marley Scates sat next to me in labs for two years. He's a neurosurgeon somewhere."

"Were you in love with him?"

"We never dated."

"Was he in love with you?"

"You ask too many questions, Lucy. You can't just ask people anything you want."

"Yes I can. They don't have to answer."

"It's offensive."

"I think I've figured out how someone got into your directory, Aunt Kay. Remember I told you about users that came with the software?"

"Yes."

"There's one called demo that has root privileges but no password assigned to it. My guess is that this is what somebody used and I'll show you what probably happened." Her fingers flew over the keyboard without pause as she talked. "What I'm doing now is going into the system administrator's menu to check out the log-in accounting. We're going to search for a specific user. In this case, root. Now we'll hit g to go and boom. There it is." She ran her finger across a line on the screen.

"On December sixteenth at five-oh-six in the afternoon, someone logged in from a device called t-t-y-fourteen. This person had root privileges and we'll assume is the person who went into your directory. I don't know what he looked at. But twenty minutes later, at five-twenty-six, he tried to send the note 'I can't find it' to t-t-y-oh-seven and inadvertently created a file. He logged out at five-thirty-two, making the total time of the session twenty-six minutes. And it doesn't appear anything was printed, by the way. I took a look at the printer spooler log, which shows files printed. I didn't see anything that caught my attention."

"Let me make sure I've got this straight. Someone tried to send a note from t-t-y-fourteen to t-t-y-oh-seven," I said.

"Yes. And I checked. Both of those devices are terminals."

"How can we determine whose office those terminals are in?" I asked.

"I'm surprised there's not a list somewhere in here. But I haven't found it yet. If all else fails, you can check the cables leading to the terminals. Usually, they're tagged. And if you're interested in my personal opinion, I don't think your computer analyst is the spy. In the first place, she knows your user name and password and would have no need to log in with demo. Also, since I assume the mini is in her office, then I also assume she uses the system terminal."

"She does."

"The device name for your system terminal is t-t-y-b."

"Good."

"Another way to figure out who did this would be to sneak into someone's office when they aren't there but are logged in. All you've got to do is go into UNIX and type 'who am I' and the system will tell you."

She pushed back her chair and got up. "I hope you're hungry. We've got chicken breasts and a chilled wild rice salad made with cashews, peppers, sesame oil. And there's bread. Is your grill in working order?"

"It's after eleven and snowing outside."

"I didn't suggest that we eat outside. I simply would like to cook the chicken on the grill."

"Where did you learn to cook?"

We were walking to the kitchen.

"Not from Mother. Why do you think I was such a little fatso?

From eating the junk she bought. Snacks, sodas, and pizza that tastes like cardboard. I have fat cells that will scream for the rest of my life because of Mother. I'll never forgive her."

"We need to talk about this afternoon, Lucy. If you hadn't come home when you did, the police would have been looking for you."

"I worked out for an hour and a half, then took a shower."

"You were gone four and a half hours."

"I had groceries to buy and a few other errands."

"Why didn't you answer the car phone?"

"I assumed it was someone trying to reach you. Plus, I've never used a car phone. I'm not twelve years old, Aunt Kay."

"I know you're not. But you don't live here and have never driven here before. I was worried."

"I'm sorry," she said.

We ate by firelight, both of us sitting on the floor around the butler's table. I had turned off lamps. Flames jumped and shadows danced as if celebrating a magic moment in the lives of my niece and me.

"What do you want for Christmas?" I asked, reaching for my wine.

"Shooting lessons," she said.

5

Lucy stayed up very late working with the computer and I did not hear her stir when I woke up to the alarm early Monday morning. Parting the curtains in my bedroom window, I looked out at powdery flakes swirling in lights burning on the patio. The snow was deep and nothing was moving in my neighborhood. After coffee and a quick scan of the paper, I got dressed and was almost to the door when I turned around. No matter that Lucy was no longer twelve years old, I could not leave without checking on her.

Slipping inside her bedroom, I found her sleeping on her side in a tangle of sheets, the duvet half on the floor. It touched me that she was wearing a sweat suit that she had gotten out of one of my drawers. I had never had another human being wish to sleep in anything of mine, and I straightened the covers, careful not to wake her.

The drive downtown was awful, and I envied workers whose offices were closed because of the snow. Those of us who had not been granted an unexpected holiday crept slowly along the interstate, skating with the slightest tap on the brakes as we peered through streaked windshields that the wipers could not keep clean. I wondered how I would explain to Margaret that my teenage niece thought our computer system was insecure. Who had gotten into my directory, and why had Jennifer Deighton been calling my number and hanging up?

I did not get to the office until half past eight, and when I walked into the morgue, I stopped midway in the corridor, puzzled. Parked at a haphazard angle near the stainless steel refrigerator door was a gurney bearing a body covered by a sheet. Checking the toe tag, I read Jennifer Deighton's name, and I looked around. There was no one inside the office or X-ray room. I opened the door to the autopsy suite and found Susan dressed in scrubs and dialing a number on the phone. She quickly hung up and greeted me with a nervous "Good morning."

"Glad you made it in." I unbuttoned my coat, regarding her curiously.

"Ben gave me a lift," she said, referring to my administrator, who owned a Jeep with four-wheel drive. "So far, we're the only three here."

"No sign of Fielding?"

"He called a few minutes ago and said he couldn't get out of his driveway. I told him we only have one case so far, but if more come in Ben can pick him up."

"Are you aware that our case is parked in the hall?"

She hesitated, blushing. "I was taking her over to X ray when the phone rang. Sorry."

"Have you weighed and measured her yet?"

"No."

"Let's do that first."

She hurried out of the autopsy suite before I could comment further. Secretaries and scientists who worked in the labs upstairs often entered and left the building through the morgue because it was convenient to the parking lot. Maintenance workers were in and out, too. Leaving a body unattended in the middle of a corridor was very poor form and could even jeopardize the case should chain of evidence be questioned in court.

Susan returned pushing the gurney, and we went to work, the stench of decomposing flesh nauseating. I fetched gloves and a plastic apron from a shelf, and clamped various forms in a clipboard. Susan was quiet and tense. When she reached up to the control panel to reset the computerized floor scale, I noticed her hands were shaking. Maybe she was suffering from morning sickness.

"Everything okay?" I asked her.

"Just a little tired."

"You sure?"

"Positive. She weighs one-eighty exactly."

I changed into my greens and Susan and I moved the body into the X-ray room across the hall, transferring it from the gurney to the table. Opening the sheet, I wedged a block under the neck to keep the head from lolling. The flesh of her throat was clean, spared from soot and burns because her chin had been tucked close to her chest while she was inside the car with the engine running. I did not see any obvious injuries, no bruises or broken fingernails. Her nose wasn't fractured. There were no cuts inside her lips and she hadn't bitten her tongue.

Susan took X rays and slipped them into the processor while I went over the front of the body with a lens. I collected a number of barely visible whitish fibers, quite possibly from the sheet or her bed covers, and found others similar to the ones on the bottoms of her socks. She wore no jewelry and was naked beneath her gown. I remembered the rumpled covers on her bed, the pillows propped against the headboard and glass of water on the table. The night of her death she had put curlers in her hair, gotten undressed, and at some point, perhaps, had been reading in bed.

Susan emerged from the developer room and leaned against the wall, supporting the small of her back with her hands.

"What's the story on this lady?" she asked. "Was she married?"

"It appears she lived alone."

"Did she work?"

"She ran a business out of her home." Something caught my eye.

"What sort of business?"

"Possibly fortune-telling of sorts." The feather was very small and sooty, clinging to Jennifer Deighton's gown in the area of her left hip. Reaching for a small plastic bag, I tried to recall if I'd noticed any feathers around her house. Perhaps the pillows on her bed were filled with feathers.

"Did you find any evidence she was into the occult?"

"Some of her neighbors seemed to think she was a witch," I said.

"Based on what?"

"There's a church near her house. Allegedly, the lights in the steeple starting going on and off after she moved in some months ago."

"You're kidding."

"I saw them go on myself when I was leaving the scene. The steeple was dark. Then suddenly it was lit up."

"Weird."

"It was weird."

"Maybe it's on a timer."

"Unlikely. Lights going on and off all night would not conserve electricity. If it's true they go on and off all night. I saw it happen only once."

Susan did not say anything.

"Possibly there's a short in the wiring." In fact, I thought as I continued to work, I would call the church. They might be unaware of the problem.

"Any strange stuff inside her house?"

"Crystals. Some unusual books."

Silence.

Then Susan said, "I wish you'd told me earlier."

"Pardon?" I glanced up. She was staring uneasily at the body. She looked pale.

"Are you sure you're feeling all right?" I asked.

"I don't like stuff like this."

"Stuff like what?"

"It's like someone having AIDS or something. I ought to be told up front. Especially now."

"It's unlikely this woman has AIDS or—"

"I should have been told. Before I touched her."

"Susan—"

"I went to school with a girl who was a witch."

I stopped what I was doing. Susan was rigid against the wall, hands pressed against her belly.

"Her name was Doreen. She belonged to a coven and our senior year she put a curse on my twin sister, Judy. Judy was killed in a car wreck two weeks before graduation."

Bewildered, I stared at her.

"You know how occult stuff creeps me out! Like that cow's tongue with needles stuck in it that the cops brought in a couple of months ago. The one wrapped up in a list of dead people's names. It was left on a grave."

"It was a prank," I reminded her calmly. "The tongue came from a grocery store, and the names were meaningless, copied from headstones in the cemetery."

"You shouldn't tamper with the satanic, prank or not." Her voice trembled. "I take evil just as seriously as God."

Susan was the daughter of a minister and had abandoned religion long ago. I'd never heard her so much as allude to Satan or mention God unless it was profanely. I'd never known her to be the least bit superstitious or unnerved by anything. She was about to cry.

"Tell you what," I said quietly. "Since it appears I'm going to be short-staffed today, if you'll answer the phones upstairs, I'll take care of things down here."

Her eyes filled with tears, and I immediately went to her.

"It's okay." Putting my arm around her, I walked her out of the room. "Come on," I said gently as she leaned against me, sobbing. "You want Ben to take you home?"

She nodded, whispering, "I'm sorry. I'm sorry."

"All you need is a little rest." I sat her in a chair inside the morgue office and reached for the phone.

⋆ ⋆ ⋆

Jennifer Deighton had inhaled no carbon monoxide or soot because by the time she had been placed inside her car she was no longer breathing. Her death was a homicide, an obvious one, and throughout the afternoon I impatiently left messages for Marino to call me. Several times I tried to check on Susan but her phone just rang and rang.

"I'm concerned," I said to Ben Stevens. "Susan's not answering her phone. When you drove her home, did she mention that she was planning to go somewhere?"

"She told me she was going to bed."

He was sitting at his desk, going through reams of computer printouts. Rock and roll played quietly from the radio on a bookcase, and he was drinking tangerine-flavored mineral water. Stevens was young, smart, and boyishly good-looking. He worked hard, and played hard in singles bars, so I had been told. I was quite certain his job as my administrator would prove to be a short step on his way to someplace better.

"Maybe she unplugged her phone so she could sleep," he said, turning on his adding machine.

"Maybe that's it."

He launched into an update on our budget woes.

Late afternoon when it was beginning to get dark out, Stevens buzzed my line.

"Susan called. She said she won't be in tomorrow. And I've got a John Deighton on hold. Says he's Jennifer Deighton's brother."

Stevens transferred the call.

"Hello. They said you did my sister's autopsy," a man mumbled. "Uh, Jennifer Deighton's my sister."

"Your name, please?"

"John Deighton. I live in Columbia, South Carolina."

I glanced up as Marino appeared in my office doorway, and motioned for him to take a chair.

"They said she hooked up a hose to her car and killed herself."

"Who said that?" I asked. "And could you speak up, please?"

He hesitated. "I don't remember the name, should've wrote it down but I was too shocked."

The man didn't sound shocked. His voice was so muffled I barely could hear what he was saying.

"Mr. Deighton, I'm very sorry," I said. "But you will have to request any information regarding her death in writing. I will also need, included with your written request, some verification that you are next of kin."

He did not respond.

"Hello?" I asked. "Hello?"

I was answered by a dial tone.

"That's strange," I said to Marino. "Are you familiar with a John Deighton who claims to be Jennifer Deighton's brother?"

"That's who that was? Shit. We're trying to reach him."

"He said someone's already notified him about her death."

"You know where he was calling from?"

"Columbia, South Carolina, supposedly. He hung up on me."

Marino didn't seem interested. "I just came from Vander's office," he said, referring to Neils Vander, the chief fingerprints examiner. "He checked out Jennifer Deighton's car, plus the books that were beside her bed and a poem that was stuck inside one of 'em. As for the sheet of blank paper that was on her bed, he hasn't gotten to that yet."

"Anything so far?"

"He lifted a few. Will run them through the computer if there's a need. Probably most of the prints are hers. Here." He placed a small paper bag on my desk. "Happy reading."

"I think you're going to want those prints run without delay," I said grimly.

A shadow passed over Marino's eyes. He massaged his temples.

"Jennifer Deighton definitely did not commit suicide," I informed him. "Her CO was less than seven percent. She had no soot in her airway. The bright pink tint of her skin was due to exposure to cold, not CO poisoning."

"Christ," he said.

Shuffling through the paperwork in front of me, I handed him a body diagram, then opened an envelope and withdrew Polaroid photographs of Jennifer Deighton's neck.

"As you can see," I went on, "there are no injuries externally."

"What about the blood on the car seat?"

"A postmortem artifact due to purging. She was beginning to decompose. I found no abrasions or contusions, no fingertip bruises. But here"—I showed him a photograph of her neck at autopsy—"she's got irregular hemorrhages in the sternocleidomastoid muscles bilaterally. She's also got a fracture of the right cornua of the hyoid. Her death was caused by asphyxia, due to pressure applied to the neck—"

Marino interrupted, loudly. "You suggesting she got yoked?"

I showed him another photograph. "She's also got some facial petechia, or pinpoint hemorrhages. These findings are consistent with yoking, yes. She's a homicide, and I might suggest that we keep this out of the newspapers as long as possible."

"You know, I didn't need this." He looked up at me with bloodshot eyes. "I got eight uncleared homicides sitting on my desk even as we speak. Henrico don't got shit on Eddie Heath, and the kid's old man calls me almost every day. Not to mention, they're having a damn drug war in Mosby Court. Merry friggin' Christmas. I didn't need this."

"Jennifer Deighton didn't need this either, Marino."

"Keep going. What else did you find?"

"She did have high blood pressure, as her neighbor Mrs. Clary suggested."

"Huh," he said, shifting his eyes away from me. "How could you tell?"

"She had left ventricular hypertrophy, or thickening of the left side of the heart."

"High blood pressure does that?"

"It does. I should find fibrinoid changes in the renal microvasculature or early nephrosclerosis. I suspect the brain will show hypertensive changes, too, in the cerebral arterioles, but I won't be able to say with certainty until I can take a look under the scope."

"You're saying kidney and brain cells get killed off when you got high blood pressure?"

"In a manner of speaking."

"Anything else?"

"Nothing significant."

"What about gastric contents?" Marino asked.

"Meat, some vegetables, partially digested."

"Alcohol or drugs?"

"No alcohol. Drug screens are under way."

"No sign of rape?"

"No injuries or other evidence of sexual assault. I swabbed her for seminal fluid but won't get those reports for a while. Even then, you can't always be sure."

Marino's face was unreadable.

"What are you after?" I finally asked.

"Well, I'm thinking about how this thing was staged. Someone went to a lot of trouble to make us think she gassed herself. But then the lady's dead before he even gets her into her car. What I'm considering is that he didn't mean to whack her inside the house. You know, he applies a choke hold, uses too much force, and she dies. So, maybe he didn't know her health was bad and that's how it happened."

I started shaking my head. "Her high blood pressure has nothing to do with it."

"Explain how she died, then."

"Say the assailant is right-handed, he brought his left arm around the front of her neck and used his right hand to pull the left wrist toward the right." I demonstrated. "This placed pressure eccentrically on her neck, resulting in fracture of the right greater cornua of the hyoid bone. The pressure collapsed her upper airway and put pressure on the carotid arteries. She would have gotten hypoxic, or air hungry. Sometimes pressure on the neck produces bradycardia, a drop in the heart rate, and the victim has an arrhythmia."

"Could you tell from her autopsy if the assailant started using a choke hold that ended up a yoking? If he was just trying to subdue her and used too much force, in other words?"

"I can't tell you that from medical findings."

"But it's possible."

"It's within the realm of possibility."

"Come on, Doc," Marino said, exasperated. "Get off the witness stand for a minute, okay? Somebody else in this office besides you and me?"

No one was. But I was unnerved. Most of my staff had not shown up for work today, and Susan had acted bizarrely. Jennifer Deighton, a stranger, apparently had been trying to call me, then was murdered, and a man who claimed to be her brother had just hung up on me. Not to mention, Marino's mood was foul. When I felt a loss of control, I became very clinical.

"Look," I said, "he very well may have used a choke hold to subdue her and ended up applying too much force, yoking her by mistake. In fact, I'll even go so far as to suggest that he simply thought he'd knocked her out and didn't know she was dead when he placed her inside her car."

"So we're dealing with a dumb shit."

"I wouldn't conclude that if I were you. But if he gets up tomorrow morning and reads in the paper that Jennifer Deighton was murdered, he may be in for the surprise of his life. He's going to wonder what he did wrong. Which is why I recommended we keep this away from the press."

"I got no problem with that. By the way, just because you didn't know Jennifer Deighton don't mean she didn't know you."

I waited for him to explain.

"I've been thinking about your hang ups. You're on TV, in the papers. Maybe she knew someone was after her, didn't know where to turn, and reached out to you for help. When she got your machine, she was too paranoid to leave a message."

"That's a very depressing thought."

"Almost everything we think in this joint is depressing." He got up from his chair.

"Do me a favor," I said. "Check her house. Tell me if you find any feather pillows, down-filled jackets, feather dusters, anything relating to feathers."

"Why?"

"I found a small feather on her gown."

"Sure. I'll let you know. Are you leaving?"

I glanced past him as I heard the elevator doors open and shut. "Was that Stevens?" I asked.

"Yeah."

"I've got a few more things to do before I go home," I said.

After Marino got on the elevator, I went to a window at the end of the hall that overlooked the parking lot in back. I wanted to make sure Ben Stevens's Jeep was gone. It was, and I watched as Marino emerged from the building, picking his way through crushed snow lit up by street lamps. He trudged to his car and stopped to vigorously shake snow off his feet, like a cat that's stepped in water, before sliding behind the wheel. God forbid that anything should violate the freshened air and Armor All of his inner sanctum. I wondered if he had plans for Christmas and was dismayed that I had not thought to invite him in for dinner. This would be his first Christmas since he and Doris had divorced.

As I made my way back down the empty hall, I ducked into each office along the way to check computer terminals. Unfortunately, no one was logged in, and the only cable tagged with a device number was Fielding's. It was neither tty07 nor tty14. Frustrated, I unlocked Margaret's office and switched on the light.

Typically, it looked as if a fierce wind had blown through, scattering papers across her desk, tipping books over in the bookcase and knocking others on the floor. Stacks of continuous-paper printouts spilled over like accordions, and indecipherable notes and telephone numbers were taped to walls and terminal screens. The minicomputer hummed like an electronic insect and lights danced across banks of modems on a shelf. Sitting in her chair before the system terminal, I slid open a drawer to my right and began rapidly walking my fingers through file tabs. I found several with promising labels such as "users" and "networking," but nothing I perused told me what I needed to know. Looking around as I thought, I noticed a thick bundle of cables that ran up the wall behind the computer and disappeared through the ceiling. Each cable was tagged.

Both tty07 and tty14 were connected directly to the computer. Unplugging tty07 first, I roamed from terminal to terminal to see which had been disconnected as a result. The terminal in Ben Stevens's office was down, then up again when I reconnected the cable. Next I set about to trace tty14, and was perplexed when the unplugging of that cable seemed to illicit no response. Terminals on the desks of my staff continued to work without pause. Then I remembered Susan. Her office was downstairs in the morgue.

Unlocking her door, I noticed two details the instant I walked into her office. There were no personal effects, such as photographs and knickknacks, to be seen, and on a book-shelf over the desk were a number of UNIX, SQL, and Word-Perfect reference guides. I vaguely recalled that Susan had signed up for several computer courses last spring. Flipping a switch to turn on her monitor, I tried to log in and was baffled when the system responded. Her terminal was still connected; it could not be tty14. And then I realized something so obvious that I might have laughed were I not horrified.

Back upstairs, I paused in my office doorway, looking in as if someone I had never met worked here. Pooled around the workstation on my desk were lab reports, call sheets, death certificates, and page proofs of a forensic pathology textbook I was editing, and the return bearing my microscope didn't look much better. Against a wall were three tall filing cabinets, and across from them a couch situated far enough away from bookcases that you could easily go around it to reach books on lower shelves. Directly behind my chair was an oak credenza I had found years earlier in the state's surplus warehouse. Its drawers had locks, making it a perfect repository for my pocketbook and active cases that were unusually sensitive. I kept the key under my phone, and I thought again of last Thursday when Susan had broken jars of formalin while I was doing Eddie Heath's autopsy.

I did not know the device number of my terminal, for there had never been occasion when it mattered. Seating myself at my desk and sliding out the keyboard drawer, I tried to log in but my keystrokes were ignored. Disconnecting tty14 had disconnected me.

"Damn," I whispered as my blood ran cold. "Damn!"

I had sent no notes to my administrator's terminal. It was not I who had typed "I can't find it." In fact, when the file was accidentally created late last Thursday afternoon, I was in the morgue. But Susan wasn't. I had given her my keys and told her to lie down on the couch in my office until she recovered from the formalin spill. Was it possible that she not only had broken into my directory but also had gone through files and the paperwork on my desk? Had she attempted to send a note to Ben Stevens because she couldn't find what they were interested in?

One of the trace evidence examiners from upstairs suddenly appeared in my doorway, startling me.

"Hello," he muttered as he looked through paperwork, his lab coat buttoned up to his chin. Pulling out a multiple-page report, he walked in and handed it to me.

"I was getting ready to leave this in your box," he said. "But since you're still here, I'll give it to you in person. I've finished examining the adhesive residue you lifted from Eddie Heath's wrists."

"Building materials?" I asked, scanning the first page of the report.

"That's right. Paint, plaster, wood, cement, asbestos, glass. Typically, we find this sort of debris in burglary cases, often on the suspects' clothing, in their cuffs, pockets, shoes, and so on."

"What about on Eddie Heath's clothes?"

"Some of this same debris was on his clothes."

"And the paints? Tell me about them."

"I found bits of paint from five different origins. Three of them are layered, meaning something was painted and repainted a number of times."

"Are the origins vehicular or residential?" I inquired.

"Only one is vehicular, an acrylic lacquer typically used as a top coat in cars manufactured by General Motors."

It could have come from the vehicle used to abduct Eddie Heath, I thought. And it could have come from anywhere.

"The color?" I inquired.

"Blue."

"Layered?"

"No."

"What about the debris from the area of pavement where the body was found? I asked Marino to get sweepings to you and he said he would."

"Sand, dirt, bits of paving material, plus the miscellaneous debris you might expect around a Dumpster. Glass, paper, ash, pollen, rust, plant material."

"That's different from what you found adhering to the residue on his wrists?"

"Yes. It would appear to me that the tape was applied and removed from his wrists in a location where there's debris from building materials and birds."

"Birds?"

"On the third page of the report," he said. "I found a lot of feather parts."

Lucy was restless and rather irritable when I got home. Clearly, she had not had enough to occupy her during the day, for she had taken it upon herself to rearrange my study. The laser printer had been moved, as had the modem and all of my computer reference guides.

"Why did you do this?" I asked.

She was in my chair, her back to me, and she replied without turning around or slowing her fingers on the keybroad. "It makes more sense this way."

"Lucy, you can't just go into someone else's office and move everything around. How would you feel if I did that to you?"

"There would be no reason to rearrange anything of mine. It's all arranged very sensibly." She stopped typing and swiveled around. "See, now you can reach the printer without getting up from the chair. Your books are right here within reach, and the modem is out of your way completely. You shouldn't set books, coffee cups, and things on top of a modem."

"Have you been in here all day?" I asked.

"Where else would I be? You took the car. I went jogging around your neighborhood. Have you ever tried to run on snow?"

Pulling up a chair, I opened my briefcase and got out the paper bag Marino had given me. "You're saying you need a car."

"I feel stranded."

"Where would you like to go?"

"To your club. I don't know where else. I'd simply like the option. What's in the bag?"

"Books and a poem Marino gave me."

"Since when is he a member of the literati?" She got up and

stretched. "I'm going to make a cup of herbal tea. Would you like some?"

"Coffee, please."

"It's bad for you," she said as she left the room.

"Oh, hell," I muttered irritably as I pulled the books and poem out of the bag and red fluorescent powder got all over my hands and clothes.

Neils Vander had done his usual thorough examination, and I had forgotten his passion for his new toy. Several months ago he had acquired an alternate light source and had retired the laser to the scrap heap. The Luma-Lite, with its "state-of-the-art three-hundred-and-fifty-watt high-intensity blue enhanced metal vapor arc lamp," as Vander lovingly described it whenever the subject came up, turned virtually invisible hairs and fibers a burning orange. Semen stains and street drug residues jumped out like solar flares, and best of all, the light could pick up fingerprints that never would have been seen in the past.

Vander had gone the gamut on Jennifer Deighton's paperback novels. They had been placed in the glass tank and exposed to vapors from Super Glue, the cyanoacrylate ester that reacts to the components of perspiration transferred by human skin. Then Vander had dusted the slick covers of the books with the red fluorescent powder that was now all over me. Finally, he had subjected the books to the cool blue scrutiny of the Luma-Lite and purpled pages with Ninhydrin. I hoped he would be rewarded for all of his trouble. My reward was to go into the bathroom and clean up with a wet washcloth.

Flipping through *Paris Trout* was unrevealing. The novel told the story of the heartless murder of a black girl, and if that was significant to Jennifer Deighton's own story, I could not imagine why. *Seth Speaks* was a spooky account of someone supposedly from another life communicating through the author. It did not really surprise me that Miss Deighton, with her otherworldly inclinations, might read such a thing. What interested me most was the poem.

It was typed on a sheet of white paper smudged purple with Ninhydrin and enclosed in a plastic bag:

Jenny

Jenny's kisses many
warmed the copper penny
wedded to her neck
with cotton string.
It was in the spring
when he had found it
on the dusty drive
beside the meadow
and given it to her.
No words of passion
spoken.
He loved her
with a token.
The meadow now is brown
and overgrown with brambles.
He is gone.
The coin asleep
is cold
down deep
in a woodland
wishing pond.

There was no date, no name of the author. The paper was creased from having been folded in quarters. I got up and went into the living room, where Lucy had set coffee and tea on the table and was stirring the fire.

"Aren't you hungry?" she asked.

"As a matter of fact, I am," I said, glancing over the poem again and wondering what it meant. Was "Jenny" Jennifer Deighton? "What would you like to eat?"

"Believe it or not, steak. But only if it's good and the cows haven't been fed a bunch of chemicals," Lucy said. "Is it possible you could bring home a car from work so I could use yours this week?"

"I generally don't bring home the state car unless I'm on call."

"You went to a scene last night when you supposedly weren't on call. You're always on call, Aunt Kay."

"All right," I said. "Why don't we do this. We'll go get the best steak in town. Afterward, we'll stop by the office and I'll drive the wagon home and you can take my car. There's still a little ice on the roads in spots. You have to promise to be extra careful."

"I've never seen your office."

"I'll show it to you if you wish."

"No way. Not at night."

"The dead can't hurt you."

"Yes, they can," Lucy said. "Dad hurt me when he died. He left me to be raised by Mom."

"Let's get our coats."

"Why is it that every time I bring up anything germane to our dysfunctional family, you change the subject?"

I headed to my bedroom for my coat. "Do you want to borrow my black leather jacket?"

"See, you're doing it again," she screamed.

We argued all the way to Ruth's Chris Steak House, and by the time I parked the car I had a headache and was completely disgusted with myself. Lucy had provoked me into raising my voice, and the only other person who could routinely do that was my mother.

"Why are you being so difficult?" I said in her ear as we were shown to a table.

"I want to talk to you and you won't let me," she said.

A waiter instantly appeared for drink orders.

"Dewar's and soda," I said.

"Sparkling water with a twist," Lucy said. "You shouldn't drink and drive."

"I'm having only one. But you're right. I'd be better off not having any. And you're being critical again. How can you expect to have friends if you talk to people this way?"

"I don't expect to have friends." She stared off. "It's others who expect me to have friends. Maybe I don't want any friends because most people bore me."

Despair pressed against my heart. "I think you want friends more than anyone I know, Lucy."

"I'm sure you think that. And you probably also think I should get married in a couple of years."

"Not at all. In fact, I sincerely hope you won't."

"While I was roaming around inside your computer today, I saw the file called 'flesh.' Why do you have a file called that?" my niece asked.

"Because I'm in the middle of a very difficult case."

"The little boy named Eddie Heath? I saw his record in the case file. He was found with no clothes on, next to a Dumpster. Someone had cut out parts of his skin."

"Lucy, you shouldn't read case records," I said as my pager went off. I unclipped it from the waistband of my skirt and glanced at the number.

"Excuse me for a moment," I said, getting up from the table as our drinks arrived.

I found a pay phone. It was almost eight P.M.

"I need to talk to you," said Neils Vander, who was still at the office. "You might want to come down here and bring by Ronnie Waddell's ten print cards."

"Why?"

"We've got an unprecedented problem. I'm about to call Marino, too."

"All right. Tell him to meet me at the morgue in a half hour."

When I returned to the table, Lucy knew by the look on my face that I was about to ruin another evening.

"I'm so sorry," I said.

"Where are we going?"

"To my office, then to the Seaboard Building." I got out my billfold.

"What's in the Seaboard Building?"

"It's where the serology, DNA, and fingerprint labs moved not so long ago. Marino's going to meet us," I said. "It's been a long time since you've seen him."

"Jerks like him don't change or get better with time."

"Lucy, that's unkind. Marino is not a jerk."

"He was last time I was here."

"You weren't exactly nice to him, either."

"I didn't call him a smartass brat."

"You called him a number of other names, as I recall, and were continually correcting his grammar."

A half hour later, I left Lucy inside the morgue office while I hurried upstairs. Unlocking the credenza, I retrieved Waddell's case file, and no sooner had I boarded the elevator when the buzzer sounded from the bay. Marino was dressed in jeans and a dark blue parka, his balding head warmed by a Richmond Braves baseball cap.

"You two remember each other, don't you?" I said. "Lucy's visiting me for Christmas and is helping out with a computer problem," I explained as we walked out into the cold night air.

The Seaboard Building was across the street from the parking lot behind the morgue and cater-cornered to the front of Main Street Station, where the Health Department's administrative offices had relocated while its former building was being stripped of asbestos. The clock in Main Street Station's tower floated high above us like a hunter's moon, and red lights atop high buildings blinked slow warnings to low-flying planes. Somewhere in the dark, a train lumbered along its tracks, the earth rumbling and creaking like a ship at sea.

Marino walked ahead of us, the tip of his cigarette glowing at intervals. He did not want Lucy here, and I knew she sensed it. When he reached the Seaboard Building, where supplies had been loaded onto boxcars around the time of the Civil War, I rang the bell outside the door. Vander appeared almost immediately to let us in.

He did not greet Marino or ask who Lucy was. If a creature from outer space were to accompany someone he trusted, Vander would not ask any questions or expect to be introduced. We followed him up a flight of stairs to the second floor, where old corridors and offices had been repainted in shades of gunmetal gray and refurnished with cherry-finished desks and bookcases and teal upholstered chairs.

"What are you working on so late?" I asked as we entered the room housing the Automated Fingerprint Identification System, known as AFIS.

"Jennifer Deighton's case," he said.

"Then what do you want with Waddell's ten print cards?" I asked, perplexed.

"I want to be sure it was Waddell you autopsied last week," Vander said bluntly.

"What the hell are you talking about?" Marino looked at him in astonishment.

"I'm getting ready to show you." Vander seated himself before the remote input terminal, which looked like an everyday PC. It was connected by modem to the State Police computer, on which resided a data base of more than six million fingerprints. He hit several keys, activating the laser printer.

"Perfect scores are few and far between, but we got one here." Vander began typing, and a bright white fingerprint filled the screen. "Right index finger, plain whorl." He pointed to the vortex of lines swirling behind glass. "A damn good partial recovered from Jennifer Deighton's house."

"Where in her house?" I asked.

"From a dining room chair. At first I wondered if there was some mistake. But apparently not." Vander continued staring at the screen, then resumed typing as he talked. "The print comes back to Ronnie Joe Waddell."

"That's impossible," I said, shocked.

"You would think so," Vander replied abstractedly.

"Did you find anything in Jennifer Deighton's house that might indicate she and Waddell were acquainted?" I asked Marino as I opened Waddell's case file.

"No."

"If you've got Waddell's prints from the morgue," Vander said to me, "we'll see how they compare to what's in AFIS."

I pulled out two manila envelopes, and it struck me wrong immediately that both weren't heavy and thick. I felt my face get hot as I opened each and found the expected photographs inside and nothing else. There was no envelope containing Waddell's ten print cards. When I looked up, everybody was looking at me.

"I don't understand this," I said, conscious of Lucy's uneasy stare.

"You don't have his prints?" Marino asked in disbelief.

I rifled through the file again. "They're not here."

"Susan usually does it, right?" he said.

"Yes. Always. She was supposed to make two sets. One for Corrections and one for us. Maybe she gave them to Fielding and he forgot to give them to me."

I got out my address book and reached for the phone. Fielding was home and knew nothing about the fingerprint cards.

"No, I didn't notice her printing him, but I don't notice half of what other people are doing down there," he said. "I just assumed she'd given the cards to you."

Dialing Susan's number next, I tried to remember seeing her get out the spoon and print cards, or rolling Waddell's fingers on the ink pad.

"Do you remember seeing Susan print Waddell?" I asked Marino as Susan's phone continued to ring.

"She didn't do it while I was there. I would have offered to help if she had."

"No answer." I hung up.

"Waddell was cremated," Vander said.

"Yes," I said.

We were silent for a moment.

Then Marino said to Lucy with unnecessary brusqueness, "You mind? We need to talk alone for a minute."

"You can sit in my office," Vander said to her. "Down the hall, last one on the right."

When she was gone, Marino said, "Waddell's supposedly been locked up ten years, and there's no way the print we got from Jennifer Deighton's chair was left ten years ago. She didn't even move into her house on Southside until a few months ago, and the dining room furniture looks brand-new. Plus, there were indentations on the carpet in the living room that make it appear a dining room chair was carried in there, maybe on the night she died. That's why I wanted the chairs dusted to begin with."

"An uncanny possibility," Vander said. "At this moment, we can't prove that the man who was executed last week was Ronnie Joe Waddell."

"Perhaps there is some other explanation for how Waddell's print ended up on a chair in Jennifer Deighton's house," I said. "For example, the penitentiary has a wood shop that makes furniture."

"Unlikely as hell," Marino said. "For one thing, they don't do woodworking or make license plates on death row. And even if they did, most civilians don't end up with prison-made furniture in their house."

"All the same," Vander said to Marino, "it would be interesting if you could track down who and where she bought her dining room set from."

"Don't worry. It's a top priority."

"Waddell's complete past arrest record, including his prints, should all be in one file at the FBI," Vander added. "I'll get a copy of their print card and retrieve the photograph of the thumbprint from Robyn Naismith's case. Where else was Waddell arrested?"

"Nowhere else," Marino said. "The only jurisdiction that will have his records should be Richmond."

"And this print found on a dining room chair is the only one you've identified?" I asked Vander.

"Of course, a number of those lifted came back to Jennifer Deighton," he said. "Particularly on the books by her bed and the folded sheet of paper—the poem. And a couple of unknown partials from her car, as you might expect, maybe left by whoever loaded groceries into her trunk or filled her tank with gas. That's all for now."

"And no luck with Eddie Heath?" I asked.

"There wasn't much to examine. The paper bag, can of soup, candy bar. I tried the Luma-Lite on his shoes and clothes. No luck."

Later, he walked us out through the bay, where locked freezers stored the blood of enough convicted felons to fill a small city, the samples awaiting entry into the Commonwealth's DNA data bank. Parked in front of the door was Jennifer Deighton's car, and it looked more pathetic than I remembered, as if it had gone into a dramatic decline since the murder of its owner. Metal along the sides was creased and dented from being repeatedly struck by other car doors. Paint was rusting in spots and scraped and gouged in others, and the vinyl top was peeling. Lucy paused to peer inside a sooty window.

"Hey, don't touch nothing," Marino said to her.

She looked levelly at him without a word, and all of us went outside.

* * *

Lucy drove off in my car and went straight to the house without waiting for Marino or me. When we walked in, she was already in my study with the door shut.

"I can see she's still Miss Congeniality," Marino said.

"You don't win any prizes tonight, either." I opened the fireplace screen and added several logs.

"She'll keep her mouth shut about what we were talking about?"

"Yes," I said wearily. "Of course."

"Yeah, well, I know you trust her, since you're her aunt. But I'm not sure it was a good idea for her to hear all that, Doc."

"I do trust Lucy. She means a lot to me. You mean a lot to me. I hope the two of you will become friends. The bar is open, or I'll be glad to put on a pot of coffee."

"Coffee would be good."

He sat on the edge of the hearth and got out his Swiss Army knife. While I made coffee, he trimmed his nails and tossed the shavings into the fire. I tried Susan's number again, but there was no answer.

"I don't think Susan took his prints," Marino said when I set the coffee tray on the butler's table. "I've been thinking while you were in the kitchen. I know she didn't do it while I was at the morgue that night, and I was there most of the time. So unless it was done right when the body was brought in, forget it."

"It wasn't done then," I said, getting more unnerved. "Corrections was out of there in minutes. The entire scene was very distracting. It was late and everybody was tired. Susan forgot, and I was too busy with what I was doing to notice."

"You hope she forgot."

I reached for my coffee.

"Something's going on with her, based on what you've been telling me. I wouldn't trust her as far as I could throw her," he said.

Right now I didn't.

"We need to talk to Benton," he said.

"You saw Waddell on the table, Marino. You saw him executed. I can't believe we can't say it was him."

"We can't say it. We could compare mug shots and your morgue photos and still not say it. I hadn't seen him since he got popped more than ten years ago. The guy they walked out to the chair was about eighty pounds heavier. His beard, mustache, and head had been shaved. Sure, there was enough resemblance that I just assumed. But I can't swear it was him."

I recalled Lucy's walking off the plane the other night. She was my niece. I had seen her but a year ago, and still I almost had not recognized her. I knew all too well how unreliable visual identifications can be.

"If someone switched inmates," I said. "And if Waddell is free and someone else was put to death, please tell me why."

Marino spooned more sugar into his coffee.

"A motive, for God's sake. Marino, what would it be?"

He looked up. "I don't know why."

Just then, the door to my study opened and both of us turned as Lucy walked out. She came into the living room and sat on the side of the hearth opposite Marino, who had his back to the fire, elbows on his knees.

"What can you tell me about AFIS?" she asked me as if Marino were not in the room.

"What is it you wish to know?" I said.

"The language. And is it run on a mainframe."

"I don't know the technical details. Why?"

"I can find out if files have been altered."

I felt Marino's eyes on me.

"You can't break into the State Police computer, Lucy."

"I probably could, but I'm not necessarily advocating that. There may be some other way to gain access."

Marino turned to her. "You're saying you could tell if Waddell's records was changed in AFIS?"

"Yes. I'm saying I could tell if his records *were* changed."

Marino's jaw muscles flexed. "Seems to me if someone was slick enough to do it, they'd be slick enough to make sure some computer nerd didn't catch on."

"I'm not a computer nerd. I'm not a nerd of any description."

They fell silent, parked on either end of the hearth like mismatched bookends.

"You can't go into AFIS," I said to Lucy.

She looked impassively at me.

"Not alone," I added. "Not unless there is a safe way to grant you access. And even if there is, I think I'd rather you stay out of it."

"I don't think you'd really rather that. If something was tampered with, you know I'd find out, Aunt Kay."

"The kid's got a god complex." Marino got up from the hearth.

Lucy said to him, "Could you hit the twelve on the clock over there on the wall? If you drew your gun right this minute and took aim?"

"I ain't interested in shooting up your aunt's house in order to prove something to you."

"Could you hit the twelve from where you're standing?"

"You're damn right."

"You're positive."

"Yeah, I'm positive."

"The lieutenant's got a god complex," Lucy said to me.

Marino turned to the fire, but not before I caught a flicker of a smile.

"All Neils Vander has is a workstation and printer," Lucy said. "He's connected to the State Police computer by modem. Has that always been the case?"

"No," I replied. "Before he moved into the new building, there was much more equipment involved."

"Describe it."

"Well, there were several different components. But the actual computer was much like the one Margaret has in her office." Realizing Lucy had not been inside Margaret's office, I added, "A mini."

Firelight cast moving shadows on her face. "I'll bet AFIS is a mainframe that isn't a mainframe. I'll bet it's a series of minis strung together, all of it connected by UNIX or some other multiuser, multitasking environment. If you got me access to the system, I could probably do it from your terminal here in the house, Aunt Kay."

"I don't want anything traced back to me," I said with feeling.

"Nothing would be traced back to you. I would dial into your computer downtown, then go through a series of gateways, set up a really complicated link. By the time all was said and done, I'd be very hard to track."

Marino headed to the bathroom.

"He acts like he lives here," Lucy said.

"Not quite," I replied.

Several minutes later, I walked Marino out. The crusty snow of the lawn seemed to radiate light, and the air was sharp in my lungs like the first hit of a menthol cigarette.

"I'd love it if you would join Lucy and me for Christmas dinner," I said from the doorway.

He hesitated, looking at his car parked on the street. "That's mighty nice of you, but I can't make it, Doc."

"I wish you did not dislike Lucy so much," I said, hurt.

"I'm tired of her treating me like a dumb shit who was born in a barn."

"Sometimes you act like a dumb shit who was born in a barn. And you haven't tried very hard to earn her respect."

"She's a spoiled Miami brat."

"When she was ten, she was a Miami brat," I said. "But she's never been spoiled. In fact, quite the opposite is true. I want you two to get along. I want that for my Christmas present."

"Who said I was giving you a Christmas present?"

"Of course you are. You're going to give me what I've just requested. And I know exactly how to make it happen."

"How?" he asked suspiciously.

"Lucy wants to learn to shoot and you just told her you could shoot the twelve off a clock. You could give her a lesson or two."

"Forget it," he said.

6

The next three days were typical for the holiday season. No one was in or returning telephone calls. Parking lots had spaces to spare, lunch hours were long, and office errands involved clandestine stops at stores, the bank, and the post office. For all practical purposes, the Commonwealth had shut down before the official holiday began. But Neils Vander was not typical by any standard. He was oblivious to time and place when he called me Christmas Eve morning.

"I'm getting started on an image enhancement over here that I think you might be interested in," he said. "The Jennifer Deighton case."

"I'm on my way," I said.

Heading down the hallway, I almost ran into Ben Stevens as he emerged from the men's room.

"I have a meeting with Vander," I said. "I shouldn't be long, and I've got my paper."

"I was just coming to see you," he said.

Reluctantly, I paused to hear what he had on his mind. I wondered if he detected that it was a struggle for me to act relaxed around him. Lucy continued to monitor our computer from my terminal at home to see if anyone attempted to access my directory again. So far, no one had.

"I had a talk with Susan this morning," Stevens said.

"How is she?"

"She's not coming back to work, Dr. Scarpetta."

I was not surprised, but I was stung that she could not tell me this herself. By now I had tried at least half a dozen times to get hold of her, and either no one answered or her husband did and offered some excuse for why Susan couldn't come to the phone.

"That's it?" I asked him. "She's simply not coming back? Did she give a reason?"

"I think she's having a tougher time with the pregnancy than she thought. I guess the job's just too much right now."

"She'll need to send a letter of resignation," I said, unable to keep the anger from my voice. "And I'll leave it to you to work out the details with Personnel. We'll need to begin looking for a replacement immediately."

"There's a hiring freeze," he reminded me as I walked off.

Outside, snow plowed along roadsides had frozen into mounds of filthy ice impossible to park on or walk across, and the sun burned wanly through portentous clouds. A streetcar carried a small brass band past, and I climbed granite steps gritty with salt as "Joy to the World" moved on. A Forensics police officer let me inside the Seaboard Building, and upstairs I found Vander inside a room bright with color monitors and ultraviolet lights. Seated at the image enhancer's workstation, he was staring intensely at something on the screen as he manipulated a mouse.

"It's not blank," he announced without so much as a "how are you." "Someone wrote something on a piece of paper that was on top of this one, or close to on top of this one. If you look hard, you can barely make out impressions."

Then I began to understand. Centered on the light table to his left was a clean sheet of white paper, and I leaned closer to take a look. The impressions were so faint that I wasn't sure if I was imagining them.

"The sheet of paper found under the crystal on Jennifer Deighton's bed?" I asked, getting excited.

He nodded, moving the mouse some more, adjusting the gray tones.

"Is this live?"

"No. The video camera's already captured the impressions and they're saved on the hard disk. But don't touch the paper. I haven't processed it for prints yet. I'm just getting started, keep your fingers crossed. Come on, come on." He was talking to the enhancer now. "I know the camera saw it fine. You gotta help us out here."

Computerized methods of image enhancement are a lesson in contrasts and conundrums. A camera can differentiate more than two hundred shades of gray, the human eye less than forty. Just because something isn't there doesn't mean it isn't there.

"Thank God with paper you don't have to worry about background noise," Vander went on as he worked. "Speeds things up considerably when you don't have to worry about that. Had a time of it the other day with a bloody print left on a bed sheet. The weave of the fabric, you know. Not so long ago the print would have been worthless. Okay." Another tint of gray washed over the area he was working on. "Now we're getting somewhere. You see it?" He pointed at slender, ghostly shapes on the upper half of the screen.

"Barely."

"What we're trying to enhance here is shadow versus eradicated writing, because nothing was written and erased here. The shadow was produced when oblique light hit the flat surface of this paper and the indentations in it—at least the video camera perceived shadow loud and clear. You and I can't see it without help. Let's try a little more enhancement of the verticals." He moved the mouse. "Darken the horizontals just a tad. Good. It's coming. Two-oh-two, dash. We've got part of a phone number."

I pulled a chair close to him and sat down. "The area code for D.C.," I said.

"I'm making out a four and a three. Or is that an eight?"

I squinted. "I think it's a three."

"That's better. You're right. Definitely a three."

He continued to work for a while and more numbers and words became visible on the screen. Then he sighed and said, "Rats. I can't get the last digit. It's just not there, but look at this before the D.C. area code. 'To' followed by a colon. And right under it is 'from' followed by another colon and another number. Eight-oh-four. That's local. This number's very unclear. A five and maybe a seven, or is that a nine?"

"I think that's going to be Jennifer Deighton's number," I said. "Her fax machine and telephone are on the same line—she had a fax machine in her office, a single-sheet feed that uses ordinary typing paper. It appears she wrote out a fax on top of this sheet of paper. What did she send? A separate document? There's no message here."

"We're not finished yet. We're getting what looks like the date now. An eleven? No, that's a seven. December seventeenth. I'm going to move down."

He moved the mouse and the arrows slid down the screen. Hitting a key, he enlarged the area he wanted to work on, then began painting it with shades of gray. I sat very still while shapes began to slowly materialize out of a literary limbo, curves here, dots there, and *t*'s boldy crossed. Vander worked silently. We barely blinked or breathed. We sat like this for an hour, words gradually getting sharper, one shade of gray contrasting with another, molecule by molecule, bit by bit. He willed them, coaxed them into existence. It was incredible. It was all there.

Exactly one week ago, barely two days before her murder, Jennifer Deighton had faxed the following message to a number in Washington, D.C.:

> Yes, I'll cooperate, but it's too late, too late, too late. Better you should come here. This is all so wrong!

When I finally looked up from the screen as Vander hit the print button, I was light-headed. My vision was temporarily blurred, adrenaline surging.

"Marino needs to see this immediately. Hopefully, we can figure out whose fax number this is, the Washington number. We've got all but the last digit. How many fax numbers can there be in Washington that are exactly like this except for the last digit?"

"Digits zero through nine." Vander raised his voice above the printer's rat-a-tat-tat. "At the most, there could be only ten. Ten numbers, fax or otherwise, exactly like this one except for the last digit."

He gave me a printout. "I'll clean it up some more and get you a better copy later," he said. "And there's one more thing. I'm not having any luck getting my hands on Ronnie Waddell's print, the photo of the bloody thumbprint recovered from Robyn Naismith's house. Every time I call Archives, I'm told they're still looking for his file."

"Remember what time of year it is. I'll bet there's hardly anybody there," I said, unable to dispel a sense of foreboding.

Back in my office, I got hold of Marino and explained what the image enhancer had discovered.

"Hell, you can forget the phone company," he said. "My contact there's already left for vacation, and nobody else is going to do shit on Christmas Eve."

"There's a chance we can figure out who she sent the fax to on our own," I said.

"I don't know how, short of sending a fax that reads 'Who are you?' and then hoping you get a fax back that reads 'Hi. I'm Jennifer Deighton's killer.' "

"It depends on if the person has a label programmed into his fax machine," I said.

"A *label?*"

"Your more sophisticated fax machines allow you to program your name or company name into the system. This label will be printed on anything you fax to someone else. But what's more significant is that the label of the person receiving the fax will also appear in the character-display window of the machine sending the fax. In other words, if I send a fax to you, in the character display of my fax machine I'll see 'Richmond Police Department' right above the fax number I've just dialed."

"You got access to a fancy fax machine? The one we got in the squad room sucks."

"I've got one here at the office."

"Well, tell me what you find out. I've gotta hit the street."

Quickly, I made up a list of ten telephone numbers, each one beginning with the six digits Vander and I had been able to make out on the sheet of paper found on Jennifer Deighton's bed. I completed each number with a zero, a one, a two, a three, and so on, then began trying them out. Only one of them was answered by an inhuman, high-pitched tone.

The fax machine was located in my computer analyst's office, and Margaret, fortunately, had begun her holiday early, too. I shut her door and sat down at her desk, thinking as the minicomputer hummed and modem lights blinked. Labels worked both ways. If I began a transmission, the label for my office was going to appear in the character-display window of the fax machine I had dialed. I would have to kill the process fast, before the transmission was completed. I hoped that by the time anyone checked the machine to see what was going on, "Office of the Chief Medical Examiner" and our number would have vanished from the window.

Inserting a blank sheet of paper into the tray, I dialed the Washington number and waited as the transmission began. Nothing materialized in the character-display window. Damn. The fax machine I had dialed did not have a label. So much for that. I killed the process and returned to my office, defeated.

I had just sat down at my desk when the telephone rang.

"Dr. Scarpetta," I answered.

"Nicholas Grueman here. Whatever you just tried to fax, it didn't transmit."

"Excuse me?" I said, stunned.

"I got nothing on this end but a blank sheet of paper with the name of your office stamped on it. Uh, error code zero-zero-one, 'please send again,' it says."

"I see," I said as the hairs on my arms raised.

"Perhaps you were trying to send an amendment to your record? I understand you took a look at the electric chair."

I did not reply.

"Very thorough of you, Dr. Scarpetta. Perhaps you learned something new about those injuries we discussed, the abrasions to the inner aspects of Mr. Waddell's arms? The *antecubital fossas*?"

"Please give me your fax number again," I said quietly.

He recited it for me. The number matched the one on my list.

"Is the fax machine in your office or do you share it with other attorneys, Mr. Grueman?"

"It's right next to my desk. No need to mark anything for my attention. Just send it on—and *do* put a rush on it please, Dr. Scarpetta. I was thinking of going home soon."

I left the office a little later, frustration having driven me out the door. I could not get Marino. There was nothing more I could do. I felt caught in a web of bizarre connections, clueless as to the point in common they shared.

On impulse I pulled into a lot on West Cary where an old man was selling wreaths and Christmas trees. He looked like a lumberjack from a fable as he sat on a stool in the midst of his small forest, the cold air fragrant with evergreen. Perhaps my shunning of the Christmas spirit finally had gotten to me. Or maybe I simply wanted a distraction. At this late date, there wasn't much of a selection, those trees passed over, misshapen or dying, each destined to sit out the season, I suspected, except for the one I chose. It would have been lovely were it not scoliotic. Decorating it proved more an orthopedic challenge than a festive ritual, but with ornaments and strands of lights strategically hung and wire straightening the problem places, it stood proudly in my living room.

"There," I said to Lucy as I stepped back to admire my work. "What do you think?"

"I think it's weird that you suddenly decided to get a tree on Christmas Eve. When was the last time you had one?"

"I suppose when I was married."

"Is that where the ornaments came from?"

"Back then I went to a lot of trouble at Christmas."

"Which is why you don't anymore."

"I'm much busier than I was back then," I said.

Lucy opened the fireplace screen and rearranged logs with the poker. "Did you and Mark ever spend Christmas together?"

"Don't you remember? We came down to see you last Christmas."

"No, you didn't. You came for three days *after* Christmas and flew home on New Year's Day."

"He was with his family on Christmas Day."

"You weren't invited?"

"No."

"Why not?"

"Mark came from an old Boston family. They had certain ways of doing things. What did you decide about this evening? Did my jacket with the black velvet collar fit?"

"I haven't tried anything. Why do we have to go to all these places?" Lucy said. "I won't know anybody."

"It's not that bad. I simply have to drop off a present to someone who's pregnant and probably not coming back to work. And I need to show the flag at a neighborhood party. I accepted the invitation before I knew you were going to be visiting. You certainly don't have to come with me."

"I'd rather stay here," she said. "I wish I could get started on AFIS."

"Patience," I told her, though I did not feel patient at all.

In the late afternoon, I left another message with the dispatcher and decided that either Marino's pager wasn't working or he was too busy to find a pay phone. Candles glowed in my neighbors' windows, an oblong moon shining high above trees. I played that Christmas music of Pavarotti and the New York Philharmonic, doing what I could to get into the proper frame of mind as I showered and dressed. The party I was to attend did not begin until seven. That gave me enough time to drop off Susan's gift and have a word with her.

She surprised me by answering the phone, and sounded reluctant and tense when I asked if I could drop by.

"Jason's out," she said, as if that mattered somehow. "He went to the mall."

"Well, I have a few things for you," I explained.

"What things?"

"Christmas things. I'm supposed to go to a party, so I won't stay long. Is that all right?"

"I guess. I mean, that's nice."

I had forgotten she lived in Southside, where I rarely went and was inclined to get lost. Traffic was worse than I had feared, the Midlothian Turnpike choked with last-minute shoppers prepared to run you off the road as they ran their Happy Holidays errands. Parking lots swarmed with cars, stores and malls so garishly lit up it was enough to make you blind. Susan's neighborhood was very dark and twice I had to pull over and turn on the interior light to read her directions. After much riding around, I finally found her tiny ranch-style house sandwiched between two others that looked exactly like it.

"Hi," I said, peering at her through leaves of the pink poinsettia in my arms.

She nervously locked the door and showed me to the living room. Pushing books and magazines aside, she set the poinsettia on the coffee table.

"How are you feeling?" I asked.

"Better. Would you like something to drink? Here, let me take your coat."

"Thanks. Nothing to drink. I can't stay but a minute." I handed her a package. "A little something I picked up when I was in San Francisco last summer." I sat on the couch.

"Wow. You really do your shopping early." She avoided my eyes as she curled up in a wing chair. "You want me to open it now?"

"Whatever you'd like."

She carefully sliced through tape with a thumbnail and slipped off the satin ribbon intact. Smoothing the paper into a neat rectangle, as if she planned to reuse it, she placed it in her lap and opened the black box.

"Oh," she said under her breath, unfolding the red silk scarf.

"I thought it would look good with your black coat," I said. "I don't know about you, but I don't like wool against my skin."

"This is beautiful. It's really thoughtful of you, Dr. Scarpetta. I've never had anybody bring me something from San Francisco before."

The expression on her face pricked my heart, and suddenly my surroundings came into sharper focus. Susan was wearing a yellow terry cloth robe, frayed at the cuffs, and a pair of black socks that I suspected belonged to her husband. Furniture was scarred and cheap, upholstery shiny. The artificial Christmas tree near the small TV was scantily decorated and missing several limbs. There were few presents underneath. Propped against a wall was a folded crib that was clearly secondhand.

Susan caught me glancing around and looked ill at ease.

"Everything is so immaculate," I said.

"You know how I am. Obsessive-compulsive."

"Thankfully. If a morgue can look terrific, ours does."

She carefully folded the scarf and returned it to its box. Pulling her robe more tightly around her, she stared silently at the poinsettia.

"Susan," I said gently, "do you want to talk about what's going on?"

She did not look at me.

"It's not like you to get upset as you did the other morning. It's not like you to miss work and then quit without so much as calling me."

She took a deep breath. "I'm really sorry. I just can't seem to handle things too well these days. I really react. Like when I was reminded of Judy."

"I know your sister's death must have been terrible for you."

"We were twins. Not identical. Judy was a lot prettier than me. That was part of the problem. Doreen was jealous of her."

"Doreen was the girl who claimed to be a witch?"

"Yes. I'm sorry. I just don't want to be around anything like that. Especially now."

"It might make you feel better to know that I called the church near Jennifer Deighton's house and was told that the steeple is illuminated with sodium vapor lights that started going bad several months ago. Apparently, no one was aware that the lights hadn't been properly repaired. That seems to be the explanation for why they blink on and off."

"When I was growing up in the church," she said, "there were pentecostals in the congregation who believed in speaking in tongues and casting out demons. I remember this man coming to dinner and talking about his encounter with demons, about lying in bed at night and hearing something breathing in the dark and books flying off shelves and slamming around the room. I was scared to death by stuff like that. I couldn't even see *The Exorcist* when it came out."

"Susan, we have to be objective and clearheaded on the job. We can't let our backgrounds, beliefs, or phobias interfere."

"You didn't grow up the daughter of a minister."

"I grew up Catholic," I said.

"Nothing's the same as growing up the daughter of a fundamentalist minister," she challenged, blinking back tears.

I did not argue.

"I think I've gotten free of old stuff, then it grabs me around the throat," she went on with difficulty. "Like there's this other person inside who messes with me."

"How are you being messed with?"

"Some things have gotten ruined."

I waited for her to elaborate, but she would not. She stared down at her hands, her eyes miserable. "It's just too much pressure," she muttered.

"What is too much pressure, Susan?"

"Work."

"How is it any different than it's ever been?" I assumed she would say that expecting a child made everything different.

"Jason doesn't think it's healthy for me. He's always thought that."

"I see."

"I come home and tell him what my day was like, and he has a real hard time with it. He says, 'Don't you realize how awful this is? There's no way it can be good for you.' He's right. I can't always shake it off anymore. I'm tired of decomposed bodies and people raped, cut up, and shot. I'm tired of dead babies and people killed in their cars. I don't want any more violence." She looked at me, her lower lip trembling. "I don't want any more death."

I thought of how difficult it was going to be to replace her. With someone new, days would be slow, the learning curve long. Worse were the perils of interviewing applicants and screening out the weirdos. Not everyone eager to work in a morgue is the paragon of normalcy. I liked Susan and I felt hurt and deeply troubled. She was not being honest with me.

"Is there anything else you'd like to tell me about?" I asked, my eyes not leaving her.

She glanced at me and I saw fear. "I can't think of anything."

I heard a car door shut.

"Jason's home," she barely said.

Our conversation had ended, and as I got up I said quietly to her, "Please contact me if you need anything, Susan. A reference, or just to talk. You know where I am."

I spoke to her husband only briefly on my way out. He was tall and well built, with curly brown hair and distant eyes. Though he was polite, I could tell he was not pleased to discover me in his house. As I drove across the river, I was shaken by the image that this struggling young couple must have of me. I was the *boss* dressed in a designer suit arriving in her Mercedes to deliver token gifts on Christmas Eve. The alienation of Susan's loyalty touched my deepest insecurities. I was no longer sure of my relationships or how I was perceived. I feared I had failed some test after Mark was killed, as if my reaction to that loss held the answer to a question in the lives of those around me. After all, I was supposed to handle death better than anyone. Dr. Kay Scarpetta, the expert. Instead, I had withdrawn, and I knew others felt the coolness around my edges no matter how friendly or thoughtful I tried to be. My staff no longer confided in me. Now it appeared security in my office had been violated, and Susan had quit.

Taking the Cary Street exit, I turned left into my neighborhood and headed for the home of Bruce Carter, a district court judge. He lived on Sulgrave, several blocks from me, and suddenly I was a child in Miami again, staring at what had seemed mansions to me then. I remembered going door-to-door with a wagon full of citrus fruit, knowing that the elegant hands doling out change belonged to unreachable people who felt pity. I remembered returning home with a pocket full of pennies and smelling the sickness in the bedroom where my father lay dying.

Windsor Farms was quietly rich, with Georgian and Tudor houses neatly arranged along streets with English names, and estates shadowed by trees and surrounded by serpentine brick walls. Private security jealously guarded the privileged, for whom burglar alarms were as common as sprinklers. Unspoken covenants were more intimidating than those in print. You did not offend your neighbors by putting up clotheslines or dropping by unannounced. You did not have to drive a Jaguar, but if your means of transportation was a rusting pickup truck or a morgue wagon, you kept it out of sight inside the garage.

At quarter past seven, I parked behind a long line of cars in front of a white-painted brick house with a slate roof. White lights were caught like tiny stars in boxwoods and spruces, and a fragrant fresh wreath hung on the red front door. Nancy Carter embraced my arrival with a gorgeous smile and arms extended to take my coat. She talked nonstop above the indecipherable language of crowds as light winked off the sequins of her long red gown. The judge's wife was a woman in her fifties refined by money into a work of well-bred art. In her youth, I suspected, she had not been pretty.

"Bruce is somewhere . . ." She glanced about. "The bar's over there."

She directed me to the living room, where the bright holiday attire of guests blended wonderfully with a large vibrant Persian rug that I suspected cost more than the house I had just visited on the other side of the river. I spotted the judge talking to a man I did not know. I scanned faces, recognizing several physicians and attorneys, a lobbyist, and the governor's chief of staff. Somehow I ended up with a Scotch and soda, and a man I had never seen before was touching my arm.

"Dr. Scarpetta? Frank Donahue," he introduced himself loudly. "A Merry Christmas to you."

"And to you," I said.

The warden, who allegedly had been ill the day Marino and I had toured the penitentiary, was small, with coarse features and thick graying hair. He was dressed like a parody of an English toastmaster in bright red tails, a ruffled white dress shirt, and a red bow tie twinkling with tiny electric lights. A glass of straight whiskey tilted perilously in one hand as he offered me the other.

He leaned close to my ear. "I was disappointed I was unable to show you around the day you came to the pen."

"One of your officers took good care of us. Thank you."

"I guess that would have been Roberts."

"I think that was his name."

"Well, it's unfortunate that you had to go to the trouble." His eyes roamed the room and he winked at someone behind me. "A lot of horse crap was what it was. You know, Waddell'd had a couple of nosebleeds in the past, and high blood pressure. Was always complaining about something. Headaches. Insomnia."

I bent my head, straining to hear.

"These guys on death row are consummate con artists. And to be honest, Waddell was one of the worst."

"I wouldn't know," I said, looking up at him.

"That's the trouble, nobody knows. No matter what you say, nobody knows except those of us who are around these guys every day."

"I'm sure."

"Waddell's so-called reformation, him turning into such a sweetheart. Sometime let me tell you about that, Dr. Scarpetta, about the way he used to brag to other inmates about what he did to that poor Naismith girl. Thought he was a real cock of the walk because he *did* a celebrity."

The room was airless and too warm. I could feel his eyes crawl over my body.

"Of course, I don't guess much surprises you, either," he said.

"No, Mr. Donahue. There isn't much that surprises me."

"To be honest, I don't know how you look at what you do every day. Especially this time of year, people killing each other and themselves, like that poor lady who committed suicide in her garage the other night after opening her Christmas presents early."

His remark caught me like an elbow in the ribs. There had been a brief story in the morning paper about Jennifer's Deighton's death, and a police source had been quoted as saying that it appeared she had opened her Christmas presents early. This might imply she had committed suicide, but there had been no statement to that effect.

"Which lady are you referring to?" I asked.

"Don't recall the name." Donahue sipped his drink, his face flushed, eyes bright and constantly moving. "Sad, real sad. Well, you'll have to visit us at our new digs in Greensville one of these days." He smiled broadly, then left me for a bosomy matron in black. He kissed her on the mouth and both of them started laughing.

I went home at the earliest opportunity, to find a fire blazing and my niece stretched out on the couch, reading. I noted several new presents under the tree.

"How was it?" she asked with a yawn.

"You were wise to stay home," I said. "Has Marino called?"

"Nope."

I tried him again, and after four rings he answered irritably.

"I hope I didn't get you too late," I apologized.

"I hope not, either. What's wrong now?"

"A lot of things are wrong. I met your friend Mr. Donahue at a party this evening."

"What a thrill."

"I wasn't impressed, and maybe I'm just paranoid, but I thought it odd he brought up Jennifer Deighton's death."

Silence.

"The other little twist," I went on, "is it appears Jennifer Deighton faxed a note to Nicholas Grueman less than two days before her murder. In it she sounded upset, and I got the impression he wanted to meet with her. She suggested he come to Richmond."

Still Marino said nothing.

"Are you there?" I asked.

"I'm thinking."

"Glad to hear it. But maybe we should think together. Sure I can't change your mind about dinner tomorrow?"

He took a deep breath. "I'd like to, Doc. But I . . ."

A female voice in the background said, "Which drawer's it in?"

Marino evidently placed his hand over the receiver and mumbled something. When he got back to me he cleared his throat.

"I'm sorry," I said. "I didn't know you had company."

"Yeah." He paused.

"I would be delighted if you and your friend would come to dinner tomorrow," I offered.

"The Sheraton's got this buffet. We was going to go to that."

"Well, there's something for you under the tree. If you change your mind, give me a call in the morning."

"I don't believe it. You broke down and got a tree? Bet it's an ugly little sucker."

"The envy of the neighborhood, thank you very much," I said. "Wish your friend a Merry Christmas for me."

7

I woke up the next morning to church bells chiming and draperies glowing with the sun. Though I'd had very little to drink the night before, I felt hung over. Lingering in bed, I fell back to sleep and saw Mark in my dreams.

When I finally got up, the kitchen was fragrant with vanilla and oranges. Lucy was grinding coffee beans.

"You're going to spoil me, and then what will I do? Merry Christmas." I kissed the top of her head, noticing an unusual bag of cereal on the counter. "What's this?"

"Cheshire muesli. A special treat. I brought my own supply. It's best with plain yogurt if you've got it, which you don't. So we'll have to settle for skim milk and bananas. Plus, we have fresh orange juice and decaffeinated French vanilla coffee. I guess we should call Mom and Grans."

While I dialed my mother's number from the kitchen, Lucy went into my study to use that extension. My sister was already at my mother's, and soon the four of us were on the line, my mother complaining at great length about the weather. It was storming fiercely in Miami, she said. Torrential rains accompanied by punishing winds had begun late Christmas Eve, the morning celebrated by a grand illumination of lightning.

"You shouldn't be on the phone during an electrical storm," I said to them. "We'll call back later."

"You're so paranoid, Kay," Dorothy chided. "You look at everything in terms of how it might kill somebody."

"Lucy, tell me about your presents," my mother interjected.

"Grans, we haven't opened them yet."

"Wow. That was really close," Dorothy exclaimed above crackling static. "The lights just flickered."

"Mom, I hope you don't have a file open on your computer," Lucy said. "Because if you do, you probably just lost whatever you were working on."

"Dorothy, did you remember to bring butter?" my mother asked.

"Damn. I knew there was something . . ."

"I must have reminded you three times last night."

"I've told you I can't remember things when you call me while I'm writing, Mother."

"Can you imagine? Christmas Eve and would you go to mass with me? No. You stay home working on that book and then forget to bring the butter."

"I'll go out and get some."

"And just what do you think will be open on Christmas morning?"

"Something will be."

I looked up as Lucy walked into the kitchen.

"I don't believe it," she whispered to me as my mother and sister continued to argue with each other.

After I hung up, Lucy and I went into my living room, where we were returned to a quiet winter morning in Virginia, bare trees still and patches of snow pristine in the shade. I did not think I could ever live in Miami again. The change of seasons was like the phases of the moon, a force that pulled me and shifted my point of view. I needed the full with the new and the nuances in between, days to be short and cold in order to appreciate spring mornings.

Lucy's present from her grandmother was a check for fifty dollars. Dorothy gave money as well, and I felt rather ashamed when Lucy opened the envelope from me and added my check to the others.

"Money seems so impersonal," I apologized.

"It's not impersonal to me because it's what I want. You just bought another meg of memory for my computer." She handed me a small, heavy gift wrapped in red-and-silver paper, and could not suppress her joy when she saw the look on my face as I opened the box and parted layers of tissue paper.

"I thought you could keep your court schedule in it," she said. "It matches your motorcycle jacket."

"Lucy, it's gorgeous." I touched the black lambskin binding of the appointment book and smoothed open its creamy pages. I thought of the Sunday she had come to town, of how late she had stayed out when I'd let her take my car to the club. I bet the sneak had gone shopping.

"And this other present here is just refills for the address section and the next calendar year." She set a smaller gift in my lap as the telephone rang.

Marino wished me a Merry Christmas and said he wanted to drop by with my "present."

"Tell Lucy she'd better dress warmly and not to wear anything tight," he said irritably.

"What are you talking about?" I puzzled.

"No tight jeans or she won't be able to get cartridges in and out of her pockets. You said she wanted to learn how to shoot. Lesson one is this morning before lunch. If she misses class, it's her damn problem. What time are we eating?"

"Between one-thirty and two. I thought you were tied up."

"Yeah, well, I untied myself. I'll be over in about twenty minutes. Tell the brat it's cold as hell outside. You want to come with us?"

"Not this time. I'll stay here and cook."

Marino's disposition was no more pleasant when he arrived at my door, and he made a great production of checking my spare revolver, a Ruger .38 with rubber grips. Depressing the thumb latch, he pushed open the cylinder and slowly spun it around, peering into each chamber. He pulled back the hammer, looked down the barrel, and then tried the trigger. While Lucy watched him in curious silence, he pontificated on the residue buildup left by the solvent I used and informed me that my Ruger probably had "spurs" that needed filing. Then he drove Lucy away in his Ford.

When they returned several hours later, their faces were rosy from the cold and Lucy proudly sported a blood blister on her trigger finger.

"How did she do?" I asked, drying my hands on my apron.

"Not bad," Marino said, looking past me. "I smell fried chicken."

"No, you don't." I took their coats. "You smell *cotoletta di tacchino alla bolognese.*"

"I did better than 'not bad,' " Lucy said. "I only missed the target twice."

"Just keep dry firing until you stop slapping the trigger. Remember, crawl the hammer back."

"I've got more soot on me than Santa after he's come down the chimney," Lucy said cheerfully. "I'm going to take a shower."

In the kitchen I poured coffee as Marino inspected a counter crowded with Marsala, fresh-grated Parmesan, prosciutto, white truffles, sautéed turkey fillets, and other assorted ingredients that were going into our meal. We went into the living room, where the fire was blazing.

"What you did was very kind," I said. "I appreciate it more than you'll ever know."

"One lesson's not enough. Maybe I can work with her a couple more times before she goes back to Florida."

"Thank you, Marino. I hope you didn't go to a lot of bother and sacrifice to change your plans."

"It was no big deal," he said curtly.

"Apparently, you decided against dinner at the Sheraton," I probed. "Your friend could have joined us."

"Something came up."

"Does she have a name?"

"Tanda."

"That's an interesting name."

Marino's face was turning crimson.

"What's Tanda like?" I asked.

"You want to know the truth, she ain't worth talking about." Abruptly, he got up and headed down the hall to the bathroom.

I'd always been careful not to quiz Marino about his personal life unless he invited me to do so. But I could not resist this time.

"How did you and Tanda meet?" I asked when he returned.

"The FOP dance."

"I think it's terrific that you're getting out and meeting new people."

"It sucks, if you really want to know. I haven't dated nobody in more than thirty years. It's like Rip Van Wrinkle waking up in another century. Women are different from what they used to be."

"How so?" I tried not to smile. Clearly, Marino did not think any of this was amusing.

"They're not simple anymore."

"Simple?"

"Yeah, like Doris. What we had wasn't complicated. Then after thirty years she suddenly splits and I have to start over. I go to this friggin' dance at the FOP because some of the guys talk me into it. I'm minding my own business when Tanda comes up to my table. Two beers later, she asks me for my phone number, if you can believe that."

"Did you give it to her?"

"I say, 'Hey, if you want to get together, you give me your number. I'll do the calling.' She asks me which zoo I escaped from, then invites me bowling. That's how it started. How it ended is her telling me she rear-ended somebody a couple weeks back and was charged with reckless driving. She wanted me to fix it."

"I'm sorry." I fetched his present from under the tree and handed it to him. "I don't know if this will help your social life or not."

He unwrapped a pair of Christmas-red suspenders and compatible silk tie.

"That's mighty nice, Doc. Geez." Getting up, he muttered in disgust, "Damn water pills," and headed to the bathroom again. Several minutes later, he returned to the hearth.

"When was your last checkup?" I asked.

"A couple weeks ago."

"And?"

"And what do you think?" he said.

"You have high blood pressure, that's what I think."

"No shit."

"What, specifically, did your doctor tell you?" I asked.

"It's one-fifty over one-ten, and my damn prostrate's enlarged. So I'm taking these water pills. Up and down all the time feeling like I gotta go and half the time I can't. If things don't get better, he says he's gonna turp me."

A *turp* was a transurethral resection of the prostate. That wasn't serious, though it wasn't much fun. Marino's blood pressure worried me. He was a prime candidate for a stroke or a heart attack.

"Plus, my ankles swell," he went on. "My feet hurt and I get these damn headaches. I've gotta quit smoking, give up coffee, lose forty pounds, cut down on stress."

"Yes, you've got to do all of those things," I said firmly. "And it doesn't look to me like you're doing any of them."

"We're only talking about changing my whole life. And you're one to talk."

"I don't have high blood pressure and I quit smoking exactly two months and five days ago. Not to mention, if I lost forty pounds I wouldn't be here."

He glared into the fire.

"Listen," I said. "Why don't we work on this together? We'll both cut back on coffee and get into exercise routines."

"I can just see you doing aerobics," he said sourly.

"I'll play tennis. You can do aerobics."

"Anybody so much as waves a pair of tights near me, they're dead."

"You're not being very cooperative, Marino."

He impatiently changed the subject. "You got a copy of the fax you told me about?"

I went to my study and returned with my briefcase. Snapping it open, I handed him the printout of the message Vander had discovered with the image enhancer.

"This was on the blank sheet of paper we found on Jennifer Deighton's bed, right?" he asked.

"That's correct."

"I still can't figure out why she had a blank sheet of paper on her bed with a crystal on top of it. What were they doing there?"

"I don't know," I said. "What about the messages on her answering machine? Anything?"

"We're still running them down. We've got a lot of people to interview." He slipped a pack of Marlboros out of his shirt pocket and blew out a loud breath of air. "Damn." He slapped the pack on top of the coffee table. "You're going to nag me every time I light up one of these now, aren't you?"

"No, I'll just stare at it. But I won't say a word."

"You remember that interview of you that was on PBS a couple months back?"

"Vaguely."

"Jennifer Deighton taped it. The tape was in her VCR and we started playing it and there you were."

"What?" I asked, amazed.

"Of course, you weren't the only thing featured on that particular program. There was also some crap about an archaeology dig and a Hollywood movie they filmed around here."

"Why would she tape me?"

"It's just another piece that's not fitting with anything else yet.

Except the calls made from her phone—the hang ups. It looks like Deighton was thinking about you before she was whacked."

"What else have you found out about her?"

"I gotta smoke. You want me to go outside?"

"Of course not."

"It gets weirder," he said. "While going through her office, we came across a divorce decree. Appears she was married in 1961, got divorced two years later, and changed her name back to Deighton. Then she moved from Florida to Richmond. The name of her ex is Willie Travers, and he's one of these health nut types—you know, into *whole* health. Hell, I can't think of the name."

"Holistic medicine?"

"That's it. Still lives in Florida, Fort Myers Beach. I got him on the phone. Hard as hell to get much out of him, but I managed to find out a few things. He says he and Miss Deighton continued feeling friendly toward each other after they split and, in fact, continued seeing each other."

"He came up here?"

"Travers said she'd go down there to see him, in Florida. They'd get together, as he put it, 'for old times' sake.' Last time she was down there was this past November, around Thanksgiving. I also pried out of him a little bit about Deighton's brother and sister. The sister's a lot younger, married, lives out West. The brother's the eldest, in his midfifties, and manages a grocery store. He had throat cancer a couple years back and his voice box was cut out."

"Wait a minute," I said.

"Yeah. You know what that sounds like. You'd know it if you heard it. No way the guy who called you at the office was John Deighton. It was somebody else who had personal reasons for being interested in Jennifer Deighton's autopsy findings. He knew enough to get the name right. He knew enough to get it straight that he's supposed to be from Columbia, South Carolina. But he didn't know about the real John Deighton's health problems, didn't know he should sound like he's talking through a machine."

"Does Travers know his ex-wife's death is a homicide?" I asked.

"I told him the medical examiner is still running tests."

"And he was in Florida when she died?"

"Allegedly. I'd like to know where your friend Nicholas Grueman was when she died."

"He has never been a friend," I said. "How will you approach him?"

"I won't for a while. You only get one shot with someone like Grueman. How old is he?"

"Somewhere in his sixties," I said.

"He a big guy?"

"I haven't seen him since I was in law school." I got up to stir the fire. "Back then Grueman's build was trim bordering on thin. I would describe his height as average."

Marino did not say anything.

"Jennifer Deighton weighed one-eighty," I reminded him. "It appears her killer yoked her and then carried her body out to her car."

"All right. So maybe Grueman had help. You want a far-out scenario? Try this one on for size. Grueman represented Ronnie Waddell, who wasn't exactly a pencil-neck. Or maybe we should say, *isn't* exactly a pencil-neck. Waddell's print was found inside Jennifer Deighton's house. Maybe Grueman did go to see her and he didn't go alone."

I stared into the fire.

"By the way, I didn't see nothing in Jennifer Deighton's house that could have been the source of the feather you found," he added. "You asked me to check."

Just then, his pager sounded. Snapping it off his belt, he squinted at the narrow screen.

"Damn," he complained, heading into the kitchen to use the phone.

"What's going . . . *What?*" I heard him say. "Oh, Christ. You sure?" He was silent for a moment. He sounded very tense when he said, "Don't bother. I'm standing fifteen feet from her."

Marino ran a red light at West Cary and Windsor Way, and headed east. Grille lights flashed and scanner lights danced in the white Ford LTD. Ten-codes crackled over the radio as I envisioned Susan curled up in the wing chair, her terry cloth robe pulled tightly around her to ward off a chill that had nothing to do with the temperature in the room. I remembered the expression on her face shifting constantly like clouds, her eyes revealing no secrets to me.

I was shivering and could not seem to catch my breath. My heart beat hard in my throat. Police had found Susan's car in an alleyway off Strawberry Street. She was in the driver's seat, dead. It was unknown what she had been doing in that part of town or what might have motivated her assailant.

"What else did she say when you talked with her last night?" Marino asked.

Nothing significant would come to mind. "She was tense," I said. "Something was bothering her."

"What? You got any guesses?"

"I don't know what." My hands shook as I fumbled with my medical bag and checked the contents again. Camera, gloves, and everything else were accounted for. I remembered Susan once saying that if anyone tried to abduct or rape her, they'd have to kill her first.

There had been a number of late afternoons when it was just the two of us cleaning up and filling out paperwork. We had had many personal conversations about being a woman and loving men, and what it would be like to be a mother. Once we had talked about death and Susan confessed she was afraid of it.

"I'm not talking about hell, either, the fire and brimstone my father preaches about—I'm not afraid of that," she said adamantly. "I'm just afraid of this being all there is."

"This isn't all there is," I said.

"How do you know?"

"Something's gone. You look at their faces and you can tell. Their energy has departed. The spirit didn't die. Just the body did."

"But how do you know?" she asked again.

Easing up on the accelerator, Marino turned onto Strawberry Street. I glanced in my side mirror. Another police car was behind us, light bar flashing red and blue. We passed restaurants and a small grocery store. Nothing was open, and the few cars out pulled over to let us pass. Near the Strawberry Street Café, the narrow street was lined with cruisers and unmarked units, and an ambulance was blocking the entrance of an alleyway. Two television trucks had parked a little farther down. Reporters moved restlessly along the perimeter cordoned off in yellow tape. Marino parked and our doors opened at the same time. Instantly, cameras pointed our way.

I watched where Marino stepped and was right behind him. Shutters whirred, film advanced, and microphones were raised. Marino's long strides did not pause and he did not answer anyone. I averted my face. Rounding the ambulance, we ducked under the tape. The old burgundy Toyota was parked head-in midway along a narrow stretch of cobblestone covered with churned-up, dirty snow. Ugly brick walls pressed in from either side and blocked out the low sun's slanted rays. Police were taking photographs, talking, and looking around. Water slowly dripped from roofs and rusting fire escapes. The smell of garbage wafted on the damp, stirring air.

It barely registered that the young Latin-looking officer talking on a portable radio was someone I had recently met. Tom Lucero watched us as he mumbled something and got off the air. From where I stood, all I could see through the Toyota's open driver's door was a left hip and arm. A shock went through me as I recognized the black wool coat, the brush-gold wedding band, and black plastic watch. Wedged between the windshield and the dash was her red medical examiner's plate.

"Tags come back to Jason Story. I guess that's her husband," Lucero said to Marino. "She's got identification on her in her purse. The name on the driver's license is Susan Dawson Story, a twenty-eight-year-old white female."

"What about money?"

"Eleven dollars in her billfold and a couple of credit cards. Nothing so far to suggest robbery. You recognize her?"

Marino leaned forward to get a better look. His jaw muscles bunched. "Yeah. I recognize her. This how the car was found?"

"We opened the driver's door. That's it," Lucero said, stuffing the portable radio in a pocket.

"The engine was off, doors unlocked?"

"They were. Like I told you on the phone, Fritz spotted the car while on routine patrol. Uh, around fifteen hundred hours, and he noticed the M.E.'s tag in the window." He glanced at me. "If you go around to the passenger's side and look in, you can see blood in the area of her right ear. Someone did a real neat job."

Marino backed away and scanned the messy snow. "Don't look like we'll have much luck with footprints."

"You got that right. It's melting like ice cream. Was when we got here."

"Any cartridge cases?"

"Zip."

"Her family know?"

"Not yet. I thought you might want to handle this one," Lucero said.

"Just make damn sure who she is and where she worked don't leak out to the media before the family knows. Jesus." Marino turned his attention to me. "What do you want to do here?"

"I don't want to touch anything inside the car," I muttered, surveying the surroundings as I got out my camera. I was alert and thinking clearly but my hands would not stop shaking. "Give me a minute to look, then let's get her on a stretcher."

"You guys ready for the doc?" Marino asked Lucero.

"We're ready."

Susan was dressed in faded blue jeans and scuffed lace-up boots, her black wool coat buttoned to her chin. My heart constricted as I noticed the red silk scarf peeking out of her collar. She wore sunglasses and leaned back in the driver's seat as if she had gotten comfortable and dozed off. On the light gray upholstery behind her neck was a reddish stain. I moved around to the other side of the car and saw the blood Lucero had mentioned. As I began taking photographs, I paused, then leaned closer to her face, detecting the faint fragrance of a distinctive masculine cologne. Her seat belt, I noted, was unfastened.

I did not touch her head until the squad had arrived and Susan's body was on a stretcher inside the back of an ambulance. I climbed in and spent several minutes looking for bullet wounds. I found one in the right temple, another in the hollow at the back of the neck, just below the hairline. I ran my gloved fingers through her chestnut hair, looking for more blood and not finding it.

Marino climbed into the back of the ambulance. "How many times was she shot?" he asked me.

"I've found two entrances. No exits, though I can feel one bullet beneath the skin over her left temporal bone."

He glanced tensely at his watch. "The Dawsons don't live too far from here. In Glenburnie."

"The Dawsons?" I peeled off my gloves.

"Her parents. I've got to talk to them. Now. Before some toad leaks something and they end up hearing about this on the damn radio or TV. I'll get a marked unit to take you home."

"No," I said. "I'll go with you. I think I should."

Streetlights were coming on as we drove away. Marino stared hard at the road, his face dangerously red.

"Damn!" he blurted, pounding his fist on the steering wheel. "Goddam! Shooting her in the head. *Shooting a pregnant woman.*"

I stared out the side window, my shattered thoughts filled with fragmented images and distortion.

I cleared my throat. "Has her husband been located?"

"No answer at their crib. Maybe he's with her parents. God, I hate this job. Christ, I don't want to do this. Merry friggin' Christmas. I knock on your door and you're screwed because I'm going to tell you something that will ruin your life."

"You have not ruined anybody's life."

"Yeah, well, get ready, 'cause I'm about to."

He turned onto Albemarle. Supercans had been rolled to the edge of the street and were surrounded by leaf bags bulging with Christmas trash. Windows glowed warmly, multicolored tree lights filling some of them. A young father was pulling his small son along the sidewalk on a fishtailing sled. They smiled and waved at us as we passed. Glenburnie was the neighborhood of middle-class families, of young professionals, single, married, and gay. In the warm months, people sat on their porches and cooked out in their yards. They had parties and hailed each other from the street.

The Dawsons' modest house was Tudor style, comfortably weathered with neatly pruned evergreens in front. Windows upstairs and down were lit up, an old station wagon parked by the curb.

The bell was answered by a woman's voice on the other side of the door. "Who is it?"

"Mrs. Dawson?"

"Yes?"

"Detective Marino, Richmond P.D. I need to talk with you," he said loudly, holding his badge up to the peephole.

Locks clicked free as my pulse raced. During my various medical rotations, I had experienced patients screaming in pain as they begged me not to let them die. I had reassured them falsely, "You're going to be just fine," as they died gripping my hand. I had said "I'm sorry" to loved ones desperate in small, airless rooms where even chaplains felt lost. But I had never delivered death to someone's door on Christmas Day.

The only resemblance I could see between Mrs. Dawson and her daughter was the strong curve of their jaws. Mrs. Dawson was sharp-featured, with short, frosted hair. She could not have weighed more than a hundred pounds and reminded me of a frightened bird. When Marino introduced me, panic filled her eyes.

"What's happened?" she barely said.

"I'm afraid I have very bad news for you, Mrs. Dawson," Marino said. "It's your daughter, Susan. I'm afraid she's been killed."

Small feet sounded in a nearby room, and a little girl appeared in a doorway to the right of us. She stopped and regarded us with wide blue eyes.

"Hailey, where's Grandpa?" Mrs. Dawson's voice quavered, her face ashen now.

"Upstairs." Hailey was a tiny tomboy in blue jeans and leather sneakers that looked brand-new. Her blonde hair shone like gold and she wore glasses to straighten a lazy left eye. I guessed she was, at the most, eight.

"You go tell him to come downstairs," Mrs. Dawson said. "And you and Charlie stay up there until I come get you."

The child hesitated in the doorway, inserting two fingers into her mouth. She stared warily at Marino and me.

"Hailey, go on now!"

Hailey left with an abrupt burst of energy.

We sat in the kitchen with Susan's mother. Her back did not touch the chair. She did not weep until her husband walked in minutes later.

"Oh, Mack," she said in a weak voice. *"Oh, Mack."* She began to sob.

He put his arm around her, pulling her close. His face blanched and he pressed his lips together as Marino explained what had happened.

"Yes, I know where Strawberry Street is," Susan's father said. "I don't know why she would have gone there. To my knowledge, it's not an area where she normally went. Nothing would have been open today. I don't know."

"Do you know where her husband, Jason Story, is?" Marino asked.

"He's here."

"Here?" Marino glanced around.

"Upstairs, asleep. Jason's not feeling well."

"The children are whose?"

"Tom and Marie's. Tom's our son. They're visiting for the holidays and left early this afternoon. For Tidewater. To visit friends. They should be home anytime." He reached for his wife's hand. "Millie, these people have a lot of questions to ask. You'd better get Jason."

"I tell you what," Marino said. "I'd rather talk to him alone for a minute. Maybe you could take me to him?"

Mrs. Dawson nodded, hiding her face in her hands.

"I think you best check on Charlie and Hailey," her husband said to her. "See if you can get your sister on the phone. Maybe she can come."

His pale blue eyes followed his wife and Marino out of the kitchen. Susan's father was tall, with fine bones, his dark brown hair thick, with very little gray. His gestures were economical, his emotions well contained. Susan had gotten her looks from him and perhaps her disposition.

"Her car is old. She has nothing of value to steal, and I know she would not have been involved. Not in drugs or anything." He searched my face.

"We don't know why this happened, Reverend Dawson."

"She was pregnant," he said, the words catching in his throat. "How could anyone?"

"I don't know," I said. "I don't know how."

He coughed. "She did not own a gun."

For a moment, I did not know what he meant. Then I realized, and reassured him, "No. The police did not find a gun. There's no evidence she did this to herself."

"The police? You aren't the police?"

"No. I'm the chief medical examiner. Kay Scarpetta."

He stared numbly at me.

"Your daughter worked for me."

"Oh. Of course. I'm sorry."

"I don't know how to comfort you," I said with difficulty. "I haven't begun to deal with this myself. But I'm going to do everything possible to find out what happened. I want you to know that."

"Susan spoke of you. She always wanted to be a doctor." He averted his gaze, blinking back tears.

"I saw her last night. Briefly, at her home." I hesitated, reluctant to probe the soft places of their lives. "Susan seemed troubled. And she has not been herself at work of late."

He swallowed, fingers laced tightly on top of the table. His knuckles were white.

"We need to pray. Would you pray with me, Dr. Scarpetta?" He held out his hand. "Please."

As his fingers wrapped firmly around mine, I could not help but think of Susan's obvious disregard for her father and distrust for what he represented. Fundamentalists frightened me, too. I felt anxious shutting my eyes and holding hands with the Reverend Mack Dawson as he thanked God for a mercy I saw no evidence of and claimed promises too late for God to keep. Opening my eyes, I withdrew my hand. For an uneasy moment I feared that Susan's father sensed my skepticism and would question my beliefs. But the fate of my soul was not foremost on his mind.

A loud voice sounded from upstairs, a muffled protest I could not make out. A chair scraped across the floor. The telephone rang and rang, and the voice rose again in a primal outcry of rage and pain. Dawson closed his eyes. He muttered something under his breath that seemed rather strange. I thought he said, "Stay in your room."

"Jason has been here the entire time," he said. I could see his pulse pounding in his temples. "I realize he can speak for himself. But I just want you to know this from me."

"You mentioned he's not feeling well."

"He woke up with a cold, the beginning of one. Susan took his temperature after lunch and encouraged him to go to bed. He would never hurt . . . Well." He coughed again. "I know the police have to ask, have to consider domestic situations. But that's not the case here."

"Reverend Dawson, what time did Susan leave the house today, and where did she say she was going?"

"She left after dinner, after Jason went to bed. I think that would have been around one-thirty or two. She said she was going over to a friend's house."

"Which friend?"

He stared past me. "A friend she went to high school with. Dianne Lee."

"Where does Dianne live?"

"Northside, near the seminary."

"Susan's car was found off Strawberry Street, not in Northside."

"I suppose if somebody . . . She could have ended up anywhere."

"It would be helpful to know if she ever made it to Dianne's house, and whose idea the visit was," I said.

He got up and started opening kitchen drawers. It took him three tries to find the telephone directory. His hands trembled as he turned pages and dialed a number. Clearing his throat several times, he asked to speak to Dianne.

"I see. What was that?" He listened for a moment. "No, no." His voice shook. "Things are not all right."

I sat quietly as he explained, and I imagined him many years earlier praying and talking on the phone as he dealt with the death of his other daughter, Judy. When he returned to the table, he confirmed what I feared. Susan had not visited her friend that afternoon, nor had there been any plan for her to do so. Her friend was not in town.

"She's with her husband's family in North Carolina," Susan's father said. "She's been there several days. Why would Susan lie? She didn't have to. I've always told her no matter what, she didn't have to lie."

"It would seem she did not want anyone to know where she was going or who she was going to see. I know that raises unhappy speculations, but we need to face them," I said gently.

He stared down at his hands.

"Were she and Jason getting along all right?"

"I don't know." He fought to regain his composure. "Dear Lord, not again." Again he whispered curiously. "Go to your room. Please go." Then he looked up at me with bloodshot eyes. "She had a twin sister. Judy died when they were in high school."

"In a car accident, yes. Susan told me. I'm so sorry."

"She's never gotten over it. She blamed God. She blamed me."

"I did not get that impression," I said. "If she blamed anyone, it seemed to be a girl named Doreen."

Dawson slipped out a handkerchief and quietly blew his nose. "Who?" he asked.

"The girl in high school who allegedly was a witch."

He shook his head.

"She supposedly put a curse on Judy?" But it was pointless to explain further. I could tell that Dawson did not know what I was talking about. We both turned as Hailey walked into the kitchen. She was cradling a baseball glove, her eyes frightened.

"What have you got there, darling?" I asked, trying to smile.

She came close to me. I could smell the new leather. The glove was tied with string, a softball in the sweet spot like a large pearl inside an oyster.

"Aunt Susan gave it to me," she said in a small voice. "You got to break it in. I have to put it under my mattress. Aunt Susan says I have to for a week."

Her grandfather reached for her and lifted her onto his lap. He buried his nose in her hair, holding her tight. "I need for you to go to your room for a little while, sugar. Will you do that for me so I can take care of things? Just for a while?"

She nodded, her eyes not leaving me.

"What are Grandma and Charlie doing?"

"Don't know." She slid off his lap and reluctantly left us.

"You said that before," I said to him.

He looked lost.

"You told her to go to her room," I said. "I heard you say that earlier, mutter something about going to your room. Who were you talking to?"

He dropped his eyes. "The child is self. Self feels intensely, cries, cannot control emotions. Sometimes it is best to send self to his room as I just did Hailey. To hold together. A trick I learned. When I was a boy I learned, had to; my father did not react well if I cried."

"It is all right to cry, Reverend Dawson."

His eyes filled with tears. I heard Marino's footsteps on the stairs. Then he strode into the kitchen and Dawson said the phrase again, in anguish, under his breath.

Marino looked at him, baffled. "I think your son's home," he said.

Susan's father began to weep uncontrollably as car doors slammed shut out front in the wintry darkness and laughter sounded from the porch.

Christmas dinner went into the trash, the evening spent pacing about the house and talking on the phone while Lucy stayed inside my study with the door shut. Arrangements had to be made. Susan's homicide had thrown the office into a state of crisis. Her case would have to be sealed, photographs kept away from those who had known her. The police would have to go through her office and her locker. They would want to interview members of my staff.

"I can't be down there," Fielding, my deputy chief, told me over the phone.

"I realize that," I said, a lump forming in my throat. "I neither expect nor want anyone down there."

"And you?"

"I have to be."

"Christ. I can't believe this has happened. I just can't believe it."

Dr. Wright, my deputy chief in Norfolk, kindly agreed to drive to Richmond early the next morning. Because it was Sunday, no one else was in the building except for Vander, who had come to assist with the Luma-Lite. Had I been emotionally capable of doing Susan's autopsy, I would have refused. The worst thing I could do for her was to jeopardize her case by having the defense question the objectivity and judgment of an expert witness who also happened to be her boss. So I sat at a desk in the morgue while Wright worked. From time to time he commented to me above the clatter of steel instruments and running water as I stared at the cinderblock wall. I did not touch any of her paperwork or label a single test tube. I did not turn around to look.

Once I asked him, "Did you smell anything on her or her clothes? A cologne of some sort?"

He stopped what he was doing and I heard him walk several steps. "Yes. Definitely around the collar of her coat and on the scarf."

"Does it smell like men's cologne to you?"

"Hmm. I think so. Yes, I'd say the fragrance is masculine. Perhaps her husband wears cologne?" Wright was near retirement age, a balding, potbellied man with a West Virginian accent. He was a very capable forensic pathologist and knew exactly what I was contemplating.

"Good question," I said. "I'll ask Marino to check it. But her husband was ill yesterday and went to bed after lunch. That doesn't mean he didn't have on cologne. It doesn't mean her brother or father didn't have on cologne that got on her collar when they hugged her."

"This looks small-caliber. No exit wounds."

I closed my eyes and listened.

"The wound in her right temple is three-sixteenths of an inch with half an inch of smoke—an incomplete pattern. A little bit of stippling and some powder but most will be lost in her hair. There's some powder in the temporalis muscle. Nothing much in bone or dura."

"Trajectory?" I asked.

"The bullet goes through the posterior aspect of the right frontal lobe, travels across anterior to basal ganglia and strikes the left temporal bone, and gets hung up in muscle under the skin. And we're talking about a plain lead bullet, uh, copper coated but not jacketed."

"And it didn't fragment?" I asked.

"No. Then we've got this second wound here at the nape of the neck. Black, burned abraded margin with muzzle mark. A little laceration about one-sixteenth of an inch at the edges. Lots of powder in the occipital muscles."

"Tight contact?"

"Yes. Looks to me like he pressed the barrel hard against her neck. The bullet enters at the junction of the foramen magnum and C-one and takes out the cervical-medullary junction. Travels right up into the pons."

"What about the angle?" I asked.

"It's angled up quite a bit. I'd say that if she was sitting in the car at the time she received this wound, she was slumped forward or had her head bowed."

"That's not the way she was found," I said. "She was leaning back in the seat."

"Then I guess he positioned her that way," Wright commented. "After he shot her. And I'd say that this shot that went through the pons was fired last. I would speculate she was already incapacitated, maybe slumped over when she was shot the second time."

At intervals I could handle it, as if we were not referring to anyone I knew. Then a tremor would go through me, tears fighting to break free. Twice I had to walk outside and stand in the parking lot in the cold. When he got to the ten-week-old fetus in her womb, a girl, I retreated to my office upstairs. According to Virginia law, the unborn child was not a person and therefore could not have been murdered because you cannot murder a nonperson.

"Two for the price of one," Marino said bitterly over the phone later in the day.

"I know," I said, digging a bottle of aspirin out of my pocketbook.

"In court the damn jurors won't be told she was pregnant. It won't be admissible, don't count he murdered a pregnant woman."

"I know," I said again. "Wright's about done. Nothing significant turned up during her external exam. No trace to speak of, nothing that jumped out. What's going on at your end?"

"Susan was definitely going through something," Marino said.

"Problems with her husband?"

"According to him, her problem was with you. He claims you were doing weird shit like calling her a lot at home, hassling her. And sometimes she'd come home from work acting half crazy, like she was scared shitless about something."

"Susan and I did not have a problem." I swallowed three aspirin with a mouthful of cold coffee.

"I'm just telling you what the guy's saying. Other thing is—and

I think you'll find this interesting—looks like we got us another feather. Not that I'm saying it links Deighton and this one, Doc, or that I'm necessarily thinking that way. But damn. Maybe we're dealing with some squirrel who wears down-filled gloves, a jacket. I don't know. It's just not typical. Only other time I've ever found feathers was when this drone broke into a crib by smashing out a window and cut his down jacket on broken glass."

My head hurt so much I felt sick to my stomach.

"What we found in Susan's car is real small—a little piece of white down," he went on. "It was clinging to the upholstery of the passenger's door. On the inside, near the floor, a couple inches below the armrest."

"Can you get that to me?" I asked.

"Yeah. What are you going to do?"

"Call Benton."

"I've been trying, dammit. I think he and the wife went out of town."

"I need to ask him if Minor Downey can help us."

"You talking about a person or a fabric softener?"

"Minor Downey with hairs and fibers at the FBI labs. His specialty is feather analysis."

"And his name's *Downey,* it really is?" Marino was incredulous.

"It really is," I said.

8

The telephone rang for a long time at the FBI's Behavioral Science Unit, located in the subterranean reaches of the Academy at Quantico. I could envision its bleak, confusing hallways and offices cluttered with the mementos of polished warriors like Benton Wesley, who had gone skiing, I was told.

"In fact, I'm the only one here at the moment," said the courteous agent who answered the phone.

"This is Dr. Kay Scarpetta and it's urgent that I reach him."

Benton Wesley returned my call almost immediately.

"Benton, where are you?" I raised my voice above terrible static.

"In my car," he said. "Connie and I spent Christmas with her family in Charlottesville. We're just west of there on our way to Hot Springs. I heard about what happened to Susan Story. God, I'm sorry. I was going to call you tonight."

"You're breaking up. I almost can't hear you."

"Hold on."

I waited impatiently for a good minute. Then he was back.

"That's better. We were in a low area. Listen, what do you need from me?"

"I need the Bureau's help with analysis of some feathers."

"No problem. I'll call Downey."

"I need to talk," I said with great reluctance, for I knew I was putting him on the spot. "I don't feel it can wait."

"Hold on."

This time the pause was not due to static. He was conferring with his wife.

"Do you ski?" His voice came back.

"It depends on who you ask."

"Connie and I are on our way to the Homestead for a couple of days. We could talk there. Can you get away?"

"I'll move heaven and earth to, and I'll bring Lucy."

"That's good. She and Connie can pal around while you and I talk. I'll see about your room when we check in. Can you bring something for me to look at?"

"Yes."

"Including whatever you've got on the Robyn Naismith case. Let's cover every base and every imagined one."

"Thank you, Benton," I said gratefully. "And please thank Connie."

I decided to leave the office immediately, and offered little explanation.

"It will be good for you," Rose said, jotting down the Homestead's number. She did not understand that my intention was not to unwind at a five-star resort. For an instant, her eyes were bright with tears as I told her to let Marino know where I was so he could contact me immediately if there were any new developments in Susan's case.

"Please don't release my whereabouts to anyone else," I added.

"Three reporters have called in the last twenty minutes," she said. "Including the *Washington Post*."

"I'm not discussing Susan's case right now. Tell them the usual, that we're waiting on lab results. Just tell them I'm out of town and unavailable."

I was haunted by images as I drove west toward the mountains. I pictured Susan in her baggy scrubs, and the faces of her mother and father as Marino told them their daughter was dead.

"Are you feeling okay?" Lucy asked. She had been looking at me every other minute since we left my house.

"I'm just preoccupied," I replied, concentrating on the road. "You're going to love skiing. I have a feeling you'll be good at it."

She silently gazed out the windshield. The sky was a washed-out denim blue, mountains rising in the distance dusted with snow.

"I'm sorry about this," I added. "It seems that every time you visit, something happens and I can't give you my full attention."

"I don't need your full attention."

"Someday you'll understand."

"Maybe I'm the same way about my work. In fact, maybe I learned from you. I'll probably be successful like you, too."

My spirit felt as heavy as lead. I was grateful that I was wearing sunglasses. I did not want Lucy to see my eyes.

"I know you love me. That's what counts. I know my mother doesn't love me," my niece said.

"Dorothy loves you as much as she is able to love anyone."

"You're absolutely right. As much as she is able to, which isn't much because I'm not a man. She only loves men."

"No, Lucy. Your mother doesn't really love men. They are a symptom of her obsessive quest of finding somebody who will make her whole. She doesn't understand that she has to make herself whole."

"The only thing 'whole' in the equation is she picks assholes every time."

"I agree that her batting average hasn't been good."

"I'm not going to live like that. I don't want to be anything like her."

"You aren't," I said.

"I read in the brochure they have skeet shooting where we're going."

"They have all sorts of things."

"Did you bring one of the revolvers?"

"You don't shoot skeet with a revolver, Lucy."

"You do if you're from Miami."

"If you don't stop yawning, you're going to get me started."

"Why didn't you bring a gun?" she persisted.

The Ruger was in my suitcase, but I did not intend to tell her that. "Why are you so worried about whether I brought a gun?" I asked.

"I want to be good at it. So good I can shoot the twelve off the clock every time I try," she said sleepily.

My heart ached as she rolled up her jacket and used it as a pillow. She lay next to me, the top of her head touching my thigh as she slept. She did not know how strongly tempted I was to send her back to Miami this minute. But I could tell she sensed my fear.

The Homestead was situated on fifteen thousand acres of forest and streams in the Allegheny Mountains, the main section of the hotel dark red brick with white-pillared colonnades. The white cupola had a clock on each of its four sides that always agreed on the time and could be read for miles, and tennis courts and golf greens were solid white with snow.

"You're in luck," I said to Lucy as gracious men in gray uniforms stepped our way. "The ski conditions are going to be terrific."

Benton Wesley had accomplished what he had promised, and we found a reservation waiting for us when we got to the front desk. He had booked a double room with glass doors opening onto a balcony overlooking the casino, and on top of a table were flowers from Connie and him. "Meet us on the slopes," the card read. "We scheduled a lesson for Lucy at three-thirty."

"We've got to hurry," I said to Lucy as we flung open suitcases. "You've got your first ski lesson in exactly forty minutes. Try these." I tossed her a pair of red ski pants, which were followed by jacket, socks, mittens, and sweater flying through the air and landing on her bed. "Don't forget your butt pack. Anything else you need we'll have to get later."

"I don't have any ski glasses," she said, pulling a bright blue turtleneck over her head. "I'll go snow-blind."

"You can use my goggles. The sun will be going down soon anyway."

By the time we caught the shuttle to the slopes, rented equipment for Lucy, and connected her with the instructor at the rope tow, it was twenty-nine minutes past three. Skiers were brilliant spots of color moving downhill, and it was only when they got close that they turned into people. I leaned forward in my boots, skis firmly wedged against the slope as I scanned lines and lifts, my hand shielding my eyes. The sun was nearing the top of trees, the snow dazzled by its touch, but shadows were spreading and the temperature was dropping quickly.

I spotted the man and woman simply because their parallel skiing was so graceful, poles lifted like feathers and barely flicking snow as they soared and turned like birds. I recognized Benton Wesley's silver hair and raised my hand. Glancing back at Connie and yelling something I could not hear, he pushed off and schussed downhill like a knife, skis so close together I doubted you could fit a piece of paper between them.

When he stopped in a spray of snow and pushed back his goggles, it suddenly occurred to me that if I did not know him I would have been watching him anyway. Black ski pants hugged well-muscled legs I had never known were beneath the trousers of his conservative suits, and the jacket he wore reminded me of a Key West sunset. His face and eyes were brightened by the cold, making his sharp features more striking than formidable. Connie eased to a stop beside him.

"It's wonderful that you're here," Wesley said, and I could never see him or hear his voice without being reminded of Mark. They had been colleagues and best friends. They could have passed for brothers.

"Where's Lucy?" Connie asked.

"Conquering the rope tow even as we speak." I pointed.

"I hope you didn't mind my signing her up for a lesson."

"Mind? I can't thank you enough for being so thoughtful. She's having the time of her life."

"I think I'll stand right here and watch her for a while," Connie said. "Then I'll be ready for something hot to drink and I have a feeling Lucy will be, too. Ben, you look like you haven't had enough."

Wesley said to me, "You up for a few quick runs?"

We exchanged remarks about nonessential matters as we moved through the line, and then were silent when the lift swung around and seated us. Wesley lowered the bar as the cable slowly pulled us toward the mountaintop. The air was numbing and deliciously clean, and filled with the quiet sounds of skis swishing and dully slapping hard-packed snow. Snow from snow machines drifted like smoke through the woods between slopes.

"I talked to Downey," he said. "He'll see you at headquarters just as soon as you can get there."

"That's good news," I said. "Benton, what have you been told?"

"Marino and I have talked several times. It appears you have several cases going on right now that aren't connected by evidence, necessarily, but by a peculiar coincidence in timing."

"I think we're dealing with more than coincidence. You know about Ronnie Waddell's print turning up in Jennifer Deighton's house."

"Yes." He stared off at a stand of evergreens backlit by the setting sun. "As I've told Marino, I'm hoping there's a logical explanation for how Waddell's print got there."

"The logical explanation may very well be that he was, at some point, inside her house."

"Then we're dealing with a situation so bizarre as to defy description, Kay. A death row convict is out on the street killing again. And we're supposed to assume someone else took his place in the chair on the night of December thirteenth. I doubt there would have been many volunteers."

"You wouldn't think so," I said.

"What do you know about Waddell's criminal history?"

"Very little."

"I interviewed him years ago, in Mecklenburg."

I glanced over at him with interest.

"I'll preface my next remarks by saying that he was not particularly cooperative in that he would not discuss Robyn Naismith's murder. He claimed that if he killed her, he didn't remember it. Not that this is unusual. Most of the violent offenders I have interviewed either claim to have poor recall, or they deny that they committed the crimes. I had a copy of Waddell's Assessment Protocol faxed to me before you got here. We'll go over it after dinner."

"Benton, I'm already glad I'm here."

He stared straight ahead, our shoulders barely touching. The slope beneath us got steeper as we rode in silence for a while. Then he said, "How are you, Kay?"

"Better. There are still moments."

"I know. There will always be moments. But fewer of them, I hope. Days, perhaps, where you don't feel it."

"Yes," I said. "There are days when I don't."

"We've got a very good lead on the group responsible. We think we know who placed the bomb."

We raised the tips of our skis and leaned forward as the lift eased us out like baby birds nudged from the nest. My legs were stiff and cold from the ride, and trails in the shade were treacherous with ice. Wesley's long white skis vanished against the snow and caught light at the same time. He danced down the slope in dazzling puffs of diamond dust, pausing every now and then to look back. I waved him on by barely lifting a pole as I made languid parallel turns and floated over moguls. Halfway into the run I was limber and warm, thoughts flying free.

When I returned to my room as it was getting dark, I discovered Marino had left a message that he would be at headquarters until five-thirty and for me to call ASAP.

"What's going on?" I said when he answered.

"Nothing that's going to make you sleep better. For starters,

Jason Story's badmouthing you to anyone who will stand still long enough to listen—including reporters."

"His rage has to go somewhere," I said, my mood darkening again.

"Well, what he's doing ain't good, but it also ain't the worst of our problems. We can't locate ten print cards for Waddell."

"Not *anywhere?*"

"You got it. We've checked his files at Richmond P.D., the State Police, and the FBI. That's every jurisdiction that should have them. No cards. Then I contacted Donahue at the pen to see if I could track down Waddell's personal effects, such as books, letters, hairbrush, toothbrush—anything that might be a source for latent prints. And guess what? Donahue says the only things Waddell's mother wanted were his watch and ring. Everything else Corrections destroyed."

I sat heavily on the edge of the bed.

"And I saved the best for last, Doc. Firearms hit paydirt and you ain't going to believe it. The bullets recovered from Eddie Heath and Susan Story was fired from the same gun, a twenty-two."

"Dear God," I said.

Downstairs in the Homestead Club, a band was playing jazz, but the audience was small and the music was not too loud to talk over. Connie had taken Lucy to a movie, leaving Wesley and me at a table in a deserted corner of the dance floor. Both of us were sipping cognac. He did not seem as physically tired as I was, but tension had returned to his face.

Reaching behind him, he took another candle from an unoccupied table and set it by two others he had claimed. The light was unsteady but adequate, and though we did not get long stares from guests, we did get glances. I supposed it seemed a strange place to work, but the lobby and dining room were not private enough, and

Wesley was much too circumspect to suggest we meet in his room or mine.

"There would seem to be a number of conflicting elements here," he said. "But human behavior is not set in stone. Waddell was in prison for ten years. We don't know how he might have changed. I would categorize Eddie Heath's murder as a sexually motivated homicide while, at first glance, Susan Story's homicide appears to be an execution, a hit."

"As if two different perpetrators are involved," I said, toying with my cognac.

He leaned forward, idly flipping through Robyn Naismith's case file. "It's interesting," he said, without looking up. "You hear so much about modus operandi, about the offender's signature. He always selects this type of victim or chooses this sort of location and prefers knives, and so on. But, in fact, this isn't always the case. Nor is the emotion of the crime always obvious. I said that Susan Story's homicide, *at first glance,* does not appear to be sexually motivated. But the more I've thought about it, the more I believe there is a sexual component. I think this killer is into piquerism."

"Robyn Naismith was stabbed multiple times," I said.

"Yes. I'd say that what was done to her is a textbook example. There was no evidence of rape—not that this means it didn't occur. But no semen. The repeated plunging of the knife in her abdomen, buttocks, and breasts was a substitute for penile penetration. Obvious piquerism. Biting is less obvious, not at all related to any oral components of the sexual act, it is my opinion, but again, a substitute for penile penetration. Teeth sinking into flesh, cannibalism, like John Joubert did to the newspaper delivery boys he murdered in Nebraska. Then we have bullets. You would not associate shootings with piquerism unless you thought about it for a moment. Then the dynamics, in some instances, become clear. Something penetrating flesh. That was the Son of Sam's thing."

"There's no evidence of piquerism in Jennifer Deighton's death."

"True. This goes back to what I was saying. There isn't always a clear pattern. Certainly, we're not talking about a clear pattern here, but there is one element that the murders of Eddie Heath, Jennifer Deighton, and Susan Story have in common. I would classify the crimes as organized."

"Not as organized with Jennifer Deighton," I pointed out. "It appears the killer attempted to disguise her death as a suicide and failed. Or perhaps he did not intend to kill her at all and got carried away with a choke hold."

"Her death before she was placed inside her car probably wasn't the plan," Wesley agreed. "But the fact is, it appears there *was* a plan. And the garden hose hooked up to the exhaust pipe was severed with a sharp tool that was never recovered. Either the killer brought his own tool or weapon to the scene, or he disposed of whatever it was he found at her house and used. That's organized behavior. But before we go too far with this, let me remind you that we don't have a twenty-two bullet or other piece of evidence that might link Jennifer Deighton's homicide with the homicides of the Heath boy and Susan."

"I think we do, Benton. Ronnie Waddell's print was recovered from a dining room chair inside Jennifer Deighton's house."

"We don't know that it was Ronnie Waddell who pumped slugs into the other two."

"Eddie Heath's body was positioned in a manner reminiscent of Robyn Naismith's case. The boy was attacked the night Ronnie Waddell was to be executed. Don't you think there's some weird thread here?"

"Let's put it this way," he said. "I don't want to think it."

"Neither of us wants to. Benton, what's your gut feeling?"

He motioned for the waitress to bring more cognac, candlelight illuminating the clean lines of his left cheekbone and chin.

"My gut feeling? Okay. I have a very bad gut feeling about all of this," he said. "I believe Ronnie Waddell is the common denominator, but I don't know what that means. A latent print recently found at a scene was identified as his, yet we can't locate his ten print cards or anything else that might effect a positive identification. He also wasn't printed at the morgue, and the person who allegedly forgot to do so has since been murdered with the same gun used on Eddie Heath. Waddell's legal counsel, Nick Grueman, apparently knew Jennifer Deighton, and in fact, it appears she faxed a message to Grueman days before she was murdered. Finally, yes, there is a subtle and peculiar similarity between Eddie Heath's and Robyn Naismith's deaths. Frankly, I can't help but wonder if the attack on Heath wasn't, for some reason, intended to be symbolic."

He waited until our drinks had been set before us, then opened a manila envelope that was attached to Robyn Naismith's case. That small act triggered something I had not thought of before.

"I had to get her photographs from Archives," I said.

Wesley glanced at me as he slipped on his glasses.

"In cases this old, the paper records have been reduced to microfilm, the printouts of which are in the file you've got. The original documents are destroyed, but we keep the original photos. They go to Archives."

"Which is what? A room in your building?"

"No, Benton. A warehouse near the state library—the same warehouse where the Bureau of Forensic Science stores evidence from its old cases."

"Vander still hasn't found the photograph of the bloody thumbprint Waddell left inside Robyn Naismith's house?"

"No," I said as Wesley met my eyes. We both knew that Vander was never going to find it.

"Christ," he said. "Who retrieved Robyn Naismith's photos for you?"

"My administrator," I replied. "Ben Stevens. He made a trip to Archives a week or so before Waddell's execution."

"Why?"

"During the final stages of the appeals process, there are always a lot of questions asked and I like to have ready access to the case or cases involved. So a trip to Archives is routine. What's a little different in the instance we're talking about is I didn't have to ask Stevens to get the photos from Archives. He volunteered."

"And that's unusual?"

"In retrospect, I must admit that it is."

"The implication," Wesley said, "is that your administrator may have volunteered because what he was really interested in was Waddell's file—or more specifically, the photograph of the bloody thumbprint that's supposed to be inside it."

"All I can say with certainty is if Stevens wanted to tamper with a file in Archives, he couldn't do so unless he had legitimate reason for visiting Archives. If, for example, it came back to me that he had been there when none of the medical examiners had made a request, it would look odd."

I went on to tell Wesley about the breach of security in my office computer, explaining that the two terminals involved were assigned to me and Stevens. While I talked, Wesley took notes. When I fell silent, he looked up at me.

"It doesn't sound as if they found what they were looking for," he said.

"My suspicion is that they didn't."

"That brings us around to the obvious question. What were they looking for?"

I slowly swirled my cognac. In the candlelight it was liquid amber, and each sip deliciously burned going down.

"Maybe something pertaining to Eddie Heath's death. I was looking for any other cases in which victims may have had bite marks or cannibalistic-type injuries, and had a file in my directory. Beyond that, I can't imagine what anyone might have been looking for."

"Do you ever keep intradepartmental memos in your directory?"

"In word processing, a subdirectory."

"Same password to access those documents?"

"Yes."

"And in word processing you would store autopsy reports and other documents pertaining to cases?"

"I would. But at the time my directory was broken into there wasn't anything sensitive on file that I can think of."

"But whoever broke in didn't necessarily know that."

"Obviously not," I said.

"What about Ronnie Waddell's autopsy report, Kay? When your directory was broken into, was his report in the computer?"

"It would have been. He was executed Monday, December thirteenth. The break-in occurred late on the afternoon of Thursday, December sixteenth, while I was doing Eddie Heath's post and Susan was upstairs in my office, supposedly resting on the couch after the formalin spill."

"Perplexing." He frowned. "Assuming Susan is the one who went into your directory, why would she be interested in Waddell's autopsy report—if that's what this is all about? She was *present* during his autopsy. What could she have read in your report that she wouldn't have already known?"

"Nothing I can think of."

"Well, let me rephrase that. What pertaining to his autopsy would she not have learned from being present the night his body was brought to the morgue? Or maybe I'd better say the night *a body* was brought to the morgue, since we're no longer so sure this individual was Waddell," he added grimly.

"She wouldn't have had access to lab reports," I said. "But the lab work wouldn't have been completed by the time my directory was broken into. Tox and HIV screens, for example, take weeks."

"And Susan would have known that."

"Certainly."

"So would your administrator."

"Absolutely."

"There must be something else," he said.

There was, but as it came to mind I could not imagine the significance. "Waddell—or whoever the inmate was—had an envelope in the back pocket of his jeans that he wanted buried with him. Fielding wouldn't have opened this envelope until he had gone upstairs with his paperwork after the post."

"So Susan couldn't have known what was inside the envelope while she was in the morgue that night?" Wesley asked with interest.

"That's right. She couldn't have."

"And was there anything of significance inside this envelope?"

"There was nothing inside but several receipts for food and tolls."

Wesley frowned. "Receipts," he repeated. "What in God's name would he have been doing with those? Do you have them here?"

"They're in his file." I got out the photocopies. "The dates are all the same, November thirtieth."

"Which should have been about the time Waddell was transported from Mecklenburg to Richmond."

"That's right. He was transported fifteen days before his execution," I said.

"We need to run down the codes on these receipts, see what locations we get. This may be important. Very important, in light of what we're contemplating."

"That Waddell is alive?"

"Yes. That somehow a switch was made and he was released. Maybe the man who went to the chair wanted these receipts in his pocket when he died because he was trying to tell us something."

"Where would he have gotten them?"

"Perhaps during the transport from Mecklenburg to Richmond, which would have been an ideal time to pull something," Wesley replied. "Maybe two men were transported, Waddell and someone else."

"You're suggesting they stopped for food?"

"Guards aren't supposed to stop for anything while transporting a death row inmate. But if some conspiracy were involved, anything could have happened. Maybe they stopped and got take-out food, and it was during this interval that Waddell was freed. Then the other inmate was taken on to Richmond and put in Waddell's cell. Think about it. How would any of the guards or anybody else at Spring Street have any way of knowing the inmate brought in wasn't Waddell?"

"He might say he wasn't, but that doesn't mean that anyone would have listened."

"I suspect they wouldn't have listened."

"What about Waddell's mother?" I asked. "Supposedly, she had a contact visit with him hours before the execution. Certainly, she would know if the inmate she saw was not her son."

"We need to verify that the contact visit occurred. But whether it did or didn't, it would have been to Mrs. Waddell's benefit to go along with any scheme. I don't imagine she wanted her son to die."

"Then you're convinced that the wrong man was executed," I said reluctantly, for there were few theories, at the moment, that I more wanted to disprove.

His answer was to open the envelope containing Robyn Naismith's photographs and slide out a thick stack of color prints that would continue to shock me no matter how many times I looked at them. He slowly shuffled through the pictorial history of her terrible death.

Then he said, "When we consider the three homicides that have just occurred, Waddell doesn't profile right."

"What are you saying, Benton? That after ten years in prison his personality changed?"

"All I can say to you is that I've heard of organized killers decompensating, flying apart. They begin to make mistakes. Bundy, for example. Toward the end he became frenzied. But what you generally don't see is a disorganized individual swinging the other way, the psychotic person becoming methodical, rational—becoming organized."

When Wesley alluded to the Bundys and Sons of Sam in the world, he did so theoretically, impersonally, as if his analyses and theories were formulated from secondary sources. He did not brag. He did not name-drop or assume the role of one who knew these criminals personally. His demeanor, therefore, was deliberately misleading.

He had, in fact, spent long, intimate hours with the likes of Theodore Bundy, David Berkowitz, Sirhan Sirhan, Richard Speck, and Charles Manson, in addition to the lesser-known black holes who had sucked light from the planet Earth. I remembered Marino telling me once that when Wesley returned from some of these pilgrimages into maximum-security penitentiaries, he would look pale and drained. It almost made him physically ill to absorb the poison of these men and endure the attachments they inevitably formed to him. Some of the worst sadists in recent history regularly wrote letters to him, sent Christmas cards, and inquired after his family. It was no small wonder that Wesley seemed like a man with a heavy burden and so often was silent. In exchange for information, he did the one thing that not one of us wants to do. He allowed the monster to connect with him.

"Was it determined that Waddell was psychotic?" I asked.

"It was determined that he was sane when he murdered Robyn Naismith." Wesley pulled out a photograph and slid it across the table to me. "But frankly, I don't think he was."

The photograph was the one I remembered most vividly, and as I studied it I could not imagine an unsuspecting soul walking in on such a scene.

Robyn Naismith's living room did not have much furniture, just several barrel chairs with dark green cushions and a chocolate-brown leather couch. A small Bakhara rug was in the middle of the parquet floor, the walls wide planks stained to look like cherry or mahogany. A console television was against the wall directly across from the front door, affording whoever entered a full frontal view of Ronnie Joe Waddell's horrible artistry.

What Robyn's friend had seen the instant she unlocked the door and pushed it open as she called out Robyn's name was a nude body sitting on the floor, back propped against the TV, skin so streaked and smeared with dried blood that the exact nature of the injuries could not be determined until later at the morgue. In the photograph, coagulating blood pooled around Robyn's buttocks looked like red-tinted tar, and tossed nearby were several bloody towels. The weapon was never found, though police did determine that a German-made stainless steel steak knife was missing from a set hanging in the kitchen, and the characteristics of the blade were consistent with her wounds.

Opening Eddie Heath's file folder, Wesley withdrew a scene diagram drawn by the Henrico County police officer who had discovered the critically wounded boy behind the vacant grocery store. Wesley placed the diagram next to the photograph of Robyn Naismith. For a moment, neither of us spoke as our eyes went back and forth from one to the other. The similarities were more pronounced than I had imagined, the positions of their bodies virtually identical, from their hands by their sides to their loosely piled clothing near their bare feet.

"I have to admit, it's eerie as hell," Wesley remarked. "It's almost as if Eddie Heath's scene is a mirror image of this one." He touched the photograph of Robyn Naismith. "Bodies positioned like rag dolls, propped against boxlike objects. A big console TV. A brown Dumpster." Spreading more photographs on the table like playing cards, he drew another from the deck. This one was a close-up of her body at the morgue, the ragged tangential circles of human bite marks apparent on her left breast and left inner thigh.

"Again, a striking similarity," he said. "Bite marks here and here corresponding closely with the areas of missing flesh on Eddie

Heath's shoulder and thigh. In other words"—he slipped off his glasses and looked up at me—"Eddie Heath was probably bitten, the flesh excised to eradicate evidence."

"Then his killer is at least somewhat familiar with forensic evidence," I said.

"Almost any felon who has spent time in prison is familiar with forensic evidence. If Waddell didn't know about bite-mark identification when he murdered Robyn Naismith, he would know about it now."

"You're talking like he's the killer again," I pointed out. "A moment ago you said he doesn't profile right."

"Ten years ago, he didn't profile right. That's all I'm asserting."

"You've got his Assessment Protocol. Can we talk about it?"

"Of course."

The Protocol was actually a forty-page FBI questionnaire filled in during a face-to-face prison interview with a violent offender.

"Flip through this yourself," Wesley said, sliding Waddell's Protocol in front of me. "I'd like to hear your thoughts without further input from me."

Wesley's interview of Ronnie Joe Waddell had taken place six years ago at death row in Mecklenburg County. The Protocol began with the expected descriptive data. Waddell's demeanor, emotional state, mannerisms, and style of conversation indicated that he was agitated and confused. Then, when Wesley had given him opportunity to ask questions, Waddell asked only one: "I saw little white flakes when we passed a window. Is it snowing or are they ashes from the incinerator?"

The date on the Protocol, I noted, was August.

Questions about how the murder might have been prevented went nowhere. Would Waddell have killed his victim in a populated area? Would he have killed her if witnesses had been present? Would anything have stopped him from killing her? Did he think that capital punishment was a deterrent? Waddell said he could not remember killing "the lady on TV." He did not know what would have stopped him from committing an act he could not recall. His only memory was of being "sticky." He said it was like waking up from a wet dream. The stickiness Ronnie Waddell experienced was not semen. It was Robyn Naismith's blood.

"His problem list sounds rather mundane," I thought out loud. "Headaches, extreme shyness, marked daydreaming, and leaving home at the age of nineteen. I don't see anything here that one might consider the usual red flags. No cruelty to animals, fire setting, assaults, et cetera."

"Keep going," Wesley said.

I scanned several more pages. "Drugs and alcohol," I said.

"If he hadn't been locked up, he would have died a junkie or gotten shot on the street," Wesley said. "And what's interesting is the substance abuse did not begin until early adulthood. I remember Waddell told me he had never tasted alcohol until he was twenty and away from home."

"He was raised on a farm?"

"In Suffolk. A fairly big farm that grew peanuts, corn, soybeans. His entire family lived on it and worked for the owners. There were four children, Ronnie Joe the youngest. Their mother was very religious and took the children to church every Sunday. No alcohol, swearing, or cigarettes. His background was very sheltered. He'd really never been off the farm until his father died and Ronnie decided to leave. He took the bus to Richmond and had little trouble getting work because of his physical strength. Breaking up asphalt with a jackhammer, lifting heavy loads, that sort of thing. My theory is he could not handle temptation when he was finally faced with it. First it was beer and wine, then marijuana. Within a year he was into cocaine and heroin, buying and selling, and stealing whatever he could get his hands on.

"When I asked him how many criminal acts he had committed that he had never been arrested for, he said he couldn't count them.

He said he was doing burglaries, breaking into cars—property crimes, in other words. Then he broke into Robyn Naismith's house and she had the misfortune of coming home while he was there."

"He wasn't described as violent, Benton," I pointed out.

"Yes. He never profiled as your typical violent offender. The defense claimed that he was made temporarily insane by drugs and alcohol. To be honest, I think this was the case. Not long before he murdered Robyn Naismith he had started getting into PCP. It is quite possible that when Waddell encountered Robyn Naismith he was completely deranged and later had little or no recollection of what he did to her."

"Do you remember what he stole, if anything?" I asked. "I wonder if there was clear evidence when he broke into her house that his intent was to commit burglary."

"The place was ransacked. We know jewelry was missing. The medicine cabinet was cleaned out and her billfold was empty. It's hard to know what else was stolen because she lived alone."

"No significant relationship?"

"A fascinating point." Wesley stared off at an old couple dancing soporifically to the husky tones of a saxophone. "Semen stains were recovered from a bed sheet and the mattress cover. The stain on the sheet had to be fresh unless Robyn didn't change her bed linens very often, and we know that Waddell was not the origin of the stains. They didn't match his blood type."

"No one who knew her ever made reference to a lover?"

"No one ever did. Obviously, there was keen interest in who this person was, and since he never contacted the police, it was suspected that she had been having an affair, possibly with one of her married colleagues or sources."

"Maybe she was," I said. "But he wasn't her killer."

"No. Ronnie Joe Waddell was her killer. Let's take a look."

I opened Waddell's file and showed Wesley the photographs of the executed inmate I had autopsied on the night of December thirteenth. "Can you tell if this is the man you interviewed six years ago?"

Wesley impassively studied the photographs, going through them one by one. He looked at close-ups of the face and back of the head, and glanced over shots of the upper body and hands. He detached a mug shot from Waddell's Assessment Protocol and began comparing as I looked on.

"I see a resemblance," I said.

"That's about as much as we can say," Wesley replied. "The mug shot's ten years old. Waddell had a beard and mustache, was very muscular but lean. His face was lean. This guy"—he pointed to one of the morgue photographs—"is shaven and much heavier. His face is much fuller. I can't say these are the same man, based on these photos."

I couldn't confirm it, either. In fact, I could think of old pictures of me that no one else would recognize.

"Do you have any suggestions about how we're going to resolve this problem?" I asked Wesley.

"I'll toss out a few things," he said, stacking the photographs and straightening the edges against the tabletop. "Your old friend Nick Grueman's some kind of player in all this, and I've been thinking about the best way to deal with him without tipping our hand. If Marino or I talk to him, he'll know instantly that something's up."

I knew where this was going and I tried to interrupt, but Wesley would not let me. "Marino's mentioned your difficulties with Grueman, that he calls and in general jerks you around. And then, of course, there is the past, your years at Georgetown. Maybe you should talk with him."

"I don't want to talk with him, Benton."

"He may have photographs of Waddell, letters, other documents. Something with Waddell's prints. Or maybe there's something he might say in the course of conversation that would be revealing. The point is, you have access to him, if you wish, through your normal activities, when the rest of us don't. And you're going to D.C. anyway to see Downey."

"NO," I said.

"It's just a thought." He looked away from me and motioned for the waitress to bring the check. "How long will Lucy be visiting you?" he asked.

"She doesn't have to be back at school until January seventh."

"I remember she's pretty good with computers."

"She's more than pretty good."

Wesley smiled a little. "So Marino's told me. He says she thinks she can help with AFIS."

"I'm sure she'd like to try." I suddenly felt protective again, and torn. I wanted to send her back to Miami, and yet I didn't.

"You may or may not remember, but Michele works for the Department of Criminal Justice Services, which assists the State Police in running AFIS," Wesley said.

"I should think that might worry you a little right now." I finished my brandy.

"There isn't a day of my life that I don't worry," he said.

The next morning a light snow began to fall as Lucy and I dressed in ski clothes that could be spotted from here to the Eiger.

"I look like a traffic cone," she said, staring at her blaze orange reflection in the mirror.

"That's right. If you get lost on a trail, it won't be hard to find you." I swallowed vitamins and two aspirin with sparkling water from the minibar.

My niece eyed my outfit, which was almost as electric as hers, and shook her head. "For someone so conservative, you certainly dress like a neon peacock for sports."

"I try not to be a stick-in-the-mud all of the time. Are you hungry?"

"Starved."

"Benton's supposed to meet us in the dining room at eight-thirty. We can go down now if you don't want to wait."

"I'm ready. Isn't Connie going to eat with us?"

"We're going to meet her on the slopes. Benton wants to talk shop first."

"I would think it must bother her to be left out," Lucy said. "Whenever he talks with anyone, it seems she isn't invited."

I locked the room door and we headed down the quiet corridor.

"I suspect Connie doesn't wish to be involved," I said in a low voice. "For her to know every detail of her husband's work would only be a burden for her."

"So he talks to you instead."

"About cases, yes."

"About work. And work is what matters most to both of you."

"Work certainly seems to dominate our lives."

"Are you and Mr. Wesley about to have an affair?"

"We're about to have breakfast." I smiled.

The Homestead's buffet was typically overwhelming. Long cloth-covered tables were laden with Virginia-cured bacon and ham, every concoction of eggs imaginable, pastries, breads, and griddle cakes. Lucy seemed immune to the temptations, and headed straight for the cereals and fresh fruit. Shamed into good behavior by her example and by my recent lecture to Marino about his health, I avoided everything I wanted, including coffee.

"People are staring at you, Aunt Kay," Lucy said under her breath.

I assumed the attention was due to our vibrant attire until I opened the morning's *Washington Post* and was shocked to discover myself on the front page. The headline read, "MURDER IN THE MORGUE," the story a lengthy account of Susan's homicide, which was accompanied by a prominently placed photograph of me arriving at the scene and looking very tense. Clearly, the reporter's major source was Susan's distraught husband, Jason, whose information painted a picture of his wife leaving her job under peculiar, if not suspicious, circumstances less than a week before her violent death.

It was asserted, for example, that Susan recently confronted me when I attempted to list her as a witness in the case of a murdered young boy, even though she had not been present during his autopsy. When Susan became ill and stayed out of work "after a formalin spill," I called her home with such frequency that she was afraid to answer the phone, then I "showed up on her doorstep the night before her murder" with a poinsettia and vague offers of favors.

"I walked into my house after Christmas shopping and there was the chief medical examiner inside my living room," Susan's husband was quoted. "She [Dr. Scarpetta] left right away, and as soon as the door shut Susan started crying. She was terrified of something but wouldn't tell me what."

As unsettling as I found Jason Story's public disparagement of me, worse was the revelation of Susan's recent financial transactions. Supposedly, two weeks before her death she paid off more than three thousand dollars in credit card bills after having deposited thirty-five hundred dollars into her checking account. The sudden windfall could not be explained. Her husband had been laid off from his sales job during the fall and Susan earned less than twenty thousand dollars a year.

"Mr. Wesley's here," Lucy said, taking the paper from me.

Wesley was dressed in black ski pants and turtleneck, a bright red jacket tucked under his arm. I could tell by the expression on his face, the firm set of his jaw, that he was aware of the news.

"Did the *Post* try to talk to you?" He pulled out a chair. "I can't believe they ran this damn thing without giving you a chance for comment."

"A reporter from the *Post* called as I was leaving the office yesterday," I replied. "He wanted to question me about Susan's homicide and I chose not to talk to him. I guess that was my chance."

"So you didn't know anything, had no forewarning about the slant of this thing."

"I was in the dark until I picked up the paper."

"It's all over the news, Kay." He met my eyes. "I heard it on television this morning. Marino called. The press in Richmond is having a field day. The implication is that Susan's murder may be connected to the medical examiner's office—that you may be involved and have suddenly left town."

"That's insane."

"How much of the article is true?" he asked.

"The facts have been completely distorted. I did call Susan's house when she didn't show up at work. I wanted to make certain she was all right, and then I needed to find out if she remembered printing Waddell at the morgue. I did go see her on Christmas Eve to give her a gift and the poinsettia. I suppose my promise of favors was when she told me she was quitting and I said for her to let me know if she needed a reference, or if there was anything I could do for her."

"What about this business of her not wanting to be listed as a witness in Eddie Heath's case?"

"That was the afternoon she broke several jars of formalin and retreated upstairs to my office. It's routine to list autopsy assistants or techs as witnesses when they assist in the posts. In this instance, Susan was present for only the external examination and was adamant about not wanting her name on Eddie Heath's autopsy report. I thought her request and demeanor were weird, but there was no confrontation."

"This article makes it look as if you were paying her off," Lucy said. "That's what I would wonder if I read this and didn't know."

"I certainly wasn't paying her off, but it sounds as if someone was," I said.

"It's all making a little more sense," Wesley said. "If this bit about her financial picture is accurate, then Susan had gotten a substantial sum of money, meaning she must have supplied a service to someone. Around this same time your computer was broken into and Susan's personality changed. She became nervous and unreliable. She avoided you as much as she could. I think she couldn't face you, Kay, because she knew she was betraying you."

I nodded, struggling for composure. Susan had gotten into something she did not know how to get out of, and it occurred to me that this might be the real explanation for why she fled from Eddie Heath's post and then from Jennifer Deighton's. Her emotional outbursts had nothing to do with witchcraft or feeling dizzy after being exposed to formalin fumes. She was panicking. She did not want to witness either case.

"Interesting," Wesley said when I voiced my theory. "If you ask what of value did Susan Story have to sell, the answer is information. If she didn't witness the posts, she had no information. And whoever was buying this information from her is quite likely the person she was going to meet on Christmas Day."

"What information would be so important that someone would be willing to pay thousands of dollars for it and then murder a pregnant woman?" Lucy asked bluntly.

We did not know, but we had a guess. The common denominator, once again, seemed to be Ronnie Joe Waddell.

"Susan didn't forget to print Waddell or whoever it was that was executed," I said. "She deliberately didn't print him."

"That's the way it looks," Wesley agreed. "Someone else asked her to conveniently forget to print him. Or to lose his cards in the event that you or another member of your staff printed him."

I thought of Ben Stevens. The bastard.

"And this brings us back to what you and I concluded last night, Kay," Wesley went on. "We need to go back to the night Waddell was supposed to have been executed and determine who it was they strapped in the chair. And a place to start is AFIS. What we want to know is if and what records were tampered with." He was talking to Lucy now. "I've got it set up for you to go through the journal tapes, if you're willing."

"I'm willing," Lucy said. "When do you want me to start?"

"You can start as soon as you want because the first step will involve only the telephone. You need to call Michele. She's a systems analyst for the Department of Criminal Justice Services and works out of the State Police headquarters. She's involved with AFIS and will go into detail with you about how everything works. Then she'll begin mounting the journal tapes so you can access them."

"She doesn't mind my doing this?" Lucy asked warily.

"On the contrary. She's thrilled. The journal tapes are nothing more than audit logs, a record of changes made to the AFIS data base. They're not readable, in other words. I think Michele called them 'hex dumps,' if that means anything to you."

"Hexadecimal, or base sixteen. Hieroglyphics, in other words," Lucy said. "It means that I'll have to decipher the data and write a program that will look for anything that's gone against the identification numbers of the records you're interested in."

"Can you do it?" Wesley asked.

"Once I figure out the code and record layout. Why doesn't the analyst you know do it herself?"

"We want to be as discreet as possible. It would attract notice if Michele suddenly abandoned her normal duties and started wading through journal tapes ten hours a day. You can work invisibly from your aunt's home computer by dialing in on a diagnostic line."

"As long as when Lucy dials in it can't be traced back to my residence," I said.

"It won't be," Wesley said.

"And no one is likely to notice that someone from the outside is dialing into the State Police computer and wading through the tapes?" I asked.

"Michele says she can maneuver it so there's no problem." Unzipping a pocket of his ski jacket, Wesley slipped out a card and gave it to Lucy. "Here are her work and home phone numbers."

"How do you know you can trust her?" Lucy asked. "If tampering has gone on, how do you know she's not involved?"

"Michele has never been good at lying. From the time she was a little girl she would stare down at her feet and turn as red as Rudolf's nose."

"You knew her when she was a little girl?" Lucy looked baffled.

"And before," Wesley said. "She's my eldest daughter."

9

After much debate, we came up with what seemed a reasonable plan. Lucy would stay at the Homestead with the Wesleys until Wednesday, allowing me a brief period to grapple with my problems without worrying about her welfare. After breakfast, I drove off in a gentle snow that by the time I reached Richmond had turned to rain.

By late afternoon, I had been to the office and the labs. I had conferred with Fielding and several of the forensic scientists, and had avoided Ben Stevens. I returned not a single reporter's call and ignored my electronic mail, for if the health commissioner had sent me a communication, I did not want to know what it said. At half past four I was filling my car with gas at an Exxon station on Grove Avenue when a white Ford LTD pulled in behind me. I watched Marino get out, hitch up his trousers, and head to the men's room. When he returned a moment later, he covertly glanced around as if worried that someone might have observed his trip to the toilet. Then he strolled over to me.

"I saw you as I was driving past," he said, jamming his hands into the pockets of his blue blazer.

"Where's your coat?" I began cleaning the front windshield.

"In the car. It gets in my way." He hunched his shoulders against the cold, raw air. "If you ain't thinking about stopping these rumors, then you'd better start thinking about it."

I irritably returned the squeegee to its container of cleaning solution. "And just what do you suggest I do, Marino? Call Jason Story and tell him I'm sorry his wife and unborn child are dead but

I would certainly appreciate it if he would vent his grief and rage elsewhere?"

"Doc, he blames you."

"After reading his quotes in the *Post,* I suspect any number of people are blaming me. He's managed to portray me as a Machiavellian bitch."

"You hungry?"

"No."

"Well, you look hungry."

I looked at him as if he'd lost his mind.

"And if something looks a certain way to me, it's my duty to check it out. So I'm giving you a choice, Doc. I can get us some Nabs and sodas from the machines over there, and we can stand out here freezing our asses off and inhaling fumes while we prevent other poor bastards from using the self-service pumps. Or we can zip over to Phil's. I'm buying either way."

Ten minutes later we were sitting in a corner booth perusing glossy illustrated menus offering everything from spaghetti to fried fish. Marino faced the dark-tinted front door and I had a perfect view of the rest rooms. He was smoking, as were most of the people around us, and I was reminded that it is hell to quit. He actually could not have selected a more ideal restaurant, considering the circumstances. Philip's Continental Lounge was an old, neighborhood establishment where patrons who had known each other all their lives continued to meet regularly for hearty food and bottled beer. The typical customer was good-natured and gregarious, and unlikely to recognize me or care unless my picture regularly appeared in the sports section of the newspaper.

"It's like this," Marino said as he closed his menu. "Jason Story believes Susan would still be alive if she'd had another job. And he's probably right. Plus, he's a loser—one of these self-centered assholes who believes everything is everybody else's fault. The truth is, he's probably more to blame for Susan's death than anyone."

"You're not suggesting that *he* killed her?"

The waitress appeared and we ordered. Grilled chicken and rice for Marino and a kosher chili dog for me, plus two diet sodas.

"I'm not suggesting that Jason shot his wife," Marino said quietly. "But he set her up for getting involved in whatever it was that precipitated her homicide. Paying the bills was Susan's responsibility, and she was under big-time financial stress."

"Unsurprisingly," I said. "Her husband had just lost his job."

"It's too bad he didn't lose his high dollar taste. We're talking Polo shirts and Britches of Georgetown slacks and silk ties. A couple weeks after he gets laid off, the jerk goes out and buys seven hundred bucks' worth of ski equipment and then heads off to Wintergreen for the weekend. Before that it was a two-hundred-dollar leather jacket and a four-hundred-dollar bicycle. So Susan's down at the morgue working like a dog and then coming home to face bills her salary won't put a dent in."

"I had no idea," I said, pained by a sudden vision of Susan sitting at her desk. Her daily ritual was to spend her lunch hour in her office, and on occasion I would join her there to chat. I remembered her generic-brand corn chips and the sale stickers on her sodas. I don't think she ever ate or drank anything she had not brought from home.

"Jason's spending habits," Marino went on, "leads to the shit he's causing you. He's badmouthing you like hell to anybody who will listen because you're a doctor-lawyer-Indian chief who drives a Mercedes and lives in a big house in Windsor Farms. I think the dumbass believes if he can somehow blame you for what happened to his wife, maybe he can get a little compensation."

"He can try until he's blue in the face."

"And he will."

Our diet drinks arrived, and I changed the subject. "I'm meeting with Downey in the morning."

Marino's eyes wandered to the television over the bar.

"Lucy's getting started on AFIS. And then I've got to do something about Ben Stevens."

"What you ought to do is get rid of him."

"Do you have any idea how difficult it is to fire a state employee?"

"They say it's easier to fire Jesus Christ," Marino said. "Unless the employee is appointed and got a grade off the charts, like you. You still ought to find some way to run the bastard off."

"Have you talked to him?"

"Oh, yeah. According to him, you're arrogant, ambitious, and strange. A real pain in the ass to work for."

"He actually said something like that?" I asked in disbelief.

"That was the drift."

"I hope someone is checking into his finances. I'd be interested to know if he's made any large deposits lately. Susan didn't get into trouble alone."

"I agree with you. I think Stevens knows a lot and is covering his tracks like crazy. By the way, I checked with Susan's bank. One of the tellers remembers her making the thirty-five-hundred-dollar deposit in *cash*. Twenties, fifties, and hundred-dollar bills that she was carrying in her purse."

"What did Stevens have to say about Susan?"

"He's saying that he really didn't know her, but that it was his impression there was some problem between you and her. In other words, he's reinforcing what's been in the news."

Our food arrived, and it was all I could do to swallow a single bite because I was so angry.

"And what about Fielding?" I said. "Does he think I'm horrible to work for?"

Marino stared off again. "He says you're very driven and he's never been able to figure you out."

"I didn't hire him to figure me out, and compared to him, I am certainly driven. Fielding is disenchanted with forensic medicine and has been for several years. He expends most of his energy in the gym."

"Doc"—Marino met my eyes—"you are driven compared to *anyone,* and most people can't figure you out. You don't exactly walk around with your heart on your sleeve. In fact, you can come across as someone who don't have feelings. You're so damn hard to read that to others who don't know you, it sometimes appears that nothing gets to you. Other cops, lawyers, they ask me about you. They want to know what you're really like, how you can do what you do every day—what the deal is. They see you as somebody who don't get close to anyone."

"And what do you tell them when they ask?" I said.

"I don't tell them a damn thing."

"Are you finished psychoanalyzing me yet, Marino?"

He lit a cigarette. "Look, I'm going to say something to you, and you ain't gonna like it. You've always been this reserved, professional lady—someone real slow to let anybody in, but once the person's there, he's there. He's got a damn friend for life and you'd do anything for him. But you've been different this past year. You've had about a hundred walls up ever since Mark got killed. For those of us around you, it's like being in a room that was once seventy degrees and suddenly the temperature's down to about fifty-five. I don't think you're even aware of it.

"So nobody's feeling all that attached to you right now. Maybe they even resent you a little bit because they feel ignored or snubbed by you. Maybe they never liked you anyway. Maybe they're just indifferent. The thing about people is, whether you're sitting on a throne or a hot seat, they're going to use your position to their advantage. And if there's no bond between you and them, that just makes it all the easier for them to try to get what they want without giving a rat's ass about what happens to you. And that's where you are. There's a lot of people who've been waiting for years to see you bleed."

"I don't intend to bleed." I pushed my plate away.

"Doc"—he blew out smoke—"you're already bleeding. And

common sense tells me that if you're swimming with sharks and start bleeding, you ought to get the hell out of the water."

"Might we converse without speaking in clichés, at least for a minute or two?"

"Hey. I can say it in Portuguese or Chinese and you're not going to listen to me."

"If you speak Portuguese or Chinese, I promise I'll listen. In fact, if you ever decide to speak English I promise I'll listen."

"Comments like that don't win you any fans. That's just what I'm talking about."

"I said it with a smile."

"I've seen you cut open bodies with a smile."

"Never. I always use a scalpel."

"Sometimes there isn't a difference between the two. I've seen your smile make defense attorneys bleed."

"If I'm such a dreadful person, why are we friends?"

"Because I've got more walls up than you do. The fact is, there's a squirrel in every tree and the water's full of sharks. All of them want a piece of us."

"Marino, you're paranoid."

"You're damn right, which is why I wish you'd lay low for a while, Doc. Really," he said.

"I can't."

"You want to know the truth, it's going to start looking like a conflict of interests for you to have anything to do with these cases. It's going to make you come off looking worse."

I said, "Susan is dead. Eddie Heath is dead. Jennifer Deighton is dead. There is corruption in my office, and we aren't certain who went to the electric chair the other week. You're suggesting I just walk away until everything somehow magically self-corrects."

Marino reached for the salt but I got it first. "Nope. But you can have all the pepper you want," I said, sliding the pepper shaker closer.

"This health crap is going to kill me," he warned. "Because one of these days I'm going to get so pissed I'm going to do everything at once. Five cigarettes going, a bourbon in one hand and a cup of coffee in the other, steak, baked potato loaded with butter, sour cream, salt. And then I'm going to blow every circuit in the box."

"No, you're not going to do any of those things," I said. "You're going to be kind to yourself and live at least as long as I do."

We were silent for a while, picking at our food.

"Doc, no offense, but just what do you think you're going to find out about damn feather parts?"

"Hopefully, their origin."

"I can save you the trouble. They came from birds," he said.

I left Marino at close to seven P.M. and returned downtown. The temperature had risen above forty, the night dark and lashing out in fits of rain violent enough to stop traffic. Sodium vapor lamps were pollen-yellow smudges behind the morgue, where the bay door was shut, every parking space vacant. Inside the building, my pulse quickened as I followed the brightly lit corridor past the autopsy suite to Susan's small office.

As I unlocked the door, I did not know what I expected to find, but I was drawn to her filing cabinet and desk drawers, to every book and old telephone message. Everything looked the same as it had before she died. Marino was quite skilled at going through someone's private space without disturbing the natural disorder of things. The telephone was still askew on the right corner of the desk, the cord twisted like a corkscrew. Scissors and two pencils with broken points were on the green paper blotter, her lab coat draped over the back of her chair. A reminder of a doctor's appointment was still taped to her computer monitor, and as I stared at the shy curves and gentle slant of her neat script, I trembled inside. Where had she gone adrift? Was it when she married Jason Story?

Or was her destruction set up much earlier than that, when she was the young daughter of a scrupulous minister, the twin left behind when her sister was killed?

Sitting in her chair, I rolled it closer to the filing cabinet and began slipping out one file after another and glancing through the contents. Most of what I perused were brochures and other printed information pertaining to surgical supplies and miscellaneous items used in the morgue. Nothing struck me as curious until I discovered that she had saved virtually every memo she had ever gotten from Fielding, but not one from Ben Stevens or me, when I knew that both of us had sent her plenty. Further searching through drawers and bookshelves produced no files for Stevens or me, and that's when I concluded that someone had taken them.

My first thought was that Marino might have carried them off. Then something else occurred to me with a jolt, and I hurried upstairs. Unlocking the door to my office, I went straight to the file drawer where I kept mundane administrative paperwork such as telephone call sheets, memos, printouts of electronic mail communications I had received, and drafts of budget proposals and long-term plans. Frantically, I rifled through folders and drawers. The thick file I was looking for was simply labeled "Memos," and in it were copies of every memo I had sent to my staff and various other agency personnel over the past several years. I searched Rose's office and carefully checked my office again. The file was gone.

"You son of a bitch," I said under my breath as I headed furiously down the hall. "You goddam son of a bitch."

Ben Stevens's office was impeccably neat and so carefully appointed that it looked like a display in a discount furniture store. His desk was a Williamsburg reproduction with bright brass pulls and a mahogany veneer, and he had brass floor lamps with dark green shades. The floor was covered with a machine-made Persian rug, the walls arranged with large prints of alpine skiers and men on thundering horses swinging polo sticks and sailors racing through snarling seas. I began by pulling Susan's personnel file. The expected job description, résumé, and other documents were inside. Absent were several memos of commendation I had written since hiring her and had added to her file myself. I began opening desk drawers, and discovered in one of them a brown vinyl kit containing toothbrush, toothpaste, razor, shaving cream, and a small bottle of cologne.

Perhaps it was the barely perceptible shift of air when the door was silently pulled open wider, or perhaps I simply sensed a presence the way an animal would. I happened to look up to find Ben Stevens standing in the doorway as I sat at his desk screwing the cap back on a bottle of Red cologne. For a long, icy moment, our eyes held and neither of us spoke. I did not feel fear. I did not feel the least bit concerned by what he had caught me doing. I felt rage.

"You're keeping unusually late hours, Ben." Zipping up his toilet kit, I returned it to its drawer. I laced my fingers on top of the blotter, my movements, my speech, deliberate and slow.

"The thing I've always liked about working after hours is there is no one else around," I said. "No distractions. No risk of someone walking in and interrupting whatever it is you are doing. No eyes or ears. Not a sound, except on rare occasion when the security guard happens to wander through. And we all know that doesn't happen often unless his attention is solicited, because he hates coming into the morgue at any time. I've never known a security guard who didn't hate that. Same goes for the cleaning crew. They won't even go downstairs, and they do as little up here as they can get away with. But that point is moot, isn't it? It's close to nine o'clock. The cleaning crew is always gone by seven-thirty.

"What intrigues me is that I did not guess before now. It never crossed my mind. Maybe that is a sad comment about how preoccupied I've been. You told the police you did not know Susan personally, yet you frequently gave her rides to and from work, such as on the snowy morning I autopsied Jennifer Deighton. I remember that Susan was very distracted on that occasion. She left the body in the middle of the corridor, and she was dialing a number on the phone and quickly hung up when I walked into the autopsy suite. I doubt she was placing a business call at seven-thirty in the morning on a day when most people weren't going to venture out of their homes because of the weather. And there was no one in the office to call—no one had gotten in yet, except you. If she were dialing your number, why would her impulse be to hide that from me? Unless you were more than her direct supervisor.

"Of course, your relationship with me is equally intriguing. We seem to get along fine, then suddenly you claim that I am the worst boss in Christendom. It makes me wonder if Jason Story is the only person talking to reporters. It's amazing, this persona I suddenly have. This image. The tyrant. The neurotic. The person who is somehow responsible for the violent death of my morgue supervisor. Susan and I had a very cordial working relationship, and until recently, Ben, so did we. But it's my word against yours, especially now, since any scrap of paper that might document what I'm saying has conveniently disappeared. And my prediction is that you have already leaked to someone that important personnel files and memorandums have vanished from the office, thus implying that I'm the one who took them. When files and memos disappear, you can say anything you want about the contents of them, can't you?"

"I don't know what you're talking about," Ben Stevens said. He moved away from the doorway but did not come close to the desk or take a chair. His face was flushed, his eyes hard with hate. "I don't know anything about any missing files or memos, but if it's true, then I can't hide that fact from the authorities, just as I can't hide the fact that I happened to stop by the office tonight to get something I'd left and discovered you rummaging through my desk."

"What did you leave, Ben?"

"I don't have to answer your questions."

"Actually, you do. You work for me, and if you come into the building late at night and I happen to know about it, I have the right to question you."

"Go ahead and put me on leave. Try to fire me. That will certainly look good for you right now."

"You are a squid, Ben."

His eyes widened and he wet his lips.

"Your efforts to sabotage me are just a lot of ink you're squirting into the water because you're panicking and want to divert attention from yourself. Did you kill Susan?"

"You're losing your goddam mind." His voice shook.

"She left her house early afternoon on Christmas Day, allegedly to meet a girlfriend. In truth, the person she was meeting was you, wasn't it? Did you know that when she was dead in her car, her coat collar and scarf smelled like men's cologne, like the Red cologne you keep in your desk so you can freshen up before you hit the bars in the Slip after work?"

"I don't know what you're talking about."

"Who was paying her?"

"Maybe you were."

"That's ridiculous," I said calmly. "You and Susan were involved in some money-making scheme, and my guess is that you are the one who initially got her involved because you knew her vulnerabilities. She probably had confided in you. You knew how to convince her to go along, and Lord knows you could use the money. Your bar tabs alone have got to blow your budget. Partying is very expensive, and I know what you get paid."

"You don't know anything."

"Ben." I lowered my voice. "Get out of it. Stop while there's still time. Tell me who's behind this."

He would not look me in the eye.

"The stakes are too high when people start dying. Do you think if you killed Susan that you'll get away with it?"

He said nothing.

"If someone else killed her, do you think you're immune, that the same thing can't happen to you?"

"You're threatening me."

"Nonsense."

"You can't prove that the cologne you smelled on Susan was mine. There's no test for something like that. You can't put a *smell* in a test tube; you can't save it," he said.

"I'm going to ask you to leave now, Ben."

He turned and walked out of his office. When I heard the elevator doors shut, I went down the hall and peered out a window overlooking the parking lot in back. I did not venture out to my car until Stevens had driven away.

The FBI Building is a concrete fortification at 9th Street and Pennsylvania Avenue in the heart of D.C., and when I arrived the following morning, it was in the wake of at least a hundred noisy schoolchildren. They brought to mind Lucy at their age as they stomped up steps, dashed to benches, and flocked restlessly about huge shrubs and potted trees. Lucy would have loved touring the laboratories, and I suddenly missed her intensely.

The babble of shrill young voices faded as if carried away from me by the wind, my step brisk and directed, for I had been here enough times to know the way. Heading toward the center of the building, I passed the courtyard, then a restricted parking area and a guard before reaching the single glass door. Inside was a lobby of tan furniture, mirrors, and flags. A photograph of the president smiled from one wall, while posted on another was a hit parade of the ten most wanted fugitives in the land.

At the escort desk, I presented my driver's license to a young agent whose demeanor was as grim as his gray suit.

"I'm Dr. Kay Scarpetta, Chief Medical Examiner of Virginia."

"Who are you here to see?"

I told him.

He compared me to my photograph, ascertained that I was not armed, placed a phone call, and gave me a badge. Unlike the Academy at Quantico, Headquarters had an ambience that seemed to starch the soul and stiffen the spine.

I had never met Special Agent Minor Downey, though the irony of his name had conjured up unfair images. He would be an effete, frail man with pale blond hair covering every inch of his body except for his head. His eyes would be weak, his skin rarely touched by the sun, and of course he would drift in and out of places and never draw attention to himself. Naturally, I was wrong. When a fit man in shirtsleeves appeared and looked straight at me, I got up from my chair.

"You must be Mr. Downey," I said.

"Dr. Scarpetta." He shook my hand. "Please call me Minor."

He was at the most forty, and attractive in a scholarly sort of way, with his rimless glasses, neatly clipped brown hair, and maroon-and-navy-striped tie. He exuded a prepossession and intellectual intensity immediately noticeable to anyone who has suffered through arduous years of postgraduate education, for I could not recall a professor from Georgetown or Johns Hopkins who did not commune with the uncommon and find it impossible to connect with pedestrian human beings.

"Why feathers?" I asked as we boarded the elevator.

"I have a friend who's an ornithologist at the Smithsonian's Museum of Natural History," he said. "When government aviation officials started getting her help with bird strikes, I got interested. You see, birds get ingested by aircraft engines and when you're going through the wreckage on the ground, you find these feather parts and want to figure out which bird caused the problem. In other words, whatever got sucked in was chewed up pretty good. A sea gull can crash a B-1 bomber, and you lose one engine to a bird strike with a wide-bodied plane full of people and you've got a problem.

Or take the case of the loon that went through the windshield of a Lear jet and decapitated the pilot. So that's part of what I do. I work on bird ingestions. We test turbines and blades by throwing in chickens. You know, can the plane survive one chicken or two?

"But birds figure into all sorts of things. Pigeon down in poop on the bottom of a suspect's shoes—was the suspect in the alleyway where the body was found or not? Or the guy who stole a Double Yellow Amazon during the course of a burglary, and we find down pieces in the back of his car that are identified as coming from a Double Yellow Amazon. Or the down feather recovered from the body of a woman who was raped and murdered. She was found in a Panasonic stereo speaker box in a Dumpster. The down looked like a small white mallard feather to me, same type of feather in the down comforter on the suspect's bed. That case was made with a feather and two hairs."

The third floor was a city block of laboratories where examiners analyzed the explosives, paint chips, pollens, tools, tires, and debris used in crimes or collected from scenes. Gas chromatography detectors, microspectrophotometers, and mainframes ran morning, noon, and night, and reference collections filled rooms with automotive paint types, duct tapes, and plastics. I followed Downey through white hallways past the DNA analysis labs, then into the Hairs and Fibers Unit where he worked. His office also functioned as a laboratory, with dark wood furniture and bookcases sharing space with countertops and microscopes. Walls and carpet were beige, and crayon drawings tacked to a bulletin board told me this internationally respected feather expert was a father.

Opening a manila envelope, I withdrew three smaller envelopes made of transparent plastic. Two contained the feathers collected from Jennifer Deighton's and Susan Story's homicides, while a third contained a slide of the gummy residue from Eddie Heath's wrists.

"This is the best one, it seems," I said, pointing out the feather I had recovered from Jennifer Deighton's nightgown.

He took it out of its envelope and said, "This is down—a breast or back feather. It's got a nice tuft on it. Good. The more feather you've got, the better." Using forceps, he stripped several of the branchlike projections or "barbs" from both sides of the shaft and, stationing himself at the stereoscopic microscope, placed them on a thin film of xylene that he had dropped on a slide. This served to separate the tiny structures, or float them out, and when he was satisfied that each barb was pristinely fanned, he touched a corner of green blotting paper to the xylene to absorb it. He added the mounting medium Flo-Texx, then a coverslip, and placed the slide under the comparison microscope, which was connected to a video camera.

"I'll start off by telling you that the feathers of all birds have basically the same structure," he said. "You've got a central shaft, barbs, which in turn branch into hairlike barbules, and you've got a broadened base, at the top of which is a pore called the superior umbilicus. The barbs are the filaments that result in the feather's *feathery* appearance, and when they're magnified you'll find they're actually like minifeathers coming out of the shaft." He turned on the monitor. "Here's a barb."

"It looks like a fern," I said.

"In many instances, yes. Now we're going to magnify it some more so we can get a good look at the barbules, for it is the features of the barbules that allow for an identification. Specifically, what we're most interested in are the nodes."

"Let me see if I've got this straight," I said. "Nodes are features of barbules, barbules are features of barbs, barbs are features of feathers, and feathers are features of birds."

"Right. And each family of birds has its own peculiar feather structure."

What I saw on the monitor's screen looked, unremarkably, like a stick figure depiction of a weed or an insect leg. Lines were connected in segments by three-dimensional triangular structures that Downey said were the nodes.

"It's the size, shape, number, and pigmentation of nodes and their placement along the barbule that are key," he patiently explained. "For example, with starlike nodes you're dealing with pigeons, ringlike nodes are chickens and turkeys, enlarged flanges with prenodal swelling are cuckoos. These"—he pointed to the screen—"are clearly triangular, so right away I know your feather is either duck or goose. Not that this should come as any great surprise. The typical origin of feathers collected in burglaries, rapes, and homicides are pillows, comforters, vests, jackets, gloves. And generally the filler in these items comprises chopped feathers and down from ducks and geese, and in cheap stuff, chickens.

"But we can definitely rule out chickens here. And I'm about to decide that your feather did not come from a goose, either."

"Why?" I asked.

"Well, the distinction would be easy if we had a whole feather. Down is tough. But based on what I'm seeing here, there are, on average, just too few nodes. Plus, they aren't located throughout the barbule but are more distal, or located more toward the end of the barbule. And that's a characteristic of ducks."

He opened a cabinet and slid out several drawers of slides.

"Let's see. I've got about sixty slides of ducks. To be on the safe side I'm going to run through all of them, eliminating as I go."

One by one he placed slides under the comparison microscope, which is basically two compound microcopes combined into one binocular unit. On the video monitor was a circular field of light divided down the middle by a fine line, the known feather specimen on one side of the line and the one we hoped to identify on the other. Rapidly, we scanned mallard, Muscovy, harlequin, scoter, ruddy, and American widgeon, and then dozens more. Downey did not have to look long at any one of them to know that the duck we sought was being elusive.

"Am I just imagining it, or is this one more delicate than the others?" I said of the feather in question.

"You're not imagining it. It's more delicate, more streamlined. See how the triangular structures don't flare out quite as much?"

"Okay. Now that you've pointed it out."

"And this is giving us an important hint about the bird. That's what's fascinating. Nature really does have a reason for things, and I'm suspicious that in this case the reason is insulation. The purpose of down is to trap air, and the finer the barbules, the more streamlined or tapered the nodes, and the more distal the location of the nodes, the more efficient the down is going to be at trapping air. When air's trapped or dead, it's like being in a small, insulated room with no ventilation. You're going to be warm."

He placed another slide on the microscope's stage, and this time I could see that we were close. The barbules were delicate, the nodes tapered and distally located.

"What have we got?" I asked.

"I've saved the prime suspects for last." He looked pleased. "Sea ducks. And top in the lineup are the eiders. Let's bump the magnification up to four hundred." He switched the objective lens, adjusted the focus, and off we went through several more slides. "Not the king or the spectacle. And I don't think it's the stellar because of the brownish pigmentation at the base of the node. Your feather doesn't have that, see?"

"I see."

"So we'll try the common eider. Okay. There's consistency in pigmentation," he said, staring intensely at the screen. "And, let's see, an average of two nodes located distally along the barbules. Plus, the streamlining for extra good insulating quality—and that's important if you're swimming around in the Arctic Ocean. I think this is it, the *Somateria mollissima,* typically found in Iceland, Norway, Alaska, and the Siberian shores. I'll run another check with SEM," he added, referring to scanning electron microscopy.

"To scan for what?"

"Salt crystals."

"Of course," I said, fascinated. "Because eider ducks are saltwater birds."

"Exactly. And interesting ones at that, a noteworthy example of exploitation. In Iceland and Norway, their breeding colonies are protected from predators and other disruptions so that people can collect the down with which the female lines her nest and covers her eggs. The down is then cleaned and sold to manufacturers."

"Manufacturers of what?"

"Typically, sleeping bags and comforters." As he talked, he was mounting several downy barbs from the feather found inside Susan Story's car.

"Jennifer Deighton had nothing like that in her house," I said. "Nothing filled with feathers at all."

"Then we're probably dealing with a secondary or tertiary transfer in which the feather got transferred to the killer who in turn transferred it to his victim. You know, this is very interesting."

The specimen was on the monitor now.

"Eider duck again," I said.

"I think so. Let's try the slide. This is from the boy?"

"Yes," I said. "From an adhesive residue on Eddie Heath's wrists."

"I'll be damned."

The microscopic debris showed up on the monitor as a fascinating variety of colors, shapes, fibers, and the familiar barbules and triangular nodes.

"Well, that puts a pretty big hole in my personal theory," Downey said. "If we're talking about three homicides that occurred at different locations and at different times."

"That's what we're talking about."

"If just one of these feathers was eider duck, then I'd be tempted to consider the possibility that it was a contaminant. You know, you see these labels that say one hundred percent acrylic and it turns out to be ninety percent acrylic and ten percent nylon. Labels lie. If the run before your acrylic sweater, for example, was a lot of nylon jackets, then the very first sweaters that come off afterward will have nylon contaminants. As you run more sweaters through, the contaminant is dissipated."

"In other words," I said, "if somebody is wearing a down-filled jacket or owns a comforter that got eider contaminants in it when it was manufactured, then the probability is almost nonexistent that this individual's jacket or comforter would be leaking only the eiderdown contaminants."

"Precisely. So we'll assume the item in question is filled with pure eiderdown, and that is extremely curious. Usually what I'm going to see in cases that come through here are your Kmart-variety jackets, gloves, or comforters filled with chicken feathers or maybe goose. Eider is a specialty item, a very exclusive shop item. A vest, jacket, comforter, or sleeping bag filled with eiderdown is going to have very low leakage, be very well made—and prohibitively expensive."

"Have you ever had eiderdown submitted as evidence before?"

"This is the first."

"Why is it so valuable?"

"The insulating qualities I've already described. But aesthetic appeal also has a lot to do with it. The common eider's down is snow-white. Most down is dingy."

"And if I purchased a specialty item filled with eiderdown, would I be aware that it's filled with this snow-white down or would the label simply say 'duck down'?"

"I'm quite sure you'd be aware of it," he said. "The label would probably say something like 'one hundred percent eiderdown.' There would have to be something that would justify the price."

"Can you run a computer check on down distributors?"

"Sure. But to state the obvious, no distributor is going to be able to tell you the eiderdown you've collected is theirs, not without the accompanying garment or item. Unfortunately, a feather isn't enough."

"I don't know," I said. "It might be."

* * *

By noon I had walked two blocks to where I had parked my car, and was inside with the heater blasting. I was so close to New Jersey Avenue that I felt like the tide being pulled by the moon. I fastened my seat belt, fiddled with the radio, and twice reached for the phone and changed my mind. It was crazy to even consider contacting Nicholas Grueman.

He won't be in anyway, I thought, reaching for the phone again and dialing.

"Grueman," the voice said.

"This is Dr. Scarpetta." I raised my voice above the heater's fan.

"Well, hello. I was just reading about you the other day. You sound like you're calling from a car phone."

"That's because I am. I happen to be in Washington."

"I'm truly flattered that you would think of me while you're passing through my humble town."

"There is nothing humble about your town, Mr. Grueman, and there is nothing social about this call. I thought you and I should discuss Ronnie Joe Waddell."

"I see. How far are you from the Law Center?"

"Ten minutes."

"I haven't eaten lunch and I don't suppose you have, either. Does it suit you if I have sandwiches sent in?"

"That would be fine," I said.

The Law Center was located some thirty-five blocks from the university's main campus, and I remembered my dismay many years before when I realized that my education would not include walking the old, shaded streets of the Heights and attending classes in fine eighteenth-century brick buildings. Instead, I was to spend three long years in a brand-new facility devoid of charm in a noisy, frantic section of D.C. My disappointment, however, did not last long. There was a certain excitement, not to mention convenience, in studying law in the shadow of the U.S. Capitol. But perhaps more significant was that I had not been a student long when I met Mark.

What I remembered most about my early encounters with Mark James during the first semester of our first year was his physical effect on me. At first I found the very sight of him unsettling, though I had no idea why. Then, as we became acquainted, his presence sent adrenaline charging through my blood. My heart would gallop and I would suddenly find myself acutely aware of his every gesture, no matter how common. For weeks, our conversations were entranced as they stretched into the early-morning hours. Our words were not elements of speech as much as they were notes to some secret inevitable crescendo, which happened one night with the dazzling unpredictability and force of an accident.

Since those days, the Law Center's physical plant had significantly grown and changed. The Criminal Justice Clinic was on the fourth floor, and when I got off the elevator there was no one in sight and offices I passed looked unoccupied. It was, after all, still the holidays, and only the relentless or desperate would be inclined to work. The door to room 418 was open, the secretary's desk vacant, the door to Grueman's inner office ajar.

Not wanting to startle him, I called out his name as I approached his door. He did not answer.

"Hello, Mr. Grueman? Are you here?" I tried again as I pushed his door open farther.

His desk was inches deep in clutter that pooled around a computer, and case files and transcripts were stacked on the floor along the base of the crowded bookcases. Left of his desk was a table bearing a printer and a fax machine that was busily sending something to someone. As I stood quietly staring around, the telephone rang three times and then stopped. Blinds were drawn in the window behind the desk, perhaps to reduce the glare on the computer screen, and leaning against the sill was a scarred and battered brown leather briefcase.

"Sorry about that." A voice behind me nearly sent me out of my shoes. "I stepped out for just a moment and was hoping I'd get back before you arrived."

Nicholas Grueman did not offer me his hand or a personal greeting of any kind. His preoccupation seemed to be returning to his chair, which he did very slowly and with the aid of a silver-topped cane.

"I would offer you coffee, but none is made when Evelyn isn't here," he said, seating himself in his judge's chair. "But the deli that will be delivering lunch shortly is bringing something to drink. I hope you can wait, and please take a chair, Dr. Scarpetta. It makes me nervous when a woman is looking down on me."

I pulled a chair closer to his desk and was amazed to realize that in the flesh Grueman was not the monster I recalled from my student days. For one thing, he seemed to have shrunk, though I suspected the more likely explanation was that I had inflated him to Mount Rushmore proportions in my imagination. I saw him now as a slight, white-haired man whose face had been carved by the years into a compelling caricature. He still wore bow ties and vests and smoked a pipe, and when he looked at me, his gray eyes were as capable of dissection as any scalpel. But I did not find them cold. They were simply unrevealing, as were mine most of the time.

"Why are you limping?" I boldly asked him.

"Gout. The disease of despots," he said without a smile. "It acts up from time to time, and please spare me any good advice or remedies. You doctors drive me to distraction with your unsolicited opinions on every subject from malfunctioning electric chairs to the food and drink I should exclude from my miserable diet."

"The electric chair did not malfunction," I said. "Not in the case I'm sure you're alluding to."

"You cannot possibly know what I am alluding to, and it seems to me that during your brief tenure here I had to admonish you more than once about your great facility for making assumptions. I regret that you did not listen to me. You are still making assumptions, though in this instance your assumption was, in fact, correct."

"Mr. Grueman, I am flattered that you remember me as a student, but I did not come here to reminisce about the wretched hours I spent in your classroom. Nor am I here to engage, again, in the mental martial arts you seem to thrive on. For the record, I will tell you that you have the distinction of being the most misogynistic and arrogant professor I encountered during my thirty-some years of formal education. And I must thank you for schooling me so well in the art of dealing with bastards, for the world is full of them and I must deal with them every day."

"I'm sure you do deal with them every day, and I haven't decided yet whether you're good at it."

"I'm not interested in your opinion on that subject. I would like you to tell me more about Ronnie Joe Waddell."

"What would you like to know beyond the obvious fact that the ultimate outcome was incorrect? How would you like politics to determine whether you are put to death, Dr. Scarpetta? Why, just look at what's happening to you now. Isn't your recent bad press politically motivated, at least in part? Every party involved has his own agenda, something to gain from disparaging you publicly. It has nothing to do with fairness or truth. So just imagine what it would be like if these same people possessed the power to deprive you of your liberty or even of your life.

"Ronnie was torn to pieces by a system that is irrational and unfair. It made no difference what earlier precedents were applied or whether claims were addressed on direct or collateral review. It made no difference what issue I raised because in this instance in your lovely Commonwealth, habeas did not serve as a deterrent designed to ensure that state trial and appellate judges conscientiously sought to conduct their proceedings in a manner consistent with established constitutional principles. God forbid that there should have been the slightest interest in constitutional violations on furthering the evolution of our thinking in some area of the law. In the three years that I fought for Ronnie, I might as well have been dancing a jig."

"What constitutional violations are you referring to?" I asked.

"How much time do you have? But let's begin with the prosecution's obvious use of peremptory challenges in a racially discriminatory manner. Ronnie's rights under the equal protection clause were violated from hell to breakfast, and prosecutorial misconduct blatantly infringed his Sixth Amendment right to a jury drawn from a fair cross section of the community. I don't suppose you saw Ronnie's trial or even know much about it since it was more than nine years ago and you were not in Virginia. The local publicity was overwhelming, and yet there was no change of venue. The jury was comprised of eight women and four men. Six of the women and two of the men were white. The four black jurors were a car salesman, a bank teller, a nurse, and a college professor. The professions of the white jurors ranged from a retired railroad switchman who still called blacks 'niggers' to a rich housewife whose only exposure to blacks was when she watched the news and saw that another one of them had shot someone in the projects. The demographics of the jury made it impossible for Ronnie to be sentenced fairly."

"And you're saying that such a constitutional impropriety or any other in Waddell's case was politically motivated? What possible political motivation could there have been for putting Ronnie Waddell to death?"

Grueman suddenly glanced toward the door. "Unless my ears deceive me, I believe lunch has arrived."

I heard rapid footsteps and paper crinkle, then a voice called out, "Yo, Nick. You in here?"

"Come on in, Joe," Grueman said without getting up from his desk.

An energetic young black man in blue jeans and tennis shoes appeared and placed two bags in front of Grueman.

"This one's got the drinks, and in here we got two sailor sandwiches, potato salad, and pickles. That's fifteen-forty."

"Keep the change. And look, Joe, I appreciate it. Don't they ever give you a vacation?"

"People don't quit eating, man. Gotta run."

Grueman distributed the food and napkins while I desperately tried to figure out what to do. I was finding myself increasingly swayed by his demeanor and words, for there was nothing shifty about him, nothing that struck me as condescending or insincere.

"What political motivation?" I asked him again as I unwrapped my sandwich.

He popped open a ginger ale and removed the top from his container of potato salad. "Several weeks ago I thought I might just get an answer to that question," he said. "But then the person who could have helped me was suddenly found dead inside her car. And I'm quite certain you know who I'm talking about, Dr. Scarpetta. Jennifer Deighton is one of your cases, and although it has yet to be publicly stated that her death is a suicide, that is what one has been led to believe. I find the timing of her death rather remarkable, if not chilling."

"Am I to understand that you knew Jennifer Deighton?" I asked as blandly as possible.

"Yes and no. I'd never met her, and our telephone conversations, what few we had, were very brief. You see, I never contacted her until after Ronnie was dead."

"From which I am also to understand that she knew Waddell."

Grueman took a bite of his sandwich and reached for his ginger ale. "She and Ronnie definitely knew each other," he said. "As you must know, Miss Deighton had a horoscope service, was into parapsychology and that sort of thing. Well, eight years ago, when Ronnie was on death row in Mecklenburg, he happened to see an advertisement for her services in some magazine. He wrote to her, initially in hopes that she could look into her crystal ball, so to speak, and tell him his future. Specifically, I think he wanted to know if he was going to die in the electric chair, and this is not an uncommon phenomenon—inmates writing psychics, palm readers, and asking about their futures, or contacting the clergy and asking for prayers. What was a little more unusual in Ronnie's case was that he and Miss Deighton apparently began an intimate correspondence that lasted until several months before his death. Then her letters to him suddenly stopped."

"Are you considering that her letters to him might have been intercepted?"

"There is no question about that. When I talked to Jennifer Deighton on the telephone, she claimed that she had continued to write to Ronnie. She also said that she had received no letters from him over the past several months, and I'm very suspicious that this is because his letters were intercepted as well."

"Why did you wait to contact her until after the execution?" I puzzled.

"I did not know about her before then. Ronnie said nothing about her to me until our last conversation, which was, perhaps, the strangest conversation I've ever had with any inmate I've represented." Grueman toyed with his sandwich and then pushed it away from him. He reached for his pipe. "I'm not sure if you're aware of this, Dr. Scarpetta, but Ronnie quit on me."

"I have no idea what you mean."

"The last time I talked with Ronnie was one week before he was to be transported from Mecklenburg to Richmond. At that time, he stated that he knew he was going to be executed and that nothing I did was going to make a difference. He said that what was going to happen to him had been set into motion since the beginning and he had accepted the inevitability of his death. He said that he was looking foward to dying and preferred that I cease pursuing federal habeas corpus relief. Then he requested that I not call him or come see him again."

"But he didn't fire you."

Grueman shot flame into the bowl of his briar pipe and sucked on the stem. "No, he did not. He simply refused to see me or talk to me on the phone."

"It would seem that this alone would have warranted a stay of execution pending a competency determination," I said.

"I tried that. I tried citing everything from *Hays* versus *Murphy* to the Lord's Prayer. The court rendered the brilliant decision that Ronnie had not asked to be executed. He'd simply stated that he looked forward to death, and the petition was denied."

"If you had no contact with Waddell in the several weeks before his execution, then how did you learn of Jennifer Deighton?"

"During my last conversation with Ronnie he made three last requests of me. The first was that I see to it that a meditation he had written was published in the newspaper days before his death. He gave this to me and I worked it out with the *Richmond Times-Dispatch*."

"I read it," I said.

"His second request—and I quote—was 'Don't let nothing happen to my friend.' And I asked him what friend he referred to, and he said, and again I quote, 'If you're a good man, look out for her. She never hurt no one.' He gave me her name and asked me not to contact her until after his death. Then I was to call and tell her how much she had meant to him. Well, of course I did not abide by that wish to the letter. I tried to contact her immediately because I knew I was losing Ronnie and I felt that something was terribly wrong. My hope was that this friend might be able to help. If they had corresponded with each other, for example, then maybe she could enlighten me."

"And did you reach her?" I asked, recalling Marino's telling me that Jennifer Deighton had been in Florida for two weeks around Thanksgiving.

"No one ever answered the phone," Grueman replied. "I tried on and off for several weeks, and then, to be frank, because of timing and health fortuities relating to the pace of litigation, the holidays, and a god-awful ambush of gout, my attention was diverted. I did not think to call Jennifer Deighton again until Ronnie was dead and I needed to contact her and convey, per Ronnie's request, that she had meant a lot to him, et cetera."

"When you had attempted to reach her earlier," I said, "did you leave messages on her answering machine?"

"It wasn't turned on. Which makes sense, in retrospect. She didn't need to return from vacation to face five hundred messages from people who can't make a decision until their horoscopes have been read. And if she left a message on her machine saying that she was out of town for two weeks, that would have been a perfect invitation for burglars."

"Then what happened when you finally reached her?"

"That was when she divulged that they had corresponded for eight years and that they loved each other. She claimed that the *truth would never be known.* I asked her what she meant but she would not tell me and got off the phone. Finally, I wrote her a letter imploring her to speak with me."

"When did you write this letter?" I asked.

"Let me see. The day after the execution. I suppose that would have been December fourteenth."

"And did she respond?"

"She did, by fax, interestingly enough. I did not know she had a fax machine, but my fax number was on my stationery. I have a copy of her fax if you would like to see it."

He shuffled through thick file folders and other paperwork on his desk. Finding the file he was looking for, he flipped through it and withdrew the fax, which I recognized instantly. "Yes, I'll cooperate," it read, "but it's too late, too late, too late. Better you should come here. This is all so wrong!" I wondered how Grueman would react if he knew that her communication with him had been re-created through image enhancement in Neils Vander's laboratory.

"Do you know what she meant? What was too late and what was so wrong?" I asked.

"Obviously, it was too late to do anything to stop Ronnie's execution since that had already occurred four days earlier. I'm not certain what she thought was so wrong, Dr. Scarpetta. You see, I have sensed for quite some time that there was something malignant about Ronnie's case. He and I never developed much of a rapport and that alone is odd. Generally, you get very close. I'm the only advocate in a system that wants you dead—the only one working for you in a system that doesn't work for you. But Ronnie was so aloof with his first attorney that this individual decided the case was hopeless and quit. Later, when I took on the case, Ronnie was just as distant. It was extraordinarily frustrating. Just when I would think he was beginning to trust me, a wall would go up. He would suddenly retreat into silence and literally begin to perspire."

"Did he seem frightened?"

"Frightened, depressed, sometimes angry."

"Are you suggesting that there was some conspiracy involved in his case and he might have told his friend about it, perhaps in one of his earlier letters to her?"

"I don't know what Jenny Deighton knew, but I suspect she knew something."

"Did Waddell refer to her as 'Jenny'?"

Grueman reached for his lighter again. "Yes."

"Did he ever mention to you a novel called *Paris Trout*?"

"That's interesting"—he looked surprised. "I haven't thought of this in quite some time, but during one of my early sessions with Ronnie several years ago, we talked about books and his poetry. He liked to read, and suggested I should read *Paris Trout*. I told him I had already read the novel, but was curious as to why he would recommend it. He said, very quietly, 'Because that's the way it works, Mr. Grueman. And there's no way you're gonna change nothing.' At the time I interpreted this to mean that he was a southern black pitted against the white man's system, and no federal habeas remedy or any other magic I might invoke during the judicial review process was going to alter his fate."

"Is this still your interpretation?"

He stared thoughtfully through a cloud of fragrant smoke. "I believe so. Why are you interested in Ronnie's recommended reading list?" He met my eyes.

"Jennifer Deighton had a copy of *Paris Trout* by her bed. Inside it was a poem that I suspect Waddell wrote for her. It's not important. I was just curious."

"But it is important or you wouldn't have inquired about it. What you're contemplating is that perhaps Ronnie recommended the novel to her for the same reason that he recommended it to me. The story, in his mind, was somehow his story. And that leads us back to the question of how much he had divulged to Miss Deighton. In other words, what secret of his did she carry with her to the grave?"

"What do you think it was, Mr. Grueman?"

"I think a very nasty indiscretion has been covered up, and for some reason Ronnie was privy to it. Maybe this relates to what goes on behind bars, that is, corruption within the prison system. I don't know but I wish I did."

"But why hide anything when you're facing death? Why not just go ahead and take your chances and talk?"

"That would be the rational thing to do, now, wouldn't it? And now that I have so patiently and generously answered your probing questions, Dr. Scarpetta, perhaps you can better understand why I have been more than a little concerned about any abuse Ronnie may have received prior to his execution. You can understand better, perhaps, my passionate opposition to capital punishment, which is cruel and unusual. You don't have to have bruises or abrasions or bleed from your nose to make it so."

"There was no evidence of physical abuse," I said. "Nor did we find drugs present. You have gotten my report."

"You are being evasive," Grueman said, knocking tobacco out of his pipe. "You are here today because you want something from me. I have given you a lot through a dialogue that I did not have to engage in. But I have been willing because I am forever in pursuit of fairness and truth, despite how I may appear to you. And there is another reason. A former student of mine is in trouble."

"If you are referring to me, then let me remind you of your own dictum. Don't make assumptions."

"I don't believe I am."

"Then I must convey acute curiosity over this sudden charitable attitude you're allegedly displaying toward a former student. In fact, Mr. Grueman, the word *charity* has never entered my mind in connection with you."

"Perhaps, then, you don't know the true meaning of the word. An act or feeling of goodwill, giving alms to the needy. Charity is giving to someone what he needs versus what you want to give him. I have always given you what you need. I gave you what you needed while you were my student, and I'm giving you what you need today, though the acts are expressed very differently because the needs are very different.

"Now I am an old man, Dr. Scarpetta, and perhaps you think I don't remember much about your days at Georgetown. But you might be surprised to hear that I remember you vividly because you were one of the most promising students I ever taught. What you did not need from me was strokes and applause. The danger for you was not that you would lose faith in yourself and your excellent mind but that you would lose yourself, period. Do you think when you looked exhausted and distracted in my class that I did not know the reason? Do you think I was unaware of your complete preoccupation with Mark James, who was mediocre by your standards, by the way? And if I appeared angry with you and very hard on you, it was because I *wanted to get your attention*. I wanted you to *get mad*. I wanted you to feel alive in the law instead of feeling only in love. I feared you would throw away a magnificent opportunity because your hormones and emotions were in overdrive. You see, we wake up one day to regret such decisions. We wake up in an empty bed with an empty day stretching before us and nothing to look forward to but empty weeks, months, and years. I was determined that you would not waste your gifts and give away your power."

I stared at him in astonishment as my face began to burn.

"I have never been sincere in my insults and lack of chivalry toward you," he went on with the same quiet intensity and precision that made him frightening in the courtroom. "These are tactics. We lawyers are famous for our tactics. They are the slices and spins we put on the ball, the angles and speed we use to bring about a certain necessary effect. At the foundation of all that I am is a sincere and passionate desire to make my students tough and pray that they make a difference in this botched-up world we live in. And I feel no disappointment in you. You are, perhaps, one of my brightest stars."

"Why are you saying all this to me?" I asked.

"Because at this time in your life, you need to know it. You are in trouble, as I've already stated. You are simply too proud to admit it."

I was silent, my thoughts engaged in a fierce debate.

"I will help you if you will allow it."

If he was telling me the truth, then it was vital that I respond in kind. I glanced toward his open door and imagined how easy it would be for anyone to walk in here. I imagined how easy it would be for someone to confront him as he hobbled to his car.

"If these incriminating stories continue to be printed in the newspaper, for example, it would behoove you to develop a few strategies—"

I interrupted him. "Mr. Grueman, when was the last time you saw Ronnie Joe Waddell?"

He paused and stared up at the ceiling. "The last time I was in his physical presence would have been at least a year ago. Typically, most of our conversations were over the phone. I would have been with him in the end had he permitted it, as I've already mentioned."

"Then you never saw him or spoke with him when he was supposedly at Spring Street awaiting execution."

"*Supposedly*? That's a curious choice of words, Dr. Scarpetta."

"We can't prove it was Waddell who was executed the night of December thirteenth."

"Certainly you're not serious." He looked amazed.

I explained all that had transpired, including that Jennifer Deighton was a homicide and Waddell's fingerprint had turned up on a dining room chair inside her home. I told him about Eddie Heath and Susan Story, and the evidence that someone had tampered with AFIS. When I was finished, Grueman was sitting very still, his eyes riveted on me.

"My Lord," he muttered.

"Your letter to Jennifer Deighton never turned up," I went on. "The police found neither that nor her original fax to you when they searched her house. Maybe someone took them. Maybe her killer burned them in her fireplace the night of her death. Or maybe she disposed of them herself because she was afraid. I do believe she was killed because of something she knew."

"And this would be why Susan Story was killed, too? Because she knew something?"

"Certainly that's possible," I said. "My point is that so far two people linked to Ronnie Waddell have been murdered. In terms of someone who might know a lot about Waddell, you would be considered high on the list."

"So you think I may be next," he said with a wry smile. "You know, perhaps my biggest grievance against the Almighty is that the difference between life and death should so often turn on timing. I consider myself forewarned, Dr. Scarpetta. But I am not foolish enough to think that if someone intends to shoot me I can successfully elude him."

"You could at least try," I said. "You could at least take precautions."

"And I shall."

"Maybe you and your wife could go on a vacation, get out of town for a while."

"Beverly has been dead for three years," he said.

"I'm very sorry, Mr. Grueman."

"She had not been well for many years—in fact, not for most of the years we were together. Now that I have no one to depend on me, I have given myself up to my proclivities. I am an incurable workaholic who wants to change the world."

"I suspect that if anyone could come close to changing it, you could."

"That is an opinion not based on any sort of fact, but I appreciate it nonetheless. And I also want to express to you my great sadness over Mark's death. I did not know him well when he was here, but he seemed to be a decent-enough fellow."

"Thank you." I got up and put on my coat. It took me a moment to find my car keys.

He got up, too. "What do we do next, Dr. Scarpetta?"

"I don't suppose you have any letters or other items from Ronnie Waddell that might be worth processing for his latent prints?"

"I have no letters, and any documents that he might have signed would have been handled by a number of people. You're welcome to try."

"I'll let you know if we have no other alternative. But there is one final thing I've been meaning to ask." We paused in the doorway. Grueman was leaning on his cane. "You mentioned that during your last conversation with Waddell, he made three last requests. One was to publish his meditation, another to call Jennifer Deighton. What was the third?"

"He wanted me to invite Norring to the execution."

"And did you?"

"Well, of course," Grueman said. "And your fine governor didn't even have the manners to RSVP."

10

It was late afternoon, and Richmond's skyline was in view when I called Rose.

"Dr. Scarpetta, where are you?" My secretary sounded frantic. "Are you in your car?"

"Yes. I'm about five minutes from downtown."

"Well, keep driving. Don't come here right now."

"What?"

"Lieutenant Marino's trying to reach you. He said if I talk to you to tell you to call him before you do anything. He said it's very, very urgent."

"Rose, what on earth are you talking about?"

"Have you been listening to the news? Did you read the afternoon paper?"

"I've been in D.C. all day. What news?"

"Frank Donahue was found dead early this afternoon."

"The prison warden? That Frank Donahue?"

"Yes."

My hands tensed on the wheel as I stared hard at the road. "What happened?"

"He was shot. He was found in his car a couple of hours ago. It's just like Susan."

"I'm on my way," I said, gliding into the left lane and accelerating.

"I really wouldn't. Fielding's already started on him. Please call Marino. You need to read the evening paper. They know about the bullets."

"They?" I said.

"Reporters. They know about the bullets linking Eddie Heath's and Susan's cases."

I called Marino's pager and told him I was on my way home. When I pulled into my garage, I went straight to the front stoop and retrieved the evening paper.

A photograph of Frank Donahue smiled above the fold. The headline read, "STATE PENITENTIARY WARDEN SLAIN." Below this was a second story featuring the photograph of another state official—me. That story's lead was that the bullets recovered from the bodies of the Heath boy and Susan had been fired from the same gun, and a number of bizarre connections seemed to link both homicides to me. In addition to the same intimations that had run in the *Post* was information much more sinister.

My fingerprints, I was stunned to read, had been recovered from an envelope containing cash that the police had found inside Susan Story's house. I had demonstrated an "unusual interest" in Eddie Heath's case by appearing at Henrico Doctor's Hospital, prior to his death, to examine his wounds. Later I had performed his autopsy, and it was at this time that Susan refused to witness his case and supposedly fled from the morgue. When she was murdered less than two weeks later, I responded to the scene, appeared unannounced at the home of her parents directly afterward to ask them questions, and insisted on being present during the autopsy.

I was not directly assigned a motive for malevolence toward anyone, but the one implied in Susan's case was as infuriating as it was amazing. I may have been making major mistakes on the job. I had neglected to print Ronnie Joe Waddell when his body came to the morgue after his execution. I recently had left the body of a homicide victim in the middle of a corridor, virtually in front of an elevator used by numerous people who worked in the building, thus seriously compromising the chain of evidence. I was described as aloof and unpredictable, with colleagues observing that my personality had begun to change after the death of my lover, Mark

James. Perhaps Susan, who had worked by my side daily, had possessed knowledge that could ruin me professionally. Perhaps I had been paying for her silence.

"My fingerprints?" I said to Marino the instant he appeared at my door. "What the hell is this business about fingerprints belonging to me?"

"Easy, Doc."

"I might just file suit this time. This has gone too far."

"I don't think you want to be filing anything right now." He got out his cigarettes as he followed me to the kitchen, where the evening paper was spread out on the table.

"Ben Stevens is behind this."

"Doc, I think what you want to do is listen to what I've got to say."

"He's got to be the source of the leak about the bullets—"

"Doc. Goddam it, shut up."

I sat down.

"My ass is in the fire, too," he said. "I'm working the cases with you, and now suddenly you've become an element. Yes, we did find an envelope in Susan's house. It was in a dresser drawer under some clothes. There were three one-hundred-dollar bills inside it. Vander processed the envelope and several latents popped up. Two of them are yours. Your prints, like mine and those of a lot of other investigators, are in AFIS for exclusionary purposes, in case we ever do a dumbshit thing like leave our prints at a scene."

"I did not leave prints at any scene. There's a logical explanation for this. There has to be. Maybe the envelope was one I touched at some point at the office or the morgue, and Susan took it home."

"It's definitely not an office envelope," Marino said. "It's about twice as wide as a legal-size envelope and made of stiff, shiny black paper. There's no writing on it."

I looked at him in disbelief as it dawned on me. "The scarf I gave her."

"What scarf?"

"Susan's Christmas present from me was a red silk scarf I bought in San Francisco. What you're describing is the envelope it was in, a glossy black envelope made of cardboard or stiff paper. The flap closed with a small gold seal. I wrapped the present myself. Of course my prints would be on it."

"So what about the three hundred dollars?" he said, avoiding my eyes.

"I don't know anything about any money."

"I'm saying, why was it in the envelope you gave her?"

"Maybe because she wanted to hide her cash in something. The envelope was handy. Maybe she didn't want to throw it away. I don't know. I had no control over what she did with something I gave her."

"Did anybody see you give her the scarf?" he asked.

"No. Her husband wasn't home when she opened my gift."

"Yeah, well, the only gift from you anyone seemed to know about was a pink poinsettia. Don't sound like Susan said a word about you giving her a scarf."

"For God's sake, she was wearing the scarf when she was shot, Marino."

"That don't tell us where it came from."

"You're about to move into the accusatory stage," I snapped.

"I'm not accusing you of nothing. Don't you get it? This is the way it goes, goddam it. You want me to baby you and pat your hand so some other cop can bust in here and broadside you with questions like this?"

He got up and began pacing the kitchen, staring at the floor, his hands in his pockets.

"Tell me about Donahue," I said quietly.

"He was shot in his ride, probably early this morning. According to his wife, he left the house around six-fifteen. Around one-thirty this afternoon, his Thunderbird was found parked at Deep Water Terminal with him in it."

"I read that much in the paper."

"Look. The less we talk about it, the better."

"Why? Are reporters going to imply that I killed him, too?"

"Where was you at six-fifteen this morning, Doc?"

"I was getting ready to leave my house and drive to Washington."

"You got any witnesses that will verify you couldn't have been cruising around Deep Water Terminal? It's not very far from the medical examiner's office, you know. Maybe two minutes."

"That's absurd."

"Get used to it. This is just the beginning. Wait until Patterson sinks his teeth into you."

Before Roy Patterson had run for Commonwealth Attorney, he had been one of the city's more combative, egotistical criminal lawyers. Back then he had never appreciated what I had to say, since in the majority of cases, medical examiner testimony does not cause jurors to think more kindly of the defendant.

"I ever told you how much Patterson hates your guts?" Marino went on. "You embarrassed him when he was a defense attorney. You sat there cool as a cat in your sharp suits and made him look like an idiot."

"He made himself look like an idiot. All I did was answer his questions."

"Not to mention, your old boyfriend Bill Boltz was one of his closest pals, and I don't even need to go into that."

"I wish you wouldn't."

"I just know Patterson's going to go after you. Shit, I bet he's a happy man right now."

"Marino, you're red as a beet. For God's sake, don't go stroking out on me."

"Let's get back to this scarf you said you gave to Susan."

"I *said* I gave to Susan?"

"What was the name of the store in San Francisco that sold it to you?" he asked.

"It wasn't a store."

He glanced sharply at me as he continued to pace.

"It was a street market. Lots of booths and stalls selling art, handmade things. Like Covent Garden," I explained.

"You got a receipt?"

"I would have had no reason to save it."

"So you don't know the name of the booth or whatever. So there's no way to verify that you bought a scarf from some artist type who uses these glossy black envelopes."

"I can't verify it."

He paced some more and I stared out the window. Clouds drifted past an oblong moon, and the dark shapes of trees moved in the wind. I got up to close the blinds.

Marino stopped pacing. "Doc, I'm going to need to go through your financial records."

I did not say anything.

"I've got to verify that you haven't made any large withdrawals of cash in recent months."

I remained silent.

"Doc, you haven't, have you?"

I got up from the table, my pulse pounding.

"You can talk to my attorney," I said.

After Marino left, I went upstairs to the cedar closet where I stored my private papers and began collecting bank statements, tax returns, and various accounting records. I thought of all the defense attorneys in Richmond who would probably be delighted if I were locked up or exiled for the rest of my days.

I was sitting in the kitchen making notes on a legal pad when my doorbell rang. I let Benton Wesley and Lucy in, and I knew instantly by their silence that it was unnecessary to tell them what was going on.

"Where's Connie?" I asked wearily.

"She's going to stay through the New Year with her family in Charlottesville."

"I'm going back to your study, Aunt Kay," Lucy said without hugging me or smiling. She left with her suitcase.

"Marino wants to go through my financial records," I said to Wesley as he followed me into the living room. "Ben Stevens is setting me up. Personnel files and copies of memos are missing from the office, and he's hoping it will appear that I took them. And Roy Patterson, according to Marino, is a happy man these days. That's the update of the hour."

"Where do you keep the Scotch?"

"I keep the good stuff in the hutch over there. Glasses are in the bar."

"I don't want to drink your good stuff."

"Well, I do." I began building a fire.

"I called your deputy chief as I was driving in. Firearms has already taken a look at the slugs that were in Donahue's brain. Winchester one-fifty-grain lead, unjacketed, twenty-two-caliber. Two of them. One went in his left cheek and traveled up through the skull, the other was a tight contact at the nape of his neck."

"Fired from the same weapon that killed the other two?"

"Yes. Do you want ice?"

"Please." I closed the screen and returned the poker to its stand. "I don't suppose any feathers were recovered from the scene or from Donahue's body."

"Not that I know of. It's clear that his assailant was standing outside the car and shot him through the open driver's window. That doesn't mean this individual wasn't inside with him earlier, but I don't think so. My guess is Donahue was supposed to meet someone at Deep Water Terminal in the parking lot. When this person arrived, Donahue rolled down his window and that was it. Did you have any luck with Downey?" He handed me my drink and settled on the couch.

"It appears that the origin of the feathers and feather particles recovered from the three other cases is common eider duck."

"A sea duck?" Wesley frowned. "The down is used in what, ski jackets, gloves?"

"Rarely. Eiderdown is extremely expensive. Your average person is not going to own anything filled with it."

I proceeded to inform Wesley of the events of the day, sparing no details as I confessed that I had spent several hours with Nicholas Grueman and did not believe he was even remotely involved in anything sinister.

"I'm glad you went to see him," Wesley said. "I was hoping you would."

"Are you surprised by how it turned out?"

"No. It makes sense the way it turned out. Grueman's predicament is somewhat similar to your own. He gets a fax from Jennifer Deighton and it looks suspicious, just as it looks suspicious that your prints were found on an envelope in Susan's dresser drawer. When violence hits close to you, you get splashed. You get dirty."

"I'm more than splashed. I feel as if I'm about to drown."

"At the moment, it seems that way. Maybe you ought to be talking to Grueman about that."

I did not reply.

"I'd want him on my side."

"I wasn't aware that you knew him."

Ice rattled quietly as Wesley sipped his drink. Brass on the hearth gleamed in the firelight. Wood popped, sending sparks swarming up the chimney.

"I know about Grueman," he said. "I know that he graduated number one from Harvard Law School, was the editor of the *Law Review,* and was offered a teaching position there but turned it down. That broke his heart. But his wife, Beverly, did not want to move from the D.C. area. Apparently, she had a lot of problems, not the least of which was a young daughter from a first marriage who was institutionalized at Saint Elizabeths at the time Grueman and Beverly met. He moved to D.C. The daughter died several years later."

"You've been running a background check on him," I said.

"Sort of."

"Since when?"

"Since I learned he had received a fax from Jennifer Deighton. By all accounts, it appears he's Mr. Clean, but someone still had to talk to him."

"That's not the only reason you suggested it to me, is it?"

"An important reason but not the only one. I thought you should go back there."

I took a deep breath. "Thank you, Benton. You are a good man with the best of intentions."

He lifted his glass to his lips and stared into the fire.

"Please don't interfere," I added.

"It's not my style."

"Of course it is. You're a pro at it. If you want to quietly steer, propel, or unplug someone from behind the scenes, you know how to do it. You know how to throw up so many obstacles and blow out so many bridges that someone like me would be lucky to find her way home."

"Marino and I are very involved in all this, Kay. Richmond P.D.'s involved. The Bureau's involved. Either we've got a psychopath out there who should have been executed or we've got somebody else who seems intent on making us think someone is out there who should have been executed."

"Marino doesn't want me involved at all," I said.

"He's in an impossible situation. He's the chief homicide investigator for the city and a member of a Bureau VICAP team, yet he's your colleague and friend. He's supposed to find out everything he can about you and what's gone on in your office. Yet his inclination is to protect you. Try to put yourself in his position."

"I will. But he needs to put himself in mine."

"That's only fair."

"The way he talks, Benton, you would think half the world has a vendetta against me and would love to see me go up in flames."

"Maybe not half the world, but there are people other than Ben Stevens who are standing around with boxes of matches and gasoline."

"Who else?"

"I can't give you names because I don't know. And I'm not going to claim that ruining you professionally is the major mission for whoever is behind all this. But I suspect it's on the agenda, if for no other reason than that the cases would be severely compromised if it appears that all evidence routed through your office is tainted. Not to mention, without you, the Commonwealth loses one of its most potent expert witnesses." He met my eyes. "You need to consider what your testimony would be worth right now. If you took the stand this minute, would you be helping or hurting Eddie Heath?"

The remark cut to the bone.

"Right this minute, I would not be helping him much. But if I default, how much will that help him or anyone?"

"That's a good question. Marino doesn't want you hurt further, Kay."

"Then perhaps you can impress upon him that the only reasonable response to such an unreasonable situation is for me to allow him to do his job while he allows me to do mine."

"Can I refresh that?" Getting up, he returned with the bottle. We didn't bother with ice.

"Benton, let's talk about the killer. In light of what's happened to Donahue, what are you thinking now?"

He set down the bottle and stirred the fire. For a moment, he stood before the fireplace, his back to me, hands in his pockets. Then he sat on the edge of the hearth, his forearms on his knees. Wesley was more restless than I had seen him in a very long time.

"If you want to know the truth, Kay, this animal scares the hell out of me."

"How is he different from other killers you have pursued?"

"I think he started out with one set of rules and then decided to change them."

"His rules or someone else's?"

"I think the rules were not his at first. Whoever was behind the conspiracy to free Waddell first made the decisions. But this guy's got his own rules now. Or maybe it would be better to say that there are no rules now. He's cunning and he's careful. So far, he's in control."

"What about motive?" I asked.

"That's hard. Maybe it would be better for me to phrase it in terms of mission or assignment. I suspect there's some method to his madness, but the madness is what turns him on. He gets off on playing with people's minds. Waddell was locked up for ten years, then suddenly the nightmare of his original crime is revisited. On the night of his execution, a boy is murdered in a sexually sadistic fashion that is reminiscent of Robyn Naismith's case. Other people start dying, and all of them are in some way connected to Waddell. Jennifer Deighton was his friend. Susan, it appears, was involved, at least tangentially, in whatever this conspiracy is. Frank Donahue was the prison warden and would have supervised the execution that occurred on the night of December thirteenth. And what is this doing to everybody else, to the other players?"

"I should think that anyone who has had any association with Ronnie Waddell, either legitimately or otherwise, would feel very threatened," I replied.

"Right. If a cop killer is on the loose and you are a cop, you know you may be next. I could walk out your door tonight and this guy's waiting in the shadows to gun me down. He could be out in his car somewhere, looking for Marino or trying to find my house. He could be fantasizing about taking out Grueman."

"Or me."

Wesley got up and began rearranging the fire again.

"Do you think it would be wise for me to send Lucy back to Miami?" I asked.

"Christ, Kay, I don't know what to tell you. She doesn't want to go home. That comes across loud and clear. You might feel better if she returned to Miami tonight. For that matter, I might feel better if you went with her. In fact, everybody—you, Marino, Grueman, Vander, Connie, Michele, me—would probably feel better if *all* of us left town. But then who would be left?"

"He would," I said. "Whoever he is."

Wesley glanced at his watch and set his glass on the coffee table. "None of us should interfere with each other," he said. "We can't afford to."

"Benton, I have to clear my name."

"It is exactly what I would do. Where do you want to start?"

"With a feather."

"Please explain."

"It's possible that this killer went out and bought some specialty item filled with eiderdown, but I'd say there's a good chance he stole it."

"That's a plausible theory."

"We can't trace the item unless we have its label or some other piece to trace back to a manufacturer, but there may be another way. Maybe something could appear in the newspaper."

"I don't think we want the killer to know he's leaking feathers everywhere. He's sure to get rid of the item in question."

"I agree. But that doesn't preclude your getting one of your journalist sources to run some trumped-up little feature about the eider duck and its prized down, and how items filled with it are so expensive that they've become a hot commodity for thieves. Maybe this could be tied in with the ski season or something."

"What? In hopes someone out there will call and say that his car was broken into and his down-filled jacket was stolen?"

"Yes. If the reporter quotes some detective who supposedly has been assigned to the thefts, this gives readers someone they can call. You know, people read a story and say, 'The same thing happened to me.' Their impulse is to help. They want to feel important. So they pick up the phone."

"I'll have to give it some thought."

"Admittedly, it's a long shot."

We began walking to the door.

"I spoke briefly with Michele before leaving the Homestead," Wesley said. "She and Lucy have already been conferring. Michele says your niece is rather frightening."

"She's been a holy terror since the day she was born."

He smiled. "Michele didn't mean it like that. She says that Lucy's intellect is frightening."

"Sometimes I worry that it's too much wattage for such a fragile vessel."

"I'm not certain she's all that fragile. Remember, I just spent the better part of two days with her. I'm very impressed with Lucy on many fronts."

"Don't you go trying to recruit her for the Bureau."

"I'll wait until she finishes college. That will take her, what? All of a year?"

Lucy did not emerge from my study until Wesley had driven off and I was carrying our glasses into the kitchen.

"Did you enjoy yourself?" I asked her.

"Sure."

"Well, I hear you got along famously with the Wesleys." I turned off the faucet and sat at the table where I'd left my legal pad.

"They're nice people."

"Rumor has it they think you're nice, too."

She opened the refrigerator door and idly stared inside. "Why was Pete here earlier?"

It seemed odd to hear Marino referred to by his first name. I supposed he and Lucy had moved from a state of cold war to détente when he had taken her shooting.

"What makes you think he was here?" I asked.

"I smelled cigarettes when I came in the house. I assume he was here unless you're smoking again." She shut the refrigerator door and came over to the table.

"I'm not smoking again, and Marino was here briefly."

"What did he want?"

"He wanted to ask me a lot of questions," I said.

"About what?"

"Why do you need to know the details?"

Her eyes moved from my face to the stack of financial files to the legal pad filled with my indecipherable penmanship. "It doesn't matter why since you obviously don't want to tell me."

"It's complicated, Lucy."

"You always say something's complicated when you want to shut me out," she said as she turned and walked away.

I felt as if my world were falling apart, the people in it scattering like dry seeds in the wind. When I watched parents with their children, I marveled over the gracefulness of their interactions and secretly feared I lacked an instinct that couldn't be learned.

I found my niece in my study sitting before the computer. Columns of numbers combined with letters of the alphabet were on the screen, and embedded here and there were fragments of what I assumed were data. She was making computations with a pencil on graph paper, and did not look up as I moved next to her.

"Lucy, your mother has had many men in and out of your house, and I am well aware of how that has made you feel. But this is not your house and I am not your mother. It is not necessary for you to feel threatened by my male colleagues and friends. It is not necessary for you to constantly be looking for evidence that some man was here, and it is unfounded for you to be suspicious of my relationship with Marino or Wesley or anyone else."

She did not respond.

I placed my hand on her shoulder. "I may not be the constant presence in your life that I wish I could be, but you are very important to me."

Erasing a number and brushing rubber particles off the paper, she said, "Are you going to get charged with a crime?"

"Of course not. I haven't committed any crimes." I leaned closer to the monitor.

"What you're looking at is a hex dump," she said.

"You were right. It's hieroglyphics."

Placing her fingers on the keyboard, Lucy began moving the cursor as she explained, "What I'm doing here is trying to get the exact position of the SID number. That's the State Identification Number, which is the unique identifier. Every person in the system has a SID number, including you, since your prints are in AFIS, too. In a fourth-generation language, like SQL, I could actually query by a column name. But in hexadecimal the language is technical and mathematical. There are no column names, only positions in the record layout. In other words, if I wanted to go to Miami, in SQL I would simply tell the computer I want to go to Miami. But in hexadecimal, I would have to say that I want to go to a position that is this many degrees north of the equator and this many degrees east of the prime meridian.

"So to extend the geographical analogy, I'm figuring out the longitude and latitude of the SID number and also of the number that indicates the record type. Then I can write a program to search for any SID number where the record is a type two, which means a deletion, or a type three, which is an update. I'll run this program through each journal tape."

"You're assuming that if a record has been tampered with, then what was changed was the SID?" I asked.

"Let's just say it would be a whole lot easier to tamper with the SID number than it would be to mess with the actual fingerprint images on the optical disk record. And that's really all you've got in AFIS—the SID number and the corresponding prints. The person's name, history, and other personal information are in his CCH, or Computerized Criminal History, which resides on CCRE, or the Central Criminal Records Exchange."

"As I understand it, the records in CCRE are matched to the prints in AFIS by the SID numbers," I said.

"Exactly."

Lucy was still working when I went to bed. I fell right to sleep, only to awaken at two A.M. I did not drift off again until five, and my alarm roused me less than an hour later. I drove downtown in the dark and listened as one of the local radio announcers gave a news update. He reported that police had questioned me, and I had refused to disclose information pertaining to my financial records. He went on to remind everyone that Susan Story had deposited thirty-five hundred dollars in her checking account just weeks before her murder.

When I got to the office, I had barely taken off my coat when Marino called.

"The damn major can't keep his mouth shut," he said right off.

"Obviously."

"Shit, I'm sorry."

"It's not your fault. I know you have to report to him."

Marino hesitated. "I need to ask you about your guns. You don't own a twenty-two, right?"

"You know all about my handguns. I have a Ruger and a Smith and Wesson. And if you pass that along to Major Cunningham, I'm sure I'll hear about it on the radio within the hour."

"Doc, he wants them submitted to the firearms lab."

For an instant, I thought Marino was joking.

"He thinks you should be willing to submit them for examination," he added. "He thinks it's a good idea to show right away that the bullets recovered from Susan, the Heath kid, and Donahue couldn't have been fired from your guns."

"Did you tell the major that the revolvers I have are *thirty-eights?*" I asked, incensed.

"Yes."

"And he knows that *twenty-two* slugs were recovered from the bodies?"

"Yeah. I went round and round with him about it."

"Well, ask him for me if he knows of an adapter that would make it possible to use twenty-two rim-fire cartridges in a thirty-eight revolver. If he does, tell him he ought to present a paper on it at the next American Academy of Forensic Sciences meeting."

"I really don't think you want me to tell him that."

"This is nothing but politics, publicity ploys. It's not even rational."

Marino did not comment.

"Look," I said evenly, "I have broken no laws. I am not submitting my financial records, firearms, or anything else to anyone until I have been appropriately advised. I understand that you must do your job, and I want you to do your job. What I want is to be left alone so I can do mine. I have three cases downstairs and Fielding's off to court."

But I was not to be left alone, and this was made clear when Marino and I concluded our conversation and Rose appeared in my office. Her face was pale, her eyes frightened.

"The governor wants to see you," she said.

"When?" I asked as my heart skipped.

"At nine."

It was already eight-forty.

"Rose, what does he want?"

"The person who called didn't say."

Fetching my coat and umbrella, I walked out into a winter rain that was just beginning to freeze. As I hurried along 14th Street, I tried to recall the last time I had spoken to Governor Joe Norring and decided it was almost a year ago at a black-tie reception at the Virginia Museum. He was Republican, Episcopalian, and held a law degree from UVA. I was Italian, Catholic, born in Miami, and schooled in the North. In my heart I was a Democrat.

The Capitol resides on Shockhoe Hill and is surrounded by an ornamental iron fence erected in the early nineteenth century to keep out trespassing cattle. The white brick building Jefferson designed is typical of his architecture, a pure symmetry of cornices and unfluted columns with Ionic capitals inspired by a Roman temple. Benches line the granite steps leading up through the grounds, and as freezing rain fell relentlessly I thought of my annual spring resolution to take a lunch hour away from my desk and sit here in the sun. But I had yet to do it. Countless days of my life had been lost to artificial light and windowless, confined spaces that defied any architectural rubric.

Inside the Capitol, I found a ladies' room and attempted to bolster my confidence by making repairs. Despite my efforts with lipstick and brush, the mirror had nothing reassuring to say. Bedraggled and unsettled, I took the elevator to the top of the Rotunda, where previous governors gaze sternly from oil portraits three floors above Houdon's marble statue of George Washington. Midway along the south wall, journalists milled about with notepads, cameras, and microphones. It did not occur to me that I was their quarry until, as I approached, video cameras were mounted on shoulders, microphones were drawn like swords, and shutters began clicking with the rapidity of automatic weapons.

"Why won't you disclose your finances?"

"Dr. Scarpetta . . ."

"Did you give money to Susan Story?"

"What kind of handgun do you own?"

"Doctor . . ."

"Is it true that personnel records have disappeared from your office?"

They chummed the water with their accusations and questions as I fixed my attention straight ahead, my thoughts paralyzed.

Microphones jabbed at my chin, bodies brushed against me, and lights flashed in my eyes. It seemed to take forever to reach the heavy mahogany door and escape into the genteel stillness behind it.

"Good morning," said the receptionist from her fine wood fortress beneath a portrait of John Tyler.

Across the room, at a desk before a window, a plainclothes Executive Protection Unit officer glanced at me, his face inscrutable.

"How did the press know about this?" I asked the receptionist.

"Pardon?" She was an older woman, dressed in tweed.

"How did they know I was meeting with the governor this morning?"

"I'm sorry. I wouldn't know."

I settled on a pale blue love seat. Walls were papered in the same pale blue; the furniture was antique, with chair seats covered in needlepoint depicting the state seal. Ten minutes slowly passed. A door opened and a young man I recognized as Norring's press secretary stepped inside and smiled at me.

"Dr. Scarpetta, the governor will see you now." He was slight of build, blond, and dressed in a navy suit and yellow suspenders.

"I apologize for making you wait. Unbelievable weather we're having. And I understand it's supposed to drop into the teens tonight. The streets will be glass in the morning."

He ushered me through one well-appointed office after another, where secretaries concentrated behind computer screens and aides moved about silently and with purpose. Knocking lightly on a formidable door, he turned the brass knob and stepped aside, chivalrously touching my back as I preceded him into the private space of the most powerful man in Virginia. Governor Norring did not get up from his padded leather chair behind his uncluttered burled walnut desk. Two chairs were arranged across from him and I was shown to one while he continued perusing a document.

"Would you like something to drink?" the press secretary asked me.

"No, thank you."

He left, softly shutting the door.

The governor placed the document on the desk and leaned back in his chair. He was a distinguished-looking man with just enough irregularity of his features to cause one to take him seriously, and he was impossible to miss when he walked into a room. Like George Washington, who was six foot two in a day of short men, Norring was well above average height, his hair thick and dark at an age when men are balding or going gray.

"Doctor, I've been wondering if there might be a way to extinguish this fire of controversy before it's completely out of control." He spoke with the soothing cadences of Virginian conversation.

"Governor Norring, I certainly hope there is."

"Then please help me understand why you are not cooperating with the police."

"I wish to seek the advice of an attorney, and have not had a chance to do so. I don't view this as a lack of cooperation."

"It certainly is your right not to incriminate yourself," he said slowly. "But the very suggestion of your invoking the Fifth only darkens the cloud of suspicion surrounding you. I'm certain you must be aware of that."

"I'm aware that I will probably be criticized no matter what I do right now. It is reasonable and prudent for me to protect myself."

"Were you making payments to your morgue supervisor, Susan Story?"

"No, sir, I was not. I have done nothing wrong."

"Dr. Scarpetta." He leaned forward in his chair and laced his fingers on top of the desk. "It is my understanding that you are unwilling to cooperate by turning over any records that might substantiate these claims you've made."

"I have not been informed that I am a suspect in any crime, nor have I received Miranda warnings. I have waived no rights. I have had no opportunity to seek counsel. At this moment, it is not my intention to open the files of my professional and personal life to the police or anyone else."

"Then, in summary, you are refusing to make full disclosure," he said.

When a state official is accused of conflict of interests or any other manner of unethical behavior, there are only two defenses, full disclosure or resignation. The latter yawned before me like an abyss. It was clear that the governor's intention was to maneuver me over the edge.

"You are a forensic pathologist of national stature and the chief medical examiner of this Commonwealth," he went on. "You've enjoyed a very distinguished career and an impeccable reputation in the law enforcement community. But in the matter before us, you are showing poor judgment. You are not being meticulous about avoiding any appearance of impropriety."

"I have been meticulous, Governor, and I have done nothing wrong," I repeated. "The facts will bear this out, but I will not discuss the matter further until I speak with an attorney. And I will not make full disclosure unless it is through him and before a judge in a sealed hearing."

"A sealed hearing?" His eyes narrowed.

"Certain details of my personal life affect individuals besides me."

"Who? Husband, children, lover? It is my understanding you have none of these, that you live alone and are—to use the cliché—wedded to your work. Just who might you be protecting?"

"Governor Norring, you are baiting me."

"No, ma'am. I'm simply looking for anything to corroborate your claims. You say you are concerned with protecting others, and I'm inquiring as to who these *others* might be. Certainly not patients. Your patients are deceased."

"I do not feel that you are being fair or impartial," I said, and I knew I sounded cold. "Nothing about this meeting was fair from the outset. I'm given twenty minutes' notice to be here and am not told the agenda—"

He interrupted. "Why, Doctor, I should think you might have guessed the agenda."

"Just as I should have guessed that our meeting was a public event."

"I understand the press came out in force." His expression did not change.

"I'd like to know how this occurred," I said heatedly.

"If you're asking if this office notified the press of our meeting, I'm telling you that we did not."

I did not respond.

"Doctor, I'm not certain you understand that as public servants we must operate by a different set of rules. In a sense, we are not allowed private lives. Or perhaps it would be better to say that if our ethics or judgment are questioned, the public has a right to examine, in some instances, the most private aspects of our existences. Whenever I am about to undertake a certain activity or even write a check, I have to ask myself if what I am doing will hold up under the most intense scrutiny."

I noticed that he scarcely used his hands when he talked, and that the fabric and design of his suit and tie were a lesson in understated extravagance. My attention darted here and there as he continued his admonition, and I knew that nothing I might do or say would save me in the end. Though I had been appointed by the health commissioner, I would not have been offered the job, nor could I last long in it without the support of the governor. The quickest way to lose that was to cause him embarrassment or conflict, which I had already accomplished. He had the power to force my resignation. I had the power to buy myself a little time by threatening to embarrass him more.

"Doctor, perhaps you would like to tell me what you would do if you were in my position?"

Beyond the window rain was mixed with sleet, and buildings in the banking district were bleak against a dreary, pewter sky. I stared at Norring in silence, then quietly spoke. "Governor Norring, I would like to think that I would not summon the chief medical examiner to my office to gratuitously insult her, both professionally and personally, and then demand of her that she surrender the rights guaranteed to every person by the Constitution.

"Further, I would like to think that I would accept this person's innocence until she had been proven guilty, and would not compromise her ethics and the Hippocratic oath she had sworn to uphold by demanding that she open confidential files to public scrutiny when doing so might do harm to herself and to others. I would like to think, Governor Norring, that I would not give an individual who has served the Commonwealth faithfully no choice but to resign for cause."

The governor absently picked up a silver fountain pen as he considered my words. For me to resign for cause after meeting with him would imply to all of the reporters waiting beyond his office door that I had quit because Norring had asked me to do something that I considered unethical.

"I have no interest in your resigning at this moment," he said coldly. "In fact, I would not accept your resignation. I am a fair man, Dr. Scarpetta, and, I hope, a wise one. And wisdom dictates that I cannot have someone performing legal autopsies on the victims of homicide when this individual, herself, is being implicated in homicide or as an accessory to it. Therefore, I think it best to relieve you with pay until this matter is resolved." He reached for the phone. "John, would you be so kind as to show the chief medical examiner out?"

Almost instantly, the smiling press secretary appeared.

As I emerged from the governor's offices, I was accosted from every direction. Flashguns went off in my eyes, and it seemed that everyone was shouting. The lead news item the rest of the day and the following morning was that the governor had temporarily relieved me of my duties until I could clear my name. An editorial conjectured that Norring had shown himself to be a gentleman, and if I were a lady I would offer to step down.

11

Friday I stayed home in front of the fire, continuing the tedious and frustrating job of making notes to myself as I attempted to document my every move over the past few weeks. Unfortunately, I was in my car driving home from the office at the time the police believed Eddie Heath was abducted from the convenience store. When Susan was murdered, I was home alone, for Marino had taken Lucy shooting. I was also by myself the early morning that Frank Donahue was shot. I had no witnesses to testify to my activities during the three murders.

Motive and modus operandi would be significantly more difficult to sell. It is very uncommon for a woman to kill execution style, and there could be no motive at all in Eddie Heath's slaying unless I were a closet sexual sadist.

I was deep in thought when Lucy called out, "I've got something."

She was seated before the computer, the chair swiveled around to one side, her feet propped up on an ottoman. In her lap were numerous sheets of paper, and to the right of the keyboard was my Smith and Wesson thirty-eight.

"Why do you have my revolver in here?" I asked uneasily.

"Pete told me to dry-fire it whenever I have a chance. So I've been practicing while running my program through the journal tapes."

I picked up the revolver, pushed the thumb latch, and checked the chambers, just to be sure.

"Though I've still got a few tapes to run through, I think I've already gotten a hit on what we're looking for," she said.

I felt a surge of optimism as I pulled up a chair.

"The journal tape for December ninth shows three interesting TUs."

"TUs?" I asked.

"Tenprint Updates," Lucy explained. "We're talking about three records. One was completely dropped or deleted. The SID number of another was altered. Then we have a third record which was a new entry made around the same time the other two were deleted or changed. I logged into CCRE and ran the SID numbers of both the altered record and the new record entered. The altered record comes back to Ronnie Joe Waddell."

"What about the new record?" I said.

"That's spooky. There's no criminal history. I entered the SID number five times and it kept coming back to 'no record found.' Do you understand the significance?"

"Without a history in CCRE, we have no way of knowing who this person is."

Lucy nodded. "Right. You've got someone's prints and SID number in AFIS, but there's no name or other personal identifiers to match him up with. And that would indicate to me that somebody dropped this person's record from CCRE. In other words, CCRE has been tampered with, too."

"Let's go back to Ronnie Waddell," I said. "Can you reconstruct what was done to his record?"

"I've got a theory. First, you need to know that the SID number is a unique identifier and has a unique index, meaning the system won't allow you to enter a duplicate value. So if, for example, I wanted to switch SID numbers with you, I'd have to delete your record first. Then, after I've changed my SID number to yours, I'd reenter your record, giving you my old SID number."

"And that's what you think happened?" I asked.

"Such a transaction would explain the TUs I've found in the journal tape for December ninth."

Four days before Waddell's execution, I thought.

"There's more," Lucy said. "On December sixteenth, Waddell's record was deleted from AFIS."

"How can that be?" I asked, baffled. "A print from Jennifer Deighton's house came back to Waddell when Vander ran it through AFIS a little over a week ago."

"AFIS crashed on December sixteenth at ten-fifty-six A.M., exactly ninety-eight minutes after Waddell's record was deleted," Lucy replied. "The data base was restored with the journal tapes, but you've got to keep in mind that a backup is done only once a day, late in the afternoon. Therefore, any changes made to the data base the morning of December sixteenth hadn't been backed up yet when the system crashed. When the data base was restored, so was Waddell's record."

"You mean someone tampered with Waddell's SID number four days before his execution? Then three days after his execution, someone deleted his record from AFIS?"

"That's the way it looks to me. What I can't figure is why the person didn't just delete his record in the first place. Why go to all the trouble to change the SID number, only to turn around and delete his entire record?"

Neils Vander had a simple answer to that when I called him moments later.

"It's not unusual for an inmate's prints to be deleted from AFIS after he's dead," Vander said. "In fact, the only reason we wouldn't delete a deceased inmate's records would be if it were possible his prints might turn up in any unsolved cases. But Waddell had been in prison for nine, ten years—he'd been out of commission too long to make it worthwhile to keep his prints on line."

"Then the deletion of his record on December sixteenth would have been routine," I said.

"Absolutely. But it would not have been routine to delete his record on December ninth, when Lucy believes his SID number was altered, because Waddell was still alive then."

"Neils, what do you think this is all about?"

"When you change somebody's SID number, Kay, in effect you have changed his identity. I may get a hit on his prints, but when I enter the corresponding SID number in CCRE, it's not his history I'm going to get. I'll either get no history at all, or the history of somebody else."

"You got a hit on a print left at Jennifer Deighton's house," I said. "You entered the corresponding SID number in CCRE and it came back to Ronnie Waddell. Yet we now have reason to believe his original SID number was changed. We really don't know who left the print on her dining room chair, do we?"

"No. And it's becoming clear that someone has gone to a lot of trouble to make sure we can't verify who that person might be. I can't prove it's not Waddell. I can't prove that it is."

Images flashed in my mind as he spoke.

"In order to verify that Waddell did not leave that print on Jennifer Deighton's chair, I need an old print of his that I can trust, one that I know couldn't have been tampered with. But I just don't know where else to look."

I envisioned dark paneling and hardwood floors, and dried blood the color of garnets.

"Her house," I muttered.

"Whose house?" Vander puzzled.

"Robyn Naismith's house," I said.

Ten years previously, when Robyn Naismith's house was processed by the police, they would not have arrived with laser or Luma-Lite. There was no such thing as DNA printing then. There was no automated fingerprint system in Virginia, no computerized means to enhance a bloody partial print left on a wall or anywhere else. Though new technology generally is irrelevant in cases that have long been closed, there are exceptions. I believed Robyn Naismith's murder was one of them.

If we could spray her house with chemicals, it was possible we could literally resurrect the scene. Blood clots, drips, drops, spatters, stains, and screams bright red. It seeps into crevices and cracks, and sneaks under cushions and floors. Though it may disappear with washing and fade with the years, it never completely goes away. Like the writing that wasn't there on the sheet of paper found on Jennifer Deighton's bed, there was blood invisible to the naked eye inside the rooms where Robyn Naismith had been accosted and killed. Unaided by technology, police had found one bloody print during the original investigation of the crime. Maybe Waddell had left more. Maybe they were still there.

Neils Vander, Benton Wesley, and I drove west toward the University of Richmond, a splendid collection of Georgian buildings surrounding a lake between Three Chopt and River roads. It was from here that Robyn Naismith had graduated with honors many years before, and her love of the area had been such that she had later bought her first home two blocks from the campus.

Her former small brick house with its mansard roof was set on a half-acre lot. I was not surprised that the site should have been ideal for a burglar. The yard was dense with trees, the back of the house dwarfed by three gigantic magnolias that completely blocked the sun. I doubted the neighbors on either side could have seen or heard anything at Robyn Naismith's house, had they been home. The morning Robyn was murdered, her neighbors were at work.

Due to the circumstances that had placed the house on the market ten years ago, the price had been low for the neighborhood. We'd discovered the university had decided to buy it for faculty housing, and had kept much of what was left inside it. Robyn had been unmarried, an only child, and her parents in northern Virginia did not want her furnishings. I suspected they could not bear to live with or even look at them. Professor Sam Potter, a bachelor who taught German, had been renting the house from his employer since its purchase.

As we gathered camera equipment, containers of chemicals, and other items from the trunk, the back door opened. An unwholesome-looking man greeted us with an uninspired good-morning.

"You need a hand with that?" Sam Potter came down the steps, sweeping his long, receding black hair out of his eyes and smoking a cigarette. He was short and pudgy, his hips wide like a woman's.

"If you want to get the box here," Vander said.

Potter dropped the cigarette to the ground and didn't bother stamping it out. We followed him up the steps and into a small kitchen with old avocado-green appliances and dozens of dirty dishes. He led us through the dining room, with laundry piled on the table, then into the living room at the front of the house. I set down what I was carrying and tried not to register my shock as I recognized the console television connected to a cable outlet in the wall, the draperies, the brown leather couch, the parquet floor, now scuffed and as dull as mud. Books and papers were scattered everywhere, and Potter began to talk as he carelessly collected them.

"As you can see, I'm not domestically inclined," he said, his German accent distinct. "I will stick these things on the dining room table for now. There," he said when he returned. "Anything else you would like me to move?" He slipped a pack of Camels from the breast pocket of his white shirt and dug a book of matches from his faded denim jeans. A pocket watch was attached to a belt loop by a leather thong, and I noticed a number of things as he slid it out to glance at the time and then lit the cigarette. His hands trembled, his fingers were swollen, and broken blood vessels covered his cheekbones and nose. He had not bothered to empty ashtrays, but he had collected bottles and glasses and had been careful to carry out the trash.

"This is fine. You don't need to move anything else," Wesley said. "If we do, we'll put it back."

"And you said this chemical you're using won't damage anything and isn't toxic to humans?"

"No, it's not hazardous. It will leave a grainy residue—similar to when salt water dries," I said to him. "We'll do our best to clean up."

"I really don't want to be here while you do this," Potter said, taking a nervous drag on the cigarette. "Can you give me an approximation of how much time it will require?"

"Hopefully, no more than two hours." Wesley was looking around the room, and though his face was completely devoid of expression, I could imagine what was going through his mind.

I took off my coat and didn't know where to put it, while Vander opened a box of film.

"Should you finish before I get back, please shut the door and make sure it's locked. I don't have an alarm to worry about." Potter went back out through the kitchen, and when he started his car it sounded like a diesel bus.

"It's a shame, really," Vander said as he lifted two bottles of chemicals from a box. "This could be a very nice house. But inside it's not much better than a lot of slums I've seen. Did you notice the scrambled eggs in the skillet on the stove? What more do you want to pick up here?" He squatted on the floor. "I don't want to mix this up until we're ready."

"I'd say we need to move as much out of here as we can. You've got the pictures, Kay?" Wesley said.

I got out Robyn Naismith's scene photographs. "You've noticed that our professor friend is living with her furniture," I said.

"Well, then we'll leave it here," Vander said as if it were common for furniture from a ten-year-old murder scene to still be in place. "But the rug's got to go. I can tell that didn't come with the house."

"How?" Wesley stared down at the blue-and-red braided rug beneath his feet. It was filthy and curling up at the edges.

"If you lift up the edge, you can see that the parquet is just as dull and scratched underneath as it is everywhere else. The rug hasn't been here long. Besides, it doesn't look very well made. I doubt it would have lasted all this time."

Spreading several photographs on the floor, I turned them this way and that until the perspectives were right and we could tell what needed to be moved. What furnishings were original to the room had been rearranged. As much as it was possible to do so, we began to re-create the scene of Robyn's death.

"Okay, the ficus tree goes over there," I said like a stage director. "Right, but slide the couch back about two more feet, Neils. And that way just a little bit more. The tree was maybe four inches from the left armrest. A little closer. That's good."

"No, it's not. The branches are over the couch."

"The tree's a little bigger now."

"I can't believe it's still alive. I'm surprised anything could live around Professor Potter except maybe bacteria or fungi."

"And the rug goes?" Wesley took off his jacket.

"Yes. She had a small runner by the front door and another small Oriental under the coffee table. Most of the floor was bare."

He got down on his hands and knees and began to roll up the rug.

I went over to the television and studied the VCR on top and the cable connection leading into the wall.

"This has got to go against the wall opposite the couch and the front door. Either of you gentlemen good with VCRs and cable connections?"

"No," they answered simultaneously.

"Then I'm left to my own devices. Here goes."

I disconnected the cable and the VCR, unplugged the TV, and carefully slid it across the bare, dusty floor. Referring to the photographs again, I moved it a few more feet until it was directly opposite the front door. Next I surveyed the walls. Potter apparently collected art and was fond of an artist whose name I could not quite make out, but it looked French. The sketches were charcoal studies of the female form with lots of curves, pink splotches, and triangles. One by one they all came down and I propped them against the walls in the dining room. By this point, the room was almost bare and I was itching from the dust.

Wesley wiped his forehead on the back of his arm. "Are we about ready?" He looked at me.

"I think so. Of course, not everything is here. She had three barrel chairs right over there." I pointed.

"They're in the bedrooms," Vander said. "Two in one bedroom and one in the other. Do you want me to bring them out?"

"Might as well."

He and Wesley carried in the chairs.

"She had a painting on that wall over there, and another one to the right of the door leading into the dining room," I pointed out. "A still life and an English landscape. So Potter couldn't live with her art but didn't seem to have a problem with anything else."

"We need to go around the house and close all blinds, shades, and curtains," Vander said. "If any light is still coming through, then tear off a section of this paper"—he pointed to a roll of heavy brown paper on the floor—"and tape it over the window."

For the next fifteen minutes, the house was filled with the sounds of footsteps, venetian blinds rattling, and scissors slicing through paper. Occasionally somebody swore loudly when the paper had been cut too short or the tape stuck to nothing but itself. I stayed in the living room and covered the glass in the front door and in the two windows facing the street. When the three of us reconvened and turned out the lights, the house was pitch-black. I could not even see my hand in front of my face.

"Perfect," Vander said as the overhead light went back on.

Putting on gloves, he set bottles of distilled water, chemicals, and two plastic spray bottles on the coffee table. "Here's the way we're going to work this," he said. "Dr. Scarpetta, you can spray while I videotape, and if an area reacts, just keep spraying it until I tell you to move on."

"What do you want me to do?" Wesley asked.

"Keep out of the way."

"What's in this stuff?" he asked as Vander unscrewed the caps from bottles of dry chemicals.

"You don't really want to know," I replied.

"I'm a big boy. You can tell me."

"The reagent's a mixture of sodium perborate, which Neils is mixing with distilled water, and three-aminophthalhydrazide and sodium carbonate," I said, getting a packet of gloves out of my pocketbook.

"And you're certain it will work on blood this old?" Wesley asked.

"Actually, aged and decomposed blood reacts better with luminol than do fresh bloodstains because the more oxidized the blood, the better. As blood ages, it becomes more strongly oxidized."

"I don't think any of the wood in here is salt treated, do you?" Vander looked around.

"I shouldn't think so." I explained to Wesley, "The biggest problem with luminol is false positives. A number of things react with it, such as copper and nickel, and the copper salts in salt-treated wood."

"It also likes rust, household bleach, iodine, and formalin," Vander added. "Plus, the peroxidases found in bananas, watermelon, citrus fruit, a number of vegetables. Also horseradish."

Wesley looked at me with a smile.

Vander opened an envelope and removed two squares of filter paper that were stained with dried, diluted blood. Then he added mixture A to B and told Wesley to hit the lights. A couple of quick sprays, and a bluish white neon glow appeared on the coffee table. It began to fade almost as quickly as it had appeared.

"Here," Vander said to me.

I felt the spray bottle touch my arm, and took hold of it. A tiny red light went on as Vander depressed the power button on the video camera; then the night vision lamp burned white and looked wherever he did like a luminescent eye.

"Where are you?" Vander's voice sounded to my left.

"I'm in the center of the room. I can feel the edge of the coffee table against my leg," I said, as if we were children playing in the dark.

"I'm way the hell out of the way." Wesley's voice carried from the direction of the dining room.

Vander's white light slowly moved toward me. I reached out and touched his shoulder. "Ready?"

"I'm recording. Start and just keep going until I tell you to stop."

I began spraying the floor around us, my finger nonstop on the trigger as a mist floated over me and shapes and geometrical configurations materialized around my feet. For an instant, it was like speeding through the dark over the illuminated grid of a city far below. Old blood trapped in the crevices of the parquet emitted a blue-white glow. I sprayed and sprayed, without having any real sense of where I was in relation to anything else, and saw footprints all over the room. I bumped against the ficus tree and dim white streaks appeared on the planter that held it. To my right smeared handprints flashed on the wall.

"Lights," Vander said.

Wesley turned on the overhead light and Vander mounted a thirty-five-millimeter camera on a tripod to keep it still. The only light available would be the fluorescence of the luminol, and the film would need a long exposure time to capture it. I retrieved a full bottle of luminol and, when the lights were out again, resumed spraying the smeared handprints on the wall while the camera captured the eerie images on film. Then we moved on. Lazy, wide swipes appeared on paneling and parquet, and the stitching on the leather couch was a neon hatch line incompletely tracing the square shapes of the cushions.

"Can you lift them out of the way?" Vander asked.

One by one I slid the cushions onto the floor and sprayed down the couch's frame. The spaces between the cushions glowed. On the backrest appeared more swipes and smears, and on the ceiling appeared a constellation of small, bright stars. It was on the old television that we got our first pyrophoric display of false positives, as metal around the dials and screen lit up and cable connecters turned the blue-white of thin milk. There was nothing remarkable about the TV, only a few smudges that might be blood, but the floor directly in front of it, where Robyn's body had been found, went crazy. The blood was so pervasive that I could see the edges of the parquet's inlays and the direction of the wood fibers constituting the grain. A drag mark feathered out several feet from the densest concentration of luminescence, and nearby was a curious pattern of tangential rings made by an object with a circumference slightly smaller than a basketball.

The search did not end in the living room. We began to follow footprints. At intervals we were forced to turn on lights, mix more luminol, and move clutter out of the way, particularly in the linguistic landfill that once had been Robyn's bedroom and now was where Professor Potter lived. The floor was several inches deep in research papers, journal articles, exams, and scores of books written in German, French, and Italian. Clothes were strewn about and draped over things so haphazardly it was as if a whirlwind had kicked up in the closet and created a vortex in the center of the room. We picked up as best we could, creating stacks and piles on the unmade double bed. Then we followed Waddell's bloody path.

It led me into the bathroom, with Vander at my heels. Shoe prints and smudges were scattered about the floor, and the same circular patterns that we had found in the living room fluoresced by the side of the bathtub. When I began spraying the walls, halfway up and on either side of the toilet, two huge handprints suddenly appeared. The video camera's light floated closer.

Then Vander's voice said excitedly, "Flip on the light."

Potter's powder room was, to say the least, as disreputably maintained as the rest of his domain. Vander almost had his nose to the wall as he scrutinized the area where the prints had appeared.

"Can you see them?"

"Umm. Maybe barely." He cocked his head to one side, then the other, squinting. "This is fantastic. You see, the wallpaper is this deep blue design, so nothing much is going to show to the naked eye. And it's plasticized or vinyl—a good surface for prints, in other words."

"Jesus," said Wesley, who was standing in the doorway of the bathroom. "The damn toilet doesn't look like it's been cleaned since he moved in. Hell, it's not even flushed."

"Even if he did mop up or wipe down the walls from time to time, you really can't get rid of every trace of blood," I said to Vander. "On a linoleum floor like this, for example, a residue gets down in the pebbly surface, and luminol is going to bring it up."

"Are you saying that if we sprayed down this place again in another ten years, the blood would still be here?" Wesley was amazed.

"The only way you could eradicate most of the blood would be to repaint everything, repaper the walls, refinish the floors, and pitch the furniture," Vander said. "If you want to get rid of absolutely every trace, you'd have to tear down the house and start over."

Wesley looked at his watch. "We've been here three and a half hours."

"Here's what I suggest we do," I said. "Benton, you and I can begin restoring the rooms to their normal state of chaos, and Neils, we'll leave you to do what you need to do."

"Fine. I'll get the Luma-Lite set up in here, and keep your fingers crossed that it can enhance the ridge detail."

We returned to the living room. While Vander carried the portable Luma-Lite and camera equipment back to the bath, Wesley and I looked around at the couch, the old TV, and the dusty, scarred floor, both of us somewhat dazed. With the lights on there was not so much as the slightest trace of the horror we had seen in the dark. On this sunny winter's afternoon, we had crawled back in time and witnessed what Ronnie Joe Waddell had done.

Wesley stood very still near the paper-covered window. "I'm afraid to sit anywhere or lean up against anything. Christ. There's blood all over this goddam house."

As I looked around, I pictured fading white in the blackness, my eyes traveling slowly from the couch, across the floor, and stopping at the TV. The couch's cushions were still on the floor where I had left them, and I squatted to take a closer look. The blood that had seeped into the brown stitching was not visible now, nor were the streaks and smears on the brown leather backrest. But a careful examination revealed something that was important but not necessarily surprising. On the side of one of the seat cushions that had been flush against the backrest I found a linear cut that was, at most, three-quarters of an inch long.

"Benton, was Waddell left-handed, by chance?"

"It seems to me he was."

"They thought he stabbed and beat her on the floor near the TV because there was so much blood around her body," I said, "but he didn't. He killed her on the couch. I think I need to go outside. If this place weren't such a sewer, I'd be tempted to pinch one of the professor's cigarettes."

"You've been good for too long," Wesley said. "An unfiltered Camel would land you on your ass. Go on and get some fresh air. I'll start cleaning up."

I left the house to the sound of paper being ripped down from the windows.

That night began the most peculiar New Year's Eve in memory for Benton Wesley, Lucy, and me. I wouldn't go so far as to say the holiday was all that odd for Neils Vander. I had talked to him at seven P.M., and he was still in his lab, but that was fairly normal for a man whose raison d'être would cease to exist were the fingerprints of two individuals ever found to be the same.

Vander had edited the scene videocassette tapes to a VCR and turned copies over to me late that afternoon. For the better part of the early evening, Wesley and I had been stationed in front of my television, taking notes and making diagrams as we slowly went through the footage. Lucy, meanwhile, was working on dinner, and came into the living room only briefly from time to time to catch a glimpse. The luminescent images on the dark screen did not seem to disturb her. At a glance, the uninitiated could not possibly know what they meant.

By eight-thirty, Wesley and I had gone through the tapes and completed our notes. We believed we had charted the course of Robyn Naismith's killer from the moment she walked into her house to Waddell's exit through the kitchen door. It was the first time in my career I had retrospectively worked the scene of a homicide that had been solved for years. But the scenario that emerged was important for one very good reason. It demonstrated, at least to our satisfaction, that what Wesley had told me at the Homestead was correct. Ronnie Joe Waddell did not fit the profile of the monster we were now tracking.

The latent smudges, smears, spatters, and spurts that we had followed were as close to an instant replay as I had ever seen in the reconstruction of a crime. Though the courts might consider much of what we determined was opinion, it did not matter. Waddell's personality did, and we felt pretty certain that we had captured it.

Because the blood we had found in other areas of the house clearly had been tracked and transferred by Waddell, it was realistic to say that his assault of Robyn Naismith was restricted to the living room, where she died. The kitchen and front doors were equipped with deadbolt locks that could not be opened without a key. Since Waddell had entered the house through a window and left through the kitchen door, it had been surmised that when Robyn returned from the store, she had come in through the kitchen. Perhaps she had not bothered to relock the door, but more likely she had not had time. It had been conjectured that while Waddell was ransacking her belongings, he heard her drive up and park behind the house. He went into the kitchen and got a steak knife from the stainless steel set hanging on a wall. When she unlocked the door, he was waiting. Chances are, he simply grabbed her first and forced her through the open doorway that led into the living room. He may have talked to her for a while. He may have demanded money. He may have been with her only moments before the confrontation became physical.

Robyn had been dressed and sitting or supine on the end of the couch near the ficus tree when Waddell struck the first blow with the knife. The blood spatters that had appeared on the backrest of the couch, the planter, and the dark paneling nearby were consistent with an arterial spurt, caused when an artery is severed. The resulting spatter pattern is reminiscent of an electrocardiogram tracing due to fluctuations of arterial blood pressure, and one has no blood pressure unless he or she is alive.

So we knew that Robyn was alive and on the couch when she was first assaulted. But it was unlikely she was still breathing when Waddell removed her clothing, which upon later examination revealed a single three-quarters-of-an-inch cut in the front of the bloodstained blouse where the knife had been plunged into her chest and moved back and forth to completely transect her aorta. Since she was stabbed many more times than that, and bitten, it was safe to conclude that most of Waddell's frenzied, piqueristic attack on her had occurred postmortem.

Then this man, who later would claim he did not remember killing "the lady on TV," suddenly woke up, in a sense. He got off her body and had second thoughts about what he had done. The absence of drag marks near the couch suggested that Waddell carried the body from the couch and laid it on the floor on the other side of the room. He dragged it into an upright position and propped it against the TV. Then he set about to clean up. The ring marks that glowed on the floor, I believed, were left by the bottom of a bucket that he carried back and forth from the body to the bathtub down the hall. Each time he returned to the living room to mop up more blood with towels, or perhaps to check on his victim as he continued raiding her belongings and drinking her booze, he again bloodied the bottom of his shoes. This explained the profusion of shoe prints wandering peripatetically throughout her house. The activities themselves explained something else. Waddell's postoffense behavior was inconsistent with that of someone who felt no remorse.

"Here he is, this uneducated farm boy who's living in the big city," Wesley explained. "He's stealing to support a drug habit that's rotting his brain. First marijuana, then heroin, coke, and finally PCP. And one morning he suddenly comes to and finds himself brutalizing the corpse of a stranger."

Logs shifted in the fire as we stared at big handprints glowing as white as chalk on the dark television screen.

"The police never found vomit in the toilet or around it," I said.

"He probably cleaned that up, too. Thank God he didn't wipe down the wall above the john. You don't lean against a wall like that unless you're commode-hugging sick."

"The prints are fairly high above the back of the toilet," I observed. "I think he vomited, and when he stood up got dizzy, lurched forward, and raised his hands just in time to prevent his head from slamming into the wall. What do you think? Remorse or was he just stoned out of his mind?"

Wesley looked at me. "Let's consider what he did with the body. He sat it upright, tried to clean it with towels, and left the clothes in a moderately neat stack on the floor near her ankles. Now, you can look at that two ways. He was lewdly displaying the body and thereby showing contempt. Or he was demonstrating what he considered caring. Personally, I think it was the latter."

"And the way Eddie Heath's body was displayed?"

"That feels different. The positioning of the boy mirrors the positioning of the woman, but something's missing."

Even as he spoke, I suddenly realized what it was. "A *mirror* image," I said to Wesley in amazement. "A mirror reflects things backward or in reverse."

He looked curiously at me.

"Remember when we were comparing Robyn Naismith's scene photographs with the diagram depicting the position of Eddie Heath's body?"

"I remember vividly."

"You said that what was done to the boy—from the bite marks to the way his body was propped against a boxy object to his clothing being left in a tidy pile nearby—was a mirror image of what had been done to Robyn. But the bite marks on Robyn's inner thigh and above her breast were on the left side of her body. While Eddie's injuries—what we believe are eradicated bite marks—were on the *right*. His right shoulder and right inner thigh."

"Okay." Wesley still looked perplexed.

"The photograph that Eddie's scene most closely resembles is the one of her nude body propped against the big console TV."

"True."

"What I'm suggesting is that maybe Eddie's killer saw the same photograph of Robyn that we did. But his perspective is based on his own body's left and right. And his right would have been Robyn's left, and his left would have been her right, because in the photograph she's facing whoever is looking on."

"That's not a pleasant thought," Wesley said as the telephone rang.

"Aunt Kay?" Lucy called out from the kitchen. "It's Mr. Vander."

"We got a confirmation," Vander's voice came over the line.

"Waddell did leave the print in Jennifer Deighton's house?" I asked.

"No, that's just it. He definitely did not."

12

Over the next few days, I retained Nicholas Grueman, delivering to him my financial records and other information he requested, the health commissioner summoned me to his office to suggest that I resign, and the publicity would not end. But I knew much that I had not known even a week before.

It was Ronnie Joe Waddell who died in the electric chair the night of December 13. Yet his identity remained alive and was wreaking havoc in the city. As best as could be determined, prior to Waddell's death his SID number in AFIS had been swapped with another's. Then the other person's SID number was dropped completely from the Central Computerized Records Exchange, or CCRE. This meant there was a violent offender at large who had no need of gloves when he committed his crimes. When his prints were run through AFIS, they would come back as a dead man's every time. We knew this nefarious individual left a wake of feathers and flecks of paint, but we could surmise almost nothing about him until January 3 of the new year.

On that morning, the *Richmond Times-Dispatch* ran a planted story about highly prized eiderdown and its appeal to thieves. At one-fourteen P.M., Officer Tom Lucero, head of the fictitious investigation, received his third call of the day.

"Hi. My name's Hilton Sullivan," the voice said loudly.

"What can I do for you, sir?" Lucero's deep voice asked.

"It's about the cases you're investigating. The eiderdown clothes and things that are supposedly hot with thieves. There was this article about it in the paper this morning. It said you're the detective."

"Right."

"Well, it really pisses me off that the cops are *so* stupid." He got louder. "It said in the paper that since Thanksgiving this and that have been stolen from stores, cars, and homes in the greater Richmond metropolitan area. You know, comforters, a sleeping bag, three ski jackets, blah, blah, blah. And the reporter quoted several people."

"What is your point, Mr. Sullivan?"

"Well, obviously the reporter got the victims' names from the cops. In other words, from you."

"It's public information."

"I don't really give a shit about that. I just want to know how come you didn't mention *this victim,* yours truly? You don't even remember my name, do you?"

"I'm sorry, sir, but I can't say that I do."

"Figures. Some fucking asshole breaks into my condo and wipes me out, and other than smearing black powder everywhere—on a day when I was dressed in white cashmere, I might add—the cops don't do a thing. I'm one of your fucking cases."

"When was your condo broken into?"

"*Don't you remember*? I'm the one who raised such a stink about my down vest. If it wasn't for me, you guys would never have even heard of eiderdown! When I told the cop that among other things my vest had been taken and it had cost me five hundred bucks *on sale,* you know what he said?"

"I have no idea, sir."

"He said, 'What's it stuffed with, cocaine?' And I said, 'No, *Sherlock.* Eider duck down.' And he looked around nervous as hell and dropped his hand close to his nine-mil. The dumb-shit really thought there was some other person in my place named *Eider* and I'd just yelled at this person to *duck down,* like I was going to pull a gun or something. At that point I just left and—"

* * *

Wesley switched off the tape recorder.

We sat in my kitchen. Lucy was working out at my club again.

"The B-and-E this Hilton Sullivan's talking about was in fact reported by him on Saturday, December eleventh. Apparently, he'd been out of town, and when he returned to his condo that Saturday afternoon, he discoverd that he'd been burglarized," Wesley explained.

"Where is his condo located?" I asked.

"Downtown on West Franklin, an old brick building with condos that start at a hundred grand. Sullivan lives on the first floor. The perpetrator got in through an unsecured window."

"No alarm system?"

"No."

"What was stolen?"

"Jewelry, money, and a twenty-two revolver. Of course, that doesn't necessarily mean that Sullivan's revolver is the one that was used to kill Eddie Heath, Susan, and Donahue. But I think we're going to find that it is, because there's no question that our guy did the B-and-E."

"Prints were recovered?"

"A number of them. The city had them, and you know how their backlog is. With all the homicides, B-and-Es aren't a top priority. In this instance, the latents had been processed and were just sitting. Pete intercepted them right after Lucero got the call. Vander's already run them through the system. He got a hit in exactly three seconds."

"Waddell again."

Wesley nodded.

"How far is Sullivan's condo from Spring Street?"

"Within walking distance. I think we know where our guy escaped from."

"You're checking out recent releases?"

"Oh, sure. But we're not going to find him in a stack of paper on somebody's desk. The warden was too careful for that. Unfortunately, he's also dead. I think he sent this inmate back out on the street, and the first thing he did was burglarize a condominium and probably find himself a set of wheels."

"Why would Donahue free an inmate?"

"My theory is that the warden needed some dirty work done. So he selected an inmate to be his personal operative and set the animal loose. But Donahue made a slight tactical error. He picked the wrong guy, because the person who's committing these killings is not going to be controlled by anyone. My suspicion, Kay, is that Donahue never intended for anyone to die, and when Jennifer Deighton turned up dead, he freaked."

"He was probably the one who called my office and identified himself as John Deighton."

"Could very well be. The point is that Donahue's intention was to have Jennifer Deighton's house ransacked because someone was looking for something—perhaps communications from Waddell. But a simple burglary isn't enough fun. The warden's little pet likes to hurt people."

I thought of the indentations in the carpet of Jennifer Deighton's living room, the injuries to her neck, and the fingerprint recovered from her dining room chair.

"He may have sat her in the middle of her living room and stood behind her with his arm yoked around her neck while he interrogated her."

"He may have done that to get her to tell him where things were. But he was being sadistic. Possibly forcing her to open her Christmas presents was also sadistic," said Wesley.

"Would someone like this go to the trouble to disguise her death as a suicide by placing her body in her car?" I asked.

"He might. This guy's been in the system. He's not interested in getting caught, and it's probably a challenge to see who he can fool. He eradicated bite marks from Eddie Heath's body. If he ransacked Jennifer Deighton's house, he left no evidence. The only evidence he left in Susan's case was two twenty-two slugs and a feather. Not to mention, the guy altered his fingerprints."

"You think that was his idea?"

"It was probably something that the warden cooked up, and swapping records with Waddell may simply have been a matter of convenience. Waddell was about to be executed. If I wanted to trade an inmate's prints with someone, I'd choose Waddell's. Either the inmate's latents are going to come back to someone who is dead or—and this is more likely—eventually the dead person's records will be purged from the State Police computers, so if my little helper is messy and leaves prints somewhere, they aren't going to be identified at all."

I stared at him, dumbfounded.

"What?" Surprise flickered in his eyes.

"Benton, do you realize what we're saying? We're sitting here talking about computer records that were altered before Waddell died. We're talking about a burglary and the murder of a little boy that were committed before Waddell was dead. In other words, the warden's operative, as you call him, was released before Waddell was executed."

"I don't believe there can be a question about that."

"Then the assumption was that Waddell was going to die," I pointed out.

"Christ." Wesley flinched. "How could anyone be certain? The governor can intervene literally at the last minute."

"Apparently, someone knew that the governor wasn't going to."

"And the only person who could know that with certainty is the governor," he finished the thought for me.

I got up and stood before the kitchen window. A male cardinal pecked sunflower seeds from the feeder and flew off in a splash of bloodred.

"Why?" I asked without turning around. "Why would the governor have a special interest in Waddell?"

"I don't know."

"If it's true, he won't want the killer caught. When people get caught, they talk."

Wesley was silent.

"Nobody involved will want this person caught. And nobody involved will want me on the scene. It will be much better if I resign or am fired—if the cases are screwed up as much as possible. Patterson is tight with Norring."

"Kay, we've got two things we don't know yet. One is motive. The other is the killer's own agenda. This guy is doing his own thing, beginning with Eddie Heath."

I turned around and faced him. "I think he began with Robyn Naismith. I believe this monster has studied her crime scene photographs, and either consciously or subconsciously re-created one of them when he assaulted Eddie Heath and propped his body against a Dumpster."

"That could very well be," Wesley said, staring off. "But how could an inmate get access to Robyn Naismith's scene photographs? Those would not be in Waddell's prison jacket."

"This may be just one more thing that Ben Stevens helped with. Remember, I told you that he was the one who got the photos from Archives. He could have had copies made. The question is *why* would the photos be relevant? Why would Donahue or someone else even ask for them?"

"Because the inmate wanted them. Maybe he demanded them. Maybe they were a reward for special services."

"That is sickening," I said with quiet anger.

"Exactly." Wesley met my eyes. "This goes back to the killer's agenda, his needs and desires. It is very possible that he'd heard a lot about Robyn's case. He may have known a lot about Waddell, and it would excite him to think about what Waddell had done to his victim. The photographs would be a turn-on to someone who has a very active and aggressive fantasy life that is devoted to violent, sexualized thought. It is not farfetched to suppose that this person incorporated the scene photographs—one or more of them—into his fantasies. And then suddenly he's free, and he sees a young boy walking in the dark to a convenience store. The fantasy becomes real. He acts it out."

"He re-created Robyn Naismith's death scene?"

"Yes."

"What do you suppose his fantasy is now?"

"Being hunted."

"By us?"

"By people like us. I'm afraid he might imagine that he is smarter than everybody else and no one can stop him. He fantasizes about games he can play and murders he might commit that would reinforce these images he entertains. And for him, fantasy is not a substitute for action but a preparation for it."

"Donahue could not have orchestrated releasing a monster like this, altering records, or anything else without help," I said.

"No. I'm sure he got key people to cooperate, like someone at State Police headquarters, maybe a records person with the city and even the Bureau. People can be bought if you have something on them. And they can be bought with cash."

"Like Susan."

"I don't think Susan was the key person. I'm more inclined to suspect that Ben Stevens was. He's out in the bars. Drinks, parties. Did you know he's into a little recreational coke when he can get it?"

"Nothing would surprise me anymore."

"I've got a few guys who have been asking a lot of questions. Your administrator has a lifestyle he can't afford. And when you screw with drugs, you end up screwing with bad people. Stevens's vices would have made him an easy mark for a dirtbag like Donahue. Donahue probably had one of his henchmen make a point of running into Stevens in a bar and they start talking. Next thing, Stevens has just been offered a way to make some pretty decent change."

"What way, exactly?"

"My guess is to make sure Waddell wasn't printed at the morgue, and to make sure the photograph of his bloody thumbprint disappeared from Archives. That was probably just the beginning."

"And he enlisted Susan."

"Who wasn't willing but had major financial problems of her own."

"So who do you think was making the payoffs?"

"They were probably handled by the same person who originally made Stevens's acquaintance and sucked him into this. One of Donahue's guys, maybe one of his guards."

I remembered the guard named Roberts who had given Marino and me the tour. I remembered how cold his eyes were.

"Saying the contact is a guard," I said, "then who was this guard meeting with? Susan or Stevens?"

"My guess is with Stevens. Stevens wasn't going to trust Susan with a lot of cash. He's going to want to shave his share off the top because dishonest people believe everybody is dishonest."

"He meets the contact and gets the cash," I said. "Then Ben would meet with Susan to give her a cut?"

"That's probably what the scenario was Christmas Day when she left her parents' house ostensibly to visit a friend. She was going to meet Stevens, only the killer got to her first."

I thought of the cologne I smelled on her collar and her scarf, and I remembered Stevens's demeanor when I'd confronted him in his office the night I was looking through his desk.

"No," I said. "That's not how it went."

Wesley just looked at me.

"Stevens has several qualities that would set Susan up for what happened," I said. "He doesn't care about anyone but himself. And he's a coward. When things get hot, he's not going to stick his neck out. His first impulse is to let someone else take the fall."

"Like he's doing in your case by badmouthing you and stealing files."

"A perfect example," I said.

"Susan deposited the thirty-five hundred dollars in early December, a couple of weeks before Jennifer Deighton's death."

"That's right."

"All right, Kay. Let's go back a bit. Susan or Stevens or both of them tried to break into your computer days after Waddell's execution. We've speculated that they were looking for something in the autopsy report that Susan could not have observed firsthand during the post."

"The envelope he wanted buried with him."

"I'm still stumped over that. The codes on the receipts do not confirm what we'd speculated about earlier—that the restaurants and tollbooths are located between Richmond and Mecklenburg, and that the receipts were from the transport that brought Waddell from Mecklenburg to Richmond fifteen days prior to his execution. Though the dates on the receipts are consistent with the time frame, the locations are not. The codes come back to the stretch of I-95 between here and Petersburg."

"You know, Benton, it very well may be that the explanation for the receipts is so simple that we've completely overlooked it," I said.

"I'm all ears."

"Whenever you go anywhere for the Bureau, I imagine you have the same routine I do when traveling for the state. You document every expense and save every receipt. If you travel often, you tend to wait until you can combine several trips on one reimbursement voucher to cut down on the paperwork. Meanwhile, you're keeping your receipts somewhere."

"All that makes good sense in terms of explaining the receipts in question," Wesley said. "Someone on the prison staff, for example, had to go to Petersburg. But how did the receipts then turn up in Waddell's back pocket?"

I thought of the envelope with its urgent plea that it accompany

Waddell to the grave. Then I recalled a detail that was as poignant as it was mundane. On the afternoon of Waddell's execution, his mother had been allowed a two-hour visit with him.

"Benton, have you talked to Ronnie Waddell's mother?"

"Pete went to see her in Suffolk several days ago. She's not feeling particularly friendly or cooperative toward people like us. In her eyes, we're the ones who sent her son to the chair."

"So she didn't reveal anything significant about Waddell's demeanor when she visited him the afternoon of his execution?"

"Based on what little she said, he was very quiet and frightened. One interesting point, though. Pete asked her what had happened to Waddell's personal effects. She said that Corrections gave her his watch and ring and explained that he had donated his books, poetry, and so on to the N-double-A-C-P."

"She didn't question that?" I asked.

"No. She seemed to think it made sense for Waddell to do that."

"Why?"

"She doesn't read or write. What's important is that she was lied to, as were we when Vander tried to track down personal effects in hopes of getting latent prints. And the origin of these lies most likely was Donahue."

"Waddell knew something," I said. "For Donahue to want every scrap of paper that Waddell had written on and every letter ever sent to him, then there must be something that Waddell knew that certain people don't want anyone else to know."

Wesley was silent.

Then he said, "What did you say is the name of the cologne Stevens wears?"

"Red."

"And you're fairly certain this is what you smelled on Susan's coat and scarf?"

"I wouldn't swear to it in court, but the fragrance is quite distinctive."

"I think it's time for Pete and me to have a little prayer meeting with your administrator."

"Good. And I think I can help get him in the proper frame of mind if you'll give me until noon tomorrow."

"What are you going to do?"

"Probably make him a very nervous man," I said.

I was working at the kitchen table early that evening when I heard Lucy drive into the garage, and I got up to greet her. She was dressed in a navy blue warm-up suit and one of my ski jackets, and was carrying a gym bag.

"I'm dirty," she said, pulling away from my hug, but not before I smelled gun smoke in her hair. Glancing down at her hands, I saw enough gunshot residues on the right one to make a trace element analyst ecstatic.

"Whoa," I said as she started to walk off. "Where is it?"

"Where's what?" she asked innocently.

"The gun."

Reluctantly, she withdrew my Smith and Wesson from her jacket pocket.

"I wasn't aware you had a license for carrying a concealed weapon," I said, taking the revolver from her and making sure it was unloaded.

"I don't need one if I'm carrying it concealed in my own house. Before that I had it on the car seat in plain view."

"That's good but not good enough," I said quietly. "Come on."

Wordlessly, she followed me to the kitchen table, and we sat down.

"You said you were going to Westwood to work out," I said.

"I know that's what I said."

"Where have you been, Lucy?"

"The Firing Line on Midlothian Turnpike. It's an indoor range."

"I know what it is. How many times have you done this?"

"Four times." She looked me straight in the eye.

"My God, Lucy."

"Well, what am I supposed to do? Pete's not going to take me anymore."

"Lieutenant Marino is very, very busy right now," I said, and the remark sounded so patronizing that I was embarrassed. "You're aware of the problems," I added.

"Sure I am. Right now he's got to stay away. And if he stays away from you, he stays away from me. So he's out on the street because there's some maniac on the loose who's killing people like your morgue supervisor and the prison warden. At least Pete can take care of himself. Me? I've been shown how to shoot one lousy time. Gee, thanks a lot. That's like giving me one tennis lesson and then entering me in Wimbledon."

"You're overreacting."

"No. The problem is you're underreacting."

"Lucy . . ."

"How would you feel if I told you that every time I come visit you, I never stop thinking about that night?"

I knew exactly which night she meant, though over the years we had managed to go on as if nothing had happened.

"I would not feel good if I knew you were upset by anything that has to do with me," I said.

"*Anything*? What happened was just *anything*?"

"Of course it wasn't just anything."

"Sometimes I wake up at night because I dream a gun is going off. Then I listen to the awful silence and remember lying there, staring into the dark. I was so scared I couldn't move, and I wet my bed. And there were sirens and red lights flashing, and neighbors coming out on their porches and looking out their windows. And you wouldn't let me see it when they carried him out, and you wouldn't let me go upstairs. I wish I had, because imagining it has been worse."

"That man is dead, Lucy. He can't hurt anyone now."

"There are others just as bad, maybe worse than him."

"I'm not going to tell you there aren't."

"What are you doing about it, then?"

"I spend my every waking moment picking up the pieces of the lives destroyed by evil people. What more do you want me to do?"

"If you let something happen to you, I promise I will hate you," my niece said.

"If something happens to me, I don't suppose it will matter who hates me. But I wouldn't want you to hate anyone because of what it would do to you."

"Well, I will hate you. I swear."

"I want you to promise me, Lucy, that you won't lie to me again."

She did not say a word.

"I don't ever want you to feel that you need to hide anything from me," I said.

"If I'd told you I wanted to go to the range, would you have let me?"

"Not without Lieutenant Marino or me."

"Aunt Kay, what if Pete can't catch him?"

"Lieutenant Marino is not the only person on the case," I said, not answering her question, because I did not know how to answer it.

"Well, I feel sorry for Pete."

"Why?"

"He has to stop whoever this person is, and he can't even talk to you."

"I imagine he's taking things in stride, Lucy. He's a pro."

"That's not what Michele says."

I glanced over at her.

"I was talking to her this morning. She says that Pete came by the house the other night to see her father. She said that Pete looks awful—his face was as red as a fire truck and he was in a horrible mood. Mr. Wesley tried to get him to go to the doctor or take some time off, but no way."

I felt miserable. I wanted to call Marino immediately, but I knew it wasn't wise. I changed the subject.

"What else have you and Michele been talking about? Anything new with the State Police computers?"

"Nothing good. We've tried everything we can think of to figure out who Waddell's SID number was switched with. But any records marked for deletion were overwritten long ago on the hard disk. And whoever is responsible for the tampering was swift enough to do full system backups after the records were altered, meaning we can't run SID numbers against an earlier version of CCRE and see who pops up. Generally, you have at least one backup that's three to six months old. But not so in this case."

"Sounds like an inside job to me."

I thought how natural it seemed to be home with Lucy. She no longer was a guest or an irascible little girl. "We need to call your mother and Grans," I said.

"Do we have to tonight?"

"No. But we do need to talk about your returning to Miami."

"Classes don't start until the seventh, and it won't make any difference if I miss the first few days."

"School is very important."

"It's also very easy."

"Then you should do something on your own to make it harder."

"Missing classes will make it harder," she said.

The next morning I called Rose at eight-thirty, when I knew a staff meeting was in progress across the hall, meaning that Ben Stevens was occupied and would not know I was on the line.

"How are things?" I asked my secretary.

"Awful. Dr. Wyatt couldn't get here from the Roanoke office

because they got snow in the mountains and the roads are bad. So yesterday Fielding had four cases with no one to help him. Plus, he was due in court and then got called to a scene. Have you talked to him?"

"We touch base when the poor man has a moment to get to the phone. This might be a good time for us to track down a few of our former fellows and see if one of them might consider coming here to help us hang on for a while. Jansen's doing private path in Charlottesville. You want to try him and see if he wants to give me a call?"

"Certainly. That's a fine idea."

"Tell me about Stevens," I said.

"He hasn't been here very much. He signs out in such an abbreviated, vague fashion that no one is ever sure where he's gone. I'm suspicious he's looking for another job."

"Remind him not to ask me for a recommendation."

"I wish you'd give him a great one so someone else would take him off our hands."

"I need for you to call the DNA lab and get Donna to do me a favor. She should have a lab request for the analysis of the fetal tissue from Susan's case."

Rose was silent. I could feel her getting upset.

"I'm sorry to bring this up," I said gently.

She took a deep breath. "When did you request the analysis?"

"The request was actually made by Dr. Wright, since he did the post. He would have his copy of the lab request at the Norfolk office, along with the case."

"You don't want me to call Norfolk and have them make a copy for us?"

"No. This can't wait, and I don't want anyone to know that I've requested a copy. I want it to appear that our office inadvertently got a copy. That's why I want you to deal directly with Donna. Ask her to pull the lab request immediately and I want you to pick it up in person."

"Then what?"

"Then put it in the box up front where all the other copies of lab requests and reports are left for sorting."

"You're sure about this?"

"Absolutely," I said.

I hung up and retrieved a telephone directory, which I was flipping through when Lucy walked into the kitchen. She was barefoot and still wearing the sweat suit she had slept in. Groggily wishing me a good morning, she began rummaging in the refrigerator as I ran my finger down a column of names. There were maybe forty listings for the name Grimes, but no Helens. Of course, when Marino had referred to the guard as Helen the Hun, he was being snide. Maybe Helen wasn't her real name at all. I noted that there were three listings with the initial H., two for the first name and one for a middle name.

"What are you doing?" Lucy asked, setting a glass of orange juice on the table and pulling out a chair.

"I'm trying to track down someone," I said, reaching for the phone.

I had no luck with any of the Grimeses I called.

"Maybe she's married," Lucy suggested.

"I don't think so." I called Directory Assistance and got the listing for the new penitentiary in Greensville.

"What makes you think she isn't?"

"Intuition." I dialed. "I'm trying to reach Helen Grimes," I said to the woman who answered.

"Are you referring to an inmate?"

"No. To one of your guards."

"Hold, please."

I was transferred.

"Watkins," a male voice mumbled.

"Helen Grimes, please," I said.

"Who?"

"Officer Helen Grimes."

"Oh. She don't work here anymore."

"Could you please tell me where I could reach her, Mr. Watkins? It's very important."

"Hold on." The phone clunked against wood. In the background, Randy Travis was singing.

Minutes later, the man returned. "We're not allowed to give out information like that, ma'am."

"That's fine, Mr. Watkins. If you give me your first name, I'll just send all this to you and you can forward it to her."

A pause. "All *what?*"

"This order she placed. I was calling to see if she wanted it mailed fourth-class or sent ground."

"What order?" He didn't sound happy.

"The set of encyclopedias she ordered. There are six boxes weighing eighteen pounds each."

"Well, you can't be sending no 'cyclopedias here."

"Then what do you suggest I do with them, Mr. Watkins? She's already made the down payment and your business address was the one she gave us."

"Shhhhooo. Hold on."

I heard paper rustle; then keys clicked on a keyboard.

"Look," the man said quickly. "The best I can do is give you a P.O. box. You just send the stuff there. Don't be sending nothing to me."

He gave me the address and abruptly hung up. The post office where Helen Grimes received her mail was in Goochland County. Next I called a bailiff I was friendly with at the Goochland courthouse. Within the hour he had looked up Helen Grimes's home address in court records, but her telephone number was unlisted. At eleven A.M., I gathered my pocketbook and coat, and found Lucy in my study.

"I've got to go out for a few hours," I said.

"You lied to whoever you were talking to on the phone." She stared into the computer screen. "You don't have any *encyclopedias* to deliver to anyone."

"You're absolutely right. I did lie."

"So sometimes it's okay to lie and sometimes it's not."

"It's never really okay, Lucy."

I left her in my chair, modem lights winking and various computer manuals open and scattered over my desk and on the floor. On the screen the cursor pulsed rapidly. I waited until I was well out of sight before slipping my Ruger into my pocketbook. Though I was licensed to carry a concealed weapon, I rarely did. Setting the alarm, I left the house through the garage and drove west until Cary Street put me on River Road. The sky was marbled varying shades of gray. I was expecting Nicholas Grueman to call any day. A bomb ticked silently in the records I had given him, and I did not look forward to what he was going to say.

Helen Grimes lived on a muddy road just west of the North Pole restaurant, and on the border of a farm. Her house looked like a small barn, with few trees on its tiny parcel of land, and window boxes clumped with dead shoots that I guessed once had been geraniums. There was no sign in front to announce who lived inside, but the old Chrysler pulled up close to the porch announced that at least somebody did.

When Helen Grimes opened her door, I could tell by her blank expression that I was about as foreign to her as my German car. Dressed in jeans and an untucked denim shirt, she planted her hands on her substantial hips and did not budge from the doorway. She seemed unbothered by the cold or who I said I was, and it wasn't until I reminded her of my visit to the penitentiary that recognition flickered in her small, probing eyes.

"Who told you where I live?" Her cheeks were flushed, and I wondered if she might hit me.

"Your address is in the court records for Goochland County."

"You shouldn't have looked for it. How would you like it if I dug up your home address?"

"If you needed my help as much as I need yours, I wouldn't mind, Helen," I said.

She just looked at me. I noticed that her hair was damp, an earlobe smudged with black dye.

"The man you worked for was murdered," I said. "Someone who worked for me was murdered. And there are others. I'm sure you've been keeping up with some of what is going on. There is reason to suspect that the person who is doing this was an inmate at Spring Street—someone who was released, perhaps around the time that Ronnie Joe Waddell was executed."

"I don't know anything about anybody being released." Her eyes drifted to the empty street behind me.

"Would you know anything about an inmate who disappeared? Someone, perhaps, who wasn't legitimately released? It seems that with the job you had you would have known who entered the penitentiary and who left."

"Nobody disappeared that I heard of."

"Why don't you work there anymore?" I asked.

"Health reasons."

I heard what sounded like a cupboard door shut from somewhere inside the space she guarded.

I kept trying. "Do you remember when Ronnie Waddell's mother came to the penitentiary to visit him on the afternoon of his execution?"

"I was there when she came in."

"You would have searched her and anything she had with her. Am I correct?"

"Yes."

"What I'm trying to determine is if Mrs. Waddell might have brought anything to give her son. I realize that visiting rules prohibit people from bringing in items for the inmates—"

"You can get permission. She got it."

"Mrs. Waddell got permission to give something to her son?"

"Helen, you're letting all the heat out," a voice sounded sweetly from behind her.

Intense blue eyes suddenly fixed on me like gun sights in the space between Helen Grimes's meaty left shoulder and the door frame. I caught a flash of a pale cheek and aquiline nose before the space was empty again. The lock rattled and the door was quietly shut behind the erstwhile prison guard. She leaned up against it, staring at me. I repeated my question.

"She did bring something for Ronnie, and it wasn't much. I called the warden for permission."

"You called Frank Donahue?"

She nodded.

"And he granted permission?"

"Like I said, it wasn't much, what she brought for him."

"Helen, what was it?"

"A picture of Jesus about the size of a postcard, and something was wrote on the back. I don't remember exactly. Something like 'I will be with you in paradise,' only the spelling was wrong. Paradise was spelled like 'pair of dice,' all run together," Helen Grimes said without a trace of a smile.

"And that was it?" I asked. "This was what she wanted to give her son before he died?"

"I told you that was it. Now, I need to go in, and I don't want you coming here again." She put her hand on the doorknob as the first few drops of rain slowly slipped from the sky and left wet spots the size of nickels on the cement stoop.

When Wesley arrived at my house later in the day, he wore a black leather pilot's jacket, a dark blue cap, and a trace of a smile.

"What's happening?" I asked as we retreated to the kitchen,

which by now had become such a common meeting place for us that he always took the same chair.

"We didn't break Stevens, but I think we put a pretty big crack in him. Your having the lab request left where he would find it did the trick. He's got good reason to fear the results of DNA testing done on fetal tissue from Susan Story's case."

"He and Susan were having an affair," I said, and it was odd that I did not object to Susan's morals. I was disappointed in her taste.

"Stevens admitted to the affair and denied everything else."

"Such as having any idea where Susan got thirty-five hundred dollars?" I said.

"He denies knowing anything about that. But we're not finished with him. A snitch of Marino's says he saw a black Jeep with a vanity plate in the area where Susan was shot and about the time we think it happened. Ben Stevens drives a black Jeep with the vanity plate '1 4 Me.' "

"Stevens didn't kill her, Benton," I said.

"No, he didn't. I think what happened is Stevens got spooked when whoever he was dealing with wanted information about Jennifer Deighton's case."

"The implication would have been pretty clear," I agreed. "Stevens knew that Jennifer Deighton was murdered."

"And coward that he is, he decides that when it is time for the next payoff, he'll let Susan handle it. Then he'll meet her directly afterward to get his share."

"By which time she's already been killed."

Wesley nodded. "I think whoever was sent to meet her shot her and kept the money. Later—maybe mere minutes later—Stevens appears in the designated spot, the alleyway off Strawberry Street."

"What you're describing is consistent with her position in the car," I said. "Originally, she had to have been slumped forward in order for the assailant to have shot her in the nape of the neck. But when she was found, she was leaning back in the seat."

"Stevens moved her."

"When he first approached the car, he wouldn't have immediately known what was wrong with her. He couldn't see her face if she were slumped forward against the steering wheel. He leaned her back in the seat."

"And then ran like hell."

"And if he'd just splashed on some of his cologne before heading out to meet her, then he would have cologne on his hands. When he leaned her back in the seat, his hands would have been in contact with her coat—probably in the area of her shoulders. That's what I smelled at the scene."

"We'll break him eventually."

"There are more important things to do, Benton," I said, and I told him about my visit with Helen Grimes and what she had said about Mrs. Waddell's last visit with her son.

"My theory," I went on, "is that Ronnie Waddell wanted the picture of Jesus buried with him, and that this may have been his last request. He puts it in an envelope and writes on it 'Urgent, extremely confidential,' and so on."

"He couldn't have done this without Donahue's permission," Wesley said. "According to protocol, the inmate's last request must be communicated to the warden."

"Right, and no matter what Donahue's been told, he's going to be too paranoid to let Waddell's body be carried off with a sealed envelope in a pocket. So he grants Waddell's request, then devises a way to see what's inside the envelope without a hassle or a stink. He decides to switch envelopes after Waddell is dead, and instructs one of his thugs to take care of it. And this is where the receipts come in."

"I was hoping you'd get around to that," Wesley said.

"I think the person made a little mistake. Let's say he's got a white envelope on his desk, and inside it are receipts from a recent trip to Petersburg. Let's say he gets a similar white envelope, tucks something innocuous inside it, and then writes the same thing on the front that Waddell had written on the envelope he wanted buried with him."

"Only the guard writes this on the wrong envelope."

"Yes. He writes it on the one containing the receipts."

"And he's going to discover this later when he looks for his receipts and finds the innocuous something inside the envelope instead."

"Precisely," I said. "And that's where Susan fits in. If I were the guard who made this mistake, I'd be very worried. The burning question for me would be whether one of the medical examiners opened that envelope in the morgue, or if the envelope was left sealed. If I, this guard, also happened to be the contact for Ben Stevens, the person forking over cash in exchange for making sure Waddell's body wasn't printed at the morgue, for example, then I'd know exactly where to turn."

"You'd contact Stevens and tell him to find out if the envelope was opened. And if so, whether its contents made anybody suspicious or inclined to go around asking questions. It's called tripping over your paranoia and ending up with many more problems than you would have had if you'd just been cool. But it would seem Stevens could have answered that question easily."

"Not so," I said. "He could ask Susan, but she didn't witness the opening of the envelope. Fielding opened it upstairs, photocopied the contents, and sent the original out with Waddell's other personal effects."

"Stevens couldn't have just pulled the case and looked at the photocopy?"

"Not unless he broke the lock on my credenza," I said.

"Then, in his mind, the only other alternative was the computer."

"Unless he asked Fielding or me. He would know better than that. Neither of us would have divulged a confidential detail like that to him or Susan or anyone else."

"Does he know enough about computers to break into your directory?"

"Not to my knowledge, but Susan had taken several courses and had UNIX books in her office."

The telephone rang and I let Lucy answer it. When she came into the kitchen, her eyes were uneasy.

"It's your lawyer, Aunt Kay."

She moved the kitchen phone within reach, and I picked it up without moving from my chair. Nicholas Grueman wasted no words on a greeting but went straight to his point.

"Dr. Scarpetta, on November twelfth you wrote a money market account check to the tune of *ten thousand dollars cash*. And I find no records in any of your bank statements that might indicate this money was deposited in any of your various accounts."

"I didn't deposit the money."

"You walked out of the bank with ten thousand dollars cash?"

"No, I did not. I wrote the check at Signet Bank, downtown, and with it purchased a cashier's check in British sterling."

"To whom was the cashier's check made out?" my former professor asked as Benton Wesley stared tensely at me.

"Mr. Grueman, the transaction was of a private nature and in no way has any bearing on my profession."

"Come now, Dr. Scarpetta. *You know* that's not good enough."

I took a deep breath.

"Certainly, you know we're going to be asked about this. Certainly, you must realize it doesn't look good that within weeks of your morgue assistant's depositing an unexplained amount of cash, you wrote a check for a large amount of cash."

I shut my eyes and ran my fingers through my hair as Wesley got up from the table and came around behind me.

"Kay"—I felt Wesley's hands on my shoulders—"for God's sake, you've got to tell him."

13

Had Grueman never been a practitioner of the law, I would not have entrusted my welfare to him. But before teaching he had been a litigator of renown, and he had done civil rights work and prosecuted mobsters for the Justice Department during the Robert Kennedy era. Now he represented clients who had no money and were condemned to die. I appreciated Grueman's seriousness and needed his cynicism.

He was not interested in trying to negotiate or protest my innocence. He refused to present the slightest shred of evidence to Marino or anyone. He told no one of the ten-thousand-dollar check, which was, he said, the worst piece of evidence against me. I was reminded of what he had taught his students on the first day of criminal law: *Just say no. Just say no. Just say no.* My former professor abided by these rules to the letter, and frustrated Roy Patterson's every effort.

Then on Thursday, January 6, Patterson called me at home and requested that I come downtown to his office to talk.

"I'm sure we can clear all this up," he said amicably. "I just need to ask you a few questions."

The implication was that if I cooperated, then something worse might be derailed, and I marveled that Patterson would consider, for even a moment, that such a shopworn maneuver would work with me. When the Commonwealth's Attorney wants to chat, he's on a fishing expedition that does not involve letting anything go. The same is true of the police. In good Gruemanian fashion, I told Patterson no, and the next morning was subpoenaed to appear before the special grand jury on January 20. This was followed by a subpoena duces tecum for my financial records. First Grueman claimed the Fifth, then filed a motion to quash the subpoena. A week later, we had no choice but to comply unless I wished to be held in contempt of court. About this same time, Governor Norring appointed Fielding acting Chief Medical Examiner of Virginia.

"There's another TV van. I just saw it go by," Lucy said from the dining room, where she stood staring out the window.

"Come on in and eat lunch," I called out to her from the kitchen. "Your soup is getting cold."

Silence.

Then, "Aunt Kay?" She sounded excited.

"What is it?"

"You'll never guess who just pulled up."

From the window over the sink, I watched the white Ford LTD park in front. The driver's door opened, and Marino climbed out. He hitched up his trousers and adjusted his tie, his eyes taking in everything around him. As I watched him follow the sidewalk to my porch, I was so powerfully touched that it startled me.

"I'm not sure if I should be glad to see you or not," I said when I opened the door.

"Hey, don't worry. I'm not here to arrest you, Doc."

"Please come in."

"Hi, Pete," Lucy said cheerfully.

"Aren't you supposed to be in school or something?"

"No."

"What? Down there in South America they give you January off?"

"That's right. Because of the bad weather," my niece said. "When it drops below seventy degrees, everything shuts down."

Marino smiled. He looked about the worst I had ever seen him.

Moments later I had built a fire in the living room, and Lucy had left to run errands.

"How have you been?" I asked.

"Are you going to make me smoke outside?"

I slid an ashtray closer to him.

"Marino, you have suitcases under your eyes, your face is flushed, and it's not warm enough in here for you to be perspiring."

"I can tell you've missed me." He pulled a dingy handkerchief from his back pocket and mopped his brow. Then he lit a cigarette and stared into the fire. "Patterson's being an asshole, Doc. He wants to scorch you."

"Let him try."

"He will, and you'd better be ready."

"He has no case against me, Marino."

"He has a fingerprint found on an envelope inside Susan's house."

"I can explain that."

"But you can't prove it, and then there's his little trump card. And I swear I shouldn't be telling you this, but I'm going to."

"What trump card?"

"You remember Tom Lucero?"

"I know who he is," I said. "I don't know him."

"Well, he can be a charmer and he's a pretty damn good cop, to be honest. Turns out he's been snooping around Signet Bank and talked up one of the tellers until she slipped him information about you. Now, he wasn't supposed to ask and she wasn't supposed to tell. But she told him she remembered you writing a big check for cash sometime before Thanksgiving. According to her, it was for ten grand."

I stared stonily at him.

"I mean, you can't really blame Lucero. He's just doing his job. But Patterson knows what to look for as he rummages through your financial records. He's going to hammer you hard when you get before the special grand jury."

I did not say a word.

"Doc." He leaned forward and met my eyes. "Don't you think you ought to talk about it?"

"No."

Getting up, he went to the fireplace and nudged the curtain open far enough to flick the cigarette inside.

"Shit, Doc," he said quietly. "I don't want you indicted."

"I shouldn't drink coffee and I know you shouldn't, but I feel like having something. Do you like hot chocolate?"

"I'll drink some coffee."

I got up to fix it. My thoughts buzzed sluggishly like a housefly in the fall. My rage had nowhere to go. I made a pot of decaf and hoped Marino would not know the difference.

"How is your blood pressure?" I asked him.

"You want to know the truth? Some days, if I was a kettle I'd be whistling."

"I don't know what I'm going to do with you."

He perched on the edge of the hearth. The fire sounded like the wind, and reflected flames danced in brass.

"For one thing," I went on, "you probably shouldn't even be here. I don't want you having any problems."

"Hey, fuck the CA, the city, the governor, and all of them," he said with sudden anger.

"Marino, we can't give in. Someone knows who this killer is. Have you talked to the officer who showed us around the penitentiary? Officer Roberts?"

"Yo. The conversation went exactly nowhere."

"Well, I didn't fare a whole lot better with your friend Helen Grimes."

"That must've been a treat."

"Are you aware that she no longer works for the pen?"

"She never did any *work* there that I know of. Helen the Hun was lazy as hell, unless she was patting down one of the lady guests. Then she got industrious. Donahue liked her, don't ask me why.

After he got whacked, she got reassigned to guard tower duty in Greensville and suddenly developed a knee problem or something."

"I have a feeling she knows a lot more than she let on," I said. "Especially if she and Donahue were friendly with each other."

Marino sipped his coffee and looked out the sliding glass doors. The ground was frosted white, and snowflakes seemed to be falling faster. I thought of the snowy night I was summoned to Jennifer Deighton's house, and images flashed in my mind of an overweight woman in curlers sitting in a chair in the middle of her living room. If the killer had interrogated her, he had done so for a reason. What was it he had been sent to find?

"Do you think the killer was after letters when he appeared at Jennifer Deighton's house?" I asked Marino.

"I think he was after something that had to do with Waddell. Letters, poems. Things he may have mailed to her over the years."

"Do you think this person found what he was looking for?"

"Let's just put it this way, he may have looked around, but he was so tidy we couldn't tell."

"Well, I don't think he found a thing," I said.

Marino looked skeptically at me as he lit another cigarette. "Based on what?"

"Based on the scene. She was in her nightgown and curlers. It appears she had been reading in bed. That doesn't sound like someone who is expecting company."

"I'll go along with that."

"Then someone appears at her door and she must have let him in, because there was no sign of forcible entry and no sign of a struggle. I think what may have happened next is this person demanded that she turn over to him whatever it was he was looking for, and she wouldn't. He gets angry, gets a chair from the dining room, and sets it in the middle of her living room. He sits her in it and basically tortures her. He asks questions, and when she doesn't tell him what he wants to hear he tightens the choke hold.

This goes on until it goes too far. He carries her out and puts her in her car."

"If he was going in and out of the kitchen, that might explain why that door was unlocked when we arrived," Marino considered.

"It might. In summary, I don't think he intended for her to die when she did, and after he tried to disguise her death he probably didn't hang around very long. Maybe he got scared, or maybe he simply lost interest in his assignment. I doubt he rummaged through her house at all, and I also doubt that he would have found anything if he had."

"We sure as hell didn't," Marino said.

"Jennifer Deighton was paranoid," I said. "She indicated to Grueman in the fax she sent him that there was something wrong about what was being done to Waddell. Apparently, she'd seen me on the news and had even tried to contact me, but continued to hang up when she got my machine."

"Are you thinking she might have had papers or something that would tell us what the hell this is all about?"

"If she had," I said, "then she was probably sufficiently frightened to get them out of her house."

"And stash them where?"

"I don't know, but maybe her ex-husband would. Didn't she visit him for two weeks the end of November?"

"Yeah." Marino looked interested. "As a matter of fact, she did."

Willie Travers had an energetic, pleasant voice over the phone when I finally reached him at the Pink Shell resort in Fort Myers Beach, Florida. But he was vague and noncommittal when I began to ask questions.

"Mr. Travers, what can I do to make you trust me?" I finally asked in despair.

"Come down here."

"That's going to be very difficult at present."

"I'd have to see you."

"Excuse me?"

"That's the way I am. If I can see you, I can read you and know if you're okay. Jenny was the same way."

"So if I come down to Fort Myers Beach and let you *read* me, you will help me?"

"Depends on what I pick up."

I made airline reservations for six-fifty the following morning. Lucy and I would fly to Miami. I would leave her with Dorothy and drive to Fort Myers Beach, where there was a very good chance I would spend a night wondering if I'd lost my mind. Chances were overwhelming that Jennifer Deighton's holistic health nut of an ex would turn out to be a great big waste of time.

Saturday, the snow had stopped when I got up at four A.M. and went into Lucy's bedroom to wake her. For a moment I listened to her breathe, then lightly touched her shoulder and whispered her name in the dark. She stirred and sat straight up. On the plane, she slept to Charlotte, then wallowed in one of her unbearable moods the rest of the way to Miami.

"I'd rather take a cab," she said, staring out the window.

"You can't take a cab, Lucy. Your mother and her friend will be looking for you."

"Good. Let them drive around the airport all day. Why can't I come with you?"

"You need to go home, and I need to drive straight to Fort Myers Beach, and then I'm going to fly from there back to Richmond. Trust me. It wouldn't be any fun."

"Being with Mother and her latest idiot isn't any fun, either."

"You don't know he's an idiot. You've never met him. Why don't you give him a chance?"

"I wish Mother would get AIDS."

"Lucy, don't say such a thing."

"She deserves it. I don't understand how she can sleep with every dickhead who takes her out to dinner and a movie. I don't understand how she can be your sister."

"Lower your voice," I whispered.

"If she missed me so much, she'd want to pick me up herself. She wouldn't want someone else around."

"That's not necessarily true," I told her. "When you fall in love someday, you'll understand better."

"What makes you think I've never been in love?" She looked furiously at me.

"Because if you had been, you would know that being in love brings out both the best and the worst in us. One day we're generous and sensitive to a fault, and the next we're not fit to shoot. Our lives become lessons in extremes."

"I wish Mother would hurry up and go through menopause."

Mid-afternoon, as I drove the Tamiami Trail in and out of the shade, I patched up the holes guilt had chewed into my conscience. Whenever I dealt with my family, I felt irritated and annoyed. Whenever I refused to deal with them, I felt the same way I had as a child, when I learned the art of running away without leaving home. In a sense, I had become my father after he died. I was the rational one who made A's and knew how to cook and handle money. I was the one who rarely cried and whose reaction to the volatility in my disintegrating home was to cool down and disperse like a vapor. Consequently, my mother and sister accused me of indifference, and I grew up harboring a secret shame that what they said was true.

I arrived in Fort Myers Beach with the air-conditioning on and the visor down to shield the sun. Water met the sky in a continuum of vibrant blue, and palms were bright green feathers atop trunks as sturdy as ostrich legs. The Pink Shell resort was the color of its name. It backed up to Estero Bay and threw its front balconies open wide to the Gulf of Mexico. Willie Travers lived in one of the cottages, but I was not due to meet him until eight P.M. Checking into a one-bedroom apartment, I literally left a trail of clothes on the floor as I snatched off my winter suit and grabbed shorts and a tennis shirt out of my bag. I was out the door and on the beach in seven minutes.

I did not know how many miles I walked, for I lost track of time, and each stretch of sand and water looked magnificently the same. I watched bobbing pelicans throw their heads back as they downed fish like shots of bourbon, and I deftly stepped around the flaccid blue balloons of beached Portuguese men-of-war. Most people I passed were old. Occasionally, the high-pitched voice of a child lifted above the roar of waves like a bit of bright paper carried by the wind. I picked up sand dollars worn smooth by the surf and leached shells reminiscent of peppermints sucked thin. I thought of Lucy and missed her again.

When most of the beach was in shade, I returned to my room. Showering and changing, I got in my car and cruised Estero Boulevard until hunger guided me like a divining rod into the parking lot of the Skipper's Galley. I ate red snapper and drank white wine while the horizon faded to a dusky blue. Soon boat lights drifted low in the darkness and I could not see the water.

By the time I found cottage 182 near the bait shop and fishing pier, I was as relaxed as I had been in a long time. When Willie Travers opened the door, it seemed we had been friends forever.

"The first order of business is refreshment. Surely you haven't eaten," he said.

I regretfully told him I had.

"Then you'll simply have to eat again."

"But I couldn't."

"I will prove you wrong within the hour. The fare is very light. Grouper grilled in butter and Key Lime juice with a generous sprinkling of fresh ground pepper. And we have seven-grain bread I make from scratch that you'll never forget as long as you live. Let's see. Oh, yes. Marinated slaw and Mexican beer."

He said all this as he popped the caps off two bottles of Dos Equis. Jennifer Deighton's former husband had to be close to eighty years old, his face as ruined by the sun as cracked mud, but the blue eyes set in it were as vital as a young man's. He smiled a lot as he talked, and was beef jerky lean. His hair reminded me of white tennis ball fuzz.

"How did you come to live here?" I asked, looking around at mounted fish on the walls and rugged furnishings.

"A couple of years ago I decided to retire and fish, so I worked out a deal with the Pink Shell. I'd run their bait shop if they'd let me rent one of the cottages at a reasonable rate."

"What was your profession before you retired?"

"Same as it is now." He smiled. "I practice holistic medicine, and you never really retire from that any more than you retire from religion. The difference is, now I work with people I want to work with, and I no longer have an office in town."

"Your definition of holistic medicine?"

"I treat the whole person, plain and simple. The point is to get people in balance." He looked appraisingly at me, set his beer down, and came over to the captain's chair where I sat. "Would you mind standing up?"

I was in a mood to be agreeable.

"Now hold out one of your arms. I don't care which one, but hold it straight out so it's parallel to the floor. That's fine. Now I'm going to ask you a question and then as you answer I'm going to try to push your arm down while you resist. Do you view yourself as the family hero?"

"No." My arm instantly yielded to his pressure and lowered like a drawbridge.

"Well, you do view yourself as the family hero. That tells me you're pretty damn hard on yourself and have been from the word *go.* All right. Now let's put your arm up again and I'm going to ask you another question. Are you good at what you do?"

"Yes."

"I'm pushing down as hard as I can and your arm is steel. So you are good at what you do."

He returned to the couch and I sat back down.

"I must admit that my medical teaching makes me somewhat skeptical," I said with a smile.

"Well, it shouldn't, because the principles are no different from what you deal with every day. Bottom line? The body doesn't lie. No matter what you tell yourself, your energy level responds to what is actually true. If your head says you aren't the family hero or you love yourself when that's not how you feel, your energy gets weak. Is this making any sense?"

"Yes."

"One of the reasons Jenny came down here once or twice a year was so I could balance her. And when she was here last, around Thanksgiving, she was so out of whack I had to work with her several hours every day."

"Did she tell you what was wrong?"

"A lot of things were wrong. She'd just moved and didn't like her neighbors, especially the ones across the street."

"The Clarys," I said.

"I suppose that was the name. The woman was a busybody and the man was a flirt until he had a stroke. Plus, Jenny's horoscope readings had gotten out of hand and were wearing her out."

"What was your opinion of this business she ran?"

"Jenny had a gift but she was spreading it too thin."

"Would you label her a psychic?"

"Nope. I wouldn't label Jenny—wouldn't even begin to try. She was into a lot of things."

I suddenly remembered the blank sheet of paper anchored by the crystal on her bed and asked Travers if he might know what that meant, or if it meant anything.

"It meant she was concentrating."

"Concentrating?" I puzzled. "On what?"

"When Jenny wanted to meditate, she would get a white sheet of paper and put a crystal on top of it. Then she would sit very still and slowly turn the crystal around and around, watching light from the facets move on the paper. That did for her what staring at the water does for me."

"Was anything else bothering her when she came to see you, Mr. Travers?"

"Call me Willie. Yes, and you know what I'm about to say. She was upset about this convict who was waiting to be executed, Ronnie Waddell. Jenny and Ronnie had been writing to each other for many years, and she just couldn't deal with the thought of him being put to death."

"Do you know if Waddell ever revealed anything to her that could have placed her in jeopardy?"

"Well, he gave her something that did."

I reached for my beer without taking my eyes off him.

"When she came down here at Thanksgiving, she brought all of the letters he had written and anything else he had sent her over the years. She wanted me to keep them down here for her."

"Why?"

"So they would be safe."

"She was worried about somebody trying to get them from her?"

"All I know is, she was spooked. She told me that during the first week of this past November, Waddell called her collect and said he was ready to die and didn't want to fight it anymore. Apparently, he was convinced nothing could save him, and he asked her to go to the farm in Suffolk and get his belongings from his mother. He said he wanted Jenny to have them, and not to worry, that his mother would understand."

"What were those belongings?" I asked.

"Just one thing." He got up. "I'm not real sure of the significance—and I'm not sure I want to be sure. So I'm going to turn it over to you, Dr. Scarpetta. You can take it on back to Virginia. Share it with the police. Do with it what you want."

"Why are you suddenly being helpful?" I asked. "Why not weeks ago?"

"Nobody bothered to come see me," he said loudly from another room. "I told you when you called that I don't deal with people over the phone."

When he returned, he set a black Hartmann briefcase at my feet. The brass lock had been pried open and the leather was scarred.

"Fact is, you'd be doing me a big favor to get this out of my life," Willie Travers said, and I could tell he meant it. "The very thought of it makes my energy bad."

The scores of letters Ronnie Waddell had written Jennifer Deighton from death row were neatly bundled in rubber bands and sorted chronologically. I skimmed through few in my hotel room that night, because their importance all but disappeared in the light of other items I found.

Inside the briefcase were legal pads filled with handwritten notes that made little sense, for they referred to cases and dilemmas of the Commonwealth from more than ten years ago. There were pens and pencils, a map of Virginia, a tin of Sucrets throat lozenges, a Vick's inhaler, and a tube of Chapstick. Still in its yellow box was an EpiPen, a .3-milligram epinephrine auto-injector routinely kept by people fatally allergic to bee stings or some foods. The prescription label was typed with the patient's name, the date, and the information that the EpiPen was one of five refills. Clearly, Waddell had stolen the briefcase from Robyn Naismith's house on the fateful morning he murdered her. It may be that he had no idea who it belonged to until he carried it off and broke the lock. Waddell discovered he had savaged a local celebrity whose lover, Joe Norring, was then the attorney general of Virginia.

* * *

"Waddell never had a chance," I said. "Not that he necessarily deserved clemency in light of the severity of his crime. But from the moment he was arrested, Norring was a worried man. He knew he had left his briefcase at Robyn's house, and he knew it had not been recovered by the police."

Why he had left his briefcase at Robyn's house was not clear, unless he'd simply forgotten it on a night that neither of them could know was her last.

"I can't even begin to imagine Norring's reaction when he heard," I said.

Wesley glanced at me over the rim of his glasses as he continued perusing paperwork. "I don't think we can imagine it. It was bad enough he had to worry about the world discovering he was having an affair, but his connection with Robyn would have instantly made him the prime suspect in her murder."

"In a way," Marino said, "he was lucky as hell Waddell took the briefcase."

"I'm sure in his mind he was unlucky either way he looked at it," I said. "If the briefcase had turned up at the scene, he was in trouble. If the briefcase was stolen, as it was, then Norring had to worry about it turning up somewhere."

Marino got the coffeepot and refilled everyone's cup. "Somebody must have done something to ensure Waddell's silence."

"Maybe." Wesley reached for the cream. "Then again, maybe Waddell never opened his mouth. My guess is he feared from the beginning that what he had stumbled upon only made matters worse for him. The briefcase could be used as a weapon, but who would it destroy? Norring or Waddell? Was Waddell going to trust the system enough to badmouth the AG? Was he going to trust the system enough years later to badmouth the governor—the only man who could spare his life?"

"So Waddell remained silent, knowing that his mother would protect what he had hidden on the farm until he was ready for someone else to have it," I said.

"Norring had ten damn years to find his briefcase," Marino said. "Why did he wait so long to start looking?"

"I suspect Norring has had Waddell watched from the beginning," Wesley said, "and that this surveillance was stepped up considerably over the past few months. The closer Waddell got to the execution, the less he had to lose, and the more likely he was to start talking. It's possible someone was monitoring his phone conversation when he called Jennifer Deighton in November. And it's possible that when word got to Norring, he panicked."

"He should have," Marino said. "I personally searched through all of Waddell's belongings when we was working the case. The guy had next to nothing, and if anything belonging to him was back on the farm, we never found it."

"And Norring would have known that," I said.

"Hell, yes," Marino said. "So he's going to know there's something strange about *belongings* from the farm being given to this friend of Waddell's. Norring starts seeing that damn briefcase in his nightmares again, and to make matters worse, he can't have someone just barge into Jennifer Deighton's house while Waddell's still alive. If something happens to her, there's no telling what Waddell will do. And the worst possibility would be if he started singing to Grueman."

"Benton," I said, "would you happen to know why Norring was carrying epinephrine? What is he allergic to?"

"Apparently, to shellfish. Apparently, he keeps EpiPens all over the place."

While they continued to talk, I checked the lasagna in the oven and opened a bottle of Kendall-Jackson. The case against Norring would take a very long time, if it could be proven at all, and I thought I understood, to a degree, how Waddell must have felt.

It wasn't until close to eleven P.M. that I called Nicholas Grueman at home.

"I'm finished in Virginia," I said. "As long as Norring is in office, he'll make sure I won't be. They've taken my life, goddam it, but I'm not giving them my soul. I plan to take the Fifth every time."

"Then you will certainly be indicted."

"Considering the bastards I'm up against, I think that's a certainty anyway."

"My, my, Dr. Scarpetta. Have you forgotten the bastard representing you? I don't know where you spent your weekend, but I spent mine in London."

I felt the blood drain from my face.

"Now, there's no guaranteeing that we can slide this around Patterson," said this man I used to think I hated, "but I'm going to move heaven and earth to get Charlie Hale on the stand."

14

January 20 was as windy as March but much colder, and the sun was blinding as I drove east on Broad Street toward the John Marshall courthouse.

"Now I will tell you something else you already know," Nicholas Grueman said. "The press is going to be churning up the water like bluefish on a feeding frenzy. You fly too low, you lose a leg. We'll walk side by side, eyes cast down, and don't turn and look at anyone no matter who it is or what he says."

"We're not going to find a parking place," I said, turning left on 9th. "I knew this would happen."

"Slow down. That good woman right there on the side is doing something. Wonderful. She's leaving, if she can ever get the wheels turned enough."

A horn blared behind me.

I glanced at my watch, then turned to Grueman like an athlete awaiting last-minute instruction from the coach. He wore a long navy blue cashmere coat and black leather gloves, his silver-topped cane leaning against the seat and a battle-scarred briefcase in his lap.

"Now remember," he said. "Your friend Mr. Patterson decides who's going in and who isn't, so we've got to depend on the jurors to intervene, and that's going to be up to you. You've got to connect with them, Kay. You've got to make friends with ten or eleven strangers the instant you walk into that room. No matter what they want to chat with you about, don't put up a wall. Be accessible."

"I understand," I said.

"We're going for broke. A deal?"

"A deal."

"Good luck, Doctor." He smiled and patted my arm.

Inside the courthouse, we were stopped by a deputy with a scanner. He went through my pocketbook and briefcase as he had a hundred times before when I had come to testify as an expert witness. But this time he said nothing to me and avoided my eyes. Grueman's cane set off the scanner, and he was the paragon of patience and courtesy as he explained that the silver top and tip would not come off, and that there truly was nothing concealed inside the dark wood shaft.

"What does he think I have here, a blowgun?" he remarked as we boarded the elevator.

The instant the doors opened on the third floor, reporters descended with the predicted predatory vigor. My counselor moved quickly for a man with gout, his strides punctuated by taps of his cane. I felt surprisingly detached and out of focus until we were inside the nearly deserted courtroom, where Benton Wesley sat in a corner with a slight young man I knew was Charlie Hale. The right side of his face was a road map of fine pink scars. When he stood and self-consciously slipped his right hand into his jacket pocket, I saw that he was missing several fingers. Dressed in an ill-fitting somber suit and tie, he glanced around while I preoccupied myself with the mechanics of being seated and sorting through my briefcase. I could not speak to him, and the three men had the presence of mind to pretend they did not notice that I was upset.

"Let's talk for a minute about what they have," Grueman said. "I believe we can count on Jason Story testifying, and Officer Lucero. And, of course, Marino. I don't know who else Patterson will include in this Star Chamber proceeding of his."

"For the record," Wesley said, looking at me, "I have spoken to Patterson. I've told him he doesn't have a case and I'll testify to that at the trial."

"We're assuming there will be no trial," Grueman said. "And

when you go in, I want you to make sure the jurors know that you talked to Patterson and told him he has no case but he insisted on going forward. Whenever he asks a question and you respond by addressing an issue that you have already addressed with him in private, I want you to say so. 'As I told you in your office,' or 'As I clearly stated when we spoke whenever it was,' et cetera, et cetera.

"It is important that the jurors know that you are not only an FBI special agent, but that you are the chief of the Behavioral Science Unit at Quantico, the purpose of which is to analyze violent crime and develop psychological profiles of the perpetrators. You may wish to state that Dr. Scarpetta in no way, shape, or form fits the profile of the perpetrator of the crime in question, and in fact, that you find the thought absurd. It is also important that you impress upon the jurors that you were Mark James's mentor and closest friend. Volunteer whatever you can because you can rest assured that Patterson isn't going to ask. Make it clear to the jurors that Charlie Hale *is here.*"

"What if they do not request me?" Charlie Hale asked.

"Then our hands are tied," Grueman replied. "As I explained when we talked in London, this is the prosecutor's show. Dr. Scarpetta has no right to present any evidence, so we have to get at least one of the jurors to invite us in through the back door."

"That's quite something," Hale said.

"You have the copies of the deposit slip and the fees you have paid?"

"Yes, sir."

"Very good. Don't wait to be asked. Just put them on the table as you're talking. And the status of your wife is the same since we spoke?"

"Yes, sir. As I told you, she's had the in vitro fertilization. So far, so good."

"Remember to get that in if you can," Grueman said.

Several minutes later, I was summoned to the jury room.

"Of course. He wants you first." Grueman got up with me.

"Then he'll call in your detractors so he can leave a bad taste in the jurors' mouths." He went as far as the door. "I will be right here when you need me."

Nodding, I went inside and took the empty chair at the head of the table. Patterson was out of the room, and I knew this was one of his gambits. He wanted me to endure the silent scrutiny of these ten strangers who held my welfare in their hands. I met the gazes of all and even exchanged smiles with a few. A serious young woman wearing bright red lipstick decided not to wait for the Commonwealth's Attorney.

"What made you decide to deal with dead people instead of the living?" she asked. "It seems a strange thing for a doctor to choose."

"It is my intense concern for the living that makes me study the dead," I said. "What we learn from the dead is for the benefit of the living, and justice is for those left behind."

"Don't it get to you?" inquired an old man with big, rough hands. The expression on his face was so sincere that he seemed in pain.

"Of course it does."

"How many years did you have to go to school after you graduated from high school?" asked a heavyset black woman.

"Seventeen years, if you include residencies and the year I was a fellow."

"Lord have mercy."

"Where all did you go?"

"To school, you mean?" I said to the thin young man wearing glasses.

"Yes, ma'am."

"Saint Michael's, Our Lady of Lourdes Academy, Cornell, Johns Hopkins, Georgetown."

"Was your daddy a doctor?"

"My father owned a small grocery store in Miami."

"Well, I'd hate to be the one paying for all that schooling." Several of the jurors laughed softly.

"I was fortunate enough to receive scholarships," I said. "Beginning with high school."

"I have an uncle who works at the Twilight Funeral Home in Norfolk," said someone else.

"Oh, come on, Barry. There really isn't a funeral home called that."

"I kid you not."

"That's nothing. We got one in Fayetteville owned by the Stiff family. Guess what it's called."

"No way."

"You're not from around here."

"I'm a native of Miami," I replied.

"Then the name Scarpetta's Spanish?"

"Actually, it's Italian."

"That's interesting. I thought all Italians were dark."

"My ancestors are from Verona in northern Italy, where a sizable segment of the population shares blood with the Savoyards, Austrians, and Swiss," I patiently explained. "Many of us are blue-eyed and blond."

"Boy, I bet you can cook."

"It's one of my favorite pastimes."

"Dr. Scarpetta, I'm not real clear on your position," said a well-dressed man who looked about my age. "Are you the chief medical examiner for Richmond?"

"For the Commonwealth. We have four district offices. Central Office here in Richmond, Tidewater in Norfolk, Western in Roanoke, and the Northern Office in Alexandria."

"So the chief just happens to be located here in Richmond?"

"Yes. That seems to make the most sense, since the medical examiner system is part of state government and Richmond is where the legislature meets," I replied as the door opened and Roy Patterson walked in.

He was a broad-shouldered, good-looking black man with close-shorn hair that was going gray. His dark blue suit was double-breasted, and his initials were embroidered on the cuffs of his pale yellow shirt. He was known for his ties, and this one looked hand painted. He greeted the jurors and was tepid toward me.

I discovered that the woman wearing the bright red lipstick was the foreman. She cleared her throat and informed me that I did not have to testify, and that anything I said could be used against me.

"I understand," I said, and I was sworn in.

Patterson hovered about my chair and offered a minimum of information about who I was, and elaborated on the power of my position and the ease with which this power could be abused.

"And who would there be to witness it?" he asked. "On many occasions there was no one to observe Dr. Scarpetta at work except for the person who was by her side virtually every day. Susan Story. You can't hear testimony from her because she and her unborn child are dead, ladies and gentlemen. But there are others you will hear from today. And they will paint for you a chilling portrait of a cold, ambitious woman, an empire builder who was making grievous mistakes on the job. First, she paid for Susan Story's silence. Then she killed for it.

"And when you hear tales of the *perfect crime,* who better able to carry it off than someone who is an expert in solving crimes? An expert would know that if you plan to shoot someone inside a vehicle, it would behoove you to choose a low-caliber weapon so you don't run the risk of bullets ricocheting. An expert would leave no telling evidence at the scene, not even spent shells. An expert would not use her own revolver—the gun or guns that friends and colleagues know she possesses. She would use something that could not be traced back to her.

"Why, she might even *borrow* a revolver from the lab, because, ladies and gentlemen, every year the courts routinely confiscate hundreds of firearms used in the commission of crimes, and some of these weapons are donated to the state firearms lab. For all we know, the twenty-two revolver that was put against the back of Susan Story's skull is, as we speak, hanging on a pegboard in the firearms lab or downstairs in the range the examiners use for test fires and where Dr. Scarpetta routinely practices shooting. And by the way, she is good enough to qualify for any police department in America. And she has killed before, though to give her credit, in the instance I'm referring to her actions were ruled to be self-defense."

I stared down at my hands folded on top of the table as the court reporter played her silent keys and Patterson went on. His rhetoric was always eloquent, though he usually did not know when to quit. When he asked me to explain the fingerprints recovered from the envelope found in Susan's dresser, he made such a big production of pointing out how unbelievable my explanation was that I suspected the reaction of some was to wonder why what I'd said *couldn't* be true. Then he got to the money.

"Is it not true, Dr. Scarpetta, that on November twelfth you appeared at the downtown branch of Signet Bank and made out a check for *cash* for the sum of ten thousand dollars?"

"That is true."

Patterson hesitated for an instant, his surprise visible. He had counted on my taking the Fifth.

"And is it true that on this occasion you did not deposit the money in any of your various accounts?"

"That is also true," I said.

"So several weeks before your morgue supervisor inexplicably deposited thirty-five hundred dollars into her checking account, you walked out of Signet Bank with ten thousand dollars cash on your person?"

"No, sir, I did not. In my financial records you should have found a copy of a cashier's check made out to the sum of seven thousand, three hundred and eighteen pounds sterling. I have my copy here." I got it out of my briefcase.

Patterson barely glanced at it as he asked the court reporter to tag it as evidence.

"Now, this is very interesting," he said. "You purchased a cashier's check made out to someone named Charles Hale. Was this some creative scheme of yours to disguise payoffs you were making to your morgue supervisor and perhaps to others? Did this individual named Charles Hale turn around and convert pounds back into dollars and route the cash elsewhere—perhaps to Susan Story?"

"No," I said. "And I never delivered the check to Charles Hale."

"You didn't?" He looked confused. "Then what did you do with it?"

"I gave it to Benton Wesley, and he saw to it that the check was delivered to Charles Hale. Benton Wesley—"

He cut me off. "The story just gets more preposterous."

"Mr. Patterson . . ."

"Who is Charles Hale?"

"I would like to finish my previous statement," I said.

"Who is Charles Hale?"

"I'd like to hear what she was trying to say," said a man in a plaid blazer.

"Please," Patterson said with a cold smile.

"I gave the cashier's check to Benton Wesley. He is a special agent for the FBI, a suspect profiler at the Behavioral Science Unit in Quantico."

A woman timidly raised her hand. "Is he the one I've read about in the papers? The one they call in when there are these awful murders like the ones in Gainesville?"

"He is the one," I said. "He is a colleague of mine. He was also the best friend of a friend of mine, Mark James, who also was a special agent for the FBI."

"Dr. Scarpetta, let's get the record straight here," Patterson said impatiently. "Mark James was more than a, quote, *friend* of yours."

"Are you asking me a question, Mr. Patterson?"

"Aside from the obvious conflict of interest involved in the chief medical examiner's sleeping with an FBI agent, the subject is nongermane. So I won't ask—"

I interrupted him. "My relationship with Mark James began in law school. There was no conflict of interest, and for the record, I object to the Commonwealth's Attorney's reference to whom I allegedly was sleeping with."

The court reporter typed on.

My hands were clasped so tightly my knuckles were white.

Patterson asked again, "Who is Charles Hale and why would you give him the equivalent of ten thousand dollars?"

Pink scars flashed in my mind, and I envisioned two fingers attached to a stump shiny with scar tissue.

"He was a ticket agent at Victoria Station in London," I said.

"Was?"

"He was on Monday, February eighteenth, when the bomb went off."

No one told me. I heard reporters on the news all day and had no idea until my phone rang on February 19 at two-forty-one A.M. It was eight-forty-one in the morning in London, and Mark had been dead for almost a day. I was so stunned as Benton Wesley tried to explain, that none of it made any sense.

"That was yesterday, I read about that yesterday. You mean it happened again?"

"The bombing happened yesterday morning during rush hour. But I just found out about Mark. Our legal attaché in London just notified me."

"You're sure? You're absolutely sure?"

"Jesus, I'm sorry, Kay."

"They've identified him with certainty?"

"With certainty."

"You're sure. I mean . . ."

"Kay. I'm at home. I can be there in an hour."

"No, no."

I was shivering all over but could not cry. I wandered through my house, moaning quietly and wringing my hands.

"But you did not know this Charles Hale prior to his being injured in the bombing, Dr. Scarpetta. Why would you give him ten thousand dollars?" Patterson dabbed his forehead with a handkerchief.

"He and his wife have wanted children and could not have them."

"And how would you know such an intimate detail about strangers?"

"Benton Wesley told me, and I responded by suggesting Bourne Hall, the leading research facility for in vitro fertilization. IVF is not covered by national health insurance."

"But you said the bombing was way back in February. You just wrote the check in November."

"I did not know about the Hales' problem until this past fall, when the FBI had a photo spread for Mr. Hale to look at and somehow learned of his difficulties. I'd told Benton long ago to let me know if there was ever anything I could do for Mr. Hale."

"Then you took it upon yourself to finance in vitro fertilization for strangers?" Patterson asked as if I'd just told him that I believed in leprechauns.

"Yes."

"Are you a *saint,* Dr. Scarpetta?"

"No."

"Then please explain your motivation."

"Charles Hale tried to help Mark."

"Tried to help him?" Patterson was pacing. "Tried to help him buy a ticket or catch a train or find the men's room? Just what is it that you mean?"

"Mark was conscious briefly, and Charles Hale was seriously injured on the ground next to him. He tried to move rubble off Mark. He talked to him, took off his jacket, and wrapped it around . . . He, uh, tried to stop the hemorrhaging. He did everything he could. There was nothing that would have saved him, but he wasn't alone. I am so grateful for that. Now there will be a new life in the world, and I am thankful I could do something in return. It helps. There is at least some meaning. No. I'm not a saint. The need was mine, too. When I helped the Hales, I was helping me."

The room was so quiet it was as if it were empty.

The woman wearing red lipstick leaned forward a little to get Patterson's attention.

"I expect Charlie Hale is way over there in England. But I wonder if we could subpoena Benton Wesley?"

"It's not necessary to subpoena either one of them," I answered. "Both of them are here."

When the foreman informed Patterson that the special grand jury had refused to indict, I was not there to see it. Nor was I present when Grueman was told. As soon as I had finished testifying, I had begun frantically looking for Marino.

"I saw him come out of the men's room maybe a half hour ago," said a uniformed officer I found smoking a cigarette by a water fountain.

"Can you try him on your radio?" I asked.

Shrugging, he unfastened his radio from his belt and asked the dispatcher to raise Marino. Marino did not respond.

I took the stairs and broke into a trot when I got outside. When I was in my car, I locked the doors and started the engine. I grabbed the phone and tried headquarters, which was directly across the street from the courthouse. While a detective in the squad room told me that Marino wasn't in, I drove through the lot in back looking for his white Ford LTD. It wasn't there. Then I pulled into an empty reserved place and called Neils Vander.

"You remember the burglary on Franklin—the prints you recently ran that matched up with Waddell?" I asked.

"The burglary in which the eiderdown vest was stolen?"

"That's the one."

"I remember it."

"Was the complainant's ten print card turned in for exclusionary purposes?"

"No, I didn't have that. Just the latents recovered from the scene."

"Thank you, Neils."

Next I called the dispatcher.

"Can you tell me if Lieutenant Marino is marked on?" I asked.

She came back to me. "He is marked on."

"Listen, please see if you can raise him and find out where he is. Tell him this is Dr. Scarpetta and it's urgent."

Maybe a minute later the dispatcher's voice came over the line. "He's at the city pumps."

"Tell him I'm two minutes from there and on my way."

The gas pumps used by the city police were located on a bleak patch of asphalt surrounded by a chain-link fence. Filling up was strictly self-service. There was no attendant, no rest room or vending machines, and the only way you were going to clean your windshield was if you brought your own paper towels and Windex. Marino was tucking his gas card in the side pouch where he always kept it when I pulled up next to him. He got out and came around to my window.

"I just heard the news on the radio." He couldn't contain his smile. "Where's Grueman? I want to shake his hand."

"I left him at the courthouse with Wesley. What happened?" I suddenly felt light-headed.

"You don't know?" he asked, incredulous. "Shit, Doc. They cut you loose, that's what happened. I can think of maybe two times in my career that a special grand jury hasn't returned with a true bill."

I took a deep breath and shook my head. "I guess I should be dancing a jig. But I don't feel like it."

"I probably wouldn't, either."

"Marino, what was the name of that man who claimed his eider-down vest was stolen?"

"Sullivan. Hilton Sullivan. Why?"

"During my testimony, Patterson made the outrageous accusation that I might have used a revolver from the firearms lab to shoot Susan. In other words, there is always a risk involved if you use your own weapon because if it's checked and it's proven that it fired the bullets, then you've got a lot of explaining to do."

"What's this got to do with Sullivan?"

"When did he move into his condo?"

"I don't know."

"If I were going to kill someone with my Ruger, it would be pretty clever of me to report it stolen to the police before I commit any crimes. Then if for some reason the gun is ever recovered—if, for example, the heat is on and I decide to toss it—the cops might trace the serial number back to me, but I can prove through the burglary report I filed that the gun was not in my possession at the time of the crime."

"Are you suggesting Sullivan falsified a report? That he staged the burglary?"

"I'm suggesting you consider that," I said. "It's convenient that he has no burglar alarm and left a window unlocked. It's convenient that he was obnoxious with the cops. I'm sure they were delighted to see him leave and weren't about to go the extra mile and get his fingerprints for exclusionary purposes. Especially since he was dressed in white and bitching about the dusting powder everywhere. My point is, how do you know that the prints in Sullivan's condo weren't left by Sullivan? He lives there. His prints would be all over the place."

"In AFIS they matched up with Waddell."

"Exactly."

"If that's the case, then why would Sullivan call the police in response to that story about eiderdown we planted in the paper?"

"As Benton said, this guy loves to play games. He loves to jerk people around. He skates on the edge for kicks."

"Shit. Let me use your phone."

He came around to the passenger's side and got in. Dialing Directory Assistance, he got the number of the building where Sullivan lived. When the superintendent was on the line, Marino asked him how long ago Hilton Sullivan had purchased his condominium.

"Well, then, who does?" Marino asked. He scribbled something on a notepad. "What's the number and what street does it face? Okay. What about his car? Yeah, if you've got it."

When Marino hung up, he looked at me. "Christ, the squirrel doesn't own the condo at all. It's owned by some businessman who rents it, and Sullivan started renting it the friggin' first week in December. He paid the deposit on the sixth, to be exact." He opened the car door, adding, "And he drives a dark blue Chevy van. An old one with no windows."

Marino followed me back to headquarters and we left my car in his parking place. We shot across Broad Street, heading toward Franklin.

"Let's hope the manager hasn't alerted him." Marino raised his voice above the roar of the engine.

He slowed down and parked in front of an eight-story brick building.

"His condo's in back," he explained, looking around. "So he shouldn't be able to see us." He reached under the seat and got out his nine-millimeter to back up the .357 in the holster under his left arm. Tucking the pistol in the back of his trousers and an extra clip in his pocket, he opened his door.

"If you're expecting a war, I'll be glad to stay in the car," I said.

"If a war starts, I'll toss you my three-fifty-seven and a couple speed loaders, and you damn better be as good a shot as Patterson's been saying you are. Stay behind me at all times." At the top of the steps, he rang the bell. "He's probably not going to be here."

Momentarily, the lock clicked free and the door opened. An elderly man with bushy gray eyebrows identified himself as the building superintendent Marino had spoken to earlier on the phone.

"Do you know if he's in?" Marino asked.

"I have no idea."

"We're going to go up and check."

"You won't be going up because he's on this floor." The superintendent pointed east. "Just follow that corridor and take the first left. It's a corner apartment at the very end. Number seventeen."

The building possessed a quiet but tired luxuriousness, reminiscent of old hotels that no one particularly wants to stay in anymore because the rooms are too small and the decor is too dark and a little frayed. I noted cigarette burns in the deep red carpet, and the stain on the paneling was almost black. Hilton Sullivan's corner apartment was announced by a small brass 17. There was no peephole, and when Marino knocked, we heard footsteps.

"Who is it?" a voice asked.

"Maintenance," Marino said. "Here to change the filter in your heater."

The door opened, and the instant I saw the piercing blue eyes in the space and they saw me, my breath caught. Hilton Sullivan tried to slam shut the door, but Marino's foot was wedged against the jamb.

"Get to the side!" Marino shouted at me as he snatched out his revolver and leaned as far away from the door's opening as he could.

I darted up the corridor as he suddenly kicked the door open wide and it slammed against the wall inside. Revolver ready, he went in, and I waited in dread for a scuffle or gunfire. Minutes went by. Then I heard Marino saying something on his portable radio. He reappeared, sweating, his face an angry red.

"I don't fucking believe it. He went out the window like a damn jackrabbit and there's not a sign of him. Goddam son of a bitch. His van's sitting right out there in the lot in back. He's off on foot somewhere. I've sent out an alert to units in the area." He wiped his face on his sleeve and struggled to catch his breath.

"I thought he was a woman," I said numbly.

"Huh?" Marino stared at me.

"When I went to see Helen Grimes, he was inside her house. He looked out the door once while we were talking on the porch. I thought it was a woman."

"Sullivan was at Helen the Hun's house?" Marino said loudly.

"I'm sure of it."

"Jesus Christ. That don't make a damn bit of sense."

But it did make sense when we began looking around Sullivan's apartment. It was elegantly furnished with antiques and fine rugs, which Marino said belonged to the owner, not to Sullivan, according to the superintendent. Jazz drifted from the bedroom, where we found Hilton Sullivan's blue down jacket on the bed next to a beige corduroy shirt and a pair of faded jeans, neatly folded. His running shoes and socks were on the rug. On the mahogany dresser were a green cap and a pair of sunglasses, and a loosely folded blue uniform shirt that still had Helen Grimes's nameplate pinned above the breast pocket. Beneath it was a large envelope of photographs that Marino went through while I silently looked on.

"Holy shit," Marino muttered every other minute.

In more than a dozen of them, Hilton Sullivan was nude and in poses of bondage, and Helen Grimes was his sadistic guard. One favorite scenario seemed to be Sullivan sitting in a chair while she played the role of interrogator, yoking him from behind or inflicting other punishments. He was an exquisitely pretty blond young man, with a lean body that I suspected was surprisingly strong. Certainly, he was agile. We found a photograph of Robyn Naismith's bloody body propped against the television in her living room, and another one of her on a steel table in the morgue. But what unnerved me more than any of this was Sullivan's face. It was absolutely devoid of expression, his eyes cold the way I imagined they would be when he killed.

"Maybe we know why Donahue liked him so much," Marino said, sliding the photographs back inside their envelope. "Someone was taking these pictures. Donahue's wife told me the warden's hobby was photography."

"Helen Grimes must know who Hilton Sullivan really is," I said as sirens wailed.

Marino peered out the window. "Good. Lucero's here."

I examined the down vest on the bed and discovered a downy white feather protruding from a minute tear in a seam.

More engines sounded. Car doors slammed shut.

"We're out of here," Marino said when Lucero arrived. "Make sure you impound his blue van." He turned to me. "Doc? You remember how to get to Helen Grimes's crib?"

"Yes."

"Let's go talk to her."

Helen Grimes did not have much to say.

When we got to her house some forty-five minutes later, we found the front door unlocked and went inside. The heat was turned up as high as it would go, and I could have been anywhere in the world and recognized the smell.

"Holy God," Marino said when he walked into the bedroom.

Her headless body was in uniform and sitting in a chair against the wall. It wasn't until three days later that the farmer across the road found the rest of her. He didn't know why anyone would have left a bowling bag in one of his fields. But he wished he had never opened it.

EPILOGUE

The yard behind my mother's Miami house was half in the shade and half in the gentle sun, and hibiscus grew in a riot of red on either side of the back screen door. Her Key Lime tree by the fence was heavy with fruit when virtually all others in the neighborhood were barren or dead. It was a fact I failed to understand, for I had not known it was possible to criticize plants into good health. I thought you had to talk nicely to them.

"Katie?" my mother called from the kitchen window. I heard water drumming into the sink. There was no point in answering.

Lucy knocked out my queen with a castle. "You know," I said, "I really hate playing chess with you."

"Then why do you keep asking me?"

"*Me* asking *you*? You force me, and one game is never enough."

"That's because I keep giving you another chance. But you blow it every time."

We were sitting across from each other at the patio table. The ice in our lemonades had melted and I felt a little sunburned.

"Katie? Will you and Lucy go out after a while and get the wine?" my mother said from the window.

I could see the shape of her head and the round outline of her face. Cupboard doors opened and shut; then the telephone sounded its high-pitched ring. It was for me, and my mother simply handed the cordless phone out the door.

"It's Benton," the familiar voice said. "I see from the papers that the weather's great down there. It's raining here and a lovely forty-five degrees."

"Don't make me homesick."

"Kay, we think we've got an ID. And by the way, someone went to a lot of trouble. Fake identifications—good ones. He was able to walk into a gun store, and rent a condo, with no questions asked."

"Where'd he get his money?"

"Family. He's probably had some stashed. Anyway, after going through prison records and talking to a lot of people, it seems that Hilton Sullivan is an alias for a thirty-one-year-old male named Temple Brooks Gault from Albany, Georgia. His father owns a pecan plantation and there's a lot of money. Gault's typical in some ways—preoccupied with guns, knives, martial arts, violent pornography. He's antisocial, et cetera."

"In what ways is he atypical?" I asked.

"His pattern would indicate that he's completely unpredictable. He doesn't really fit any profile, Kay. This guy's off the charts. If something strikes his fancy, he just does it. He's consummately narcissistic and vain—his hair, for example. He highlights it himself. We found the bleach, rinses, and so on in his apartment. Some of his inconsistencies are, well, weird."

"Such as?"

"He was driving this beat-up old van that was once owned by a housepainter. Doesn't appear Gault ever washed it or bothered to clean it out, not even after he murdered Eddie Heath inside the thing. We've got some pretty promising trace, by the way, and blood that's consistent with Eddie's type. That's disorganized. Yet Gault also apparently eradicated bite marks and had his fingerprints changed. That's as organized as hell."

"Benton, what is his history?"

"A manslaughter conviction. Two and a half years ago he got angry with a man in a bar and kicked him in the head. This was in Abingdon, Virginia. Gault, by the way, has a black belt in karate."

"Any new developments on locating him?" I watched Lucy set up the chessboard.

"None. But for all of us involved in the cases, I'll say what I've said before. This guy's absolutely without fear. He's very much guided by impulse and is, therefore, troublesome to second-guess."

"I understand."

"Just make sure you exercise the appropriate precautions at all times."

There were no appropriate precautions against someone like this, I thought.

"All of us need to be alert."

"I understand," I said again.

"Donahue had no idea what he unleashed. Or better put, Norring didn't. Though I don't believe our good governor handpicked this dirtbag. He just wanted his damn briefcase and probably gave Donahue the necessary funds and told him to take care of it. We're not going to get any hard time for Norring. He's been too careful and too many people aren't around to talk." He paused, adding, "Of course, there's your attorney and me."

"What do you mean?"

"I've been clear—in a subtle way, of course—that it would be a damn shame if something got leaked about the briefcase stolen from Robyn Naismith's house. Grueman had a little tête-à-tête with him, too, and reports that Norring looked a little queasy when it was mentioned that it must have been a harrowing experience when he drove himself to the ER the night before Robyn's death."

By checking old newspaper clips and talking to contacts in various ERs around the city, I had discovered that the night before Robyn's murder, Norring had been treated at Henrico Doctor's emergency room after administering epinephrine to himself by injection in his left thigh. Apparently, he had suffered a severe allergic reaction to Chinese food, cartons for which I recalled from police reports had been found in Robyn Naismith's trash. My theory was that shrimp or some other shellfish had inadvertently gotten mixed in with spring rolls or something else he and Robyn had eaten for dinner. He had begun to go into anaphylactic shock, had used one of his EpiPens—perhaps one he'd kept at Robyn's house—and then had driven himself to the hospital. In his great distress, he had left without his briefcase.

"I just want Norring as far away from me as possible," I said.

"Well, it seems he's been suffering health problems of late and has decided it would be wise to resign and look for something less stressful in the private sector. Perhaps on the West Coast. I'm quite certain he won't bother you. Ben Stevens won't bother you. For one thing, he—like Norring—is too busy looking over his shoulder for Gault. Let's see. Last I heard, Stevens was in Detroit. Did you know?"

"Did you threaten him, too?"

"Kay, I never threaten anyone."

"Benton, you're one of the most threatening people I've ever met."

"Does that mean you won't work with me?"

Lucy was drumming her fingers on top of the table and leaning her cheek against her fist.

"Work with you?" I asked.

"That's really why I'm calling, and I know you'll need to think about it. But we'd like you to come on board as a consultant to the Behavioral Science Unit. We're just talking a couple of days a month—as a rule. Of course, there will be times when things get a little crazy. You'll review the medical and forensic details of cases to assist us in working up the profiles. Your interpretations would be very useful. And besides, you probably know that Dr. Elsevier, who has been serving as our consulting forensic pathologist for the past five years, is retiring as of June one."

Lucy poured her lemonade on the grass, got up, and began stretching.

"Benton, I'll have to think about it. For one thing, my office is still in shambles. Give me a little time to hire a new morgue supervisor and administrator and get things back on track. When do you need to know?"

"By March?"

"Fair enough. Lucy says hello."

When I hung up, Lucy looked defiantly at me. "Why do you say something like that when it isn't true? I didn't say hello to him."

"But you desperately wanted to." I got up. "I could tell."

"Katie?" My mother was in the window again. "You really should come in. You've been outside all afternoon. Did you remember to put on sun block?"

"We're in the *shade,* Grans," Lucy called out. "Remember this *huge* ficus tree back here?"

"What time did your mother say she was coming over?" my mother asked her granddaughter.

"As soon as she and what's-his-name finish screwing, they'll be here."

My mother's face disappeared from the window and water drummed in the sink again.

"Lucy!" I whispered.

She yawned and wandered to the edge of the yard to catch an elusive ray of sun. Turning her face to it, she closed her eyes.

"You're going to do it, aren't you, Aunt Kay?" she said.

"Do what?"

"Whatever Mr. Wesley was asking you to do."

I began putting the chess game back in its box.

"Your silence is a very loud answer," my niece said. "I know you. You're going to do it."

"Come on," I said. "Let's go get the wine."

"Only if I get to drink some."

"Only if you're not driving anywhere tonight."

She slipped her arm around my waist and we went inside the house.

ABOUT THE AUTHOR

An award-winning former crime reporter for the *Charlotte Observer,* Patricia Cornwell spent six years working for the Virginia Chief Medical Examiner's Office and as a volunteer police officer before she wrote her first Dr. Kay Scarpetta novel, *Postmortem,* which received outstanding international acclaim and made her the only author ever to win five major mystery awards in a single year on both sides of the Atlantic for a first novel. Eleven subsequent Scarpetta novels became international bestsellers, together with *Food to Die For* and *Scarpetta's Winter Table.* She is a graduate of Davidson College in North Carolina and the author of three police procedural novels, *A Time for Remembering*—a biography of Ruth Graham, wife of the evangelist; *Portrait of a Serial Killer: Jack the Ripper—Case Closed;* and *Life's Little Fable,* a book for children. She lives in Greenwich, Connecticut, and New York City, and she supports several institutions that are concerned with forensic research, victims' support, and animal rescue.